Rosie grew up in the Scottish Highlands before moving to Melbourne, and now lives with her family in Southport, North West England. Writing as Rachael Lucas, she is the author of four women's fiction novels, published by Pan Macmillan, as well as two YA novels, published by Macmillan Children's Books.

We Met in December

ROSIE CURTIS

avon.

Published by AVON
A division of HarperCollins*Publishers* Ltd
1 London Bridge Street
London SE1 9GF
www.harpercollins.co.uk

A Paperback Original 2019

First published in Great Britain by HarperCollins*Publishers* 2019

Typeset in Sabon 10.75/15 pt by
Palimpsest Book Production Limited, Falkirk, Stirlingshire
Printed and bound in UK by CPI Group (UK) Ltd, Croydon CR0 4YY

To Archie, with all my love
(and thank you for all the cups of tea, darling).

PROLOGUE

Jess

22nd December

Christmas and London are a match made in heaven. There's a man on the street corner selling hot chestnuts by the bag, filling the air with the smell of cinnamon and vanilla. The ornate wooden windows of Liberty are glittering with lights and decorations. I stop to look at a huge tree swathed in ribbons and hung with a million dancing fairy lights and—

'Watch out!'

A woman crashes into me, giving me a furious look and weaving past, muttering loudly about bloody tourists.

I am not a tourist, I think. I am – or will be, in just a couple of hours – an official Londoner. I step out of the way of the thronging crowds, pasting myself against a carved wooden window frame, and watch as a sea of people scurry past.

I add 'stop dead on the pavement' to my mental list of Things London People Never Do. I know that already, really, but it's easy to forget when everything is so sparkly and festive. I pause for a moment and take a photo to share on my Instagram stories, because it's just so ridiculously perfect and my life has been so beige and boring for months – it's lovely to have something interesting to put on there. And then I take another of the street scene, because it's just so . . . London-y and Christmassy and perfect.

I look at the flowers in the doorway of Liberty, thinking that it would be a nice idea to take Becky some as a thank you (again) for offering me a room in a house that would otherwise be completely out of my reach. There doesn't seem to be a price anywhere though, which I think is weird, then I hear my Nanna Beth's voice saying, *If you have to ask, you can't afford it*. But they're only flowers, surely. How expensive can a bunch of flowers be?

'Can I help you?' The girl behind the faux-Victorian wooden flower stall looks at me. She's tiny and has huge brown eyes that match the expensive-looking Liberty of London apron she's wearing.

'I was wondering how much these are?' I lift up a ready-prepared bouquet – deep red roses mingled with silver-grey foliage and white lilies streaked with lime green, still not quite open. They're wrapped in thick, luxurious waxed paper and sealed with a gold Liberty sticker. They'll make the perfect thank you present for Becky.

The girl chews her gum for a moment and looks at me, taking in the fluffy pink coat I bought for my big move (if I'm going to be a London creative, I thought I should wear something that suits my new job), along with my denim pinafore, blue tights and my trusty silver Doc Marten boots. When I got off the train from Bournemouth earlier I felt quirky and artistic, but now under her supercilious stare I think perhaps I look like a kids' TV presenter.

'Forty-seven pounds,' she says. 'And five pounds extra if you want our gift-wrapping service.'

Ouch. That's a week's worth of my new food budget. I put the flowers back in the stylish metal bucket. I think Becky would understand.

'I like your coat,' she says, as I start to slink off. I turn, surprised, and smile a thank you.

'It's from eBay,' I tell her, patting my fluffy arm.

'Cool. It's really nice.' The girl lowers her voice, conspiratorially. 'I couldn't afford the flowers either, if it helps. There's a stall a couple of minutes away on Noel Street – he always has decent flowers.'

She waves her hand briefly in the air, but then another customer appears and she turns to them, greeting them with a cheerful smile.

'Thanks,' I say, in her general direction, but she's not listening.

So I take my phone out. My sense of direction is absolutely hopeless, and I still can't work out how people find their way around London. I've worked out bits of it, but

I can't seem to join them up. It takes me three tries, but I make it to Noel Street in the end. There I find a round-faced man wearing a Santa hat, singing along to Christmas songs from a Bluetooth speaker. His stall is piled high with fruit and veg, and – phew – surrounding it is a rainbow array of flowers, which look to my uneducated eye just as nice as the ones from round the corner at Liberty. Well, almost as nice. A bit gaudy maybe, but I can't afford to be fussy on my new London wages.

Five minutes later I'm back on Oxford Street looking at the Christmas lights with a bunch of (considerably cheaper) red roses, their cellophane wrapping crinkling in my arms. The lights – strung from one side of the street to the other – sparkle against the sky, which ten minutes ago had been the usual English winter grey, but now has shifted to an ominous bruised purple. I'm trying to figure out if it's easier to jump on a bus or get the tube to Notting Hill to meet Becky and my new house-mates. I'm standing on a street corner peering at Google Maps again when the first hailstones hit me on the head. And – *ow* – they really sting.

In seconds the packed streets empty, as everyone ducks into the nearest shop or doorway to shelter, clutching their shopping bags tightly. Only the smug umbrella holders and the hardy few carry on, marching down pavements now clear of tourists and Christmas shoppers. The tyres of the red buses and black taxis hiss on the tarmac and the hailstones hammer on the metal awning over our heads. I'm crammed with a handful of shoppers in the doorway of – I look up to see a shiny brass plaque on the wall – NMC Inc, and then I frown at the screen of my phone once again.

'Are you lost?' a man says. He has Scandinavian-looking blond hair and a dark blue scarf wrapped round his neck. He's got a bit of an accent and now he's indicating my phone with a finger. 'Where are you trying to go?'

'Notting Hill,' I say, feeling like I've stepped into a film for a moment. Christmas is everywhere and there's a tiny split second where the noticing-things part of my brain is looking at me from the outside. The thing about being addicted to a certain kind of romantic movie is that you're always half-expecting that your life might just suddenly take a turn for the better. And handsome Scandinavian types who look a bit like Jaime Lannister are pretty much up there on my list of good things.

'I'm not sure which bus to get,' I say. 'Because I usually get the tube, but my friend said it was easy from here. Easy if you've got a sense of direction, I think. Which I definitely have not.'

And then I find myself telling this complete stranger, who has opened the Citymapper app on his phone and is tapping rapidly: 'I'm picking up the keys for my new house.' I can hear the little note of pride in my voice.

'Nice,' he says, smiling. He points to the bus stop on the opposite side of the road. 'If you get the 94, it'll take you straight to Notting Hill Gate. It'll take a bit longer than the tube, but on the other hand, it's a lovely view if you're new to the area.'

5

'Thanks,' I say. I'm not doing a great job at trying to look like a well-established local, then. A fresh torrent of hailstones batters the canopy above us. 'Might just wait a moment.'

'That's very wise.'

Obviously if this was one of those movies with woolly hats and kissing in the snow and hard-bitten business-women remembering the true meaning of Christmas, at this point we'd start a conversation, and he'd follow me onto the bus, and – well, you know the score. But this is not a movie, I am one hundred per cent single, and despite being as much of a sucker for a Richard Curtis movie as the next hopeless romantic, I remind myself that I am one hundred per cent not looking for anyone else. Because this is my new start, and my new life, and I am doing it On My Own.

The hail stops, and I try my best to stride across the road in the manner of an independent London girl living her best life, aware that the handsome Scandinavian person is watching and (obviously) thinking that I am the one that got away and wondering if he'll ever see me again. What actually happens is I almost get knocked flat by a bloke on a Deliveroo bike, fumble to find my card to swipe it when I get on the bus, and when I do climb the stairs and sit down on a seat, I look across the road to see the handsome Jaime Lannister lookalike beaming with delight as his boyfriend appears from behind the door of NMC Inc in an expensive-looking coat, kisses him on the mouth and runs an affectionate hand through his lovely blond hair. Ah well. It's just as well I'm not looking.

I sit wedged in against the window of the bus, wiping away condensation with my fluffy pink sleeve so I can stare out of the window all the way to Notting Hill. I watch as we pass Hyde Park, the huge trees' bare, branches reaching up to the grey sky. The bus stops, disgorging passengers, and I watch as a woman dressed in a red coat with a fur collar climbs out of a shiny black taxi, her arms full of expensive-looking paper shopping bags.

And then we pull away and I watch as the buildings get smaller and the grey sky gets bigger, and the bus takes me to my new house and my new life. I smile at a woman when she gets on and sits beside me, and I don't even mind that she opens up an absolutely honking tuna sandwich from M&S and eats it. Nothing is going to get in the way of this moment, because I've got a job in London and a room in a house-share I couldn't even begin to imagine. I squish my hands into fists of excitement when I see the words *Notting Hill Gate* flash up on the information board on the bus. I press the bell – my bell – and my heart gives a little skip of excitement as the bus pulls to a stop. This is London, I think. And now, London is home.

CHAPTER ONE

Jess

22nd December, 15 Albany Road, Notting Hill

I pause for a minute outside the house and look up, still not quite believing that this terraced mansion is home. It's huge, slightly shabby, and has an air of faded grandeur. Six wide stone steps lead to a broad wooden front door, painted a jaunty red that is faded in places and chipped away to a pale, dusky pink. Each window on the road is topped with ornate stuccoed decorations – the ones on our house are a bit chipped and scruffy-looking, but somehow it just makes the place look more welcoming, as if it's full of history.

Next door on one side is freshly decorated, the black paint of the windowsills gleaming. They've got window boxes at every window, crammed full of pansies and evergreen plants. I can see a huge Christmas tree tastefully decorated with millions of starry lights, topped with a huge metal star. There's a little red bicycle chained to the railings and a pair of wellies just inside the porch. This must be the investment banker neighbours Becky talked about. The mansion on the other side has been turned into flats, and there's a row of doorbells beside a blue front door.

I rush up the steps and lift the heavy brass door-knocker.

'You don't have to knock,' Becky says, beaming as she opens the door. 'This is home!'

'I do, because you haven't given me a key yet.' I love Becky.

'Ah.' Becky takes my bag and hangs it on a huge wooden coat hook just inside the door, which looks like it's been there forever. There's a massive black umbrella with a carved wooden handle hanging beside my bag.

'Used to be my grandpa's,' she says, absent-mindedly running a hand down it. 'This place is like a bloody museum.'

'I can't believe it's yours.'

'Me neither.' Becky shakes her head and beckons me through to the kitchen. 'Now wait here two seconds, and I'll give you the tour.'

I stand where I've been put, at the edge of a huge kitchen-slash-dining-room space, which has been here so long that it's come back into fashion. It's all cork tiles and dangling spider plants and a huge white sink, which is full of ice and bottles of beer.

I think Nanna Beth would be impressed with this. With all of it. I've taken the leap.

'Life is for living, Jessica, and this place is all very well, but it's like God's waiting room,' she'd once said, giving a cackle of laughter and inclining her head towards the window, where a flotilla of mobility scooters had passed by, ridden by grey-haired elderly people covered over with zipped-up waterproof covers. The seaside town I'd grown up in wasn't actually as bad as all that, but it was true: things had changed. Grandpa had passed away, and Nanna Beth had sold the house and invested her money in a little flat in a new sheltered housing development where there was no room for me, not because she was throwing me out, but because – as she'd said, looking at me shrewdly – it was time to go. I'd been living in a sort of stasis since things had ended with my ex-boyfriend Neil.

Weirdly, the catalyst for all this change had been being offered a promotion in the marketing company where I worked. If I'd taken it, it would have been a job for life. I could have afforded to buy a little house by the sea and upgraded my car for something nice, and I'd have carried on living the life I'd been living since I graduated from university and somehow gravitated back home when all my friends spread their wings and headed for the bright lights of London, or New York, or – well, Sarah ended up in Inverness, so I suppose we didn't quite all end up somewhere exotic.

But Nanna Beth had derailed me and challenged me with the task of getting out and grabbing life with both hands, which is pretty tricky for someone like me. I tend to take the approach that you should hold life with one hand, and keep the other one spare just in case of emergencies. And yet here I am, an hour early (very me) for a housewarming party for the gang of people that Becky has gathered together to share this rambling, dilapidated old house in Notting Hill that *her* grandparents left her when they passed away.

'I still can't believe this place is yours,' I repeat, as I balance on the edge of the pale pink velvet sofa. It's hidden under a flotilla of cushions. The arm of the sofa creaks alarmingly, and I stand up, just in case it's about to give way underneath my weight.

Becky shakes her head. '*You* can't? Imagine how I feel.'

'And your mum *really* didn't object to your grandparents leaving you their house in their will?'

She shakes her head and pops open the two bottles of beer she's holding, handing me one. 'She's quite happy where she is. And you know she's all *property is theft* and that sort of thing.'

'True.' I take a swig of beer and look at the framed photographs on the wall. A little girl in Mary-Jane shoes with a serious face looks out at us, disapprovingly. 'She's keeping her eye on you: look.'

Becky shudders. 'Don't. She wanted me to come to Islay for a Christmas of meditation and chanting, but I managed to persuade her that I'd be better off coming when the weather was a bit nicer.'

Becky's mum had been a mythical figure to all of us at university. She'd been a model in her youth, and then eschewed all material things and moved to an ethical

12

living commune on the island of Islay when Becky was sixteen. Becky had stayed behind to finish her exams with a family friend, and horrified her mother by going into not just law, but corporate law of all things. Relations had been slightly strained for quite a while, but she'd spent some time in meditative silence, apparently, and now they got on really well – as long as they had a few hundred miles between them.

I look at the photograph of Becky's mum – she must only be about seven. She looks back at me with an intense stare, and I think that if anyone can save the planet, it's very possibly her. Anyway, I raise my bottle to her in a silent thank you. If she'd contested the will, Becky might not have inherited this place, and she wouldn't have offered me a room at £400 a month, which wouldn't have got me space in a broom closet anywhere else in commutable distance of King's Cross, where my new job was situated.

'Just going to get out of this jacket,' Becky says, looking down at her work clothes; then she disappears for a moment and I'm left looking around. The house is old-fashioned, stuffed full of the sort of mid-century furniture that would sell for vast amounts of money on eBay – there's an Ercol dresser in the sitting room and dining chairs that look like they've come straight out of Heal's. I take a photo of the huge potted plant that looms in the corner like a triffid, and then I wander into the hall. It's huge and airy, with a polished wooden banister that twirls round and up to the third floor where there's a skylight – dark just now, because it's midwinter, but I bet it fills this space with light in the

13

middle of summer. There's a huge wooden coat stand with a mirror by the interior door, and a porch with ceramic tiles worn through years of footsteps passing over them. The place must be 150 years old, at least. And – I push the sitting room door open – there's enough space for everyone to collapse on the sofas in a Sunday-ish sort of way. The paintings on the walls are draped with brightly coloured tinsel and fairy lights, and there's a Christmas tree on the side table, decked with multi-coloured lights and hung with a selection of baubles, which look—

'Hideous, aren't they?' Becky's voice sounds over my shoulder. 'I couldn't resist. They're from the pound shop so I just went to town a bit. If you can't be tacky at Christmas, when can you?'

'I love it,' I say, and I do. Becky disappears back into the kitchen and I can hear the sound of her warbling out of tune to Mariah Carey and the clattering of plates and saucepans. I stand in the hallway and look at this amazing house that I couldn't afford in a million years, and I think back to about two months ago when I saw an advert for my dream job in publishing come up and wondered if I should take the chance and apply. And how Nanna Beth had said, 'Nothing ventured, lovey – you never know what's around the corner . . .'

An hour later and we're in the kitchen and everything's been laid out so it looks perfect for the housewarming party.

'Stop!' I put a hand up in the air.

Becky stops dead and I leap between her and the massive old oak table in the kitchen. Her face registers alarm as I reach into the back pocket of my jeans and then she rolls her eyes as she realises what I'm doing.

With my free hand, I reach across, straightening a plate and moving a piece of tinsel so it sits jauntily beside the jewel-bright heaps of salsa and guacamole. 'There.'

Leaning over, I take a photo from above and step back, letting her put the tray of tequila shots down on the table.

'Since when were you the Instagram queen?' Becky tucks back a strand of hair that's escaped from behind her ear. She's had it cut into a sleek graduated bob, which makes her look like a proper grown-up, especially as she's still dressed in her work clothes of grey slim-fitting trousers and a pale blouse made of silky stuff, which I would definitely have spilled coffee on within an hour. But she's here at 6.30 p.m. looking as if she's just got out of the shower, instead of having battled her way home through London traffic after a long day doing corporate law stuff. I've taken off my pink fluffy coat because it was making me feel like a dislodged tree bauble, or a pom-pom, in comparison to Becky's minimalist chic.

'Hardly,' I say, fiddling with a filter and making the photo look nice before hashtagging it and hitting share. 'I just thought it'd be nice to show everyone back home what it's like living in London.'

'And make a point of what a lovely time you're having even though they all think you're insane to give up a

15

promotion in Bournemouth for a pay cut up here?' she says.

I nod, and pick up a tortilla chip, breaking it in half. 'That too,' I admit, making a face. 'And Nanna Beth is on there too – she's got herself an iPhone contract. I'm her only Instagram follower so far.'

'She's going to be sharing selfies with all the hot doctors in the nursing home, isn't she?' Becky snorts with laughter.

I turn the phone so she can see it. @nanna_beth1939 has posted a string of photos of her new ground-floor flat in the sheltered accommodation unit she's moved into.

'Oh, bless,' says Becky, taking my phone so she can have a closer look. 'Look, she's got that wooden carving you bought her in Cyprus on the mantelpiece.'

I peer over her shoulder. 'Ahh, that's nice.' I'm hit by a wave of guilt that I'm going to be up here and she's going to be down there. I've spent the last year living in her house, ever since Grandpa died, and it's going to be weird not having her there every night when I get home from work.

'She'll be fine,' says Becky, as if reading my thoughts. She clicks the phone off and puts it down on the table. 'And it's not as if you're miles away. It's a train ride, that's all.'

'I know. Just feels weird leaving her to the tender mercies of Mum.'

Becky makes a face. 'Yeah, well, she's not exactly . . . well, she wasn't at the front of the queue when they were giving out the nurturing quota, was she?'

I snort. My mother is many things, but maternal is

not one of them. I mean she's lovely, in her own way. But I'm not sure she'll remember to pop round every couple of days and check Nanna Beth's doing okay in her new place. Anyway. I square my shoulders and think of what Nanna Beth told me when she'd pressed a roll of twenty-pound notes into my hand yesterday morning. It was time for me to step out into the big world and let her do her own thing. Slightly odd role reversal, I know, but our family's always been a bit unusual.

In the kitchen, Becky's still singing out of tune and lighting the tiny tea-light candles that are scattered around. Even when we were living in university halls, she managed to make her room look good.

There's a clatter as someone opens the door, and a gust of air blows a couple of Christmas cards off the top of the fridge. I bend down and pick them up, catching the one-sided conversation that's going on in the hall.

'You said you'd be able to get away.' It must be Emma, the girl Becky's found to take another one of the rooms.

There's a long pause and I hover by the kitchen door, wondering if I should pop my head round and say hello. Becky's stirring spiced chicken and peppers, filling the room with a smell that makes my stomach growl. I haven't eaten since breakfast.

'What about me?' Emma says. My eyes widen. I shouldn't be listening in, but I'm a sucker for a bit of drama. I fiddle with my phone, trying to look as if I'm busy and not just eavesdropping. Emma's voice is in that middle ground, somewhere between angry and upset.

17

'I don't care what *she's* doing,' she says, and this time she's not keeping her voice down. 'I'm not waiting around forever.'

Becky turns round, frying pan in hand. She raises her eyebrows and looks towards the door. 'Uh-oh, trouble in paradise by the sound of it.'

I nod, and lower my voice. 'What's the story?'

Becky puts a finger to her lips. 'Tell you later. But it's very Emma. It'll be all over and they'll be loved up before you know it.'

A moment later, Emma appears in the room, her eyes sparkling in that suspiciously bright way that mine do if I've been crying and I'm trying to look like everything's okay.

'Hi, hello,' she says, and leans over and kisses me on the cheek.

'Sorry, just had to take a quick work call. You know what it's like. They pay us nothing, and expect us to be on call 24/7.'

I smile in a way that I hope suggests I haven't heard a thing.

'Emma, this is Jess, the university friend I told you about. She's taking the room on the first floor.'

'Lovely to meet you, Jess. God I need a drink,' says Emma, picking up one of the little shot glasses of tequila. I'm about to pass her a lemon slice, but she's too quick for me. The whole thing is gone in a second, and she winces in disgust. 'Ugh. Revolting. I hate tequila.' She takes another one and downs it as well. 'Cheers.'

I'm still holding the lemon slice in mid-air when the kitchen door opens again.

'Sorry I'm late,' says a low voice. I look up, and almost drop my phone in shock.

Standing in the doorway, taking up quite a lot of it, is a man. The kind of man that makes you feel like your stomach just fell through the floor. I mean I say that, but Emma's scrolling through her phone and Becky's running hot water over the fajita saucepan, so maybe they're immune or something but – wow.

I press my lips together, mainly to check that my mouth isn't actually hanging open. I suspect my eyes are cartoon circles though, and I can't press them shut without looking a bit weird, so I just sort of stand there, making a kind of mental inventory.

Scruff of beard – check. Broad, muscular shoulders – check. Twinkly eyes – check. Bottle of tequila in hand. He's wearing a grey shirt and a pair of jeans and he's got a scarf hanging round his neck and . . .

'Hey. You must be Jess,' he says, stepping towards me. He reaches out a hand to shake mine, and then leans forward to kiss me on the cheek in greeting. 'I'm Alex.'

He smells fresh, his cheek cold from the winter air against mine. I catch a faint scent of cedar wood and notice as he steps back that his sleeves are rolled up, showing off the sort of forearms that look as if he chops wood or does something outdoorsy for a living, only we're in the middle of Notting Hill and that's unlikely.

There's a moment where I think I've forgotten how

19

to speak, which is slightly awkward as I'm basically standing there like the human embodiment of the heart eyes emoji, suppressing the urge to put one hand to my cheek (because: phwoar, basically) and the other on his, to check he's real (because: well, ditto). And then I remember that I'm sensible, level-headed Jess, and this is my new house and my new life and the number one rule that Becky told us all about in the welcome email was NO COUPLES. Which is absolutely fine, because I'm here to work and definitely absolutely not to fall in love at first sight with gorgeous men with cute beards holding tequila bottles.

'Hi.' I shove my phone back in the pocket of my jeans and try to force myself to do something practical, so I press my hands together in a workmanlike manner and say in an artificially bright voice, 'That's everyone, isn't it?'

I turn to Becky, who's halfway through what she'd later explain was a test fajita, a dollop of sour cream on her chin. She wipes it off, and tries to talk with her mouth full, so it comes out a bit muffled.

'Everyone except Rob.'

I watch Emma, who has helped herself to another drink, but she's added a mixer this time and she's actually drinking it, not downing it in one. She's sitting on the edge of the table, her long legs stretched out and crossed at the ankles. 'Ah, yes. The mysterious Rob,' she says, arching an eyebrow and smiling. She reaches over and takes a handful of tortilla chips. 'Have you met him, Jess? I'm beginning to think maybe he's a figment of Becky's imagination.'

'Yeah, Becky,' says Alex. He shoves the bottle on the wonky wooden shelf over the kitchen sink and grabs a plate, turning to look at her, jokingly. 'What's the story with Rob?'

'He is real, I promise you.' Becky shakes her head, laughing.

'Of course. Man of few words and many knives.' Emma points to the kitchen counter. 'Where are they, Becky? They were there the other day when I had breakfast then they disappeared.'

But Becky has her head in the freezer, trying to find a bag of ice, and doesn't reply.

I take a look at Emma while she's occupied with assembling a fajita wrap. She's properly beautiful. She has a very attractive, angular face, with an aquiline nose and huge doe eyes. She looks like she's made to swan about in Notting Hill, hanging out in expensive restaurants, being treated to expensive lunches. I pull up a chair at the big table and have a moment of feeling scruffy, freckled, and very suburban. Almost like someone who's been living with their grandparents and working in an office in a seaside town a million miles from London, which isn't surprising.

'So what we know is this: Rob's a chef, which means he works really long hours and we never see him because he's home when we're all out at work, and then out when we get back,' Emma begins. 'He turned up the other day, dumped all this expensive-looking kitchen kit on the table, then looked at his watch and said he had to run.'

'Then I put his stuff in the big larder cupboard,' Becky continues, banging a bag of ice against the edge of the table until the cubes separate. 'Because three blocks of intimidating kitchen knives sitting out on the work surface was going to give me nightmares and I had visions of a serial killer turning up and murdering us all in our beds.'

'I think a serial killer would probably have their own kit, don't you?' Alex says, looking thoughtful.

The three of them look at each other and laugh and I do too, but a split second behind. It's weird – like being back at school or when you start a new job and you have that new-girl feeling when you've missed the boat a little bit. I watch as Alex, Emma and Becky make themselves fajitas from the food laid out on the table.

'Dig in, Jess,' Becky says, shoving the bowl of guacamole towards me.

I'm still reeling a bit from the unexpected handsomeness of Alex, and trying not to look at him. Except I can't help taking a sneaky look when I think he won't notice, and he glances in my direction and our eyes meet and I think that there's a very strong possibility that I might inadvertently shout 'PHWOAR' by mistake because really he is very handsome indeed and the other two seem to be completely oblivious.

Becky's telling a story about something that happened at work and the two of them are listening and laughing. Becky's always been the most sociable of my university friends. We met in fresher's week and we've been friends ever since. I studied English lit, she studied law, but whereas I left and found myself back in Bournemouth working for a perfectly nice, safe little marketing company, and ensconced in a relationship with Neil, Becks headed to London where she got a job with a law firm and started working her way up the ladder. And then it all went slightly pear-shaped for me back home, and it turned out to be a (mostly) good thing and now, I still can't believe that this – I look out the window at the rainy street below, cars splashing past and the streetlights lighting everything with an orange glow – is my new life.

I let the evening wash over me for a while, and because they're all so chatty, nobody really notices that I'm not saying much. Emma hands me a drink. She's still in work clothes – very neat in expensive-looking boots and a shirt dress printed all over with tiny foxes.

'So. When are you joining us?' she asks.

She's very formal, I think, watching her as I take a sip. Alex and Becky have whizzed up some sort of pomegranate cocktail with the ice and tequila he brought. It tastes like something you'd drink by the pool, instead of on a rainy December evening in London.

'Not until after New Year. I've got a holiday booked with friends – we're going skiing.'

'Ooh, lovely. Christmas skiing.' She looks impressed.

'It's not quite as fancy as it sounds. My friend Gen got a last-minute deal through a contact of hers, so we're going to Val d'Isère on a coach.'

Gen's friend – an actor, like her – was working in a call centre for a travel company when the deal had come through. We'd been making promises to each other for years that we'd go skiing again, after a school trip to Andorra a million years ago, and when this came up it felt like the perfect time. As soon as I'd said yes, the prospect of living every moment on a twenty-one-hour-long coach ride had started to pall slightly, but that was a minor detail.

'Ouch.' Emma looked sympathetic. 'That's a whole day on a coach. Still, it'll be worth it for all the apres-ski and the gorgeous posh ski totty. You might meet a millionaire.'

I steal a quick look in Alex's direction, thinking that actually, I'd be quite happy with someone like him, thank you very much, but give Emma a smile of agreement. 'You never know.'

Becky fiddles with her phone, changing the music. She's wrapped some silvery Christmas ribbon around her head like a halo, and starts singing along as Michael Bublé begins crooning from the speaker on the shelf above the sink.

'Oh God, Becks,' I groan. 'Do we have to have Bublé *again*?'

'It's Christmas,' she says, pulling me up by the waist and waltzing me out of the kitchen door and into the hall. She puts a finger to her lips, shushing me before I can protest. The hall is painted an odd shade, somewhere between violet and grey, and hung with a collection of floral paintings that must've belonged to Becky's grandparents. There's a huge spiky-leaved plant towering over us in the corner by the stairs. I dodge sideways before Becky waltzes me straight into it.

'What d'you reckon?' Her voice is an urgent whisper.

'They seem nice.' I try to sound non-committal when what I want to know is why on earth she'd omitted to mention that one of our flatmates was ridiculously gorgeous. 'How'd you know Emma again?' I ask.

'Oh, she's one of those friend-of-a-friend people. You know, you're in the same pubs, vaguely know each other through a WhatsApp group, that sort of thing. I can't remember how we met in the first place. But she was looking for somewhere because the girl she was flat-sharing was moving her boyfriend in, and I had one room left. I'd already sorted you and Alex—' my stomach does a disobedient sort of swooping thing '—and it just seemed like she'd be a nice addition. Everyone's pretty chilled out, so it should be quite a nice laid-back sort of house.'

'She seems nice,' I say, lamely.

'God, I must pee,' says Becky, and leaves me standing in the hallway.

I hadn't noticed, but the carpet looks like someone threw up on a giraffe – it's yellow and brown with greenish swirls and it clashes so badly with the lilac walls that it must have been the height of fashion at some point in the 1970s. Nobody could choose that colour scheme just randomly, surely?

I head back to the kitchen, realising that I'm feeling a bit fuzzy round the edges. Emma's kicked off her boots now, and she's sitting at the table chatting animatedly to Alex, who is sitting opposite. He pushes out the dining chair next to him, beckoning me to join them.

'Come and get something else to eat.'

He passes me a plate stacked high with tortillas. I think perhaps it'll soak up some of the alcohol.

'So how do you know Becky?' He stretches across the table for the cheese, placing it between me and Emma.

I take a tortilla and spread it with sour cream. 'I feel like I should make something up that doesn't make me sound as tragic as this will.'

Alex raises an eyebrow. He really does have a very nice face. Emma gets up and goes and throws a load of ice and stuff in the blender, shouting, 'Sorry,' as she turns it on, drowning out my words as I'm about to start explaining.

Emma tips a pink slush into our glasses and Alex tastes it, pulling a face. 'Bloody hell, that's like rocket fuel. I'll make the next one, or we'll all end up with alcohol poisoning.'

'We met at uni,' I say, starting again. 'I was crying in the loos because I'd just dumped my boyfriend back home for someone who'd promptly cheated on me a week later.'

Emma laughs, but not unkindly. 'Oh God, we've all been there.' She picks at some slices of red pepper while I'm stacking a tortilla wrap with chicken and cheese and more sour cream, just for good measure. I roll it up and realise there's no way of eating it that doesn't involve half of it falling down the front of my top and

26

the other half spilling all over my chin, so I end up sort of dangling it in mid-air.

'So I took her out, bought her three vodka and limes, and told her the secret was to go out and lay his ghost,' Becky chimes in. I hadn't even noticed her coming back.

'The best way to get over someone is to get under someone else?' Emma says, taking a drink. She's one of those people who manages to just radiate cool. If I'd said that I'd have blushed extravagantly and probably got my words all tangled up into the bargain.

'I think so,' I say. 'I wish I could remember lines like that. I never think of the right thing to say until hours later, when I'm lying in bed reliving the whole conversation.'

'God, me too.' Alex looks at me and does an upside-down sort of smile, and the sides of his eyes crinkle a bit as he looks directly at me. I feel like we're on the same team for a second. It's nice. He lifts up the tequila bottle, waving it in Emma's direction. 'Oh go on,' he says. 'Throw caution to the wind. D'you want to make another one of those – whatever it was you just made?'

I feel like the world is starting to sway gently – or maybe I am. But I'm just the right sort of happily pissed where I feel like the edges have been blurred a bit and I don't feel as self-conscious as I usually do.

The other half a bottle of tequila later and we've managed to persuade Becky to put on something other than Christmas music. We're all sitting round the table, which is scattered with empty plates. The window isn't even open, but we can hear a gang of teenagers passing,

27

singing Christmas carols and laughing loudly. I get up and look outside, marvelling at the idea that outside there are eight million people, all living London lives, and in just a couple of weeks I'm going to be one of them. It's just an ordinary street, but to me it feels full of magic and promise.

I turn around to look at my new housemates. Emma's on her phone again, absent-mindedly twirling a lock of hair around her finger. I notice she has long, manicured red nails.

Alex looks up at me and grins. 'D'you think you can cope with living with us lot?' He starts stacking plates.

'No,' says Becky, firmly, tapping him on the hand. 'I'll do it in the morning. This is a get-to-know-each-other evening. When we're all in and settled, we can sort out a kitchen rota and all that boring stuff, but tonight is margaritas. The night is young. Let's play the name game.'

'Oh my God.' I roll my eyes at her. There's a point in every evening when she insists we do this. Before anyone else realises what's happening, she's got a packet of Post-it Notes out and she's handing them out. 'Everyone has to write the name of someone famous and stick it on the forehead of the person to their left.'

'And to think Rob's missing this,' says Alex, pressing the Post-it Note to my forehead. 'D'you want another drink?'

I feel distinctly head-spinny already, but I nod. This is my new London life. I can drink tequila and have avocado on toast and be cool. Well, cool-ish. Cooler than I was living back home. Not that there's anything wrong with back home, of course. I swallow a little gulp of sadness that sneaks up on me out of nowhere – just thinking about leaving Nanna Beth back there and me being all the way up here. She's already lost Grandpa, and now I'm going, too.

'Oh my God,' says Becky, seeing the name written on my forehead. She snorts with laughter.

'Am I a woman?' I say, when it's my turn.

'You're a phenomenon, I think you'd say,' Alex replies, grinning at me.

Emma guesses hers almost straight away (I think she's pleased she got to be Meghan Markle) and in no time there's just me and Alex, trying desperately to work out who we are.

'Do I have a unique blond hairstyle?'

We snort with laughter.

'Am I a megalomaniac? Am I the best president ever in the history of presidents? Is this the biggest Post-it Note, bigger and better than any Post-it Notes that have ever been before?'

Alex has already guessed, but he's making us laugh so hard with his terrible Donald Trump impressions that we're all doubled over, and mine falls off my forehead and onto the ground where I can't help sneaking a peek.

'Am I . . . Kim Kardashian?' I sit up, triumphant, waving the Post-it Note in the air.

'Yes.' Becky takes it from me. 'You're totally cheating, but you are definitely Kim Kardashian.'

'And I am definitely going to bed.' Emma pushes her

29

chair away from the table and stands up, looking at the kitchen clock. 'It's almost eleven, and I've got a killer day tomorrow. Back-to-back meetings.'

'But how can you leave us when we're just getting started?' Alex is standing by the sink now, brandishing a bottle of Prosecco and some sort of pink liqueur. 'I was going to make one of my signature cocktails.' He rummages in the fridge. I can't help but notice his nice arms again – I've always had a thing about nice arms, the kind that look like they'd wrap you up and make you feel safe. Oh, and the way that when he reaches up to get some orange juice from the top shelf his T-shirt rucks up, showing a strip of faintly tanned skin.

But I am absolutely not looking at any of this, because I am here to work, and he is my new housemate, and there will be none of that here. I blame the tequila for making my imagination run away with me.

But if I *was* looking . . .

'Night, all.' Emma picks up her phone and heads off. 'Have a great holiday, Jess. See you in the New Year.'

'You got any more ice, Becky?' Alex asks as he looks in the freezer.

'Nope.'

I know she's told us not to clear up, but I'm absent-mindedly piling plates and tipping leftover salsa into the bin. It's a distraction. The alternative is sitting with my chin in my hands staring with undisguised admiration at Alex, and that wouldn't be a good look.

'God I'm dying for some chocolate. I tell you what,

30

I'll go get some and grab some ice from Tesco Express while I'm at it.'

'We'll clean up.' Alex stands up from the freezer and turns around. 'And then I'll make cocktails. You don't think Rob will mind that we've borrowed his blender thing to crush ice?'

I pull a face. 'I dunno. I think it's knives chefs are funny about. Anyway, that thing's a monster. As long as we clean it out, I'm sure he won't object.'

Alex pokes an experimental finger at the huge behemoth of a blender standing on the worktop. It roars into life for a second and he steps backwards.

'Bloody hell. That thing could take your arm off.'

'Back in a sec,' Becky says, wrapping a scarf around her face and pulling on a bobble hat.

'Don't freeze,' I say, looking out the window. 'Oh look, the rain's turned to snow.'

'Really?' Alex and Becky join me, looking out. The snow is falling in flurries, swirling in the spotlight glow of the street lamp outside the front of our new home. It's disappearing as soon as it hits the wet pavement, but it looks gorgeously Christmassy and romantic nonetheless. For a moment we all stand in silence, watching it, all lost in our own thoughts.

Michael Blooming Bublé is playing in the background again.

It only takes me and Alex a moment to clear up the table, shoving the rubbish and recycling in the bins, and loading up the ancient dishwasher.

'My last place didn't have one,' Alex says, unwrapping a dishwasher tablet and shoving it in. 'This thing might be prehistoric, but it's a luxury. No more waking up in the morning to last night's dishes.'

'Were you in a house-share before?' I ask.

He pauses for a second. 'Mmm, sort of.'

I get the feeling there's more to it than he's saying, but I don't want to push it.

'And you used to work with Becky?'

I am standing by the sink, rinsing my hands, aware he's standing close beside me and putting glasses back on the shelf. I can feel the heat of his body and it makes the tiny hairs on my arms stand up. This is the tequila talking, I think. Tequila, and the fact that I have been single for a year and the only reason I fancy him is because I've been told there's no relationships allowed in this house so my brain is being contrary. He is Alex, a friend of my friend Becky, and my new housemate. And he is one hundred per cent off limits. I take a step sideways, drying my hands on the dishtowel and spending an excessive amount of time hanging it back up, neatly.

'I used to work with Becky, yeah,' says Alex, after a long pause.

I turn around.

'Turns out that thirty is the perfect time to have my first *oh my God what am I doing with my life* crisis.'

I find myself smiling. 'Me too.'

'So she's found herself a houseful of strays. That's very Becky, isn't it? She likes to think she's all corporate law and hard as nails, but I reckon she's just as much of an old hippy as her mum. So what brings you here?' he asks.

'Oh God. It's a long story.'

Alex takes four limes from the fridge, then passes me two and a kitchen knife. 'Chop these, then, and tell all. It makes me feel better to know I'm not the only one making what everyone thinks is the biggest mistake of my life.'

He's taken a lemon zester and made a stack of bright green furls of lime zest, and he's putting them all together in a little grassy heap. I realise I've stopped chopping and I'm staring at his hands like some sort of weirdo.

'So I did English literature at uni. I've always loved books, and I used to dream of living in London and working in a publishing house, but it just seemed like you had to know someone in the business or have enough money to get an internship and work for nothing, and I had student loans to pay off, and bills to pay, and . . .' I pause, thinking of the responsibility of making sure that Nanna Beth and Grandpa were okay, because my mum was never around. I take a deep breath. 'Anyway, so I'd pretty much given up on that idea – I did look, but the money was terrible, and there was no way I could afford anywhere in London to live that wasn't basically a broom cupboard.'

He laughs. 'I actually know someone who lived in a cupboard. His bed literally folded down at night, then he'd fold it up, close the door, and go off to work.'

'Exactly.' Our eyes meet for a second and we laugh at the idea of it. London is strange.

'And then Becky came along?'

'Not quite. Basically, I was helping look after my grandpa and then he died.'

'Oh.' He turns to look at me, his brown eyes gentle. 'I'm sorry.'

I shake my head and curl my fingers into my palm, because I'm still at the stage where tears sneak up unexpectedly, and alcohol helps them along. 'It's okay. Anyway, my grandma – Nanna Beth – decided that she wanted to move into a sheltered accommodation place, and I'd been staying in their spare room.' I smile, as I always do, thinking about her. Everyone should have a grandma like mine. 'And then – when I'd moved back in with my mother, temporarily, Becky called and asked if I'd be interested in joining her house-share. My Nanna Beth kept telling me I should follow my dreams and do what I really wanted to because we only get one life, and I was trying to convince myself that actually, I was perfectly happy. Then I saw a job in *The Bookseller* – because I couldn't help looking, even though I knew it wasn't ever going to happen – and I thought I'd apply even though I had no chance, and I still can't believe they've given me it. And—' I stop and draw breath. It's all come out in a huge garbled sentence, just the same way that it all happened. 'One minute there I was thinking about it, and wondering how I was going to find somewhere to live and deal with my mother, and then next thing—'

'Here we are. That feels like fate,' Alex says, finishing my spoken and unspoken sentences.

34

'It does, a bit,' I say, trying to make a joke of it. 'What about you?'

'Oh I was all set. Law career on the up, nice – tiny – flat in Stokey, the lot. But I knew something was missing.'

I chop the limes into pieces, waiting for him to carry on.

'Anyway, I kept going for a while, but it was nagging away at me. I went into law to make a difference, but I realised that most of my life was going to be spent behind a desk pushing paper around, and it was boring me to death. And – some stuff happened.' He pauses for a second, and then says. 'And here *I* am.'

'So you're not doing law now?'

He shakes his head. 'No. That's how I knew Becky – we worked together. But unlike most other people, she was brilliant when I told her I was giving up. You need a friend like that on your side.'

'I agree,' I say, thinking of her insistence that I come and stay here, and the ridiculously low rent she'd suggested. I'd looked up Rightmove to see how much it would cost to rent a place like this, and I'd almost fainted. Basically a month's rent for a house this size was my annual publishing salary. When I'd mentioned it, Becky had just snorted and said something about redressing the balance, which had sounded suspiciously like something her mother would have said, so maybe the hippy stuff had rubbed off a bit after all.

'So,' I say, wincing slightly as a bit of lime juice squirts up and hits me in the face. 'What are you doing now?'

'Training to be a nurse,' Alex says.

'No way.' I put down the knife and look at him. 'That's amazing.'

'Yeah.' Alex gives me that same lopsided smile and looks relieved. 'That's not quite the reaction I got when I told people. It was more like: *Oh my God, why are you giving up a job that pays megabucks to be treated like crap, working for a failing NHS?*'

Not only is he gorgeous, but he's noble and ethical as well. He's like a unicorn, or something.

'Well I think what you're doing is brilliant.'

Alex tips the limes into a cocktail shaker and looks at me, his face serious. 'Thanks, Jess.'

I feel a bit wibbly. Like we've had a bit of a moment here together. Like we've bonded.

I pass him a glass, and we drink our cocktails and look out of the window at the Notting Hill street. He looks at me for a moment, just as I'm glancing at him.

For a second, our eyes meet again, and something inside me gives the sort of fizzing sensation that I've read about in books (oh, so many books) and never once felt in real life, not even in the four years I was with Neil, and he and I had talking about getting *married*.

I'm almost thirty, and I'd pretty much accepted that my secret love of terrible, brilliant, curl-up-on-the-sofa romantic movies had somehow cursed me. And yet here I was, looking directly into the chocolate-drop eyes of a man who looked like I'd ordered him online from the romantic movie store.

CHAPTER TWO

Jess

2nd January, Val d'Isère

'You got room in your case for these?'

My oldest friend Gen throws a bulging Tesco bag at me and I miss the catch. It bounces off the bed of the room we've been sharing for the last week and falls to the floor. I bend down to get it and emit a groan of pain. Everything hurts, and my head feels as if someone has hit me with a snowboard. I shouldn't have had that last cocktail last night. Or the one before. I stand up, holding the bag at arm's length. It smells like something died in it.

'What is it?'

'Don't ask.' Gen shakes her head. She should be even more hungover than me, but she somehow manages to look glowing and healthy, her skin bronzed after a week on the slopes where mine is scarlet and wind-chapped.

She's tied her hair back with a band, but spirals of red curls have already escaped and are framing her face. She's wearing an assortment of hideously clashing Nineties-style apres-ski clothes she found in a charity shop, and somehow it looks amazing on her.

I peer inside the bag and hold my nose. 'Ugh, honking ski socks.'

'If they ask if you packed your bag yourself, just say yes,' Gen says.

'And take responsibility for those?' I shove them in a corner of my case. 'They could probably walk home to London by themselves. Actually, I'm going to keep them,' I say, teasing Gen. 'When you're a famous actress, someone will pay a fortune for them.'

'Someone would pay a fortune for them now. There's a whole market for smelly socks on eBay,' says Sophie, who doesn't miss a trick when it comes to money stuff.

'That's disgusting.' I wrinkle my nose at the thought. Being Soph, and therefore revoltingly efficient, she's already got her bag packed, and is sitting cross-legged on her bed, back against the wall, scrolling through her phone. 'Oh my God, Jess, that photo of us you've posted on Instagram is terrible. It looks like one of my legs is about to snap off.'

'It's not that easy to do a selfie on a ski lift,' I say, peering at her screen to remind myself. 'I was convinced I was going to drop the phone into a ravine.'

'Then you could have got Fabien to zoom down off piste and rescue it,' says Gen, making a dreamy face as she mentions our gorgeous ski instructor. 'He definitely had the hots for you, Jess.'

'Shut up,' I groan. She's been going on about it all week, and I still haven't admitted to them that I've been daydreaming – and, if I'm honest, night-dreaming – about Alex, and accidental meetings in the kitchen where I'm dressed in a pair of cute PJ bottoms and a little vest top, my hair knotted up in a messy bun, just reaching into the fridge to get myself a glass of orange juice when his hands are on either side of my waist and he spins me round and looks at me with those incredible eyes and says . . .

'Jess?' Gen nudges me. 'You've been on another bloody planet all week. Come on, spill.'

I shake my head and zip up my suitcase. 'Just thinking, that's all.'

My phone bleeps and I look down at it. Both Gen and Sophie pick up their phones at the same time.

'Delay in coach pick-up,' we read in unison. 'You will now be collected from your hotel reception approximately two hours later than the scheduled time.'

'Oh God,' Soph groans. 'We could have gone skiing this morning after all.'

'Not without skis, we couldn't,' I point out, reasonably. 'We handed them back, remember?'

'Well, we can leave our bags here and go and have one last *vin chaud* at least.'

My stomach gives a warning lurch at the prospect. 'D'you not think we had enough of those yesterday?'

'And the day before, but one more won't hurt,' says Sophie, and we drag our cases down to reception and leave them behind the desk, collecting little tokens in exchange as they're locked away.

Outside there's no sign of the sun and the sky is thick with pale clouds, tinged with the faintest hint of violet. More snow on the way, it said on the forecast, after a week that had been absolutely gorgeous. The sun had shone so brightly that we'd sat at the piste café having lunch outside most days with our ski coats off, listening to the thudding bass of dance music, our skis standing upright in the snow. It feels sad to be leaving Val d'Isère, with its throng of holiday guests, swooshing past in their expensive-looking ski garb, heading up the chair lifts for another day of fun. We take a seat at the little wooden chairs outside the hotel and stretch our legs out in the sunshine. It's strange to be back in normal clothes, after a week of clomping around in heavy ski boots.

Celebrating New Year – and New Year's Day – in a ski resort has been amazing, but my liver feels like it needs to go on a rest cure. Not to mention my legs, which are aching so much I'm walking like a robot, and covered in bruises from a pretty spectacular fall when the aforementioned Handsome Fabien, the instructor we'd clubbed together to pay for, had tried to get us to go down a run that ended with *'une petit noir'*, except his idea of a little black run looked like a vertical drop. Sophie and Gen, who'd had more time on skis than me, managed to make it down in one piece. I'd landed at the bottom, on my bottom, followed unceremoniously by one ski clonking me on the head (thank goodness for helmets) while the other one sailed past, over the edge of the piste and into the trees.

The waiter brings our order – hot chocolate laced with cream and a dash of rum for me and Gen, *vin chaud* for Sophie.

'It's amazing that we're all in the same place at the same time at the beginning of a year,' I say.

'Can't remember the last time that happened.' Sophie twirls a beer mat between her fingers, looking thoughtful. 'Wonder what we'll be doing this time next year?'

'Maybe I'll have had my big break,' says Gen, who has been saying that since she started drama classes back when we were in primary school.

'This is the year,' Sophie says, sounding determined. 'Rich and I are settling down. I'm going to be thirty. It's time. And I'm knocking these on the head, too.' She taps her glass with a neatly manicured finger.

'You're giving up drinking?' I look at Gen, and Gen looks at me, and together we look at Sophie.

'I don't want to take any risks.'

'You're not even thirty. *Nobody* has children when they're this age. You're the only person I know who is like a proper grown-up, Soph,' I say.

Gen nods. 'They'll make the house untidy and you'll have loads of plastic crap everywhere and you'll end up being one of those people who pisses everyone off in Pizza

41

Express because you turn up with a baby that screams the place down when we're all trying to have a nice hangover meal on Tesco points.'

'Thanks,' says Sophie, drily. 'I can't believe you spent so many years working as a mother's help. You're literally the most un-maternal person I've ever met.'

'I am not,' Gen protests, unconvincingly. 'I just don't understand why anyone would want to subject themselves to parenthood.'

'That's what she means,' I say.

'I am still here,' Sophie points out. 'As in sitting right here. Anyway, I won't have the sort of baby that screams in restaurants. If it does, I'll take it outside or something. But I've got it all planned out . . .'

There's a split second where Gen and I look at each other and make a face, and Sophie mutters something unrepeatable under her breath before we all laugh and she carries on. 'I'll get married this year. Then I want three kids and I want them before I turn forty.' She's actually counting this out on her fingers. 'If I have a two-year age gap, that's—'

'Soph, you're so *organised*.' Gen snorts with laughter. 'I don't even have a bloody house of my own, and you're planning everything out. I bet you've got a spreadsheet on Excel with all this stuff.'

'Shut up.' Sophie blushes a bit so we know that she absolutely does.

'Anyway, changing the subject.' Sophie purses her lips, but she's trying not to laugh. 'I'm so excited, Jess. I can't believe we're all going to be in the same city. We can do lunches and go to the cinema and lovely girly stuff.'

'We can help you do fertility dances, or whatever it is you have to do to get pregnant,' says Gen, helpfully.

'Did you miss that class at school?' I say, and Sophie snorts. 'It's not fertility dances that get the job done.'

We all snigger, like we're thirteen again in science class with the biology teacher drawing pictures on the whiteboard.

'Ooh, we could help you find a wedding dress, Soph.' I'm imagining a montage of us, movie-style, all sitting around in the changing room of a wedding shop while she pops in and out with various different flouncy meringues on before she appears, radiant, in The Perfect Dress.

Sophie wrinkles her nose and looks a bit pink in the face. 'I've actually chosen one already.'

'No way.' My vision evaporates.

'Oh my God! I didn't know it was official!' Gen shrieks with excitement.

'It's not. But it's so gorgeous I decided it had to be The One.'

'Oh my God, this is so exciting,' says Gen, clapping her hands together. 'Have you got a photo of it on your phone?'

'I thought marriage was a tool created by the patriarchy to suppress women?' Sophie raises an eyebrow, keeping her phone curled tightly in her palm.

'Yes, yes, it is, but that doesn't mean I can't appreciate

a bit of dressing up, and that's basically what a wedding is, isn't it?'

Sophie opens her phone and scrolls down to show us a photo of the most perfect, understated, gorgeous dress. It's absolutely her, and I can see why she's fallen for it.

'Let's hope Rich doesn't have other plans,' Gen teased.

'Yeah, he might have run off with the girl in the flat next door while I've been away,' Sophie jokes, but we all knew there was no way that would happen. Rich and Sophie were the poster couple – the ones that were solid as a rock, the ones you could always rely on. Gen called them Mum and Dad sometimes, and I think Sophie secretly liked it. She's always wanted to be settled down, ever since we were little and playing together at primary school. Rich is the perfect match for her, and it was always a matter of when, not if, they'd get married. She met him at university and they've been smug (not) marrieds ever since. I reach over and give her arm a little squeeze.

'I'm so pleased for you, Soph. And I can't wait to be on Aunty Jess duty.'

Gen pulls a face, but we both know she's only teasing. She's happy for Soph even though she wouldn't like to be in her shoes. Her passion has always been acting, ever since the first time she stood on stage and played the starring role in *Bugsy Malone* in our primary school production. She's worked her backside off to get where she is – she may not be famous, but she's had a few decent roles in theatre productions off the West End, and it's just a matter of time before she gets her big break. Gen believes in herself, that's half the battle, I think.

'And what about you, Jess?' Sophie looks at me thoughtfully.

'You're not still in mourning after Neil-gate, are you?'

'Gen,' says Sophie, 'if she was, she's hardly going to tell us now, is she?'

I shake my head. 'No, I am one hundred per cent definitely not in mourning over the end of my relationship with Neil.'

'Even though your mum thought he was *the perfect catch*?' Gen looks at me.

I shudder. 'Especially not because of that.'

I hadn't even been that upset when I found out he was cheating on me with someone else from the office – just slightly miffed that it was going to make work pretty awkward. After the initial shock of finding them together, I'd realised that I didn't really feel anything. That was a pretty good sign that it had run its course.

'Your mum just wants you settled down and happy,' Sophie says, kindly.

'Yeah,' I say, 'and she thinks because Neil dumped me for whatshername from accounts that I'm a complete failure as a human being.'

'That's not strictly true,' says Sophie, trying to make me feel better.

'Yes it is,' says Gen, who knows my mother as well as I do. 'She's weirdly fixated on the idea of Jess getting married and buying a nice house and having two-point-four children and a dog. Probably because she did the opposite.'

When I split up with Neil Mum had been absolutely horrified that I'd 'let him slip through my fingers'. I never knew my dad – she's never talked about him, and there's just a blank space on my birth certificate where his name should be – and she's absolutely determined that my life will be far more conventional than hers. It's weird.

'What's she saying about you moving to London?' Gen says.

'She's hoping I might meet a nice man and settle down.'

'Ironic,' Gen snorts, 'that your mother never did it but she wants it for you.'

'It's called transference,' Sophie says, thoughtfully. 'Or something like that. It's about wanting to live her life through yours, vicariously.'

'It's called being a total nightmare,' I say, scooping off some of the whipped cream on my drink with a spoon, and licking it.

'Oh she's not that bad,' says Gen, who has a soft spot for my mother because she's a fellow thespian. My mother's an actress too, but she's never made it to London. Instead she travels a bit, and she tries various schemes to keep money coming in, in between jobs working as a voice-over artist or being an extra on film sets. She's never really been the maternal type. It's lucky I've got my Nanna Beth to make up for it.

'No,' I concede. 'I think it'll be a lot easier to have a relationship with her when I'm ninety miles away in London than when she's breathing down my neck the whole time wanting to know what I'm doing with my life.'

The strange thing about Mum is that despite being unconventional herself, she's completely hooked on the idea of me doing a Soph and getting married, popping out a couple of grandchildren, and finding a nice house in the suburbs. It's weird. It also means she was Not Happy when Neil and I split up, and she thinks my plans for a new life in London are impractical and faintly ridiculous. I quote. Not that I'm still chuntering to myself over her saying it, of course.

'She'll be wanting regular relationship updates,' Gen says.

'There won't be any,' Sophie points out, shooting a quick look at Gen, 'because Becky has decreed that there's to be no relationships in the house.'

'She can't do that.'

'She can do whatever she bloody well wants if she's renting Jess a room in Notting Hill for £400 a month. I'd take a vow of chastity for that.' Gen takes a sip of her drink.

'Yeah but even so—' I watch Sophie giving Gen a fleeting look.

Sophie and Gen have met Becky a few times. They get on okay, in that way that friends do when you try and combine one part of your life with another part. I'm hoping that now we're all going to be in the same place they'll get to know each other a bit more, and even get on a bit.

'She isn't banning me from having sex with anyone,' I say. 'Just that there's to be no inter-house relationship stuff.'

'Just as well. You've got the whole of London at your disposal. You downloaded Tinder yet?' Gen asks. She curls one of her ginger ringlets around her finger, then lets it go so it springs back into place. Gen's never had a bad hair day in her life.

'Ugh, no.' I shudder. 'The thing is I'm not really a Tinder sort of person.'

'Mmm.' Sophie nods. I wonder what she means by that.

I sigh. 'Anyway the thing is there's a bit of a problem with Becky's whole plan. I mean, there's being practical, and then there's – well, do you believe in fate?'

Gen cups her chin in both hands and leans forward. 'Tell me more.'

'I totally do,' says Sophie. 'I mean look at me and Rich.'

I think about the two of them and catch a glimpse of Gen, who doesn't say a word but there's a split second when her nostrils flare, which is always a tell with her, and I know she's thinking *Sophie and Rich*, the most practical couple in the world?

'Come on,' Gen urges. 'Spill.' She looks at Sophie and they look back at me.

'It's not – I mean it couldn't go anywhere. I'm just being silly,' I begin. 'It's, um, Alex.'

'Ahhh,' they say, and exchange another glance.

'What d'you mean, *ahh*?' I cup my hot chocolate in both hands, holding it in front of me defensively.

'Oh, just Alex . . . as in the new housemate you've casually mentioned about fifteen times a day for the last week?' Sophie's eyebrows lift and she gives a snort of laughter.

'No,' says Gen, totally straight-faced. '*Alex*, as in the guy who's training as a nurse and isn't that amazing because he's given up being a *lawyer* to do something that really *matters* . . .'

'Shut up, you two.' I can feel my cheeks are going pink, and put my hands against them so my face is all squashed up, and I make a silly fish face at them to make them laugh and hide my blushes. I feel like I'm about fourteen again.

'Yeah, we wondered how long it'd be before you actually admitted to us that you've got a massive grade-A crush on him. I mean it's been pretty obvious. But—' Gen pauses to beckon the waiter, before asking, 'how does that work with Becky's no-relationships rule in the house?'

'I'm pretty sure that's not enforceable,' says Sophie, her brow furrowing. She's a stickler for rules and regulations and things. She takes out her phone.

'Don't google it,' I say, warningly, and she puts her mobile back on the table, making a face because I've caught her out. 'Becky's totally right. It would never ever work. Plus, I'm starting a new job, and I've got a brand-new life to be getting on with.'

'Yeah, and gorgeous men who wear nurses' scrubs and walk into your life completely out of the blue are ten a penny in London,' Sophie says.

'Totally.' Gen nods, earnestly. 'That's why I've been single for bloody eternity, and why you haven't had sex since Sad Matthew.'

'Don't,' I say, covering my whole face in my hands now. I'd had an accidental one-night stand with Matthew-from-school after Neil and I split up, and every time he got pissed he'd text long, drunken messages telling me how he thought we were the perfect couple, and how it wasn't too late. In the end, I'd blocked him, feeling only about five per cent guilty. The rest of me was deliriously happy to have him out of my hair.

'Anyway. You can't let him just slip through your fingers.' Gen looks up at the waiter and asks for some more drinks and a plate of chips to share. It's half ten in the morning and my stomach contracts with horror at the thought.

'He's hardly going to slip through my fingers. He's sleeping in the room next door.'

'And Becky's on the second floor. She'll never know,' says Gen, waggling her eyebrows. 'You can just sneak into his room after dark. That's quite romantic.'

'Or creepy,' said Sophie, pulling a face. 'Honestly, I'm sure Becky would be fine. Maybe when she said no couples, she probably meant it as in *no couples moving into the flat*, not that you all had to take a vow of chastity when you signed the lease.'

I make a face. I think Becky was pretty bloody unequivocal about it. 'I think that's probably just as well. I think keeping a vow of chastity with him in the room next door might be pretty much impossible.'

I think of Alex reaching up to get something from the cupboard and the sight of his bare skin underneath his T-shirt and the way it felt when I was standing beside him and my arms were all prickly with goose bumps and I give a tiny shiver of anticipation. Maybe when I go back, the best thing to do would just be to get it out in the open. Ask him out for a drink. There's nothing wrong with asking someone out for a drink, is there? And if it happens to lead to something else, well . . .

CHAPTER THREE

Jess

3rd January, London

I think there is a strong possibility that my body is going to be bent into this position forever. We've been on a coach for twenty-one hours, and I can't remember who I am. When I stand up, everything aches. I took a travel sickness pill and I've slept groggily for so long that I have to count on my fingers to work out what day it is. Victoria Coach Station doesn't look any more glamorous at 5.30 a.m. than it does in the middle of the day – in fact, it probably looks worse without people all around. It smells cold and damp and grey, but inside I feel a tiny fizz of excitement that I'm back home – that London, the city I've always loved, is home.

I've done what feels like the scariest thing of all in changing career when I was perfectly safe and secure. My stomach contracts when I think about it and all the things that could go wrong. It's a bit of a weird leap from managing a marketing company to working as Operations Manager for a publishing house where I'll be in charge of making sure books go from finished manuscripts to products on the shelves. It's still weird to think of books as products, if I'm completely truthful. I look at the posters on the bus station hoardings – half of them are for books. Someone like me helped that to happen. It feels like a huge, pretty terrifying responsibility. I swallow and turn back to the girls, who are organising their bags.

'I want ALL the details on what happens when you get back,' Gen says, hugging me goodbye before she hops in an Uber.

'Come for dinner next Friday?' Sophie kisses me on the cheek. Rich's waiting by the road to give her a lift home. Getting up at five in the morning to collect her from the coach is the most Rich thing he could do.

'Sure you don't want a lift?'

I shake my head. There's an early morning bus in ten minutes, and I want to stand up while I wait, stretch my legs, and think about what I'm going to do when I get home. And then I beam with happiness at a flock of unsuspecting pigeons. I think this year is going to be pretty bloody amazing.

Even though I'm so tired I feel like a zombie I can't help smiling to myself as the bus makes its way along the streets. London looks so pretty, dusted with the finest icing-sugar coating of frost. It sparkles on the top of stone walls and expensive-looking black railings, making the red telephone boxes look picture-postcard pretty. This is home. I squeeze my arms around myself, because I can't quite believe it's true. I feel warm and sleepy in my thick ski coat. My head leans against the cool of the bus window and I watch the city coming to life.

Two early-morning runners, clad in thermals with reflective stripes, zoom past as we wait for a traffic light to turn from red to green. Christmas trees still light up the windows of houses, which makes me happy. I always feel sad for the trees I see lying waiting for collection on the kerbside, piled up with heaps of black rubbish bags. When I have a house of my own, I'm going to have a tree in every room and the whole place lit up with millions of tiny, starry white lights. I think about growing up and how I used to decorate my bedroom, and how my mum couldn't wait to take the decorations down because she hated the mess and how Nanna and Grandpa used to make up for it with a tree they always let me decorate, hung with trinkets I'd made at primary school and riotous rainbows of tinsel. And then as we turn down into Church Street, my mind skips forward, imagining this time next year, and all of us celebrating Christmas in the house in Albany Road. Rob could cook – there had to be an advantage to living with a chef, surely – and I'd be there, dressed in something clinging and sexy, and—

I look out of the window, and realise I'm at Ladbroke Grove. After I get off the bus, I grab my bag and bump it along the street, the wheels sounding loud in the early morning silence. And then I turn the corner, and there's the street sign that announces I'm home. Albany Road. I live in London now, I say to myself quietly, stepping back to take it all in.

'Watch it!'

A man looms out of nowhere on a bike and speeds off, his wheel lights flashing. He's muttering something and I don't think it's very polite, somehow. But nothing is going to take the tarnish off this moment. The house is in darkness and I climb the stone steps, lifting the suitcase up so it doesn't make a noise. I'm aware that it's early and I don't want to wake anyone up. I stand at the huge red-panelled door for a moment.

I turn the key in the lock and open the door slowly. There's a sidelight on in the hall, and a pile of junk mail on the wooden dresser. Hanging on a hook there's a battered straw hat covered in tinsel. There's a tired-looking plastic Christmas tree, and three empty wine bottles that look like they've been dumped on the floor by the door, waiting to go out in the recycling bin. The house smells of stale beer and leftover pizza, like a student flat. I guess the New Year celebrations must have been ongoing. I creep upstairs and open the door to my room. Becky has made up the bed (I love her so much for that at this moment that I could run upstairs and hug her, but something tells me she wouldn't appreciate that) and the curtains are drawn.

I dump my case and my bag, and sit down on the edge of the bed for a moment. I feel completely wide awake, and as I sit there I realise that next door, with

56

only a wall between us, is Alex. And – I hear a clonking noise, and the sound of footsteps – I realise he's awake. I could go and say hi. That would be perfectly normal, if he's awake. I mean admittedly it's – I check my watch – quarter past six in the morning, but maybe he's an early bird. I might just pop to the loo, and if I happen to bump into him . . . well, that's just coincidence, isn't it? Totally normal coincidence.

(Yes, I'll check my face in the mirror while I'm in there, wipe the eyeliner smudges from underneath my eyes, and fluff up my hair. I do that every time I go to the loo. Doesn't everyone?)

I open my bedroom door, and his door opens at exactly the same time. My heart gives a massive thump against my ribcage. This is *meant to be.*

And then *Emma* walks out, and heads towards the bathroom. She doesn't turn around, so she doesn't see me, and as the bathroom door closes I recoil backwards into my room like a snail into its shell, then floomp onto the bed with a groan. Why on earth is Emma coming out of Alex's room? If they've swapped bedrooms, that means he's across the other side of the stairwell, and I've been stealthily listening to her getting ready for work. She's exactly the sort of person who *would* get up at six a.m. She's probably done yoga already, and now she's going to drink some green juice and meditate before she does an hour of paperwork then goes into the office. She's a proper grown-up.

And then I realise that I'm still desperate for the loo,

so I stand up and open my bedroom door, just as Emma walks out of the bathroom.

'Oh! Jess. Hi,' she says in a whisper, smiling with her perfect teeth. 'Have you just got back? Did you have a lovely time?'

'It was amazing,' I say, and then I open my mouth again to ask if they've swapped rooms in my absence, and close it when I realise that she's walking past me, in a kimono-style dressing gown made of some sort of swishy silk material, and heading for the bedroom at the end of the hall. Her bedroom.

I lean back against the door of my room, and it sinks in. Emma, our beautiful housemate, has spent the night with Alex.

CHAPTER FOUR

Alex

3rd January

Oh. My. God. My head feels like someone used it as a punchbag. I reach down the side of the bed where Past Me has thoughtfully left half a bottle of Coke. It's completely flat and tastes like crap, but it washes down the double dose of ibuprofen and paracetamol I'm hoping might crack this hangover. What the hell was I thinking last night? Today's going to be a killer – a twelve-hour shift in A&E, full of half-pissed Christmas casualties (and that's just the staff). Oh bollocks – and I've just remembered that effing assignment I was supposed to do last night on Modern Nursing Practices and the *Something of Something*.

I rub my chin. And I need to get my beard sorted before I tip over into looking like someone who's been lost in a cave for a month. God, I should've been working that essay last night and yet instead I found myself sharing a bottle of red with Emma. And another one. And – I open one eye carefully, because it feels like someone's shining lasers in my direction – how the hell did I end up in bed with her, when I'd made a resolution that the last time was the Last Time? Capital letters, no going back.

I stumble to the bathroom and stand under the shower for ages, trying to wash off the hangover and straighten my head out. I didn't even mean to start something with Emma. In fact – I run my hands through my hair and groan again – it's probably best to not think of it as a *something* at all. Definitely not the sort of something that would get in the way of Becky's no-couples rule. After all, we're just two people, who'd ended up in a bit of a situation, and who were looking for the same thing. People do that sort of thing all the time.

Not me, admittedly, because I've never been a one-night stand sort of guy, but then – well, that all got screwed up last year when Alice walked out and I swore I was going to focus on work and absolutely definitely not on relationships. Not that I was planning on being a player or anything – that's not me, either. Just that I was going to focus on work, and studying, and leave the complications out of it. That's why Becky's no-relationships rule didn't make me flinch, even if it did seem a bit weird. To be honest with you, I'd have taken a vow of chastity for the next five years if it meant I could get a place like this for the ridiculously low rent she was willing to take.

Just as well she didn't make me take one, mind you. I switch off the shower and think back on how it all happened as I'm drying myself off.

I'd been working a late shift, and when I'd got home at eleven the house was empty. Rummaging through the fridge, I'd found a beer, cracked it open and sat down at the table, scrolling through my phone. The thing was just about falling over with a million notifications from friends – half of whom I hadn't heard from in ages because of the whole Alice thing – sending mass WhatsApp invites to New Year's celebrations. The old me would've been up for it, but the new Alex – wrecked after a night working supply as an HCA on A&E – couldn't think of anything worse. As I went to put my phone down, another notification had buzzed through. It was a text from Jonno:

We're in the Pig and Bucket. Come and find us when you've finished playing doctors and nurses. Fizz on ice.

Oh, piss off, I thought, and chucked the phone across the table. The joke was wearing a bit thin at this point. I've heard a million and one variations on the doctors and nurses theme, countless boring jokes about male nurses, and I still get the odd bemused message from former uni friends who'd heard through the grapevine I'd given up a perfectly good burgeoning law career to retrain as a nurse.

'Hi,' Emma had said, and I'd looked up. I had to admit she looked pretty bloody amazing. The cut of the dress emphasised the curve of her waist and cinched her breasts up so they were balanced, like two scoops of ice cream, spilling over the top of her dress. I looked away rapidly. Note to self: do not look in direction of chest. I stared down and picked at the label of my beer. She threw her keys on the table and sat on a chair, looking disconsolate.

'Bad night?' I asked.

'Shitty.' She screwed up her face. 'I hate New Year. Too much enforced jollity.'

'D'you want a beer? I think there's a couple left in the fridge.'

She nodded. 'Yes please.'

I got up, fetching one for her and another for me out of the fridge, and cracking them open.

She hooked a long strand of hair back behind her ear, and took a sip of beer from the bottle. 'I knew it would be a disaster. Work friends, and a load of people I didn't want to see. Well, one person, to be completely honest.' She grimaced again. 'My ex.'

God I could sympathise there. I'd been avoiding all social gatherings where there was a chance I'd bump into Alice for ages now. It made the whole division of friendships thing quite easy, mind you. Alice got pretty much everyone, and I got – well, most of them were work colleagues, so it wasn't a major deal. And I'd made a couple of good friends on the course, which really helped . . .

'Sorry, you were saying?' I said, realising I'd drifted into my own thoughts. 'So you work with him? That must be awkward.'

Emma pulled a face. 'Sort of. He's in the same building, and our companies work side by side, so he's always sort of – there. Which is how I ended up in a relationship with him. But he's still very married, despite his insistence that he was going to leave her.'

'Oh God, that old line.'

'Yeah. Exactly.' She fiddled with her keys, spinning each one round on the ring, before putting them carefully back on the table. 'Anyway, much as I am over him – and I am . . .'

As she trailed off, I raised my eyebrows, giving her a look. 'Really?'

'Totally. But you know what? Not the sort of over him that I want to spend my New Year's Eve watching him with his wife, drinking champagne and casting glances in my direction. I'm not some bit on the side, which is what I told him in the first place. Anyway.' She took another swig of beer, then got up, heading for the fridge. 'It's almost midnight. We can celebrate here, instead.'

She pulled out a bottle of champagne. I'd seen it in the fridge and wondered who owned it – my guess was right. Emma looked like the sort of person who'd drink posh champagne. Becky was a tequila girl, Rob would have to be around at some point to have left champagne in the fridge, and so far he hasn't been, and Jess hadn't moved in yet. The champagne was an expensive brand, the kind we used to open to celebrate successes in the office. Now I was on a student loan though, and living on my savings, it was beer all the way. Cheap beer, at that.

'Want some?'

I nodded. 'Yes please.'

She found two glasses and popped the cork. 'Let's put some music on. Alexa, play some New Year's music.'

'Here's a playlist for New Year's music,' said the speaker. Ed Sheeran started playing and we both shouted 'Alexa, stop!' at the same time, laughing.

'I'll find something on my phone,' Emma said.

A couple of glasses – and some debate over Emma's dodgy taste in music – later, we decided to go through to the sitting room to watch the New Year celebrations on television at midnight. As if by agreement, we both flopped down on the sofa. Emma kicked off her heels and curled up her legs underneath her. In the background, a band was playing music at Edinburgh Castle with a horde of familiar TV faces standing at the side of the screen, trying to look animated. They were clearly freezing cold.

'So what about you?' Emma said. 'I know you said you were living with someone before. Are *you* still friends?'

I gave a groan and stretched my arms out above my head until various joints creaked. I really needed to get to the gym. 'Not really,' I replied.

'Hard, isn't it? I don't know many people who stay friends with their ex.'

'Yeah.'

Emma poured another glass of champagne for us both. 'The thing is, Alice signed up for the lawyer boyfriend, lots of money, and a nice house.' I looked around at the tattered Seventies décor and raised my eyebrows at Emma. 'This isn't exactly her sort of thing. We had a place in Stoke Newington – a nice little flat. It was pretty much all mapped out – two-point-four children, dog, cat, move out to the suburbs eventually . . .'

'Ugh,' Emma said, making a face. 'That sounds like hell.'

'Everyone says that,' I said, spinning my glass round on my knee, slowly. 'Thing is, I think I'm a bit of a romantic at heart. I wanted the whole thing.'

'That's quite sweet,' Emma said. 'Even if it's my idea of hell. I don't even like being responsible for a potted plant.'

'Yeah, well, we were engaged and everything. Then we had some family stuff happen, and I realised that actually I didn't want to carry on doing law. I wanted to do something that made a difference. That's how I ended up getting into nursing.'

'That's fair enough.'

'Yeah. Not for Alice, it turned out. She'd had our future all mapped out, and my giving up the well-paid job with prospects for a career in a failing NHS wasn't on her to-do list.'

'So when you gave up on law, she gave up on you?'

'Yeah,' I said, and took a large swig of champagne. 'Pretty much.'

Emma reached over, putting a hand on my leg. 'I'm sorry. That's pretty brutal.'

'Thanks,' I said, and looked down at Emma's hand, which hovered there for a second. And I'd like to say that we carried on watching the television and then went to our separate beds after the bells struck midnight and that was that. But no. Turned out I was only human, after all, and that after a bottle of champagne and some sort of dodgy liqueur from the back of the kitchen cupboard, and some pretty direct flirting from Emma, my resolve to stay celibate and focus completely on my studies was – well, it wasn't as steely as all that. And afterwards, when I was lying on the bed watching her fastening her bra and slipping the impossibly tight red dress back on, Emma had turned to me and smiled.

'Nobody needs to know this ever happened,' she'd said.

'Not a soul,' I'd agreed. 'Becky would murder us, for one thing.'

'Nice though,' she'd said, and given a wicked little smile that had made me want to pull her back into bed.

Bloody hell.

And then last night it happened *again*.

I wipe the mirror in the bathroom and look at myself through the condensation. Still look like the same old me – bit knackered, perhaps, because I've been up shagging half the night – but no, definitely still the same old Alex. I raise my eyebrows at Mirror Me and suppress a snort of laughter. It's the most out-of-character thing I've ever done. I try and imagine the faces of Jack and Lucy when I tell them. Jack and Lucy are my two best friends back home in Canterbury (who conveniently got off with each other a couple of years back, meaning that now they live together and I can see both of them in one go when I go back to visit). They're always telling me to get on dating apps and have a rebound shag to get over Alice. Well, I guess I've done it. Didn't even have to download Tinder.

I wrap the towel round my waist and head back to my bedroom, opening the window even though it's freezing cold outside. It's ridiculously early in the morning and the house is almost completely silent, but I can hear noises, I think. Sounds like someone's moving boxes in the room next door. Jess? I check the calendar hanging on the wall. God, yes, it's the third. She must've arrived overnight – I put a hand over my mouth – God, I hope she didn't arrive when we were . . .

No. We'd have heard the door, wouldn't we? She must've arrived when I was in the shower.

I pull on jeans and a clean T-shirt, running my hand back through my hair to shove it into place. Even if Jess had heard, she wasn't likely to say anything. It didn't have to be a big deal. Even if I have to have a conversation with Becky about the whole no-couples thing . . . well, it's not like we're actually a couple.

This is all completely new ground for me, though, and it's weird. Jack and Lucy always took the piss out of me for being an old romantic, but the thing is, what happened with Alice really took the wind out of my sails. I loved her, and I thought we were going to do the whole married, house, kids, dogs thing – especially the dogs, I've always wanted a golden retriever – but it floored me completely when she told me it was over. I was a complete mess for ages, but I've got a grip now. I'm just not putting myself in that place again for a long time. Relationships are not for me.

I'm glad Jess is back. Now the house is full, it feels sort of . . . complete, somehow. I'm sure she said she's not starting work until the second week of January. Maybe I'll see if she fancies coming for a walk tomorrow, to find her feet a bit. It'll be nice to have a friend who's a girl, and not a girlfriend. I miss Lucy's point of view on things – since she and Jack got together they basically come as a package.

I lace up my boots and I think about Jess chopping limes and chatting to me in the kitchen. Grudgingly, I have to admit to myself that in another life, Jess would be completely my type. She's funny and she's interesting, and I love the fact that she's doing the same as me: taking the plunge to try something new and start life over again. It'd be good to have a partner in crime. It makes it seem less terrifying, somehow.

CHAPTER FIVE

Jess

10th January

'What's with you and the whole Instagram thing?' Alex asks.

He's walking behind me on a narrow pavement in Covent Garden when I stop dead. He almost crashes into the back of me. I turn around, before he's stepped back, and we're so close we're almost touching. I stumble backwards, knocking into the wooden shutter of the cheese shop.

'Sorry,' I say, but he's laughing.

'It's fine. I just . . . What're you even taking a photo of?'

I motion to the alleyway to our left. 'I love stuff like that. Little hidden doorways and things.'

'Right.'

'Let me just . . .' I fiddle with the phone then hit share. 'Sorry. Done now.'

'Shall we stop for lunch?' he asks.

'Yeah.' I point to the sign that beckons us through the little alleyway. 'There's a café upstairs there, in Neal's Yard.'

We climb the stairs, which are rainbowed with a million postcards and posters, advertising everything from toddler gymnastics to Chakra Rebalancing.

'D'you get your chakras rebalanced often?' Alex grins.

'Never. That's probably why I'm so clumsy.'

'Maybe they should start offering it on the NHS.'

The café's cramped and the staff seem slightly frazzled, which feels at odds with the whole hippy Zen vibe it's giving off from the signs outside. We find an empty table. The uneven walls are painted with thick white paint, and woven hangings are displayed on a rail with price tags underneath. I lean forward, thinking I must have read it wrong, but no.

'They want £120 for that?' I nudge Alex and his eyes widen in surprise. He passes me a menu. We both look at it in silence for a moment.

'Hi, people,' says a tall woman with her braids tied back in a thick ponytail. 'Do you need time to have a think, or are you ready to order?'

I catch Alex's eye and I can tell he's trying not to laugh, because the menu is – well, it's not Starbucks, that's for sure.

'Can we have a couple of moments?'

'Sure. I'll leave you some of this for now. It's rose-quartz-infused water.'

She puts a carafe down on the table. There's a pink crystal sitting at the bottom of it. We both contemplate it for a moment before Alex drops his head in his hands.

'If we weren't so bloody British, we'd get up and leave,' he says.

'I know.'

'Instead, we're going to have to have a rice milk latte and a—' he looks down at the menu and frowns '—spiralised courgette and carrot hummus open sandwich on pressed raw grain bread?'

'I dunno, I quite fancy the radish and sprout salad,' I say.

'I want a cinnamon and raisin bagel, and a large bucket of coffee.'

I groan at the thought of it. 'I wouldn't say no to a bacon roll.'

'Maybe we could get one on the way back.'

'Ready to order?' The woman has returned, and – being too polite to leave – we request our food, then sit back and look at the clientele. There's a woman with two scruffy-haired children who've been freed from their pushchair. They're climbing over the cushions on the bench to draw pictures with thick crayons.

'Cute.' Alex looks over at them.

'I bet they're called Hephzibah and Moon Unit, or something.' I take a look at them, trying not to catch their eye in case they come over and start making conversation. I find small children slightly alarming.

'No way.' Alex shakes his head. 'Myrtle and Theodore,

and they go to a Steiner school and her husband earns shitloads working as an investment banker.'

'Like the ones next door to us? You reckon?'

'Totally.'

We've seen the family from next door going in and out a few times. They've got two nannies, I think, and a gardener, and a fleet of cleaning people who come in every morning. The children go off to school wearing the kind of expensive-looking woollen coats and hats that suggest they're at a posh private school.

'They must think we're lowering the tone, don't you think?'

Alex grins. 'What, Becky and her random collection of low-rent waifs and strays?'

After the waitress brings our food, Alex takes a bite of his open-topped sandwich and makes a face. 'God, this is disgusting.'

'It is a bit weird,' I say, picking a radish off the top of mine and biting into it. It's got some sort of lime dressing on it. I steer the conversation back to Becky and the house. 'I don't think Becky knows what to do with the house, so it seemed like the easiest thing to do.'

'Have you looked at the price of houses on our street?' Alex raises an eyebrow.

I nod. 'Have you?'

'She's like – literally beyond your wildest dreams rich. She could sell that and give up work forever.' He sits back, giving up on the sandwich.

'Not if she wanted to live in London.' I carry on dissecting my food.

'True. Anyway we better not go putting ideas in her head when we've just signed a lease, or we'll be screwed. There's no way I could afford a place in central London on what I've got.'

'Me neither.'

We sit back in silence, watching the children as they try and climb out of their chairs and escape.

It's only been a week, but Alex and I have got into a bit of a routine with our Exploring London walks. He's had some time off, and it's been nice to wander about and find my bearings a bit. I still reckon I could get lost quite easily, but I'm beginning to join bits of the city up and make sense of it. My first day is next Monday – and I'm being extremely noble about the fact that there's *something* going on with him and Emma. Although I'm not sure what that something is – I haven't heard any more nocturnal happenings but I can't be sure. I'm just repressing all thoughts about how gorgeous he is.

He gets up to use the loo, climbing out of the tiny space in the corner where our table's situated. A woman with a baby in a backpack asks him to help reach the highchair that is hanging folded on the wall behind us, and I try very hard not to notice as he reaches up, showing a strip of slightly tanned skin and the edge of his boxers peeking out underneath his jeans. Okay, I've repressed *almost* all thoughts. I am human, after all, and living with the nicest man you could imagine who just happens

73

to be sleeping – on the quiet – with one of your other housemates isn't quite as easy as you'd think. I grit my teeth and make a face, surprising the waitress, who looks at me with a confused expression.

CHAPTER SIX

Jess

14th January

The office of Elder Branch Publishing is smaller than I remember from my interview. Or maybe I just expanded it in my imagination in the six long weeks between being offered the job and waiting to start. Anyway, the nice thing is that it's as bookish as I remember. And when I walk in, an office full of heads shoot up, meerkat-style, and my face goes very red.

'Ah, Jessica,' Veronica greets me. Veronica is the publisher, which I've learned means she's basically where the buck stops. She's very nice, very posh, and very busy. I don't correct her and tell her it's Jess, because she's quite fierce and I'm extremely nervous.

'So, as you'll know, as Operations Manager you're responsible for keeping all the publications on track, but of course you got the job, so we can be certain that you're going to be absolutely wonderful. This is Sara. She'll show you the ropes.'

Sara gives me a tour of the office. She's tall and thin, in a flowery dress, and opaque mustard-yellow tights that match her cardigan. In fact everyone in the office seems to be wearing a variation on the same outfit. Most of them are in a meeting, but the handful I've met have that shiny, expensive-looking hair that comes from being well-nourished and brought up with lots of healthy outdoor activities. They've all got the same accent too – sort of home counties crossed with London – and I'm feeling distinctly suburban. Sara's hair is held back from her face with a Kirby grip, which she takes out and puts back in about five times in the process of our conversation.

'So, basically your job is just to make sure you keep all of us in line, hahaha,' she snorts, as if the idea is slightly unlikely.

'Not all of us are as disorganised as you,' says a voice from the other side of my desk. A head pops up. 'Hiya. I'm Jav.'

She's tall and slender in a pair of black trousers and a jade green tunic, her long black hair hanging down her back. Her desk is neatly stacked with books and thick printed manuscripts, a pencil case from The Strand bookstore in New York, and a reusable coffee cup. It looks exactly like you'd expect an editor's desk to look.

'Jess,' I reply, with a little wave.

'Jav likes to put us all to shame by terrifying her authors into delivering on time.'

Jav raises her eyes skyward. 'I just happen to be efficient, that's all.'

Unlike the rest of my colleagues, she's got an accent from somewhere up north – Manchester or somewhere around there – and I warm to her instantly. Not just because she's efficient, although I have to be honest and admit that's a bit of a plus. I've been used to working at my own pace in the past, and I'm a bit apprehensive about my work performance now hanging on whether a manuscript gets delivered on time or if a publishing schedule goes awry. I swallow and try and look as if I'm super confident.

Sara steps back and gives a ta-dah sort of wave in the direction of my desk. It's empty, with a desktop computer and a leftover stack of Post-it Notes sitting beside the keyboard. Someone's already left me three proof copies of books that aren't out until next summer. I look at the covers and can't help thinking how nice it would be to climb into one of them and—

'Right,' I say, tapping the top of my desktop monitor in what I hope is an authoritative manner, 'I better get to work.'

'I've left email logins on a Post-it Note – you can change your password and stuff, obviously, and there's a meeting about the Tiny Fish publicity campaign at half ten. You should pop in, meet the rest of the team.'

Jav pushes her chair sideways when Sara leaves, and swings herself round.

'Just shout if there's anything you need.' She tucks a stray lock of black hair back behind her ear. 'I know it's

a bit scary on the first day, especially when you're not
– well—' she lowers her voice '—one of the posh lot,
but they're all very sweet really.'

'Oh God. How did it go?' Becky drops her bag beside
me on the kitchen table with a crash. I'm sitting with my
head in my hands, my hair hiding my face, so I can see
why she's thinking the worst. I lift my face up to see her
looking at me, head on one side, like a concerned sparrow.

'Oh, it was fine. I'm just so tired that I can't move.
You know what it's like when you start a new job –
you've got so much stuff to remember and your brain
gets overloaded. I could literally fall asleep here.'

'That's not a good idea,' she says, briskly. 'We're
supposed to be going to Pilates, remember?'

'Oh my God. I can't.'

'It'll be good for you.'

'I don't want to engage my core and strengthen my
glutes. I want to lie on the sofa with a tub of Ben and
Jerry's and watch crap on TV.'

'You can do that afterwards. It's not on until nine.'

'You know what I mean.'

She hooks me under the elbow and tugs me up to
standing. 'Come on, I'm not going on my own. Last time
I did that creepy Charles tried to hit on me afterwards.'

'FINE,' I say, yawning so hard my jaw cracks.

The thing about living in Notting Hill is that even the
most basic gym class is super posh. There's a string of
black Range Rovers parked outside the fitness studio,

and inside everyone's Lululemoned from head to toe. I'm in a bog-standard pair of sports leggings from JD Sports and a vest top, so I hide at the back of the room so nobody notices me, taking a yoga mat and parking myself in the corner beside a young mum who has a sleeping baby in a carrier. Becky's standing at the door answering a last-minute call when the instructor walks in.

'Hello, everyone.' She's a cheerful looking Australian woman of about forty-five, with the figure of an eighteen-year-old. Her buttocks are so perky that they look like they need their own morning TV show. She tosses her water bottle to the side of the room and claps her hands. Her ponytail swings. Oh God, I think, this is shaping up to be a torture session.

'Now then,' she says, giving me a welcoming smile. 'We're going to shake things up slightly this evening, for those of you who like to hide in the corners. Pull your mats back a couple of feet.'

Everyone does as they're told. There's a very quiet murmur of dissent, but nobody's brave enough to speak up.

'Excellent. So the back row is now the front row, and the front row is the back.' She looks very pleased with herself.

I don't know who's more disappointed – the Lycra-clad goddesses who like to show off in front of everyone, or the scruffy reprobates like me who are now centre stage. I'm pretty certain my knickers have gone up my bum and now I can't hoick them back out.

I haven't been to a gym class since school, when Miss Bates the terrifying PE teacher used to make us do yoga with a side order of military-style barked instructions. Now I'm standing beside my mat wondering what exactly I'm expected to do.

We start off lying down, and it all seems very restful and soothing. But the next thing I know we're on our sides doing something with our legs that's making me want to cry. I'm not the only one. Just as we shift positions, the baby starts screaming at the top of his lungs, and there's a brief – but oh God, much appreciated – pause as his mother hisses an apology and gathers him up and exits, trailing muslin cloths and water bottles, her yoga mat unravelling behind her. I eye the clock. Another half an hour to go and then I can escape.

'Keep those heels together. We want to feel those glutes engaging,' she says, cheerfully.

My glutes feel like they've been set on fire and I don't think I'll ever be able to sit down again. This is torture.

It's possible it'll go down in history as the longest half hour of my life. I've seen Pilates classes before, and I always thought they looked pretty gentle – like exercise classes for people who can't be bothered getting all sweaty. Except now I'm lying face down on the floor with my arms by my sides, doing what looks like the tiniest little movement. I wait until the instructor has passed by me and flop my arms down onto the mat, and lie there quietly, like roadkill.

Next morning, I wake up with the alarm and sit up with a yelp of pain.

Last night, as we'd walked home Becky had said, cheerfully, 'You're not going to be able to walk tomorrow.'

Bloody *hell* she wasn't joking.

'You all right?'

I bump into Alex as he's coming out of the bathroom, wrapped in a grey dressing gown. He's towelling his hair and looking amused.

'No I am not all right. Becky took me to a torture chamber last night and now I can't actually walk, and I've got three meetings in a row this morning.'

'You need to come for a walk to loosen yourself up. You free on Friday afternoon?'

I nod. 'Ow.'

'It hurts to nod?'

Stupidly, I nod again. 'Apparently. Ow. Anyway, yes I am free. Well, I'm working, but we all get Friday afternoons off to work from home, so . . . as long as I catch up over the weekend, I think that's fair enough.'

Alex looks at me, one eyebrow cocked slightly.

I press my lips closed. God, I can't half go on. 'Yes.'

'Excellent. I'm free at one. Want to meet me here and we can go for a wander?'

CHAPTER SEVEN

Alex

18th January

I meet Jess after lunch. She's still in work clothes – a pair of dark grey trousers, black boots and a soft red jumper, which is an improvement on my work uniform. I've been living in scrubs for the last week on a placement in the paeds ward, and it wasn't until I got home last night that I realised I had a teddy bear sticker stuck to the side of my beard. I'd like to think nobody noticed, but knowing the staff of Paddington Ward, I suspect they thought it was amusing.

'You okay?'

'Yes,' she says, but it's in that sort of brittle, not very convincing kind of way.

'What's up?'

'Just one of those days. Loads of work stuff.'

'We don't have to do this if you'd rather get on?'

She shakes her head. 'No, I need the fresh air. Just that first week of work thing. I feel like I haven't a clue what I'm doing.'

We start walking.

'So how did you end up knowing your way round London so well?' Jess asks as she pulls her hat down a bit further on her head. It's weird that January's often colder than December – even though December is the month most associated with winter and snow. It feels a bit like it might snow now – the sky's a funny sort of yellow-grey colour.

'My dad worked here for years. He used to get the train up, and when I was old enough I'd come up with him in the holidays and just sort of wander around.'

Jess looks at me sideways like I'm a weirdo. 'On your own?'

I pull a face. 'Yeah.'

'That is a *bit* weird. What did you do?'

'I wanted to be an architect like him. So I'd wander about and look at stuff. I always had a Travelcard, so I could go wherever I wanted – within reason. Plus I wasn't a baby – I was fifteen, sixteen.' I tail off a bit. It does sound a bit weird, come to think of it. 'Anyway. The good thing is that I didn't become an architect, because it turns out I'm pretty hopeless at precision stuff.'

'That's good to know. I'll avoid you if you're wielding a scalpel in future.'

'You know what I mean. Architecture's all about the detail. I'm more slapdash and that'll do.'

She grins at me. 'All right. So how did you go from

wannabe architect to lawyer to student nurse?' she asks.

'Ah.' We pause and wait for the lights to change at a crossing. There's a coffee shop opposite. 'I'm dying for a coffee. Shall we get one to take out?'

'Sure.'

Two takeaway lattes later, we set off again. I'm explaining how I fell into studying law because it seemed like a sensible thing to do, and Jess is nodding vigorously.

'That's like me with the marketing job. I finished my degree and went back home to work out what to do, and I saw the advert and the next thing I knew I'd applied.'

'And then you got the job and the next thing you knew the rest of your life was all mapped out?'

She nods again. 'Exactly!'

'That's what happened to me. I thought I'd do law, then maybe do a postgrad in something else, do a job that made a difference. But I kind of got caught up in the whole job thing by mistake, and of course I'd met Alice by then . . .'

'Your girlfriend?'

'Ex.'

'Sorry. That's what I meant.'

'And it just all sort of slotted together. And it would've been fine, except then my dad got sick, and then he died.'

'Oh.' Jess puts a hand on my arm as we stop at another crossing. She squeezes it gently. 'I'm sorry.'

I shake my head. It's taken me time to be able to talk about it so calmly. There were times when someone being kind would bring tears springing to my eyes. Grief is weird like that. But now I feel like – well, I guess I've made my peace with it. And somehow, I feel like Dad would be quite impressed that I'd decided to do something I felt passionate about, just like he did.

'It's okay. But the thing was, watching him, it made me realise I'd always wanted to do something that was going to make a difference and sitting in an office doing corporate law shit wasn't going to do that. The nurses in the oncology unit – they were amazing when my dad was in their care.'

We've stopped now, and somehow we're sitting on a wooden bench that looks down Elgin Avenue. Buses trundle past and heave to a halt at the stop a few metres away, spilling out a sea of people who scatter in different directions in the late afternoon greyness. It's so cold I can see Jess's breath as she looks at me over the top of her coffee cup.

'So, that's what made you want to do it?' she asks.

'Yeah.' I take a sip of almost-cold coffee, make a face and lower it again. 'Only it turned out that unravelling the life I'd made wasn't as easy as all that.'

'Tell me about it. So, what happened?'

'Well, I got talking to one of the Macmillan nurses after Dad died when she was picking up some of the stuff we'd had at the house – equipment, and things like that. I thought she'd think I was crazy, but it turned out she'd only done her training a few years before herself – and she was almost forty.'

'So you jacked in your high-flying career and got a place at uni.'

'And now here I am. I mean, it wasn't that much of a high-flying career, to be fair. And I had some savings and some money that Dad left me, so I thought I might as well just go for it.'

'Exactly.' I notice Jess is sitting with her hands inside her sleeves. It's cold, and sitting still makes it seem even more so. 'Shall we keep going?' Jess stands up.

'Where are we going? The suspense is killing me,' Jess says.

We turn the corner and I nod my head towards the sign on the edge of the road. It's a second before she gets it.

'Abbey Road? Like the Beatles' Abbey Road?'

'That's the one.'

'I didn't even know it was a real thing.' She laughs.

'Ah, my dad would be turning in his grave at that.' I stop and point to the building opposite, and the famous doorway. 'He took me here when I was little. He was a massive Beatles fan.'

Jess has her phone out and she's taking a photo for Instagram (of course).

'Oh look, there's loads of pictures of a wall with writing on it somewhere round here.' She shows me her phone, and under #abbeyroad on Instagram, there they are. I spin round and point to the wall behind us. 'This one?'

'Oh, that's amazing.' She bends down and starts taking photographs. I watch her, thinking about the first time my dad brought me here. He was a massive music fan. Not just the Beatles. He loved all kinds of music. When he died, Mum passed his entire vinyl collection on to me. It's all still stacked on shelves back home in Kent, though – there's so much of it it'd take up half my room in Notting Hill, and Alice wasn't ever that keen on it. I dream of getting an old record player and having them all with me one day.

'It wasn't just the Beatles that recorded here,' I say.

'No?' Jess says, straightening up.

'Loads of others. Amy Winehouse, Oasis, Radiohead . . .'

'Ooh, let's cross over and have a look. We might see someone famous.'

We join a group of frozen-looking Japanese tourists who are taking photographs of the outside of the building. There's a buzz of excitement when the door opens, but we all give a deflated sigh when a middle-aged bloke with a bomber jacket walks out.

'You can take my photo if you like,' he says, chuckling as he strides off towards his car.

Jess heads off out when we get home. I'm at the too-tired-to-sleep stage, and end up sitting up watching crap on television until I doze off. It's half two in the morning when I wake up and stagger into the hallway to find Emma pulling off a pair of vertiginous heels and throwing them on the floor.

'Hi,' she says. 'Fancy meeting you here.' She arches an eyebrow, and – it's ridiculous – there's something about her complete lack of artifice and the fact that there are precisely no strings attached that make it just too easy.

CHAPTER EIGHT

Jess

4th February

'Hello, lovey.'

I'm having a bit of a wobble when Nanna Beth calls. It's nothing, really, but somehow she manages to pick that up in about two seconds flat. I sit on the edge of the bed and listen to her telling me how life is going in the sheltered accommodation.

'So Clara who lives in number twelve had a party to celebrate her eighty-fifth, and caused ructions because she had all the family round including the great-grand-children *on bicycles*.'

I raise my eyebrows. 'I thought rule number twenty-three subsection five or whatever it was said strictly no bikes?'

'Exactly.' I can picture her face and it makes my heart feel warm. Listening to her is almost as good as having one of her hugs. I must get down there soon.

'So anyway Fiona, the accommodation supervisor, was fine with it, and then there was a big fuss because that old trout next door complained.'

I giggle.

'So what's happening in the Big Smoke? Any exciting news?'

'Well,' I say, wriggling backwards on the bed and curling my feet underneath me, 'I told you last time that I finally met Rob. He's been giving us lessons in baking sourdough bread.'

'That's the chef one, am I right?'

'Yes.' I nod, even though she can't see me. 'We've got to feed this starter thing – it's basically like flour and water mixed into a paste – and then leave the bread dough to prove overnight. Only nobody fed the starter and the bread turned out more like a brick than anything else.'

'I'll give you my recipe,' Nanna says, comfortingly. 'It's none of that new-fangled sourdough stuff, just a good old-fashioned loaf.'

I think of Rob telling us how sourdough was the most ancient method of baking in his gruff Scottish accent, and decide I'll just leave that bit out. My foray into baking has given me a whole new level of respect for the people that run Le Pain Quotidien. Imagine making all those loaves every day? The responsibility must be terrifying.

'And what's happening with your mum?'

'Mum?' I realise with a start that I haven't heard from her in ages. I've always been a bit out of sight, out of mind, for Mum, particularly when she's busy. I think maybe it's rubbed off on me a bit. I really ought to call her.

'Haven't seen her for about a week,' Nanna Beth tells me. 'She was telling me all about this job she's found selling something online. She's caught up with some project or other. You know what she's like.'

I sigh. I do. She's forever finding money-making schemes that are going to solve all our problems – or just hers, nowadays. The trouble is that every one of them so far has involved her ploughing a load of money in '*as an investment*' and none of it ever seems to come back.

'Remember the lifestyle coaching or whatever it was?' Nanna chuckles.

'And the meditation teacher training?' I laugh, thinking about how many times my mother's been utterly convinced about something that was going to make her fortune. Six months sitting in a dusty church hall three nights a week soon put an end to that one, and she was on to the next thing. I bite my thumbnail.

'Oh, I forgot,' says Nanna Beth. 'She said she was going for a cabaret job on one of the cruise ships when I spoke to her last.'

'Did she?' I say, sitting up sharply. How the hell is she going to look out for Nanna if she's halfway round the world on the *Disney Princess* or whatever it is?

'Anyway, enough about that. I want to hear all about your exciting new job. How's it going? Any nice men on the scene?'

I suppress a sigh. Nanna Beth doesn't miss a trick.

'What's happening with that nice-sounding lad? The one who's been taking you out?'

I drop my voice slightly. 'Alex? There's nothing going on there. We're just friends.'

'Pfft,' she says.

'We are. Honestly. He's got something going on with one of the other girls in the house.'

'Hmm,' she sounds mildly disapproving. 'Sounds like a bit of a ladies' man.'

I choke back a giggle. Alex is the most unlikely ladies' man I've ever met. I think it's that – coupled with the fact that I met him once and basically fabricated an entire romance in my head because I've spent too long watching romantic movies – that makes the whole thing with him and Emma bearable. Plus from what he's said – not much, admittedly – I get the feeling that the break-up he had with his ex was pretty brutal.

'He's definitely not that.'

'Well you mind yourself, my love. After all that business with Neil, I don't want you rushing into something else too quickly.'

'There is no chance of that,' I say.

'Right then. I'm going to get off, because it's almost time for *Coronation Street* and I'm dying to know what happens to Steve.'

'I'll see you soon, Nanna.'

'That would be lovely. Lots of love to you.' She blows kisses down the phone and hangs up.

Afterwards, I curl up in bed and watch *La La Land*

on my iPad. I've bought some noise-cancelling headphones just in case of any incidents next door. I've literally no idea how much of a *thing* the whole thing is, but I'm not taking any chances.

Later that night, I'm tiptoeing downstairs to make a cup of hot chocolate because I can't sleep when I bump into Emma coming upstairs. She's wearing a dressing gown and holding a bottle of white wine and two glasses. She gives me a look I can't quite decipher – I'm not sure if she's feeling weird about me noticing the two glasses, or hoping I won't tell Becky there's something going on. I give a sort of sympathetic smile (I have no idea why).

When I make the hot chocolate, I add a large slug from the bottle of leftover spiced Christmas rum that's been sitting by the sink for weeks and head upstairs to climb into bed, putting my headphones firmly over my ears.

CHAPTER NINE

Jess

10th February

I've been living in Notting Hill for a month now, and Alex has been as good as his word. He's showing me his London, piece by piece, like a jigsaw, and I'm falling even more in love. With *London*, I should add, not with him. Definitely not with him. Not even a tiny little bit. Not even one atom of my romance-loving, musical-addicted, happy-ever-after body is longing to throw myself into his arms and say *pick me, you idiot*. Because that would be completely pointless and I am not a fool. He spins round again, thrusting his hands in the pockets of his jeans so I can see his bottom (which is an exceptionally nice specimen – just saying, purely objectively). Well, perhaps I am a little bit of a fool.

Because the thing is, I can't help thinking that if I hadn't gone on that bloody skiing holiday, which was admittedly lovely, perhaps Alex wouldn't have got off with the beautiful, effortlessly glamorous, high-flying Emma the night before I got back. And instead of lying with my head under two pillows gritting my teeth and trying not to listen to the sounds of them *definitely* not being a couple in the room next door, I could be in there. Literally.

As it is, I feel like a complete fool. And Alex hasn't a clue. He's so sweet. Whenever he's got time off, he's taking me on adventures around London, showing off his favourite places to me. And he loves this city so much that even if I didn't already, he would have converted me.

And he's got no idea I know something's going on with him and Emma. The weird thing is, they're perfectly civil to each other in the house the rest of the time, so it's like nothing's going on and it's all in my head. Except I'd have to be pretty screwed up to be imagining that.

'It's called fuckbuddies,' Gen said to me on the phone earlier in the week, as if she was explaining something very simple to a child of about four years old.

'I know what it *is*,' I said. 'I just didn't think it was actually a thing.'

'God Jess, you are so naïve sometimes. Of course it's a thing. Look at me and Marco.'

'Marco from the Ballet?'

'Yes.' I could picture her rolling her eyes.

'I thought you two were just friends.'

'With benefits,' Gen said, with a dirty sort of chuckle. 'When it suited me. Or him.'

'But what if it suited you and not him? How did you know when he'd be in the right mood? What happened if he turned up and you were like, "No thanks, I'm wearing a face mask and watching reruns of *Gilmore Girls*"?'

'Jess, you are illustrating precisely why you have never been, and probably never will be, the sort of person who has a friend with any sort of benefits.'

'I could,' I said, feeling a bit injured. 'If I wanted to. Which I don't.'

'Sure, Jess,' said Gen, laughing, but not unkindly. 'You're a total hearts and flowers romantic. And that's okay.'

After we'd ended the call, I looked at myself in the mirror. I tried a sexy sort of pout, and held my hair up off my face to try to imagine what it'd be like to be the sort of person – someone like Emma – who can just have sex with whoever she feels like and then get up the next morning and ask them to pass the cornflakes without feeling even the slightest bit awkward. I pulled a face at the thought, and let my hair drop back down to my shoulders. You know what, I said to myself, maybe it's okay if I'm just not that sort of person.

'And here we have the lesser-spotted tourist,' Alex says in a David Attenborough voice, turning around on his heel and walking backwards, facing me.

It's a Sunday afternoon and miraculously he's not working. A week has gone by and I've hardly seen Alex because he's been working nights and sleeping in the daytime. He's not just doing his placement, but he's doing some bank work as a healthcare assistant as well to earn a bit of extra money. He looks hollow-eyed with exhaustion.

Right on cue, he yawns widely. 'God, I'm sorry.'

'You should probably be asleep,' I point out, reasonably. 'Not wandering around showing me slightly interesting parts of London.'

'Yeah but I can't just work all day and sleep all night,' he says, then bursts out laughing realising his mistake.

'You could. Like the rest of the sane world. Only you've decided on a noble vocation where you get precisely no sleep and work ridiculous hours instead.'

He laughs, his bright eyes twinkling in a way that is disturbingly sexy, and I look down at the squashed, end-of-winter grass and scuff it with the toe of my boot. I know how it feels.

I look sideways at Alex as we're walking. He's checking his email on his phone and not really paying attention, so he doesn't notice. I'm trying to size him up and decide if he's *that sort of person*, or if he's just going along with it and half-hoping Emma might want to make something more permanent out of their arrangement. I can't tell.

I think I'm doing quite a good job of dealing with the fact that I can't actually get away from the one that got away (as I think of him, quietly, when nobody's looking) because he lives in the bedroom next to mine, and we've got a twelve-month bloody lease. Not that I'd want to move out, even if I could afford it. I love living there, and

I like him, and Becky, and – weird as this might sound, given their nocturnal habits – I like Emma, too. And Rob, even though I don't see him very often. We're a weird mix, but we work really well as housemates. I take a deep breath. I'll just have to focus all my romantic thoughts in the direction of Sophie and Rich's future wedding.

'Do you want to see something really interesting?' Alex says, out of the blue, as two small children zoom past on scooters, their mothers following close behind with tiny babies in prams. We've been walking along in a peaceable sort of silence for a while now.

'Really interesting?' I look at him sideways. 'You're not overselling this are you?'

He shakes his head and laughs. 'Yeah, all right. It's a bit interesting.'

'Oh go on then.'

'It's down here. Bit of a walk.'

'I'm not in any rush.'

'So this is what I was going to show you.' Alex steps aside and points between a gap in the railings.

'Oh my God, it's a miniature graveyard. You are seriously weird.' I lean in closer, peering at the little stone graves.

'It's a pet cemetery.'

'Yikes. Like the film?'

'I hope not.' He laughs. 'It's been closed to the public for years now – but there are about three hundred pets from the turn of the last century buried there.'

'That's creepy. Imagine if they all come to life and London's taken over by spooky little pet zombies.'

He shakes his head with a rueful smile. '*You* are seriously weird, Jess.'

Before long, we're meandering down the paths along the Serpentine. After a while we find a bench and sit down for a rest.

'It's funny,' I say, looking at the jumble of people I can see. 'In between the tourists, there are people just living their lives here. This is their park.'

He nods, thoughtfully. 'And of course—' he gets up, holding out a hand to help me up '—down that end, you can hang out and spot Kate Middleton and her kids – or the Duchess of Cambridge, I should say – sometimes.'

'Seriously?'

'Yeah. I guess she has to try and live a normal life some of the time.'

We start walking up towards home – my sense of direction is improving a bit now we're walking everywhere. It's funny, because when you don't live in London and you go everywhere by tube, the city feels completely different. It's actually not that big, when you start walking around.

'There,' Alex says, pointing to the huge, ornate building that is Kensington Palace. 'That's their house. Well, not all of it. There's loads of other random royals in there too. But they've got a little flat with about fifteen bedrooms down the side. I've seen her once, pushing a pushchair and walking a dog.'

'No way.' I realise I sound like an overawed tourist, but the idea of bumping into the royal family when I'm out for a stroll just seems completely bonkers.

'I don't think it happens that often, if you were planning on hanging out all day on the off chance.'

I give a little snort. 'As if,' I say. And then we keep walking, but my head swivels left and I have a little daydream about what I'd do if I bumped into the Duchess of Cambridge one sunny afternoon.

The trouble with me is I've always been a daydreamer. Always been a sucker for a romantic film, always loved a book with a good old-fashioned happy ever after ending. And now I'm working for a publisher that specialises in that sort of story and I'm as happy as a pig in – well, rose petals might be a nicer way of putting it. I had no idea that working for a publishing company meant I'd be given as many free books as I could get my hands on. The shelf in my room is groaning with advance reading copies – early editions of books, offered to reviewers, librarians and booksellers.

'Let's go back down this way. Fancy something to eat?'

My stomach growls in answer. 'Definitely.'

Crossing the road out of Hyde Park, we head down towards Portobello Road, and the smell hits us almost as we turn the corner onto the street. The fizz and spit of burgers being cooked mingles with the sweet scent of cinnamon buns from the bakery stall, and sour-spiced olives and paella in a huge frying pan.

'What d'you fancy?'

'Everything.' I laugh.

'Bockwurst, genuine German sausages, get your sausages here,' shouts a voice, and I turn to the right, seeing a market stallholder handing one over. 'Mustard and sauce over there, love,' he says to the woman, who gives a nod of thanks.

'What can I get you, love?' he asks as he turns to me.

We take our sausages and sit down on the stone wall outside the Electric Cinema. At last the beginnings of spring are showing themselves. There are crocuses peeping through the earth in wooden window boxes, and bright yellow daffodils standing proudly in the garden beside us. Portobello Road is a riot of noise and colour, alive with people and bustle and everything I love about London. I sit there with Alex by my side, and we eat our sausages, and we watch the world go by in a companionable silence.

'There's a place I'd like to show you,' Alex says, as we stand up after we've finished eating. He looks at me, his expression concerned. 'Unless you want to get back? We've been ages.'

I shake my head. What I want to say is that I'd be quite happy walking the streets of London every day with him, because I think he is lovely. What I do say is: 'No, I'm not in any rush to get back.' And off we go.

We walk to Little Venice, which looks exactly like you'd think from the name. It's like an oasis of calm in the middle of the city – canals lined with pubs and cafés, willow trees dipping their branches in the water, and colourful narrowboats moored by the canal-side.

'I've always wanted to live in one of those,' I say,

peering in the window. A small child presses her nose against the window from inside and I laugh.

'Me too,' says Alex. 'This is the café I wanted to show you.'

It's not posh. The curtains are faded gingham and outside there are a couple of rickety wooden tables and chairs.

'They do the best coffee – and breakfast – around here. I love it. And you can sit and watch the world go by.'

'Yes please.' I pull out a chair – it's freezing cold, but there are thick red fleece blankets hanging on the back. I wrap one around my knees and sit, watching. It reminds me more of Amsterdam than Venice, in a funny way.

I watch the sun streaking the sky pale coral pink and red as it begins to set. After a few minutes, Alex reappears with two flat whites, each with a pretty heart on the top. I pull my phone out and take a photo, adding it to my Instagram story.

'I like your Instagram.' Alex stirs sugar into his coffee, and the heart disappears from the froth. 'It's like you see all the good bits in London.'

'Thanks.' I sip my drink and look out at the people on the canal. The little girl we saw earlier has climbed out of the narrowboat now. She's wearing a thick padded coat and wellie boots, waiting for her dad to get her bike. She stamps her feet and catches my eye, jumping in a puddle and laughing. 'I like sharing the nice bits.'

'That's a good way of looking at life,' he says, smiling at me in a way that makes his eyes crinkle and my heart give a disobedient thud.

'It's partly a way of saving up memories, and it's also because I like sharing them with my Nanna Beth.'

'And your mum? Is she an Instagram addict as well?'

I shake my head, laughing. 'Definitely not. My mother only likes to do stuff when there's applause at the end of it. Put her on stage and she's quite happy. There's not enough feedback from online stuff.'

'She's an actress?'

I want to say no, she's a drama queen, but that's not really fair. I had a long, rambling voicemail from her earlier, complaining that she's had to go over and help Nanna Beth when she's got a performance tomorrow and she should be saving her voice. The performance Mum was talking about is the local theatre's rendition of *Chicago*, but nonetheless . . . apparently she's been working on it for weeks now.

'She's a part-time actress, yeah. Never quite made it to the West End, but she's done a few bits on television and stuff like that.'

'Wow. That's amazing.'

'She's hoping to get a job on one of the cruise ships, so she'll be away for ages.'

'That'll be weird for you,' Alex says, looking up at me through his dark fringe.

I shake my head. 'She was always away a lot when I was growing up.'

'With work?' He looks at me, head slightly to one side, his expression thoughtful.

'Um,' I frown a bit and fiddle with the wooden coffee

stirrer. It's not something I talk about very often, but there's something about Alex that makes me feel it's safe to open up. 'She wasn't great at the whole birthdays and Christmases thing, so my grandparents kind of picked up the slack there. And sometimes she had boyfriends who weren't that keen on children – well, on me – so I ended up spending more and more time with my grandparents, until it ended up being pretty much a permanent fixture.'

'Wow.' He sort of sits back a bit, looking at me. 'That must've been hard then. I mean, when your grandpa died, it was like losing a parent.'

I chew my lip and look across at where the little girl is playing. She and her dad are heading off down the canal-side now. She's meandering on her bike, unsteady on two wheels, and he's got his hand at the small of her back, protecting and guiding her. I blink hard, because for a strange half-second I feel tears stinging at my eyes.

'Yeah.' I look down at the table for a moment, gathering myself, then look up at Alex. He's got such a kind face. 'It was hard, because it was like we lost him twice – first when the dementia set in, and then again when he died.'

Alex nods. 'I get it. When my dad died I felt guilty because the first thing I felt was relief. He'd been sick for ages – and cancer just seemed to change him. He wasn't the same person at the end.'

'That's exactly it.' I let out a sigh. 'And so you decided to retrain as a nurse.'

He nods. 'I know everyone thinks it's insane. It's just – I saw the difference they made to Dad. To everyone in the ward. And I watched him fading away and I thought about all the stuff he'd done, and how he made a difference – the buildings he worked on are actual, concrete things. There's a children's hospice in Liverpool that he worked on, and they took the parents' and the children's views into account when they built it, because he said that mattered.' He looks away then for a moment, and I reach across the table, forgetting myself, and put a hand on his arm. He looks back and his eyes are shining with tears, which he wipes away with a sleeve, making a self-deprecating face. 'Sorry.'

'God, don't be. That's so lovely.'

'Yeah. I haven't ever really talked about that, you know?' He rubs his nose for a moment and then picks up the other wooden stirrer and starts snapping it into tiny pieces. 'Thing is I wanted to do something worthwhile. Corporate law wasn't it. I want to do something that I can be proud of, if . . .' He tails off.

'I get it.'

He looks at me then, holding my gaze for a second. My hand's still on his arm and I move it away, feeling suddenly shy.

He smiles and stands up, holding his hand out to me to pull me up to standing. 'I'm glad you do.'

We walk home together through the gathering dark of the February evening. There's still the tiniest hint of spring streaking across the sky as the night falls, and I feel happy. Properly, straightforwardly happy. It's a good feeling.

When we get back, the house is in uproar. Emma is standing on one of the kitchen chairs, holding a loaf of our home-made sourdough bread and swearing profusely.

'Um,' says Alex, looking at me and raising his eyebrows. 'Hi?'

'There's a – *thing* – eating my bread.'

I look at Alex and burst out laughing. 'You didn't take a bite after working a long shift yesterday?'

'Not guilty.'

'It's no' one of us,' says a gruff voice from downstairs. Rob emerges from the hall, brandishing two old-fashioned mousetraps. He's a short, bearded, red-haired man – older than the rest of us – probably in his forties. Rob looks and sounds so Scottish that I always expect him to be wearing a kilt. 'I think we've got a wee bit of a mouse problem.' He puts the mousetraps down on the table and holds his hand out to me. 'Hello, stranger,' he says, with a welcoming smile. 'Long time no see.'

'A mouse?' Nanna Beth gives a snort of laughter as I tell her the latest on what's been happening in the house. I'm curled up on the bed, a fleecy blanket over my knees because it's freezing cold and there's something wrong with the heating. It feels good to hear her voice, and I feel a wave of longing.

'You need to put some peanut butter on a trap. They can't resist it.'

'Then we'll have a squished mouse to deal with.' I shudder at the prospect.

'Oh for heaven's sake, girl. You're made of tougher stuff than that.'

I pull a face, but don't say anything.

'So you seem to be quite settled in with the housemates now.'

'I am. Work's a bit . . .' I try and think of the right word, but can't. 'It's all a bit new, that's all.'

It's like trying to stuff an octopus in a string bag; that's what it's like. When I was working at the marketing company, everything went according to plan – admittedly mainly because I was doing most of it. But here, now – well. I'm reliant on authors delivering manuscripts on time, editors getting their work done on time, the vagaries of cover designers and delivery dates and all sorts of things. It's like Jenga, only with books. If one thing goes wrong, the whole tower falls apart. This week an author decided the book she was working on wasn't right, and that she wanted to rewrite the whole thing. Trouble is, we've got production all set up and it's meant to be going to print in eight weeks. I go to bed worrying about printing schedules and wake up with my teeth gritted.

Nanna Beth makes a slight snorting noise. 'You sound a bit stressed out to me, my love. Maybe you need some sea air and some of my cherry scones.'

I sag slightly. The thought of both of those *and* a comforting hug from her makes me feel about ten years old again, and I ache with homesickness like I did at that age when we went on a school trip to Wales for a week.

'Oh God, I do. In fact, I'm going to come down and see you next weekend, if you're free.'

'Oh, that would be nice, lovey, but I'm going on a coach trip to Hastings.'

I sag a bit more.

'The weekend after, perhaps?' she says, cheerfully. 'I've got a chess competition, but that's only Saturday afternoon. You can have a nice bath or go for a walk along the prom with your mum.'

'You've got a better social life than me,' I say, and I'm not even joking. Since moving into the sheltered housing complex, she's been busier than I've ever known her. It makes me wonder if she's been storing all this social energy up for all the years she was married to Grandpa. And then it hits me – she's lonely.

'You're okay, though?' I ask, concerned.

'Me? Right as rain.'

'You're not – not missing Grandpa too much?'

The last couple of years when he was at home, and the dementia was making it harder and harder for him to manage, had been tough on her. I'd lived there, determined to help as much as I could, especially as Mum had – par for the course with her – checked out and gone travelling with a new boyfriend she'd met. She didn't really do responsibility. It's not that she didn't care, it's more that she – well, she's always been sort of focused on herself.

'No, lovey. I mean I miss him, of course, but he wouldn't have wanted to carry on like that. It's a blessing, in a horrible way.'

'I know.' I think of Grandpa before, when he was well, pottering around the garden in his slippers and a woolly jumper, dead-heading roses and sorting out the shed that was his pride and joy. I try not to think about him sitting, lost in a world of his own, staring into space for hours on end.

'Anyway, enough of that. What else is happening with you?' she asks.

I tell her a slightly filtered version of how it's really going at work, and how I managed to survive a meeting with a load of important people without screwing it up. I don't mention Alex, or how I'd taken to sleeping with earplugs in just in case I accidentally overhear him and Emma in the room next to mine, or how I'm grateful for the solid Victorian walls that muffle most of the noise even though they unfortunately make this place freezing cold on days like today.

And then I hang up, because she's got to get going to her chair yoga class, and I hug my knees and I smile to myself, because somehow, at twenty-nine and seventy-nine, the two of us are doing okay in our new lives.

CHAPTER TEN

Alex

14th February

Valentine's Day is *everywhere* this year, even more than usual. I can't decide if it's that confirmation bias thing, or if we're just going full on Hallmark, but it feels like the entire city of London is festooned with pink ribbons and covered in love hearts, and to be perfectly honest with you, it's a bit much. I've had a really shitty day, and I'm well and truly over all of it.

I pull my beanie hat down low over my head as I make my way up the station steps.

'Bunch of flowers for the girlfriend, love?' a woman outside Notting Hill Gate tube station asks. She's standing with two huge buckets of red roses and thrusts one in my direction. I shake my head.

'No thanks,' I say.

'Or boyfriend?' she calls, hopefully.

'Not that either,' I mutter, waiting for the lights to change, looking across the road where there's another stall drowning in a sea of red roses, teddy-bear-shaped balloons, bouquets of flowers, and ribbons tied to everything.

It was a genius idea of Becky's to turn the house into a sort of anti-Valentine celebration with plenty of wine, pizza, and a horror movie or two. Thank God I don't have to get up in the morning either. I've done a week of nights – again – and a weekend. Nobody told me nursing was going to be easy, but my God, I am so tired. And today was a really crappy day, too. We lost a patient, which happens, but this one came completely out of the blue. It's a million times harder when you're working on the paeds ward and it's a child. I shake my head and try and wipe the faces of her parents out of my head. Valentine's Day was always going to be synonymous with the most painful memory for them.

I stop at Tesco Express on the corner and pick up a bottle of red wine and some tubes of Pringles. All I want to do is get the 14th of February out of the way and forget Valentine's Day exists.

This morning I'd sat on the tube on the way into work, staring mindlessly at the adverts opposite, avoiding the gaze of the woman sitting across from me, thinking about last year. It was hard not to reflect on how different life had been. I'd taken Alice for a surprise dinner to Clos Maggiore in Covent Garden, and we'd both known why. Yeah, it was more than a little bit clichéd and cheesy, but I thought that was what romance was supposed to be about. We'd passed forkfuls of food to each other, a waiter had lit a candle between us and smiled knowingly, and the whole evening had gone exactly as planned. We'd shared a crème brûlée – two spoons and one bowl – not fighting over the last mouthful but me politely telling her she could have it even though it was my favourite. God, if that wasn't love, I don't know what is. I'd kill for a crème brûlée normally.

Everything, Alice had said afterwards, had been perfect. And then I'd got down on one knee on a tiny side street sprinkled with a million fairy lights (I'd even chosen the location, scouting it out beforehand) and asked her to marry me. She'd said yes before I'd even got the ring out of the box. And then I'd kissed her and she'd called her parents as we walked home, waking them from an early night in their neat Georgian house in Surrey. They'd been delighted, and feigned surprise. And if I'd climbed into bed that night with a vague sense of unease, well, I'd told myself it was probably indigestion. The cracks were there, spreading invisibly. I think I'd just hoped if I tried hard enough I could make it all okay again.

It had only been a few weeks after the proposal that I told Alice I'd been offered a place. God, she'd been so *disappointed* in me. It was the first time I'd seen that side of her. She'd been humouring me all along, hoping I'd get a grip and stop having some sort of third-of-life crisis.

'Can't you just do voluntary work or donate some money to charity?' she'd said, trying to brush it off.

'I can't – it's not that simple,' I'd replied.

'You don't have to make up for your dad dying by giving up your life and becoming a nurse,' she'd said, trying to keep her voice even. I remember spreading my hands out on the table, looking down at them, wondering if she just needed a chance to get her head around the idea and get used to it.

'It's not that. I want to do something that makes a difference. I want to work with people.'

'Why don't you train as a doctor then? At least that's . . .' She'd paused, and the words had hung, unspoken, in the air.

'I don't want to be a doctor, that's why.'

'But you'd get a half-decent salary, at least.' She'd barely been able to disguise how cross she was.

But the idea had been nagging away at me since those long weeks we spent in the hospital with Dad. It wouldn't leave me alone. I wanted to be a nurse. I was going to be a nurse. And if Alice couldn't get her head round it now, well, she'd get there in the end.

Weeks had passed, and Alice hadn't said anything about my plans; it's clear now she was hoping it would all go away. Occasionally she'd throw me the odd barbed comment about playing nurses, but other than that she carried on as normal. It was a bit weird, when I look back on it.

When it was clear the idea wasn't going away, particularly after I'd taken up the offer for the place on the course, she started throwing out every objection under the sun. A change in career would throw our perfectly ordered life into chaos, she'd said. She'd been making noises about having babies, and made it clear that there was no way that'd be happening if I was earning a nurse's salary. We wouldn't be able to carry on paying the rent on our pretty little place in Stoke Newington with me not earning. She became shrill and angry, yelling at me that I was putting her future in jeopardy just because I was having some sort of crisis. And the relationship that had seemed so solid had slowly but inexorably begun to show those tiny cracks, which soon turned into gaping huge chasms.

The one thing I know is that I didn't blame Alice. In a way, I almost felt that I'd lured her into getting engaged under false pretences. She'd bought into a lifestyle as well as a relationship, and then I'd decided – on what seemed to her like a whim – to take that lifestyle away.

I turn the corner onto Albany Road, still lost in my thoughts.

'Hi,' Becky says when she pulls the door open back at the house.

I've had all this stuff going through my head and I need to have a shower, gather my thoughts, try and wipe it all away. God I hate Valentine's Bloody Day.

I don't know why I find myself upstairs in my room, rummaging through balled-up socks and crumpled boxers, reaching right to the back until my hand finds the small, solid box. There it is – a tangible reminder of the life I left behind. And when I look up at my face reflected in the mirror I realise I look knackered. Also, I really need to get a haircut. I rub my face with both hands, before giving a huge yawn. What I really need is to get a decent night's sleep.

A couple of hours later, we're all sprawled on the sofas, so stuffed with Domino's pizza we can hardly move. Rob isn't there, of course – Valentine's Day being one of the big nights in the restaurant biz, with people like Alice and me last year keeping them in business.

'My God,' says Becky, rubbing her stomach as if she's six months pregnant. 'I swear I'm having a pizza baby.'

'I'm never eating pizza again.' Jess leans forward, taking a slice of Hawaiian from the cardboard box. 'After this bit, I mean. This is my last hurrah.'

'Pineapple on pizza is beyond disgusting,' says Emma, looking at Becky for back-up.

Jess sits back and takes an extra big mouthful to prove that she's wrong, making us all laugh. I watch as she curls her long legs underneath her, sitting tailor-style on the huge soft sofa cushions. And then – realising what I'm doing – I look away. She looks at the pizza, thoughtfully.

'Pineapple's the best bit.'

'You are so disgusting,' says Emma, walking across the room to get another bottle of red wine. 'Drink, anyone?'

'I'm with Jess. Team Pineapple forever.'

I take a piece of pizza in solidarity with Jess. Reaching across, she holds out her hand for a high five and then flashes me a beam of gratitude.

There's a general groan of disgust from the other two. Jess gives me a sideways look and a cheeky, conspiratorial grin, before taking the hairband from her wrist and – as

I've seen her do so many times before out of habit as we've been walking around London on our exploring trips – twists up her long, dark hair into a messy knot at the top of her head. I'd half expected to get back and find she wasn't here this evening, after what happened yesterday.

I'd got home from a long shift at the hospital, and found Jess sitting at the kitchen table with a couple of friends. They'd been screaming with laughter over photographs on Tinder, with – incongruously – a pile of open *Bride* magazines spread all over the table.

Jess had looked from me, to the table, to and back, to meet my look of confusion.

'Alex, this is my friend Gen I told you about, and this—' she motioned to both of them, but I'd already recognised them from Jess's descriptions '—this is Sophie.'

Sophie was blonde and very pretty, with her hair tied back from her face in a ponytail. I'm not sure how but she somehow managed to look as organised as Jess has told me she is. I think it was just because she seemed so neat. She looked like she'd never had a scruffy day in her life. Meanwhile, Gen was in a pair of rainbow-coloured trousers with a black vest top, and her wild red curls were pushed back from her face with a navy blue fisherman's cap. The look shouldn't have worked, but somehow it did. She looked exactly like you'd imagine someone in the theatre should look.

'We're trying to find a nice young chap for Jess,' Gen said, looking at me with huge, very direct blue eyes. She had a mischievous look on her face, as if she knew

117

something I didn't. It made me feel slightly unnerved. I went to the fridge, opened a bottle of orange juice, and poured myself a glass.

I looked down at the wedding magazines and then at Jess, who rolled her eyes.

'And you're moving straight from choosing someone on Tinder to planning the wedding?' I took a long drink of juice, then put the glass down on the kitchen counter.

'I'm not planning on marrying anyone right now,' Jess said, laughing. She gathered up the magazines and put them in a neat stack. 'These are for Soph. She *is* getting married.'

'And these two are terrified in case I'm going to force them to wear some sort of hideous meringue dress as bridesmaids,' Sophie said.

'Please, God, no,' said Gen, raising her eyes heavenward.

'He's quite nice,' Sophie said, leaning over Gen's shoulder and looking at her phone screen. 'Wonky nose, though.'

'Oh my God, this is hideous.' Jess hit the home button on the phone and the screen went blank.

I felt a bit weird. Maybe it was just the excess of female energy in the room or something, or the way Gen was looking at me as if she was sizing me up, but I didn't like the idea of Jess on Tinder. There are loads of really dodgy characters out there.

The truth was there's something inside me that feels slightly discomfited by the idea of Jess – London walking buddy, housemate, fan of midnight toast-and-Marmite snacks and chats over the kitchen table – dating anyone.

I have absolutely no right to feel like that for about eight million reasons. One, because I'd made an executive decision at the beginning of this year that I wasn't getting involved with anyone. And two, because of the whole Emma thing. Not that it's a thing, but it's basically my belt-and-braces guard against getting into a relationship with anyone else. I'm not the sort of person who'd mess around with more than one person at a time, even if it was all completely no strings attached. And it's the perfect solution to avoid me getting caught up in a relationship and messing up my nursing course and my – already pretty screwed up – heart.

I knew all of that made me a hypocrite and an idiot, so what I needed was to duck out of this situation ASAP. 'I'll leave you three to it,' I said, grabbing a can of Coke from the fridge so I wouldn't have to come in and interrupt them again later.

But now here we are, at the end of our alternative Valentine's evening. We've given up on the terrible horror film, which wasn't even scary, and ended up watching a really freaky episode of *The Haunting of Hill House* on Netflix, and chatting about ghost stories we've heard, trying to think of scarier and scarier ones until we're all completely spooked.

'I'm going to be too scared to fall asleep tonight, at this rate,' Jess says, getting up from the sofa. 'I'm going to bed before I completely terrify myself.'

'Yeah, me too,' I say, and stand up, picking up an empty pizza box. Jess stacks another two in my arms.

'Can you put them outside?' she says, pulling a face. 'There's no way I'm going out there in the dark now.'

'The man in black might get you,' says Emma, in a creepy voice.

'I'll do it, don't worry,' I say.

'Phew.' Jess mops her brow, then gives a wave from the sitting room door. 'Right, night all.'

I turn and say goodnight, and Emma flicks a glance over her shoulder. It's a split-second look, but I know what she's thinking. However, I'm stuffed with pizza and I've had way more wine than I should have. She raises her eyebrows slightly, and I give a slight shake of my head. I like Emma – she doesn't take life too seriously. She's got a body to die for and she's bloody hot in bed. And she knows what she wants. But the thing is, if I fuck this up I'll be out of a house, and that matters more than anything else.

I head out to put the boxes in the recycling and the howl of foxes somewhere nearby makes the hairs on the back of my neck stand on end.

When I go upstairs, the bathroom door's open, but the light's still on, so I push it open carefully. Jess is standing there, hair knotted off her face in a bun, carefully putting toothpaste on her toothbrush.

'Oh sorry, I'll come back in a sec,' I say.

Jess shakes her head. 'It's fine, I'm just brushing my teeth.'

She hands me the toothpaste and I pick up my brush, and somehow we're standing there side by side – me in

120

my trackies and T-shirt, her in a pair of mismatched PJs – brushing our teeth. She waggles her eyebrows at me in the mirror, making me laugh, which is harder than you'd think when you've got a toothbrush in your mouth.

'Night then,' I say, once we've finished, and she's heading out to her bedroom. I contemplate a shower before bed, but decide I'll have one in the morning. I lie under the covers, thinking that I've made the right move in not sleeping with Emma tonight. I find myself wondering about Jess lying in the room next to mine, hoping she's not too freaked out by the ghost stories to sleep. I close my eyes and, exhausted after the impossibly long day I've had, I'm gone.

CHAPTER ELEVEN

Jess

12th March

'Welcome to my new house.'

Gen's standing on her bed. She reaches up and pushes the glitter ball that hangs from the ceiling so it twirls, casting squares of light that bounce and reflect off the walls, the furniture and us.

Gen's always lived in, well, unusual places. She spent a summer after university living in a silent meditation retreat in Bali, sleeping in a hut and sweeping bugs off the floor before bed every night. The concept of the irrepressible Gen, the human embodiment of a can of Coke that's been shaken up then opened, keeping her mouth shut for a week at a time was pretty much unthinkable to me. But she said afterwards that she'd loved it, and that it had really helped her acting. That made sense. She's so dedicated to acting that she'd do pretty much anything if she thought it would make a difference – including, it would seem, saving money by sleeping in assorted battered-looking disused buildings to save money for more classes. Her large residence had been a mansion house – huge, grand and with a sweeping staircase that belonged on a movie set – that was waiting for redevelopment.

When she'd told Sophie and me that her new place was an ex-nightclub, I thought perhaps she'd be sleeping in a converted office or something, not on the dance floor.

Gen jumps down, and beckons me to follow her. 'I'll make us a coffee. Come this way.'

I climb wooden stairs lined with faded posters that have been plastered to the wall, their edges curled and peeling. Familiar faces look back at me, ghosts of the musical past. The place smells dark and cool and – if you inhale and close your eyes – you can almost imagine the thudding of the bass and the throngs of excited, wild-eyed clubbers ricocheting off each other on the dance floor, arms in the air.

'They've made a little kitchen for us, here – look.' Gen opens the door, proudly, and I walk inside what was clearly once the manager's office. It's got a brand-new IKEA unit, with a hob, a sink, and a fridge and washing machine. But it's clearly still a room that's pretending to be something it's not. Gen switches on the kettle.

Life as a live-in guardian isn't for the faint-hearted. The properties are vacant, so it can be a bit spooky and weird – basically, you're making sure the building isn't taken over by squatters. Gen heard about it from an actor friend while she was working on a play about a year ago. Before that, she'd done what most people do when they're trying to make their way in London – she'd lived in a tiny, cramped house-share, in a bedroom that was once a walk-in cupboard, with no window and a door she had to keep propped open at night so she didn't overheat or worse still suffocate. It was grim. Then she found herself looking up live-in guardians, and discovered that – as long as you didn't mind being relatively impermanent, and could cope with living pretty much anywhere in central London – you could get by paying about half what you'd normally pay for the area. It's still more than I'm paying Becky, but I'm in a very weird – totally miraculous – position.

'What d'you think?' Gen asks as she clatters spoons, spilling sugar and wiping it up, before handing me a coffee.

'It's . . . interesting,' I say.

'Cheap. And the other guy who is sharing it is pretty low-profile. Nice to know I'm not on my own here, though. We've had a couple of pissed people banging on the door in the middle of the night. I reckon they thought the club was still open. Ancient clubbing dinosaurs from another time . . .' She grins, sipping her coffee.

'I don't think I could cope with moving every few months, though.' I think about Albany Road and feel a wave of gratitude for Becky. She could have put that place on the market and sold it for millions. I still don't know what came over her when she decided to gather us lot together and let us stay there for a ridiculously low rent. As it is, my new publishing salary isn't stretching very far. By the time I've paid rent and my share of the bills, there's not an awful lot of money left. February wasn't so bad because it's a short month, but March has barely started and I'm already feeling the pinch a bit.

'I don't mind moving if it means I get to stay here. London's so bloody expensive.'

'We could move back to Bournemouth,' I say, waiting for her reaction.

'No chance in hell. I'd rather live on 20p noodles from Tesco for the rest of my life.'

'I think that's what's going to happen to me. Payday's only just gone, and I'm absolutely skint already.'

She looks at me, brows knitted together. 'I thought your snazzy job in publishing was paying really well?'

'Yeah.' I nod. 'In Bournemouth terms, maybe. Not so much in London.'

'It's fine as long as you don't want to go anywhere or do anything.' Gen lifts her mug up. 'Even a coffee's more expensive here. Not to mention drinks . . .'

'Yeah. I was invited on a night out to celebrate some-one's leaving do the other day, but I turned it down when I looked up the menu. Cocktails were about £18 each.'

'Is everyone you work with loaded then?' Gen swivels herself round on the old black office chair, spinning herself like a child visiting a parent's workplace.

'I don't know. Maybe they've got private incomes or something. I reckon half of them are subsidised by parents, and the other half are like me. Jav didn't go on the night out, either.'

Jav and I have taken to going off to the café down the back street behind our office for lunch a couple of times a week. It's full of plaster-splattered workers from the building they're redeveloping round the corner, but they do a pretty decent soup and sandwich for the same price as a glass of freshly squeezed orange juice from the posh restaurant below our building.

Jav's nice, and I relate to her because she comes from a housing estate in Peterborough, and doesn't have parents in the business. There are an awful lot of people in the office who seem to have found their way into the job because of someone knowing someone. The MD of the company is so posh that when he talks I have to focus very hard to work out what he's actually saying. He doesn't just have a plum in his mouth – I reckon he's got several fruit trees.

'Jess?'

I shake my head. Gen's been talking and I've been lost in my thoughts.

'If you're struggling, maybe you should give notice at Becky's place and sign up to become a live-in guardian? I know you said the rent's cheap, but this is *really* cheap.'

I shake my head. I haven't actually told her how much I'm paying, because I feel a bit guilty that she's been struggling for ages to get by and then I just landed on my feet.

'I like it there. And the rent's not expensive. It's just I keep buying coffees and stuff and they're so bloody ridiculous. I was walking with Alex the other day in Bloomsbury and we went past a place that was charging £5.50 for a flat white.'

Gen whistles. 'That's ridiculous.'

'I know.'

'You need to get a flask,' she says. 'More to the point, what's with all the *walking with Alex* stuff?'

I make a face. 'Nothing. He's just showing me London.'

'Thought you said he came from Kent?'

'He does. He just used to spend a lot of time here as a teenager with his dad, and he's got a really good memory for places and stuff, and you know what I'm like with directions.'

'Completely, unimaginably hopeless?'

I nod. 'And it's really helping. I made it home on foot the other day without getting lost once. It's nice – like joining up a jigsaw puzzle. And that's why everyone wears trainers with their office stuff. I couldn't work it out at first.'

'Yep.' Gen waggles a foot. She's always in huge, chunky trainers. 'It's easier to walk most of the time instead of waiting for a bus or fighting your way through the tube. Nice that Alex is taking the time to show you round,' she says, giving me a sly, sideways look, one eyebrow crooked upwards. 'Out of the goodness of his heart?'

I feel my cheeks going slightly pink. 'There's nothing going on. He's completely wrapped up in work, and I get the feeling that whatever he's got going on with Emma is exactly what he wants – no complications.'

'What about Becky's no-relationships rule?'

'I don't think she knows there's anything going on.'

'Oh my God. So you're the keeper of the secret? Does he know you know?'

I pull an awkward face. 'Don't think so. Emma doesn't realise I saw her coming out of his room that morning, and there's nobody but me on our floor.'

'You should say something. Drop a little hint.'

'God, Gen, no. That would be awful.'

'Right. So you're just going to quietly carry on living with the man of your dreams while he's banging your flatmate on the QT and not say a word.'

'He is *not* the man of my dreams.'

'He so is. I've seen him. And I've seen the way you looked at each other. I reckon he's got the hots for you, too. Why else would he be spending his non-existent time trawling over London showing you how to get from A to B when Google Maps exists?'

'I can't work Google Maps, you know that,' I say, only half joking. Whichever way I start walking, I always end up going the wrong way. It happened the other day at work when I was supposed to pop out to a bookshop near the office. Fifteen minutes later, I'd walked in a circle and still hadn't found it.

'That is *so* not my point, and you know it.'

Gen takes a sip of her coffee and narrows her eyes slightly, in that way she does when she's convinced she's right about something. I don't say anything.

There's a pause. I stand up and look around the little kitchen, and Gen spins round on the chair again. A couple of times she opens her mouth to speak, and then – uncharacteristically – closes it.

'Gen?' I sit back down, looking at her. 'What's up?'

She rubs her finger and thumb together. It's an anxious habit she's had as long as I've known her. Before a performance on stage, she stands in the wings doing it unthinkingly. I look down at her hand and up at her face. She realises what she's doing and lifts both hands up in a gesture of confusion.

'It's Soph. This wedding stuff. The baby stuff. All of it.'

Sophie's on the verge of something called the two-week wait. Apparently, it's something to do with waiting to see if her and Rich's attempts at getting pregnant have been successful. Our group chat has become a little bit . . . medical, these days.

'You mean you don't want to know how many times she and Rich have had sex?' I say.

Gen makes a slightly disgusted noise. 'No. I love her, but she's treating this exactly the same way she treated exams at school, and it's a bit TMI. And she's obsessing over wedding dresses and it's like there she is, on the verge of becoming a Proper Grown-Up. And I feel a bit shit. I'm living in—' she waves her arm, indicating the converted club manager's office that is her kitchen '—well, in this. Still hoping for my big break, still scrabbling to survive from one month to the next, still having to tap my parents for money when I'm skint and with credit cards up to my eyeballs.'

I totally get it. Admittedly I can't tap my mother for money, because she's always been skint and – oh God, I've just realised it's Mother's Day at the end of the month. I must check and see if it falls before payday. She's going to expect flowers, and wine. Mainly wine. I wonder if she'd mind if I skipped the flower bit.

I remember we're talking about Sophie. Now there's someone who likes things *just so*. Always has. If she has children, she's going to be calling Interflora to make sure they send reminders a week before every occasion.

'Soph's always been like that, though,' I say.

We both fall silent for a moment. I think of Sophie at primary school, her pencil case filled with neatly sharpened coloured pencils, ruler and strawberry-scented eraser, writing her name neatly at the top of her exercise book. Meanwhile, Gen and I would be scrabbling around at our desks, trying to find a pencil sharpener and rummaging in our bags for our crumpled, half-finished homework.

'She's just – naturally organised,' I conclude.

'It just feels like our ski trip was the last hurrah,' Gen says, looking a bit sad. 'I don't want to grow up.'

'Don't worry, Peter Pan.' I reach over and squeeze her hand. 'I'm always here to make you feel like a normal, functioning adult. I can't even manage to get relationships right.'

Speak of the devil, Sophie messages us a moment later, asking if we want to meet up on the South Bank for a drink later on – her treat.

*

'I need a bit of moral support,' she explains when we meet her a couple of hours later, shifting out of the way so the waiter can put our drinks down. 'Thanks,' she says, with a smile. The bar looks out over the Thames. We're protected from the still-cold spring weather by a wall of glass, but we can watch the people scurrying about like ants on the Embankment. I gaze out of the window for a moment, but Sophie gives a large sigh, drawing my attention back to her.

'What's up?' Gen puts her chin in her hand.

'Well, I'm not pregnant, that's what's up.'

I don't know a whole lot about trying to get pregnant. To be honest, I've spent the last decade trying to *avoid* it. The way we're taught at school, you'd think you just had to sit on the same sofa as a man to end up up the duff, so the idea that it's a bit of a challenge is news to me.

'You've had two goes,' says Gen, trying to be consoling. It's never been her strong point. 'I think it probably takes more than that. Look at all those people that have years of IVF.'

I spin my head round and give her A Look.

Sophie gives a wail. 'Oh my God, what if that happens to me?'

'I'm sure it won't,' I say, reassuringly. 'I think you probably just need to not stress about it. And have sex lots.'

'I have been. Rich says he's feeling a bit worn out. And I'm bloody exhausted. I fell asleep at work the other day.'

'That might be a sign you need to cool it a bit. Maybe

132

focus on the wedding stuff instead?' Gen flicks a glance in my direction. 'Have you got any ideas for our dresses yet?'

Sophie shakes her head. 'We haven't actually made it official yet.' She waves a naked left hand.

'You're not getting married?'

She shakes her head vigorously. 'Oh we are, it's just we haven't had the official Will You Marry Me bit.'

'Did you just instruct Rich he was getting married, Soph?' Gen gives her a look.

'I did not.' She looks offended. 'He did have *some* say in it.'

Gen gives a snort. The waiter arrives with a tray of drinks – gin and tonic for me, a beer for Gen, and a large vodka and tonic for Sophie.

'Cheers,' she says, clinking our glasses.

'What happened to not drinking?'

'Oh, bollocks to it. Just for tonight, anyway.' She takes a large swig and gives a happy sigh. 'God, that's good.'

A couple of drinks later and Sophie's feeling much better. She's visibly relaxed, and it reminds me that in amongst all the other stuff – finding my way through this new job, the house stuff (which is what I'm calling it and definitely not the Alex stuff) – it's so nice to have both my oldest friends living right here in the same city. I beam at them and they smile back.

'I love you two,' I say. 'And that's not the gin talking.'

We order another round of drinks. Thank goodness Sophie's paying, because this place is astronomically expensive.

'You should order the most tight-fitting, slinky, unforgiving wedding dress you can find,' I say, thoughtfully. 'I bet if you tempt fate you'll be preggers before you know it, and you'll have to have a bump-extension sewn in.'

'Or you can get a Meghan Markle style dress?' Gen's one hundred per cent Team Meghan and a bit obsessed. 'She looked like she'd left room for expansion in hers.'

'D'you think?' Sophie perks up a bit. I'm scrolling through Instagram to find photos of Meghan's dress, and before we know it, Sophie's writing lists and making plans and normal Sophie service is resumed. I catch Gen's eye over the top of Sophie's head as she scribbles down a list of wedding dress designers in her ever-present notebook, and we exchange grins. Friend duty complete.

CHAPTER TWELVE

Jess

30th March, Bournemouth

I'm on the train heading south to the seaside. It's Mother's Day on Sunday, so I'm staying with Mum and spending the day with Nanna Beth. It's only the second time I've been home since I moved – the last flying visit having to fit in around Nanna Beth's chess tournament. I hadn't factored in the cost of train journeys when I said I'd be back to visit as often as I could. But I speak to Nanna Beth on the phone all the time, and she's still swapping Instagram photos with me. She's developed a bit of a following: I showed her how to add hashtags to her posts, and it turns out there's a whole world of elderly people out there sharing their photos. Who knew? Jav keeps joking there's a book in it. She's following her, and now her grandma in Mumbai and Nanna Beth are Instagram friends too.

Nanna Beth's got a bit of an eye – I'm scrolling through her photos as we rumble out of the edges of London, past tired old buildings and graffiti-covered industrial units. The train stops and I snap a photo of a faded ghost sign and share it. Nanna B loves them.

The train pulls into Bournemouth and it feels like stepping into a pair of comfy old slippers after a long day in heels. I can smell the sea in the air and the sky stretches out huge in that way you only get at the seaside. I don't even have to think about where I'm going, which is such a relief after the constant map-checking that characterises my London life. I'm still trying to find my way around the city. But here – home – my feet carry me along the road towards the prom and I turn left at the end, crossing over to walk along the pavement beside the edge of the little stony cliff that drops down to the beach path. It takes half an hour, but I'm not in any rush. Every step I take, every breath of salty air I breathe in, I feel like I'm unwinding. I hadn't realised how much I missed being by the seaside.

I turn left and walk up the little street where Mum lives now. There's a row of doorbells, and her name's there, on a faded sticker. I push the buzzer and there's a pause before the front door clicks open automatically to allow me in.

'I could have been a mass murderer,' I say, as she opens the door to her flat and kisses me on the cheek. She's dyed her hair a dark burgundy-red and cut it into a jaw-length bob. It emphasises her high cheekbones and makes her look ridiculously young for her age.

'Sorry I can't stay. I have to rush. I've got rehearsal at twelve.'

Mum's opening words aren't the usual 'Darling! It's lovely to see you!' that a daughter might expect. It's just as well I'm used to her. But she's always been a bit – well, lacking in the traditional maternal side of things. She was amazing if I needed a costume in the school play, mind you. She bustles past, giving me a vague kiss on the cheek, and taking the flowers I'm holding.

'For me? You shouldn't have. Thanks, lovely.'

She sniffs them and tosses them aside on the table by the front door, and picks up her keys.

'Pop them in water for me, will you? I won't be back until after the performance because we've got loads to do to prep, but you'll be okay with Nanna Beth, won't you? There's probably something in the fridge for dinner if you have a look.'

And she's gone.

Growing up I got the distinct impression my mum would have been happier if she'd had Gen as a daughter. I was boring and bookish. Gen was like Mum – a rainbow of drama and glamour who made everyone look when she walked into the room. I didn't doubt for a second that she loved me, but she was always slightly disappointed that I wasn't as exciting as she'd hoped. She wanted a mini me, a second chance at fame. She was always desperate to hear how Gen was getting on.

'That could've been me, you know, if it hadn't been for parenthood getting in the way,' she'd say, unthinkingly. I guess I have learned some acting skills from her – the ability to remain impassive in situations like that, for one.

'Don't worry yourself, lovey,' Nanna Beth would always say. 'She doesn't realise what she's saying. She loves you very much.'

I look around the flat Mum's been renting since I've moved out. It's five floors up on a side road near the promenade, and the walls are painted a dull, uninspiring grey. She's covered them with posters from Vaudeville shows, huge colourful ones with high-kicking dancers festooned with feathers and glittering, tiny outfits. There are boxes stacked up against one wall.

I look at my reflection in the huge full-length mirror. I'm wearing a grey pinafore, a green cardigan and red shoes. I look about five. I can almost hear Becky's voice in my head, making a comment about the hidden psychological meaning behind the outfit I'm wearing. She's obsessed with power dressing and the effect of clothes at the moment, and I realise that dressing like a child on a trip home to see my mother is probably quite telling.

But I don't dwell on it, because she's disappeared for the day and I'm off to the sheltered housing place to see Nanna Beth. I run a brush over my hair and leave my overnight bag on the sofa. I'm about to head out the door when I think I'd probably better check there *is* something to eat in the fridge.

A dried-up lemon, an empty pack of low-fat butter substitute, a cracked, ancient piece of cheddar, and a bottle of Evian. I decide I'll pick something up on the way back.

I head out of Mum's flat and towards the seafront and the sheltered accommodation complex where Nanna Beth lives now. It gives me a pang when I walk past the street where her old house stands – there's a new family living there, all Grandpa's roses pulled up out of the front garden and a car parking spot tarmacked in their place. But my heart lifts when I see the brightly painted sign for Boscombe View. There's a couple of people in the garden, bickering happily over some wooden planters, holding a trowel each. It felt like the right place for Nanna as soon as we set eyes on it. I look across the car park, and she's standing at the window of her little apartment, waving through the glass.

'Darling,' Nanna Beth is at the door. She beckons me inside. Since I was there last, they've hung all her old pictures on the walls, and she's somehow managed to make the little sitting room feel completely like home. The green velvet sofa is up against the back wall, with the imitation painting of Constable's 'The Hay Wain' framed above it. The mantelpiece is crowded with photographs of me, Mum, Grandpa and Nanna Beth herself, and various great-aunts and second cousins I met as a child but don't really remember, but who are oddly familiar after years of their photos surrounding me.

'Sit down. You must be tired out after that journey,' Nanna Beth says.

I do as I'm told, and listen as she gently potters around

in the little kitchen at the end of the hall. I can hear the kettle going on and the sounds of her warming the teapot. The familiar clunk of the biscuit tin she's owned forever opening up, and the rustle of aluminium foil being taken off a plate of ham sandwiches she'll have made up earlier.

'Here we are,' she says as she returns with a tray.

We settle down with food and tea. It feels warm and safe, the way it always has. I look up at a photo of Grandpa in his gardening cardigan, a spade in his hand.

'He'd be proud of you, you know that.' Nanna follows my gaze. 'It takes a lot of courage to follow your dream, you know. So how's it going?'

I think for a moment. I've been in the job for over two months now, and I still feel like I'm finding my feet. 'Okay. Ish.'

'Bit of a change to working for Neil, I expect,' she says, with a chuckle. We'd met at work and sort of fallen together. There were definite pluses and minuses to working for your partner. I can't really think what the pluses were. The minuses were that when I found out he was sleeping with Claire from accounts, it was pretty hard to maintain a civil working environment. God, it doesn't matter how hard this new job is or how much of a learning curve I'm on (and right now it feels like I'm never going to get the hang of it) anything had to be better than working in that environment.

'It's so . . . fast.' I try and explain what it's like, but it's hard. 'And then so slow. It's like trying to herd cats, getting a book from start to finish.'

'Still enjoying it though? I bet you've got them all under control,' she says, and I think of Jav, who I'd left on Friday evening working on the final proofs of a book that was already a month late. It had to be finished quickly, because it was nominated for romance of the year in one of the glossy magazines, and the books editor had been on the phone asking hopefully if there were finished copies available. Jav had managed to stall her, and she'd messaged me at midnight to say she'd finally got things sorted out. Publishing is a lot like being a swan. You look very sleek and posh from the outside, but there's an awful lot of furious paddling going on underneath. And a lot of mud.

'I'm getting there,' I say, after a pause. She raises an eyebrow and looks at me over the top of her teacup.

'Rome wasn't built in a day. You've found a new house, and you're settling into a new life. Any other interesting news you want to share?'

'Becky's had a promotion. And Gen's up for a role in the new Cameron Mackintosh show at the Apollo. If she gets that, she's really going places.'

'Gen's going places, no matter what.' Nanna smiles fondly. She's always had a soft spot for Gen. I think she sees Mum in her.

'What's happening with Mum?' I ask. 'You know she's hopeless at keeping in touch.' The only thing I'd heard from her recently was that she didn't get the cruise ship work she'd been hoping for.

'Well, she's met some bloke from the theatre who's

doing some sort of pyramid selling thing, and she's convinced that she's going to make her fortune.'

'Again?' I say, realising that must be why the sitting room of Mum's flat was stacked with cardboard boxes.

'Again,' she says and our eyes meet. 'You know your mum; she's a sucker for a get-rich scheme and even more for a man with a good line of patter.'

I nod. Nanna settles back on her new chair – it's an upright one with an extending footrest, and sturdy arm supports. She puts a cushion on her lap and pats it. A moment later, as if summoned, Phoebe, her calico cat, appears. She hops onto Nanna's lap with a chirrup.

Nanna switches on the television. 'You don't mind if I just turn on the news? I want to see what's happening.'

She and Grandpa said this after every lunch. Sandwiches and soup at twelve-thirty, a sit-down, the news on, and one or other of them would doze off for quarter of an hour then act surprised, as if it didn't happen like clock-work every afternoon. It is nice that, even a year on from Grandpa's death, she is still doing the same little routines. It makes me feel safe, somehow. I eat another sandwich – they're sliced into little triangles, a throwback from when I was little and I used to ask for them that way in my packed lunch. Nanna watches the news, intently. She's always been fascinated by politics and mutters under her breath when a clip of Prime Minister's Questions appears on the screen. I suppress a smile, and drink my tea.

Sure enough, ten minutes later she's dozed off. I take

the plates and cups through to the tiny kitchen and wash them in the sink. She's already rinsed off the aluminium foil and left it to dry on the draining board – she's from the generation of make do and mend. I go back through to the sitting room and she's snoring gently. It's only then that I realise that she looks so much older, all of a sudden. But it can't have just happened. I suppose going away and coming back has brought it into relief. A knot of anxiety twists in my stomach at the thought of losing her and I hold on to the back of the sofa, gripping the edge of it with my fingers until my knuckles whiten.

'Dear me,' she says, waking with a start. 'I must have dropped off.'

I laugh, and the moment is broken.

'Let's go to the community centre,' she says, 'and I'll introduce you to Cyril, my new friend. He's setting up a mindfulness circle – used to be a bit of an old hippy, if you ask me. He's very nice.'

I look at her sideways. 'Oh yes?'

'Shush. He's just a friend. I'm far too old for that sort of thing.' She levers herself out of the armchair.

We walk to the community centre, which I recognise from Nanna's Instagram photographs. It's funny piecing it all together – makes me realise how much she must enjoy seeing the photos of my life in London. I resolve to take more. I've been slacking off a bit, because life seems to have been nothing but the commute to work, slaving over a hot desk all day, commuting home again, collapsing in front of Netflix, and then bed.

'This is Cyril,' Nanna Beth says, having taken me straight over to a man once we arrive at the centre.

I can see he was probably quite handsome in his day. He's got a kind face, and is dressed in a soft houndstooth checked shirt and a smart navy blue sweater.

'Ah, Jess, I've heard all about you. I'm a bit of a fan.'

'You are?' I say, surprised.

'I am. Anyone who brings a smile to Beth's face the way you do must be a pretty good sort, in my opinion.'

I look sideways at Nanna Beth and realise with amusement that she's gone a little bit pink. She ducks her head, laughing, and says, 'Oh, Cyril, you are a charmer.'

Cyril chuckles, sounding pleased with himself – but not in a smarmy way. It's nice for her to have something good in her life after all those years of looking after Grandpa with his dementia.

'I'm going to take Jess for a walk along the prom, and get an ice cream. You're never too old for an ice cream with your nanna, are you,' she says, squeezing my arm. I shake my head.

'Do you want to join us?'

'Ice cream, in March?' Cyril shakes his head and does a mock shiver. It's sunny outside, but there's still a definite chill in the air. But ice cream on the prom is our thing, and we've always done it no matter what the weather. 'Absolutely not. I'm sure you two girls have lots to catch up on, and I've got plenty to be going on with here.'

I swear if he could have had a cartoon twinkle in his eye, he would have. Nanna positively skips out of the community centre on my arm. I can't help wondering if I'll be as sprightly as she is at seventy-nine.

It occurs to me as we're wandering along the prom with ice cream cones, admiring the massed plantings of daffodils in their huge pots by the shelters, that Nanna's got a more interesting love life going on than I do. Something Sophie said the other day comes back to me – she pointed out in the bar the other day that I needed to get back on the horse. I said I'd think about it. And as I stand in the queue waiting for ice creams, I do. Maybe I should take the plunge and try dating again. It can't do any harm, can it? We've got a half-populated Tinder profile sitting there. Maybe – ugh. I grimace. I can't face the dick pics and the endless stream of weirdos sending messages. I've heard so many horror stories.

'No nice young men on the scene?' Nanna asks, looking at me over her glasses. It's as if she can read my mind.

I shake my head.

'None.'

'The trouble with you, lovey, is you've got a streak of your mother in you.'

I step back, stunned. Mum and I couldn't *be* more different. 'Me? And Mum?'

'Both old romantics, the pair of you. She's always dreamed that someone's going to come and sweep her off her feet, take her away from all this. That's why she's addicted to the drama of being on stage. And you're the same in your own way – hooked on those romantic films.'

I look at her, feeling my brows gathering in a frown of confusion.

'I don't think I'm like Mum at all,' I say, then eat some more ice cream and think about what she's said. I like it better when Nanna and I talk about day-to-day stuff, when she doesn't make me confront unpleasant realities. Today it's as if someone's taken her filter off. Maybe it's an age thing.

'I *definitely* don't want someone to sweep me off my feet,' I say, firmly. 'I've seen more than enough of that with Mum. She's been swept off her feet by so many dodgy con artists that I'm surprised she even knows whether she's the right way up or not.'

'No, but you'd like a nice happy ever after, wouldn't you?'

I let my guard down a little at that. 'A bit,' I concede.

'What about that nice Alex boy, then? I can't help noticing you're spending a lot of time with him.'

'As *friends*, Nanna. That's all.'

She gives me an old-fashioned look. 'Just friends?'

'Definitely. It's nice to have someone showing me London – that's it.'

'Hrmm,' she says, and then changes the subject, in a way that makes it clear she doesn't believe me for a second.

CHAPTER THIRTEEN

Alex

31st March, London

'Stick the kettle on, Alex, I'm gasping for a cuppa.'

I hear Becky call, and the slam of the door, thud of her bag full of papers on the dresser, clatter of her keys landing in the dish she keeps beside the half-dead geranium that's keeling over on a stand in the hall.

Jess got back from a weekend in Bournemouth an hour or so ago. I was sleeping off a night shift when I heard her coming upstairs and the sound of the shower turning on. It's nice that she's back. I don't know why, but I like it when everyone's here. I fill the kettle and put it on to boil, absent-mindedly picking up some dishes from the draining board and stacking them on the shelf. The dishwasher's on the blink again – I got home at half ten this morning to find it had sicked up grey water all over the floor, and I stood for about five night-shift-fuzzy minutes trying to decide if the right thing to do would be to a) pretend I hadn't seen it and leave it for someone else to deal with or b) unload the half-washed dishes and stack them up by the sink. In the end, I'd given a fairly hefty sigh then got on with it. Meanwhile, someone else had clearly washed them and left them to dry – most likely Rob. He was a stickler for a tidy kitchen.

With the dishes sorted and the surfaces wiped, I sit down at the kitchen table with a couple of pieces of toast. I'm so tired I feel like I've got jet lag, only without the exotic holiday to show for it. And with tiredness comes all the feelings I try to keep squashed down with work and the gym and all the other stuff people do to get a handle on emotional crap. I feel a bit shit that I haven't been able to make it back down to Kent for Mother's Day today, because I worked a late shift yesterday and I've got an assignment due next week that I've barely started, so I blew way more money than I can afford sending Mum a massive bunch of flowers. And then I went for a run, even though I was completely knackered. It helped, a bit. Not as much as the delicious three hours of sleep I've just had, mind you.

The guilt's worse now that Dad's gone, of course. My big sister Mel's in finance, and she's working in New York on secondment, which is a pretty reasonable excuse not to be able to make it, but it feels a bit crap to be an hour away on the train and stuck here in London because I've got an assignment to get done and I've worked a weekend shift. It's weird. I knew that we'd be thrown straight into placements in our first year, but I thought there'd be a bit more time to – I dunno. Breathe, maybe?

Nursing's way more all-consuming than law. I can't help thinking of all the friends who took the piss when I told them I was leaving. They thought I couldn't hack the pace at work, but the irony is nursing is way more pressurised than anything I experienced in law. If I'm not writing essays or studying for never-ending maths tests for medication dosage formulas, I'm cramming in a couple of agency shifts to get a bit of extra money coming in. Thank God for Becky – if she hadn't offered me a room in this place, I'd have spent every last penny on rent before I'd reached the end of my first year. As it is, money's tight. Rob's promised to give us another lesson in baking our own bread one day this week – he's got a couple of days off, and nothing to do in them, he says – so perhaps I can save some money by making all my own sandwiches from scratch.

'Look what I've got.' Becky appears in the kitchen, wearing a fluffy cat onesie. I assume she's been upstairs to change in record time, rather than going to Costco wearing it.

Jess appears moments after. She looks tired as well – it's like we've all got sleeping sickness. She puts a hand to her mouth, suppressing a massive yawn.

'Cock Soup?' I say, peering at the sachet Becky's holding. She snorts with laughter.

'It was on special offer. I got loads of noodles, too. We can split the cost.'

'Soup, made from cocks,' I say slowly.

Becky starts laughing. 'I like a nice cock in my soup,' she manages.

I don't know why, but for some reason Becky goes into hysterics and it's contagious. It's a good five minutes before we stop laughing, and my stomach muscles are killing me.

'I am *not* eating that,' Jess says, wiping her eyes.

'It's good for you. Packed with—' Becky turns the pack over and scans the ingredients '—monosodium glutamate and chicken flavouring. Mmm.'

'I'd rather starve,' Jess says.

'You're going to have to, unless you've got any other plans for making the rest of your crappy paycheque stretch.' Becky throws her a packet.

'I bet it's not that bad. Try it. Delicious salty goodness.'

'Don't start that again.'

Emma comes in at that point. She's looking pissed off about something, and she doesn't stay in the kitchen long before heading upstairs telling us she's going to have a bath. I hang around, watching as Becky checks the kitchen cupboards for signs of the mouse, even though I know I should go upstairs and get to work on the assignment that's due next week. In the end, I compromise and get my laptop and my notes and take them into the sitting room where Rob's watching the Arsenal match.

'They're playing like shit, man,' he says, offering me a beer.

'I shouldn't, I've got work to do,' I say, shaking my

head, but he gives me a sceptical look and extends his arm a bit further, waggling the bottle under my nose.

'Go on, then. You've twisted my arm.'

Predictably I end up spending more time watching the match than I do on the assignment. Rob's easy company, which helps. He's not one of those blokes who watches the football and screams at the TV – probably because it's not his team playing (he's a Liverpool supporter), but also because he's pretty laid-back by nature, as I'm discovering now we're spending more time together. His odd hours and mine seem to overlap, so we're spending more time than I expected just hanging out, cooking and watching television.

'How's it going?' He indicates the printouts and the laptop, now sitting on the coffee table.

'Good,' I say.

'You're not missing the legal stuff?'

'God, no.' I shake my head vigorously.

'I reckon when you start a career as an adult, you've got more of an idea what you're getting yourself into,' he says, in his gruff Glaswegian burr. 'I used to work in construction management,' he continues.

'Really?' I ask, trying not to sound surprised. He doesn't really look the type.

'Aye. Gave it all up and went back to college when I was about the same age you are now. Everyone thought I was off my head.'

'And no regrets?'

He gives a deep laugh. 'I wouldnae mind doing a few

less split shifts, but they come wi' the job. I bet you'd no' say no to a nine to five nursing job if one came up when you graduated.'

'They're rarer than hen's teeth,' I say.

'Aye, exactly. But you wouldn't give it up, would you?'

I shake my head again. 'Definitely not.'

'Weird, isn't it? I guess that's why they talk about vocations. You must've been born to it and it just took a while to find out.'

I think about the nurses in the hospital when Dad was sick, and the palliative care nurses in the day hospice in his final days: their kindness and the way they always seemed to hold it together no matter what was going on.

I recall a recent shift when I'd had a really hard night working as an HCA on a geriatric ward, doing a bit of agency work, and I'd been covered from head to toe in – well, let's just say I pretty much had to hose myself down afterwards. One of the nurses had got wind of the fact that I was a career changer and she'd been pretty catty about it. I'd been given all the crappy jobs – literally – but there was no way I was being accused of being 'too posh to wash' by the others on shift. So, I rolled up my sleeves and got on with it. By the end of the evening, the entire ward had been given a personal hygiene wash – head to toe, and everything else in between – and the sarky nurse had buttoned it.

Rob's right. Placements are long, the essays are never-ending, but I still don't regret it one bit.

Becky pops her head round the door. She's all dressed up, and tells us she's off to meet some friends from work. The fact that it's a Sunday night means nothing to her – she's always up for a night out. I pick up my assignment and head upstairs, saying goodnight to Rob, quietly convinced that I've done the right thing. It's a good feeling.

CHAPTER FOURTEEN

Jess

6th April

'I've chosen a dress,' says Sophie, brandishing a magazine at us.

We're sitting in gorgeous yellow sunshine on the little balcony of Sophie and Rich's flat in East London, where you can almost see the canal if you lean over at a precarious angle and peer between the houses in front. There's just about enough room for the three of us, as long as we don't try and move too fast.

'I took your advice – can't remember which one of you said it, but I've gone for the slinkiest one I could find. If that doesn't get me pregnant, I don't know what will.'

'If you think that's what makes you pregnant, it's not surprising it's not happened yet,' says Gen, drily. She looks up at the magazine. 'Ooh, very nice.'

It's a gorgeous, dark cream dress and it will suit Sophie's slender figure perfectly. 'I love it,' I agree.

'Anyway,' Gen says, tapping on the table with her finger, as if calling us back to order, 'let's get back to the task in hand. Which is *get Jess a shag*, in case anyone's forgotten.'

'Excuse me,' I yelp. 'I want a date. I'm not after a one-night stand.'

Sophie leans over and looks at my phone screen, where we've finally uploaded a decent photo to my Tinder profile, and we're trying to work out what to put on my bio. We used Gen's one before to look through profiles, but now I've – well, they've – decided that I need to get out there.

'You should get a dog. I was running in the park the other morning and I saw loads of good-looking men with dogs,' says Sophie.

'Should you be running in your condition?' Gen looks at her thoughtfully, tapping a pen against her teeth.

'What condition?' I spin round to look at Sophie. 'Have I missed a memo?'

She shakes her head. 'Still in the waiting period. Or hopefully *not* period.'

'Yeah, but you might jog it out of place or something,' says Gen, waving an arm, vaguely.

'I can't put my life on hold because I'm trying to get pregnant,' says Sophie. 'Anyway I've got a good feeling about this month. I did a headstand after sex on day fourteen.'

156

I glance at Gen, who looks faintly disgusted.

'TMI,' we both say, in unison.

'Soz,' says Sophie, shrugging.

There's a For Sale sign hanging from the railings in front of us. When Soph decides she wants something, she doesn't hang about. She's decided she wants a wedding ring, two-point-four children, a dog, and a house in the suburbs. And by sheer force of nature (and a few headstands) she'll get it. She always does.

Rich pops out to the balcony to kiss Sophie goodbye.

'Just nipping up to the gym,' he says, dropping a kiss on the top of her head. 'See you two later.'

I flick a glance in Gen's direction, wondering if she's thinking what I'm thinking. I know way more about Rich's sex life than I feel is necessary. Meanwhile, my sex life is completely dead in the water, and I'm pretty sure that Alex and Emma hooked up again the other night. Not that I've a problem with that, of course, because we're *friends* and that's perfectly nice. But I did kind of hope maybe it had fizzled out.

The most logical conclusion is to do as the saying goes, and get over him by getting under someone else. Or on top of. I'm not fussy, really. So, I've done it. Committed to signing up for online dating, starting with Tinder, because it's free, and the idea of paying for online dating seems a bit – well, it doesn't really matter what it seems, the truth is I'm skint.

'Why don't you just put something nice in your bio: "likes long walks and lazy Sundays drinking coffee and reading the papers"?' Sophie suggests, as if it's that easy to bag a man.

'Yeah, that'll definitely do it,' Gen says, giving me a bug-eyed stare.

'What's wrong with that?' Sophie sounds slightly offended.

'It's just a bit – sad.'

'But it's true. She does like walks and Sundays and coffee and all that stuff. Don't you, Jess?' She looks to me for confirmation. I feel torn.

'I do,' I say, hesitantly. 'It's just a bit . . .'

'Clichéd,' says Gen, firmly.

'Oh.' Sophie sags a little bit in her chair.

'Oh God,' Gen looks slightly shame-faced. 'Hang on, you met Rich at uni. I was feeling guilty in case I'd exposed your secret Tinder technique.'

'Yes, we met in the debating club, remember?'

Gen and I exchange glances. Nope, don't remember that at all, but it couldn't be more Sophie if she tried.

I should channel her, I think, and then I'd meet someone nice. My thoughts float in the direction of Alex, and I realise that if I was Sophie I'd probably just channel my thoughts in the direction of him, and he'd realise that he was looking for a relationship after all, and definitely wasn't after a no-strings-attached shag-fest with Emma. I wrinkle my nose at the thought.

'You all right?' Gen looks at me with concern.

'I've heard some horror stories about Tinder,' I say quickly (it's the first thing that springs to mind, and it's true at least). 'What if I end up being chopped into pieces by an axe murderer?'

'That could happen any day of the week regardless of dating apps,' says Sophie, reassuringly. She even squeezes my arm to underline what she's saying, her face creased into a little frown of kindness.

'Right, well, that's comforting,' I say.

'They're more likely to be married players, looking for a bit on the side,' says Gen.

'Nice,' I say in despair.

'Well, they're not *all*. I mean there are *some* decent men left out there. There must be,' Gen adds.

I look down at my screen, feeling faintly sick at the thought of my photo being out there, and my face being swiped left (or was it right? God, I better find that out) on a whim.

'One of the girls at work was telling me that she got a match the other day,' I tell them. 'He was a really nice-looking guy, really good job working as an investment banker, et cetera, et cetera, et cetera. Two messages in, the formalities over with, and he asked her what she was doing. "Just having a coffee and thinking about heading to the shops for a bit of a wander," she said. "What about you?"' I grimaced, thinking about poor Jav's face when she'd been telling us over lunch.

'And he replied: "Just cracking one off over your photograph".'

'Ugh.' Sophie's nose wrinkles in disgust. 'And that was supposed to be a come-on?'

'A come-over,' Gen said, also looking a bit queasy. 'This is why I intend to remain single forever. I'm not putting myself through all that crap.'

'Uh, thanks, Gen,' I say.

'Sorry.'

'I'm not sure I'm ready for this.' I pick up the phone. There's a photograph of a nice-looking man with dark brown hair and green eyes looking back at me. 'Oh.'

Gen snatches the phone back. 'Exactly.' She swipes at the screen.

'Oh my God, did you swipe him away?'

'Nope.' Gen puts the phone back down on the table, looking triumphant. 'I just took your Tinder virginity.'

'Ewww,' I say, feeling slightly sick. The phone buzzes and I pick it up.

'Oh my God, he's replied.' Gen gives a squeak of glee and high-fives Sophie. 'Get in.'

I look up and catch a glimpse of my face in the mirror. It looks more horrified than excited, but they don't seem to have noticed that.

CHAPTER FIFTEEN

Jess

13th April

And so, that's how I end up standing – one week, and a lot of surprisingly saucy Tinder chat (which I have to confess I liked more than I expected, so maybe I'm not as much of a prude as I thought) later – by the bridge leading to a riverboat on the Thames, dressed in one of Sophie's mega-expensive dresses, sheltering under Rob's golf umbrella in the pouring rain. Theo, my date, has told me to meet him here instead of the bar we were meant to be at, because he's running late. I guess that's what happens when you work in the city and you're a high-flying investment banker type. I peer through the sheets of rain, trying to see if I can spot him through the crowds. There's a mixture of people dressed up and heading into the party boat, drenched tourists with raincoats, and pissed-off-looking commuters making their way back home.

He'd left it late to tell me about the change of plans. I'd stood in the bar looking around for him for a while, scanning the place in case he was one of those people who didn't look anything like his picture. But then a waiter had come up and asked if I wanted a table, so I'd said yes (because I'm a strong independent woman and I don't mind sitting alone at a table in a crowded bar drinking a glass of red wine that costs £15). But then the glass of wine – which I'd been eking out for as long as I could – ran out, and he still hadn't turned up. And just as I was paying the bill and thinking that literally everyone in the entire place knew that I'd been stood up (because who goes to a bar dressed in a peacock-blue body-con dress with expensive hair and ridiculous really-hard-to-walk-in shoes for a casual solo drink?) my phone buzzed. And it was Theo, full of apologies, asking me to jump in an Uber and telling me he'd sort it out when I got there.

As first dates go, this is pretty bloody spectacular. I'm his plus-one at a masquerade ball, and despite the rain and the wind and the feeling that I might actually freeze to death if he doesn't turn up soon, I'm so excited I could burst. And I can't wait to get my hands on him, if I'm honest. He's gorgeous, charming, has an amazing job in investment banking, and a pretty good line in chat. I think I might have struck lucky the first time. It has to happen to some people, doesn't it? I mean statistically speaking, for all those people kissing frogs there has to be a one-in-a-million chance that I'll be the one who ends up with the prince?

I wrap the long coat Sophie has lent me around my chest, trying to keep the rain out. Emma's been really sweet, and done my hair up in a gorgeous mass of curls and so many kirby grips I won't have a clue how to get it down tomorrow morning, but that's the last thing on my mind. I don't even care (well, all right, a tiny bit, but I'm going to let that go) that I'm pretty sure I heard her creeping out of Alex's room yesterday morning. It might've been my imagination, anyway.

Oh come on, come on . . . It's five past seven, and Theo said he'd be here at five to. I'm standing in the rain, watching as glowing couples and groups of chatting people make their way across the little bridge and onto the boat. The railings are strung with fairy lights, which are swaying in the wind, and for a second it's as if I'm looking at myself from the outside, and it feels like I'm at the start of a movie.

And then I spot him. Hmm. All right, he's shorter than I imagined, but definitely still cute. And he's meandering along, talking on the phone – probably some terribly busy and important investment banking call, which is why he isn't rushing, because otherwise he'd get out of breath – and as he sees me he raises an arm in greeting, and ends the call.

'Jess,' Theo says, kissing me on the mouth. He smells of whisky and I realise in a second that he's already more than a little bit drunk. His eyes are crossing slightly, and he's swaying – and not just because we're being buffeted by the wind. 'Sorry I'm a bit late, got caught up in a –

thing.' His jaw is stubbled and he looks hollow-eyed and exhausted. 'You look lovely.'

He starts walking up the gangway towards the boat, and I realise I'm still standing, half expecting him to take the arm of my now-sodden coat. I hurry after him.

'I'll take your coat, madam,' says a man in a white jacket as we step onto the riverboat. He hands us each a black mask. Mine is trimmed with tiny diamante sparkles, which glitter in the light. Theo's is plain black. He slips his on immediately and his eyes gleam out at me.

'The ladies are just over there, if you want to—' He gives me an up and down look, and I suddenly feel very not-London and a bit scruffy, then checks his phone. He catches a glimpse of someone over my shoulder and waves at them. 'You nip to the loo, and I'll get you a drink. Don't forget your mask.'

A second later, he's gone. I go to the bathroom and look at myself in the mirror, fixing my lipstick – which I've chewed off, biting my lip in anticipation and nerves waiting for him to arrive – and try to tame my hair, which has come loose in the wind and rain so that lots of dark tendrils are fluffing around the edges of my face. I hook the mask on and look at myself once more.

I feel excited, and glamorous, and I tell myself that this is all very romantic. Me, at a masked ball, in London, with an investment banker as my date. A slightly drunk one, but nonetheless.

I climb the stairs and realise that while I've been down there they've loosed the boat from its moorings, and

164

we're sailing. The floor is swaying slightly beneath my feet.

The space is thronging with people, and I stand for a moment, trying to work out which one of the hundred or so men in black tie and a plain black mask is Theo.

'There you are,' he says, over my shoulder. I turn around and he's holding a bottle of expensive champagne with a glass already poured for me. He takes a slug from the bottle. 'Thought you'd gone overboard.'

'Thanks,' I say as I take the glass and sip it, looking around. The women are wearing vibrant-coloured dresses covered in sequins and sparkles. Sophie's clingy peacock dress, which had felt so expensive before I left, now makes me feel a little bit drab, like a moth in comparison to their iridescent, dazzling butterfly garb.

'Theo!' A woman in a very short purple dress trimmed with feathers grabs his arm and he turns, taking another drink from the bottle of champagne. 'There you are,' she says. 'And who is this?' She looks at me, expectantly.

'This is Jess,' Theo answers.

'Hello,' I say, wondering if I should extend my hand for her to shake, or clink glasses, or what the etiquette is in these situations. She gives me a faint half-smile and turns, noticing someone else in the crowd.

'Jack!'

'My boss,' says Theo. He reaches forward and fingers the sparkling strap of my dress. 'You look gorgeous.'

'Thanks.'

I think he must've had quite a lot to drink already. His

165

voice is slurred and thick. 'Just got to do a bit of mingling, that sort of thing. You'll be okay here for a moment, yeah?'

I stand beside the bar, holding my glass of champagne, and try to look like I'm just casually people-watching, in the manner of a person who is happy in their own company. After ten minutes, Theo reappears, looking suspiciously bright-eyed. 'Jess. Sorry. Want to come upstairs?' he says.

We climb up the narrow metal staircase and onto the covered deck. The rain and wind have dropped, and the air smells fresh and clean. London sparkles, the lights on the embankment glittering like strings of jewels. The London Eye glows in the darkening blue sky and the buildings are a rainbow of lights silhouetted against the night. I turn to murmur something about how pretty it is to Theo, and realise he's gone – again. This is not going according to plan, and I'm on a bloody boat.

Help, I message Gen and Sophie.

What's happened? Sophie replies, instantly. *Man overboard?*

I shift out of the way as a couple, clearly very drunk, rebound against me, giggling, then disappear behind a pillar.

No. Man AWOL.

There's a moment before Sophie replies.

Oh my God, he stood you up?

No, I tap into my phone, as another drunk man in a mask steps on my foot as he walks past. I glare at him, but I think he's probably too pissed to notice.

166

Worse. He's here, he's pissed, and I've lost him on a bloody boat.

I go back downstairs, feeling like a complete idiot. An hour later, I've learned more than I needed to know about investment banking from that bloke in the office who nobody wants to talk to (there's always one), who has cornered me and downloaded the contents of his brain onto me. Occasionally I see Theo, who's clearly forgotten I even exist, passing by, always with a bottle in hand, rapidly reaching the staggering stage of drunkenness.

I excuse myself, leaving the office bore talking to another victim who'd found themselves in the corner of doom. And when I come out of the loo, I see what has to be the perfect end to a perfect date. Theo is standing, one arm propping himself up against the wall, the other burrowing like a ferret inside the front of a woman's dress, with his tongue halfway down her throat. I contemplate getting a drink and pouring it over his head, but I can't be bothered climbing the stairs and going to the bar, so I leave him there, and chalk it up to experience.

I see I have a message: *How's it going?*

God, I love Sophie. I think she's feeling guilty that my first Tinder date has turned out to be such a nightmare.

Well, he's now getting off with someone else, and I'm trapped on the boat from hell.

Where are you?

I message her the location.

I'm somewhere near Vauxhall.

Leave it with me, she replies.

A few minutes later, she messages again. Bless her, she's looked up the boat, worked out where the next stop on the Thames is, and has booked me an Uber. I really do love her.

'All right?' says the Uber driver as I climb in, having finally escaped the boat.

'I've had better evenings,' I say, sitting back against the seat and shaking my head in despair.

I get home forty-five minutes later, having messaged thanks in about fifteen different languages to Sophie, and rummage in my bag for the keys to the front door. I'm just about to put the key in the lock when the door opens and I stagger forward slightly, straight into Alex.

'Whoops,' says Alex.

'Sorry,' I say, steadying myself against the door.

He raises an eyebrow and gives that lopsided smile that makes my knees – bloody disobedient knees, which I wish would learn to behave themselves – go a bit weak. 'Good night, was it?'

I splutter. 'Hardly.'

'You coming in, then?'

CHAPTER SIXTEEN

Alex

13th April

Normal people would probably take advantage of the first Saturday night off in what felt like forever to go out and get hammered. Normal people – I think, as I stretch luxuriously, revelling in the fact that I've got the entire sitting room to myself and the house is empty – don't work the sort of week I've just worked. I put my feet up on the coffee table and sink into the battered pink sofa. This is exactly what I need.

'There's been an explosion in the Heart Surgery ward,' says a voice, urgently. No, I have no idea why watching a hospital drama on a Saturday night is my idea of relaxation but it's the kind of mindless thing I need right now. It bears precisely no relation to my experiences so far of hospital life, but I quite like it for that. For one thing, they're always using their phones in the ward.

Everyone knows there's generally only one spot in the entire hospital where you can get 4G service, and it's usually down a corridor near a supplies cupboard. You can always find them if you're in a hospital – just look for the spot where a disparate collection of NHS Trust staff are hovering, fingers tapping furiously, catching up on group chats or making plans for the end of their shift. Take it from me. It's the most useful information I've learned so far.

So, the plan is this: Sunday off, after six days working on the trot. Lie-in, lazy, scrambled eggs and toast sort of morning, followed by a walk around Hyde Park with Jess. The blossom's gorgeous this time of year, and we can have a wander up to look at Buckingham Palace, maybe do the Royal Mews, and be tourists for the day. That's assuming she comes home, of course. When she'd headed out earlier she looked – well. I'd had a moment when I'd had to remind myself sharply that just because I was used to hanging out with her in jeans, a hoody and her Converse, didn't mean she couldn't scrub up and look frankly amazing for a date. I'd made a bit of a joke out of it, and to be honest I was still feeling a bit guilty that I hadn't been generous enough to just tell her how great she'd looked. Emma had done Jess's hair, and her eyes were huge and smoky with dark shadow all around them. She'd looked amazing.

Thinking of Emma reminds me of what had happened next. I had nipped upstairs to get my phone charger and overheard Emma talking on the phone, her door ajar.

'Yeah, I don't know what I'm doing now. I think this evening I'm having a night in.'

There was a pause, and Emma had laughed. 'I suppose, yes. Boyfriend . . . no.'

I knew I shouldn't be listening, but that didn't stop me. It was as if time stood still for a second.

A tinkly laugh. 'Yeah. Yes. You'll meet him eventually, I promise. I'm working on it. Playing it cool.'

I don't know what made me listen. Some sort of weird sixth sense she was talking about me – or us, not that there was an *us*. At least, I hadn't thought there was. We'd had several *this is nothing serious, definitely just a bit of fun* type conversations.

'Yeah, I'd love you to meet him. I might see if he fancies dinner next week – I mean that might be a bit soon, but—'

There was a silence and then Emma laughed, and I realised that no, hang on, she was clearly talking about someone else. She must've met someone. I puffed out a breath, which was half a sigh of relief and half – well, nobody wants to feel like they've just been given the silent heave-ho without even being consulted, do they? Emma said something else I couldn't catch, and then laughed again.

'Yes, he's cute. Used to be a lawyer. He's training to be a nurse.'

I looked down at the skin on my knuckles, which was turning white as I gripped the stair wall. Who was Emma talking to? And – God. I felt my face invert in a grimace.

The deal we'd both agreed was that it was nothing more than a friends with benefits sort of thing. Nobody getting too involved, nobody getting hurt.

I'd crept back downstairs, keen to make sure she didn't realise I'd overheard.

In the end, half an hour later, Emma had popped her head around the kitchen door and said she was off out for last-minute drinks with a friend, and that maybe she'd see me later, if I was still up.

We'd slept together for the first time on New Year's Eve, and now it's April. I suppose it was naïve of me to think something could stay so casual for that long. It's not Emma. She's lovely. But after Alice – no way. Signing up for my new career meant walking away from a relationship I thought was for life, and I'm not taking that sort of risk again, not now, with years of training to do. I'm just starting to feel that, actually, I'm okay on my own, and I'm getting over the whole Alice thing.

I let myself think about Alice, which is something I don't often do. I'm over her – but I don't want to leap into anything else and end up in the same place all over again. If Emma is starting to think there's something more to this, I'm going to have to knock it on the head, gently. But – I rub my face in confusion – how the hell do I do that without causing ructions in the house-share?

This is exactly what Becky had meant with her no-relationships rule. It wasn't the being in a relationship that was the problem, it's the end of them when it all gets messy. And Emma's the sort of girl who likes things done her way.

Just as the credits begin to roll on my overdramatic hospital drama, I hear a commotion at the door. I figure it's probably someone at the wrong house. I get to the door and pull it open and there's a moment when Jess sort of falls through and crashes against me with a little 'oomph' noise of surprise. Her hair is damp and curling round her face in little strands, and all the dark eye make-up she'd had on is smudged. She takes a step back. Her coat's splattered with huge raindrops.

'Good night, was it?' I can't help smiling at her. She looks so cross.

'Hardly.'

'You coming in then?' She wipes her feet on the mat. 'So the date didn't go well?'

'Not exactly. I'm bloody freezing. If this was an April shower, I don't like it.'

She steps past me and shrugs off her coat, revealing the bluey-green dress she's got on underneath. I avert my eyes, as if she's undressing, not pulling off a pair of black heeled boots. And then she's Jess-sized again, standing in a pair of black tights on the carpet.

'Want me to put the kettle on?' I ask when I notice she's shivering.

'Give it five minutes. I'm going to run up and get out of this—' she motions to the dress '—have a quick shower to defrost, and put on something that doesn't make me feel like I'm dressing up.'

While Jess changes, I put the kettle on for tea, then make toast, buttering it thickly and spreading it with her favourite marmalade. And then I put it all on a tray, and take it into the sitting room. A moment later, Jess reappears, looking more like her usual self in a pair of checked flannel pyjama bottoms, and a light grey teddy-bear fleece top. Her hair and make-up are still in place, so she looks incongruous – like an actress after a performance on the West End stage.

'Oh my God. I think I love you,' she says, seeing the tea and toast. 'You're a mind reader.'

I hand her a mug. 'I figured you might be cold even after the shower.'

I watch as she creates the little nest she always makes when she sits watching television, wrapping her fingers around the mug and curling up on the sofa like a cat. She pulls a fluffy blanket down and wraps it over her legs, building a cushion fort around her, and almost purrs with happiness.

Then she takes a sip of tea, and pulls a face of absolute horror.

'Are you all right?' I ask, thinking maybe I've put salt in her tea instead of sugar.

'I am never, ever going on a Tinder date again,' she says.

I'm not sure why I feel something that is suspiciously like relief. She's my friend, nothing more. And I need to get a grip. It's nothing to do with me what – or how – she dates.

'What happened?' I say, carefully.

'Oh God,' Jess says, then regales me with the tale of Theo turning up plastered, dumping her in a corner, then getting off with someone else – making me roar with laughter.

'I honestly think dating is some sort of torture,' I say.

'You're not joking.' Jess pulls the blanket up towards her nose and turns to face me, laughing. She wipes a smudge of black mascara stuff from underneath her eye.

'I bet you can't beat that, though?'

'Mine's quite tame compared to that,' I say. 'I went on a blind date organised by a friend from uni once, when I'd just started working at the law firm. We were working such long hours, it was impossible to meet anyone.'

'Go on. So what happened?' Jess shuffles slightly on the sofa, so a cushion drops onto the floor. I pick it up and hand it back, and she hugs it, looking at me expectantly.

'Well, you know how everyone always has the old made-up emergency call thing?'

'You mean when you tell your friends to ring up and invent a disaster so you can make a quick exit?'

I nod.

'I was sitting in a bar in Clerkenwell, waiting for this girl to turn up. She walked up to the window, looked in, spotted me, picked up her phone and pretended to take a call.'

'What happened then?'

'She never came back.'

'Oh, Alex, you poor thing.' Jess reaches out and pats

me on the thigh. 'I wouldn't have left you sitting there like a lemon, I promise.' Her eyes are soulful. 'So what did you do?'

'Waited an hour, ate my entire body weight in olives, then went home.'

'And she definitely wasn't coming back? It wasn't an actual emergency or anything?'

I shake my head. 'Apparently she took one look and decided *no thanks*.'

'Brutal.' Jess gives a low whistle.

'Yeah, not great for the self-esteem.'

'That's dating in London for you,' Jess says, picking up the remote control and fiddling with it. 'But then you met Alice, and it all worked out okay in the end.'

'Well, okay until she dumped me, yeah. I mean basically great, apart from the whole thanks but no thanks element.'

I look at her with a dubious expression and she claps a hand to her mouth, realising what she's said.

'Oh my God, Alex.' Jess is laughing in horror. 'I am so sorry.'

We end up staying up for hours, watching a rom com that Jess has found on Netflix, drinking gallons of tea and eating toast. At one point Emma comes home, looks into the sitting room and says hi. I feel like a bit of a shit because I give her a quick wave of hello and Jess carries on talking. I don't know what to do about the whole Emma thing, and I don't want to think about it this evening. I just shove it to the back of my mind, and decide I'll leave it there until tomorrow.

CHAPTER SEVENTEEN

Alex

28th April

A few weeks pass. I still haven't worked out what to do about the whole Emma situation. Right now I'm opting for the very mature, completely self-aware *ignore the whole thing and hope it'll go away* approach. Emma hasn't been around that much, which helps. I think she's got a lot on with work. I've got a mountain of assignments to do, and another placement coming up, so the days pretty much pass without me even being aware what's going on. I'm still finding time to take the odd walk with Jess, but she's got loads going on at work as well. It's like the nicer the weather gets, and the more we'd want to actually enjoy it, the less time there is for us to get outside, which is a shame because I've been thinking maybe I could ask Jess for some advice on what to do about Emma.

But not this weekend – because whatever the weather, we're all outside for the whole of Sunday. Well, me, Jess and Becky, anyway. Matt, one of my old friends from when I worked with Becky, has been living with stage four leukaemia for the last year, and a couple of friends are running the London Marathon to raise money for Cancer Research.

'All you have to do is stand by the side of the road in Shadwell at the official cheering point for a few hours and gee up the runners,' Becky said, when she roped the rest of the house in. Jess is well up for it. Turns out she watches the marathon every year, so being there for the actual thing is really exciting for her. I volunteered last year in the St John's Ambulance tent, so I'm slightly less excited and slightly more aware that getting from our side of London to Shadwell on Marathon day is a feat in itself.

'It's really good of you guys to come along,' says Harry, the charity stand organiser. We're spread out across three folding trestle tables, with boxes of bottled water, bowls of jelly babies and packs of energy gel all ready to go. Jess dances around, banging the inflatable noisemakers together, trying them out.

'You might want to save that for later,' says Harry, grinning. He's an old hand at this. He tells us he's been running the cheering station here for the last ten years, since he recovered from leukaemia himself.

'Least I could do,' he says, with a self-deprecating grin.

'Lazy bugger,' says a woman who introduces herself as Andrea, Harry's wife. 'You could at least run the bloody marathon like I did.'

She's dressed from head to toe in the charity colours, with a ridiculous inflatable hat on her head. She's short and round and clearly the power behind Harry. Throughout the morning, I watch him glancing to her for approval regularly. She teases him incessantly and he winds her up. They're obviously mad about each other.

There's a long, long gap after the first runners go through, shooting past in seconds, following their pace-makers, and the wheelchair athletes, who move so fast that Jess almost misses the whole pack because she's gone to the loo.

'So what happens now?' Jess sits down on a folding chair and shades her eyes, looking up at Andrea.

'We wait.' Andrea tapes down a sign that's come loose.

'Sounds a bit ominous.'

Andrea nods emphatically. 'Rained the morning I ran it. I got soaked at the start, then had to run the whole thing in a damp T-shirt. And I lost five toenails.'

'Yowch.' Jess pulls a face. 'How did that happen?'

'It's fairly standard – 26.2 miles is a long old way to run.'

'Can't believe you did it. That's amazing,' Jess says, looking incredibly impressed.

'I can't either. It was bloody knackering,' Andrea says, then gives a snort of laughter. 'But it seemed a hell of a lot easier than going through six rounds of chemo like he did.' She nods in the direction of Harry, who is tying balloons full of helium to the side of the charity banner.

'I love watching the Marathon,' Jess says. 'Especially that bit at the beginning where you see everyone's stories and it makes you cry.'

'Oh God,' Becky says as finally she appears. She's been staying with a friend in Poplar, so she's on foot, wearing a baseball cap and sunglasses to protect her eyes from the already-bright sunshine. She pinches a couple of jelly-babies. 'Has she told you about how she sits there every year to watch the runners, weeping and eating toast?'

'Shut up, you,' Jess says, going pink.

'True though,' Becky says. 'God I am so hungover. I need a saline drip. You haven't learned to do that yet, have you, Alex?'

'I don't have one handy, no,' I say. 'And I don't think the medical tent would be that impressed if you turned up and told them you needed rehydration.'

'I'm going to go and find some full-fat Coke then. I need to be in full-on cheering mode for the lads from work.'

I nip to the loo and when I get back I stand for a moment, watching Jess chatting to Becky. I've been trying to work out how to talk to her about the whole thing with Emma – I mean if we're friends, there's no reason why I shouldn't be telling her, but at the same time, it feels – awkward. I don't want to mention it in front of Becky though, because of her whole no relationships thing – not that it *is* a relationship. That's kind of the whole point.

'Ready?' Andrea turns to me, and the moment is lost. From then on we're caught in a strange mixture of cheering then waiting, waiting then cheering.

The Mass Race runners come through first – super fit amateur athletes who zoom past us wearing our charity colours, grabbing a drink and tossing it to one side before pelting on down the road in search of a personal best time.

'I'm waiting for the people in fancy dress.' Jess peers into the distance again. 'I can't believe the noise.'

'That's why I said earlier that you'd soon have enough of it.' Harry grins and rattles the noisemakers near her ear. She ducks away, laughing.

Becky isn't joking when she says Jess cries at the runners. When the charity runners start coming through with the names of the people they're running for and their photos printed on the backs of their T-shirts, Jess basically starts sobbing and doesn't stop. Becky teases her about it incessantly.

'Shut up,' Jess says, wiping her face with both hands. Any make-up she had on is long gone. She blows her nose on a spare bit of kitchen roll from Andrea's picnic bag. 'I can't help it. It's just so . . .' and she points to a woman who's half-walking, half-jogging with "This one's for you, Dad" on the back of her T-shirt. And just like that, my heart cracks and I feel tears streaming down my face, too. I wipe them away, ineffectually. Jess hands me one of her tissues, silently, and bumps the side of my arm with hers.

*

'I feel like *I've* run a marathon after all that,' Becky says, hours later, as we fold up the last of the tables and high-five the other supporters. She blows us a kiss and heads off before we do, because she's left her stuff at her friend's place.

The tractors and clearing-up lorries have passed by now, following a handful of stragglers – some who were walking, some clearly baking hot in heavy fancy dress costumes. It's a long way to go dressed as Big Bird on a sunny day. Still, Big Bird gave us a cheery wave.

'You can do it,' Jess shouted, clapping as the last few people made their way past. They had another five and a bit miles to go, and they looked completely wiped out. But they brightened when she cheered them. I picked up my noisemaker and gave them a rattle, and together we called out their names.

'Come on, Brian, you can do it!'

'Go on, Sarah!'

'Jamie! Not long to go now.'

Without thinking, I put an arm around Jess's shoulders as we cheered the couple who were shuffling along in a tandem bicycle costume and as they passed it turned into a funny, awkward sort of hug and I think Jess's tears must be contagious because I saw they were running for our charity and I thought of Matt sitting at home watching the television and I had to wipe the tears away from my face again.

'Gets to us all in the end,' said Harry, clapping me on

the back. He dropped an arm around my shoulder and squeezed me. 'Get yourselves off for a drink.'

Jess went to collect her rucksack and Harry gave me a look. 'Got a good one there, son.'

'Oh she's not my—' I began, but he'd turned away before I could finish the sentence.

CHAPTER EIGHTEEN

Jess

3rd May

I look up at the sky, cerulean blue and cloudless, and feel the heat of the sun on my face. It could be the middle of August, instead of May. A little practical voice pops up in my head, and points out that I should probably be wearing sunscreen. I stop for a second and rummage in my bag – I'm sure there's some in there somewhere.

'It's better in May, before the summer holiday tourists appear,' Alex says. We're in Regent's Park near the zoo. We haven't been out for a walk for a while, or really out together at all since the Marathon; I've been flat out with work, and Alex has started a placement in the geriatric ward. He's been doing nights, which seems to be when they all die, grimly enough, so I'm cautious about asking how it's going because every tale seems to start with 'we lost another one last night . . .' I don't know how he does it and stays cheerful. It's weird. I can't imagine what would make anyone want to be a nurse, but I'm very glad that whatever it is makes people do it.

'I'm so tired I could sleep for a week,' says Alex.

'We can lie on the grass for a bit. We don't have to walk ten miles a day if you don't want to.'

He stops and looks at the grass. Newly mown, it looks quite tempting.

'Just for a bit?'

'Just for a bit,' I agree.

We lie down on the grass, side by side, and look up at the sky.

'When I was little I used to lie on the beach with my grandpa and spot shapes in the clouds,' I said. I'd forgotten that until now, looking up at a vaguely snowman-shaped cloud, hovering above us.

'*Do you want to build a snowman . . .*' sings Alex.

'You've spent too much time doing agency work on the kids' ward.'

'Tell me about it. I reckon I know the entire plot of *Frozen* inside out.'

'Does it even have a plot?' I ask.

He turns his head to look at me. 'Have a plot? I'll have you know there are academics right now arguing the toss over whether *Frozen* is a feminist tract or if it's inherently problematic because of its depiction of the trolls.'

'Seriously?'

He nods. 'Seriously.'

'I think I need to watch it and find out.'

'Deal.' He turns his head and looks back up at the sky. The air is heavy with the scent of candyfloss machines, bitter coffee, and the faint waft of something distinctly animal-ish from the zoo.

'Roaaaar!'

Something flies past our heads and I roll over onto my side just as Alex does, so we are looking straight at each other. His eyebrows gather in a frown, but he's laughing. He rolls over, and pushes himself up to standing.

'What the hell was that?' I scramble up, brushing newly cut grass off my legs.

'Low-flying zoo escapee?' he asks.

I point across the park. 'I think I've found the culprit.'

A small child is holding on to a remote control, trying inexpertly to fly a tiny plane, and making sound effects at the same time.

'Timmy, don't fly that so close to the people,' his mother shrieks as she runs toward him, grabbing the remote control, but it's too late. The plane, which zipped over our heads a second ago, has crashed straight into the newspaper an elderly and grumpy-looking man is reading, while sitting in a striped deckchair. He shuffles the paper and looks at us all over his glasses. Both Alex and I turn away, trying not to giggle.

'Let's get out of here before we get into trouble,' Alex says.

We walk along the edge of the zoo fence, looking up at the netting that hangs over the high rails, keeping us out and the animals in.

A giraffe peers over the fence at us, chewing thoughtfully.

'Oh look,' I point to her.

Alex looks up, shading his eyes. 'Hello, gorgeous.'

'She's lovely, isn't she?'

'Might be a he. I don't know how you tell with giraffes.'

'Sorry. Hello, gorgeous giraffe of indeterminate gender,' I say, laughing. Alex has his hands in the pockets of his jeans, and he gives me a gentle nudge with his shoulder.

'Fancy an ice cream?' he asks.

'God, yes.'

He points to the stall on the other side of the park. 'Race you.'

'What are you, five years old?' I ask, but he's already gone. I get there ages after him, realising as I stand with my hands on my knees and my lungs feeling like they're on fire that maybe it's time I got some proper exercise.

'Sorry,' Alex says, from above where I'm bent over. I take a breath in and unfurl myself, standing up to look him in the eye. He hands me an ice cream, swirled with raspberry sauce and covered in rainbow sprinkles.

'For this ' I take it from him and lick a trail of ice cream that's dripping down the side of the cone '—I will forgive you. This time.'

'How's your friend Gen getting on with her property guardian thing?'

'Oh—' I look up. He remembers so much detail. Alex pays attention to little things, I've noticed. He's the only one in the house who remembers how everyone takes their tea and coffee and doesn't have to ask. It's nice. 'I forgot I told you about that. She's fine, I think. A glitter ball in the bedroom is very much her style.'

'I wanted to ask your advice about something,' Alex says, as we start walking again. I look at him sideways. He's biting the edge of his ice cream cone, frowning in concentration as he twirls it round. I've never seen anyone eat an ice cream like that.

'Go on.' I scuff my toe on the gravel of the path. A flock of tourists fly past us on Boris Bikes, shrieking with laughter, and we jump out of the way.

'It's about Emma.'

Oh.

No.

My ice cream becomes very interesting and I look at it intently, hoping that I haven't gone red in the face. Alex stops, turning to look at me. I try to put it off, but I have to look him in the eye and I swallow as I do so. 'Emma?' I say, breezily. 'What about her?'

'Well, the thing is . . .' He tails off, biting his thumb-nail and gazing into the middle distance, back towards the zoo animals. I see the tall shape of the giraffe reaching up to take a mouthful of leaves from one of the trees. A plane flies past, with an advert hanging from the back of it, old-fashioned style. Bees are humming, and children are shrieking, and gravel is scrunching, and I'm waiting for him to say something, and then it all comes out in a jumble of words.

'I don't know if you know . . .' He pushes a hand through his hair. 'I don't want it to be awkward.'

'It's fine,' I say, airily. 'I mean, I think everyone must have some idea, so it's not going to be a major deal. And I'm sure you'll be very happy. You make a nice couple.' I think I've done quite a good job of that. Might be better to stop talking now, mind you. I press my lips together before any more words escape.

He runs a hand through his hair again, making it stand on end. I half want to laugh, but I also want to burst into tears and shout *it's not fair* like a child and run away. I like him, and he likes me, and we get on and make each other laugh and I've never seen him and Emma laughing together, and why does it have to be the case that I'm always the—

'We're *not* together,' he says firmly. 'And I don't want us to be. That's the problem.'

'Ohhh.' I raise my eyebrows, trying to look sage, and knowledgeable, and definitely not relieved. I'm not sure how well I manage it.

'Thing is, she mentioned something about me on the phone to a friend the other week and I – God I feel really awkward saying this. I'm not being a massive ego on legs. I just got the feeling that she's wanting more than . . .'

He screws up his face and goes a bit pink in the cheeks, then bites his lip, waiting for me to say something.

'Oh, but Emma's lovely,' I say, magnanimously. I can afford to be nice now. God, am I a bitch? I make a mental note to ask Gen and Sophie if they think I am.

'She is. I don't want to screw things up,' Alex says.

'God, no.' I think of Albany Road and try to imagine

190

someone else moving into Alex's room. We've all become accustomed to each other, and anyway, I don't want Alex moving anywhere. Not if his relationship with Emma's definitely off the cards.

'I'm sure it'll be fine. Just explain to her you don't want to be caught up in anything serious just now, or something like that.'

He looks serious then for a moment. 'We *had* that conversation at the start. It was her idea, actually. Maybe I need to make sure she realises it now. I think it's time to just knock it on the head.'

'Yes,' I say. We start strolling along beside the lake, watching the swans and the ducks swimming along, enjoying the sunshine.

Ooh, I think, maybe this means there's a chance after all. Not now, of course. But this was already the start of a beautiful friendship . . . maybe it could lead to something more.

But then Alex drops the bombshell, and I remember that being a daydreaming romantic doesn't mean the world's going to fall into place just to suit me.

'Thing is,' Alex says, thoughtfully, 'I'm just not ready to be in a relationship with anyone.' He sighs. 'Oh, I don't know. I got a reminder email the other day about my upcoming wedding.'

I open my mouth and shut it again. I'm not sure what the correct response to that is.

I go with 'I'm sorry.'

'Oh, don't be,' he says, turning to look at me and

smiling so his lovely crinkly eyes twinkle in a way that makes my knees go a bit funny. 'I mean it was clearly not meant to be with me and Alice. She wanted the whole package. House, money, lawyer husband, kids . . .'

'She could have had the almost-package,' I point out.

'Alice wasn't really an almost sort of person. She's a bit like your Sophie.'

'Ah,' I say. It all falls into place a bit then, and I think that maybe it's time I got a grip and recognised that neither Alice nor Emma were anything like me, and therefore I am very definitely not Alex's type, and that I should move on, in a very grown-up and sensible manner. To hide my face, I pull out my phone and take a photograph of two swans resting by a bush, their long necks intertwined. Even they're paired off, I think, crossly.

Later I meet Sophie for an emergency dinner summit. I'm all ready to dump all my feelings of angst and woe on her, but as soon as I walk into the pasta restaurant we love, I see her sitting at the table with her chin in her hand, looking glum.

'You okay?' I shove my bag under the table and look at her intently.

She nods. She's got her pale blonde hair tied up in a sleek ponytail, and her clothes and make-up are immaculate, as always. If you didn't know her, you wouldn't have a clue anything was wrong. But I could see that something was troubling her.

'It's not Rich, is it?'

She shakes her head. A waiter appears and asks what we want to drink.

'I'll have a glass of the Montepulciano d'Abruzzo,' I say, handing him back the menu.

'Lemonade, please,' says Soph.

I raise my eyebrows.

'That's what's wrong.' Sophie gives a gusty sigh. 'I'm doing all the right things. I even did that bloody head-stand again in bed last month after we had sex, because I read a thing on Mumsnet that said it can help you get pregnant.'

'Oh my God. You're not?' I pick up the wrong end of the stick completely. 'Is that why you're drinking lemonade?'

Sophie pleats the tablecloth with her fingers and looks at me. For a moment, her habitual cool and measured manner are replaced with an expression of genuine concern.

'You know, I just thought maybe it'd save time if I got pregnant now, and we'd be married in autumn, and then I could take maternity leave in the next tax year.'

I realise my mistake and blush. She's not pregnant after all. 'Oh my God Soph, you can't organise your life like that. Babies don't just come on demand . . . I don't think.'

'It's not organising,' she says, sounding slightly cross. 'It's more like multi-tasking.'

The waiter reappears with our drinks, and she sticks a paper straw in hers, sucking it gloomily. 'It's the first thing in my life that hasn't been under my control.'

God, I think about my chaotic life. The weeks between one payday and the next. The fact I'm utterly besotted with a man who thinks I'm well and truly in the friend zone. The fact that it's been ages since I saw my mother who was last sighted stacking essential oil equipment on the kitchen table and announcing that it was going to make her a fortune, and that I'm living in a subsidised house-share and if Becky decided to pull the rug out from under me I'd be screwed. 'I don't think I have anything in my life that *is* under my control.'

Sophie smiles ruefully at this. 'I suppose I should get a grip and stop complaining, really, shouldn't I?'

I shake my head. 'It's not that easy, though, is it?' I say. 'It's weird. Remember when we were little kids, and we thought being grown up meant having all the answers? Now we're almost thirty, and I feel like I haven't a clue what I'm doing.'

'Me neither,' says Sophie. She pushes back her chair. 'I must just run to the loo. If he comes while I'm gone, tell him I want the carbonara with some green salad on the side. No dressing.'

I watch her making her way across the room. With her long ponytail of blonde hair, height and long, long legs, she's always attracted attention. The waiter watches her with unashamed admiration before coming over to our table when I meet his eye.

'Your friend, she is very beautiful lady.'

I agree.

Very beautiful, and a slightly painful, jab-in-the-ribs

reminder of just how far I have to go in my life to start to feel like a fully functioning adult. How many years will it be before I even begin thinking about having a baby? I try to imagine it – I haven't even really given it much thought, and yet I am turning thirty this year. God, if I had a baby at, say, thirty-seven – I start doing sums in my head, and rapidly extend them to my fingers – I'd be fifty-seven by the time it turned twenty. That sounded like a lifetime away.

I think when Gen and Soph and I were young, we'd all been quite certain that by this age we'd all be settled and happy. Domestic bliss felt like a lifetime away for me. I guess that's what happens when you start all over again at the age of almost thirty.

CHAPTER NINETEEN

Alex

10th May

I get on the train to Canterbury. Not sure why it feels like the right thing to do, but it's been nagging at me. I dunno, maybe I'm reading too much into it, but the last couple of times we've spoken on the phone Mum's sounded a bit fragile: keen to tell me how busy she is, and how much she's got on.

I stare out of the window as the train pulls away, watching the familiar landmarks. I've sat on this same train countless times. An older man in an expensive-looking suit clears his throat in the chair opposite and spreads his newspaper over the table, and I feel a stab of grief. Weird how it hits you. It's not the anniversaries or the birthdays, it's the way a stranger shakes their newspaper open, or a song on the radio at the nurses' station, that reminds you of what you've lost. I rub my face with both hands, screwing up my eyes and then opening them wide. I can't remember not being tired. Everything's just a blur of —

I wake up as we pull into the station at Canterbury, because someone knocks me on the shoulder with their bag as they're pulling it down from the racks overhead.

'Sorry, mate.'

'You've done me a favour,' I say gratefully. I stand up, blearily, and pull my ticket out of my pocket as I get off the train.

I see my mother before she sees me – she's sitting in the car, waiting in the pick-up area beside the car park.

'Hello, darling,' she says, and gives me a kiss on the cheek.

'Mum.'

'I thought we could get a bit of lunch before we head home – go to the Red Lion?' she says, and we pull out of the car park.

The pub's busy, despite it being a weekday. We squeeze into a table in the corner and scan the menus.

'I spoke to Gwen the other day,' my mum says, casually.

I sit up and put the menu down. Mum carries on looking through the lunch options, as if we didn't both know that she was going to have the same thing she always has when she comes here – ploughman's lunch, no pickled onion, and half a pint of shandy.

'What for?' I ask.

I feel weirdly uncomfortable about that. Alice's mum was nice enough, but the idea of her ringing is . . . weird.

Is it weird? Maybe it's perfectly normal for them to stay in touch.

'You were going to marry her,' Mum says, clearly reading my thoughts. 'They would have been family. I thought it was nice.'

I make a vague noise of agreement. The last time I'd seen Alice had been anything but nice; we'd had a massive argument, where she'd made it more than clear that I was throwing my life away, ruining hers, and giving up a good career to (and I quote) *piss about wiping people's backsides for the rest of my life*.

I go up to the bar and place our order. We chat about mundane things for a while, then when our food arrives, Mum launches into a long list of all the things she's doing to keep herself busy. She's got a pretty full-on job as a social worker for the local council, so I'm a bit worried she's filling every second with things to avoid dealing with how she's feeling.

'I'm not overstretching myself, darling,' she says, when I suggest she might need a bit more down time. She looks at me for a moment. 'Have you just done a module on grief, or something like that?'

My mouth twists into a smile despite myself. 'Yes, I might have – but that doesn't mean I'm not right.'

'Your dad's health took up a lot of my time for the two years before he died. I had to give up pretty much everything apart from work and hospital visits, and then caring for him, and taking him to and from the hospice . . .'

'I know.'

'I still don't see how all of that – that dreadful time – made you want to give up a perfectly good career.'

'You know this.' I try and keep my voice level. I feel like I've had this conversation a million times over and it's like every time I see her – or anyone else in the family – they listen, then hit the reset button in their minds as soon as they walk away. The only person who actually gets it is Mel, my sister, but she's in New York, working her arse off on a secondment. Which reminds me, I must give her a call. WhatsApp is all very well, but it'd be nice to get a shot of her calm, measured approach to life, just to remind me I'm not insane.

'You're a social worker,' I say as I butter a bread roll, then look at her. 'You chose a job where you see some of the worst things in our community and deal with them on a daily basis.'

'Yes, but I'm making a difference,' she says.

I push my chair back in surprise and look at her, both hands pressed against the edge of the table. 'And I'm not?'

'Dad still died, didn't he?'

'Not because of nurses. He didn't die because the nurses did something wrong.'

She shakes her head. 'I just don't understand how you'd want to spend your life in one of those places.' She shudders then, and her face drops. 'Hospitals. They're like a prison.'

'It's nothing like that. We make a difference. That's

why I do it – that's why I'm doing it. I can't believe you'd honestly think that.'

'I'm sorry, Alex,' she says. She dips her head for a moment and when she looks up at me there are tears shining in her eyes, threatening to spill over and trickle down her cheeks. 'I just – I go cold thinking about Dad in there. And the doctor telling us there was nothing they could do. And . . .'

The threatened tears leak out and she dabs at them with a paper napkin, unrolling a knife and fork to get to it, and leaving them lying askew on the table.

'It's not a bad job. We're not in the habit of killing people off.'

'It just makes me so sad to think of you spending every day somewhere so depressing.'

'It's not depressing,' I say.

I think of the orthopaedic ward where I'd been doing agency work the other day, where three elderly women – all broken hips – were exchanging stories on how they'd got their injuries. Margaret, aged ninety-one, had been halfway up a ladder redecorating her dining room when she'd lost her footing and fallen. They were full of life and laughter and they'd spent the entire day winding me up. I got the usual good-humoured male nurse jokes of course – if I had a tenner for every one of those, I'd be able to retire before I even graduated – but they were a lovely lot. And when a girl of about twenty had turned up – tearful and clearly in a lot of pain – with a badly broken leg from an ice-skating competition, they'd all cheered her up, making jokes across the little four-person side ward. That sort of thing – that's what makes it worth it.

'Well,' says my mother, sounding a bit dubious. 'As long as you're happy.'

'I am,' I say.

She chats about her pottery class and the outdoor swimming club she's joined, and I listen and make the right noises. I think if I told her about Margaret and the girls in the orthopaedic ward, she'd probably get it, but I can't face it. I'm tired of trying to convince people that I've done the right thing when there are others out there who don't need to be told. Look at Jess. She understands. She gave up a good job and stability and all the rest of it to follow her dream of working in publishing. I shake my head and bring my focus back to what my mother's saying.

'She's okay then?' Mel's on the phone from New York as I'm sitting on the train back to London, later that evening. She's about to go into a lunchtime meeting when she takes my call, and I'm trying to keep my voice down and not be one of those wankers making a call at the top of my voice.

'Yeah, she's good. I think you'd say she's keeping busy.'

'Sounded a bit manic to me.'

'Nah,' I say back, even though it's exactly what I was worried about. 'She's fine. Just getting on with stuff.'

'How about you?' Mel asks.

'All right. Tired. Always tired.'

'Quit moaning,' Mel says, laughing. 'You chose this. You could've been sitting at a desk between meetings with your feet up, looking out over Manhattan like I am.'

'No thanks,' I say honestly. I picture it and can't think of anything worse.

'How's the house working out? Still in the honeymoon period with your fellow residents?'

'Pretty much. Everyone's pretty easy-going so it's no stress.'

'And what's the deal with *Emma*?'

Gah, I wish I'd never mentioned it to her. Every time I speak to Mel she winds me up about my 'house romance'.

'Nothing. I need to knock it on the head properly. I've got way too much on to be getting caught up in relationship stuff.'

'I knew it,' she crows. 'You are *so* not the friends with benefits sort. You've always been way too straight.'

'I am not,' I protest, but I know she's right.

'You so are. That's how you ended up with Alice. If you hadn't taken an uncharacteristic left turn and given up your job you'd be well on the way to domestic bliss in Surrey.'

'Shut up,' I say, laughing.

'Got to go,' Mel says suddenly. 'I can see them heading into the meeting room. Message me and let me know what happens with the whole Emma thing. She might go psycho on you and screw up your domestic bliss.'

203

I put the phone down on the table in front of me and close my eyes. I think Mel's reading way too much into this.

I hope she is, anyway.

CHAPTER TWENTY

Jess

3rd June

'You know when you don't notice something's missing until you realise it's not there?'

There's a long pause while Gen takes in what I've just said.

'Right,' she says, slowly. 'You're going to have to run that by me again.'

'Sorry,' I say, tucking my phone between chin and shoulder as I rip open the post that's addressed to me. Junk mail, junk mail, credit card bill . . . 'I mean—' I pause for a second, making sure there's nobody else home, but the house is silent, and there's none of the usual detritus in the hall that tells me my housemates are back from work '—I think something's going on with Emma and Alex.'

There's a moment where Gen processes what I've just

said. 'What, like they've been secretly shagging for six months?'

'No,' I say. 'Not just that, I mean like there's a bit of a weird atmosphere. I think maybe he's already broken things off with her. He walked into the kitchen the other day and she walked out.'

'Maybe she'd finished in there and he was just walking in?' Gen asked.

'No, it's more than that. Maybe she's really upset with him, even though he said it was her idea for them to be casual.'

I shove the letters in the recycling bin. Then I bend over and fish out the credit card bill. Tempting as it would be to leave it there, I don't think it would do my credit rating any good.

'And the thing is – apart from that I haven't seen Emma around for ages.'

'Hmmm,' said Gen. 'But you don't see thingy – what's his name? The chef guy much either. And you don't think there's something going on with him.'

'He works split shifts. It's different.'

'You're very interested in what's going on with Alex for someone who's not interested in what's going on with Alex,' she says, in that very familiar, arch, Gen-like tone.

'I am not. I just happen to work in publishing, so I'm particularly interested in stories.'

'Yeah, whatever,' she says, and I can picture her smiling.

There's a clatter of keys in the lock and I look up. It's Becky, home uncharacteristically early from work.

'Better go,' I say to Gen. 'I'll message you later, okay?'

'Don't forget. I want updates on this non-existent drama.'

Moments later, with a dramatic sigh, Becky drops her bags on the floor and collapses on the stairs. 'God I'm so tired,' she says as she lays her head down for a second. 'There's no way I can make it up two flights. I'm just going to have to sleep here – ugh.'

'What is it?' I ask.

She lifts her head up again, making a disgusted face. 'We really need to sort out some sort of cleaning rota. These stairs are covered in fluff and random stuff.'

'I'll hoover them in a bit. Coffee?' I point to the kitchen. 'D'you want me to put the kettle on?'

She shakes her head. 'I'm trying to give up caffeine.'

'Are you insane? You work about twenty-three hours a day. You can't survive without caffeine.'

'How's the celery juice looking?'

'Beyond disgusting. I'll make you a peppermint tea.' I leave her lying there looking like a deflated jellyfish on the bottom stair and head into the kitchen to boil the kettle. The fridge absolutely honks. I grab the milk, close the door quickly, and make my coffee and pour water over Becky's expensive-looking peppermint tea bag.

'There's something dying in the fridge,' I say, going back to the hall and handing her a mug. She sniffs it and takes a huge sip, making ecstatic noises.

'It's Rob.'

'In the fridge?'

'No, it's Rob's stuff. He was given some enormously posh French cheeses from a salesman, and he's brought them home because – oh, something complicated. Anyway, they're in the fridge. He said he was bringing home some artisan bread and stuff and we could have it for dinner, if anyone was around.'

My stomach rumbles at the thought, and it would be nice to get to know Rob better. Six months into our lease and Rob's still a bit of a mystery. We sort of adjusted to him being here but not here pretty early on. When the rest of us are hanging out in the evenings, shovelling in Ben and Jerry's and watching Netflix movies, he's out doing chef things until midnight, by which time we're usually staggering off to bed. He lies on the sofa reading the sports pages (he's a massive football fan) and unwinding until about two a.m. Then when we get up, he's fast asleep downstairs in the cellar. It's a bit like living with a Hobbit, only one who's really good at cooking and occasionally brings home leftovers to die for.

And really stinking cheese.

I take a sip of my coffee, and—

'Ugh.' I look down at my mug realising I've handed Becky my coffee and I've got her peppermint and fennel stuff. It tastes like someone dipped a pair of used socks in muddy water.

'I wondered when you'd notice,' Becky says, holding the mug tightly in both hands.

'I've got your tea.'

'And I—' she takes another sip, eyes closed in bliss, a

beatific smile on her face '—have your delicious, sleep-depriving, adrenal whatsit-damaging, blood-pressure-raising coffee.'

I reach across, laughing. She's not letting go of that mug any time soon.

'Gerroff,' growls Becky. 'This is mine.'

I make another cup, and we flop on the sofas in the sitting room. We'd made all sorts of plans to sort the place out when we all first moved in, but somehow none of us had done anything. It always felt a bit like sitting in your grandma's sitting room as a result. I notice that the potted plant on the windowsill is looking like it's in danger of dying of thirst.

'How's work? You must be feeling quite settled in now?' Becky asks as she flexes her foot against the arm of the sofa, leaning her head backwards. Something gives an alarming crack. 'God, I'm falling to pieces.'

'Was that you?' I say, alarmed. 'I thought it was the furniture.'

'No, definitely me. That's why I'm trying to do this healthy eating thing. This job is bloody exhausting. I'm not surprised Alex gave it up for an easy life working as a nurse.'

We both laugh.

'So go on then, spill the beans. Any exciting gossip from the glamorous world of publishing? I was expecting a lot more invites to posh book launches and meeting famous people.'

'Yeah, me too,' I say.

'Not enjoying it?'

'Oh, I am. I really like it. I mean it's way more pressur-ised than I expected – I think I was imagining us all drifting about reading books and discussing literature, and it's not like that at all, but – yeah.' I nod. 'I feel like I've found my feet a bit. It helps that a couple of new people have started, so I'm not the new girl any more. And Jav's lovely.'

'You should invite her round sometime. We could have a house party. A housewarming. My God, why haven't we had a proper housewarming?' Becky says.

'Because we're only ever all in the same place at once about twice a month, and that's usually a Saturday lunch-time?'

'Oh. Yeah. That.' Becky flips through the pages of one of Emma's magazines. She buys them all – *Vogue, Marie Claire, Tatler* . . .

'Look, there's a launch for Nigella Lawson's latest book. Why aren't you going to stuff like that?'

'Because I work for a tiny publisher who mostly does romance, and we don't do stuff like that.'

'You should. You'd get loads of publicity. And I'd get to meet—' she peers at the photographs on the social pages of *Tatler* '—Robert Pattinson. D'you think he sparkles in real life?'

'I do not. And your sad *Twilight* addiction needs to be addressed. I saw you'd been watching the whole series again on Netflix.'

'It's comfort watching. I'm mega stressed with work. There's a load of exams coming up.'

'More exams? I thought you were finished with all that.'

'No, these are different exams. Professional development stuff. It's never-ending.'

'Weird to think of Alex doing all that,' I say, casually.

Becky curls her feet up underneath her. 'Alex? He was really good. Got one of the best degrees in our year, I think. Everyone's still stunned he gave it up.'

'He seems to really like nursing though,' I say, and I wonder how he's getting on with his new placement. He's moved on to a new one now, working in a retirement home on Primrose Hill.

'You know he'd be getting married this weekend?'

'Oh of course,' I say, remembering Alex mentioning it the other week, but it hadn't really sunk in.

She reaches across to the coffee table and takes one of the chocolates that Rob left there last night with a Post-it Note saying *help yourself*. She indicates the box with her head. 'Want one?'

'No thanks,' I say, trying to imagine scruffy, laid-back Alex buttoned up in a suit and tie, watching the mythical Alice walk up the aisle towards him. 'What was she like?' I ask.

'Alice?' Becky chews for a moment, making exaggerated faces, then swallows and carries on. 'Sorry, toffee stuck in teeth. She was very nice. Bit posh, in that Home Counties long swishy hair way. Mummy and Daddy had two Labradors and she probably went to Pony Club.'

'Really? I can't imagine Alex with someone like that. He seems way too down to earth.'

211

'Yeah, but she wasn't stuck up. I mean she was nice. Just – well, I think that she'd pretty much planned out their future, and I don't think Alex buggering off to train as a nurse and earn approximately a quarter of what he was on as a corporate lawyer was on her wall planner.'

'Whatever happened to *for richer, for poorer*?' I ask.

Becky gives a snort of laughter. 'In London? Are you joking?'

I think about the amount of money she'd be getting if she rented this place out, or sold it.

'You're the one sitting on a gold mine,' I point out. 'I'm surprised you haven't got a string of handsome young gold-diggers beating a path to your door.'

'Nobody knows I own it, that's why,' she says.

'I've had so many people asking how I can afford to live in Notting Hill.'

'Yeah, me too.' She laughs. 'What do you tell them?'

'I say I'm staying with a family member.'

'Me too.'

'How's your mum?' I ask. 'Haven't heard anything about her for ages.'

'Oh, she's completely off-grid now. They've rigged up some machine on the island to make electricity by cycling on an exercise bike.'

'Talking of which,' I say, 'I must give you my share of the bill.'

'Yeah, we'll sort it out at the weekend,' Becky says. 'I was thinking – Alex is off this Saturday, which would have been the big day. D'you fancy coming with me and we'll take him out? Take his mind off things a bit? Emma's away this weekend and I think Rob's working, so it'd just be the three of us.'

My heart gives a little skip of happiness at the thought of spending the day with him, which is slightly pathetic. I really need to get a grip.

'I think that's a brilliant idea.'

CHAPTER TWENTY-ONE

Jess

8th June

'A boat?' Alex is standing in the kitchen in his socks and a crumpled, faded grey T-shirt. His jeans are slung low on his waist and when he clasps his hands together and raises them above his head in a stretch that turns into a yawn, I see a faint trail of dark hair that travels from his navel downwards to . . .

I look away and pick up a cloth, wiping the kitchen sink, which is already clean. 'Yeah,' I say, rinsing the cloth and folding it and hanging it up to dry on the tap. 'Me and you and Becky. Emma's away this weekend.'

'Come on,' Becky says, appearing in her dressing gown. 'It'll be fun.'

'It's all fun until someone drowns in a hideous boating accident,' says Alex, grimly. But his mouth lifts in a smile and he nods, slowly.

'All right. I think you two are insane. But all right.'

'Excellent,' says Becky, giving him a high five.

As he's leaving the kitchen he turns, a hand on the door, his early-morning hair rumpled. He scratches his beard and looks from Becky to me, a slow smile stretching across his face. 'Thanks, guys. I appreciate it.'

'I *told* you he'd think it was a good idea,' Becky says in a whisper, as we hear his feet on the last – squeaky – stair.

'What are you two brewing up?'

I look at Rob, who has walked into the room and headed straight for the fridge. 'Oh hello,' I say. 'It's the scarlet pimpernel.' Our anticipated cheese night didn't happen in the end, because Rob was called in to work to cover someone else's shift.

'One of these days I'm going to have a week off,' he says, in his deep Glasgow accent. 'And you'll be complaining ah'm under your feet.'

'I think it's a myth. You basically work 365 days a year as far as I can see,' teases Becky.

'I'll have you know I've got today off to make up for going in on Monday, and I've got no plans.'

'Ooh,' Becky says, glancing at me. 'Do you want some?'

'Depends what they are.' Rob grins. 'You're no' wanting me to do DIY or something like that?'

She beckons him over. Looking pleased to be included, he comes and sits down, and listens while we explain that we're on a mission to keep Alex's mind off what today should have been.

'I'd love that. And then mebbe when we get back I could make something nice for dinner. What about a curry? Alex likes curry, doesn't he?'

'Definitely.'

'Right. What time are we leaving?'

Becky looks at the clock. 'Oh God, not for ages yet. About half twelve?'

'Great.' Rob rubs his hands together. 'I'm away to the shop to get some bits and pieces for dinner. I'll make a feast that'll blow his socks off. He won't have a chance to think about whatshername when I'm done.'

In the time it takes me and Becky to get showered, find something to wear, and bumble around the house in a Saturday-morning sort of way, Rob has been out to the market on Portobello Road, picked up huge bagfuls of meat and the freshest of veg, and he's standing at the kitchen worktop chopping onions and garlic with lightning precision. Despite his huge hands, the knife moves so quickly I can't quite take it in.

'I thought you were making dinner later?' I pinch a piece of chopped red pepper.

'Aye,' he says, slapping my hand and laughing. 'I'm just leaving this lot to marinate for a few hours.'

I peer inside the fridge and it's stuffed full of various dishes, covered over with cling film, and smelling delicious already.

'Right.' He scrapes a heap of chopped-up stuff into a Pyrex dish, mixes it with what looks like some chunks of fish, and covers them over.

'Can I help?' I feel a bit useless standing there when the master is at work. He shakes his head.

'Nah, that's it all done.' He runs the tap and washes his hands, shoving the prep stuff in the dishwasher and turning it on. 'You guys ready?'

We walk down to Paddington where the boats are moored. There's a little queue – families and tourists all waiting to get on board their boats. Everyone seems to be feeling the same as we are – slightly nervous and a bit giggly. I'm trying very hard not to worry about all the six million things that could go wrong. I'm not really a boat person. I'm surprised to discover that Becky knows exactly what she's doing. She ushers us all onto a boat and we sit down. I'm peering around, looking for oars.

'It's electric,' she says, laughing. She sits down at the back, and expertly steers us away from Merchant Square and the throngs of tourists who are milling around. There are loads of boats on the water, and yet somehow Becky manages to smoothly dodge out of the way, and before we know it we're sailing along, the sun reflecting on the water. I'm glad I've brought my sunglasses. Alex is wearing his, too, and Rob – his pale freckled arms covered in sun cream – is wearing a baseball cap, and sitting at the steering end of the boat – I think it's the stern, or maybe it's the bow; one of those, anyway – with Becky. It's clear he's dying to have a turn.

I sit sideways on, my knees almost brushing against Alex's jeans. He's gazing out at the water, lost in thought.

'It's so quiet,' he says, after a while.

Rob and Becky are chatting away about cooking stuff. I'm watching the way the long arms of the weeping willow branches reach down, their leaves swishing gently in the breeze. Families with dogs and pushchairs are walking along the canal-side and I think about Sophie and her trying-to-get-pregnant headstand and it makes me laugh.

Alex pulls his glasses off and looks at me suspiciously, his mouth turning up in amusement. 'What's the joke?'

I put a hand up to my mouth, hiding my smile. 'Don't ask.'

'I'm glad we came out,' Alex says, nudging my knee gently with his. 'Thanks.'

'It was Becky's idea. She thought you might want to be distracted today, because . . .' I tail off, taking my sunglasses off, too, and chewing on the arm of them. I look at him and push my hair back from my face.

'I wanted to talk to you,' Alex begins, in a low voice, changing the subject. 'I'm really sorry if I put you on the spot the other week, asking you about Emma.'

'It's fine,' I say, putting my glasses back on and tucking my hair behind my ears.

'Look.' Alex points over my shoulder. 'There's our café.'

I turn, carefully (I don't want to fall out of the boat) and see we've reached Little Venice, and I can see the little pavement café where we stopped for coffee after our first walk together. It's become a bit of a routine for us now, to end there after our walks and have a flat white and a chocolate brownie. I try to ignore the way it makes my toes go all curly inside my Converse that he called it *our café*.

'Anyway,' he carries on, and I turn around to look at him again. 'I just wanted you to know that I really appreciated you listening. And I've broken things off – well, not that it was a thing, really, but you know what I mean – with Emma.' His voice is low.

'How did she take it?' I ask. No wonder the house has felt a bit weird.

'Fine.' He clears his throat. 'Well, fine-ish.'

'Is that why she's been a bit low-profile?'

He nods, and picks at a loose thread on his jeans, pulling it until it snaps and then twisting it absent-mindedly between his fingers. 'She went back to stay with her parents.'

'God.' I try and think when I saw her last. 'I knew she was going away but hadn't realised where to.'

'Yeah.'

A boat passes us, and we all laugh at two spaniels wearing doggy life jackets who are sitting on the table, their owners holding hands and steering the boat together.

'D'you want a go, Jess?' Becky motions to the tiller. Or is it the rudder? Whatever.

I shake my head. 'I think the fact I don't know if it's a tiller or a rudder is probably a good reason to stay where I am.'

'Alex?' Becky asks.

'Go on, then.' He grins at me and they perform a

slightly dodgy manoeuvre that makes the boat wobble alarmingly.

'Next stop—' he shades his eyes and peers ahead '— The Pirate Castle.'

'The Pirate Castle? As in an actual castle?' I ask.

'Nope.' He laughs. 'It's actually a charity that do stuff on boats with kids from disadvantaged backgrounds.'

'How do you know so much about it?' We sail past and there's a group of kids in life jackets climbing onto a boat.

'The company I used to work for did some fundraising for them.'

'So they weren't just about corporate greed?' I tease him.

'No, they did some good stuff.' He pushes his hair back from his face. 'I mean there was a fair old amount of corporate crap in there as well.'

I think about my ill-fated date with whatshisname, the investment banker. That was on a boat, too. I seem to be floating my way through my first year in London.

And then we're back at London Zoo, the enclosure a huge geometric shape that stretches high above the trees.

'D'you think we'll see our giraffe again?' Alex peers upwards.

A group of people sunbathing on the top of a house-boat raise their glasses to us as we pass them, and Becky takes out a pack of beers from the bag she'd stowed under the table.

'Cheers,' we say, clinking the necks of our bottles together.

We float on, lazily, up to Camden Lock, where there's a traffic jam of boats, and back round again, heading towards home. My stomach rumbles so loudly that it makes Alex laugh.

'Shall we go and get food after this?' he asks. He doesn't know that Rob's been hard at work all morning, creating a feast for us to have when we get back. I look at Rob, raising my eyebrows in query. He nods, subtly.

'Why don't you two go and get a snack when we drop this back at the pontoon, and Rob and I will head back?'

If I didn't know Becky better, I'd swear she was trying to put us in a situation where we were forced together, alone. But a) Becky's not a matchmaking sort (she's way too practical for that) and b) that's not what today is about. We're supposed to be taking Alex's mind off his not-wedding. And she's got absolutely no idea how I feel about him. I think I've done a pretty good job of hiding it. I hope I have, anyway.

We get off near Primrose Hill and meander back across the park, stopping to pick up sandwiches, which we eat, sitting on the grass, legs crossed, facing each other. The sun is still bursting out of the sky. It's the perfect day for a wedding, I think. Alex is quiet. I wonder if he's thinking the same thing. I lie back on the grass, looking up at the sky, soaking up the heat.

He lies down beside me, so close I can feel the fizz of my skin prickling at his proximity. My heart hasn't got the *there's nothing going on* memo and is currently banging very loudly in my ears.

'Weird, isn't it?' he says, still looking at the sky. He shades his eyes against the sun.

'What?'

He reaches out, so the side of his arm just brushes against mine. I feel a whole rainbow of butterflies burst into life in my stomach.

'What might have been. Near misses.'

I think he's talking about the wedding. He's definitely talking about the wedding. Isn't he?

I lie there, keeping very still.

And then he reaches out, and for a second his little finger touches mine. I can't work out if it's an accident or not. I don't pull my hand away. I just lie there, looking up at the clouds, wondering how the tiniest bit of physical contact can leave me feeling like someone shot a bolt of electricity from my head to my feet. I'm fizzing like I'd glow in the dark.

CHAPTER TWENTY-TWO

Alex

8th June

What the hell am I doing?

We walk back to Albany Road together in what I hope is a friendly sort of silence.

All I did is reach out and touch her finger, for God's sake. The voice in my head comes back with a fairly reasonable counter-argument.

You're single *for a reason*. You're not getting caught up in anything with Emma *for a reason*.

Two different reasons, I argue with myself.

It's surprisingly hard to conduct a balanced and reasonable argument with your own inner voice. The truth is I really like Jess. Like her enough that I'm not going to screw up a friendship, and enough that I'm not getting myself caught up in a relationship when I've got enough going on with work and study right now, and after what happened with Alice – well, I promised myself I wouldn't even go there until I finished my nursing course.

It's not the same with Emma, my unhelpful inner voice says.

Hang on, I think. Weren't you on the other side a minute ago?

It's complicated, says the inner voice.

I groan out loud.

'You okay?' Jess's voice makes me start. I'd half-forgotten she was there.

'Yeah, just thinking about work stuff.'

'I thought maybe it was, you know—' She hesitates for a bit. 'Alice. The wedding?'

I shake my head. 'No,' I say firmly. 'Definitely not that.'

We turn the corner and get onto Albany Road. One of the kids from the house two doors down has set up a lemonade stall. They've got a table out on the pavement, and a stack of paper cups. A sign says, *Lemonade £4 a cup*.

'Bloody hell,' I say under my breath to Jess. 'Definitely London prices.'

One of the children looks up at me. She's got light brown hair and very piercing bright blue eyes. 'The lemons are organic, and the sugar.'

'Of course they are,' says Jess, snorting with laughter. Only in Notting Hill. 'I'm really sorry, I haven't got any money on me.'

'That's okay,' says the smaller of the two children.

'We're going to make some more so you can come back later.'

When we're out of earshot and walking up the steps to our house, we both burst out laughing.

'Well, you've got to give it to them. They're enterprising.'

'Those kids' school fees probably cost more a term than I make in a year.' Jess giggles. 'Not surprised they're enterprising. Their dad'll own half the property in Notting Hill. He's a private landlord.'

We're still laughing when the front door opens. I thought Emma had gone home, but she's there, with a look on her face that I can't read. I open my mouth to say hello and then close it again.

Despite Emma's cool welcome, I can't help noticing that the house smells warm and fragrant with spices. There's a sizzling noise coming from the kitchen. And over that, I can hear the sound of Rob singing as he cooks something amazing.

I walk down the hall and into the kitchen.

'All right, you two?' Rob looks up, wooden spoon in hand, an apron tied round his waist. He looks in his element, and he's beaming happily, a bottle of white wine half drunk beside the hob.

The back door's open, and light from the little garden is spilling into the kitchen. I can see the overgrown vines hanging over the doorway, and the light dappling through the leaves. It looks pretty idyllic – the perfect day for a lazy, sunny afternoon in the garden. We've hardly used it so far – mainly because it's so overgrown that none of us know where to start.

'Gorgeous day, isn't it?' says Emma from behind us, in her smooth, deep voice. She's looking at me curiously. I step out of the way to let her and Jess through.

'We should have Pimm's on a day like this. I bet there's mint in the garden. Have you looked?' Jess says. She clearly hasn't picked up on the weird atmosphere.

Becky appears from the garden with a piece of leaf caught in her hair. And she's standing between the back door and the kitchen. 'Ah,' she says. 'I wondered when you two were going to get back.'

And then there's a rustle as someone moves one of the vines out of the way and a shape – silhouetted against the sunlight so it takes a moment for me to recognise it – stands for a moment in the doorway.

'I told you he wouldn't be long,' says Emma, in an artificially cheerful voice.

'Hello, Alex,' says Alice.

CHAPTER TWENTY-THREE

Jess

8th June

So this is a bit awkward. I flick a glance in Becky's direction and she manages to articulate, with widened eyes, a vague gesture with her hands, and a flare of her nostrils that no, she doesn't have a clue what's going on, either.

I watch Alex, trying to look as if I'm not watching him. He steps across the kitchen and puts a hand to Alice's waist, kissing her warmly on the cheek. Emma lifts an eyebrow almost imperceptibly.

'Jess, this is Alice,' says Alex.

And I reach out a hand – why on earth do I do that? It seems weirdly formal, but I don't know her well enough to kiss her and it feels like I have to do *something*. Alice takes it and we shake in greeting. Alex gives me an odd, sideways look.

'Very nice to meet you, Alice,' I say. 'I've heard a lot

about you,' I add. Becky, standing behind her, widens her eyes at that and gives me A Look.

'You have?' Alice tilts her head slightly, smiling. 'I hope it's not all bad.'

'Gosh, no,' I say, aware I'm digging myself into a hole. 'All very good in fact. Lovely.'

Becky's nostrils flare.

'Why don't I go to the shop and get some Pimm's? I was just saying it's the sort of afternoon you should be drinking Pimm's.'

I turn around and head for the door.

'I'll come with you,' says Becky, hotfooting it out of the kitchen.

'What the hell?' I say when we get outside.

'I have no idea. Literally none,' Becky replies. 'Has she come back to say she's made a terrible mistake and she wants him back?'

I almost say '*Bloody hell, I hope not*', but manage to turn it into a cough and then a much more appropriate: 'Maybe she thought she should pay her respects, or something?'

'To their non-marriage?' Becky snorts with laughter again.

'I don't know. What kind of weirdo turns up on their not-wedding day and randomly appears from the garden in the middle of our Keep Alex's Mind Off Things mission? Is this the sort of thing she always does?'

'I dunno. I only met her a few times at work events. She always seemed quite nice, in a sort of horsey, Surrey,

I've-got-posh-parents sort of way. Bit like Alex used to be.'

'Did he?' I ask, surprised.

'God, yeah.'

I stop suddenly in the street and someone walking crashes into me from behind, swears, and then carries on, making a detour round me. I'm still not very good at the not-stopping-on-London-streets thing.

'Alex doesn't seem like a posh sort of person. He's . . .'

'He's lovely, yeah. But before his dad died he was much more like your stereotypical law type. Nice suit, pretty girlfriend, liked a night out at the Sloaney Pony.'

Despite having heard about the 'old Alex' a few times, I struggle to reconcile the laid-back, slightly scruffy, bearded, permanently exhausted Alex with the image she's creating.

'That's really weird. I can't imagine that at all.'

'I don't think Alice could imagine him the way he is now. She'd have that beard off him in about five seconds flat, for one thing.'

After picking up Pimm's, cucumber, a punnet of strawberries and some lemonade, we head back to Albany Road.

'What d'you think's going on in there?' Becky nods towards our house as we approach.

'Have you got any change yet?' says the little girl from the lemonade stall.

'Sorry, no,' I say. 'Unless you take credit cards?'

She giggles. 'I did ask Daddy if he'd let us but he said no.'

'You'll have to catch me after payday, then,' I say, only half joking. I'm still lurching precariously from one month to the other. Becky's paid for the Pimm's, which is just as well because I've pretty much run out of money and there's still quite a lot of the month left. I clock the expensive-looking car parked opposite our house and wonder if it belongs to Alice.

'Is that . . .?'

Becky nods. 'Yep. You can see how downgrading to hoofing it on the tube on a student loan wasn't really her style.'

Inside, Rob's dishing up spiced chicken kebabs on a bed of colourful salad leaves. There's no sign of Emma, or Alex, or Alice, for that matter. I can't help feeling angry that we've arranged a day to take his mind off something and Alice has come along and put a massive spanner in the works.

'They're outside in the garden.' Rob nods his head towards the door.

'I'll make the Pimm's,' says Becky, quickly. 'You go and size up the atmosphere out there.'

Surprisingly, Emma's on her hands and knees, pulling up weeds from a flower border. She's gathered quite a pile, heaped up beside her.

'I didn't have you down as a gardener,' I say, nodding at the pair of battered-looking green gardening gloves she's wearing.

'They're not mine. Think they must've belonged to Becky's gran. But yeah, I love gardening. Used to help my dad out at the allotment all the time. I still do, when I go home.'

Well, this day just gets weirder.

Meanwhile, Alex and Alice are sitting at a faded wooden picnic table. It's worn smooth and silver with age.

'Come and join us,' says Alex, patting the bench beside him. I slide myself into the narrow gap and sit down, not too close to him, and look at Alice. She seems perfectly composed, sitting with her hands folded neatly in front of her, a glass of Rob's wine half drunk on the table.

Well, I think. This is going to be a bit of an awkward afternoon.

'Pimm's, anyone?' says Becky, in a sing-song voice.

'God, yes,' I say, falling on a glass with as much enthusiasm as one of our marathon runners at the support table reaching for water. I take a slightly too-large sip and cough.

But of course, we're British, and what we do best is awkward, slightly stilted social gatherings. Rob insists there's more than enough food for everyone, so we spend a perfectly polite and charming evening around the battered old garden table celebrating Alex's not-wedding with the wife that never was.

CHAPTER TWENTY-FOUR

Jess

28th June

'It's lovely to hear you,' says Nanna. Her voice makes me smile as I walk along the narrow road towards Pimlico, where we're meeting for a wedding dress trying-on session. Gen's supposed to be meeting me at Starbucks, but she's texting a series of updates from the bus she's on, which seems to be stuck behind some sort of impromptu protest march. Her messages beep in my ear as I talk to Nanna and walk.

'So what's happening with you?'

'I'm off to play dressing up with the girls.'

'Ooh, lovely. Has she set a date?' Nanna loves a wedding – and a funeral. In fact she loves any sort of occasion where you can dress up and wear a nice hat. I step off the pavement to make way for a man carrying two buckets filled with flowers, then step back hastily as a black cab beeps loudly.

'No, she hasn't set a date – it's most un-Sophie-like. I'm not sure what she's doing.'

'That doesn't sound like her at all.'

'It's the baby stuff. I think she's all over the place, trying to plan something that can't be planned and it's making her computer brain malfunction.'

'Babies come when they're ready,' says Nanna Beth, soothingly.

'So everyone keeps telling her. She's threatened to behead the next person who tells her to relax.'

'It's not really Sophie's thing, is it?'

'Definitely not. Ooh, Nanna – I'd better go. Gen's just getting off the bus opposite. I can see her waving.'

'Give her my love, sweetheart.'

I blow a kiss down the phone and shove it back in my bag, waving to Gen. She's got a purple scarf wrapped around her hair and huge, ornate silver earrings that jangle and glitter in the light. I don't know how she does it – if I dressed like her, I'd look like I'd been raiding a dressing-up box.

'Hi,' Gen says, kissing me on the cheek and giving me a hug. 'Are you ready to be meringued?'

'There's no way she's going to put us in something hideous.'

'I don't care if she does as long as she hurries up and gets here. What kind of shop is by appointment only anyway?'

'A royal one?' Gen hops up and down. 'How the hell can it be this cold? It's nearly July.'

'It was sunny when I left the house this morning.'

'Well it's bloody well not now.' Gen starts doing actual star jumps in the middle of the pavement. A little girl walks past, holding on to her mother's hand, turning round to look as they walk away. Gen pokes her tongue out at her, making her giggle.

'Mummy, that lady has a shiny thing on her tongue,' I hear the girl saying in wonder as they turn the corner.

Right then – thankfully, because I'm beginning to think there's a danger we'll freeze to the spot – Sophie arrives. It's not like her to be late.

'Sorry,' she says, shoving her phone in her bag. She pulls her cardigan tightly round her chest against the cold. 'God it's cold round here in the shade, isn't it?'

'You're not bloody joking.'

She rings a bell and the door opens. I have to confess that I'm a sucker for a wedding dress shop. There's something about all that tulle and sparkly stuff. Even Gen gives a little *ooh* of surprise.

'This is lovely.'

'Welcome to Briarwood Bridal.' The woman who owns the shop is tall, with her hair cut in a severe black bob. She's dressed in the sort of angular, expensive-looking linen stuff that designers seem to favour.

'This place looks *seriously* expensive,' Gen whispers to me, as Sophie disappears with the woman into a back room.

'Can I get you two ladies a glass of Prosecco while you're waiting?'

I wasn't aware there was more waiting happening, but if there is, there might as well be Prosecco with it. I nod.

There's a lot of rustling and we've almost finished our Prosecco when the severe-looking woman calls us through. Sophie – who appears to be about a foot taller than normal – is standing in the middle of the room looking pleased with herself.

'What d'you think?'

She looks absolutely gorgeous. The dress looks even better on her than it did in the magazine, and it goes in and out in exactly the right places.

'If you're not pregnant by the time your wedding day comes, that dress ought to do it,' says Gen, giving a filthy wolf whistle that earns her an even filthier look from the owner of the bridal shop. I shoot Gen the sort of look that hopefully says *shut up*.

'Well,' says Gen, defensively. 'You are trying to get up the duff, aren't you?'

Sophie gives her a steely look and says nothing. She's so stressed out at the moment, even by Sophie standards.

'I thought we were here to try on bridesmaid dresses,' Gen says looking aggrieved.

'We're just going to take some measurements now, madam.' Bob-woman unrolls a measuring tape and approaches Gen. Gen, being an old hand at costume measurements for the stage, holds out a hand, palm flat in a STOP gesture. 'I can tell you mine right now,' she says, parroting them off instantly. The woman inclines her head, looking slightly mollified. I lift my arms up as she measures my bust, waist and hips, feeling like I'm getting measured for school uniform. Sophie dismounts from the low stool she's been standing on and sashays off to get changed with the aid of the tea-making girl.

Afterwards we go to the cinema then for a drink. Sophie sneaks a look at her phone before, during and after the film to see if Rich has been in touch.

'Have you two had a fight or something?'

'He's just being an arse,' says Sophie. She plaits her long hair down one shoulder, which is what she's always done when she's feeling anxious, so I know there's something going on.

'What's up?' Gen cocks her head sideways. She might be loud and boisterous but she's a good person to have on your side. 'Do you need us to go and rough him up a bit?'

Sophie laughs. 'No. He's just – it's just – well, it's been seven months now and I'm still not pregnant.'

I look at Gen. I've never really contemplated that sort of thing, so I've no idea how long it normally takes. Like I said, we were brought up to believe getting pregnant happened the second you went anywhere *near* a male person. Maybe those sex education classes weren't completely accurate.

'Seven months isn't that long,' says Gen, kindly. 'I read somewhere it can take the average person twelve months to get pregnant. Plus, you're stressing about it, and the wedding stuff, and work, and you've got the flat on the market. I mean basically all you need to do is have a bereavement and you've ticked off the four most stressful things a person can do.'

'I know.' Sophie sighs. 'I can't even get Rich to agree to a wedding date.'

Gen shoots me a sideways look. 'You don't mean . . .'

Sophie shakes her head. 'He's had this idea that he doesn't want a big fuss.'

I can feel my eyes widening into saucer shapes. Sophie's basically been planning her wedding since she was about nine.

'And how do you feel about that?'

I'm surprised when she shrugs. 'I dunno, actually. You know when you've always had your mind set on an idea, then someone comes along and says something and you realise that actually . . .' She tails off, taking a sip of her drink through a straw and gazing out of the window.

Gen glances over at me and subtly raises an eyebrow.

'Well, there's no need to think about any of that stuff right now.'

Sophie gives a gusty sigh. 'It's like telling someone not to think of a pink elephant,' she says. 'What's the first thing you think of?'

'All right. So we'll have to distract you. We just have to find you a project,' I say.

I go to the loo and when I get back I'm pleased to see Gen and Sophie are laughing about something and Sophie looks happier than she has done in ages. I head home once I finish my drink, because I've got plans to hang out with Becky tomorrow morning, and we agree to meet up for lunch on Wednesday.

Back at Albany Road, the house is surprisingly quiet. There's usually someone pootling around the kitchen making toast or curled up on the sofa watching television, but it's completely deserted. Alex's hoody is hanging on the end of the banister. It's weird that I have barely seen him since the day Alice turned up. Except I have to remind myself it is completely not-weird. Alex is just a friend. A housemate. But since his finger touched the side of mine, I've managed to reignite the world's biggest and most ridiculously unrequited crush. I need to get a grip. Plus he's probably back with Alice.

Alice, who seems perfectly nice. Alice who – as his ex-almost-wife – has rather more claim to him than I do as his housemate. And even Emma seems relatively unscathed – in fact, she was off on a date with a friend of a friend last night, as she confided when we met in the hall. It's ridiculous. I am ridiculous. This needs to stop.

CHAPTER TWENTY-FIVE

Jess

1st July

I wake up at half five in the morning for some reason, probably because the sun's shining through my curtains, spilling warm yellow light on my face. On a whim, I decide to go for a run. I throw on my ancient leggings and a T-shirt, and rummage under the bed until I find my trainers. They're a bit battered, but they'll do. I leave my phone behind, because I need to clear my head and stopping to check Instagram every five minutes isn't going to do that. I tie my hair up in a high ponytail that swishes as I walk.

I set off at a gentle jog from our place, feeling quite dynamic. That lasts until I hit the end of Albany Road, by which time my lungs feel like two exploding balloons in my chest. I stop for a moment, hands on my knees, doubled over and wheezing. God, I'm unfit.

But there's something quite nice about being out in London at this time of the morning with no phone and nothing to do but take in the sights. I run along towards Holland Park where the pavements widen and the houses are gleaming white, the railings shiny black and the cars outside are massive brand-new Range Rovers. It gets a bit easier, somehow, as I keep going. And then I circle back, heading up Portobello Road, which is a hive of activity already. The stallholders are clanking bits of metal and laughing as they assemble their stalls. Boxes of fruit and veg and huge buckets of flowers spill out everywhere, echoing the rainbow colours of the buildings, and I feel a lovely glow of happiness and love for this amazing place I get to call home. This must be the runner's high they talk about – or maybe I'm just delirious.

'Is this a mirage?' Rob says when he opens the door, before bursting out laughing.

'Shut up, you,' I say, collapsing in a heap on the bottom stair.

'I'm only kidding,' he says. 'D'you want a drink? Looks like you need one.'

I nod, gratefully. Once I've drunk an espresso and my breathing has returned to almost normal, I stand up and catch a glimpse of myself in the hall mirror. In my head I've looked cute and sporty, my hair swishing back and forth as I jog along the streets of Notting Hill. The reality is distinctly less glamorous. My ponytail has slipped to one side, my face is an alarming brick-red colour, and I have two half-moons of sweat under each arm.

'If you ever want a running partner,' Rob says, in his gruff Scottish voice, 'just ask. I did the marathon a couple of years ago.'

Still looking at myself in the mirror, I watch as my eyes widen in horror. I've managed to jog-walk about two miles and it's taken me ages. The idea of running twenty-six miles is completely insane. That's what public transport is for. Except there's a little voice in my head that points out that all the runners we cheered on in April must've started somewhere, and after all, I've told myself I'm going to make some changes in my life.

I peel off my horribly sweaty clothes and dump them in the laundry basket. After I've showered, I lie back on the bed, wrapped in a towel. I could sleep for a week, but I've got about twenty minutes before I need to get going if I'm going to get to work on time. Maybe I'll just have one more minute.

CHAPTER TWENTY-SIX

Jess

3rd July

'You?' Gen splutters, when I tell her and Sophie about my new running regime . . . of all of two days. Sophie, also laughing, pats her on the back. It's Wednesday lunchtime and we're sitting in a café in the city.

'Why not?'

'You're just not exactly – well, come on, Jess. The last time you ran anywhere was probably when you found out Tesco had reduced all the Christmas chocolate to half price last January.'

I'm slightly offended at just how funny Gen and Sophie find the idea of me running. 'I'm actually quite fit, I'll have you know,' I lie.

'Well,' Sophie says, looking at Gen then me. 'As you're on a mission to turn your life around, we've got a proposition for you.'

She's got that glint in her eye that I recognise, and I groan.

I'm about to be organised.

'So, Gen and I were talking about your lack of love life—'

I glare at Gen, who is trying to look angelic and chewing on the crust of her toasted sandwich. 'Sorry,' she mouths, pulling a face with her mouth still full. 'She needed a project.'

'I didn't mean *me*,' I say, scowling. But I can't deny it, Sophie's looking far more like her old self.

'You've tried one date. It was a disaster, but you can't just fall off the horse and stay there. You need to get back on.'

Sophie's tone is firm, like a primary school teacher encouraging a recalcitrant pupil to join in with a PE class.

'Honestly,' I say, trying to sound assertive, 'I'm fine. Loads of work stuff going on, lots of friends, I've got my running—' I've been twice, but that definitely counts '—and I really just don't want to . . .' I tail off.

'You don't want to end up stranded on a riverboat party cruise while some banking wanker gets off with someone else under your nose?' Gen looks at me, her huge blue eyes wide, eyebrows lifted.

'Exactly.'

'And that's why we've decided to stage an intervention.'

'I'm beginning to feel slightly nervous.'

Sophie shakes her head, and her pale blonde hair lifts

and settles back down, still perfectly neat. 'No need. We've found you The Perfect Man.'

'There's no such thing,' I say.

'Ah,' says Sophie, pulling her phone out of her bag, 'there is. Look.'

'I'm not signing up for online dating again. I had to delete Tinder – every time I looked at it there were dodgy messages from perverts, telling me what they'd like to do to me, or what they were doing to themselves, or worse. And the photographs?' I shudder dramatically.

'Will you stop talking for *one* second?' Sophie pushes her phone across to me and I pick it up.

There's a photograph on her screen. I zoom in on the picture so I can see it more clearly. It's a blond man with dark brown eyes. He's holding a bottle of beer and standing next to Sophie. They look a bit like a pair of Danish twins. Both tall, healthy-looking, blond, and with impossibly good teeth. Weirdly, he reminds me a bit of the man I saw in the hailstorm that day before Christmas. Only presumably Sophie isn't trying to set me up with someone who already has a boyfriend.

'Who's that?' I ask.

'James.' Sophie takes the phone away, looking slightly smug. I reach across, grabbing it back and zooming in on the photo again. He looks nice. Friendly.

'Is he gay?' I ask.

'I beg your pardon?' Sophie takes the phone back, laughing. 'Thought you weren't interested.'

'I'm not,' I say. He does look quite nice though. 'What's the catch?'

'No catch,' says Gen. She's doodling absent-mindedly on the expensive-looking menu, drawing groups of tiny little daisies. A waitress comes past and swipes it from her hands, giving her a disapproving look.

'Would you like anything else?' she says to Gen, who's already wolfed down her sandwich.

'I'd like another coffee, please – decaf, thanks.' Sophie smiles up at her.

'I'll have a diet Coke, thanks,' says Gen.

I look out of the window and watch as a couple of tourists wander by, hand-in-hand. It's weird, but recently everywhere I've looked people seem to be loved up and I've felt like a spare part, sitting in cafés watching the world go by and with a vague sense that my life is going by too, and if I don't do anything about it, I'm going to wake up one morning and find I'm forty-five, still single, and still wondering what I'm going to be when I grow up. I square my shoulders and turn back to look at Sophie.

'So what's the deal with James?'

'He works in the marketing department with me. Really lovely. Single – no skeletons in the closet. As soon as he was transferred in last month I thought he'd be perfect for you.'

'Okay,' I say, feeling bold. 'Where do I sign?'

Sophie blushes slightly and looks sideways at Gen.

'Ah. Well,' she says, pulling a face, 'I have to confess

I sort of organised a blind date for the two of you for next Friday.'

'You did *what?*' I reel backwards, my head banging off the window. 'Ouch.'

'That's what she meant by an intervention,' Gen says, wryly. She shifts over slightly as the waitress returns with our order.

'What if I'd said no?' I ask.

'But you didn't, did you?' Sophie looks very pleased with herself.

'A blind date, though?' I grimace.

'Don't knock it,' says Sophie. 'Worked for Harry and Meghan, didn't it?'

I roll my eyes. She's got a point though, I guess.

'Fine,' I say, and they high-five and say *yes* in unison.

CHAPTER TWENTY-SEVEN

Alex

5th July

'Bloody hell,' my sister says.

Mel's just flown in from New York. She's here for four days for a series of meetings. I've come out of a two-hour lecture, brain reeling with stuff I need to learn for an exam next week, and she's waiting for me outside the university entrance.

'Hello to you too.'

'I don't have time for niceties. I'm too busy and important for stuff like that.' She waggles an expensive-looking briefcase at me. 'Got a meeting at four. You're lucky I can fit you in.'

'Thanks,' I say, shaking my head and laughing.

I'd mentioned I'd seen Alice, and of course she wants to know all the details, so I tell her the sorry story over lunch at a café nearby.

'And she turned up completely out of the blue?' Mel asks. 'You didn't have even an inkling she was planning it?'

'Not a clue. I got back from a day out with friends, and we walked into Albany Road, and there she was.'

'Bloody hell,' Mel says again. She's not exactly helping.

'I was hoping you might have some sort of wise counsel. I can say "bloody hell" myself.'

'All right. So, let me get this straight. She turns up, plonks herself down on a garden bench, and tells you she's made a terrible mistake and wants to start things up again?'

'Pretty much, yeah.'

'And? Were you tempted?'

I shake my head. 'Not even a bit.'

'God, poor Alice. What a nightmare.'

'Yeah.'

'What d'you think brought it on?'

'Oh God, loads of things. Well, she started off just casually saying she'd been thinking that maybe she hadn't been fair.'

Mel gives a thoughtful nod. 'Reasonable point.'

'She wanted us to go out for dinner. All I could think was that I had a shitload of coursework to do before Monday morning, and Rob had cooked a meal for everyone and I didn't want to be rude to a mate.'

'Romance isn't dead then,' says Mel, drily.

'Look I didn't plan any of this. Anyway she insisted we go out the next day and said she'd pay. Then we had dinner and talked.'

'How did it go?'

I shrug. 'Not great. I mean for one thing, when she said she'd pay, she clearly didn't actually expect me to go through with that. We had a bit of a silent standoff when the bill arrived.'

'What did you do?' Mel asks.

'I paid.'

'Alex, you've got sod-all money. I bet it wasn't Pizza Hut either.'

Alice always did have expensive tastes. A bottle of red and two courses in the Grapevine in Holland Park cost me the best part of two weeks' food budget.

'I felt like it was the least I could do,' I say.

'She turned up on your doorstep.'

'Yeah, I know, but . . .'

'So what did she say? I bet she hates the beard, right?'

I laugh. 'She did make a comment, yeah.'

'And I'm guessing she's still not over the whole lawyer to nurse thing?'

I shake my head. 'Nope. I mean, she knew it was coming. It's not like I went to work one day with a briefcase and wearing a suit and turned up the next morning dressed in scrubs and carrying a thermometer. Anyway,' I say, fiddling with the edge of my plate, 'She came back, said she missed me, said we could make a go of things.'

Mel makes a dubious noise.

'I didn't want to make her feel bad.'

'Oh my God, so you decided to just flannel her with a load of "it's not you it's me" bullshit?'

'No.' God, sometimes talking to my sister is painful. She's hit the mark.

'Anyway, she went back home to her parents' place that night. She wanted to go for a walk the next day, so we did. I talked about work, and she tried to understand what I loved about it.'

There was a point when we were wandering along through Covent Garden when it felt like Alice was really listening. But it came back round to money, and how I was willing to give up everything that mattered just for the sake of a job, and that's when I realised that we're just fundamentally different in the way we see life.

'And then what happened? I'm dying to know,' Mel says, and I shoot her a sideways look because I can't work out if she's being sarcastic.

'So where have you left things?'

I rub my jaw. It was weird. When Alice had ended things, I'd been pretty crushed. It felt like the one person who was supposed to get me, and understand why I wanted to do something that would make a difference, just didn't. I'd been pretty devastated by it. And then she came back and I felt – nothing.

'I think she wanted to give me another chance to change my mind,' I say.

'About her or about the job?'

'Both. I think she was hoping I'd got the whole thing out of my system and maybe I'd just realise I'd made a terrible mistake. She did use the words "life crisis" several times.'

'To be fair,' Mel says, wiping coffee off her upper lip. 'We've all used those words. Normal people don't bin off a perfectly good law career to spend their lives wip—'

'Fuck's sake, Mel. For the millionth time.'

'All right, don't get touchy,' she says. 'I know you don't just wipe people's arses.'

I let out a sigh of irritation.

'So, how *did* you leave it?'

'I saw her before I got on the train down here. We had coffee at the station – she was off to a meeting – and we pretty much said our goodbyes.'

'What d'you think triggered her change of heart?'

'The wedding date thing, I reckon.'

'So what happens now?' Mel checks the time on the wall clock. 'And make it the short version. I've got about fifteen minutes left before I have to scarper.'

'Nothing. I get on with work, and get these assignments done.' I point to the folders on the table beside us.

CHAPTER TWENTY-EIGHT

Jess

5th July

James is – exactly as Sophie said – absolutely charming, and even better-looking in the flesh. I get to Polpo five minutes late, hoping desperately that he's the sort of person who turns up early, and that I'm not going to be sitting there looking tragic for half an hour and nursing a drink while the bar staff look at me with knowing glances. And I'm in luck.

'Hi,' he says, standing up as I arrive. He leans across, putting a hand on my arm, and kisses me on the cheek. He smells of something spicy and woody and sort of lemony. It's nice.

We order a bottle of red and look at the menu. The waiters are just the right level of helpful and take our order of a few sharing plates. For some reason, I don't feel nervous or butterflies-ish, and we chat about work, and Soph – laughing about the fact that she's such a super-organised perfectionist – and he tells me about growing up in Yorkshire. He's got a lovely accent.

'Here we are,' says the waiter, bringing a tray of assorted dishes and setting them on the table in front of us. It looks amazing.

'I don't know where to start,' James says, picking up the bottle and pouring some more into our glasses.

'These are amazing.' I pass him a tiny little piece of sausage wrapped in pieces of dried tomato.

'Try this.' He offers a little arancini ball, and our fingers touch as he passes it to me before I put it in my mouth. It's weird. I don't feel that nervous buzz I've experienced with Alex, but it's nice being with him. It's easy, and relaxed.

When I go to the bathroom, I check my messages and both Gen and Sophie have been in touch, dying to know how I'm getting on.

I like him, I say, standing by the mirrors.

EXCELLENT news, Sophie types. I bet she's planning a new side hustle as a dating service as we speak.

'We've finished this wine, somehow,' James says when I return, lifting up the bottle and shaking it from side to side. We've eaten all the food, too.

'We could get cocktails,' I say, spying a list on a board by the bar. 'Unless you want to get back?'

He shakes his head and looks at me directly with his nice, kind brown eyes. 'I'm not in any rush, are you?'

'Not at all.' I smile at him, and we order two negronis.

And then we drink another three, and as I stand up from the table – he's paid the bill, and refused to take my share – I realise I feel more than a little bit fuzzy round the edges. Outside it's not quite dark, the sky hazed a pale-around-the-edges blue, the moon a perfect half-circle.

'Thanks for a lovely night,' I say.

'D'you want to call a cab?' James looks down the street, scanning for black cabs.

'I'll just get the bus.'

He offers to walk me to the bus stop. We wander along, side by side, arms occasionally brushing. It's still warm, the heat of the day radiating from the pavement and the walls of the buildings.

'I love London at this time of night,' he says.

'I love London full stop.'

'I think when you're not from here, you really appreciate what an amazing place it is to live.'

I nod. 'I've been exploring since I moved here at the beginning of the year,' I say. I don't mention that I've been covering the city on foot with the housemate I have a crush on. It's been a while since we've been for a walk together – he's been doing loads of agency work, and – I shake my head, realising that I shouldn't be thinking about him when I'm on a real-life actual date with a handsome Yorkshireman. 'And there's so much to discover,' I say, sounding like a tour guide. 'History everywhere.'

'That's exactly how I feel,' James says. We reach my stop and I see the bus is approaching.

'Right, well, I better get going. I've had a really good night,' James says.

'Me too,' I say, again. I'm not actually sure how you do this whole dating thing. It's been so long that I'm completely out of practice.

'Do you – I mean would you—' He starts, then clears his throat. 'Would you like to go out again? With me, I mean?'

And something about the awkwardness of the situation makes us both laugh. I nod. 'Yes, please,' I say. 'I'd like that a lot.'

'I'll message you,' he says.

My bus arrives, and I climb on. When I get to my seat and look back, I see he's still standing there, waiting until I leave to make sure I'm on board safely.

CHAPTER TWENTY-NINE

Alex

1st August

I've had a couple of weeks back home hanging out with Lucy and Sam (who are so loved up, I can't decide if it's inspiring or nauseating, or possibly a bit of both) and I've gone straight back into two back-to-back weeks of night shifts, so I'm feeling a bit like Albany Road's nothing more than a place to sleep before I stagger out of bed and back to work again. I feel like the living dead, but I'll give hospital work this – it never stops being interesting. I'm doing agency work to get some money in the bank before the next semester starts. St Thomas's Hospital is huge and confusing, and I've got lost about five times already. The weird thing is I know that another few shifts and I'll have the entire place mapped in my head, permanently. I don't know how it works, but it does.

'Hello, darlin',' says a voice from the waiting area. I give a vague smile but don't engage. I've got a load of overnight reports to hand over, and if I don't get them in before the shift changes I'm going to end up hovering around for an hour like I did yesterday.

'I said "hello",' says the voice, again. It belongs to a woman wearing a hospital gown and a pair of tired-looking fleece-lined slippers. Her mouse-brown hair is suspiciously flat on one side, as if she's just got out of bed.

'Where have you come from?' I ask. We've got a wanderer, I suspect. I check her arm. 'You didn't have an ID band on, did you?'

'Took it off,' she says. 'They make me itch.'

I can't help smiling. She's feisty, I'll give her that. But we're in a hospital the size of a small village, and I've got a lost soul to sort out.

'So where did you come from – can you remember?' I ask.

'Not sure,' she said, and gives a cackle of laughter. 'These places all look the same. Don't you agree?'

I look at the chairs, the neutral walls, and the posters urging us to wash our hands and use hand gel between patients and I think that I could be pretty much anywhere in any London hospital.

'Yes, they are all much of a muchness, aren't they?'

'Are you a doctor?' she asks.

'Nurse.' I frown and peer down the corridor, trying to see if I can spot anyone. Can't leave her sitting alone

264

when she's clearly vulnerable, but at the same time, I'm going to get a bollocking if I go AWOL with these reports.

'Nurse?' She clicked her tongue. 'Male nurses. Well I never.' She looks pleased at this. I smile politely.

'Excuse me,' I say when I see a pink-clad Healthcare Assistant appear from inside some double doors. 'I've got a patient here, and—'

'She's not one of ours, I don't think,' says the HCA.

'She's AWOL, I think.'

'Wait there two secs,' the HCA says, and disappears, returning a few seconds later with a hospital-issue wheel-chair. 'I bet we can relocate her.'

Before long, we've traced her back to the ward she'd come from. She's not that old – pain can disorient you – and I watch as she's installed safely back in her bed. She hadn't gone far.

'Turned left at the loos instead of right. Happens all the time,' says the ward sister, wearily. 'We've got massive signs, but nobody ever looks at them.'

I head back down the never-ending corridors, but the patient's face stays with me for the rest of the shift, in that way people do, sometimes, even though we're supposed to retain professional detachment at all times. I remember it being mentioned in one of the first classes we had – that we had to find our own way of distancing ourselves. It's not that easy, though – especially when you see someone like her, wandering, alone – I don't know why it got to me. Maybe just that moment of realising that the old cliché about life being short really is true?

Back home, hours later, dead on my feet and bleary-eyed, I'm in the kitchen ripping off the plastic on a microwave meal for two, tipping it onto a plate, when Rob comes in with a couple of dirty mugs.

'That crap's no good for you, man,' he says. He shoves the mugs in the dishwasher and turns to look at me. 'You need some decent food inside you when you're working those long shifts. Believe me, I know.'

'It's better than Becky's Cock Soup,' I say.

There are still about fifteen packets of the stuff in the cupboard. It's become a standing joke. We've tried adding vegetables, throwing in noodles, even mixing it with a tin of sweetcorn. It's still absolutely disgusting, but come the week before payday, we're not too proud to give it another go.

The microwave curry tastes pretty grim. The chicken's somehow spongy and rubbery, and the rice has dried up in parts and is rock hard. But I'm exhausted and starving hungry and there's nothing else to eat, so it'll have to do. Once I've had a sleep I'll nip out and get some shopping.

'You working tonight?' I say, looking at Rob.

'Night off. Thought I might go and see that new Marvel film at the cinema if you fancy it.'

'I'd love to, but I can guarantee you that within five minutes of the opening credits, I'd be fast asleep. I feel like I haven't stopped for days.'

'I've been meaning to ask what the story is. You sort things out with that Alice lassie?' He grins. 'Wee bit awkward getting home to find your ex standing in the kitchen.'

'Just a bit.' I nod. 'Anyway, I've cleared the air with her, at least.'

'So you're just friends now?' Rob asks.

'Well, as much as you can ever be. Civil, I think, is probably as good as we're going to get. She's still not over me giving up law for nursing, no matter how much she's tried to convince herself it didn't matter.'

'Aye,' says Rob, sagely. 'Not easy to get your head round something like that. My ex-wife couldn't cope with my long hours working in the restaurant. Not many can. It's a killer, but I couldn't give it up.'

'Did she give you an ultimatum?' I ask, looking up with interest. I had no idea he'd been married. I don't know much about him at all, really. Rob doesn't talk about himself much, although I've found him chatting away to Becky a few times in the kitchen when I've got in from work. But Becky's like that – she could strike up a conversation in a room full of statues. Probably has, knowing her.

'No, but if she had . . . I cannae tell you which I'd have chosen. I bloody love my job. I spent years working in construction, and paid a fortune to retrain. You've got to follow your heart, haven't you?'

These words, coming from the stocky, gruff Scotsman make me smile. He's right, though.

Of course, what I've not mentioned to him, or to Becky, or to anyone – and I'm not sure why – is that it turns out that after we split, Alice had had a semi-serious fling with Paul, who I used to work with. I think it was them splitting up that was the catalyst for her getting back in touch. It's weird because he was one of the ones from the office who'd sort of kept in touch – for a bit, at least. We'd been out for drinks a few times since leaving, and yet he'd never mentioned it. Not that I'm in any position to comment, given what happened with Emma.

God, relationships are complicated. I head upstairs, pull the curtains, and climb under the covers. Sleeping after night shifts is a killer in the summer. It's so hot that I've got to leave the window open, but there's music blaring and car horns beeping and kids off school yelling at each other in the gardens, and there's no way I can possibly sleep with all that going on . . .

Weird thing is it's not Emma or Alice who get caught up in my daytime dreams when I'm tangled in the sheets, dozing, trying to catch up after night shifts. It's Jess. My subconscious is an awkward bugger.

When it becomes clear I'm not falling asleep any time soon, I shove off the sheet and climb out of bed, heading for the kitchen. I need caffeine, and fast.

Talking of the devil, Jess appears in the kitchen, her nose smattered with new freckles from the August sun outside, her hair in long waves around her shoulders. She's wearing a pretty flower-patterned sundress and flip-flops, her sunglasses balanced on the top of her head. She's standing in the doorway as a reminder that no, I wasn't imagining it. It is her I've been dreaming about. God, my subconscious needs to get a grip. A second later, the universe throws an ice-cold bucket of water over my subconscious when Jess steps further into the room followed by a tall, fair-haired, Scandinavian-looking bloke.

'Oh! Alex.' She goes a bit pink. 'This is James.'

I've only been gone a couple of weeks. Where the hell has this James sprung from? I realise I'm probably staring and extend a hand. James shakes it – firmly.

'Hi. I'm Alex, Jess's housemate.' Obviously I'm her housemate – that's why I'm standing here with bare feet and wearing track pants and a T-shirt.

'Ah, right,' he says, looking pleased he knows which one I am. 'You're the walking one.'

'That's right.' Jess beams.

I make polite small talk for a few more moments, then make my excuses. I pull the door of my bedroom closed and look out of the window at Albany Road and the sea of houses that stretches out as far as I can see. My stomach contracts with something I really don't want to acknowledge. I can't be jealous because Jess has met someone. We're friends, that's all. Yes, we flirted that first night in December when we met, and yes, we'd become friends as we walked miles together over the city. That's perfectly normal.

I think for a second about that briefest of touches, lying on the grass, staring up at the sky. I really need to get a grip. It was nothing. There's a soft thud as Jess's bedroom door closes, and I grimace. I'm not staying around to find out what will happen next. I grab a towel and head for the shower, determined to stand under needles of burning hot water until I've cleared my head, and then for as long as I can. Hopefully that way I can avoid whatever's going on in the room next door.

CHAPTER THIRTY

Jess

10th September.

There's the first hint of autumn in the air as we walk to Sophie and Rich's place for dinner. A light breeze blows, and a few yellow-brown leaves eddy and swirl on the street as we get off the tube. They feel at odds with the warm weather. London seems to hold on to summer longer than other places, making more of the season. The shop windows, though, are already full of mannequins wearing long winter coats, wrapped in hats and scarves. It'll be Hallowe'en next, and then Guy Fawkes Night, and—

'You look like you're miles away,' says James, swinging my hand as we wait at the traffic lights. 'What are you thinking about?'

'Oh, Christmas, and stuff like that,' I say, shaking myself back to reality. 'Just daydreaming.'

James squeezes my hand and smiles at me. 'You're organised.'

I run my thumb over the top of his hand, and hope my face doesn't give things away. I wasn't thinking about Christmas. I was thinking about Alex and Alice, and what might be going on with them, and wondering why I was thinking about it when I was holding hands with a perfectly nice man.

Before long, we're standing outside Sophie's place waiting for her to open the door. James leans over and drops a kiss on the top of my head. 'You smell lovely,' he says, inhaling the scent of expensive Aveda shampoo that I've splurged on.

'Aww, look at you two,' Sophie says as she opens the door and catches him with his face buried in my hair. 'You have to admit,' she says, almost unbelievably smugly, taking our coats, 'I'm pretty shit-hot at matchmaking.'

James looks at me and rolls his eyes. He's used to Sophie, working with her in the office every day. And of course, I've known her forever. She likes nothing more than being proved right, and James and I seem to make the perfect couple. Everyone says so, after all.

'Come through, you guys,' says Rich, drying his hands on a tea towel and slinging it over his shoulder. 'I've just put the starters in. It won't be long.'

The sitting room is spotlessly tidy, of course. Sophie's hung a huge spider plant in one corner and it trails down, skimming the edges of the bookcase where all her books

272

are neatly ordered by colour. The whole house looks like something from an interiors magazine. I make a mental note to snap a photo of the little grouping of cacti and old Observer's Books spotter's guides she has sitting on a side table for Instagram. Nanna Beth would love that.

'Hi, you two,' Gen says as we enter. Gen has brought along an actor friend called Malcolm. He's tall, willowy, and despite the late-summer sun, wearing a trilby and a floaty long raincoat. He has a drooping, strangely clown-like face and reminds me of a bloodhound.

Gen has a habit – I think it's an acting thing – of taking on the mannerisms and personality of the person she's seeing. So tonight she's dressed in similarly floppy clothes, with two long scarves hanging around her neck. She's sitting on the sofa beside Malcolm, draping her legs over his, and fiddling with one of his long, Byronic curls. He doesn't seem to say much.

'Did you get that report done, Soph?' James asks as he takes my coat and hangs it up. It's all very comfortable, in a strange sort of way. Because James knows Sophie from work, we don't have the usual 'introducing a new boyfriend to your mates and hoping he'll get on with them' thing. Sophie approves of James completely, and of course Rich – silent and easy-going, currently doing something with the starter in the kitchen – is happy to go along with whatever Sophie thinks.

'Yeah. I had to stay behind for three hours, but it's been put to bed.'

'How's work, Jess? Are you still enjoying it?' Gen

stretches, raising her arms up in the air and balling her fists.

I nod, and take a seat next to James on a sofa. It's been a steep learning curve for the last nine months and I'm exhausted. I need a proper holiday. James made some vague noises about going away somewhere next year, and the idea of us having a next year together – well, it felt quite nice.

'Drink?' Sophie leans down between mine and James's shoulders, beaming contentedly. She loves playing hostess.

'I'd love a beer, please,' says James.

'Can I have one too?'

'Coming up.'

Malcolm gives a huge yawn, echoing Gen's a moment ago, stretching his arms up in the air. His huge clown-like face elongates and his eyes close. I look at James sideways. I get the feeling that perhaps this is all a little bit too tame and suburban for Malcolm. I sit back in the chair and take the beer Sophie hands me, looking around. It's weird to think that nine months ago we were sitting looking at the mountains on our ski trip, talking about how things might change over the next year. And now, here's Gen with Malcolm and me with James. It's all very neat and lovely. I shift a little on the sofa and James turns, giving me a look of concern.

'You all right, hon?'

I freeze slightly. He's never used that term with me before and I'd be quite happy if he never did so again. I am not a 'hon'.

Gen notices and snorts with laughter. 'You're going to have to break the spell, James, or she'll be frozen in that position of abject horror all night.'

'What did I do?' James looks genuinely anguished. His brow furrows and he runs a hand through his thick blond thatch of hair.

'I'm just not a very "hon" sort of person.'

'She's more of a darling, aren't you, darling?' Gen grins.

'What about poppet?' Malcolm raises his chin slightly and looks at me thoughtfully. 'You're quite posh. You seem a bit of a poppet to me.'

'Posh? Jess?' Sophie says.

'Excuse me,' I say, 'I am sitting right here.'

'Poshly.' Gen reaches for a crisp.

'I didn't say I was posh, Malcolm said I was posh.'

'James is posh,' Gen says, decisively. 'I bet your parents sent you to boarding school and you have an Aga and all that stuff.'

'My God,' he says, but he's laughing. He puts his hands up. 'Guilty as charged. Yes, my parents have an Aga. No, I didn't go to boarding school.'

'And did they call you poppet or hon?'

'Neither. Always James.'

'Exactly.' Gen looks pleased with herself.

'I'm just not a cute names sort of person, that's all,' I say.

With all that out of the way, we have dinner – prawn curry and a million side dishes, all prepared by Rich, who is a brilliant cook – and spend the rest of the night talking about the plot of a film we've all watched on Netflix. By the time we get home, I'm so full of curry and wine I feel like I have to be rolled upstairs to bed.

CHAPTER THIRTY-ONE

Jess

11th September

The next morning, so early that the birds are only just starting to stir and the streets are quiet and empty, I kiss James goodbye on the doorstep. I don't remember him getting into bed after he jumped in the shower when we got home. I think I was so full of food I basically passed out.

'I'll see you later,' he says, curling a hand into my hair and pressing a final kiss on my forehead.

He's reliable, he's handsome, he's solvent, and he calls when he says he will. My God, he reminds me of that Taylor Swift song. And my friends love him. I think of Alex for a second and then shake my head.

He's basically the perfect boyfriend. I watch him striding down Albany Road, turning to wave goodbye before he disappears out of view.

I turn around and head back upstairs. There's a moment when I pause outside my bedroom, one hand on the door, and I look across at Alex's door. I wonder if he's asleep, or if he's lying staring at the ceiling like I used to when he was sharing a bed with Emma. I shake myself. Of course he's not.

Alex

I put a hand up to lift my phone and check the time. A groan of exhaustion escapes almost unbidden. It's half five. I'd been woken in the middle of the night by the thud of Jess's bedroom door closing, and the sound of soft laughter, followed by silence. So I'd put a pillow over my head, determined to block out the sound – and the idea – of Jess in bed with James.

I roll over and stare at the ceiling, hands behind my head. James is a nice enough bloke, as far as I can see. Easy-going, stable, a proper grown-up – all the usual stuff. We've exchanged pleasantries in the kitchen a couple of times over the past few weeks since Jess started seeing him, and I think I've done a pretty good job of hiding how I feel. Feeling *anything* wasn't on my list of things to achieve this year. I'm not quite sure how Jess snuck in under the radar, but I have, in fact, decided the best way to deal with it is to just face up to their relationship head on (because Jess is a friend, and therefore I am – like a good friend – very happy that she has met someone nice), so I've suggested to Jess that she bring

James on one of our London walks. We're going to head up to Hampstead at the weekend and take a wander round. We'll have something to talk about, a set route, and an end point at the pub, where I can have a pint with them, then leave them to it and head back home to my room.

And then I'll have a cold shower or punch a pillow or something like that. Yep, completely sorted. Everything is under control.

CHAPTER THIRTY-TWO

Alex

15th September

All we have to do is take a walk around Hampstead. Normally, we would set off from home, jumping on the bus or the tube as necessary, grabbing a coffee on the way, and then walking, soaking up the atmosphere. But this time, with James joining us, Jess has switched things around. I think she's probably feeling a bit edgy about it. Maybe I'm reading too much into it. Anyway, she's suggested we meet at Kenwood House instead, and set off from there.

'You off out?' Emma says when we meet in the hall as I come downstairs.

I nod. 'You look nice. Off somewhere interesting?'

Emma flips her long dark hair over her shoulders and smiles. She knows she looks good. I like her for that. 'A third date, actually.'

'Nice.' Is this awkward? I wonder. But, you know what? I think maybe it's okay.

'Yeah.' She looks at me for half a moment with an odd expression on her face, and then she grins. 'He's a lawyer, funnily enough.'

She's dressed beautifully as ever, her hair hanging in a shiny curtain down her back. There's a rumble of music from downstairs – Rob must've woken up from his post-work sleep, and be getting ready to head off to the restaurant. I pick up the pile of letters and rifle through them, checking none are for me – which thankfully they're not, as all I seem to get is junk mail and credit card bills – and stack them neatly on the dresser in the hall.

'Anyway,' she starts, pausing to run lipstick around her lips, looking at me in the mirror in the hall. I look back at her reflection for a second.

'You all right?' I ask.

She nods. 'You?'

I nod as well. It's the nearest we're going to get to a *well that was nice while it lasted, but that's it* conversation.

She picks up her keys and puts them in her expensive-looking red leather bag. 'I better get going. We're having lunch at the Granary this afternoon.'

She slings her bag over her shoulder, opens the door, and heads down the stairs and onto the street.

I sit on the overground train heading towards Stratford, head against the window, staring out but not really taking in what I'm seeing. It's only when the woman sitting

282

opposite drops her bag on my foot that I glance up, realising I've almost missed my stop.

'Sorry, excuse me,' I say, climbing out of the seat and heading for the exit. I check my watch – I don't want to get there early and be hovering outside Kenwood House like a loser. I nip into the bakery beside the station and get a sandwich and a can of Coke, and eat them sitting at the entrance to the Heath, before setting off through the trees.

It feels like everyone in London's here today – dogs on extendable leads getting tangled round each other, and little kids on training bikes being chased downhill by exasperated-looking parents. I march up towards Kenwood House – I haven't been there for ages, and it was one of the places I'd planned to show Jess on our walks. I just hadn't banked on James being there, too. It comes into sight – huge and magnificent at the crest of the hill – and I wonder what it'd be like to live in a place like that. Mind you, I bet people think that about our place. I've had more than my fair share of raised eyebrows at college when I've told them I live on Albany Road. I wonder how long it'll be before Becky sells the place? I can't imagine her keeping it as a house-share when it's worth millions.

I walk around the edge of the house to the place where we've arranged to meet, and—

'Alex, there you are.'

Jess is tying her shoelace. She looks up and beams at me and I feel something in my stomach give a sort of flip. I can't help it – I grin back. Realising James is standing just to one side of her, I reach out a hand and shake his hand in greeting.

'Hi,' I say.

'This is gorgeous,' says James. 'I've never been here before.'

'Pretty nice, isn't it? There's a gallery inside,' I say, realising as I do that James is the sort of person who'll probably want to go in. I've nothing against art per se, but the prospect of wandering around a stately home looking at paintings doesn't exactly fill me with joy.

'And a collection of shoe buckles,' says Jess. 'I've googled. Anyway, shall we walk?'

'Let's go,' James says, heartily. I realise this is probably as awkward for him as it is for me.

We set off through the gardens of the house. Jess stops to take a photograph of the Henry Moore sculpture, (because in Jess's world if you haven't Instagrammed it, did it really happen?) and while she's standing with her phone, trying to get the perfect angle, James and I are left standing side by side, making conversation.

'So I gather you two have been walking miles all over London?' James says, looking at me intently. He's very . . . solid. Golden. Like – oh my God, he's like a Golden Retriever. Sort of healthy and sturdy and reliable. I have no idea why that just popped into my head, and now it won't go away. The irony is that Jess would normally find that kind of comment funny, but under the circumstances . . .

'Well,' I begin, sounding very serious because I'm trying

not to think about James as a Golden Retriever in a suit and tie, 'it started because Jess didn't know her way around.'

'And Alex knows it really well because he spent loads of time here when his dad used to come up here for work.' Jess appears beside us and finishes my sentence, looking at me sideways and smiling. She hooks a strand of hair behind her ear. She's wearing a jumper and a dress that is patterned all over with tiny little rosebuds, and the necklace she told me her Nanna Beth gave her as a good luck charm before she moved up here. I blink hard and look away, wondering if I've been staring.

'And Alex just seems to know loads of history about the places we've been,' she continues, as if I haven't just been gazing at her for what felt like ages. Maybe it was only a couple of seconds. Maybe – no, definitely – I need to get a grip.

'That's only because I'm a complete geek, with a weird memory for random stuff,' I add.

'It's not random. If it wasn't for you, I'd never have discovered the delight that is the Hyde Park pet cemetery.' She laughs.

'I thought you'd like it here because of the whole *Notting Hill* thing.' I wave an arm down in the direction of the sweep of grass where a scene from the movie was shot.

'Ahh,' sighs Jess, happily. 'If only a young Hugh Grant would materialise in front of us right now.'

'What would you do?' I raise an eyebrow.

'Go scarlet in the face and hide behind a tree, of

course. I mean in my fantasy world I'd introduce myself and he'd fall madly in love with me, but—'

James clears his throat. 'I was thinking we could walk down to the Pergola – there's a lovely view over the city from there.'

Jess shoots me a quick look. I make a face. I'm not sure her Richard Curtis movie daydreams are really James's thing. He's going to need to get used to them, mind you. It's a standing joke in the house that every time we turn on Netflix in the sitting room we're asked if we want to carry on watching one of them. She's completely addicted.

'That sounds good, doesn't it, Alex?'

I nod. And we start walking – James slightly in front, because he's got a printed-out map, even though it's not exactly difficult to find, and if we keep walking in a straight line we'll get there. I don't say anything. Jess hovers somewhere between the two of us. This is – awkward. I feel like the third wheel on a date, only a date that isn't even going all that well. 'Um,' I start to say, trying to think of something intelligent and interesting to say that'll get James talking – and then a gust of wind blows a kid's plastic kite right through the middle of the three of us and we duck out of the way. James grabs it and walks over to the little boy and his parents, bending down to his level to hand it over. He smiles and shows James a handful of pebbles he's collected and stuffed in his pockets. The parents get involved, and I watch as he chats to them, probably about the weather and other suitable topics, and when he stands up and dusts down his trousers he looks across at us and smiles, and the little boy does, too.

'Well, he's good with children,' I say, with an eyebrow raised.

'Shut it, you.' Jess shoves me with an elbow.

'I'm just saying. Good marriage material, and all that.' Why on earth did I say that? Why am I trying to push her into his arms? Oh, God. I give myself a shake.

'Well, don't,' she says, looking a bit cross.

'Talking of children,' I say, 'what's happening with Sophie?'

'Nothing,' says Jess. She gives me a look that quite clearly says '*Stop talking*'. I turn around to see that James has rejoined us. At first I can't figure out what Jess is worried about, then I realise, shit. Shit. James works with Sophie and he probably overheard me.

'What's happening with Sophie?' James repeats.

'Just a party she's organising for her niece. I was helping her make plans.' Jess covers up quickly. I don't think James even thinks about it, mind you. He's looking at the map, brow furrowed. I lean across and show him where we are, pointing in the direction of the Pergola.

'There's a road in the way,' says James.

'Yeah, we just have to cross there and walk down a bit past the Spaniards – it's an old pub, been there since the sixteenth century – and then we're back on the heath again.

Jess is trailing behind, looking more at her phone than the scenery. I try and think of something to say to James, but somehow he reminds me so much of the life I left behind that I find it really weird. I hadn't really noticed that I'd changed – I mean, I know Alice talked about it, but I still felt like the old Alex, on the whole. But here's James, talking about someone at work who'd just bought a house in the Highlands and a trip to Goa he was planning for Christmas, and it all feels like a world I used to know, but it's so far removed from my own life that I can hardly recognise it.

We're distracted – thankfully – by a group of Basset Hounds that are lumbering along just in front of their owners. They flock around our legs, long tails wagging, noses sniffing in case we've got any spare dog treats hanging around. It breaks the ice a bit, which is just as well because this walk feels like it's going to last a lifetime.

And then Jess's phone rings. 'Gen! Hi! Oh how funny, I was just thinking about you.'

James fiddles with the sleeve of his shirt, adjusting the buttons. I lean back against a wall, pushing my sunglasses up my nose so I can watch Jess without being seen. I am almost one hundred per cent certain that Gen's call was a set-up. Jess's tone is just a little bit too perky for it to be realistic.

Jess hangs up, sticking her phone back in the pocket of her jeans.

'Gen's just around the corner in the Spaniards having drinks, isn't that amazing?'

'Really?' James looks surprised. 'What's she doing up here? This isn't her neck of the woods, is it?'

'Oh,' Jess says, airily. 'Perhaps she just fancied a change?'

I tip my sunglasses down a fraction with a finger, looking

at Jess over the top of the lenses. She catches my gaze for the briefest of moments. Her eyes dart away from mine, and her mouth twitches in the way it does whenever she's trying not to laugh. I look the other way and smile.

Outside in the beer garden of the Spaniards, Gen's sitting at a wooden table with a tall, rather pissed-off-looking man in a long, drooping sort of coat that matches his long, drooping hair and face – like one of the Basset Hounds we've just seen. The other tables are full of tourists, cameras hanging round their necks and guide books and maps spread out between their drinks.

'Alex!' Gen stands up and kisses me on the cheek. She smells of apple shampoo and chewing gum. Her red curls are a wild halo around her face. 'Fancy meeting you here.'

'Fancy,' I say, drily. 'Shall I get us some drinks?'

'I'll get them,' says James, taking his wallet out of his pocket. 'What do you guys want?'

Gen and her lugubrious-looking boyfriend ponder for a moment, which gives me time to make a rapid escape plan.

I pull my phone out of my pocket, scrolling down the screen and frowning in an exaggerated manner, before firing off a rapid text.

'Alex? Drink?' James looks over at me. He's so solid and wholesome. All he needs is a tail to wag and he'd be off.

I shake my head sorrowfully. 'Sorry, guys, something's come up.' I wave the phone as evidence. 'Just had a message. I've got to get across town. Work stuff.'

Jess gives me a very sharp look. I look back, my expression one of injured innocence, and raise a hand in farewell, vaulting over the wooden fence of the beer garden, striding off in the direction of the tube.

Jess

I don't for one second believe that Alex had something come up at work. For one thing, he's not working today. For another, he was clearly finding it as excruciatingly awkward as I was. Introducing boyfriends to existing friends is bloody hard work. Even more so when the existing friend is – well, I'm not even going to go there. James is lovely, and charming, and when I get back from the loo he's sitting chatting quite happily to Gen and her boyfriend. There, you see. Perfect boyfriend material. And objectively speaking, he's good-looking too, in a sort of posh boy way. I mean not that I'm being objective. I should be being subjective. But – oh, you know what I mean. It's just . . .

I can't help wondering if the emergency text – if there even was one – has something to do with the whole Alice thing. He hasn't said anything more about it but I wonder if she's still on the scene, somehow. And then I have to remind myself that it's nothing to do with me, because I'm with James, and Alex can do what he wants. He's a friend, that's all. And there's no reason at all why a friend wouldn't send a text to ask if everything's okay, is there?

CHAPTER THIRTY-THREE

Jess

2nd October

'We've got a meeting at half eleven.' Camilla, operations director, pops her head over my desk. The open-plan office is buzzing with noise and industry because one of the biggest publishing trade fairs – Frankfurt – is coming up, and we have several big books going on sale. I've been so wrapped up in work that I haven't seen James all week, and we're supposed to be going to the cinema straight after work tonight. I secretly wonder if he'd notice if I just had a two-hour nap instead of watching the film. Even though I got home late from work and planned to go straight to bed, everyone in the house stayed up last night in the kitchen playing a killer game of cards, sharing a bottle – well, several – of wine and ordering pizza at midnight. I've had maybe four hours sleep, everything aches, and my head feels like someone's used it as a punchbag. When my phone buzzes on my desk, I pick it up, fully expecting it to be James, but it's my mother.

Nanna Beth not so well. Call me.

It feels like my stomach has just dropped through the floor. I put the phone back on the desk face down so I don't have to see the message, and stand up automatically, pushing my chair back. My hands are on the desk, my knuckles stark white. I take a shaky breath.

'Jess,' says a voice behind me kindly. 'You okay?'

I turn around, still holding on to the desk. It's Camilla.

'You look like you've seen a ghost. Are you feeling okay?'

'Just had a message to say my Nanna Beth isn't feeling well.' I look at the photo montage of the two of us on my desk. Pictures of me when I was a tiny baby perched on her knee, another of us arm in arm when I was ten and got a pair of roller skates for Christmas. There's a photo of her standing at Cardiff Uni the day I graduated, with Becky grinning in the background. I feel a bit sick and sit back down in the chair.

'Let me get you a glass of water,' says Camilla.

I look at the clock. It's twenty past eleven. Almost time for our meeting.

'Here you are.' She hands me the water, and – oddly – a tissue. 'Now, what can we do?'

I shake my head. 'We've got a meeting at half past.'

'You don't need to be in a meeting,' Camilla says, gently. 'Do you need to go home and see her?'

I turn the phone over and press the home button, looking again at the stark words lit up against a background of me, Gen and Sophie in ski clothes, laughing in the snow at New Year. I feel sick with guilt that I've moved to London and haven't been to visit Nanna Beth as often as I should have.

'I think maybe I do.'

'Okay. Leave it with me. We can give you some leave. Now why don't you get home and sort things out, pack a bag, and get on the train down to – where is it?'

'Bournemouth,' I say, my voice sounding strange and faint and far away.

As soon as I get off the train I'm aware of the sea not far off. There's something in the air – an openness in the big sky that stretches out over our heads – and of course the ozone smell of the beach. I jump in a taxi, and head straight to the hospital with my overnight bag over my shoulder.

Going home for a few days because Nanna Beth isn't well, I've texted Becky. Her reply – I check the clock, realising she's probably just finished work – flashes up as I'm sitting in the taxi.

You poor chick. Send her my love. Keep me posted.

I will, I reply.

When I get to the hospital I stand for a moment, not sure where to go. It crosses my mind – irrationally – that if Alex was here, he'd know. I head for the reception desk at A&E and they tell me she's been triaged and is in a cubicle. I follow the receptionist's instructions and make my way through the swinging doors into a corridor throning with people. There's a young woman sitting on a plastic chair, a drip hanging from her arm. A youngish couple are sitting looking pale-faced and worried, holding a baby. I hear my mother before I see her.

'This is ridiculous,' she's saying. 'We've been here eight hours and she hasn't been admitted to a ward. How much longer do you think it'll be?'

A small woman in a pink hospital tunic, her braids tied back from her face with a wide band, looks at me as I peer around the curtain. She scribbles something on a clipboard and replaces it at the end of the bed, smiling at Nanna Beth before she slips out of the door.

'Hello, duck,' says Nanna Beth, faintly. Her skin is bluish pale and her eyes have bruised shadows underneath. 'Your mother is causing a fuss.'

I lean over the bed, putting my hand on hers, feeling the papery, whisper-thin skin and squeezing her hand gently. I kiss her cheek and smell the familiar scent of Nivea face cream and Elnett hairspray. I lift my head.

'Honestly,' my mother is saying, looking irritated, 'this is absolutely ridiculous. Hello, darling.' She leans across and gives me a peck on the cheek.

'Now you're here, Jess, I'm just going to go outside and make a couple of calls. I'm supposed to be performing this evening.'

'That's fine,' I say, exchanging glances with Nanna. She's well enough to roll her eyes, so I think that maybe things aren't as bad as they seem.

Mum slips out of the cubicle and I sit down on the chair next to Nanna Beth's bed, still holding her hand.

'So what's been going on?'

'Oh, it's something to do with my heart.'

I look at her, alarmed.

'Nothing to worry about. A bit of angina, something like that.'

'They wouldn't have rushed you in here if it wasn't something to worry about.'

She tuts. 'I just need a bit of medicine and I'll be right as rain. Now, I want you to tell me all about what's been going on since I saw you last. How's that nice Alex doing?'

We talk about what I've been getting up to in London, and after a while, Nanna's eyes close and she drifts off to sleep. I take my phone out of my bag. I'm not sure you're even supposed to use them in hospitals, but I check to see if I have any messages. The first one reads:

Any news? Thinking of you. Xx

Of course, James has been in touch already. I messaged him from the train, telling him what was going on.

Hey, says a WhatsApp from Alex. I watch as the dots form on the screen, suggesting he's typing another message. They disappear, and then reappear. And then the rest of the message comes through. *Becky told me what's going on. Hope your Nanna Beth's okay – from what you've said, she's a trooper. Let me know if there's anything I can do? X*

295

I smile.

A nurse appears.

'Hello, Mrs Collins,' she says, gently. Nanna's eyes flicker open. 'We've found a bed for you upstairs, so we're just sorting out some paperwork and we're going to get you admitted. Are you the next of kin?' she says, turning to me. Mum's still on the phone somewhere, so I nod. 'Yes. I'm her granddaughter.'

'Okay, well, you can go with her up to ward 12. Do you know if your grandma has a bag with her? There's a WRVS shop down by reception if you need to pick up a toothbrush and a flannel and that sort of thing.'

I point to the flowery bag that's sitting under my chair. I wonder whether it was Mum or the staff at the sheltered accommodation who packed it. Hopefully not Mum, or half the stuff Nanna needs will be missing. 'Yes, she's got a bag. I'll check it when we get upstairs.'

It's another hour before a porter comes and helps Nanna into a wheelchair. Mum has come back and told me she hasn't been able to get the understudy to take over in her play. She looks pale and anxious, her lipstick chewed off and her hair's sticking up at the back. I reach across and smooth it and she jumps.

'Sorry.' She puts a hand to her hair.

'It was sticking up.' I chew my lip. There's a clattering in the background somewhere as if someone's dropped something. I glance at Mum and she shakes her head slightly as if to say not to worry.

Mum hastily says goodbye and leaves for the theatre.

'You're a good girl,' says Nanna Beth, faintly. She looks small in her nightie and dressing gown – as if she's shrunk in the last few months.

'Come on then, love,' says the porter cheerfully. 'We'll have you upstairs in no time.'

Ward 12 is a small room with six beds in it. All but one of them are occupied, and it must be visiting time because almost all of them have family members sitting around. There are get well cards and balloons and boxes of chocolates sitting on top of the side tables, and a low murmur of conversation. A nurse arrives and helps Nanna out of her chair and into bed while the porter wheels the chair away.

'You're in the best ward,' the nurse says in a warm, deep voice that sounds like honey. Nanna, who can't resist a good-looking man, beams up at him as she allows him to tuck the sheets around her waist and plump up pillows behind her back. 'We'll take good care of you here, don't you worry.'

I watch as he walks away, whistling. It makes me think of Alex, and how he must be with the patients on his ward. He's working on orthopaedics right now, he told me the other day, and it's basically nothing but elderly people with broken hips. Oh and one mother of four with a broken ankle. She did it playing roller derby, apparently, and she said she was quite enjoying the peace and quiet.

Nanna Beth has closed her eyes again.

I take the opportunity to message Alex back.

She's in a ward. Mum's gone to the theatre.

A moment later, Alex replies.

You must be exhausted. Where are you sleeping?

Mum's place, I suppose. x

His answer flashes straight back.

When I said let me know if there's anything I can do, I meant it. x

Alex has heard enough stories about my childhood as we've walked around London to know exactly why the prospect of staying with Mum doesn't exactly fill me with joy. I spent most of my life growing up at Nanna and Granddad's little house, because Mum was almost never around. If she wasn't off with one boyfriend or another, she was on some hare-brained money-making scheme. She'd only been seventeen when I was born, and she'd been happy to let my grandparents bring me up.

'Hello, lovey,' says a different nurse, walking into the room. 'Just going to take some observations.' She picks up a clipboard and writes something down, taking Nanna's pulse and blood pressure.

'It's all go here,' Nanna says, faintly.

'Do you know what's happening?' I ask. 'How long will she be in?' I feel a bit stranded, waiting for something to happen.

'We've got Beth on some medication, which should lower her blood pressure. The doctor will be here tomorrow morning and do her rounds. She'll take it from there.'

'What about tonight?' I look at the clock. It's already half seven.

'Well, visiting hours are over at seven forty-five,' the nurse says, checking her watch, 'but you can come back tomorrow.'

I feel a wave of anxiety wash over me. 'What if Nanna needs me?'

'Don't you worry,' Nanna Beth says, reaching her hand over and squeezing mine, gently. 'I'm in the right place. You get back to your Mum's place and I'll see you tomorrow morning. And don't you worry about the cat – she's being looked after.'

I feel weird leaving her there. She looks small and faded and old against the bright white sheets, and my stomach contracts in fear at the smells and sounds of the hospital as I make my way down flights of stairs to the entrance. I can't bear the thought of losing her.

My mother's sent a text, at least, telling me that she's going to be at the performance until eleven, and that the key is under the stone cat on the front step. She's moved again, to a flat in a scruffy-looking part of town, and I have to check the map on my phone to make sure I'm on the right street. I climb yet more stairs – she's on the third floor, overlooking rooftops and a distant view of the sea. I peer out of the window in the sitting room, looking at the dark autumn sky. Winter is creeping in. I shiver, wrapping my arms around myself. There's a gas heater and I switch it on, clicking the button five times before it sparks into life.

I wander around the empty flat, noticing bits and pieces that Mum has brought with her from one house to the next. A green china mermaid, a painting of a naked woman gazing out of a window. Battered old tea, coffee and sugar canisters. I fill the kettle and switch it on, checking in the fridge for milk. Amazingly, there is some, and when I sniff it, it's even fresh.

I make a cup of tea, rummage around in the cupboard in her room to find a blanket, and curl up on the sofa to watch television, and worry about Nanna.

James texts to ask how it's going. I reply vaguely, explaining that Nanna's fine, Mum's off at a performance, and everything will hopefully become clearer in the morning. He's all for coming down tonight, but the thought of trying to negotiate Mum meeting him, and dealing with everything that's going on – I'm just too tired, and I can't face it. But as I put the phone down and my stomach growls – making me realise I haven't eaten since this morning – I can feel fear curling into the room like overnight mist from the sea. I don't want Nanna to die. I've already lost Grandpa.

My phone buzzes again.

You surviving?

It's Alex. I reply straight away.

I've left her in a ward full of old people, I type. *And I'm worried I'm going to lose her. I've hardly got any family.*

She'll be okay. His message comes through quickly. *You're made of pretty strong stuff. You've always said that comes from your Nanna Beth. What have they said?*

They've given her some medication and the doctor will be there tomorrow.

Are you going to be there?

Should I be?

Definitely. Get there for visiting hours – I had a look for you, they start at ten. The doctors won't do their rounds until after then, so you can just tell them you want to be in on the conversation. Get your nanna to say she wants you there.

I breathe a sigh of relief. It's nice to have someone onside who knows what they're talking about, and it occurs to me that Alex has such a kind, reassuring manner that he must make a really good nurse.

I will, I write. And then add, *Thanks – I really appreciate it. Xxx*

That's what friends are for, he replies. Another text appears a second later. It's just one single x.

CHAPTER THIRTY-FOUR

Jess

3rd October, Bournemouth

I'm woken by the phone the next morning at seven-thirty. I must've fallen asleep on the spare-room bed in my clothes – I'm still covered over by the blanket, my head awkwardly positioned on a velvet cushion. I grab my mobile, answering before I've even had time to register who's calling.

'Jess,' says Sophie, sounding breathless. 'Sorry to ring you so early but I'm in back-to-back meetings all day and I wanted to know what was happening with Nanna B.'

Sophie's known Nanna almost all her life, too.

'I'll know more once I've been into hospital.'

'Message me,' she says, urgently. 'I'll keep James updated. Is he coming down?'

I feel my face gathering in a frown. 'Coming down where?'

'Bournemouth. Don't you think it might be an idea to have him there for moral support?'

'I dunno.' I lift the covers and swing my legs out of bed, feeling the soft rug that used to be in my childhood bedroom beneath my bare feet. 'He said something last night about coming down, but I feel like it's just another thing to have to deal with. Plus – you know – family stuff, is complicated,' I say, lamely.

'And James is your boyfriend. If something like this happened, Rich would be there for me.'

'Yeah but you and Rich live together. You're like a proper couple.

Sophie speaks very slowly and clearly, as if she's talking to someone who finds it difficult to understand basic concepts. 'Yes, and stuff like this is what brings you to-gether. I bet James would want to come down and keep you company.'

'And meet Mum?'

Sophie makes a noise between a groan and a snort. 'Mmm, yeah, well, there is that – that's the downside.'

'Tell me about it.' I rub sleep out of my eyes, and my jaw cracks as a huge yawn escapes my mouth.

'Well, he's going to have to meet her sometime,' Sophie says, reasonably. 'No time like the present, and all that.'

'I'll see,' I say, non-committally, and we say goodbye and hang up.

Later that morning, sitting by Nanna's bed waiting for the doctor to do her rounds I get a message from James.

Spoke to Soph at work. I'm going to come down tomorrow. No arguments.

I type *No, please don't* then look at it for a moment. Am I being unfair? He wants to be there for support. That's what relationships are supposed to be about, aren't they? I delete the words and look at the blinking cursor.

Bloody Sophie. I know she thinks she's doing the right thing, but – I give an exasperated sigh. It's just – it's not the right time. I can hear her saying brightly, 'There's never a right time, Jess,' and I feel slightly murderous. I'm still looking at the phone, contemplating my reply to James when the doctor appears.

The doctor makes us all feel better. I hadn't realised that I was basically holding my breath, but as she explains that Nanna's blood pressure has been up and they're giving her pills to keep it under control, but they're going to monitor her for a few days, I feel my shoulders dropping in relief. It's going to be a few days though, before they let her go back to the sheltered accommodation. She's not that happy about that.

'I bet that Maureen steals my favourite chair by the window in the lounge,' she says, crossly.

'There must be other seats, Mum,' says my mother, opening some get-well cards and placing them on the bedside table. I notice she doesn't read them. Later, I'll take each one and read the messages out to Nanna, who likes to keep tabs on stuff like that.

I go down to the WRVS café with Mum to have some lunch. The visiting hours are fairly relaxed, but we're expected to make ourselves scarce at lunchtime. The hospital's too far out of town to make it worth going in, so instead we sit and eat pale ham sandwiches and drink dark tannin-infused tea, and watch the other relatives as they do the same.

You'd love it here, I write to Alex. *It's people-watching heaven.*

Exactly why I love this job, he replies, five minutes later. *Hope it's going okay. Did she have a good night?*

Really good, I reply. *In fact, she's already started flirting with the male nurse,* I joke, thinking of the nurse from the night before.

Oh yeah, that happens to me all the time.

I bet it does, I type without thinking. Then I blush slightly, because the thought of Alex in his work clothes and the idea of him turning up at my bedside pops into my head and even though nobody else knows what I'm thinking, I feel like – God, what am I *doing*?

'Is that James you're texting?' Mum asks, looking at me with interest.

I'm caught between trying to explain the situation with Alex, and having her not believe for one second we're just friends, or telling a small white lie. I decide to settle for the easy option, and say it's James.

CHAPTER THIRTY-FIVE

Jess

4th October, Bournemouth

Nanna's clearly feeling better the next afternoon, because she's asked me to bring in her favourite red lipstick and a comb.

She puts on a crochet bedjacket, neatens her hair and puts lipstick on, so she looks much more like herself. We're talking about the other patients on her ward when I hear Mum. She's out in the corridor talking to the good-looking male nurse – she gives the tinkling laugh I recognise as her in flirt mode.

'Well this *is* a surprise,' she says, as she re-enters the little ward, pausing for a moment in the doorway as if she's waiting for applause. She gives a little flourish of her hands as James – looking slightly uncomfortable – steps into the room behind her.

'So I found this young man in the corridor, looking

for you.' She raises an approving eyebrow and gives a wide smile. 'Jess, you didn't tell me how *handsome* he was. James, this is my mother, Beth.'

I stand up, and Mum – apparently oblivious to the fact that we're in a hospital ward and not the foyer of a theatre after curtain fall – gives the whole room the benefit of her widest smile. She always perks up when there's a good-looking man around.

'Hi,' says James, leaning over to give me a kiss, which lands on my temple. He looks slightly wide-eyed, as if he hadn't quite been expecting the full Mum treatment. Nobody usually is. She gestures to the chair on the other side of Nanna Beth's bed, her armful of bangles jingling. 'James, do have a sit-down. You must be tired after working this morning and then driving down all this way. Was the traffic awful?'

'Not too bad.'

'Hello, James,' says Nanna Beth. She smooths down the white cotton sheet over her lap and looks at me for a moment. It's a look that says *well, you kept this one quiet.*

'I thought I'd better come and see if there was anything I could do,' says James. He's still in a suit, the top button of his shirt undone and his tie off. He looks pretty good, actually. I notice the granddaughter of the woman opposite eyeing him up and I feel a little surge of pride that I have a handsome boyfriend in a suit and a whole life in London and all that stuff. I catch his eye and he gives me a quick smile, before turning to Nanna Beth.

'So how are you feeling? I'm sorry we're meeting in these circumstances.'

'Not too bad,' she says. She definitely looks brighter. Mum's looking perky, as well. I – on the other hand – haven't had a second to brush my hair, am wearing no make-up, and the same top I've had on for the last three days because I forgot to pack anything besides pyjamas, knickers, and a toothbrush.

Half an hour later, when James has left the ward to go and get some bits and pieces from the shop (on a mission that was clearly made up by Mum, just so she could pass verdict), I sit on the side of Nanna's bed biting my thumbnail and listening to the two of them talking.

'He's very nice,' Mum says, looking as pleased with herself as if she'd selected James herself. She takes a little compact mirror out of her bag and applies some more fuchsia lipstick, then fluffs up her hair.

'Charming,' agrees Nanna. 'And so kind and helpful. Nice of him to go to the shop, wasn't it, Jess, darling?'

I bite the inside of my cheek, not quite sure why their praise of James makes me feel uncomfortable. In the end, I wander out into the corridor to go to the loo, and to see if I can catch him when he returns. But someone's using the bathroom, and I have to wait, standing reading NHS posters about hand washing and patient care policies, until I eventually get in.

When I look at myself in the mirror I realise I look even worse than I thought. I run water over my hands and comb them through my hair, turning my head upside

309

down and shaking it to try and make it look less lank. The trouble with the new Dyson hand driers is you can't exactly stick your head under one and wake your hair up. I settle for washing my face and drying it with a green hospital-issue paper towel, and rubbing my teeth – which feel grotty – with another one. When I come back out I can hear Mum laughing before I see her, so it's no surprise to discover that James is in there, standing at the end of Nanna's bed, holding a bottle of lemon barley water and some sandwiches from the hospital shop.

'Oh, and I brought you these,' James says. He hands Mum a box of chocolates, and Nanna a crossword book. How on earth has he worked out that she loves them in that short space of time? It must be a lucky guess. Mum is over-the-top delighted and Nanna claps her hands.

'Thank goodness. I'm bored out of my mind already, stuck in here.' She chuckles and he pulls a pen out of his jacket pocket.

'He's thought of everything, Jess.' Nanna Beth beams at me. 'You've chosen well there.'

He's nice to my mother; he's charming to my grandmother. Even the grumpy nurse in charge has found him an extra chair so nobody has to perch on the end of the bed. He's a massive hit with both generations. He's basically the perfect boyfriend. So why, I ask myself, as I surreptitiously turn my phone over to check for messages, am I looking to see if Alex has been in touch?

CHAPTER THIRTY-SIX

Jess

5th October, Bournemouth

I've been thinking, Alex has typed, *that you and me should go on another exploring trip when you get back.*

We're sitting on the sofa at Mum's place the next morning. We've slept in the little spare room bed, crammed together like sardines in a tin, and I'm exhausted and dreaming of my own bed. James is sipping a mug of coffee and reading the local newspaper, his long legs concertinaed in the tiny space. He looks a bit like someone's tried to put a giant in a doll's house. I watch him for a moment, looking out of the corner of my eye. He thinks I'm replying to work emails. I *am* replying to work emails. I just happen to be looking at a message from Alex and trying to work out why – when I have a handsome, eligible, kind, et cetera, et cetera, et cetera boyfriend sitting here in my mum's house – I'm more excited by the prospect of walking around London in the October drizzle than I am about being here.

I decide that maybe I'm just being fickle. But – I turn the phone over in my hands, pondering – I do like our wanders. And Alex makes me laugh. And it's important to have male friends when you're in a relationship.

I'd like that.

There's a pause when I see the dots on the screen, indicating he's writing something, and then they disappear. I wait a moment, but nothing comes.

? I type, waiting for his response.

Just, maybe we should skip inviting anyone else this time?

My insides give a disobedient little fizz, as if I've had a tiny electric shock. I'm not doing anything wrong, I tell myself, and I can feel the corners of my lips tugging upwards in a secret little smile as I tap out a reply.

Definitely.

And then I put the phone down on the table and turn towards James. He puts down the paper and gazes at me with his huge, soft brown eyes.

'You okay?'

I nod.

'And you're going to cope—' he pauses, glancing in the direction of Mum's bedroom, where she's still sleeping '—when I go back tonight?'

'Definitely.'

As if he's summoned her, Mum appears from the

bedroom, wrapped in a purple satin dressing gown. She rubs her face, and gives a huge, over-exaggerated yawn.

'Morning, James,' she says. She can't see my face, and I give him A Look – nostrils flaring and eyes wide. Mum has always been very much male focused, and with James around I've been relegated to a sort of incidental character, a bit-part player without a speaking part.

'Do we have anything for breakfast?' She opens the kitchen cupboard and closes it again, making a little noise of disappointment. It's as if she's forgotten that we're her guests, and she's the one responsible for catering.

'I noticed there was a deli on the corner when I moved the car last night. I thought I'd pop over and get us some pastries,' says James, unfolding himself and standing up, towering over me as I sit on the low, uncomfortable sofa.

'Oh, you are an angel,' Mum says, beaming at him. 'Isn't he a doll, Jess?'

'Absolutely,' I say, deadpan. James flashes me a look. He thinks I'm too hard on her. I haven't told him that much about growing up with her around – or rather, growing up at Nanna and Grandpa's house with Mum not around. It's weird that I've shared so much of this with Alex, but I think there's something about walking that makes it easier to talk about stuff. Anyway, I think he's got a more realistic view of what life with my mother was like.

'I'll be back in a couple of minutes,' James says, picking up the keys. 'I'll let myself back in.'

'He's *very* nice,' Mum says, for the fiftieth time,

watching as I put on the kettle and wipe up the kitchen surface from the night before. She'd clearly come in from a performance and made tea and a vodka and orange (or two) and the worktop is covered with a sticky layer of crumbs and juice that has dried into a rough layer.

'He is,' I agree, scrubbing at a particularly sticky bit.

'You should take a leaf out of Sophie's book,' she continues.

'Mum,' I begin, warningly. I know where this is going, because I've been hearing it since I was eight years old. I adore Soph, but my mother has been using her as a poster girl for as long as I can remember. Childishly, I want to point out that Sophie's in the midst of some sort of super early life crisis, because she and Rich still can't agree on what they want their wedding to be, so they've reached stalemate. But I don't say anything.

'I'm just saying,' she says, pouting slightly, her tone bruised. 'You're always looking for something to be offended by. Sophie's got a good job, nice house, she's trying for a baby – you're not getting any younger, Jess.'

'I'm not even thirty.' I'm trying to keep my tone level. How can she be so different to Nanna Beth?

'And he's a good-looking young man. *Very* good-looking,' she purrs, in a way that makes me feel slightly uncomfortable.

'This is 2019. I don't have to snare a man before it's too late. I'm not going to be on the shelf if I'm still single when I turn thirty. I've just started a brand-new job.'

'Well yes of course,' she says, shaking her head as if

I'm the one being unreasonable. 'I'm just saying, if I were you I'd put a ring on it before it's too late.'

She gives a little shimmy, and heads for the bathroom, humming Beyoncé. I stand there, open-mouthed, fuming.

When James walks in a few moments later, I'm still recovering.

He puts the paper bags full of pastries down on the table and turns to me, smiling with his lovely white perfect teeth. I go over and kiss him, taking him by surprise.

'What was that for?' He takes me by the shoulders and steps back, looking at me as if he's taking me in. I look back at him. He is a nice man, I think.

'Just because,' I say, and I hug him, wrapping my arms around his broad back and gazing out at the rooftops that lead to the sea. He feels safe, and solid, and like he's not going anywhere. Maybe that's a good thing, I think, looking sideways at Mum's place. Maybe that's what I should be aiming for.

And then Mum's phone rings.

'Yes. Oh, right. Yes. Of course.' Her face blanches whiter and whiter as she speaks until there are just two spots of high colour on each cheekbone, and something in my stomach drops down to the floor and I realise I'm clenching both hands into fists.

'Of course. Yes. We'll be there straight away.'

'Mum?' I squeeze the word out.

'We need to get a taxi to the hospital.'

'I've got the car,' says James, picking up his car keys.

315

'Of course. I need my bag,' says Mum, her words mechanical and stiff. 'Jess?'

'I'm ready.'

I don't even want to ask what's happened. If I don't ask, it can't be the worst thing. It *can't* be the worst thing.

Nanna's lying in a bed in the Coronary Care Unit. I see her through the window. She looks tiny, propped up in bed with wires coming from her arms. When the nurse takes us into the room I spin round, as if to walk away from it all, covering my face with my hands. It's Mum who puts a hand on my arm and says, 'Come on, love.' I turn back, and we walk in together.

The room is oddly silent. I don't know what I was expecting: beeps and machines and all the sounds you think of when you watch this sort of thing on *Casualty* on television, not just this weird, deathly silence. Mum sits down on the chair beside the bed and looks to the nurse as if to ask permission to hold Nanna's hand. The nurse who is checking something on the machine smiles and gives a brief nod. He looks exhausted.

'She's just sleeping. We did a procedure last night to unblock an artery and put in a stent.'

I glance up at him, horrified. 'Heart surgery?'

'Not the way you're thinking,' he says, gently. 'We went in through her arm, and removed the blockage that way. She should be okay to go home in a few days, although there'll be rehab and some lifestyle changes—'

'I'll look after you, don't worry,' says Mum, squeezing

316

Nanna Beth's hand. The nurse gives another reassuring smile and leaves us.

I watch him heading down the ward, checking the time on his watch. I stand at the other side of Nanna Beth's bed, stroking her fingers. There's a cannula coming out of her hand, and wires coming out of her arm. Across the way, in another bed, there's another woman, half awake, being helped upright by a nurse. It's weird to think of Alex in the same situation, doing that day in, day out. I wish there was reception in here. I want to message him and ask what he knows about all of this. I feel scared and powerless and—

'Hello,' Nanna Beth croaks.

'My God, you gave us a fright,' says Mum.

Nanna looks at me through heavy lidded eyes. 'Sorry,' she says. Her voice is not much more than a whisper. 'Didn't mean to cause a fuss.'

CHAPTER THIRTY-SEVEN

Alex

6th October, London

I'm so tired that I could just lie down here and have an emergency nap. The words on the screen of my iPad are swimming in front of my eyes. I'm supposed to be working on an essay, but my brain's gone on strike.

On a plus note, things at home are a bit less fraught. Now the whole Emma thing is over – and I've firmly ended my brief dalliance with being the sort of bloke who has a friend with benefits – I feel like I can breathe a bit. I mean it's all very well in theory, but it just wasn't me at all. Not even recovering-from-a-break-up me.

'Can't believe you got a first in that essay,' Jameela says, throwing her bag down on the floor of the nurses' station. I jump, because my overtired nerves are jangling on high alert at the moment, and she gives a snort of laughter.

She looks as shattered as I feel. Sometimes I think if

it wasn't for the others who are all in the same boat I'd struggle to believe this job wasn't just some sort of nightmare. We're all so tired we could fall asleep standing up, and we've got assignments coming out of our ears.

I watch her peeling off layers of coat, scarf and cardigan. She shoves them in her locker in a ball and, reaching over, grabs the cup of stewed tea I'm holding, then takes a slurp.

'Oi,' I say, laughing.

'I'm bloody freezing. And you got a first. Maybe if I nick your tea I'll soak up some of your magic.'

'Doubt it,' I joke.

We're waiting for one of the senior nursing team to appear and take us on an observation in theatre. My stomach's churning with excitement and nerves. The familiar ritual of boiling kettle, teabag in cup, milk and sugar steadies me. Before I'd started working in the hospital I'd taken tea with nothing more than a splash of milk. Now, working long hours, never quite sure when the next break is coming, I heap sugar in for extra calories to keep me going. We all do.

I make another cup and pass it to Jameela. 'Here. How did you do in the essay, then?'

'Sixty-eight.'

'That's basically a first.'

'No prizes for coming second.' She rolls her eyes.

I watch as Jameela sips her tea, flicking her hijab back over her shoulder.

'So what's happening at your place?' she asks.

'Nothing much.'

She gives me a meaningful look. 'Everything sorted with Emma?'

Jameela's a good listener. I told her the whole story one long boring night – she and I have ended up on the same rotation and it's made a real difference to have someone who actually gets how I'm feeling. And who doesn't mind if I doze off mid-sentence.

'Nope. She's got someone else. I've accepted my new life as a permanent singleton. Anyway, all that sneaking around in the middle of the night was a bit like being seventeen and on a school trip.'

'That sounds quite exciting.'

'It loses the novelty pretty bloody fast. No, I'm focusing on this—' I wave in the general direction of the ward '—and on getting decent grades.'

Jameela takes another sip of tea and looks at me for a moment. 'How's Jess?' she asks.

'Fine.'

'Fine?' She gives me a look.

'Fine. Well, she's in Bournemouth seeing her gran, who's had some blood pressure issues.' I take a green paper towel and dry the mug, hanging it back on the rack. I've been trying not to think about Jess down there in Bournemouth, with the perfect, super-capable James there for moral support. When they're not sitting hand in hand by Nanna Beth's bedside, they're probably taking romantic walks on the beach.

'And no news from Alice?'

321

I look at her sideways and arch an eyebrow. 'This is like the Spanish Inquisition.'

'Sorry. Your life's way more interesting than mine at the mo. Mine is basically work, study, sleep, work.'

I nod. 'Yeah. Mine is basically that with a bit of screwed-up relationship stuff added in. As for Alice, no. Nothing much. The odd text. But I don't think you can go backwards, you know?'

'God, yes.' Jameela sounds emphatic. 'Been there. It's like trying to revive someone who's come in DoA.'

'Nice image.'

'Sorry. I swear my entire life is nursing-focused since I started this course.' Jameela yawns so widely that the last words are smothered with her hand.

'All right?'

That evening I almost jump out of my skin as I walk into the sitting room after my shift and hear a voice from the dark. 'Rob,' I say, once I've got my bearings. 'God, I forget you're here half the time.'

'Cheers,' says Rob, sardonically. He lifts his legs off the coffee table so I can head over to the battered beige armchair beside the television. 'What's up? You look like you've had a shit day.'

'Just, y'know, life stuff.'

'Anything I can help with?' Rob leans forward. He turns the volume down on the television and inclines his head towards the door, and the rest of the house. 'Woman trouble?'

322

Does *everyone* know what went on with me and Emma?

'I dunno,' I say, picking up a cushion and hugging it. 'I was talking about Alice today at work and I got out of a surgery observation – open heart, ironically – and there was a message from her. I guess she's at a bit of a crossroads – she was seeing someone for a bit and it didn't work out.'

'Ah.' Rob nods briefly. 'That's a tricky one. You dinnae want to be the fallback guy.'

'Alice wants more than I've got. Not in a bad way – I mean I don't think she was only after my money when we met, but she thought she was marrying into a lifestyle. She wants kids, a nice house in the suburbs, all that sort of thing.'

'And you don't?'

Unbidden, an image of Jess pops into my head, laughing at something as we're walking along the canal path at Little Venice. I need to get a grip.

'I wouldn't say I don't, but I'm never going to be able to give Alice what she wanted, and – she's a nice girl, and all, but—'

'She's no' the one?'

'Exactly.'

Rob looks thoughtful. 'Well, you don't want to settle. I tried that, and here I am at forty-four, living in a basement with you lot.'

'What happened?' I ask.

'Oh, I liked her a lot; she was a nice lassie. We moved down here when I got the job as a commis chef at my

323

first restaurant, and when things started falling apart we tried to fix it by getting married.'

'And it didn't work out?'

He shakes his head. 'Nah. She headed back to Glasgow, and I signed over the wee flat we had up there to her. Felt like I owed her that much.'

'So that's how you ended up here?'

'Yep. No property, no savings, not a bean to ma name. But I'd still rather have that than be stuck in a marriage where we were both miserable. You need to actually like the person you're with, no' just fancy the pants off them.'

'You're right.'

'Aye.' Rob looks at me, steadily. 'Mind you remember that. It's important.'

Suddenly, Becky crashes into the room. 'What's going on in here?' she asks.

'Just men's talk.' Rob waggles his eyebrows.

'Oh God, right, football and all that crap.' Becky laughs, looking at the screen where the weekend football fixture list is playing. It's a pretty good cover.

'Aye, something like that,' Rob says.

'Well, I have a treat in store, if you're not busy. A client's just delivered a massive crate of wine as a thank you, so I think we should celebrate the fact that we've made it to the end of the week – assuming none of you are doing anything tonight?'

'Nope,' I say. 'Well, I'd been planning an early night, and a bit of studying. But it won't take much to convince me to work on the assignment in the morning.'

'Or the afternoon, if you're hungover. But this is good wine,' Becky says, pulling a bottle out of the crate, 'and I was reading a thing today that said that you shouldn't get hangovers from expensive wine, so we can test it out. Rob, are you about?'

'I am.'

'Not working?' I ask, surprised.

'I've knackered my ankle.' He indicates the leg that was propped up on the table. 'Can't stand up for longer than about five minutes, and it's so manic in the kitchen on the weekends that I'm a liability, so I've been signed off sick for a couple of days.'

'We can have a party,' said Becky, looking cheerful. 'I've just helped on a case that looks like it's going to the High Court and we're going to win.'

She looks triumphant and exhilarated, the same expression on her face as I'd seen on the surgeon's earlier when they'd successfully completed a bypass operation. It was weird – instead of making me envious, it just underlines the fact that I don't miss law one bit. Doesn't make me want to be a surgeon, either, mind you.

'Em,' Becky calls up the stairs. 'Are you in?' She's opened the wine and is thrusting glasses into everyone's hands. 'Has anyone heard from Jess today?'

'She's coming back in a few days, I think.' I sip the red wine. It tastes expensive, and it's the kind that goes down way too easily, especially after the week I've had. I sit back and put my feet up on the coffee table.

'Shame she's not here for this,' said Becky, as Emma

comes down the stairs. I can see her through the open door of the sitting room. She's dressed for a lazy evening in a pair of cut-off jeans and a fluffy grey cardigan over a tiny white vest top. She pauses for a moment.

'This banister is seriously wobbly,' she says.

'The whole place is crumbling,' says Becky. 'Anyone any good at DIY?'

'I'll have a look at it tomorrow,' Rob says.

'With your foot?' Becky laughs.

'With my eyes.'

'I mean, should you be doing house repairs in your state?'

He chuckles. 'I know what you meant. I promise, I'll be safe.'

'Alex, want a top-up?' Becky pours more wine into my glass and hands one to Emma.

'It's Jess's birthday next Saturday. We should do something to cheer her up.' Becky curls up on the sofa beside Emma and Rob.

'Good thinking. Assuming she's free, of course,' I say.

I don't mention our plans to get together for a walk sometime soon. I haven't heard from her since yesterday, actually, which is weird. She's normally messaging stupid jokes or sharing things she's seen that she knows will make me laugh, although now James is on the scene that's tailed off a bit, obviously.

'I'm out of the loop a bit here. Is Jess okay? What's been going on?' Emma looks at Becky.

'Oh her gran's been sick, and she's been away. Didn't you notice?'

Emma shakes her head. 'I've been so busy with work, I thought we just hadn't crossed paths for a bit.'

It's weird how we can all scatter for days – weeks even – without really seeing much of each other. I watch Rob chatting to Becky about how to make the perfect chilli, arguing over recipes online, debating about whether dark chocolate is the perfect addition or an abomination. Emma catches my eye and raises her eyebrows heavenward.

We watch a crappy Netflix thriller and drink more wine. I nip out to get some snacks, realising halfway down Albany Road on my way to the corner shop that it definitely feels like winter's coming early, and a T-shirt and joggers is not enough to keep me warm. By the time I get back home my fingers and toes are like ice and the sitting room's empty.

'The secret's in the chopping.' Rob's preparing a very late-night dish of chilli-spiked vegetables and shredded beef. Becky's standing beside him, measuring out rice into a jug and boiling the kettle.

'They're doing competitive cooking again,' says Emma, passing me the wine.

We watch and wait, drinking and chatting. They work well together, despite the constant bantering half-arguments, and at quarter to midnight – all of us pretty much completely pissed – we're sitting down to dinner in the cosy, dilapidated kitchen.

CHAPTER THIRTY-EIGHT

Jess

7th October, Bournemouth

It's midnight. James is back in London, and I'm staying a bit longer, just because of the operation, and because I want to know Nanna Beth's okay before I leave. The people have been lovely at work – I think because they know she's like a mum to me. I said I'd take the time off unpaid, but got an email back telling me not to be so silly. I'll just have to work twice as hard when I get back. Meanwhile, the doctor and the nurses all keep telling us she'll be fine, and that she's doing well, but it doesn't seem to matter how many times I hear it.

I want to text Alex for reassurance, have him tell me she's going to be okay, and that I'm worrying about nothing. I can't take much more time off work. You don't get compassionate leave for grandparents, even if they're the ones who brought you up. I lie staring at the ceiling in Mum's flat, watching the hours go by on the clock, which ticks loudly on the mantelpiece, and wonder if I'll ever fall asleep.

Alex
7th October, London

'Morning.'

My eyes, which have been slowly and cautiously opening in the excruciatingly bright daylight, pop open in shock at the sound of a voice in my ear.

I close them again and screw my face up, because I think maybe I imagined it. But then I open them, and nope, there's a face beside mine on the pillow. And this isn't my pillow. It smells faintly of roses and the sunlight from the window's coming in at the wrong angle.

Emma rolls over to her side and props herself up on one elbow, and her hair falls down in a tangle. She pulls the cover up slightly, and I realise that she's got bare shoulders, which means it's more than likely the rest of her is bare as well.

I rack my brains. We were in the kitchen eating chilli wrap things, and there was wine, and . . .

'We drank the rest of the tequila. Did slammers. Don't you remember?' Emma says, clearly seeing my confused expression. She looks unperturbed.

'I—'

Vague recollections of Rob and Becky having a sword

330

fight with wooden spoons. Dancing. Music playing. It's slowly coming back to me.

'I feel like death,' says Emma, cheerfully. 'Thank God I've got today off. D'you fancy going out for breakfast to recover?'

I lie very still for a moment trying to piece it together. Rob juggling limes. Becky disappearing somewhere – probably to pass out due to an excess of wine and tequila. What a killer combination. I shift slightly in bed. It feels like my brain has come loose and is banging against my skull.

'Oh God,' I say.

'You all right?' Emma says.

I have a horrible moment of clarity. After Becky disappeared, Rob had tossed me the limes as he left the room, hobbling on his dodgy ankle. And Emma said, 'If life gives you limes, drink tequila,' and we'd finished the bottle, and . . .

For fuck's sake. Why on earth did I let my bloody libido drag me by the scruff of the neck up the stairs and into Emma's bedroom?

'I'm really sorry, Em,' I say, wriggling out of bed and grabbing my boxers and jeans, which are lying in a heap on the floor. 'I can't do this.'

'Breakfast?' She rolls over to face me, sitting up in bed and wrapping the duvet around her body. She looks like she's just woken up after an eight-hour sleep. If it was anyone else, she'd have the decency to look hungover.

'No.' I haul up my jeans, buttoning the fly. My T-shirt's

inside out and hanging over the bedside lamp. Bloody hell. 'Us,' I say, voice muffled from inside the T-shirt as I pull it on. This isn't who I am. It's not who I want to be. It's not about Emma – I like her a lot – and it's not about anyone else, either. It's just . . .

'Oh come on, Alex,' says Emma, in a cool voice. 'I'm not asking for your hand in marriage. We got pissed; we had sex.'

'Shh,' I say, putting a finger to my lips.

Emma laughs for a moment and then looks at me as if she's sizing me up, raising her chin slightly, her eyes narrowing almost imperceptibly.

'Jess isn't here, don't worry.'

'What d'you mean?' I say.

'Nothing.' She rolls over, lying on her back and staring at the ceiling. 'Just passing comment.'

'There's nothing going on with me and Jess.'

'Never said there was.'

I feel like a complete arsehole.

'It's just sex, Alex,' she says, in a clear voice, as I open the door to leave. I feel my cheeks stinging red. I am *so* shit at this whole relationship/no relationship thing.

Something's got to change. I stand in the shower, letting it run almost cold to try and wash off the hangover and the crappy feeling that I've made an idiot of myself. Afterwards I pick up my keys and my phone and head out into the autumnal drizzle. I walk up to the café in Little Venice, picking up a property paper on the way past the estate agent and sit brooding over the prices of

332

houses until my coffee goes cold and I have to order another.

'Anything to eat?' Lona, the café owner, looks at me appraisingly. 'You look like you could do with something to soak up a hangover. Panini? Some soup?'

I thank her and order a panini, then sit in the corner by the window, looking out at the crowds of people bustling past wrapped up against a weirdly early cold snap. The leaves have turned already, and the slender poplar trees are already half-bare, their long branches reaching up to the sky like slender fingers. It's going to be a cold winter.

'Here you are, my love.' Lona slides a plate in front of me, the panini steaming hot. 'And I've made you another coffee on the house. You look like you've got the cares of the world on your shoulders.'

'Something like that,' I say. 'Thank you.'

I wait for my food to cool and stare into space. Something has to change. I saw Becky before I left, and she looked seriously shifty. She gave me an odd look and sidled past me in the hallway. I'm pretty sure she's guessed something is up. I've been taking the piss with the whole *no-relationships* thing, carrying on with Emma the way I have. I can't help wondering if it's time for a fresh start. I've screwed this up. Abeo and Oli, two of my friends from work, said the other day they were looking for a new place. We'd be on placements loads more in second year, and maybe living with other nurses would make more sense. But even if we found a grotty place the rent would be sky high compared to Becky's house.

Maybe I should look into that guardian thing that Jess's friend Gen does. But she moves house every few months, flitting from one place to the next quite happily. I've got enough going on with shifting placements. I want to feel settled, or at least feel like I can unpack my things and not be waiting for the next move all the time, especially with college stress going on as well.

I drop my head into my hands, closing my eyes and giving a quiet groan of desperation. Why the hell did I end up in bed with Emma? I don't even *like* her – well, not like *that*. I mean she's a lovely girl and everything. But – shit. The truth is, every time this happens, it feels like I'm doing a pretty good job of sabotaging something. I'm not sure what.

I look down at my phone. There's a message from Jess.

I am now a cardiac expert. Coming home to grill you and see if I know more than you do.

That wouldn't be hard, I type back in reply.

Feeling a bit better about leaving NB today – she asked for her lipstick to put on because the handsome nurse is on shift again, so think she's feeling better. X

Glad to hear it.

Oh and she patted the handsome nurse on the thigh in a slightly saucy manner earlier.

[eyeroll emoji] Yep, that's a sign she's on the mend. Happens to me all the time. x

I had no idea you were so popular. x

You'd be surprised.

I scroll through eBay as I'm eating. Jess's birthday's

coming up and I've had a brainwave – if I can find her a signed copy of *One Day*, I think she'd love it. Only reasonably priced signed copies are not that easy to come by. I disappear down an eBay rabbit hole of personalised *Game of Thrones* T-shirts and diamante dog collars, eating absent-mindedly. There's no sign of one on there or anywhere else online, so I finish lunch, and take a walk up to the second-hand bookshop. Despite my lack of success online, I have a good feeling they'll have a copy – they've got pretty much everything under the sun stacked up on the shelves there.

'*One Day*, you say?' The bookseller puts down the magazine he's reading.

'Yes. It's for my friend. It's her favourite.'

I've rummaged through the shelves, with no luck.

'As it happens, you've come to the right place.' He stands up, dusting off his sleeves in a curiously thoughtful manner. He's wearing tiny, silver-rimmed glasses and looks like he's stepped out of another century.

He beckons to me to follow him, through a little doorway and into a smaller room, where the air is heavy with that dusty, sweet, old-book smell. He waves to one of the shelves with a flourish.

'A whole shelf of David Nicholls books, right here. All signed.'

'Wouldn't they be better off out on the shelves in the actual shop?'

'Sell them through a book website,' he explains, shaking his head.

He wraps it up and I head out of the shop. I sit down when I get back to the house and find myself getting caught up in the story. I can see why she loves it, but God, it's like a jab in the ribs. All missed opportunities and second chances – appropriate under the circumstances.

By the time I get up, it's dark. I look out of the window to see a girl walking down Albany Road and for a second I think it's Jess and my heart leaps, but then she turns to check the traffic before she crosses the road and I realise that no, it's nothing like her. And I don't know why, but my brain spins me back to last December when we first met. God, I screwed up there. She'd laughed and wound tinsel round her hair, and we'd chatted about everything and nothing over fajitas and tequila. I could have been in a completely different situation if I hadn't been such an arse. If I hadn't fallen into bed with Emma – I groan and run my hands through my hair. If this year's taught me one thing, it's that I'm not ever going to be a casual fling sort of person. It's just too bloody complicated.

I keep thinking about what Rob said. He almost made me believe that if something was meant to be, it was worth all the struggle and the mess and the heartache. And with someone like Jess, I don't think I'd have to choose between the job and the relationship. She'd get it.

Sod it. When Jess gets back, I'm going to ask her if she'll come on that walk we've been planning, and then we can end up back at our favourite café, and Lona can make us a hot chocolate with rum. And I can give her the book, and – the idea makes me feel a bit sick – maybe I can find a way to tell her how I feel.

CHAPTER THIRTY-NINE

Alex

11th October

The week drags past. This module we're on is the most boring one so far – all health and safety issues in the workplace and risk assessments and protocols. I spend most of the time half-listening in lectures, doodling in the margins of my notepad, and feeling sick at the thought of seeing Jess.

And then Friday comes and I come back from college to find the front door open. Jess's red and white striped key ring is lying on the dresser, and her coat's hanging on the end of the banister. I try and act casual, taking the stairs one at a time. I don't want to look like I'm hurtling up there to see her but I realise I've got butter-flies in my stomach. God, this is ridiculous.

I knock on the door and wait a second.

'Hello?' Jess says from within.

'It's me.'

'Alex!' She grins as I push the door open, popping my head round.

'Bloody hell,' I say. 'You're organised. Unpacking already? I always leave my case shoved under the bed for days after I get back from being away. Weeks, sometime.' *Shut up, you fool, you're gibbering nonsense.*

'Oh.' A strange expression flits across her face. She bites her lower lip and looks up at me. A long strand of hair curls across her face. 'I'm not unpacking. I'm packing.'

Her hair's escaping from a loose ponytail and falling in wavy tendrils around her face. She's wearing a huge fluffy jumper that hangs off one shoulder and her legs are folded underneath her. She looks adorable, and slightly frazzled, and I can't read the expression on her face at all.

'Packing? Didn't you just get back? Is your Nanna Beth okay?'

'She's fine. Really good, actually.' Her face brightens into a smile, and she adds, 'She's been misbehaving again.'

'She's going to get into trouble,' I say.

'I'm just glad she's back to herself. She's doing really well.'

'Oh that's good news. You must be relieved,' I say, conscious I sound stilted, formal.

'I am.'

'So what's the case for?' I ask.

She blushes slightly and drops her gaze. 'James. He

booked us a surprise trip for my birthday weekend. We're
going to Venice – tonight.'

Jess

I don't think – if I'm really, truly honest with myself –
I'd have let myself be as excited about James's
announcement, if it wasn't for something Becky said. Or
rather, what she didn't say.

Having dumped my stuff at the bottom of the stairs,
I had walked into the kitchen just as she made a slightly
pointed comment about *the other night* to Emma.

'I don't know what you're talking about,' Emma had
said, popping an olive into her mouth. She was standing
by the fridge, still wearing her coat. She'd turned around,
spotting me, and closed the fridge.

Becky was standing with her back to me. 'Just
saying, you and Alex sloped off without even saying
goodnight. Rob and I came back into the kitchen and
the two of you had buggered off. It's not exactly subtle,
is it?'

'Are you sure?' Emma sounded unconvincing. 'God.
I was so pissed I don't even remember. Oh, hi Jess.'

Becky spun around and looked at me with an odd
expression.

'When was this?' I tried to keep my tone of voice
casual. I felt a strange sort of dropping in my stomach.

'Oh we all had far too much to drink one night when
you were away, and it all got a bit messy.' Becky lifted

341

her chin slightly. Emma shot her a look. It was one of those looks – the *let's not mention this now* kind.

'Sounds like a good night.' I'd cleared my throat. 'I really need to get my stuff organised,' I'd said, making a rapid exit. I could hear my heart thudding in my ears.

When I got up to my room I'd flopped down on the bed with a groan. If things were back on between Emma and Alex, it was a fairly obvious sign. I needed to stop half-wondering if there was something between us, and work out what it was I wanted in my own life. And if a weekend in Venice wasn't a good way to start that, I didn't know what was. I opened my wardrobe and tried to decide what to pack.

'Oh my God, that's the most romantic thing EVER.'

Sophie hadn't even waited to message back when I shared the news on our little group chat. She'd dropped everything and called. I was on the train back from Bournemouth. I have to admit that it's sweet that James couldn't resist the urge to tell me before he saw me in person at the station when I got home to London.

'How are you feeling?' I said.

'Like death.'

Oh yes. There's another thing – a pretty big one – that happened this week. It's clearly some sort of cosmic shift, or something. I can't believe it's happened. Sophie is actually pregnant. Eight weeks, which is early – I know that much, although I'm a bit hazy on the rest of the details – but she couldn't resist telling us. Sometimes I find myself wondering if she'd carried on doing headstands after sex, and if that had been the thing that had done the trick. It's a pretty weird image to have in your head.

'I feel like I've got travel sickness but I'm not moving.'

'That sounds awful,' I said.

'Ah, but it'll be worth it,' Soph replied, in a dreamy voice. I could already imagine Gen's sardonic comments. It's weird that we're friends when we're all so different. I guess that's why it works. Plus I bet Gen's going to be the best aunty you can imagine to Sophie's baby. She'll be taking it for exotic days out and introducing it to all her thespian friends at the theatre.

'So what are you taking to wear? Where are you staying? Oh my God, you don't think he's going to get down on one knee, do you?'

I felt a leaden thud of fear in my stomach at that. 'God, I hope not. I hardly know him.'

'Jess!' Sophie chided me.

'I don't mean "I hope not" like that, just . . .' I felt a weird sensation at the idea of it. I mean I like James, and everything, but – the idea of settling down fills me with a vague sense of terror.

'But he's lovely,' Sophie said. I know she's very keen that we end up together. It's very Sophie to want me to be with someone she's selected specifically for me.

'Oh yeah, yeah,' I replied, nodding so vigorously that the woman sitting opposite me on the train looked at me as if I'd lost the plot. 'Totally lovely. I just don't think we're quite there yet.'

I half-listened to Sophie chatting happily about odd, alien things, like nursery school waiting lists and house purchase timetables, making the right noises in the right places, staring out of the window as we passed the backs of suburban houses. The gardens follow a pattern. Untidy, stacked with miniature bikes and plastic toys and a huge trampoline on the grass. Neatly kept, with a greenhouse, tidy borders edged with hedges. Scruffy and chaotic, with uncut lawns and shaggy, overgrown hedges.

That's what our garden in Albany Road looks like. Becky's been saying she's going to hire someone to sort it out for ages, but it's funny, we all forget it's there. Sophie's going to be joining the trampoline and plastic toy society before long. When I think of that, I feel a pang of something I can't put my finger on – it's not jealousy, though. More the sense that she's going to disappear out of our lives. I resolved to call her and Gen when I get back from Venice and sort out a night out, maybe dinner or something, and we can catch up. It's ridiculous that we're all living in the same place and we go weeks and weeks without seeing each other.

Shortly after I'd finished talking to Sophie, the train ground to a halt at Waterloo and I'd bumped my bag out, walking up the platform towards the gate. As I was showing my ticket, I saw James, taller and blonder than almost anyone else, like a huge Viking (if Vikings wore suits and had neat, well-kept haircuts). His face beamed with a huge smile of welcome and I thought to myself how lucky I am to be loved by someone who feels so safe, and solid, and sweet. He wrapped his arms around me.

'I didn't want to be one of those people who does the whole *pack your bag, we're going on a surprise trip* thing,' he'd explained, taking my case and wheeling it along as we headed for the tube. 'But I thought you'd had enough stress, and you could do with a break.'

He'd stayed on the tube and I'd kissed him goodbye, heading back to Queensway where I got off and bumped my case along the streets to Albany Road. There was a parcel in the porch, and I'd picked it up and opened the door, balancing it under my chin. Inside the house had smelled faintly of one of Emma's expensive scented candles.

It's weird. We've been living together for almost a year and I still feel like I know nothing about her. I've spent hours standing in the kitchen, helping Rob prep vegetables and learning how to cook some of his favourite dishes. Alex and I have walked so far over London that our Fitbits have given us all kinds of badges for effort. Becky – well, she's never here because she's always working, but I know her so well from uni that it doesn't count. But somehow, Emma and I have always kept each other at arm's length. I guess it's the Alex thing – not that there's an Alex thing from my perspective, I remind myself. We're just friends.

I told her I was off to Venice with James and she looked genuinely delighted for me.

'Oh, it's gorgeous. Hang on – I've been a couple of times with my ex,' she said, running up the stairs. 'I've got a couple of really good guidebooks.'

And then, once I'd gone into my room to get my stuff together, Alex appeared. And there was a moment when my heart leapt as his head popped round the side of the door and he stood there chatting to me. I felt weird, somehow, telling him I was going away with James. But he was his usual self, and waved me goodbye and wished me a happy birthday when it comes. I need to get over myself. And him. I've created a whole *thing* between us when there's nothing there, and there's a real live James who was messaging me that second. I clicked on my phone screen to read his message, telling myself to forget about Alex once and for all.

So now we're sitting in Terminal 5, drinking Prosecco and eating cashew nuts and looking at Emma's guide-books.

'We have to do a gondola trip,' James says, pointing out a photograph on one of the pages. 'You can't go to Venice without doing that.'

I make a non-committal noise. There's something a bit weird, I've always thought, about sitting on a boat looking self-consciously romantic while a bloke stands at the end, trying not to look at you.

'How's Sophie?' James asks.

'Says she feels sick.' I've told James Sophie is pregnant – I checked it would be okay when she called and she said she didn't mind, but she's not telling anyone else at work.

'I'll cover her back in meetings,' he says, kindly.

We get on the plane; British Airways, of course. I don't know why I guessed it would be, but it's very James. We sit back and relax whilst they come round with champagne. It's a bit of a change from my last flight, which was a Ryanair last-minute job to Madrid with the girls.

And then, once the flight and taxi are out of the way, we arrive in Venice, and it is so – Venice-y. I mean Venetian. I *mean*, it's not like one of those cities where you get there and there are two streets that look like the brochure and the rest of it's all Holiday Inns and high-rises and dodgy-looking side roads. Literally everywhere you look it's so beautiful that it makes my heart ache. It's the most romantic city in the world.

Our hotel room is huge.

'D'you like it?'

James stands behind me as I look out onto the sparkling water of the canal. I can feel his breath in my hair. He wraps his arms around my waist.

'It's gorgeous. More than gorgeous.'

I turn around and he kisses me gently. 'I'm going to have a shower,' he says, dropping one more kiss on my temple before he goes. I turn back to look at the view, and a huge yawn escapes from somewhere deep inside me. I take a photo and share it on Instagram. Nanna Beth likes it straight away and leaves a comment:

Love you very much xxx

I feel tears prickling at the corners of my eyes. It's been such a long week, and I am so tired. Nanna's back in her sheltered accommodation, only with a carer popping in once a day just to make sure she's okay. She's got a ton of medication to take each morning and evening, but she's sorted it all out with neat little pillboxes – it's very her. But oh, I miss her. I wish I could be there – wish I didn't have to be so far away. Wish I wasn't so tired . . .

CHAPTER FORTY

Jess

12th October, Venice

When I wake up, it's with a start. And I realise it's morning, and the bed's empty. It's my birthday, and I'm in Venice, and I'm completely alone. It's not exactly what I'd been thinking of when James said we were having a weekend in a lovely hotel. I roll over, lifting the duvet just in case he's hidden underneath.

Shit.

'James?'

Silence.

I look in the bathroom and there's a hotel branded Post-it Note on the mirror.

Gone for a wander. Thought I'd let you sleep. J x

I think about breakfast in bed or a lazy brunch in a café,

349

and sigh as I switch on the little hotel kettle and make myself a cup of instant coffee. It'll have to do for now. When I look on the desk, James being James, he's left a fold-out travel map on the dressing table, and a note of where he's planning to be. He'd give Sophie a run for her money in the organisation stakes. I shake my head, laughing at how similar they are, and head for the shower.

Jess
13th October

Even on a grey October Sunday afternoon, the Piazza san Marco is heaving with tourists – and pigeons.

I drop a piece of the pastry I'm eating on the run on the ground.

'Shoo,' says James, as one hops up beside him when we stop to look at a carving on the wall.

I look at the pigeon and I swear it winks at me. It takes the piece of pastry and hops off, looking pleased with itself. I shiver, and pull the collar of my coat more tightly around my neck. I don't know why I'd expected it to be warm, but I've brought nothing but unsuitable clothes. The drizzle is relentless, and James's desire to inspect every building and tell me historic facts is . . . well, it leaves something to be desired. They do say you don't really get to know someone until you go away on holiday with them, and so far I've established that James is a *lot* more interested in Venetian architecture than I am.

I look longingly at a café with roaring patio heaters glowing in the doorway, and squeeze his hand.

'D'you think maybe it's time for a drink?'

Thankfully, he agrees, and as soon as we approach, the waiter takes my coat and pulls out my chair. We're in a covered dining area, and the plastic roof is rattling in the wind. A long stream of rainwater pours from the corner, splattering into a puddle, which is starting to seep underneath and spread below the chairs opposite us. It feels as if we're living underwater. I don't think I've ever been anywhere so damp in my life.

'Negroni?' James looks at me, his eyebrows questioning. I nod. He's been in a weird mood all afternoon. There's something about going away with someone – away from all the distractions of everyday life, from friends, and familiar places around you – that really underlines how your relationship is faring.

Or . . . *isn't*?

After I got up yesterday, and once I'd managed to get lost twice trying to find my way to the restaurant where we'd agreed to have lunch (Google Maps and I are officially on non-speaking terms again), we did the gondola trip that everyone has to do when they visit Venice. James told the gondolier it was my birthday, and he insisted on serenading me, which was – well, I think James thought it was romantic. If I'm truthful it was just mortifying. It finally stopped raining in the afternoon for an hour or two, and we went to a café and I sat, feeling awkward and self-conscious, trying to make conversation.

Somehow that pissed him off, and he was offhand and a bit moody for a while afterwards, as we squelched our way around sodden pavements, stopping for coffee again to try and dry off. The rain started about twelve hours after we arrived, and it hadn't stopped. We'd gone to bed after dinner, and I'd fallen asleep in James's arms and thought that actually it was rather nice. Then we'd woken up this morning, and I'd found him sitting, guide-book in hand, writing a list of places we could go. I made a joke about no more architecture spotting, and he'd been a tiny bit huffy about it.

'Cheers,' says James now, lifting his glass to mine. He looks at me with his big, soulful eyes, and seems to relax a little bit.

'Thanks so much for bringing me,' I say, taking a gulp of negroni. God, it's strong. He watches me, smiling fondly. An elderly couple sit down at the table across from us.

'I brought her here fifty years ago,' the man says, leaning over and smiling. 'We've come back for our anniversary weekend.'

James's eyes meet mine briefly and I am hit by a sudden panic.

'Just nipping to the loo,' I say.

'What if they come back to order?' James asks.

'Oh,' I say, clambering out of the chair and knocking over a candle holder at the table behind me, 'just tell them to hang on. Or get a pizza, or something.'

'What kind of pizza?' James calls after me, but I've

352

slipped through the plastic door and I'm standing in the Piazza San Marco, looking at tourists and Venetian people dashing, coats over their heads, trying to get out of the rain, which is landing in huge splashy drops on my head, covering my shoulders, dripping down my nose.

'Are you lost, *bella*?' The waiter appears, holding an umbrella over me. My reputation precedes me.

'Just looking for the loo. I mean the bathroom. Toilet?'

'Ah.' He beckons for me to follow him. 'This way.'

Standing in front of the mirror, I look at my mascara-smudged face. My hair has gone flop in the rain and is hanging in tragic limp strands. My heart is thumping because I have this terrible lingering sense of horror that something's going to happen. I put a hand to each cheek and hold them there, gazing at my own reflection. The feeling of trepidation doesn't go away.

What if James *has* brought me to Venice to propose?

I realise with absolute, incontrovertible certainty that I can't say yes. Not just because I've known him for about five minutes, but because he brings all his travel documents in a see-through plastic folder. And because he gets up the morning we arrive and goes for a walk instead of staying under the covers like any sane, normal person. And because he's – oh, God. Just because he's him. I love Sophie to death, but he's like the male version of her. And there is no way I could ever live with her. I think Rich needs a bloody medal.

I wash my face, wiping away the smudges of mascara with a paper towel, and run my fingers through my hair.

And then I square my shoulders, brace myself, and return to the Piazza, where James is sitting, waiting quite patiently, for my return. He's reading a guidebook. Obviously.

The waiter reappears and takes our order. I can't think what I want, because there are so many things on offer that my brain's on shutdown. Plus my heart is thumping with anticipation, and not in a good way. I choose a small margherita pizza, because it seems the simplest thing to go for.

James leans in, lowering his voice. I sit back slightly, curling my fingers into my palms. It's not him, I say to myself, it's me. He's lovely. I'm just . . . I don't know what I am.

'I wanted to talk to you about something,' he begins. I pick up a napkin and shake it out, taking it by the corners and folding it into neat squares.

'I wondered – I mean, the thing is – you said your lease is coming up soon. And I know you like living there, and Becky's your friend, and everything, but—' it feels like everyone in the room is holding their breath, waiting for him to carry on talking '—I've seen a really nice flat, and I wondered if you'd like to move in with me.'

There's a second where I exhale, and I feel so dizzy that it's as if I'm a balloon that's just been untied, and I can see myself whizzing round in circles, high above the Piazza San Marco, all the air flying out of me until I collapse back down, completely deflated, in my chair. Sitting opposite James – charming, nice, Golden Retriever James, with his big chocolate button eyes and his helpful, kindly nature, and his broad dependable shoulders and his good job. I look at him, and feel my shoulders sag with relief and guilt and a million other things I can't put a name on.

'I can't,' I say eventually.

'What do you mean, you can't? Have you signed another lease?' He looks at me, and I feel like I just kicked a puppy. But it's really just hit me. I'm thirty, and life is happening all around me. And I can't spend any more of it doing what looks like the right thing just to keep some imaginary observer happy. I've only got one life and I want to start living it, now.

'No,' I say, and I feel a bit sad, but not so sad I'd spend the rest of my life with someone who is nice enough, but not enough. 'I just . . . can't.'

The journey home is pretty hideous. James sits beside me, drinking gin and tonic and studiously reading the in-flight magazine and not saying much. I try to make things better by making stupid, pointless observations, and being extra lovely to the cabin crew, as if somehow that'll make up for the fact that I've just dumped James in the most romantic city in the world because I want . . .

What is it that I want?

We fly over London, the lights illuminating the darkness like a million tiny sparkles, and when we pass through passport control James turns to me, shouldering his bag, and says stiffly, 'I think maybe we could leave it from here?'

And I nod.

He strides off, his long legs eating up the floor of the airport, and I make my way back towards the station, and the tube, and home to Albany Road.

My phone buzzes with notifications as I get off the tube and the Wi-Fi connects. A million messages from work friends and Sophie and Gen, asking if I've had a gorgeous time, updating me on what's been going on, telling me they can't wait to hear all about it.

And there's a message from Becky, sent to the house group chat, calling for a team meeting.

When I walk into Albany Road there's a really weird, hushed atmosphere. Everyone – apart from Rob, who's (predictably) working – is sitting round the kitchen table, drinking coffee or tea. They look up at me expectantly.

'Nice time?' Alex says, first.

'Venice was gorgeous,' I say, truthfully. 'Lots and lots of water.' Also truthful.

'Loved your photos,' says Becky. 'Looks like you had the most amazing time.'

'It's so romantic,' Emma sighs. She glances across at Alex, and I can't read her expression. I want to tell them that what they see on Instagram isn't necessarily representative of my real life, and remind them that the main reason I share the photos isn't to try and become Insta-famous or to get free stuff. It's because it's an easy way of sending a little pictorial *hello* to Nanna Beth and my friends from wherever I am, whatever time of day it is. And I suppose there's a bit of me that's felt like I had a point to prove – after all, I walked away from my life in Bournemouth and moved to London to have the dream career and the amazing house in Notting Hill, and all of that.

'Right. We're here for an extraordinary meeting,' Becky says, steepling her fingers and clearing her throat, 'because one of us is leaving the fold.'

I look at everyone. Before I have time to start trying to size up who it is, Becky laughs, and carries on.

'Alex is leaving to share a place with some of his friends from the nursing course, so we need to put our heads together and see if we can find someone to replace him.'

'Shouldn't be too hard,' Alex says, laughing and looking a bit uncomfortable. I try to catch his eye, but he looks down at the table.

'Have you got a place yet?' Emma says.

'Not quite,' says Alex. 'Got a couple of places to look at though.'

'I might know someone,' Emma says. 'She's a friend from work.'

'Do I know her?' Becky asks, looking interested.

I watch Alex, who is drinking his tea and looking out of the window. It's as if he's distancing himself already. I can't help wondering with a sinking feeling if he's moving out so he can make it easier for him and Emma to actually get together. Once again, I've gone away and come back to find that Alex has slipped through my fingers. Or the idea of him, anyway. I have to remind myself that all of this has been in my own bloody head. I need to get over myself and stop believing my life is going to turn out like a romantic movie.

It turns out Becky vaguely knows the girl through another friend at work, so it looks like the deal might already be done.

I stand up, faking a yawn. 'I'm really sorry,' I say, picking up my bag. 'I'm so tired, and I've got work in the morning. After a week and a half off, God knows what I've got waiting for me.'

I walk out of the room without looking back.

CHAPTER FORTY-ONE

Alex

20th November

Turns out it's not that easy finding a place in London. We've been trying for the last month but every time we think we've found somewhere that's the right price (cheap) and the right size (basically not a postage stamp) someone's got in before us with references and deposit. It's a full-time job trying to find somewhere, and we're all trying to juggle college work, agency shifts, and being in the same place at the same time. But I think at last we've done it.

The flat in Stockwell seems tiny compared to Albany Road. We take a final look at it as the letting agency guy stands in the hallway. The whole flat is approximately the size of the kitchen and dining room at Albany Road. The windows look out over a landscape that's grey and depressing. I give myself a shake, reminding myself that it's pissing down with rain on a gloomy November afternoon, and anywhere would look miserable under those circumstances.

'Everyone happy?' The estate agent does a sort of shuffling motion, bobbing his head. He's wearing a shiny grey suit and smells of Lynx Africa. It reminds me of school changing rooms.

'Yep.' I look at the boys and we all nod.

'Excellent.' He puts out a hand. 'Let's shake. I like to shake on a deal.'

We all go through the motions. I suppress a yawn, because I'm exhausted after working a night shift.

'Assuming your references work out okay, you three can be in just before Christmas.'

We're going to be working shifts, so the fact that the sitting room is the size of a cupboard is a minor detail. It's pretty unlikely we'll ever be in the room at the same time.

We all stand and watch as the letting agency guy – who's probably only twenty-one, at most – wanders back to his little car, branded with the name of the agency. He's already on the phone, organising his next deal. He gets in and drives off, giving us a wave as he passes.

It's not exactly Notting Hill. Walking back to get the tube we skirt a massive heap of rubbish waiting for collection, and pass a house with broken railings, and half a bicycle chained to a lamp-post outside. Music's blaring from a window and a man wearing a vest is hanging out shouting down to a boy on a bike below.

He circles, then disappears. It all feels a bit like something from a crime drama, and I half expect a flotilla of police cars to appear, blue lights on, and police officers to leap out and start surrounding the place. Still, it's all we can afford. And at least I'm getting out of my current house-share situation. Living in the same house as Jess has just brought it home to me that there's no way we can carry on the way we were before.

We walk down the road towards Stockwell. Some parts of it are unrecognisable now they've been poshed up, but it doesn't take long before you're in streets that look the way they've done for decades. Tattered shop hoardings and windows held together with thick layers of fly-posted adverts are interspersed with metal shutters graffitied with ornate spray-painted tags. We walk past a betting shop, which already has multi-coloured lights strung across the doorway and we hear a blast of 'Step into Christmas'. It's not even December. It gets stuck in my head and the words jam there, reminding me of this time last year when we were moving into Albany Road and I was still getting over Alice. It feels like light years ago. She sent me an email the other day, just to let me know she'd got back together with Paul, and that she hoped I was okay with that. I sent her a reply wishing them both well, and I meant it. I'm glad she's happy.

'Where are you headed now?' Abeo asks, checking his phone as we stand at the crossing, waiting for the lights to change. A recycling lorry groans and clatters past. It's got fairy lights strung across the dashboard and the driver's wearing a red and white Santa hat. I feel like the whole of London is lit up for Christmas. It's weird, then, that it feels like something inside me has been switched off.

'Back to my place,' I say, correcting myself mentally: *my old place*. I'll have to get used to the Victoria line, and find myself another café to hang out in on a Sunday morning. But it won't be the same without Jess. I've only seen her fleetingly since she got back from Venice – work is manic, by all accounts, and she'd messaged saying she'd have to put off the farewell walk we planned for Sunday morning. I chew my lip. I think she's probably avoiding me, and that makes perfect sense. Instead she'll probably be spending it tucked up in bed at James's place.

'Cheer up, mate,' a gang of suits say as they run past, tinsel round their shoulders, knocking me backwards. It looks like someone's cloned our estate agent. There's about ten of them, all in shiny-looking suits, ties loosened. They must be on an early Christmas lunch. A very early one. One of them pauses and drapes their piece of tinsel over my head, shouting, 'It's nearly Christmas, have a mince pie.'

God, London is oppressively cheerful at this time of year. I feel like the bloody Grinch. I must get a grip and stop moping. It's pathetic.

When I get back to Albany Road the house is deserted. There's a pile of post on the mat in the porch – mostly junk, none of it addressed to me. I stack it on the dresser and wonder if I should bother getting my mail redirected, or if I should just pop round once in a while and pick it up. That'll mean risking bumping into Jess. That's a good thing, and a bad one.

In the kitchen it looks like everyone's rushed out as usual. Someone's left the lid half-fastened on a carton of milk and it's fallen over sideways, leaving a leaky puddle on the fridge shelf. I pick it up, wipe up the mess, and bang the fridge shut. It never closes on the first attempt.

Upstairs, Jess's door's open. I pause for a moment outside her room, looking in at the unmade bed, the jumble of clothes on the chair beside her bed, and the snaking wires of hairdryer and straighteners tangled on the carpet. And then I notice the light of the straighteners is glowing green – she must've left them on in her rush to get out of the door and get to work on time. They're balanced on a pile of paper – she's always leaving stuff like that lying around – and I stand on the threshold, wondering what to do. Is it weird to go in? I can't ignore it. I decide to send a message to the house group chat. It's been quiet there for ages.

Just standing outside your door, Jess, and you've left your straighteners on.

Bloody hell, Jess 😖, Becky shoots back.

Excuse me, Jess types, (I feel a little jolt of something. And then I shake my head. For God's sake.) *You did it the other day, Beck. Can you switch them off, Alex? Thank youuuu x*

I step in, carefully, and unplug them from the wall.

For the briefest of moments I look around at Jess's things – at her framed *When Harry met Sally* picture on the wall, and her fluffy pink coat thing. There's a striped woollen rug thing on the end of the bed, and a teetering pile of books on her bedside table. I step out of the room, realising that it'll probably be the last time I'm in there. It feels very final.

CHAPTER FORTY-TWO

Alex

18th December

There's a week to go before Christmas and I need to study for end-of-term exams. The prospect of lying in bed listening to Jess and James together isn't exactly appealing. I decide I might as well just head back, see my mum, get some decent work done and enjoy some meals I don't have to cook myself before next term starts. I pick up my notes and textbooks, and shove them in an overnight bag with a bunch of T-shirts, jeans and stuff. I message Mum to make sure she's okay with me turning up out of the blue. She doesn't reply. I think given past performance she'll probably be okay with it, and I pull the door on Albany Road closed behind me.

I always forget how full-on Christmas is in Canterbury. The market stalls are crammed with cinnamon-scented lebkuchen and painted wooden toys. Pubs are stuffed with people in striped Breton tops and deck shoes sipping mulled wine and having leisurely lunches. The university has broken up for the end of term, but the place is still full of students. And my mother is at home, where she's gone all out with a massive eight-foot fir tree decorated with tasteful silver baubles. She has a house full of guests from her art class.

'It's so lovely to have you here, darling,' she says as she shuts the door behind me, then pulls me in for a hug. The kitchen is jammed with people who all seem to know who I am. I'm touched that she seems to have got her head round the idea of nursing at last, and she's proudly telling everyone that yes, this is Alex, and yes, he's the one who's retraining as a nurse. It's sweet, if a little bit overwhelming. Eventually I escape upstairs. Mel texts to say she's checking in to make sure I'm surviving.

I point out that she owes me one. Or several.

20th December

I don't even manage a week before it all gets too much. I hadn't made any promises about staying for the whole of the holidays because of work. Mum's already got plans to spend the whole of Christmas Day helping at the soup kitchen in town, so I don't have to feel guilty about dropping her in it and leaving her alone. She seems pretty easy-going about it.

'You could always stay here for Christmas, darling,' she says, standing in the doorway watching as I shove things back into the overnight bag. 'I'll be back by six. Or you could come and help. They might need a spare nurse.'

I shake my head. 'It's all right, honestly. I need to go and say goodbye properly to the guys in the house and get myself settled in the new place.'

'What about Christmas?' She looked concerned. 'I hate to think of you sitting there in that place all by yourself when there's a perfectly good bed down here. And I've got the Bridge Club gang coming around on Boxing Day for a buffet.'

'I won't be alone, honestly.'

I don't have a clue if anyone's going to be around over Christmas. I'm half thinking I might just pick up some agency shifts and get a bit of money behind me before term starts. Thanks to Becky's ridiculously low rent, I've managed to keep a hold of a decent chunk of my back-up savings, but once I move they're going to be dwindling away rapidly. If I work all over the holidays, not only will I have a decent chunk of money behind me, but I'll have managed to avoid any awkward encounters with Jess and James too. Bonus. I'm a genius.

I head back home – well, home for now – to Albany Road and manage to lose the time leading up to Christmas in work and revision. Rob's working really long hours, Emma's nowhere to be seen, I think because we've both been skirting around each other a bit, and Becky's gone on a trip up north to see her parents, so there's a weird sense of anti-climax.

As I get to my room, I get a call to say that Abeo, Oli and I passed the landlord's reference checks without event. It feels a bit strange and final. We just need to sort a hire van so we can move in three days before Christmas, and then nip to IKEA and pick up the essentials. The thing I'd taken for granted living in Becky's place was that the house was fully furnished, with everything her grandparents had left there. We didn't have to buy so much as a can opener. I think I took a lot of things for granted in Albany Road.

Jess

The Christmas work lunch is legendary, apparently. Everyone comes, and they hire a whole restaurant and take it over for the afternoon. But I'm just not in the mood. A waiter passes as I'm escaping to the bathroom, offering me some sort of twiddly-looking canapé. I shake my head and lock myself in the cubicle, sitting down on the top of the loo seat. Elton John's playing through the speakers, and I listen as two of the women from editorial come in, chatting about an author they've had a nightmare time with. I sit, silent and patient, and they wash their hands, reapply their lipstick, and leave, still grumbling about how late he was delivering his last manuscript, and how it had screwed everything up for next spring.

Once I'm sure it's quiet, I let myself out of the cubicle and wash my hands and face, looking at myself in the mirror. I look tired, and a bit miserable. It's Christmas,

I'm living in London, and this is everything I ever dreamed of. I think about this time last year and how I was giddy with excitement, wide-eyed, ready to soak it all up. Right now I'd like to just slink off somewhere on my own and have a rest. It's probably just end-of-year tiredness, I tell myself, squaring my shoulders as I look at myself in the mirror. I add another layer of red lipstick as a protective barrier.

I make my way back downstairs and lean over the shoulder of Jav, who is wearing a purple Christmas crown.

'I'm feeling a bit sick,' I say, quietly. 'I don't want a massive fuss, so I'm just going to sneak off now before they do pudding. Will you let people know if they ask?'

She nods, waving the glass of Prosecco in her hand. 'You sure you don't just need another one of these?'

'Definitely not.' I shake my head.

As soon as I get outside into the fresh air I feel more human. I check the map on my phone to make sure I'm walking in the right direction, and decide I'll set off home through Hyde Park.

The bare trees are silhouetted against a silver-grey sky. Dogs scamper past, their owners carrying long plastic ball throwers and dressed warmly against the December cold. I'm in a dress covered in tiny, Christmassy stars, with my big red coat over the top. I've changed my work shoes for trainers, carrying them over my shoulders in a rucksack. I watch a couple walking past, his arm around her waist, and I feel a pang of guilt. Sophie says James has been fine at work, but I still wonder if I should have let him down more gently. But I think about Nanna Beth, and how she told me to remember I only have one life and that I should leave it with as few regrets as possible. It's funny, but as much as Mum and Nanna Beth seemed to like him, I didn't love him – I mean *I* liked him, and he felt safe and secure, and all those things . . . but I definitely didn't love him. And being together with the wrong person was a million times worse than being single.

I walk past the bike hire rack where Alex and I hired Boris Bikes on one of our first outings together. I feel like he's been avoiding me, but when I tried to skirt around the question with Becky – trying to make it sound as casual as possible, she just made non-committal noises about him going back to his Mum's place to study.

'We've got someone coming to have a look at the room,' she'd reminded me that morning over breakfast. I'd looked up, confused.

'What about the girl Emma knew?'

'Mmm,' Becky had said, looking dubious. 'Dan's a friend from work. He's split up with his boyfriend and he's staying on a friend's sofa. I'd be doing him a favour. And after the whole – ' she'd raised her eyes towards the ceiling and waggled a finger back and forth, motioning in the direction of Alex and Emma's rooms '—Well, the whole *situation*, I think we want minimal drama, don't you?'

My eyes widened in surprise, and Emma had met my

gaze with a knowing look. I'd had no idea she'd known what was going on.

I stop to sit on a bench. My breath clouds in puffs in the freezing air. A family walk past, the children dragging sticks, the parents doubled over with laughter at their antics. That's the kind of family I want, I find myself thinking. And then it hits me. It's almost Christmas, and I'm here, alone, in London. I've got nobody. Publishing is full of women and gay men as far as I can see, so the chances of meeting someone at work are non-existent, and there's *nothing* on this planet that's going to convince me to try online dating again.

I'll just have to spend the rest of my life alone. Maybe I'll get some cats. Or a dog. Except I'm never going to be able to afford to buy a place. I give a massive, gusty sigh. Maybe I should just jack all this stuff in and go back to Bournemouth. If I went back to marketing, I could get a decent job and save up a deposit. I could even – I grimace at the prospect – move back in with Mum for a bit while I save.

I'd have to be pretty bloody desperate for that. I watch as two swans circle gracefully on the pond, and I pull out my phone to take a photo, editing it quickly then uploading it to Instagram. Sophie likes it almost immediately, and leaves a comment underneath.

That doesn't look like a publishing party.

I type a private message back.

I ducked out. Couldn't face it.

What're you up to now? Soph types.

Heading home. Having a bit of a walk and a think.

Sounds better than my afternoon, she types, after a moment's pause. *I've been on the bathroom floor hugging the loo for the last four hours. This is hideous.*

I look over at Kensington Palace as I walk towards Albany Road and think of the Duchess of Cambridge and her hyperemesis gravidarum. Imagine being in the public eye like that and just wanting to lie on the bathroom tiles dying quietly, but instead having to get up, plaster on a happy face, and shake people's hands. When I get closer, I realise there's a huge pine tree outside the Orangery at the palace, dotted with a million fairy lights.

There's a street vendor wearing a thick woollen cap and fingerless gloves, selling hot chestnuts. He offers me some, and I take out some money and buy a little bagful, stuffing them in the pocket of my coat. They glow in there, keeping me warm, as I head back to Albany Road. But something tugs my feet in another direction. I walk past shops lit up with decorations and buy a copy of the *Big Issue* from the man who stands outside Queensway station. My phone rings, and I almost drop it in surprise when I see it's Mum.

'Hello, love,' she says, 'I can't talk long.' She always starts calls like that. I don't know why she doesn't call when she's not busy, but she seems to like living her life pressed up to the edges of things.

'Hi,' I say, holding the phone with one hand and pressing the button at the traffic lights with the other. A little girl looks at me crossly and presses it again.

'I was supposed to do that, wasn't I, Mummy?'

I look at the mother and pull an apologetic face. She shakes her head, laughing. 'It's not a problem, honestly,' she says, taking the little girl by the hand and pushing the pram across the road.

'What's happening with Nanna Beth?' I ask.

'Oh she's fine, absolutely fine. I told her you and James might be coming down at Christmas to see her.'

'Just me,' I say, quietly. I walk past wildly expensive double-fronted houses with huge real Christmas trees in the bay of each matching window.

'Oh that's a pity,' says Mum, and she sounds genuinely distraught. 'What's James doing?'

'I don't know,' I say.

'What do you mean?' There's another pause, and I can almost hear her brain cogs whirring. 'Oh no, Jess. He hasn't finished with you?'

I give a snort, which I hope she can't hear.

'No, Mum, I finished it,' I say.

'For goodness' sake. Whatever for?'

She sounds completely astounded. There's no way on this earth that my mother, who likes to know which side her bread is buttered on, and who dreams of finding a nice, solid, stable sort of chap to rely on, could ever imagine ending things with someone like James.

'I just didn't think it was going to work out.'

'You didn't give it enough time,' she says, flatly.

'No, I just realised that I didn't actually love him. He's nice, but you can't just marry nice, and that's what I would have ended up doing.'

373

'Oh, Jess,' she says, again. 'What are you going to do now?'

'I dunno,' I say, stopping at the edge of Little Venice and looking at the canals. The late afternoon light is glowing on the water and it looks as if someone's spilled a pot of gold, which is floating on the top of the water, flashing dazzling soft light everywhere. I want to take a photograph before the sun drops down behind the buildings in the west.

It's weird. All this build-up to my glamorous new life in London, and I suspect I'll end up sharing Christmas lunch with Nanna Beth and Cyril and my mother (unless she got a better offer) in the sheltered accommodation dining room.

I say my goodbyes, and hang up. I snap several photographs and head for the café where Alex and I always liked to sit and share an after-walk coffee and a brownie. It's half three, and it closes at half four in the winter, just before it gets properly dark.

'Hello, my love,' says Lona, the owner. 'What are you after? Where's Alex?'

I shrug. 'Not sure, actually.'

'Haven't seen you two for a while. Have you had a falling-out?'

'No,' I say, taking a cup of coffee and tipping in sugar. 'Just busy with work and stuff. You know Alex is moving across town?'

She nods, thoughtfully. 'He's a nice boy.'

'He is,' I agree. But Becky let slip that things might be back on with him and Emma, and things are moving on. I wonder if maybe I should, too. Becky's never there, and while I like Rob, he's not around that much. Whoever moves in, it's going to feel pretty strange. I realise I'm going to miss Alex.

Maybe I should just head home for a bit. I sip my coffee and look out at the canal. Maybe I'm just having a wobble, because it's been almost a year and I still feel a bit like the new girl at work.

I look at my phone, and see a new message from Gen. *Oh my God I got the part. I GOT THE PART.*

This is it for Gen – I just know it. It's a part in a West End show, and she's absolutely made for it. I feel a lump in my throat and realise that there's a tear sneaking down my cheek. I wipe it away with my sleeve. I'm so, so bloody proud of her.

CONGRATULATIONS! That's amazing! You're brilliant and you deserve this. Love you xxx, I reply.

Gen this is just the beginning. You are an absolute STAR xxx Sophie types. And then there's more coming. She's still typing something, then a moment later the little notification changes from 'Sophie is typing' to 'Sophie is recording'. I frown at the screen.

A second later a voice message pops up on our group chat.

'Hi,' says Sophie, 'It's me.' There's a pause. 'I mean obviously it's me. Anyway listen I have a confession to make and I was going to tell you today and you got in first with exciting news, Gen – congratulations by the way – so I thought actually maybe it's the day for it.'

And she gives a laugh, which sounds most unlike her. 'The thing is me and Rich did a thing today. A spontaneous thing. Well it wasn't that spontaneous really because we had to book it two weeks in advance but we didn't tell a soul – oh God, sorry, I'm gabbling – but we got MARRIED.' The last word comes out as a sort of shriek and then there's a giggle and the message ends.

I hit the record button.

'Bloody *hell*, Sophie. You did what? I mean congratulations! Oh my God.' I hit send, then add as an afterthought, 'I thought you were throwing up?'

Gen's typing a message.

OH MY GOD I MUST BE DREAMING.

Nope! Sophie types a reply. *You know how much Rich was dragging his heels over the whole setting a date thing. Well, we talked and it turned out that all he wanted to do was get married and not do the whole big wedding thing. Oh – and I am throwing up. But it's much nicer doing it in Paris.*

But you've been planning this since you were like NINE, Gen types.

PARIS??? I tap out.

There's another pause while Sophie records another message.

'I can't be bothered to type it,' Sophie says, and I can hear Rich laughing in the background. 'We're on the way to Paris on the train for a honeymoon. Turns out that being spontaneous is quite fun, actually. Love you both, speak to you when I get back . . .'

And she types in a string of kisses.

I sit back and put my phone down and for a second I think I'm going to cry again. I don't know what's wrong with me today. It feels like everyone is moving on except me. Yet again I wonder if I should just give up trying to be a London person, and head back to Bournemouth with my tail between my legs. I've got a million and one old school friends back there, and Gen and Soph visit all the time. Sophie's even muttered once or twice about moving back, because you get so much more house for your money, and she likes the idea of the baby living by the sea. But I don't know.

I begin to type a message to Becky, just to see how it feels if I see it written down.

Hi Beck, I begin. *I've been thinking that maybe London life isn't for me. I've decided to hand in my notice on the room, and head back to the beach.*

Alex

How anyone could amass so much random stuff in the space of a year is pretty amazing. I shove a pile of scrappy course notes into a box, and tip the contents of my desk drawer out to see if there's anything in there worth salvaging.

'All right, mate?'

I look up to see Rob in the doorway. He's in chef's trousers and a black T-shirt, and he's growing a beard. He's looking good. Happy.

377

'No' going to be the same without you here. D'you reckon you'll come back and see us now and then?'

I grin up at him, touched. Not only has Rob given me a decent bit of life advice here and there, he's also taught me how to make a mean lamb jalfrezi and all the trimmings.

'Now and then,' I say, feeling a bit sad, knowing it's not that likely. I can't face coming back to see Jess and James all loved up and cosy. It already feels weird, because I haven't seen her in weeks. I miss our talks. London felt different when I was sharing it with her – as if I was seeing it for the first time all over again. But – I shake myself, mentally – that's over. 'But I've got a really busy year coming up with college.'

'Aye,' Rob says, nodding. 'I bet. Have you seen Jess recently?'

'Not really,' I say, looking down at the stuff on my desk. I pick up a jade green stone I was given at a fortune-telling stall when Jess and I were wandering around Camden, and I shove it in my pocket.

'You know her trip to Venice didn't go all that well?'

My head snaps up and I look at Rob, saying more sharply than I mean to, 'What d'you mean? Is she okay?'

'Oh she's fine, I think. Wee bit quiet. Less of the romantic break, more of the break-up.'

My heart bangs against my ribs. 'Break-up?' It feels as if the blood is rushing in my ears.

'Aye.' Rob looks at me, levelly. 'Told me a while ago when we were having breakfast. We were talking about this and that, and she just came out with it. Said she realised she didn't feel anything for him but friendship, so when he asked her to move in, she gave him the heave-ho.'

'Ouch,' I say, to cover my elation.

He nods. 'Aye. Anyway—' Rob sticks his hand out, and I stand up and make as if to shake it, but he pulls me into a bear hug and slaps me firmly on the back. As he lets go, he murmurs in his gruff Glasgow accent, 'Reckon you should be having a wee think about telling Jess how you feel.'

'Me?' I'm surprised that Rob seems to have picked up on what's going on – or should I say, what's *not* going on. I sigh.

'Aye. You. No point missing the boat, eh? I'll see you later, pal.'

And with a wave of his arm, Rob pulls the door closed behind him and leaves me standing in a sea of cardboard boxes and half-packed bags, my mind whirling in confusion.

I pick up my phone and scan my messages. The last one I got from Jess was a photo of a terrier in a Christmas sweater walking on a lead in Hyde Park a couple of days ago. No message, just the photo and a laughing face.

Maybe I should message her now. And say what?

Oh hi, I hear you've dumped James . . . what about it? Hardly. My heart seems to have gone into overdrive and it's banging so loud in my chest I feel like it's about to crash out. Of course—

I click on Instagram, checking to see if she's updated

379

her whereabouts. I'm always teasing her that she can't resist documenting every second of her day.

'If a serial killer was after you,' I've told her, 'all they'd have to do is check Instagram and they'd be on to you in a second.'

I scroll down the main page and her face flashes up on the screen. Sure enough, there's a photograph – I zoom in on the picture, looking at the golden light on the water, and the sun setting over the canal at Little Venice: 3.30 p.m., the time stamp underneath says. It's ten to four now. Surely she'll still be there?

I grab my wallet and pull the bedroom door behind me. I hurtle down the stairs two at a time, almost tripping over my own feet, and yank the front door open. Then I have a brainwave and run back up the stairs and into my room. I grab the book I never got the chance to give her and shove it in the back pocket of my jeans, before hurtling back out of the door again.

Outside on Albany Road the light's already fading, and the sky's a strange blue, tinged with orange. It's freezing cold. My breath clouds as I sprint up the street, jumping over a pile of cardboard boxes folded up by the red letterbox, and head towards Little Venice. The strains of carol singers on the corner of Talbot Road drift towards me as I stop for a minute, doubled over, catching my breath. God, I really need to get back to the gym.

'Mummy,' says a little girl, wrapped up against the cold in a bright red woollen coat, 'do you think Father Christmas gets cold living at the North Pole?'

'Definitely not,' I say, straightening up and looking at the solemn-faced little girl. 'I think he's got a nice warm coat like yours to keep him toasty.'

'Exactly,' said the mother, giving me a conspiratorial smile. 'See. That nice man knows, too. Everyone knows.'

I set off again at a jog. The streetlights are on, and cars line up with red buses and chunky black London cabs along Delamere Terrace as I head towards the trees and water of Little Venice. Running to the end of the road, I stand on the footpath and shade my eyes, realising that tiny pinprick flakes of snow are starting to fall.

Is that – I screw up my eyes—

It's definitely her.

'Jess!'

I can see her, sitting outside despite the freezing cold, a black bobble hat on her dark hair, a thick scarf wrapped around her neck. She's in her red coat, and she stands out in the crowds of people – as if she's the only one there. She's standing up, putting something in her bag.

'Jess!' I call again, and she half-turns, as if she'd almost heard, but isn't quite sure.

Jess

I shove my phone back in my bag and stand up, putting the coffee cup and sugar sachets back on my tray. I can't decide what to do.

And then I think I hear someone calling my name. I

381

look around, wondering if I'm imagining things. And a second later, more urgently, I hear it once more.

'*Jess!*'

Standing at the top of the road is Alex, his T-shirt hanging out from under the huge blue sweater he wears around the house, no coat on despite the fact it's zero degrees and starting to snow. My heart feels as if someone's shot it with about a million volts of electricity and I walk towards him as he weaves his way through the meandering tourists, bumping into them and apologising, his face – his lovely face – one huge ridiculous grin of happiness.

We reach each other and stand on the canal path, beside the houseboat we've both said we'd love to live in, and we stare at each other for a moment.

'Hi,' says Alex, after a moment.

'How did you know where I was?'

'You leave a trail,' he says, and reaches across, unfurling one of the tassels of my scarf. 'I got you a birthday present. I mean, I'm sorry it's late, but—' he says, pulling a book out of his back pocket. He hands it to me. It's wrapped up in brown paper and string. I tug at it and the wrapping comes away.

'Look inside,' he says.

It's a signed copy of *One Day*. I feel my cheeks going all pink with happiness. 'That's so lovely.'

'Is it okay? I thought . . .' He looks a bit shy.

I look up at the sky. 'It's snowing,' I say, for no reason at all. As if he hasn't noticed. As if it actually matters. My brain isn't working properly.

He nods. 'The thing is, I spoke to Rob,' he starts to say.

He's gazing at me intently. I put a hand to my face.

'Have I got chocolate on my nose, or something?' I ask.

He shakes his head. 'You broke up with James.'

I nod. Something inside me gives a gigantic whoosh, as if I'm a firework display and someone's lit the first match. It's freezing cold, but I drop my gloves on the footpath beside the canal and take a step towards him. My heart is going to explode in a moment and I think if I don't just do something about it right now I don't know what'll happen—

'What about – I mean . . .' I open my mouth and try and find a way to say what I want to, but there doesn't seem to be a way to ask.

'Emma?' He reads my mind. I nod.

'Friends.'

I raise my eyebrows slightly.

'It wasn't ever really a thing. I mean we're friends. That's all. I mean the thing is, it couldn't be, because . . .' He stops and puts the heels of his hands to his forehead, closing his eyes, as if he's trying to concentrate. 'Because the thing is—'

'What is the thing, Alex?' My heart is beating so loudly in my ears that the outside world seems to have just disappeared. I watch as he bends down and picks up my gloves, holding them in one hand.

He's closer to me now, so close that I think it's possible

that he can hear the sound of my heart banging in my chest.

'The thing is—' He takes a breath and looks at me with those huge brown eyes. 'I love you, Jess.'

My breath catches in my throat. A couple walk past and I see them looking at each other and one says 'aww' to the other. There's a snowflake on Alex's eyebrow and I reach forward to brush it off and he catches my hand in his and there's a moment where I feel like all the snowflakes in the world have paused, just for a second, and I look into Alex's face – and I see his beard and his melty brown eyes and the way one eyebrow sticks up untidily and his hair is scattered with snow and—

'That's funny.' And I don't know why but I feel like my whole face is one huge beam of happiness. 'Because I love you, too.'

And I stand on tiptoe and for a second I brush a kiss on the side of his mouth and I breathe in the familiar scent of him and I think my legs might give way. And then he drops my gloves and I drop my bag and he pulls me close so I can feel that underneath his jumper his heart is thumping even harder than mine, and we kiss. And the snow starts falling again, and I don't even notice. I reach my hands inside the warmth of his jumper and feel the skin of his back under his shirt and it's burning hot.

'Your hands are bloody freezing,' he says, pulling back and laughing.

'I think maybe we should go home,' I say. And I take his hand, and we walk back through the darkness, past the cinnamon-scented coffee stall, and through the shortcut past the Dog and Ferret, where they're playing 'Last Christmas' on the speakers and we hear a blast of it when someone pushes the door open. And he looks at me and swings my hand for a second, and smiles.

EPILOGUE

Jess

One Year Later

'You sure you want to give up the room?' Becky says, still dressed in her work clothes, which look incongruous because she's got a Santa hat balanced on the top of her hair. The kitchen's covered in paper chains, which I can't stop making. I found a kit in the craft shop round the corner, and it's very therapeutic. Alex said earlier that he's worried that if anyone stands still for too long they'll be decorated with baubles and strung up with Christmas lights. I can't help it. We've been together a year, and I'm so revoltingly happy that I even make myself slightly queasy sometimes. Nanna Beth's doing really well. She's completely Team Alex – in fact she loves him to bits, probably because she's got her very own male nurse to harass. And even my mother – grudgingly, because she still secretly thinks James was a better bet – has conceded that Alex and I seem very happy together.

'Yes. I definitely want to give up the room,' I say. If someone takes it over and has as good an introduction to London as I've had, they'll be lucky. I look around the kitchen, which is still as tumbledown and dilapidated as it always was. I've loved living at Albany Road, but it's time to move on.

'We could put up with a couple if it was you two, I reckon,' she says, looking across at Rob. He nods. I look at Alex fleetingly. There's something in the air. I've suspected for a while that maybe she and Rob are more than just friends, but they still haven't gone public, and I'm not going to be the one to push her to admit to anything if she's not ready – I mean, it took us long enough. But if they're just good friends, they're *very* good friends. And I love watching the way they wind each other up, and the way they spend hours in the kitchen cooking Sunday roasts. They're like the parents of the house.

'Well we're going to have two rooms to fill, then,' Becky says, looking at Rob.

'Two?' I frown.

'Oh, Emma's moving out in January – didn't I tell you? She's off to manage the entertainments section on a cruise ship.'

When we first came out and told everyone about our relationship, I'd been nervous about her reaction. She'd been a little bit frosty to start with, but it only lasted a few days. I tried to talk to her about it but she shook her head and told me that it hadn't ever been anything more than a hook up with Alex, and that she hoped we'd be very happy together. And that – amazingly – was that. Things had been pretty much plain sailing after that.

'A cruise ship?' I look at Alex, who is sitting at the kitchen table where we first met in December last year. This time, though, he's not making margaritas, but scrolling through his phone looking at online baby shops. He makes an impressed sort of face. I half wonder if she'll end up working alongside my mum, if she ever manages to get her dream job.

'If you and me and Gen club together,' he says, thoughtfully, 'we could get this for Lottie as a christening present.'

Becky peers down at the screen. 'A rocking horse? Didn't you say she was only six months old, Alex?'

'Yeah, but Jess and Gen are joint godmothers. They should get something she can keep.'

'You're such a softy,' says Becky, ruffling his hair. He ducks away, laughing.

'I think it's a lovely idea.' I drop a hand on the back of his neck, feeling the heat of his skin underneath my fingertips. And then I want to leave the kitchen and head upstairs with him as soon as I can. I take my hand away, trying to focus on what we're supposed to be doing.

'Becky, did they get in touch about doing references for our new place?' Alex asks.

'Yeah, it's all done. Can I see the pics again?'

I click on the link on my phone. I've saved a load of photos, but I won't be uploading them anywhere until we've got the keys in our hands. It's the tiniest flat you can imagine, one bedroom and a kitchen/sitting room in Queen's Park, the closest we could get to Little Venice, which is always going to be special to us.

'It looks so sweet,' Becky coos, looking back at Alex.

'How long do you have left 'til you qualify?'

'Another year.'

I look at him then back at Becky. It's going to be tight, but I don't care. 'But I've been promoted, so we'll manage – just.'

'I get the feeling you two would be okay whatever happened, anyway.' Rob looks pleased with himself. He's still revelling in his Cupid role, a year later.

Alex swivels round in his chair and looks up at me. 'I think you're right,' he says to Rob, but I'm the one who gets the full benefit of those gorgeous chocolate-drop eyes. He gives me the ghost of a wink.

'Took you long enough to work it out,' Becky teases. 'I thought you two would be perfect for each other the moment you met.'

'We were,' I say. Alex stands up, taking my hand, and as I finish my sentence we're disappearing out of the room.

'It just took us a while to figure it out.'

Acknowledgements

Like Alex, when I was a teenager I spent a lot of time wandering around London while my dad was working, so it's been absolutely lovely to write a whole book about one of my favourite places in the world. Huge thanks to everyone in the hardworking Avon gang for being so welcoming, and making this book such a joy to write – particular thanks to my brilliant editor, Rachel Faulkner-Willcocks. Thanks also to Amanda Preston, brilliant agent, moral support and cheerleader. You deserve a medal.

To the Millionaires, Hooters, and the Book Camp gang – thank you all for keeping me (relatively) sane, making me laugh with publishing gossip, and for celebrating with me every time I think I'm finished a book, and then again when it's finally done. You are all the best.

To my gorgeous children Verity, Rosie, Archie, Jude

and Rory – I love you enormously, and I'm so proud of the kind, lovely, thoughtful people you are. Sorry we've had pasta for dinner eight million times this year, but on the plus side, at least it's not risotto. Also please tidy your rooms. (If I put it down on paper, maybe you'll listen.)

To my family – Ross, Zoe, Mae, Mum, Chris – and my dear friends – Jax, Elise and Rhiannon – who put up with my vagueness, disorganisation and promises to call back when I've finished one more chapter, I love you all.

To my dogs, Mabel, Martha and Tilly – love and ear rubs. (But do please stop eating the furniture/chasing the guinea pigs/barking when I'm trying to edit.)

Last of all and most importantly – to you, reading this. Thank you for picking up this story. I hope you enjoyed reading Alex and Jess's story as much as I enjoyed writing it!

WHAT THE DOG SAW

And Other Adventures

MALCOLM GLADWELL

PENGUIN BOOKS

For Henry and David

PENGUIN BOOKS

Published by the Penguin Group
Penguin Books Ltd, 80 Strand, London WC2R ORL, England
Penguin Group (USA), Inc., 375 Hudson Street, New York, New York 10014, USA
Penguin Group (Canada), 90 Eglinton Avenue East, Suite 700, Toronto, Ontario, Canada M4P 2Y3
(a division of Pearson Penguin Canada Inc.)
Penguin Ireland, 25 St Stephen's Green, Dublin 2, Ireland (a division of Penguin Books Ltd)
Penguin Group (Australia), 250 Camberwell Road, Camberwell, Victoria 3124, Australia
(a division of Pearson Australia Group Pty Ltd)
Penguin Books India Pvt Ltd, 11 Community Centre, Panchsheel Park, New Delhi – 110 017, India
Penguin Group (NZ), 67 Apollo Drive, Rosedale, North Shore 0632, New Zealand
(a division of Pearson New Zealand Ltd)
Penguin Books (South Africa) (Pty) Ltd, 24 Sturdee Avenue, Rosebank, Johannesburg 2196, South Africa

Penguin Books Ltd, Registered Offices: 80 Strand, London WC2R ORL, England

www.penguin.com

First published in the United States by Little, Brown and Company 2009
First published in Great Britain by Allen Lane 2009
Published in Penguin Books 2010

019

Copyright © Malcolm Gladwell, 2009

The moral right of the author has been asserted

These essays were originally published in *The New Yorker*

Printed in Great Britain by Clays Ltd, St Ives plc

A CIP catalogue record for this book is available from the British Library

978-0-141-04480-4

www.greenpenguin.co.uk

MIX
Paper from
responsible sources
FSC
www.fsc.org   FSC™ C018179

Penguin Books is committed to a sustainable
future for our business, our readers and our planet.
This book is made from Forest Stewardship
Council™ certified paper.

Contents

Preface

1.

When I was a small child, I used to sneak into my father's study and leaf through the papers on his desk. He is a mathematician. He wrote on graph paper, in pencil—long rows of neatly written numbers and figures. I would sit on the edge of his chair and look at each page with puzzlement and wonder. It seemed miraculous, first of all, that he got paid for what seemed, at the time, like gibberish. But more important, I couldn't get over the fact that someone whom I loved so dearly did something every day, inside his own head, that I could not begin to understand.

This was actually a version of what I would later learn psychologists call the *other minds* problem. One-year-olds think that if they like Goldfish Crackers, then Mommy and Daddy must like Goldfish Crackers, too: they have not grasped the idea that what is inside their head is different from what is inside everyone else's head. Sooner or later, though, children come to understand that Mommy and Daddy don't necessarily like Goldfish, too, and that

moment is one of the great cognitive milestones of human development. Why is a two-year-old so terrible? Because she is systematically testing the fascinating and, to her, utterly novel notion that something that gives her pleasure might not actually give someone else pleasure—and the truth is that as adults we never lose that fascination. What is the first thing that we want to know when we meet someone who is a doctor at a social occasion? It isn't "What do you do?" We know, sort of, what a doctor does. Instead, we want to know what it means to be with sick people all day long. We want to know what it *feels like* to be a doctor, because we're quite sure that it doesn't feel at all like what it means to sit at a computer all day long, or teach school, or sell cars. Such questions are not dumb or obvious. Curiosity about the interior life of other people's day-to-day work is one of the most fundamental of human impulses, and that same impulse is what led to the writing you now hold in your hands.

2.

All the pieces in *What the Dog Saw* come from the pages of *The New Yorker,* where I have been a staff writer since 1996. Out of the countless articles I've written over that period, these are my favorites. I've grouped them into three categories. The first section is about obsessives and what I like to call *minor* geniuses—not Einstein and Winston Churchill and Nelson Mandela and the other towering architects of the world in which we live, but people like Ron Popeil, who sold the Chop-O-Matic, and Shirley Polykoff, who famously asked, "Does she or doesn't she?

Only her hairdresser knows for sure." The second section is devoted to theories, to ways of organizing experience. How should we think about homelessness, or financial scandals, or a disaster like the crash of the *Challenger*? The third section wonders about the predictions we make about people. How do we know whether someone is bad, or smart, or capable of doing something really well? As you will see, I'm skeptical about how accurately we can make any of those judgments.

In the best of these pieces, what we think isn't the issue. Instead, I'm more interested in describing what people who think about homelessness or ketchup or financial scandals think about homelessness or ketchup or financial scandals. I don't know what to conclude about the *Challenger* crash. It's gibberish to me—neatly printed indecipherable lines of numbers and figures on graph paper. But what if we look at that problem through someone else's eyes, from inside someone else's head?

You will, for example, come across an article in which I try to understand the difference between choking and panicking. The piece was inspired by John F. Kennedy Jr.'s fatal plane crash in July of 1999. He was a novice pilot in bad weather who "lost the horizon" (as pilots like to say) and went into a spiral dive. To understand what he experienced, I had a pilot take me up in the same kind of plane that Kennedy flew, in the same kind of weather, and I had him take us into a spiral dive. It wasn't a gimmick. It was a necessity. I wanted to understand what crashing a plane that way *felt* like, because if you want to make sense of that crash, it's simply not enough to just know what Kennedy did. "The Picture Problem" is

about how to make sense of satellite images, like the pictures the Bush administration thought it had of Saddam Hussein's weapons of mass destruction. I got started on that topic because I spent an afternoon with a radiologist looking at mammograms, and halfway through—completely unprompted—he mentioned that he imagined that the problems people like him had in reading breast X-rays were a lot like the problems people in the CIA had in reading satellite photos. I wanted to know what went on inside his head, and he wanted to know what went on inside the heads of CIA officers. I remember, at that moment, feeling absolutely giddy. Then there's the article after which this book is named. It's a profile of Cesar Millan, the so-called dog whisperer. Millan can calm the angriest and most troubled of animals with the touch of his hand. What goes on inside Millan's head as he does that? That was what inspired me to write the piece. But after I got halfway through my reporting, I realized there was an even better question: When Millan performs his magic, what goes on inside the *dog's* head? That's what we really want to know—what the dog saw.

3.

The question I get asked most often is, Where do you get your ideas? I never do a good job of answering that. I usually say something vague about how people tell me things, or my editor, Henry, gives me a book that gets me thinking, or I say that I just plain don't remember. When I was putting together this collection, I thought I'd try to figure that out once and for all. There is, for example, a long and somewhat eccentric piece in this book on why

no has ever come up with a ketchup to rival Heinz. (How do we feel when we eat ketchup?) That idea came from my friend Dave, who is in the grocery business. We have lunch every now and again, and he is the kind of person who thinks about things like that. (Dave also has some fascinating theories about melons, but that's an idea I'm saving for later.) Another article, called "True Colors," is about the women who pioneered the hair color market. I got started on that because I somehow got it in my head that it would be fun to write about shampoo. (I think I was desperate for a story.) Many interviews later, an exasperated Madison Avenue type said to me, "Why on earth are you writing about shampoo? Hair color is much more interesting." And so it is.

The trick to finding ideas is to convince yourself that everyone and everything has a story to tell. I say *trick* but what I really mean is *challenge,* because it's a very hard thing to do. Our instinct as humans, after all, is to assume that most things are not interesting. We flip through the channels on the television and reject ten before we settle on one. We go to a bookstore and look at twenty novels before we pick the one we want. We filter and rank and judge. We *have to*. There's just so much out there. But if you want to be a writer, you have to fight that instinct every day. Shampoo doesn't seem interesting? Well, dammit, it must be, and if it isn't, I have to believe that it will ultimately lead me to something that is. (I'll let you judge whether I'm right in that instance.)

The other trick to finding ideas is figuring out the difference between power and knowledge. Of all the people whom you'll meet in this volume, very few of them are powerful, or even famous. When I said that I'm most

interested in minor geniuses, that's what I meant. You don't start at the top if you want to find the story. You start in the middle, because it's the people in the middle who do the actual work in the world. My friend Dave, who taught me about ketchup, is a middle guy. He's *worked on* ketchup. That's how he knows about it. People at the top are self-conscious about what they say (and rightfully so) because they have position and privilege to protect—and self-consciousness is the enemy of "interestingness." In "The Pitchman" you'll meet Arnold Morris, who gave me the pitch for the "Dial-O-Matic" vegetable slicer one summer day in his kitchen on the Jersey Shore: "Come on over, folks. I'm going to show you the most amazing slicing machine you have ever seen in your life," he began. He picked up a package of barbecue spices and used it as a prop. "Take a look at this!" He held it in the air as if he were holding up a Tiffany vase.

He held it in the air as if he were holding up a Tiffany vase. That's where you find stories, in someone's kitchen on the Jersey Shore.

4.

Growing up, I never wanted to be a writer. I wanted to be a lawyer, and then in my last year of college, I decided I wanted to be in advertising. I applied to eighteen advertising agencies in the city of Toronto and received eighteen rejection letters, which I taped in a row on my wall. (I still have them somewhere.) I thought about graduate school, but my grades weren't quite good enough. I applied for a fellowship to go somewhere exotic for a year and was rejected. Writing was the thing I ended up doing by

default, for the simple reason that it took me forever to realize that writing could be a *job*. Jobs were things that were serious and daunting. Writing was fun.

After college, I worked for six months at a little magazine in Indiana called the *American Spectator*. I moved to Washington, DC, and freelanced for a few years, and eventually caught on with the *Washington Post*—and from there came to *The New Yorker*. Along the way, writing has never ceased to be fun, and I hope that buoyant spirit is evident in these pieces. Nothing frustrates me more than someone who reads something of mine or anyone else's and says, angrily, "I don't buy it." Why are they angry? Good writing does not succeed or fail on the strength of its ability to persuade. Not the kind of writing that you'll find in this book, anyway. It succeeds or fails on the strength of its ability to engage you, to make you think, to give you a glimpse into someone else's head—even if in the end you conclude that someone else's head is not a place you'd really like to be. I've called these pieces adventures, because that's what they are intended to be. Enjoy yourself.

PART ONE

OBSESSIVES, PIONEERS, AND OTHER VARIETIES OF MINOR GENIUS

"To a worm in horseradish, the world is horseradish."

The Pitchman

RON POPEIL AND THE CONQUEST

OF THE AMERICAN KITCHEN

1.

The extraordinary story of the Ronco Showtime Rotisserie & BBQ begins with Nathan Morris, the son of the shoemaker and cantor Kidders Morris, who came over from the Old Country in the 1880s, and settled in Asbury Park, New Jersey. Nathan Morris was a pitchman. He worked the boardwalk and the five-and-dimes and county fairs up and down the Atlantic coast, selling kitchen gadgets made by Acme Metal, out of Newark. In the early forties, Nathan set up N. K. Morris Manufacturing — turning out the KwiKi-Pi and the Morris Metric Slicer — and perhaps because it was the Depression and job prospects were dim, or perhaps because Nathan Morris made such a compelling case for his new profession, one by one the members of his family followed him into the business. His sons Lester Morris and Arnold (the Knife) Morris became his pitchmen. He set up his brother-in-law Irving Rosenbloom, who was to make a fortune on Long Island in plastic goods, including a hand grater

of such excellence that Nathan paid homage to it with his own Dutch Kitchen Shredder Grater. He partnered with his brother Al, whose own sons worked the boardwalk, alongside a gangly Irishman by the name of Ed McMahon. Then, one summer just before the war, Nathan took on as an apprentice his nephew Samuel Jacob Popeil. S.J., as he was known, was so inspired by his uncle Nathan that he went on to found Popeil Brothers, based in Chicago, and brought the world the Dial-O-Matic, the Chop-O-Matic, and the Veg-O-Matic. S. J. Popeil had two sons. The elder was Jerry, who died young. The younger is familiar to anyone who has ever watched an infomercial on late-night television. His name is Ron Popeil.

In the postwar years, many people made the kitchen their life's work. There were the Klinghoffers of New York, one of whom, Leon, died tragically in 1985, during the *Achille Lauro* incident, when he was pushed overboard in his wheelchair by Palestinian terrorists. They made the Roto-Broil 400, back in the fifties, an early rotisserie for the home, which was pitched by Lester Morris. There was Lewis Salton, who escaped the Nazis with an English stamp from his father's collection and parlayed it into an appliance factory in the Bronx. He brought the world the Salton Hotray — a sort of precursor to the microwave — and today Salton, Inc., sells the George Foreman Grill.

But no rival quite matched the Morris-Popeil clan. They were the first family of the American kitchen. They married beautiful women and made fortunes and stole ideas from one another and lay awake at night thinking of a way to chop an onion so that the only tears you shed were tears of joy. They believed that it was a mistake to separate

product development from marketing, as most of their contemporaries did, because to them the two were indistinguishable: the object that sold best was the one that sold itself. They were spirited, brilliant men. And Ron Popeil was the most brilliant and spirited of them all. He was the family's Joseph, exiled to the wilderness by his father only to come back and make more money than the rest of the family combined. He was a pioneer in taking the secrets of the boardwalk pitchmen to the television screen. And, of all the kitchen gadgets in the Morris-Popeil pantheon, nothing has ever been quite so ingenious in its design, or so broad in its appeal, or so perfectly representative of the Morris-Popeil belief in the interrelation of the pitch and the object being pitched, as the Ronco Showtime Rotisserie & BBQ, the countertop oven that can be bought for four payments of $39.95 and may be, dollar for dollar, the finest kitchen appliance ever made.

2.

Ron Popeil is a handsome man, thick through the chest and shoulders, with a leonine head and striking, oversize features. He is in his midsixties and lives in Beverly Hills, halfway up Coldwater Canyon, in a sprawling bungalow with a stand of avocado trees and a vegetable garden out back. In his habits Popeil is, by Beverly Hills standards, old school. He carries his own bags. He has been known to eat at Denny's. He wears T-shirts and sweatpants. As often as twice a day, he can be found buying poultry or fish or meat at one of the local grocery stores — in particular Costco, which he favors because the chickens there are $0.99 a pound, as opposed to a $1.49 at standard supermarkets.

Whatever he buys, he brings back to his kitchen, a vast room overlooking the canyon, with an array of industrial appliances, a collection of fifteen hundred bottles of olive oil, and, in the corner, an oil painting of him, his fourth wife, Robin (a former Frederick's of Hollywood model), and their baby daughter, Contessa. On paper, Popeil owns a company called Ronco Inventions, which has two hundred employees and a couple of warehouses in Chatsworth, California, but the heart of Ronco is really Ron working out of his house, and many of the key players are really just friends of Ron's who work out of their houses, too, and who gather in Ron's kitchen when, every now and again, Ron cooks a soup and wants to talk things over.

In the last thirty years, Ron has invented a succession of kitchen gadgets, among them the Ronco Electric Food Dehydrator and the Popeil Automatic Pasta and Sausage Maker, which featured a thrust bearing made of the same material used in bulletproof glass. He works steadily, guided by flashes of inspiration. In August of 2000, for instance, he suddenly realized what product should follow the Showtime Rotisserie. He and his right-hand man, Alan Backus, had been working on a bread-and-batter machine, which would take up to ten pounds of chicken wings or scallops or shrimp or fish fillets and do all the work — combining the eggs, the flour, the bread-crumbs — in a few minutes, without dirtying either the cook's hands or the machine. "Alan goes to Korea, where we have some big orders coming through," Ron explained recently over lunch — a hamburger, medium-well, with fries — in the VIP booth by the door in the Polo Lounge, at the Beverly Hills Hotel. "I call Alan on the phone. I wake him up. It was two in the morning there. And these

are my exact words: 'Stop. Do not pursue the bread-and-batter machine. I will pick it up later. This other project needs to come first.'" The other project, his inspiration, was a device capable of smoking meats indoors without creating odors that can suffuse the air and permeate furniture. Ron had a version of the indoor smoker on his porch — "a Rube Goldberg kind of thing" that he'd worked on a year earlier — and, on a whim, he cooked a chicken in it. "That chicken was so good that I said to myself" — and with his left hand Ron began to pound on the table — "This is the best chicken sandwich I have ever had in my life." He turned to me: "How many times have you had a smoked-turkey sandwich? Maybe you have a smoked-turkey or a smoked-chicken sandwich once every six months. Once! How many times have you had smoked salmon? Aah. More. I'm going to say you come across smoked salmon as an hors d'oeuvre or an entrée once every three months. Baby-back ribs? Depends on which restaurant you order ribs at. Smoked sausage, same thing. You touch on smoked food" — he leaned in and poked my arm for emphasis — "but I know one thing, Malcolm. You don't have a smoker."

The idea for the Showtime came about in the same way. Ron was at Costco when he suddenly realized that there was a long line of customers waiting to buy chickens from the in-store rotisserie ovens. They touched on rotisserie chicken, but Ron knew one thing: they did not have a rotisserie oven. Ron went home and called Backus. Together, they bought a glass aquarium, a motor, a heating element, a spit rod, and a handful of other spare parts, and began tinkering. Ron wanted something big enough for a fifteen-pound turkey but small enough to fit into

the space between the base of an average kitchen cupboard and the countertop. He didn't want a thermostat, because thermostats break, and the constant clicking on and off of the heat prevents the even, crispy browning that he felt was essential. And the spit rod had to rotate on the horizontal axis, not the vertical axis, because if you cooked a chicken or a side of beef on the vertical axis the top would dry out and the juices would drain to the bottom. Roderick Dorman, Ron's patent attorney, says that when he went over to Coldwater Canyon he often saw five or six prototypes on the kitchen counter, lined up in a row. Ron would have a chicken in each of them, so that he could compare the consistency of the flesh and the browning of the skin, and wonder if, say, there was a way to rotate a shish kebab as it approached the heating element so that the inner side of the kebab would get as brown as the outer part. By the time Ron finished, the Showtime prompted no fewer than two dozen patent applications. It was equipped with the most powerful motor in its class. It had a drip tray coated with a nonstick ceramic, which was easily cleaned, and the oven would still work even after it had been dropped on a concrete or stone surface ten times in succession, from a distance of three feet. To Ron, there was no question that it made the best chicken he had ever had in his life.

It was then that Ron filmed a television infomercial for the Showtime, twenty-eight minutes and thirty seconds in length. It was shot live before a studio audience, and aired for the first time on August 8, 1998. It has run ever since, often in the wee hours of the morning, or on obscure cable stations, alongside the get-rich schemes and the *Three's Company* reruns. The response to it has been such that

within the next three years total sales of the Showtime should exceed a billion dollars. Ron Popeil didn't use a single focus group. He had no market researchers, R&D teams, public-relations advisers, Madison Avenue advertising companies, or business consultants. He did what the Morrises and the Popeils had been doing for most of the century, and what all the experts said couldn't be done in the modern economy. He dreamed up something new in his kitchen and went out and pitched it himself.

3.

Nathan Morris, Ron Popeil's great-uncle, looked a lot like Cary Grant. He wore a straw boater. He played the ukulele, drove a convertible, and composed melodies for the piano. He ran his business out of a low-slung, whitewashed building on Ridge Avenue, near Asbury Park, with a little annex in the back where he did pioneering work with Teflon. He had certain eccentricities, such as a phobia he developed about traveling beyond Asbury Park without the presence of a doctor. He feuded with his brother Al, who subsequently left in a huff for Atlantic City, and then with his nephew S. J. Popeil, whom Nathan considered insufficiently grateful for the start he had given him in the kitchen-gadget business. That second feud led to a climactic legal showdown over S. J. Popeil's Chop-O-Matic, a food preparer with a pleated, W-shaped blade rotated by a special clutch mechanism. The Chop-O-Matic was ideal for making coleslaw and chopped liver, and when Morris introduced a strikingly similar product, called the Roto-Chop, S. J. Popeil sued his uncle for patent infringement. (As it happened, the Chop-O-Matic itself seemed to have

been inspired by the Blitzhacker, from Switzerland, and S.J. later lost a patent judgment to the Swiss.)

The two squared off in Trenton, in May of 1958, in a courtroom jammed with Morrises and Popeils. When the trial opened, Nathan Morris was on the stand, being cross-examined by his nephew's attorneys, who were out to show him that he was no more than a huckster and a copycat. At a key point in the questioning, the judge suddenly burst in. "He took the index finger of his right hand and he pointed it at Morris," Jack Dominik, Popeil's longtime patent lawyer, recalls, "and as long as I live I will never forget what he said. 'I know you! You're a pitchman! I've seen you on the boardwalk!' And Morris pointed his index finger back at the judge and shouted, 'No! I'm a manufacturer. I'm a dignified manufacturer, and I work with the most eminent of counsel!'" (Nathan Morris, according to Dominik, was the kind of man who referred to everyone he worked with as eminent.) "At that moment," Dominik goes on, "Uncle Nat's face was getting red and the judge's was getting redder, so a recess was called." What happened later that day is best described in Dominik's unpublished manuscript, "The Inventions of Samuel Joseph Popeil by Jack E. Dominik — His Patent Lawyer." Nathan Morris had a sudden heart attack, and S.J. was guilt-stricken. "Sobbing ensued," Dominik writes. "Remorse set in. The next day, the case was settled. Thereafter, Uncle Nat's recovery from his previous day's heart attack was nothing short of a miracle."

Nathan Morris was a performer, like so many of his relatives, and pitching was, first and foremost, a performance. It's said that Nathan's nephew Archie (the Pitchman's Pitchman) Morris once sold, over a long afternoon,

gadget after gadget to a well-dressed man. At the end of the day, Archie watched the man walk away, stop and peer into his bag, and then dump the whole lot into a nearby garbage can. The Morrises were that good. "My cousins could sell you an empty box," Ron says.

The last of the Morrises to be active in the pitching business is Arnold (the Knife) Morris, so named because of his extraordinary skill with the Sharpcut, the forerunner of the Ginsu. He is in his early seventies, a cheerful, impish man with a round face and a few wisps of white hair, and a trademark move whereby, after cutting a tomato into neat, regular slices, he deftly lines the pieces up in an even row against the flat edge of the blade. Today, he lives in Ocean Township, a few miles from Asbury Park, with Phyllis, his wife of twenty-nine years, whom he refers to (with the same irresistible conviction that he might use to describe, say, the Feather Touch Knife) as "the prettiest girl in Asbury Park." One morning recently, he sat in his study and launched into a pitch for the Dial-O-Matic, a slicer produced by S. J. Popeil some forty years ago.

"Come on over, folks. I'm going to show you the most amazing slicing machine you have ever seen in your life," he began. Phyllis, sitting nearby, beamed with pride. He picked up a package of barbecue spices, which Ron Popeil sells alongside his Showtime Rotisserie, and used it as a prop. "Take a look at this!" He held it in the air as if he were holding up a Tiffany vase. He talked about the machine's prowess at cutting potatoes, then onions, then tomatoes. His voice, a marvelous instrument inflected with the rhythms of the Jersey Shore, took on a sing-song quality: "How many cut tomatoes like this? You stab it. You jab it. The juices run down your elbow. With

the Dial-O-Matic, you do it a little differently. You put it in the machine and you wiggle" — he mimed fixing the tomato to the bed of the machine. "The tomato! Lady! The tomato! The more you wiggle, the more you get. The tomato! Lady! Every slice comes out perfectly, not a seed out of place. But the thing I love my Dial-O-Matic for is coleslaw. My mother-in-law used to take her cabbage and do this." He made a series of wild stabs at an imaginary cabbage. "I thought she was going to commit suicide. Oh, boy, did I pray — that she wouldn't slip! Don't get me wrong. I love my mother-in-law. It's her daughter I can't figure out. You take the cabbage. Cut it in half. Coleslaw, hot slaw. Pot slaw. Liberty slaw. It comes out like shredded wheat…"

It was a vaudeville monologue, except that Arnold wasn't merely entertaining; he was selling. "You can take a pitchman and make a great actor out of him, but you cannot take an actor and always make a great pitchman out of him," he says. The pitchman must make you applaud and take out your money. He must be able to execute what in pitchman's parlance is called "the turn" — the perilous, crucial moment where he goes from entertainer to businessman. If, out of a crowd of fifty, twenty-five people come forward to buy, the true pitchman sells to only twenty of them. To the remaining five, he says, "Wait! There's something else I want to show you!" Then he starts his pitch again, with slight variations, and the remaining four or five become the inner core of the next crowd, hemmed in by the people around them, and so eager to pay their money and be on their way that they start the selling frenzy all over again. The turn requires the management of expectation. That's why Arnold always kept

a pineapple tantalizingly perched on his stand. "For forty years, I've been promising to show people how to cut the pineapple, and I've never cut it once," he says. "It got to the point where a pitchman friend of mine went out and bought himself a plastic pineapple. Why would you cut the pineapple? It cost a couple bucks. And if you cut it they'd leave." Arnold says that he once hired some guys to pitch a vegetable slicer for him at a fair in Danbury, Connecticut, and became so annoyed at their lackadaisical attitude that he took over the demonstration himself. They were, he says, waiting for him to fail: he had never worked that particular slicer before and, sure enough, he was massacring the vegetables. Still, in a single pitch he took in $200. "Their eyes popped out of their heads," Arnold recalls. "They said, 'We don't understand it. You don't even know how to work the damn machine.' I said, 'But I know how to do one thing better than you.' They said, 'What's that?' I said, 'I know how to ask for the money.' And that's the secret to the whole damn business."

4.

Ron Popeil started pitching his father's kitchen gadgets at the Maxwell Street flea market in Chicago, in the midfifties. He was thirteen. Every morning, he would arrive at the market at five and prepare fifty pounds each of onions, cabbages, and carrots, and a hundred pounds of potatoes. He sold from six in the morning until four in the afternoon, bringing in as much as $500 a day. In his late teens, he started doing the state- and county-fair circuit, and then he scored a prime spot in the Woolworth's at State and Washington, in the Loop, which at the time was the

top-grossing Woolworth's store in the country. He was making more than the manager of the store, selling the Chop-O-Matic and the Dial-O-Matic. He dined at the Pump Room and wore a Rolex and rented $150-a-night hotel suites. In pictures from the period, he is beautiful, with thick dark hair and blue-green eyes and sensuous lips, and, several years later, when he moved his office to 919 Michigan Avenue, he was called the Paul Newman of the Playboy Building. Mel Korey, a friend of Ron's from college and his first business partner, remembers the time he went to see Ron pitch the Chop-O-Matic at the State Street Woolworth's. "He was mesmerizing," Korey says. "There were secretaries who would take their lunch break at Woolworth's to watch him because he was so good-looking. He would go into the turn, and people would just come running." Several years ago, Ron's friend Steve Wynn, the founder of the Mirage resorts, went to visit Michael Milken in prison. They were near a television, and happened to catch one of Ron's infomercials just as he was doing the countdown, a routine taken straight from the boardwalk, where he says, "You're not going to spend two hundred dollars, not a hundred and eighty dollars, not one-seventy, not one-sixty..." It's a standard pitchman's gimmick: it sounds dramatic only because the starting price is set way up high. But something about the way Ron did it was irresistible. As he got lower and lower, Wynn and Milken — who probably know as much about profit margins as anyone in America — cried out in unison, "Stop, Ron! Stop!"

Was Ron the best? The only attempt to settle the question definitively was made some forty years ago when Ron and Arnold were working a knife set at the Eastern States

Exposition, in West Springfield, Massachusetts. A third man, Frosty Wishon, who was a legend in his own right, was there, too. "Frosty was a well-dressed, articulate individual and a good salesman," Ron says. "But he thought he was the best. So I said, 'Well, guys, we've got a ten-day show, eleven, maybe twelve hours a day. We'll each do a rotation, and we'll compare how much we sell." In Morris-Popeil lore, this is known as "the shoot-out," and no one has ever forgotten the outcome. Ron beat Arnold, but only by a whisker — no more than a few hundred dollars. Frosty Wishon, meanwhile, sold only half as much as either of his rivals. "You have no idea the pressure Frosty was under," Ron continues. "He came up to me at the end of the show and said, 'Ron, I will never work with you again as long as I live.'"

No doubt Frosty Wishon was a charming and persuasive person, but he assumed that this was enough — that the rules of pitching were the same as the rules of celebrity endorsement. When Michael Jordan pitches McDonald's hamburgers, Michael Jordan is the star. But when Ron Popeil or Arnold Morris pitched, say, the Chop-O-Matic, his gift was to make the Chop-O-Matic the star. It was, after all, an innovation. It represented a different way of dicing onions and chopping liver: it required consumers to rethink the way they went about their business in the kitchen. Like most great innovations, it was disruptive. And how do you persuade people to disrupt their lives? Not merely by ingratiation or sincerity, and not by being famous or beautiful. You have to explain the invention to customers — not once or twice but three or four times, with a different twist each time. You have to show them exactly how it works and why it works, and make them

follow your hands as you chop liver with it, and then tell them precisely how it fits into their routine, and, finally, sell them on the paradoxical fact that, revolutionary as the gadget is, it's not at all hard to use.

Thirty years ago, the videocassette recorder came on the market, and it was a disruptive product, too: it was supposed to make it possible to tape a television show so that no one would ever again be chained to the prime-time schedule. Yet, as ubiquitous as the VCR became, it was seldom put to that purpose. That's because the VCR was never pitched: no one ever explained the gadget to American consumers — not once or twice but three or four times — and no one showed them exactly how it worked or how it would fit into their routine, and no pair of hands guided them through every step of the process. All the VCR-makers did was hand over the box with a smile and a pat on the back, tossing in an instruction manual for good measure. Any pitchman could have told you that wasn't going to do it.

Once, when I was over at Ron's house in Coldwater Canyon, sitting on one of the high stools in his kitchen, he showed me what real pitching is all about. He was talking about how he had just had dinner with the actor Ron Silver, who was playing Ron's friend Robert Shapiro in a new movie about the O. J. Simpson trial. "They shave the back of Ron Silver's head so that he's got a bald spot, because, you know, Bob Shapiro's got a bald spot back there, too," Ron said. "So I say to him, 'You've gotta get GLH.'" GLH, one of Ron's earlier products, is an aerosol spray designed to thicken the hair and cover up bald spots. "I told him, 'It will make you look good. When you've got to do the scene, you shampoo it out.'"

At this point, the average salesman would have stopped. The story was an aside, no more. We had been discussing the Showtime Rotisserie, and on the counter behind us was a Showtime cooking a chicken and next to it a Showtime cooking baby-back ribs, and on the table in front of him Ron's pasta maker was working, and he was frying some garlic so that we could have a little lunch. But now that he had told me about GLH, it was unthinkable that he would not also show me its wonders. He walked quickly over to a table at the other side of the room, talking as he went. "People always ask me, 'Ron, where did you get that name GLH?' I made it up. Great-Looking Hair." He picked up a can. "We make it in nine different colors. This is silver-black." He picked up a hand mirror and angled it above his head so that he could see his bald spot. "Now, the first thing I'll do is spray it where I don't need it." He shook the can and began spraying the crown of his head, talking all the while. "Then I'll go to the area itself." He pointed to his bald spot. "Right here. OK. Now I'll let that dry. Brushing is fifty percent of the way it's going to look." He began brushing vigorously, and suddenly Ron Popeil had what looked like a complete head of hair. "Wow," I said. Ron glowed. "And you tell me 'Wow.' That's what everyone says. 'Wow.' That's what people say who use it. 'Wow.' If you go outside" — he grabbed me by the arm and pulled me out onto the deck — "if you are in bright sunlight or daylight, you cannot tell that I have a big bald spot in the back of my head. It really looks like hair, but it's not hair. It's quite a product. It's incredible. Any shampoo will take it out. You know who would be a great candidate for this? Al Gore. You want to see how it feels?" Ron inclined the back of his head toward me. I had

said, "Wow," and had looked at his hair inside and out-side, but the pitchman in Ron Popeil wasn't satisfied. I had to feel the back of his head. I did. It felt just like real hair.

<h2 style="text-align:center">5.</h2>

Ron Popeil inherited more than the pitching tradition of Nathan Morris. He was very much the son of S. J. Popeil, and that fact, too, goes a long way toward explaining the success of the Showtime Rotisserie. S.J. had a ten-room apartment high in the Drake Towers, near the top of Chi-cago's Magnificent Mile. He had a chauffeured Cadil-lac limousine with a car phone, a rarity in those days, which he delighted in showing off (as in "I'm calling you from the car"). He wore three-piece suits and loved to play the piano. He smoked cigars and scowled a lot and made funny little grunting noises as he talked. He kept his money in T-bills. His philosophy was expressed in a series of epigrams: To his attorney, "If they push you far enough, sue"; to his son, "It's not how much you spend, it's how much you make." And, to a designer who expressed doubts about the utility of one of his greatest hits, the Pocket Fisherman, "It's not for using; it's for giving." In 1974, S.J.'s second wife, Eloise, decided to have him killed, so she hired two hit men — one of whom, aptly, went by the name of Mr. Peeler. At the time, she was living at the Popeil estate in Newport Beach with her two daugh-ters and her boyfriend, a thirty-seven-year-old machin-ist. When, at Eloise's trial, S.J. was questioned about the machinist, he replied, "I was kind of happy to have him take her off my hands." That was vintage S.J. But eleven months later, after Eloise got out of prison, S.J. married

her again. That was vintage S.J., too. As a former colleague of his puts it, "He was a strange bird."

S. J. Popeil was a tinkerer. In the middle of the night, he would wake up and make frantic sketches on a pad he kept on his bedside table. He would disappear into his kitchen for hours and make a huge mess, and come out with a faraway look on his face. He loved standing behind his machinists, peering over their shoulders while they were assembling one of his prototypes. In the late forties and early fifties, he worked almost exclusively in plastic, reinterpreting kitchen basics with a subtle, modernist flair. "Popeil Brothers made these beautiful plastic flour sifters," Tim Samuelson, a curator at the Chicago Historical Society and a leading authority on the Popeil legacy, says. "They would use contrasting colors, or a combination of opaque plastic with a translucent swirl plastic." Samuelson became fascinated with all things Popeil after he acquired an original Popeil Brothers doughnut maker, in red-and-white plastic, which he felt "had beautiful lines"; to this day, in the kitchen of his Hyde Park high-rise, he uses the Chop-O-Matic in the preparation of salad ingredients. "There was always a little twist to what he did," Samuelson goes on. "Take the Popeil automatic egg turner. It looks like a regular spatula, but if you squeeze the handle the blade turns just enough to flip a fried egg."

Walter Herbst, a designer whose firm worked with Popeil Brothers for many years, says that S.J.'s modus operandi was to "come up with a holistic theme. He'd arrive in the morning with it. It would be something like" — Herbst assumes S.J.'s gruff voice — "'We need a better way to shred cabbage.' It was a passion, an absolute goddam passion. One morning, he must have been

eating grapefruit, because he comes to work and calls me and says, 'We need a better way to cut grapefruit!'" The idea they came up with was a double-bladed paring knife, with the blades separated by a fraction of an inch so that both sides of the grapefruit membrane could be cut simultaneously. "There was a little grocery store a few blocks away," Herbst says. "So S.J. sends the chauffeur out for grapefruit. How many? Six. Well, over the period of a couple of weeks, six turns to twelve and twelve turns to twenty, until we were cutting thirty to forty grapefruits a day. I don't know if that little grocery store ever knew what happened."

S. J. Popeil's finest invention was undoubtedly the Veg-O-Matic, which came on the market in 1960 and was essentially a food processor, a Cuisinart without the motor. The heart of the gadget was a series of slender, sharp blades strung like guitar strings across two Teflon-coated metal rings, which were made in Woodstock, Illinois, from 364 Alcoa, a special grade of aluminum. When the rings were aligned one on top of the other so that the blades ran parallel, a potato or an onion pushed through would come out in perfect slices. If the top ring was rotated, the blades formed a crosshatch, and a potato or an onion pushed through would come out diced. The rings were housed in a handsome plastic assembly, with a plunger to push the vegetables through the blades. Technically, the Veg-O-Matic was a triumph: the method of creating blades strong enough to withstand the assault of vegetables received a US patent. But from a marketing perspective it posed a problem. S.J.'s products had hitherto been sold by pitchmen armed with a mound of vegetables meant to carry them through a day's worth of

demonstrations. But the Veg-O-Matic was too good. In a single minute, according to the calculations of Popeil Brothers, it could produce 120 egg wedges, 300 cucumber slices, 1,150 potato shoestrings, or 3,000 onion dices. It could go through what used to be a day's worth of vegetables in a matter of minutes. The pitchman could no longer afford to pitch to just a hundred people at a time; he had to pitch to a hundred thousand. The Veg-O-Matic needed to be sold on television, and one of the very first pitchmen to grasp this fact was Ron Popeil.

In the summer of 1964, just after the Veg-O-Matic was introduced, Mel Korey joined forces with Ron Popeil in a company called Ronco. They shot a commercial for the Veg-O-Matic for $500, a straightforward pitch shrunk to two minutes, and set out from Chicago for the surrounding towns of the Midwest. They cold-called local department stores and persuaded them to carry the Veg-O-Matic on guaranteed sale, which meant that whatever the stores didn't sell could be returned. Then they visited the local television station and bought a two- or three-week run of the cheapest airtime they could find, praying that it would be enough to drive traffic to the store. "We got Veg-O-Matics wholesale for $3.42," Korey says. "They retailed for $9.95, and we sold them to the stores for $7.46, which meant that we had four dollars to play with. If I spent a hundred dollars on television, I had to sell twenty-five Veg-O-Matics to break even." It was clear, in those days, that you could use television to sell kitchen products if you were Procter & Gamble. It wasn't so clear that this would work if you were Mel Korey and Ron Popeil, two pitchmen barely out of their teens selling a combination slicer-dicer that no one had ever heard of. They were taking a

wild gamble, and, to their amazement, it paid off. "They had a store in Butte, Montana — Hennessy's," Korey goes on, thinking back to those first improbable years. "Back then, people there were still wearing peacoats. The city was mostly bars. It had just a few three-story buildings. There were twenty-seven thousand people, and one TV station. I had the Veg-O-Matic, and I go to the store, and they said, 'We'll take a case. We don't have a lot of traffic here.' I go to the TV station and the place is a dump. The only salesperson was going blind and deaf. So I do a schedule. For five weeks, I spend three hundred and fifty dollars. I figure if I sell a hundred and seventy-four machines — six cases — I'm happy. I go back to Chicago, and I walk into the office one morning and the phone is ringing. They said, 'We sold out. You've got to fly us another six cases of Veg-O-Matics.' The next week, on Monday, the phone rings. It's Butte again: 'We've got a hundred and fifty oversold.' I fly him another six cases. Every few days after that, whenever the phone rang we'd look at each other and say, 'Butte, Montana.'" Even today, decades later, Korey can scarcely believe it. "How many homes in total in that town? Maybe several thousand? We ended up selling two thousand five hundred Veg-O-Matics in five weeks!"

Why did the Veg-O-Matic sell so well? Doubtless, Americans were eager for a better way of slicing vegetables. But it was more than that: the Veg-O-Matic represented a perfect marriage between the medium (television) and the message (the gadget). The Veg-O-Matic was, in the relevant sense, utterly transparent. You took the potato and you pushed it through the Teflon-coated rings and — voilà! — you had French fries. There were no but-

tons being pressed, no hidden and intimidating gears: you could show-and-tell the Veg-O-Matic in a two-minute spot and allay everyone's fears about a daunting new technology. More specifically, you could train the camera on the machine and compel viewers to pay total attention to the product you were selling. TV allowed you to do even more effectively what the best pitchmen strove to do in live demonstrations — make the product the star.

6.

This was a lesson Ron Popeil never forgot. In his infomercial for the Showtime Rotisserie, he opens not with himself but with a series of shots of meat and poultry, glistening almost obscenely as they rotate in the Showtime. A voice-over describes each shot: a "delicious six-pound chicken," a "succulent whole duckling," a "mouthwatering pork-loin roast..." Only then do we meet Ron, in a sports coat and jeans. He explains the problems of conventional barbecues, how messy and unpleasant they are. He bangs a hammer against the door of the Showtime, to demonstrate its strength. He deftly trusses a chicken, impales it on the patented two-pronged Showtime spit rod, and puts it into the oven. Then he repeats the process with a pair of chickens, salmon steaks garnished with lemon and dill, and a rib roast. All the time, the camera is on his hands, which are in constant motion, manipulating the Showtime apparatus gracefully, with his calming voice leading viewers through every step: "All I'm going to do here is slide it through like this. It goes in very easily. I'll match it up over here. What I'd like to do is take some herbs and spices here. All I'll do is slide it back. Raise up my glass

door here. I'll turn it to a little over an hour.... Just set it and forget it."

Why does this work so well? Because the Showtime — like the Veg-O-Matic before it — was designed to be the star. From the very beginning, Ron insisted that the entire door be a clear pane of glass, and that it slant back to let in the maximum amount of light, so that the chicken or the turkey or the baby-back ribs turning inside would be visible at all times. Alan Backus says that after the first version of the Showtime came out Ron began obsessing over the quality and evenness of the browning and became convinced that the rotation speed of the spit wasn't quite right. The original machine moved at four revolutions per minute. Ron set up a comparison test in his kitchen, cooking chicken after chicken at varying speeds until he determined that the optimal speed of rotation was actually six r.p.m. One can imagine a bright-eyed MBA clutching a sheaf of focus-group reports and arguing that Ronco was really selling convenience and healthful living, and that it was foolish to spend hundreds of thousands of dollars retooling production in search of a more even golden brown. But Ron understood that the perfect brown is important for the same reason that the slanted glass door is important: because in every respect the design of the product must support the transparency and effectiveness of its performance during a demonstration — the better it looks onstage, the easier it is for the pitchman to go into the turn and ask for the money.

If Ron had been the one to introduce the VCR, in other words, he would not simply have sold it in an infomercial. He would also have changed the VCR itself, so that it made sense in an infomercial. The clock, for example, wouldn't be

digital. (The haplessly blinking unset clock has, of course, become a symbol of frustration.) The tape wouldn't be inserted behind a hidden door — it would be out in plain view, just like the chicken in the rotisserie, so that if it was recording you could see the spools turn. The controls wouldn't be discreet buttons; they would be large, and they would make a reassuring click as they were pushed up and down, and each step of the taping process would be identified with a big, obvious numeral so that you could set it and forget it. And would it be a slender black, low-profile box? Of course not. Ours is a culture in which the term "black box" is synonymous with incomprehensibility. Ron's VCR would be in red-and-white plastic, both opaque and translucent swirl, or maybe 364 Alcoa aluminum, painted in some bold primary color, and it would sit on top of the television, not below it, so that when your neighbor or your friend came over he would spot it immediately and say, "Wow, you have one of those Ronco Tape-O-Matics!"

7.

Ron Popeil did not have a happy childhood. "I remember baking a potato. It must have been when I was four or five years old," he told me. We were in his kitchen, and had just sampled some baby-back ribs from the Showtime. It had taken some time to draw the memories out of him, because he is not one to dwell on the past. "I couldn't get that baked potato into my stomach fast enough, because I was so hungry." Ron is normally in constant motion, moving his hands, chopping food, bustling back and forth. But now he was still. His parents split up when he was very young. S.J. went off to Chicago. His mother disappeared.

He and his older brother, Jerry, were shipped off to a boarding school in upstate New York. "I remember seeing my mother on one occasion. I don't remember seeing my father, ever, until I moved to Chicago, at thirteen. When I was in the boarding school, the thing I remember was a Sunday when the parents visited the children, and my parents never came. Even knowing that they weren't going to show up, I walked out to the perimeter and looked out over the farmland, and there was this road." He made an undulating motion with his hand to suggest a road stretching off into the distance. "I remember standing on the road crying, looking for the movement of a car miles away, hoping that it was my mother and father. And they never came. That's all I remember about boarding school." Ron remained perfectly still. "I don't remember ever having a birthday party in my life. I remember that my grandparents took us out and we moved to Florida. My grandfather used to tie me down in bed — my hands, my wrists, and my feet. Why? Because I had a habit of turning over on my stomach and bumping my head either up and down or side to side. Why? How? I don't know the answers. But I was spread-eagle, on my back, and if I was able to twist over and do it my grandfather would wake up at night and come in and beat the hell out of me." Ron stopped, and then added, "I never liked him. I never knew my mother or her parents or any of that family. That's it. Not an awful lot to remember. Obviously, other things took place. But they have been erased."

When Ron came to Chicago, at thirteen, with his grandparents, he was put to work in the Popeil Brothers factory — but only on the weekends, when his father wasn't there. "Canned salmon and white bread for lunch, that was

the diet," he recalls. "Did I live with my father? Never. I lived with my grandparents." When he became a pitchman, his father gave him just one advantage: he extended his son credit. Mel Korey says that he once drove Ron home from college and dropped him off at his father's apartment. "He had a key to the apartment, and when he walked in his dad was in bed already. His dad said, 'Is that you, Ron?' And Ron said, 'Yeah.' And his dad never came out. And by the next morning Ron still hadn't seen him." Later, when Ron went into business for himself, he was persona non grata around Popeil Brothers. "Ronnie was never allowed in the place after that," one of S.J.'s former associates recalls. "He was never let in the front door. He was never allowed to be part of anything." My father, Ron says simply, "was all business. I didn't know him personally."

Here is a man who constructed his life in the image of his father — who went into the same business, who applied the same relentless attention to the workings of the kitchen, who got his start by selling his father's own products — and where was his father? "You know, they could have done wonders together," Korey says, shaking his head. "I remember one time we talked with K-tel about joining forces, and they said that we would be a war machine — that was their word. Well, Ron and his dad, they could have been a war machine." For all that, it is hard to find in Ron even a trace of bitterness. Once, I asked him, "Who are your inspirations?" The first name came easily: his good friend Steve Wynn. He was silent for a moment, and then he added, "My father." Despite everything, Ron clearly found in his father's example a tradition of irresistible value. And what did Ron do with that tradition? He transcended it. He created the Showtime, which

is indisputably a better gadget, dollar for dollar, than the Morris Metric Slicer, the Dutch Kitchen Shredder Grater, the Chop-O-Matic, and the Veg-O-Matic combined.

When I was in Ocean Township, visiting Arnold Morris, he took me to the local Jewish cemetery, Chesed Shel Ames, on a small hilltop just outside town. We drove slowly through the town's poorer sections in Arnold's white Mercedes. It was a rainy day. At the cemetery, a man stood out front in an undershirt, drinking a beer. We entered through a little rusty gate. "This is where it all starts," Arnold said, by which he meant that everyone — the whole spirited, squabbling clan — was buried here. We walked up and down the rows until we found, off in a corner, the Morris headstones. There was Nathan Morris, of the straw boater and the opportune heart attack, and next to him his wife, Betty. A few rows over was the family patriarch, Kidders Morris, and his wife, and a few rows from there Irving Rosenbloom, who made a fortune in plastic goods out on Long Island. Then all the Popeils, in tidy rows: Ron's grandfather Isadore, who was as mean as a snake, and his wife, Mary; S.J., who turned a cold shoulder to his own son; Ron's brother, Jerry, who died young. Ron was from them, but he was not of them. Arnold walked slowly among the tombstones, the rain dancing off his baseball cap, and then he said something that seemed perfectly right. "You know, I'll bet you you'll never find Ronnie here."

8.

One Saturday night, Ron Popeil arrived at the headquarters of the television shopping network QVC, a

vast gleaming complex nestled in the woods of suburban Philadelphia. Ron is a regular on QVC. He supplements his infomercials with occasional appearances on the network, and, for twenty-four hours beginning that midnight, QVC had granted him eight live slots, starting with a special "Ronco" hour between midnight and 1 a.m. Ron was traveling with his daughter Shannon, who had got her start in the business selling the Ronco Electric Food Dehydrator on the fair circuit, and the plan was that the two of them would alternate throughout the day. They were pitching a Digital Jog Dial version of the Showtime, in black, available for one day only, at a "special value" of $129.72.

In the studio, Ron had set up eighteen Digital Jog Dial Showtimes on five wood-paneled gurneys. From Los Angeles, he had sent, via Federal Express, dozens of Styrofoam containers with enough meat for each of the day's airings: eight fifteen-pound turkeys, seventy-two hamburgers, eight legs of lamb, eight ducks, thirty-odd chickens, two dozen or so Rock Cornish game hens, and on and on, supplementing them with garnishes, trout, and some sausage bought that morning at three Philadelphia-area supermarkets. QVC's target was thirty-seven thousand machines, meaning that it hoped to gross about $4.5 million during the twenty-four hours — a huge day, even by the network's standards. Ron seemed tense. He barked at the team of QVC producers and cameramen bustling around the room. He fussed over the hero plates — the ready-made dinners that he would use to showcase meat taken straight from the oven. "Guys, this is impossible," he said, peering at a tray of mashed potatoes and gravy. "The level of gravy must be higher." He was limping a

little. "You know, there's a lot of pressure on you," he said wearily. "'How did Ron do? Is he still the best?'"

With just a few minutes to go, Ron ducked into the greenroom next to the studio to put GLH in his hair: a few aerosol bursts, followed by vigorous brushing. "Where is God right now?" his co-host, Rick Domeier, yelled out, looking around theatrically for his guest star. "Is God backstage?" Ron then appeared, resplendent in a chef's coat, and the cameras began to roll. He sliced open a leg of lamb. He played with the dial of the new digital Showtime. He admired the crispy, succulent skin of the duck. He discussed the virtues of the new food-warming feature — where the machine would rotate at low heat for up to four hours after the meat was cooked in order to keep the juices moving — and, all the while, bantered so convincingly with viewers calling in on the testimonial line that it was as if he were back mesmerizing the secretaries in the Woolworth's at State and Washington.

In the greenroom, there were two computer monitors. The first displayed a line graph charting the number of calls that came in at any given second. The second was an electronic ledger showing the total sales up to that point. As Ron took flight, one by one, people left the studio to gather around the computers. Shannon Popeil came first. It was 12:40 a.m. In the studio, Ron was slicing onions with one of his father's Dial-O-Matics. She looked at the second monitor and gave a little gasp. Forty minutes in, and Ron had already passed $700,000. A QVC manager walked in. It was 12:48 a.m., and Ron was roaring on: $837,650. "It can't be!" he cried out. "That's unbelievable!" Two QVC producers came over. One of them pointed at the first monitor, which was graphing the call

volume. "Jump," he called out. "Jump!" There were only a few minutes left. Ron was extolling the virtues of the oven one final time, and, sure enough, the line began to take a sharp turn upward, as all over America viewers took out their wallets. The numbers on the second screen began to change in a blur of recalculation — rising in increments of $129.72 plus shipping and taxes. "You know, we're going to hit a million dollars, just on the first hour," one of the QVC guys said, and there was awe in his voice. It was one thing to talk about how Ron was the best there ever was, after all, but quite another to see proof of it, before your very eyes. At that moment, on the other side of the room, the door opened, and a man appeared, stooped and drawn but with a smile on his face. It was Ron Popeil, who invented a better rotisserie in his kitchen and went out and pitched it himself. There was a hush, and then the whole room stood up and cheered.*

October 30, 2000

The Ketchup Conundrum

MUSTARD NOW COMES IN DOZENS OF
VARIETIES. WHY HAS KETCHUP
STAYED THE SAME?

1.

Many years ago, one mustard dominated the supermarket shelves: French's. It came in a plastic bottle. People
used it on hot dogs and bologna. It was a yellow mustard, made from ground white mustard seed with tur-
meric and vinegar, which gave it a mild, slightly metallic
taste. If you looked hard in the grocery store, you might
find something in the specialty-foods section called Grey
Poupon, which was Dijon mustard, made from the more
pungent brown mustard seed. In the early seventies,
Grey Poupon was no more than a hundred-thousand-
dollar-a-year business. Few people knew what it was or
how it tasted, or had any particular desire for an alternative to French's or the runner-up, Gulden's. Then one
day the Heublein Company, which owned Grey Poupon,
discovered something remarkable: if you gave people a
mustard taste test, a significant number had only to try
Grey Poupon once to switch from yellow mustard. In

the food world that almost never happens; even among the most successful food brands, only about one in a hundred has that kind of conversion rate. Grey Poupon was magic.

So Heublein put Grey Poupon in a bigger glass jar, with an enameled label and enough of a whiff of Frenchness to make it seem as if it were still being made in Europe (it was made in Hartford, Connecticut, from Canadian mustard seed and white wine). The company ran tasteful print ads in upscale food magazines. They put the mustard in little foil packets and distributed them with airplane meals — which was a brand-new idea at the time. Then they hired the Manhattan ad agency Lowe Marschalk to do something, on a modest budget, for television. The agency came back with an idea: A Rolls-Royce is driving down a country road. There's a man in the backseat in a suit with a plate of beef on a silver tray. He nods to the chauffeur, who opens the glove compartment. Then comes what is known in the business as the *reveal*. The chauffeur hands back a jar of Grey Poupon. Another Rolls-Royce pulls up alongside. A man leans his head out the window. "Pardon me. Would you have any Grey Poupon?"

In the cities where the ads ran, sales of Grey Poupon leaped 40 to 50 percent, and whenever Heublein bought airtime in new cities sales jumped by 40 to 50 percent again. Grocery stores put Grey Poupon next to French's and Gulden's. By the end of the 1980s Grey Poupon was the most powerful brand in mustard. "The tagline in the commercial was that this was one of life's finer pleasures," Larry Elegant, who wrote the original Grey Poupon spot, says, "and that, along with the Rolls-Royce, seemed to impart to people's minds that this was something truly different and superior."

The rise of Grey Poupon proved that the American supermarket shopper was willing to pay more — in this case $3.99 instead of $1.49 for eight ounces — as long as what they were buying carried with it an air of sophistication and complex aromatics. Its success showed, furthermore, that the boundaries of taste and custom were not fixed: that just because mustard had always been yellow didn't mean that consumers would use only yellow mustard. It is because of Grey Poupon that the standard American supermarket today has an entire mustard section. And it is because of Grey Poupon that a man named Jim Wigon decided, four years ago, to enter the ketchup business. Isn't the ketchup business today exactly where mustard was thirty years ago? There is Heinz and, far behind, Hunt's and Del Monte and a handful of private-label brands. Jim Wigon wanted to create the Grey Poupon of ketchup.

Wigon is from Boston. He's a thickset man in his fifties, with a full salt-and-pepper beard. He runs his ketchup business — under the brand World's Best Ketchup — out of the catering business of his partner, Nick Schiarizzi, in Norwood, Massachusetts, just off Route 1, in a low-slung building behind an industrial-equipment-rental shop. He starts with red peppers, Spanish onions, garlic, and a high-end tomato paste. Basil is chopped by hand, because the buffalo chopper bruises the leaves. He uses maple syrup, not corn syrup, which gives him a quarter of the sugar of Heinz. He pours his ketchup into a clear glass ten-ounce jar, and sells it for three times the price of Heinz, and for the past few years he has crisscrossed the country, peddling World's Best in six flavors — regular, sweet,

dill, garlic, caramelized onion, and basil — to specialty grocery stores and supermarkets. If you were in Zabar's on Manhattan's Upper West Side a few months ago, you would have seen him at the front of the store, in a spot between the sushi and the gefilte fish. He was wearing a World's Best baseball cap, a white shirt, and a red-stained apron. In front of him, on a small table, was a silver tureen filled with miniature chicken and beef meatballs, a box of toothpicks, and a dozen or so open jars of his ketchup. "Try my ketchup!" Wigon said, over and over, to anyone who passed. "If you don't try it, you're doomed to eat Heinz the rest of your life."

In the same aisle at Zabar's that day two other demonstrations were going on, so that people were starting at one end with free chicken sausage, sampling a slice of prosciutto, and then pausing at the World's Best stand before heading for the cash register. They would look down at the array of open jars, and Wigon would impale a meatball on a toothpick, dip it in one of his ketchups, and hand it to them with a flourish. The ratio of tomato solids to liquid in World's Best is much higher than in Heinz, and the maple syrup gives it an unmistakable sweet kick. Invariably, people would close their eyes, just for a moment, and do a subtle double take. Some of them would look slightly perplexed and walk away, and others would nod and pick up a jar. "You know why you like it so much?" he would say, in his broad Boston accent, to the customers who seemed most impressed. "Because you've been eating bad ketchup all your life!" Jim Wigon had a simple vision: build a better ketchup — the way Grey Poupon built a better mustard — and the world will beat a path to your door. If only it were that easy.

2.

The story of World's Best Ketchup cannot properly be told without a man from White Plains, New York, named Howard Moskowitz. Moskowitz is sixty, short and round, with graying hair and huge gold-rimmed glasses. When he talks, he favors the Socratic monologue — a series of questions that he poses to himself, then answers, punctuated by "ahhh" and much vigorous nodding. He is a lineal descendant of the legendary eighteenth-century Hasidic rabbi known as the Seer of Lublin. He keeps a parrot. At Harvard, he wrote his doctoral dissertation on psychophysics, and all the rooms on the ground floor of his food-testing and market-research business are named after famous psychophysicists. ("Have you ever heard of the name Rose Marie Pangborn? Ahhh. She was a professor at Davis. Very famous. This is the Pangborn kitchen.") Moskowitz is a man of uncommon exuberance and persuasiveness: if he had been your freshman statistics professor, you would today be a statistician. "My favorite writer? Gibbon," he burst out, when we met not long ago. He had just been holding forth on the subject of sodium solutions. "Right now I'm working my way through the Hales history of the Byzantine Empire. Holy shit! Everything is easy until you get to the Byzantine Empire. It's impossible. One emperor is always killing the others, and everyone has five wives or three husbands. It's very Byzantine."

Moskowitz set up shop in the seventies, and one of his first clients was Pepsi. The artificial sweetener aspartame had just become available, and Pepsi wanted Moskowitz to figure out the perfect amount of sweetener for a can of Diet Pepsi. Pepsi knew that anything below 8 percent

sweetness was not sweet enough and anything over 12 percent was too sweet. So Moskowitz did the logical thing. He made up experimental batches of Diet Pepsi with every conceivable degree of sweetness — 8 percent, 8.25 percent, 8.5, and on and on up to 12 — gave them to hundreds of people, and looked for the concentration that people liked the most. But the data were a mess — there wasn't a pattern — and one day, sitting in a diner, Moskowitz realized why. They had been asking the wrong question. There was no such thing as the perfect Diet Pepsi. They should have been looking for the perfect Diet Pepsis.

It took a long time for the food world to catch up with Howard Moskowitz. He knocked on doors and tried to explain his idea about the plural nature of perfection, and no one answered. He spoke at food-industry conferences, and audiences shrugged. But he could think of nothing else. "It's like that Yiddish expression," he says. "Do you know it? To a worm in horseradish, the world is horseradish!" Then, in 1986, he got a call from the Campbell's Soup Company. They were in the spaghetti-sauce business, going up against Ragú with their Prego brand. Prego was a little thicker than Ragú, with diced tomatoes as opposed to Ragú's purée, and, Campbell's thought, had better pasta adherence. But, for all that, Prego was in a slump, and Campbell's was desperate for new ideas.

Standard practice in the food industry would have been to convene a focus group and ask spaghetti eaters what they wanted. But Moskowitz does not believe that consumers — even spaghetti lovers — know what they desire if what they desire does not yet exist. "The mind," as Moskowitz is fond of saying, "knows not what the tongue wants." Instead, working with the Campbell's kitchens,

he came up with forty-five varieties of spaghetti sauce. These were designed to differ in every conceivable way: spiciness, sweetness, tartness, saltiness, thickness, aroma, mouth feel, cost of ingredients, and so forth. He had a trained panel of food tasters analyze each of those varieties in depth. Then he took the prototypes on the road — to New York, Chicago, Los Angeles, and Jacksonville — and asked people in groups of twenty-five to eat between eight and ten small bowls of different spaghetti sauces over two hours and rate them on a scale of one to a hundred. When Moskowitz charted the results, he saw that everyone had a slightly different definition of what a perfect spaghetti sauce tasted like. If you sifted carefully through the data, though, you could find patterns, and Moskowitz learned that most people's preferences fell into one of three broad groups: plain, spicy, and extra-chunky, and of those three the last was the most important. Why? Because at the time there was no extra-chunky spaghetti sauce in the supermarket. Over the next decade, that new category proved to be worth hundreds of millions of dollars to Prego. "We all said, 'Wow!'" Monica Wood, who was then the head of market research for Campbell's, recalls. "Here there was this third segment — people who liked their spaghetti sauce with lots of stuff in it — and it was completely untapped. So in about 1989 or 1990 we launched Prego extra-chunky. It was extraordinarily successful."

It may be hard today, twenty years later — when every brand seems to come in multiple varieties — to appreciate how much of a breakthrough this was. In those years, people in the food industry carried around in their heads the notion of a platonic dish — the version of a dish that looked and tasted absolutely right. At Ragú and Prego,

they had been striving for the platonic spaghetti sauce, and the platonic spaghetti sauce was thin and blended because that's the way they thought it was done in Italy. Cooking, on the industrial level, was consumed with the search for human universals. Once you start looking for the sources of human variability, though, the old orthodoxy goes out the window. Howard Moskowitz stood up to the Platonists and said there are no universals.

Moskowitz still has a version of the computer model he used for Prego. It has all the coded results from the consumer taste tests and the expert tastings, split into the three categories (plain, spicy, and extra-chunky) and linked up with the actual ingredients list on a spreadsheet. "You know how they have a computer model for building an aircraft," Moskowitz said as he pulled up the program on his computer. "This is a model for building spaghetti sauce. Look, every variable is here." He pointed at column after column of ratings. "So here are the ingredients. I'm a brand manager for Prego. I want to optimize one of the segments. Let's start with Segment 1." In Moskowitz's program, the three spaghetti-sauce groups were labeled Segment 1, Segment 2, and Segment 3. He typed in a few commands, instructing the computer to give him the formulation that would score the highest with those people in Segment 1. The answer appeared almost immediately: a specific recipe that, according to Moskowitz's data, produced a score of 78 from the people in Segment 1. But that same formulation didn't do nearly as well with those in Segment 2 and Segment 3. They scored it 67 and 57, respectively. Moskowitz started again, this time asking the computer to optimize for Segment 2. This time the ratings came in at 82, but now Segment 1 had fallen 10

points, to 68. "See what happens?" he said. "If I make one group happier, I piss off another group. We did this for coffee with General Foods, and we found that if you create only one product, the best you can get across all the segments is a 60 — if you're lucky. That's if you were to treat everybody as one big happy family. But if I do the sensory segmentation, I can get 70, 71, 72. Is that big? Ahhh. It's a very big difference. In coffee, a 71 is something you'll die for."

When Jim Wigon set up shop that day in Zabar's, then, his operating assumption was that there ought to be some segment of the population that preferred a ketchup made with Stanislaus tomato paste and hand-chopped basil and maple syrup. That's the Moskowitz theory. But there is theory and there is practice. By the end of that long day, Wigon had sold ninety jars. But he'd also got two parking tickets and had to pay for a hotel room, so he wasn't going home with money in his pocket. For the year, Wigon estimates, he'll sell fifty thousand jars — which, in the universe of condiments, is no more than a blip. "I haven't drawn a paycheck in five years," Wigon said as he impaled another meatball on a toothpick. "My wife is killing me." And it isn't just World's Best that is struggling. In the gourmet-ketchup world, there is River Run and Uncle Dave's, from Vermont, and Muir Glen Organic and Mrs. Tomato Head Roasted Garlic Peppercorn Catsup, in California, and dozens of others — and every year Heinz's overwhelming share of the ketchup market just grows.

It is possible, of course, that ketchup is waiting for its own version of that Rolls-Royce commercial, or the discovery of the ketchup equivalent of extra-chunky — the

magic formula that will satisfy an unmet need. It is also possible, however, that the rules of Howard Moskowitz, which apply to Grey Poupon and Prego spaghetti sauce and to olive oil and salad dressing and virtually everything else in the supermarket, don't apply to ketchup.

3.

Tomato ketchup is a nineteenth-century creation — the union of the English tradition of fruit and vegetable sauces and the growing American infatuation with the tomato. But what we know today as ketchup emerged out of a debate that raged in the first years of the last century over benzoate, a preservative widely used in late-nineteenth-century condiments. Harvey Washington Wiley, the chief of the Bureau of Chemistry in the Department of Agriculture from 1883 to 1912, came to believe that benzoates were not safe, and the result was an argument that split the ketchup world in half. On one side was the ketchup establishment, which believed that it was impossible to make ketchup without benzoate and that benzoate was not harmful in the amounts used. On the other side was a renegade band of ketchup manufacturers, who believed that the preservative puzzle could be solved with the application of culinary science. The dominant nineteenth-century ketchups were thin and watery, in part because they were made from unripe tomatoes, which are low in the complex carbohydrates known as pectin, which add body to a sauce. But what if you made ketchup from ripe tomatoes, giving it the density it needed to resist degradation? Nineteenth-century ketchups had a strong tomato taste, with just a light vinegar touch. The renegades argued

that by greatly increasing the amount of vinegar, in effect protecting the tomatoes by pickling them, they were making a superior ketchup: safer, purer, and better tasting. They offered a money-back guarantee in the event of spoilage. They charged more for their product, convinced that the public would pay more for a better ketchup, and they were right. The benzoate ketchups disappeared. The leader of the renegade band was an entrepreneur out of Pittsburgh named Henry J. Heinz.

The world's leading expert on ketchup's early years is Andrew F. Smith, a substantial man, well over six feet, with a graying mustache and short wavy black hair. Smith is a scholar, trained as a political scientist, intent on bringing rigor to the world of food. When we met for lunch not long ago at the restaurant Savoy in SoHo (chosen because of the excellence of its hamburger and French fries, and because Savoy makes its own ketchup — a dark, peppery, and viscous variety served in a white porcelain saucer), Smith was in the throes of examining the origins of the croissant for the upcoming *Oxford Encyclopedia of Food and Drink in America*, of which he is the editor-in-chief. Was the croissant invented in 1683, by the Viennese, in celebration of their defeat of the invading Turks? Or in 1686, by the residents of Budapest, to celebrate *their* defeat of the Turks? Both explanations would explain its distinctive crescent shape — since it would make a certain cultural sense (particularly for the Viennese) to consecrate their battlefield triumphs in the form of pastry. But the only reference Smith could find to either story was in the *Larousse Gastronomique* of 1938. "It just doesn't check out," he said, shaking his head wearily.

Smith's specialty is the tomato, however, and over

the course of many scholarly articles and books — "The History of Home-Made Anglo-American Tomato Ketchup," for *Petits Propos Culinaires,* for example, and "The Great Tomato Pill War of the 1830s," for *The Connecticut Historical Society Bulletin* — Smith has argued that some critical portion of the history of culinary civilization could be told through this fruit. Cortez brought tomatoes to Europe from the New World, and they inexorably insinuated themselves into the world's cuisines. The Italians substituted the tomato for eggplant. In northern India, it went into curries and chutneys. "The biggest tomato producer in the world today?" Smith paused, for dramatic effect. "China. You don't think of tomato being a part of Chinese cuisine, and it wasn't ten years ago. But it is now." Smith dipped one of my French fries into the homemade sauce. "It has that raw taste," he said, with a look of intense concentration. "It's fresh ketchup. You can taste the tomato." Ketchup was, to his mind, the most nearly perfect of all the tomato's manifestations. It was inexpensive, which meant that it had a firm lock on the mass market, and it was a condiment, not an ingredient, which meant that it could be applied at the discretion of the food eater, not the food preparer. "There's a quote from Elizabeth Rozin I've always loved," he said. Rozin is the food theorist who wrote the essay "Ketchup and the Collective Unconscious," and Smith used her conclusion as the epigraph of his ketchup book: ketchup may well be "the only true culinary expression of the melting pot, and...its special and unprecedented ability to provide something for everyone makes it the Esperanto of cuisine." Here is where Henry Heinz and the benzoate battle were so important: in defeating the condiment Old Guard, he was

the one who changed the flavor of ketchup in a way that made it universal.

4.

There are five known fundamental tastes in the human palate: salty, sweet, sour, bitter, and umami. Umami is the proteiny, full-bodied taste of chicken soup, or cured meat, or fish stock, or aged cheese, or mother's milk, or soy sauce, or mushrooms, or seaweed, or cooked tomato. "Umami adds body," Gary Beauchamp, who heads the Monell Chemical Senses Center, in Philadelphia, says. "If you add it to a soup, it makes the soup seem like it's thicker — it gives it sensory heft. It turns a soup from salt water into a food." When Heinz moved to ripe tomatoes and increased the percentage of tomato solids, he made ketchup, first and foremost, a potent source of umami. Then he dramatically increased the concentration of vinegar, so that his ketchup had twice the acidity of most other ketchups; now ketchup was sour, another of the fundamental tastes. The post-benzoate ketchups also doubled the concentration of sugar — so now ketchup was also sweet — and all along ketchup had been salty and bitter. These are not trivial issues. Give a baby soup, and then soup with MSG (an amino-acid salt that is pure umami), and the baby will go back for the MSG soup every time, the same way a baby will always prefer water with sugar to water alone. Salt and sugar and umami are primal signals about the food we are eating — about how dense it is in calories, for example, or, in the case of umami, about the presence of proteins and amino acids. What Heinz had done was come up with a condiment that pushed all

five of these primal buttons. The taste of Heinz's ketchup began at the tip of the tongue, where our receptors for sweet and salty first appear, moved along the sides, where sour notes seem the strongest, then hit the back of the tongue, for umami and bitter, in one long crescendo. How many things in the supermarket run the sensory spectrum like this?

A number of years ago, the H. J. Heinz Company did an extensive market-research project in which researchers went into people's homes and watched the way they used ketchup. "I remember sitting in one of those households," Casey Keller, who was until recently the chief growth officer for Heinz, says. "There was a three-year-old and a six-year-old, and what happened was that the kids asked for ketchup and Mom brought it out. It was a forty-ounce bottle. And the three-year-old went to grab it himself, and Mom intercepted the bottle and said, 'No, you're not going to do that.' She physically took the bottle away and doled out a little dollop. You could see that the whole thing was a bummer." For Heinz, Keller says, that moment was an epiphany. A typical five-year-old consumes about 60 percent more ketchup than a typical forty-year-old, and the company realized that it needed to put ketchup in a bottle that a toddler could control. "If you are four — and I have a four-year-old — he doesn't get to choose what he eats for dinner, in most cases," Keller says. "But the one thing he can control is ketchup. It's the one part of the food experience that he can customize and personalize." As a result, Heinz came out with the so-called EZ Squirt bottle, made out of soft plastic with a conical nozzle. In homes where the EZ Squirt is used, ketchup consumption has grown by as much as 12 percent.

There is another lesson in that household scene, though. Small children tend to be neophobic: once they hit two or three, they shrink from new tastes. That makes sense, evolutionarily, because through much of human history that is the age at which children would have first begun to gather and forage for themselves, and those who strayed from what was known and trusted would never have survived. There the three-year-old was, confronted with something strange on his plate — tuna fish, perhaps, or Brussels sprouts — and he wanted to alter his food in some way that made the unfamiliar familiar. He wanted to subdue the contents of his plate. And so he turned to ketchup, because, alone among the condiments on the table, ketchup could deliver sweet and sour and salty and bitter and umami, all at once.

5.

A few months after Jim Wigon's visit to Zabar's, Edgar Chambers IV, who runs the sensory-analysis center at Kansas State University, conducted a joint assessment of World's Best and Heinz. He has seventeen trained tasters on his staff, and they work for academia and industry, answering the often difficult question of what a given substance tastes like. It is demanding work. Immediately after conducting the ketchup study, Chambers dispatched a team to Bangkok to do an analysis of fruit — bananas, mangoes, rose apples, and sweet tamarind. Others were detailed to soy and kimchi in South Korea, and Chambers's wife led a delegation to Italy to analyze ice cream.

The ketchup tasting took place over four hours, on two consecutive mornings. Six tasters sat around a large,

round table with a lazy Susan in the middle. In front of each panelist were two one-ounce cups, one filled with Heinz ketchup and one filled with World's Best. They would work along fourteen dimensions of flavor and texture, in accordance with the standard fifteen-point scale used by the food world. The flavor components would be divided two ways: elements picked up by the tongue and elements picked up by the nose. A very ripe peach, for example, tastes sweet but it also smells sweet — which is a very different aspect of sweetness. Vinegar has a sour taste but also a pungency, a vapor that rises up the back of the nose and fills the mouth when you breathe out. To aid in the rating process, the tasters surrounded themselves with little bowls of sweet and sour and salty solutions, and portions of Contadina tomato paste, Hunt's tomato sauce, and Campbell's tomato juice, all of which represent different concentrations of tomato-ness.

After breaking the ketchup down into its component parts, the testers assessed the critical dimension of "amplitude," the word sensory experts use to describe flavors that are well blended and balanced, that "bloom" in the mouth. "The difference between high and low amplitude is the difference between my son and a great pianist playing 'Ode to Joy' on the piano," Chambers says. "They are playing the same notes, but they blend better with the great pianist." Pepperidge Farm shortbread cookies are considered to have high amplitude. So are Hellmann's mayonnaise and Sara Lee poundcake. When something is high in amplitude, all its constituent elements converge into a single gestalt. You can't isolate the elements of an iconic, high-amplitude flavor like Coca-Cola or Pepsi. But you can with one of those private-label colas that you get

in the supermarket. "The thing about Coke and Pepsi is that they are absolutely gorgeous," Judy Heylmun, a vice president of Sensory Spectrum, Inc., in Chatham, New Jersey, says. "They have beautiful notes — all flavors are in balance. It's very hard to do that well. Usually, when you taste a store cola it's" — and here she made a series of *pik! pik! pik!* sounds — "all the notes are kind of spiky, and usually the citrus is the first thing to spike out. And then the cinnamon. Citrus and brown spice notes are top notes and very volatile, as opposed to vanilla, which is very dark and deep. A really cheap store brand will have a big, fat cinnamon note sitting on top of everything."

Some of the cheaper ketchups are the same way. Ketchup aficionados say that there's a disquieting unevenness to the tomato notes in Del Monte ketchup: tomatoes vary, in acidity and sweetness and the ratio of solids to liquid, according to the seed variety used, the time of year they are harvested, the soil in which they are grown, and the weather during the growing season. Unless all those variables are tightly controlled, one batch of ketchup can end up too watery and another can be too strong. Or try one of the numerous private-label brands that make up the bottom of the ketchup market and pay attention to the spice mix; you may well find yourself conscious of the clove note or overwhelmed by a hit of garlic. Generic colas and ketchups have what Moskowitz calls a hook — a sensory attribute that you can single out, and ultimately tire of.

The tasting began with a plastic spoon. Upon consideration, it was decided that the analysis would be helped if the ketchups were tasted on French fries, so a batch of fries was cooked up and distributed around the table.

Each tester, according to protocol, took the fries one by one, dipped them into the cup — all the way, right to the bottom — bit off the portion covered in ketchup, and then contemplated the evidence of their senses. For Heinz, the critical flavor components — vinegar, salt, tomato ID (overall tomato-ness), sweet, and bitter — were judged to be present in roughly equal concentrations, and those elements, in turn, were judged to be well blended. The World's Best, though, "had a completely different view, a different profile, from the Heinz," Chambers said. It had a much stronger hit of sweet aromatics — 4.0 to 2.5 — and outstripped Heinz on tomato ID by a resounding 9 to 5.5. But there was less salt, and no discernible vinegar. "The other comment from the panel was that these elements were really not blended at all," Chambers went on. "The World's Best product had really low amplitude." According to Joyce Buchholz, one of the panelists, when the group judged aftertaste, "it seemed like a certain flavor would hang over longer in the case of World's Best — that cooked-tomatoey flavor."

But what was Jim Wigon to do? To compete against Heinz, he had to try something dramatic, like substituting maple syrup for corn syrup, ramping up the tomato solids. That made for an unusual and daring flavor. World's Best Dill ketchup on fried catfish, for instance, is a marvelous thing. But it also meant that his ketchup wasn't as sensorily complete as Heinz, and he was paying a heavy price in amplitude. "Our conclusion was mainly this," Buchholz said. "We felt that World's Best seemed to be more like a sauce." She was trying to be helpful.

There is an exception, then, to the Moskowitz rule. Today there are thirty-six varieties of Ragú spaghetti

sauce, under six rubrics — Old World Style, Chunky Garden Style, Robusto, Light, Cheese Creations, and Rich & Meaty — which means that there is very nearly an optimal spaghetti sauce for every man, woman, and child in America. Measured against the monotony that confronted Howard Moskowitz twenty years ago, this is progress. Happiness, in one sense, is a function of how closely our world conforms to the infinite variety of human preference. But that makes it easy to forget that sometimes happiness can be found in having what we've always had and everyone else is having. "Back in the seventies, someone else — I think it was Ragú — tried to do an 'Italian'-style ketchup," Moskowitz said. "They failed miserably." It was a conundrum: what was true about a yellow condiment that went on hot dogs was not true about a tomato condiment that went on hamburgers, and what was true about tomato sauce when you added visible solids and put it in a jar was somehow not true about tomato sauce when you added vinegar and sugar and put it in a bottle. Moskowitz shrugged. "I guess ketchup is ketchup."

September 6, 2004

Blowing Up

HOW NASSIM TALEB TURNED THE
INEVITABILITY OF DISASTER INTO AN
INVESTMENT STRATEGY

1.

One day in 1996, a Wall Street trader named Nassim Nicholas Taleb went to see Victor Niederhoffer. Victor Niederhoffer was one of the most successful money managers in the country. He lived and worked out of a thirteen-acre compound in Fairfield County, Connecticut, and when Taleb drove up that day from his home in Larchmont he had to give his name at the gate, and then make his way down a long, curving driveway. Niederhoffer had a squash court and a tennis court and a swimming pool and a colossal, faux-alpine mansion in which virtually every square inch of space was covered with eighteenth- and nineteenth-century American folk art. In those days, he played tennis regularly with the billionaire financier George Soros. He had just written a best-selling book, *The Education of a Speculator,* dedicated to his father, Artie Niederhoffer, a police officer from Coney Island. He had a huge and eclectic library and a seemingly insatiable desire for knowledge.

When Niederhoffer went to Harvard as an undergraduate, he showed up for the very first squash practice and announced that he would someday be the best in that sport; and, sure enough, he soon beat the legendary Shariff Khan to win the US Open squash championship. That was the kind of man Niederhoffer was. He had heard of Taleb's growing reputation in the esoteric field of options trading and summoned him to Connecticut. Taleb was in awe.

"He didn't talk much, so I observed him," Taleb recalls. "I spent seven hours watching him trade. Everyone else in his office was in his twenties, and he was in his fifties, and he had the most energy of them all. Then, after the markets closed, he went out to hit a thousand backhands on the tennis court." Taleb is Greek-Orthodox Lebanese and his first language was French, and in his pronunciation the name Niederhoffer comes out as the slightly more exotic Nie*der*-hoffer. "Here was a guy living in a mansion with thousands of books, and that was my dream as a child," Taleb went on. "He was part chevalier, part scholar. My respect for him was intense." There was just one problem, however, and it is the key to understanding the strange path that Nassim Taleb has chosen, and the position he now holds as Wall Street's principal dissident. Despite his envy and admiration, he did not want to be Victor Niederhoffer — not then, not now, and not even for a moment in between. For when he looked around him, at the books and the tennis court and the folk art on the walls — when he contemplated the countless millions that Niederhoffer had made over the years — he could not escape the thought that it might all have been the result of sheer dumb luck.

Taleb knew how heretical that thought was. Wall Street was dedicated to the principle that when it came to playing

the markets there was such a thing as expertise, that skill and insight mattered in investing just as skill and insight mattered in surgery and golf and flying fighter jets. Those who had the foresight to grasp the role that software would play in the modern world bought Microsoft in 1985 and made a fortune. Those who understood the psychology of investment bubbles sold their tech stocks at the end of 1999 and escaped the Nasdaq crash. Warren Buffett was known as the "sage of Omaha" because it seemed incontrovertible that if you started with nothing and ended up with billions, then you had to be smarter than everyone else: Buffett was successful for a reason. Yet how could you know, Taleb wondered, whether that reason was responsible for someone's success, or simply a rationalization invented after the fact? George Soros seemed to be successful for a reason, too. He used to say that he followed something called *the theory of reflexivity.* But then, later, Soros wrote that in most situations his theory "is so feeble that it can be safely ignored." An old trading partner of Taleb's, a man named Jean-Manuel Rozan, once spent an entire afternoon arguing about the stock market with Soros. Soros was vehemently bearish, and he had an elaborate theory to explain why, which turned out to be entirely wrong. The stock market boomed. Two years later, Rozan ran into Soros at a tennis tournament. "Do you remember our conversation?" Rozan asked. "I recall it very well," Soros replied. "I changed my mind, and made an absolute fortune." He changed his mind! The truest thing about Soros seemed to be what his son Robert had once said:

My father will sit down and give you theories to explain why he does this or that. But I remember seeing it as a kid and thinking, Jesus Christ, at least half of this is bullshit.

I mean, you know the reason he changes his position on the market or whatever is because his back starts killing him. It has nothing to do with reason. He literally goes into a spasm, and it's this early warning sign.

For Taleb, then, the question why someone was a success in the financial marketplace was vexing. Taleb could do the arithmetic in his head. Suppose that there were ten thousand investment managers out there, which is not an outlandish number, and that every year half of them, entirely by chance, made money and half of them, entirely by chance, lost money. And suppose that every year, the losers were tossed out and the game was replayed with those who remained. At the end of five years, there would be three hundred and thirteen people who had made money in every one of those years, and after ten years there would be nine people who had made money every single year in a row, all out of pure luck. Niederhoffer, like Buffett and Soros, was a brilliant man. He had a PhD in economics from the University of Chicago. He had pioneered the idea that through close mathematical analysis of patterns in the market an investor could identify profitable anomalies. But who was to say that he wasn't one of those lucky nine? And who was to say that in the eleventh year Niederhoffer would be one of the unlucky ones, who suddenly lost it all, who suddenly, as they say on Wall Street, "blew up"?

Taleb remembered his childhood in Lebanon and watching his country turn, as he puts it, from "paradise to hell" in six months. His family once owned vast tracts of land in northern Lebanon. All of that was gone. He remembered his grandfather, the former deputy prime minister of Lebanon and the son of a deputy prime minister of Lebanon and a

man of great personal dignity, living out his days in a dowdy apartment in Athens. That was the problem with a world in which there was so much uncertainty about why things ended up the way they did: you never knew whether one day your luck would turn and it would all be washed away.

So here is what Taleb took from Niederhoffer. He saw that Niederhoffer was a serious athlete, and he decided that he would be, too. He would bicycle to work and exercise in the gym. Niederhoffer was a staunch empiricist who turned to Taleb that day in Connecticut and said to him sternly, "Everything that can be tested must be tested," and so when Taleb started his own hedge fund, a few years later, he called it Empirica. But that is where it stopped. Nassim Taleb decided that he could not pursue an investment strategy that had any chance of blowing up.

2.

Nassim Taleb is a tall, muscular man in his early forties, with a salt-and-pepper beard and a balding head. His eyebrows are heavy and his nose is long. His skin has the olive hue of the Levant. He is a man of moods, and when his world turns dark the eyebrows come together and the eyes narrow and it is as if he were giving off an electrical charge. It is said, by some of his friends, that he looks like Salman Rushdie, although at his office his staff have pinned to the bulletin board a photograph of a mullah they swear is Taleb's long-lost twin, while Taleb himself maintains, wholly implausibly, that he resembles Sean Connery. He lives in a four-bedroom Tudor with twenty-six Russian Orthodox icons, nineteen Roman heads, and four thousand books, and he rises at dawn to spend an hour

writing. He is the author of two books, the first a technical and highly regarded work on derivatives, and the second a treatise entitled *Fooled by Randomness,* which is to conventional Wall Street wisdom approximately what Martin Luther's Ninety-five Theses were to the Catholic Church. Some afternoons, he drives into the city and attends a philosophy lecture at City University. During the school year, in the evenings, he teaches a graduate course in finance at New York University, after which he can often be found at the bar at Odeon Café in Tribeca, holding forth, say, on the finer points of stochastic volatility or his veneration of the Greek poet C. P. Cavafy.

Taleb runs Empirica Capital out of an anonymous concrete office park somewhere in the woods outside Greenwich, Connecticut. His offices consist, principally, of a trading floor about the size of a Manhattan studio apartment. Taleb sits in one corner, in front of a laptop, surrounded by the rest of his team — Mark Spitznagel, the chief trader; another trader, named Danny Tosto; a programmer named Winn Martin; and a graduate student named Pallop Angsupun. Mark Spitznagel is perhaps thirty. Winn, Danny, and Pallop look as if they belong in high school. The room has an overstuffed bookshelf in one corner, and a television muted and tuned to CNBC. There are two ancient Greek heads, one next to Taleb's computer and the other, somewhat bafflingly, on the floor, next to the door, as if it were being set out for the trash. There is almost nothing on the walls, except for a slightly battered poster for an exhibition of Greek artifacts, the snapshot of the mullah, and a small pen-and-ink drawing of the patron saint of Empirica Capital, the philosopher Karl Popper.

On a recent spring morning, the staff of Empirica were

concerned with solving a thorny problem having to do with the square root of n, where n is a given number of random set of observations, and what relation n might have to a speculator's confidence in his estimations. Taleb was up at a whiteboard by the door, his marker squeaking furiously as he scribbled possible solutions. Spitznagel and Pallop looked on intently. Spitznagel is blond and from the Midwest and does yoga: in contrast to Taleb, he exudes a certain laconic levelheadedness. In a bar, Taleb would pick a fight. Spitznagel would break it up. Pallop is of Thai extraction and is doing a PhD in financial mathematics at Princeton. He has longish black hair and a slightly quizzical air. "Pallop is very lazy," Taleb will remark, to no one in particular, several times over the course of the day, although this is said with such affection that it suggests that *laziness*, in the Talebian nomenclature, is a synonym for genius. Pallop's computer was untouched and he often turned his chair around so that he faced completely away from his desk. He was reading a book by the cognitive psychologists Amos Tversky and Daniel Kahneman, whose arguments, he said a bit disappointedly, were "not really quantifiable." The three argued back and forth about the solution. It appeared that Taleb might be wrong, but before the matter could be resolved the markets opened. Taleb returned to his desk and began to bicker with Spitznagel about what exactly would be put on the company boom box. Spitznagel plays the piano and the French horn and has appointed himself the Empirica DJ. He wanted to play Mahler, and Taleb does not like Mahler. "Mahler is not good for volatility," Taleb complained. "Bach is good. *St. Matthew's Passion*!" Taleb gestured toward Spitznagel, who was wearing a gray woolen turtleneck. "Look at him. He wants to be like von Karajan,

like someone who wants to live in a castle. Technically superior to the rest of us. No chitchatting. Top skier. That's Mark!" As Spitznagel rolled his eyes, a man whom Taleb refers to, somewhat mysteriously, as Dr. Wu wandered in. Dr. Wu works for another hedge fund, down the hall, and is said to be brilliant. He is thin and squints through black-rimmed glasses. He was asked his opinion on the square root of n but declined to answer. "Dr. Wu comes here for intellectual kicks and to borrow books and to talk music with Mark," Taleb explained after their visitor had drifted away. He added darkly, "Dr. Wu is a Mahlerian."

Empirica follows a very particular investment strategy. It trades options, which is to say that it deals not in stocks and bonds but with bets on stocks and bonds. Imagine, for example, that General Motors stock is trading at $50, and imagine that you are a major investor on Wall Street. An options trader comes up to you with a proposition. What if, within the next three months, he decides to sell you a share of GM at $45? How much would you charge for agreeing to buy it at that price? You would look at the history of GM and see that in a three-month period it has rarely dropped 10 percent, and obviously the trader is only going to make you buy his GM at $45 if the stock drops below that point. So you say you'll make that promise, or sell that option, for a relatively small fee, say, a dime. You are betting on the high probability that GM stock will stay relatively calm over the next three months, and if you are right, you'll pocket the dime as pure profit. The trader, on the other hand, is betting on the unlikely event that GM stock will drop a lot, and if that happens, his profits are potentially huge. If the trader bought a million options from you at a dime each and GM drops to $35, he'll buy a million shares at $35 and turn

around and force you to buy them at $45, making himself suddenly very rich and you substantially poorer.

That particular transaction is called, in the argot of Wall Street, an *out-of-the-money option*. But an option can be configured in a vast number of ways. You could sell the trader a GM option at $30, or, if you wanted to bet against GM stock going up, you could sell a GM option at $60. You could sell or buy options on bonds, on the S&P index, on foreign currencies, or mortgages, or on the relationship among any number of financial instruments of your choice; you can bet on the market booming, or the market crashing, or the market staying the same. Options allow investors to gamble heavily and turn one dollar into ten. They also allow investors to hedge their risk. The reason your pension fund may not be wiped out in the next crash is that it has protected itself by buying options. What drives the options game is the notion that the risks represented by all of these bets can be quantified; that by looking at the past behavior of GM, you can figure out the exact chance of GM hitting $45 in the next three months, and whether at $1 that option is a good or a bad investment. The process is a lot like the way insurance companies analyze actuarial statistics in order to figure out how much to charge for a life-insurance premium, and to make those calculations every investment bank has, on staff, a team of PhDs, physicists from Russia, applied mathematicians from China, and computer scientists from India. On Wall Street, those PhDs are called *quants*.

Nassim Taleb and his team at Empirica are quants. But they reject the quant orthodoxy, because they don't believe that things like the stock market behave in the way that physical phenomena like mortality statistics do. Physical

events, whether death rates or poker games, are the predictable function of a limited and stable set of factors, and
tend to follow what statisticians call a *normal distribution,* a bell curve. But do the ups and downs of the market follow a bell curve? The economist Eugene Fama once
studied stock prices and pointed out that if they followed
a normal distribution, you'd expect a really big jump, what
he specified as a movement five standard deviations from
the mean, once every seven thousand years. In fact, jumps
of that magnitude happen in the stock market every three
or four years, because investors don't behave with any kind
of statistical orderliness. They change their mind. They do
stupid things. They copy one another. They panic. Fama
concluded that if you charted the ups and downs of the
stock market, the graph would have a "fat tail," meaning
that at the upper and lower ends of the distribution there
would be many more outlying events than statisticians used
to modeling the physical world would have imagined.

In the summer of 1997, Taleb predicted that hedge funds
like Long Term Capital Management were headed for trouble because they did not understand this notion of fat tails.
Just a year later, LTCM sold an extraordinary number of
options, because its computer models told it that the markets ought to be calming down. And what happened? The
Russian government defaulted on its bonds; the markets
went crazy; and in a matter of weeks LTCM was finished.
Spitznagel, Taleb's head trader, says that he recently heard
one of the former top executives of LTCM give a lecture
in which he defended the gamble that the fund had made.
"What he said was, 'Look, when I drive home every night
in the fall I see all these leaves scattered around the base of
the trees,'" Spitznagel recounts. "There is a statistical dis-

tribution that governs the way they fall, and I can be pretty accurate in figuring out what that distribution is going to be. But one day I came home and the leaves were in little piles. Does that falsify my theory that there are statistical rules governing how leaves fall? No. It was a man-made event." In other words, the Russians, by defaulting on their bonds, did something that they were not supposed to do, a once-in-a-lifetime, rule-breaking event. But this, to Taleb, is just the point: in the markets, unlike in the physical universe, the rules of the game can be changed. Central banks can decide to default on government-backed securities.

One of Taleb's earliest Wall Street mentors was a short-tempered Frenchman named Jean-Patrice, who dressed like a peacock and had an almost neurotic obsession with risk. Jean-Patrice would call Taleb from Regine's at three in the morning, or take a meeting in a Paris nightclub, sipping champagne and surrounded by scantily clad women, and once Jean-Patrice asked Taleb what would happen to his positions if a plane crashed into his building. Taleb was young then and brushed him aside. It seemed absurd. But nothing, Taleb soon realized, is absurd. Taleb likes to quote David Hume: "No amount of observations of white swans can allow the inference that all swans are white, but the observation of a single black swan is sufficient to refute that conclusion." Because LTCM had never seen a black swan in Russia, it thought no Russian black swans existed. Taleb, by contrast, has constructed a trading philosophy predicated entirely on the existence of black swans, on the possibility of some random, unexpected event sweeping the markets. He never sells options, then. He only buys them. He's never the one who can lose a great deal of money if GM stock suddenly plunges. Nor

does he ever bet on the market moving in one direction or another. That would require Taleb to assume that he understands the market, and he doesn't. He hasn't Warren Buffett's confidence. So he buys options on both sides, on the possibility of the market moving both up and down. And he doesn't bet on minor fluctuations in the market. Why bother? If everyone else is vastly underestimating the possibility of rare events, then an option on GM at, say, $40 is going to be undervalued. So Taleb buys out-of-the-money options by the truckload. He buys them for hundreds of different stocks, and if they expire before he gets to use them, he simply buys more. Taleb doesn't even invest in stocks, not for Empirica and not for his own personal account. Buying a stock, unlike buying an option, is a gamble that the future will represent an improved version of the past. And who knows whether that will be true? So all of Taleb's personal wealth, and the hundreds of millions that Empirica has in reserve, is in Treasury bills. Few on Wall Street have taken the practice of buying options to such extremes. But if anything completely out of the ordinary happens to the stock market, if some random event sends a jolt through all of Wall Street and pushes GM to, say, $20, Nassim Taleb will not end up in a dowdy apartment in Athens. He will be rich.

Not long ago, Taleb went to a dinner in a French restaurant just north of Wall Street. The people at the dinner were all quants: men with bulging pockets and open-collared shirts and the serene and slightly detached air of those who daydream in numbers. Taleb sat at the end of the table, drinking pastis and discussing French literature. There was a chess grand master at the table, with a shock of white hair, who had once been one of Anatoly Karpov's teachers,

and another man who over the course of his career had worked, in order, at Stanford University, Exxon, Los Alamos National Laboratory, Morgan Stanley, and a boutique French investment bank. They talked about mathematics and chess and fretted about one of their party who had not yet arrived and who had the reputation, as one of the quants worriedly said, of "not being able to find the bathroom." When the check came, it was given to a man who worked in risk management at a big Wall Street bank, and he stared at it for a long time, with a slight mixture of perplexity and amusement, as if he could not remember what it was like to deal with a mathematical problem of such banality. The men at the table were in a business that was formally about mathematics but was really about epistemology, because to sell or to buy an option requires each party to confront the question of what it is he truly knows. Taleb buys options because he is certain that, at root, he knows nothing, or, more precisely, that other people believe they know more than they do. But there were plenty of people around that table who sold options, who thought that if you were smart enough to set the price of the option properly, you could win so many of those $1 bets on General Motors that, even if the stock ever did dip below $45, you'd still come out far ahead. They believe that the world is a place where, at the end of the day, leaves fall more or less in a predictable pattern.

The distinction between these two sides is the divide that emerged between Taleb and Niederhoffer all those years ago in Connecticut. Niederhoffer's hero is the nineteenth-century scientist Francis Galton. Niederhoffer called his eldest daughter Galt, and there is a full-length portrait of Galton in his library. Galton was a statistician and a social scientist (and a geneticist and a meteorologist), and if he

was your hero, you believed that by marshaling empirical evidence, by aggregating data points, you could learn whatever it was you needed to know. Taleb's hero, on the other hand, is Karl Popper, who said that you could not know with any certainty that a proposition was true; you could only know that it was not true. Taleb makes much of what he learned from Niederhoffer, but Niederhoffer insists that his example was wasted on Taleb. "In one of his cases, Rumpole of the Bailey talked about being tried by the bishop who doesn't believe in God," Niederhoffer says. "Nassim is the empiricist who doesn't believe in empiricism." What is it that you claim to learn from experience, if you believe that experience cannot be trusted? Today, Niederhoffer makes a lot of his money selling options, and more often than not the person to whom he sells those options is Nassim Taleb. If one of them is up a dollar one day, in other words, that dollar is likely to have come from the other. The teacher and pupil have become predator and prey.

3.

Years ago, Nassim Taleb worked at the investment bank First Boston, and one of the things that puzzled him was what he saw as the mindless industry of the trading floor. A trader was supposed to come in every morning and buy and sell things, and on the basis of how much money he made buying and selling he was given a bonus. If he went too many weeks without showing a profit, his peers would start to look at him funny, and if he went too many months without showing a profit, he would be gone. The traders were for the most part well educated and wore Savile Row suits and Ferragamo ties. They dove into the

markets with a frantic urgency. They read the *Wall Street Journal* closely and gathered around the television to catch breaking news. "The Fed did this, the Prime Minister of Spain did that," Taleb recalls. "The Italian Finance Minister says there will be no competitive devaluation, this number is higher than expected, Abby Cohen just said this." It was a scene that Taleb did not understand.

"He was always so conceptual about what he was doing," says Howard Savery, who was Taleb's assistant at the French bank Indosuez in the 1980s. "He used to drive our floor trader (his name was Tim) crazy. Floor traders are used to precision: "Sell a hundred futures at eighty-seven." Nassim would pick up the phone and say, "Tim, sell some." And Tim would say, "How many?" And he would say, "Oh, a social amount." It was like saying, "I don't have a number in mind, I just know I want to sell." There would be these heated arguments in French, screaming arguments. Then everyone would go out to dinner and have fun. Nassim and his group had this attitude that we're not interested in knowing what the new trade number is. When everyone else was leaning over their desks, listening closely to the latest figures, Nassim would make a big scene of walking out of the room."

At Empirica, then, there are no *Wall Street Journals* to be found. There is very little active trading, because the options that the fund owns are selected by computer. Most of those options will be useful only if the market does something dramatic, and, of course, on most days the market doesn't. So the job of Taleb and his team is to wait and to think. They analyze the company's trading policies, back-test various strategies, and construct ever more sophisticated computer models of options pricing. Danny, in the

corner, occasionally types things into the computer. Pallop looks dreamily off into the distance. Spitznagel takes calls from traders, and toggles back and forth between screens on his computer. Taleb answers e-mails and calls one of the firm's brokers in Chicago, affecting, as he does, the kind of Brooklyn accent that people from Brooklyn would have if they were actually from northern Lebanon: "Howyou-doin?" It is closer to a classroom than to a trading floor.

"Pallop, did you introspect?" Taleb calls out as he wanders back in from lunch. Pallop is asked what his PhD is about. "Pretty much this," he says, waving a languid hand around the room.

"It looks like we will have to write it for him," Taleb chimes in, "because Pollop is very lazy."

What Empirica has done is to invert the traditional psychology of investing. You and I, if we invest conventionally in the market, have a fairly large chance of making a small amount of money in a given day from dividends or interest or the general upward trend of the market. We have almost no chance of making a large amount of money in one day, and there is a very small, but real, possibility that if the market collapses we could blow up. We accept that distribution of risks because, for fundamental reasons, it feels right. In the book that Pallop was reading by Kahneman and Tversky, for example, there is a description of a simple experiment, where a group of people were told to imagine that they had $300. They were then given a choice between (a) receiving another $100 or (b) tossing a coin, where if they won they got $200 and if they lost they got nothing. Most of us, it turns out, prefer (a) to (b). But then Kahneman and Tversky did a second experiment. They told people to imagine that they had $500 and then

asked them if they would rather (c) give up $100 or (d) toss a coin and pay $200 if they lost and nothing at all if they won. Most of us now prefer (d) to (c). What is interesting about those four choices is that, from a probabilistic standpoint, they are identical. Nonetheless, we have strong preferences among them. Why? Because we're more willing to gamble when it comes to losses, but are risk averse when it comes to our gains. That's why we like small daily winnings in the stock market, even if that requires that we risk losing everything in a crash.

At Empirica, by contrast, every day brings a small but real possibility that they'll make a huge amount of money in a day; no chance that they'll blow up; and a very large possibility that they'll lose a small amount of money. All those dollar, and fifty-cent, and nickel options that Empirica has accumulated, few of which will ever be used, soon begin to add up. By looking at a particular column on the computer screens showing Empirica's positions, anyone at the firm can tell you precisely how much money Empirica has lost or made so far that day. At 11:30 a.m., for instance, they had recovered just 28 percent of the money they had spent that day on options. By 12:30, they had recovered 40 percent, meaning that the day was not yet half over and Empirica was already in the red to the tune of several hundred thousand dollars. The day before that, it had made back 85 percent of its money; the day before that, 48 percent; the day before that, 65 percent; and the day before that also 65 percent; and, in fact, with a few notable exceptions — like the few days when the market reopened after September 11 — Empirica has done nothing but lose money since last April. "We cannot blow up, we can only bleed to death," Taleb says, and bleeding to

death, absorbing the pain of steady losses, is precisely what human beings are hardwired to avoid. "Say you've got a guy who is long on Russian bonds," Savery says. "He's making money every day. One day, lightning strikes and he loses five times what he made. Still, on three hundred and sixty-four out of three hundred and sixty-five days he was very happily making money. It's much harder to be the other guy, the guy losing money three hundred and sixty-four days out of three hundred and sixty-five, because you start questioning yourself. Am I ever going to make it back? Am I really right? What if it takes ten years? Will I even be sane ten years from now?" What the normal trader gets from his daily winnings is feedback, the pleasing illusion of progress. At Empirica, there is no feedback. "It's like you're playing the piano for ten years and you still can't play 'Chopsticks,'" Spitznagel say, "and the only thing you have to keep you going is the belief that one day you'll wake up and play like Rachmaninoff." Was it easy knowing that Niederhoffer — who represented everything they thought was wrong — was out there getting rich while they were bleeding away? Of course it wasn't. If you watched Taleb closely that day, you could see the little ways in which the steady drip of losses takes a toll. He glanced a bit too much at the Bloomberg. He leaned forward a bit too often to see the daily loss count. He succumbs to an array of superstitious tics. If the going is good, he parks in the same space every day; he turned against Mahler because he associates Mahler with the last year's long dry spell. "Nassim says all the time that he needs me there, and I believe him," Spitznagel says. He is there to remind Taleb that there is a point to waiting, to help Taleb resist the very human impulse to abandon

everything and stanch the pain of losing. "Mark is my cop," Taleb says. So is Pallop: he is there to remind Taleb that Empirica has the intellectual edge.

"The key is not having the ideas but having the recipe to deal with your ideas," Taleb says. "We don't need moralizing. We need a set of tricks." His trick is a protocol that stipulates precisely what has to be done in every situation. "We built the protocol, and the reason we did was to tell the guys, Don't listen to me, listen to the protocol. Now, I have the right to change the protocol, but there is a protocol to changing the protocol. We have to be hard on ourselves to do what we do. The bias we see in Niederhoffer we see in ourselves." At the quant dinner, Taleb devoured his roll, and as the busboy came around with more rolls Taleb shouted out, "No, no!" and blocked his plate. It was a never-ending struggle, this battle between head and heart. When the waiter came around with wine, he hastily covered the glass with his hand. When the time came to order, he asked for steak frites — "without the frites, please!" — and then immediately tried to hedge his choice by negotiating with the person next to him for a fraction of his frites.

The psychologist Walter Mischel has done a series of experiments where he puts a young child in a room and places two cookies in front of him, one small and one large. The child is told that if he wants the small cookie he need only ring a bell and the experimenter will come back into the room and give it to him. If he wants the better treat, though, he has to wait until the experimenter returns on his own, which might be anytime in the next twenty minutes. Mischel has videotapes of six-year-olds sitting in the room by themselves, staring at the cookies, trying to persuade themselves to wait. One girl starts to

sing to herself. She whispers what seems to be the instructions — that she can have the big cookie if she can only wait. She closes her eyes. Then she turns her back on the cookies. Another little boy swings his legs violently back and forth, and then picks up the bell and examines it, trying to do anything but think about the cookie he could get by ringing it. The tapes document the beginnings of discipline and self-control — the techniques we learn to keep our impulses in check — and to watch all the children desperately distracting themselves is to experience the shock of recognition: that's Nassim Taleb!

There is something else as well that helps to explain Taleb's resolve — more than the tics and the systems and the self-denying ordinances. It happened a year or so before he went to see Niederhoffer. Taleb had been working as a trader at the Chicago Mercantile Exchange, and he'd developed a persistently hoarse throat. At first, he thought nothing of it: a hoarse throat was an occupational hazard of spending every day in the pit. Finally, when he moved back to New York, he went to see a doctor, in one of those Upper East Side prewar buildings with a glamorous facade. Taleb sat in the office, staring out at the plain brick of the courtyard, reading the medical diplomas on the wall over and over, waiting and waiting for the verdict. The doctor returned and spoke in a low, grave voice: "I got the pathology report. It's not as bad as it sounds." But, of course, it was: he had throat cancer. Taleb's mind shut down. He left the office. It was raining outside. He walked and walked and ended up at a medical library. There he read frantically about his disease, the rainwater forming a puddle under his feet. It made no sense. Throat cancer was the disease of someone who has spent a lifetime smoking heavily. But Taleb was young,

and he barely smoked at all. His risk of getting throat cancer was something like one in a hundred thousand, almost unimaginably small. He was a black swan! The cancer is now beaten, but the memory of it is also Taleb's secret, because once you have been a black swan — not just seen one but lived and faced death as one — it becomes easier to imagine another on the horizon.

As the day came to an end, Taleb and his team turned their attention once again to the problem of the square root of n. Taleb was back at the whiteboard. Spitznagel was looking on. Pallop was idly peeling a banana. Outside, the sun was beginning to settle behind the trees. "You do a conversion to $p1$ and $p2$," Taleb said. His marker was once again squeaking across the whiteboard. "We say we have a Gaussian distribution, and you have the market switching from a low-volume regime to a high-volume. $P21$. $P22$. You have your igon value." He frowned and stared at his handiwork. The markets were now closed. Empirica had lost money, which meant that somewhere off in the woods of Connecticut Niederhoffer had no doubt made money. That hurt, but if you steeled yourself and thought about the problem at hand, and kept in mind that someday the market would do something utterly unexpected because in the world we live in something utterly unexpected always happens, then the hurt was not so bad. Taleb eyed his equations on the whiteboard and arched an eyebrow. It was a very difficult problem. "Where is Dr. Wu? Should we call in Dr. Wu?"

4.

A year after Nassim Taleb came to visit him, Victor Niederhoffer blew up. He sold a very large number of options

on the S&P index, taking millions of dollars from other traders in exchange for promising to buy a basket of stocks from them at current prices, if the market ever fell. It was an unhedged bet, or what was called on Wall Street a *naked put*, meaning that he bet everyone on one outcome: he bet in favor of the large probability of making a small amount of money, and against the small probability of losing a large amount of money — and he lost. On October 27, 1997, the market plummeted 8 percent, and all of the many, many people who had bought those options from Niederhoffer came calling all at once, demanding that he buy back their stocks at pre-crash prices. He ran through $130,000,000 — his cash reserves, his savings, his other stocks — and when his broker came and asked for still more, he didn't have it. In a day, one of the most successful hedge funds in America was wiped out. Niederhoffer had to shut down his firm. He had to mortgage his house. He had to borrow money from his children. He had to call Sotheby's and sell his prized silver collection — the massive nineteenth-century Brazilian "sculptural group of victory" made for the Visconde De Figueirdeo, the massive silver bowl designed in 1887 by Tiffany & Co. for the James Gordon Bennett Cup yacht race, and on and on. He stayed away from the auction. He couldn't bear to watch.

"It was one of the worst things that has ever happened to me in my life, right up there with the death of those closest to me," Niederhoffer said recently. It was a Saturday in March, and he was in the library of his enormous house. Two weary-looking dogs wandered in and out. He is a tall man, an athlete, thick through the upper body and trunk, with a long, imposing face and baleful, hooded eyes. He was shoeless. One collar on his shirt was twisted

inward, and he looked away as he talked. "I let down my friends. I lost my business. I was a major money manager. Now I pretty much have had to start from ground zero." He paused. "Five years have passed. The beaver builds a dam. The river washes it away, so he tries to build a better foundation, and I think I have. But I'm always mindful of the possibility of more failures." In the distance, there was a knock on the door. It was a man named Milton Bond, an artist who had come to present Niederhoffer with a painting he had done of Moby Dick ramming the *Pequod*. It was in the folk-art style that Niederhoffer likes so much, and he went to meet Bond in the foyer, kneeling down in front of the painting as Bond unwrapped it. Niederhoffer has other paintings of the *Pequod* in his house, and paintings of the *Essex,* the ship on which Melville's story was based. In his office, on a prominent wall, is a painting of the *Titanic.* They were, he said, his way of staying humble. "One of the reasons I've paid lots of attention to the *Essex* is that it turns out that the captain of the *Essex,* as soon as he got back to Nantucket, was given another job," Niederhoffer said. "They thought he did a good job in getting back after the ship was rammed. The captain was asked, 'How could people give you another ship?' And he said, 'I guess on the theory that lightning doesn't strike twice.' It was a fairly random thing. But then he was given the other ship, and that one foundered, too. Got stuck in the ice. At that time, he was a lost man. He wouldn't even let them save him. They had to forcibly remove him from the ship. He spent the rest of his life as a janitor in Nantucket. He became what on Wall Street they call a ghost." Niederhoffer was back in his study now, his lanky body stretched out, his feet up on the table, his eyes a little rheumy. "You

see? I can't afford to fail a second time. Then I'll be a total washout. That's the significance of the *Pequod*."

A month or so before Niederhoffer blew up, Taleb had dinner with him at a restaurant in Westport, and Niederhoffer told him that he had been selling naked puts. You can imagine the two of them across the table from each other, Niederhoffer explaining that his bet was an acceptable risk, that the odds of the market going down so heavily that he would be wiped out were minuscule, and Taleb listening and shaking his head, and thinking about black swans. "I was depressed when I left him," Taleb said. "Here is a guy who goes out and hits a thousand backhands. He plays chess like his life depends on it. Here is a guy who, whatever he wants to do when he wakes up in the morning, he ends up doing better than anyone else. Whatever he wakes up in the morning and decides to do, he did better than anyone else. I was talking to my hero..." This was the reason Taleb didn't want to be Niederhoffer when Niederhoffer was at his height — the reason he didn't want the silver and the house and the tennis matches with George Soros. He could see all too clearly where it all might end up. In his mind's eye, he could envision Niederhoffer borrowing money from his children, and selling off his silver, and talking in a hollow voice about letting down his friends, and Taleb did not know if he had the strength to live with that possibility. Unlike Niederhoffer, Taleb never thought he was invincible. You couldn't if you had watched your homeland blow up, and had been the one person in a hundred thousand who gets throat cancer, and so for Taleb there was never any alternative to the painful process of insuring himself against catastrophe.

This kind of caution does not seem heroic, of course. It seems like the joyless prudence of the accountant and the Sunday school teacher. The truth is that we are drawn to the Niederhoffers of this world because we are all, at heart, like Niederhoffer: we associate the willingness to risk great failure — and the ability to climb back from catastrophe — with courage. But in this we are wrong. That is the lesson of Taleb and Niederhoffer, and also the lesson of our volatile times. There is more courage and heroism in defying the human impulse, in taking the purposeful and painful steps to prepare for the unimaginable.

In the fall of 2001, Niederhoffer sold a large number of options, betting that the markets would be quiet, and they were, until out of nowhere two planes crashed into the World Trade Center. "I was exposed. It was nip and tuck." Niederhoffer shook his head, because there was no way to have anticipated September 11. "That was a totally unexpected event."*

April 22 and 29, 2002

---

* Taleb has since become famous. His second book — published a few years after this profile — was called *The Black Swan,* and it became an enormous bestseller. And the financial crisis of 2008–2009 made a staggering amount of money for his fund. I ran into him at a conference in the spring of 2009, in the midst of the financial turmoil. "We have billions under management now," he said, "and we still know nothing." Typical Nassim. When I was reporting this piece, we would have lunches that would last for hours. The delight I took in his company was offset only by the dread I felt at the prospect of transcribing all those hours of tapes. Neiderhoffer, by the way, has lost and made and lost a number of other fortunes in the intervening years.

True Colors

HAIR DYE AND THE HIDDEN HISTORY
OF POSTWAR AMERICA

1.

During the Depression — long before she became one of
the most famous copywriters of her day — Shirley Polykoff
met a man named George Halperin. He was the son of an
Orthodox rabbi from Reading, Pennsylvania, and soon
after they began courting he took her home for Passover
to meet his family. They ate roast chicken, tzimmes, and
sponge cake, and Polykoff hit it off with Rabbi Halperin,
who was warm and funny. George's mother was another
story. She was Old World Orthodox, with severe, tightly
pulled back hair; no one was good enough for her son.

"How'd I do, George?" Shirley asked as soon as
they got in the car for the drive home. "Did your mother
like me?"

He was evasive. "My sister Mildred thought you were
great."

"That's nice, George," she said. "But what did your
mother say?"

There was a pause. "She says you paint your hair." Another pause. "Well, do you?"

Shirley Polykoff was humiliated. In her mind she could hear her future mother-in-law: *Fahrbt zi der huer? Oder fahrbt zi nisht?* Does she color her hair? Or doesn't she?

The answer, of course, was that she did. Shirley Polykoff always dyed her hair, even in the days when the only women who went blond were chorus girls and hookers. At home in Brooklyn, starting when she was fifteen, she would go to Mr. Nicholas's beauty salon, one flight up, and he would "lighten the back" until all traces of her natural brown were gone. She thought she ought to be a blonde — or, to be more precise, she thought that the decision about whether she could be a blonde was rightfully hers, and not God's. Shirley dressed in deep oranges and deep reds and creamy beiges and royal hues. She wore purple suede and aqua silk, and was the kind of person who might take a couture jacket home and embroider some new detail on it. Once, in the days when she had her own advertising agency, she was on her way to Memphis to make a presentation to Maybelline and her taxi broke down in the middle of the expressway. She jumped out and flagged down a Pepsi-Cola truck, and the truck driver told her he had picked her up because he'd never seen anyone quite like her before. "Shirley would wear three outfits, all at once, and each one of them would look great," Dick Huebner, who was her creative director, says. She was flamboyant and brilliant and vain in an irresistible way, and it was her conviction that none of those qualities went with brown hair. The kind of person she spent her life turning herself into did not go with brown hair. Shirley's parents

were Hyman Polykoff, small-time necktie merchant, and Rose Polykoff, housewife and mother, of East New York and Flatbush, by way of the Ukraine. Shirley ended up on Park Avenue at Eighty-second. "If you asked my mother 'Are you proud to be Jewish?' she would have said yes," her daughter, Alix Nelson Frick, says. "She wasn't trying to pass. But she believed in the dream, and the dream was that you could acquire all the accouterments of the established affluent class, which included a certain breeding and a certain kind of look. Her idea was that you should be whatever you want to be, including being a blonde."

In 1956, when Shirley Polykoff was a junior copywriter at Foote, Cone & Belding, she was given the Clairol account. The product the company was launching was Miss Clairol, the first hair-color bath that made it possible to lighten, tint, condition, and shampoo at home, in a single step — to take, say, Topaz (for a champagne blond) or Moon Gold (for a medium ash), apply it in a peroxide solution directly to the hair, and get results in twenty minutes. When the Clairol sales team demonstrated their new product at the International Beauty Show, in the old Statler Hotel, across from Madison Square Garden, thousands of assembled beauticians jammed the hall and watched, openmouthed, demonstration after demonstration. "They were astonished," recalls Bruce Gelb, who ran Clairol for years, along with his father, Lawrence, and his brother Richard. "This was to the world of hair color what computers were to the world of adding machines. The sales guys had to bring buckets of water and do the rinsing off in front of everyone, because the hairdressers in the crowd were convinced we were doing something to the models behind the scenes."

Miss Clairol gave American women the ability, for the first time, to color their hair quickly and easily at home. But there was still the stigma — the prospect of the disapproving mother-in-law. Shirley Polykoff knew immediately what she wanted to say, because if she believed that a woman had a right to be a blonde, she also believed that a woman ought to be able to exercise that right with discretion. "Does she or doesn't she?" she wrote, translating from the Yiddish to the English. "Only her hairdresser knows for sure." Clairol bought thirteen ad pages in *Life* in the fall of 1956, and Miss Clairol took off like a bird. That was the beginning. For Nice 'n Easy, Clairol's breakthrough shampoo-in hair color, she wrote, "The closer he gets, the better you look." For Lady Clairol, the cream-and-bleach combination that brought silver and platinum shades to Middle America, she wrote, "Is it true blondes have more fun?" and then, even more memorably, "If I've only one life, let me live it as a blonde!" (In the summer of 1962, just before *The Feminine Mystique* was published, Betty Friedan was, in the words of her biographer, so "bewitched" by that phrase that she bleached her hair.) Shirley Polykoff wrote the lines; Clairol perfected the product. And from the fifties to the seventies, when Polykoff gave up the account, the number of American women coloring their hair rose from 7 percent to more than 40 percent.

Today, when women go from brown to blond to red to black and back again without blinking, we think of hair-color products the way we think of lipstick. On drugstore shelves there are bottles and bottles of hair-color products with names like Hydrience and Excellence and Preference and Natural Instincts and Loving Care and Nice 'n

Easy, and so on, each in dozens of different shades. Feria, the new, youth-oriented brand from L'Oréal, comes in Chocolate Cherry and Champagne Cocktail — colors that don't ask "Does she or doesn't she?" but blithely assume "Yes, she does." Hair dye is now a billion-dollar-a-year commodity.

Yet there was a time, not so long ago — between, roughly speaking, the start of Eisenhower's administration and the end of Carter's — when hair color meant something. Lines like "Does she or doesn't she?" or the famous 1973 slogan for L'Oréal's Preference — "Because I'm worth it" — were as instantly memorable as "Winston tastes good like a cigarette should" or "Things go better with Coke." They lingered long after advertising usually does and entered the language; they somehow managed to take on meanings well outside their stated intention. Between the fifties and the seventies, women entered the workplace, fought for social emancipation, got the Pill, and changed what they did with their hair. To examine the hair-color campaigns of the period is to see, quite unexpectedly, all these things as bound up together, the profound with the seemingly trivial. In writing the history of women in the postwar era, did we forget something important? Did we leave out hair?

2.

When the "Does she or doesn't she?" campaign first ran, in 1956, most advertisements that were aimed at women tended to be high glamour — "cherries in the snow, fire and ice," as Bruce Gelb puts it. But Shirley Polykoff insisted

that the models for the Miss Clairol campaign be more like the girl next door — "Shirtwaist types instead of glamour gowns," she wrote in her original memo to Clairol. "Cashmere-sweater-over-the-shoulder types. Like larger-than-life portraits of the proverbial girl on the block who's a little prettier than your wife and lives in a house slightly nicer than yours." The model had to be a Doris Day type — not a Jayne Mansfield — because the idea was to make hair color as respectable and mainstream as possible. One of the earliest "Does she or doesn't she?" television commercials featured a housewife in the kitchen preparing hors d'oeuvres for a party. She is slender and pretty and wearing a black cocktail dress and an apron. Her husband comes in, kisses her on the lips, approvingly pats her very blond hair, then holds the kitchen door for her as she takes the tray of hors d'oeuvres out for her guests. It is an exquisitely choreographed domestic tableau, down to the little dip the housewife performs as she hits the kitchen light switch with her elbow on her way out the door. In one of the early print ads — which were shot by Richard Avedon and then by Irving Penn — a woman with strawberry-blond hair is lying on the grass, holding a dandelion between her fingers, and lying next to her is a girl of about eight or nine. What's striking is that the little girl's hair is the same shade of blond as her mother's. The "Does she or doesn't she?" print ads always included a child with the mother to undercut the sexual undertones of the slogan — to make it clear that mothers were using Miss Clairol, and not just "fast" women — and, most of all, to provide a precise color match. Who could ever guess, given the comparison, that Mom's shade came out of a bottle?

The Polykoff campaigns were a sensation. Letters poured in to Clairol. "Thank you for changing my life," read one, which was circulated around the company and used as the theme for a national sales meeting. "My boyfriend, Harold, and I were keeping company for five years but he never wanted to set a date. This made me very nervous. I am twenty-eight and my mother kept saying soon it would be too late for me." Then, the letter writer said, she saw a Clairol ad in the subway. She dyed her hair blond, and "that is how I am in Bermuda now on my honeymoon with Harold." Polykoff was sent a copy with a memo: "It's almost too good to be true!" With her sentimental idyll of blond mother and child, Shirley Polykoff had created something iconic.

"My mother wanted to be that woman in the picture," Polykoff's daughter, Frick, says. "She was wedded to the notion of that suburban, tastefully dressed, well-coddled matron who was an adornment to her husband, a loving mother, a long-suffering wife, a person who never overshadowed him. She wanted the blond child. In fact, I was blond as a kid, but when I was about thirteen my hair got darker and my mother started bleaching it." Of course — and this is the contradiction central to those early Clairol campaigns — Shirley Polykoff wasn't really that kind of woman at all. She always had a career. She never moved to the suburbs. "She maintained that women were supposed to be feminine, and not too dogmatic and not overshadow their husband, but she greatly overshadowed my father, who was a very pure, unaggressive, intellectual type," Frick says. "She was very flamboyant, very emotional, very dominating."

One of the stories Polykoff told about herself repeatedly — and that even appeared after her death in her *New York Times* obituary — was that she felt that a woman never ought to make more than her husband, and that only after George's death, in the early sixties, would she let Foote, Cone & Belding raise her salary to its deserved level. "That's part of the legend, but it isn't the truth," Frick says. "The ideal was always as vividly real to her as whatever actual parallel reality she might be living. She never wavered in her belief in that dream, even if you would point out to her some of the fallacies of that dream, or the weaknesses, or the internal contradictions, or the fact that she herself didn't really live her life that way." For Shirley Polykoff, the color of her hair was a kind of useful fiction, a way of bridging the contradiction between the kind of woman she was and the kind of woman she felt she ought to be. It was a way of having it all. She wanted to look and feel like Doris Day without having to be Doris Day. In twenty-seven years of marriage, during which she bore two children, she spent exactly two weeks as a housewife, every day of which was a domestic and culinary disaster. "Listen, sweetie," an exasperated George finally told her. "You make a lousy little woman in the kitchen." She went back to work the following Monday.

This notion of the useful fiction — of looking the part without being the part — had a particular resonance for the America of Shirley Polykoff's generation. As a teenager, Shirley Polykoff tried to get a position as a clerk at an insurance agency and failed. Then she tried again, at another firm, applying as Shirley Miller. This time, she got the job. Her husband, George, also knew the value of

appearances. The week Polykoff first met him, she was dazzled by his worldly sophistication, his knowledge of out-of-the-way places in Europe, his exquisite taste in fine food and wine. The second week, she learned that his expertise was all show, derived from reading the *Times*. The truth was that George had started his career loading boxes in the basement of Macy's by day and studying law at night. He was a faker, just as, in a certain sense, she was, because to be Jewish — or Irish or Italian or African-American or, for that matter, a woman of the fifties caught up in the first faint stirrings of feminism — was to be compelled to fake it in a thousand small ways, to pass as one thing when, deep inside, you were something else. "That's the kind of pressure that comes from the immigrants' arriving and thinking that they don't look right, that they are kind of funny-looking and maybe shorter than everyone else, and their clothes aren't expensive," Frick says. "That's why many of them began to sew, so they could imitate the patterns of the day. You were making yourself over. You were turning yourself into an American." Frick, who is also in advertising (she's the chairman of Spier NY), is a forcefully intelligent woman, who speaks of her mother with honesty and affection. "There were all those phrases that came to fruition at that time — you know, 'clothes make the man' and 'first impressions count.'" So the question "Does she or doesn't she?" wasn't just about how no one could ever really know what you were doing. It was about how no one could ever really know who you were. It really meant not "Does she?" but "Is she?" It really meant "Is she a contented homemaker or a feminist, a Jew or a Gentile — or isn't she?"

3.

In 1973, Ilon Specht was working as a copywriter at the McCann-Erickson advertising agency, in New York. She was a twenty-three-year-old college dropout from California. She was rebellious, unconventional, and independent, and she had come East to work on Madison Avenue, because that's where people like that went to work back then. "It was a different business in those days," Susan Schermer, a longtime friend of Specht's, says. "It was the seventies. People were wearing feathers to work." At her previous agency, while she was still in her teens, Specht had written a famous television commercial for the Peace Corps. (Single shot. No cuts. A young couple lying on the beach. "It's a big, wide wonderful world" is playing on a radio. Voice-over recites a series of horrible facts about less fortunate parts of the world: in the Middle East half the children die before their sixth birthday, and so forth. A news broadcast is announced as the song ends, and the woman on the beach changes the station.)

"Ilon? Omigod! She was one of the craziest people I ever worked with," Ira Madris, another colleague from those years, recalls, using the word *crazy* as the highest of compliments. "And brilliant. And dogmatic. And highly creative. We all believed back then that having a certain degree of neurosis made you interesting. Ilon had a degree of neurosis that made her very interesting."

At McCann, Ilon Specht was working with L'Oréal, a French company that was trying to challenge Clairol's dominance in the American hair-color market. L'Oréal had originally wanted to do a series of comparison spots, presenting research proving that their new

product — Preference — was technologically superior to
Nice 'n Easy because it delivered a more natural, translucent color. But at the last minute the campaign was killed
because the research hadn't been done in the United States.
At McCann, there was panic. "We were four weeks before
air date and we had nothing — nada," Michael Sennott, a
staffer who was also working on the account, says. The
creative team locked itself away: Specht, Madris — who
was the art director on the account — and a handful of
others. "We were sitting in this big office," Specht recalls.
"And everyone was discussing what the ad should be.
They wanted to do something with a woman sitting by a
window, and the wind blowing through the curtains. You
know, one of those fake places with big, glamorous curtains. The woman was a complete object. I don't think she
even spoke. They just didn't get it. We were in there for
hours."

Ilon Specht has long, thick black hair, held in a loose
knot at the top of her head, and lipstick the color of mara-
schino cherries. She talks fast and loud, and swivels in her
chair as she speaks, and when people walk by her office
they sometimes bang on her door, as if the best way to
get her attention is to be as loud and emphatic as she is.
Reminiscing not long ago about the seventies, she spoke
about the strangeness of corporate clients in shiny suits
who would say that all the women in the office looked like
models. She spoke about what it meant to be young in a
business dominated by older men, and about what it felt
like to write a line of copy that used the word *woman* and
have someone cross it out and write *girl*.

"I was a twenty-three-year-old girl — a woman," she
said. "What would my state of mind have been? I could just

see that they had this traditional view of women, and my feeling was that I'm not writing an ad about looking good for men, which is what it seems to me that they were doing. I just thought, Fuck you. I sat down and did it, in five minutes. It was very personal. I can recite to you the whole commercial, because I was so angry when I wrote it."

Specht sat stock still and lowered her voice: "I use the most expensive hair color in the world. Preference, by L'Oréal. It's not that I care about money. It's that I care about my hair. It's not just the color. I expect great color. What's worth more to me is the way my hair feels. Smooth and silky but with body. It feels good against my neck. Actually, I don't mind spending more for L'Oréal. Because I'm" — and here Specht took her fist and struck her chest — "worth it."

The power of the commercial was originally thought to lie in its subtle justification of the fact that Preference cost ten cents more than Nice 'n Easy. But it quickly became obvious that the last line was the one that counted. On the strength of "Because I'm worth it," Preference began stealing market share from Clairol. In the 1980s, Preference surpassed Nice 'n Easy as the leading hair-color brand in the country, and in 1997 L'Oréal took the phrase and made it the slogan for the whole company. An astonishing 71 percent of American women can now identify that phrase as the L'Oréal signature, which, for a slogan — as opposed to a brand name — is almost without precedent.

4.

From the very beginning, the Preference campaign was unusual. Polykoff's Clairol spots had male voice-overs.

In the L'Oréal ads, the model herself spoke, directly and personally. Polykoff's commercials were "other-directed" — they were about what the group was saying ("Does she or doesn't she?") or what a husband might think ("The closer he gets, the better you look"). Specht's line was what a woman says to herself. Even in the choice of models, the two campaigns diverged. Polykoff wanted fresh, girl-next-door types. McCann and L'Oréal wanted models who somehow embodied the complicated mixture of strength and vulnerability implied by "Because I'm worth it." In the late seventies, Meredith Baxter Birney was the brand spokeswoman. At that time, she was playing a recently divorced mom going to law school on the TV drama *Family*. McCann scheduled her spots during *Dallas* and other shows featuring so-called silk blouse women — women of strength and independence. Then came Cybill Shepherd, at the height of her run as the brash, independent Maddie on *Moonlighting*, in the eighties. She, in turn, was followed by Heather Locklear, the tough and sexy star of the 1990s hit *Melrose Place*. All the L'Oréal spokeswomen are blondes, but blondes of a particular type. In his brilliant 1995 book, *Big Hair: A Journey into the Transformation of Self*, the Canadian anthropologist Grant McCracken argued for something he calls the "blondness periodic table," in which blondes are divided into six categories: the *bombshell blonde* (Mae West, Marilyn Monroe), the *sunny blonde* (Doris Day, Goldie Hawn), the *brassy blonde* (Candice Bergen), the *dangerous blonde* (Sharon Stone), the *society blonde* (C. Z. Guest), and the *cool blonde* (Marlene Dietrich, Grace Kelly). L'Oréal's innovation was to carve out a niche for itself in between the sunny blondes — the "simple, mild,

and innocent" blondes — and the smart, bold, brassy blondes, who, in McCracken's words, "do not mediate their feelings or modulate their voices."

This is not an easy sensibility to capture. Countless actresses have auditioned for L'Oréal over the years and been turned down. "There was one casting we did with Brigitte Bardot," Ira Madris recalls (this was for another L'Oréal product), "and Brigitte, being who she is, had the damnedest time saying that line. There was something inside of her that didn't believe it. It didn't have any conviction." Of course it didn't: Bardot is bombshell, not sassy. Clairol made a run at the Preference sensibility for itself, hiring Linda Evans in the eighties as the pitchwoman for Ultress, the brand aimed at Preference's upscale positioning. This didn't work, either. Evans, who played the adoring wife of Blake Carrington on *Dynasty,* was too sunny. ("The hardest thing she did on that show," Michael Sennott says, perhaps a bit unfairly, "was rearrange the flowers.")

Even if you got the blonde right, though, there was still the matter of the slogan. For a Miss Clairol campaign in the seventies, Polykoff wrote a series of spots with the tag line "This I do for me." But "This I do for me" was at best a halfhearted approximation of "Because I'm worth it" — particularly for a brand that had spent its first twenty years saying something entirely different. "My mother thought there was something too brazen about 'I'm worth it,'" Frick told me. "She was always concerned with what people around her might think. She could never have come out with that bald-faced an equation between hair color and self-esteem."

The truth is that Polykoff's sensibility — which found

freedom in assimilation — had been overtaken by events. In one of Polykoff's "Is it true blondes have more fun?" commercials for Lady Clairol in the sixties, for example, there is a moment that by 1973 must have been painful to watch. A young woman, radiantly blond, is by a lake, being swung around in the air by a darkly handsome young man. His arms are around her waist. Her arms are around his neck, her shoes off, her face aglow. The voice-over is male, deep and sonorous. "Chances are," the voice says, "she'd have gotten the young man anyhow, but you'll never convince her of that." Here was the downside to Shirley Polykoff's world. You could get what you wanted by faking it, but then you would never know whether it was you or the bit of fakery that made the difference. You ran the risk of losing sight of who you really were. Shirley Polykoff knew that the all-American life was worth it, and that "he" — the handsome man by the lake, or the reluctant boyfriend who finally whisks you off to Bermuda — was worth it. But, by the end of the sixties, women wanted to know that they were worth it, too.

5.

Why are Shirley Polykoff and Ilon Specht important? That seems like a question that can easily be answered in the details of their campaigns. They were brilliant copywriters, who managed in the space of a phrase to capture the particular feminist sensibilities of the day. They are an example of a strange moment in American social history when hair dye somehow got tangled up in the politics of assimilation and feminism and self-esteem. But in a certain way their stories are about much more: they are about the relation-

ship we have to the products we buy, and about the slow realization among advertisers that unless they understood the psychological particulars of that relationship — unless they could dignify the transactions of everyday life by granting them meaning — they could not hope to reach the modern consumer. Shirley Polykoff and Ilon Specht perfected a certain genre of advertising that did just this, and one way to understand the Madison Avenue revolution of the postwar era is as a collective attempt to define and extend that genre. The revolution was led by a handful of social scientists, chief among whom was an elegant, Viennese-trained psychologist by the name of Herta Herzog. What did Herta Herzog know? She knew — or, at least, she thought she knew — the theory behind the success of slogans like "Does she or doesn't she?" and "Because I'm worth it," and that makes Herta Herzog, in the end, every bit as important as Shirley Polykoff and Ilon Specht.

Herzog worked at a small advertising agency called Jack Tinker & Partners, and people who were in the business in those days speak of Tinker the way baseball fans talk about the 1927 Yankees. Tinker was the brainchild of the legendary adman Marion Harper, who came to believe that the agency he was running, McCann-Erickson, was too big and unwieldy to be able to consider things properly. His solution was to pluck a handful of the very best and brightest from McCann and set them up, first in the Waldorf Towers (in the suite directly below the Duke and Duchess of Windsor's and directly above General Douglas MacArthur's) and then, more permanently, in the Dorset Hotel, on West Fifty-fourth Street, overlooking the Museum of Modern Art. The Tinker Group rented the penthouse, complete with a huge terrace,

Venetian-tiled floors, a double-height living room, an antique French polished-pewter bar, a marble fireplace, spectacular skyline views, and a rotating exhibit of modern art (hung by the partners for motivational purposes), with everything — walls, carpets, ceilings, furnishings — a bright, dazzling white. It was supposed to be a think tank, but Tinker was so successful so fast that clients were soon lined up outside the door. When Buick wanted a name for its new luxury coupe, the Tinker Group came up with Riviera. When Bulova wanted a name for its new quartz watch, Tinker suggested Accutron. Tinker also worked with Coca-Cola and Exxon and Westinghouse and countless others, whose names — according to the strict standards of secrecy observed by the group — they would not divulge. Tinker started with four partners and a single phone. But by the end of the sixties it had taken over eight floors of the Dorset.

What distinguished Tinker was its particular reliance on the methodology known as motivational research, which was brought to Madison Avenue in the 1940s by a cadre of European intellectuals trained at the University of Vienna. Advertising research up until that point had been concerned with counting heads — with recording who was buying what. But the motivational researchers were concerned with why: Why do people buy what they do? What motivates them when they shop? The researchers devised surveys, with hundreds of questions, based on Freudian dynamic psychology. They used hypnosis, the Rosenzweig Picture-Frustration Study, role-playing, and Rorschach blots, and they invented what we now call the focus group. There was Paul Lazarsfeld, one of the giants of twentieth-century sociology, who devised something

called the Lazarsfeld-Stanton Program Analyzer, a little device with buttons to record precisely the emotional responses of research subjects. There was Hans Zeisel, who had been a patient of Alfred Adler's in Vienna and went to work at McCann-Erickson. There was Ernest Dichter, who had studied under Lazarsfeld at the Psychological Institute in Vienna and who did consulting for hundreds of the major corporations of the day. And there was Tinker's Herta Herzog, perhaps the most accomplished motivational researcher of all, who trained dozens of interviewers in the Viennese method and sent them out to analyze the psyche of the American consumer.

"For Puerto Rican rum once, Herta wanted to do a study of why people drink, to tap into that below-the-surface kind of thing," Rena Bartos, a former advertising executive who worked with Herta in the early days, recalls. "We would invite someone out to drink and they would order whatever they normally order, and we would administer a psychological test. Then we'd do it again at the very end of the discussion, after the drinks. The point was to see how people's personality was altered under the influence of alcohol." Herzog helped choose the name of Oasis cigarettes, because her psychological research suggested that the name — with its connotations of cool, bubbling springs — would have the greatest appeal to the orally fixated smoker.

"Herta was graceful and gentle and articulate," Herbert Krugman, who worked closely with Herzog in those years, says. "She had enormous insights. Alka-Seltzer was a client of ours, and they were discussing new approaches for the next commercial. She said, 'You show a hand dropping an Alka-Seltzer tablet into a glass of water. Why not

show the hand dropping two? You'll double sales.' And that's just what happened. Herta was the gray eminence. Everybody worshipped her."

After retiring from Tinker, Herzog moved back to Europe, first to Germany and then to Austria, her homeland. She wrote an analysis of the TV show *Dallas* for the academic journal *Society*. She taught college courses on communications theory. She conducted a study on the Holocaust for the Vidal Sassoon Center for the Study of Anti-Semitism, in Jerusalem. Today, she lives in the mountain village of Leutasch, half an hour's hard drive up into the Alps from Innsbruck, in a white picturebook cottage with a sharply pitched roof. She is a small woman, slender and composed, her once dark hair now streaked with gray. She speaks in short, clipped, precise sentences, in flawless, though heavily accented, English. If you put her in a room with Shirley Polykoff and Ilon Specht, the two of them would talk and talk and wave their long, bejeweled fingers in the air, and she would sit unobtrusively in the corner and listen. "Marion Harper hired me to do qualitative research — the qualitative interview, which was the specialty that had been developed in Vienna at the Österreichische Wirtschaftspsychologische Forschungsstelle," Herzog told me. "It was interviewing not with direct questions and answers but where you open some subject of the discussion relevant to the topic and then let it go. You have the interviewer not talk but simply help the person with little questions like 'And anything else?' As an interviewer, you are not supposed to influence me. You are merely trying to help me. It was a lot like the psychoanalytic method." Herzog was sitting, ramrod straight, in a chair in her living room. She was

wearing a pair of black slacks and a heavy brown sweater to protect her against the Alpine chill. Behind her was row upon row of bookshelves, filled with the books of a postwar literary and intellectual life: Mailer in German, Reisman in English. Open and facedown on a long couch perpendicular to her chair was the latest issue of the psychoanalytic journal *Psyche*. "Later on, I added all kinds of psychological things to the process, such as word-association tests, or figure drawings with a story. Suppose you are my respondent and the subject is soap. I've already talked to you about soap. What you see in it. Why you buy it. What you like about it. Dislike about it. Then at the end of the interview I say, 'Please draw me a figure — anything you want — and after the figure is drawn tell me a story about the figure.'"

When Herzog asked her subjects to draw a figure at the end of an interview, she was trying to extract some kind of narrative from them, something that would shed light on their unstated desires. She was conducting, as she says, a psychoanalytic session. But she wouldn't ask about hair-color products in order to find out about you, the way a psychoanalyst might; she would ask about you in order to learn about hair-color products. She saw that the psychoanalytic interview could go both ways. You could use the techniques of healing to figure out the secrets of selling. "Does she or doesn't she?" and "Because I'm worth it" did the same thing: they not only carried a powerful and redemptive message, but — and this was their real triumph — they succeeded in attaching that message to a five-dollar bottle of hair dye. The lasting contribution of motivational research to Madison Avenue was to prove that you could do this for just about anything — that the products and the commercial

messages with which we surround ourselves are as much a part of the psychological furniture of our lives as the relationships and emotions and experiences that are normally the subject of psychoanalytic inquiry.

"There is one thing we did at Tinker that I remember well," Herzog told me, returning to the theme of one of her, and Tinker's, coups. "I found out that people were using Alka-Seltzer for stomach upset, but also for headaches," Herzog said. "We learned that the stomach ache was the kind of ache where many people tended to say 'It was my fault.' Alka-Seltzer had been mostly advertised in those days as a cure for overeating, and overeating is something you have done. But the headache is quite different. It is something imposed on you." This was, to Herzog, the classic psychological insight. It revealed Alka-Seltzer users to be divided into two apparently incompatible camps — the culprit and the victim — and it suggested that the company had been wooing one at the expense of the other. More important, it suggested that advertisers, with the right choice of words, could resolve that psychological dilemma with one or, better yet, two little white tablets. Herzog allowed herself a small smile. "So I said the nice thing would be if you could find something that combines these two elements. The copywriter came up with 'the blahs.'" Herzog repeated the phrase, *the blahs,* because it was so beautiful. "The blahs was not one thing or the other — it was not the stomach or the head. It was both."

6.

This notion of household products as psychological furniture is, when you think about it, a radical idea. When

we give an account of how we got to where we are, we're inclined to credit the philosophical over the physical, and the products of art over the products of commerce. In the list of sixties social heroes, there are musicians and poets and civil-rights activists and sports figures. Herzog's implication is that such a high-minded list is incomplete. What, say, of Vidal Sassoon? In the same period, he gave the world the Shape, the Acute Angle, and the One-Eyed Ungaro. In the old "cosmology of cosmetology," McCracken writes, "the client counted only as a plinth...the conveyor of the cut." But Sassoon made individualization the hallmark of the haircut, liberating women's hair from the hair styles of the times — from, as McCracken puts it, those "preposterous bits of rococo shrubbery that took their substance from permanents, their form from rollers, and their rigidity from hair spray." In the Herzogian world view, the reasons we might give to dismiss Sassoon's revolution — that all he was dispensing was a haircut, that it took just half an hour, that it affects only the way you look, that you will need another like it in a month — are the very reasons that Sassoon is important. If a revolution is not accessible, tangible, and replicable, how on earth can it be a revolution?

"Because I'm worth it" and "Does she or doesn't she?" were powerful, then, precisely because they were commercials, for commercials come with products attached, and products offer something that songs and poems and political movements and radical ideologies do not, which is an immediate and affordable means of transformation. "We discovered in the first few years of the 'Because I'm worth it' campaign that we were getting more than our fair share of new users to the category — women who

were just beginning to color their hair," Sennott told me. "And within that group we were getting those undergoing life changes, which usually meant divorce. We had far more women who were getting divorced than Clairol had. Their children had grown, and something had happened, and they were reinventing themselves." They felt different, and Ilon Specht gave them the means to look different — and do we really know which came first, or even how to separate the two? They changed their lives and their hair. But it wasn't one thing or the other. It was both.

7.

In the midnineties, the spokesperson for Clairol's Nice 'n Easy was Julia Louis-Dreyfus, better known as Elaine from *Seinfeld*. In the Clairol tradition, she is the girl next door — a postmodern Doris Day. But the spots themselves could not be less like the original Polykoff campaigns for Miss Clairol. In the best of them, Louis-Dreyfus says to the dark-haired woman in front of her on a city bus, "You know, you'd look great as a blonde." Louis-Dreyfus then shampoos in Nice 'n Easy Shade 104 right then and there, to the gasps and cheers of the other passengers. It is Shirley Polykoff turned upside down: funny, not serious; public, not covert.

L'Oréal, too, has changed. Meredith Baxter Birney said "Because I'm worth it" with an earnestness appropriate to the line. By the time Cybill Shepherd became the brand spokeswoman, in the eighties, it was almost flip — a nod to the materialism of the times — and today, with Heather Locklear, the spots have a lush, indulgent feel. "New Preference by L'Oréal," she says in one of the current commercials. "Pass it on. You're worth it." The "because" — which

gave Ilon Specht's original punch line such emphasis — is gone. The forceful *I'm* has been replaced by *you're*. The Clairol and L'Oréal campaigns have converged. According to the Spectra marketing firm, there are almost exactly as many Preference users as Nice 'n Easy users who earn between fifty thousand and seventy-five thousand dollars a year, listen to religious radio, rent their apartments, watch the Weather Channel, bought more than six books last year, are fans of professional football, and belong to a union.

But it is a tribute to Ilon Specht and Shirley Polykoff's legacy that there is still a real difference between the two brands. It's not that there are Clairol women or L'Oréal women. It's something a little subtler. As Herzog knew, all of us, when it comes to constructing our sense of self, borrow bits and pieces, ideas and phrases, rituals and products from the world around us — over-the-counter ethnicities that shape, in some small but meaningful way, our identities. Our religion matters, the music we listen to matters, the clothes we wear matter, the food we eat matters — and our brand of hair dye matters, too. Carol Hamilton, L'Oréal's vice president of marketing, says she can walk into a hair-color focus group and instantly distinguish the Clairol users from the L'Oréal users. "The L'Oréal user always exhibits a greater air of confidence, and she usually looks better — not just her hair color, but she always has spent a little more time putting on her makeup, styling her hair," Hamilton told me. "Her clothing is a little bit more fashion-forward. Absolutely, I can tell the difference." Jeanne Matson, Hamilton's counterpart at Clairol, says she can do the same thing. "Oh, yes," Matson told me. "There's no doubt. The Clairol woman would represent more the American-beauty icon, more naturalness. But it's more of a beauty for

me, as opposed to a beauty for the external world. L'Oréal users tend to be a bit more aloof. There is a certain warmth you see in the Clairol people. They interact with each other more. They'll say, 'I use Shade 101.' And someone else will say, 'Ah, I do, too!' There is this big exchange."

These are not exactly the brand personalities laid down by Polykoff and Specht, because this is 1999, and not 1956 or 1973. The complexities of Polykoff's artifice have been muted. Specht's anger has turned to glamour. We have been left with just a few bars of the original melody. But even that is enough to ensure that "Because I'm worth it" will never be confused with "Does she or doesn't she?" Specht says, "It meant I know you don't think I'm worth it, because that's what it was with the guys in the room. They were going to take a woman and make her the object. I was defensive and defiant. I thought, I'll fight you. Don't you tell me what I am. You've been telling me what I am for generations." As she said *fight*, she extended the middle finger of her right hand. Shirley Polykoff would never have given anyone the finger. She was too busy exulting in the possibilities for self-invention in her America — a land where a single woman could dye her hair and end up lying on a beach with a ring on her finger. At her retirement party, in 1973, Polykoff reminded the assembled executives of Clairol and of Foote, Cone & Belding about the avalanche of mail that arrived after their early campaigns: "Remember that letter from the girl who got to a Bermuda honeymoon by becoming a blonde?"

Everybody did.

"Well," she said, with what we can only imagine was a certain sweet vindication, "I wrote it."

March 22, 1999

John Rock's Error

WHAT THE INVENTOR OF THE BIRTH
CONTROL PILL DIDN'T KNOW ABOUT
WOMEN'S HEALTH

1.

John Rock was christened in 1890 at the Church of the Immaculate Conception in Marlborough, Massachusetts, and married by Cardinal William O'Connell, of Boston. He had five children and nineteen grandchildren. A crucifix hung above his desk, and nearly every day of his adult life he attended the 7 a.m. Mass at St. Mary's in Brookline. Rock, his friends would say, was in love with his church. He was also one of the inventors of the birth-control pill, and it was his conviction that his faith and his vocation were perfectly compatible. To anyone who disagreed he would simply repeat the words spoken to him as a child by his hometown priest: "John, always stick to your conscience. Never let anyone else keep it for you. And I mean anyone else." Even when Monsignor Francis W. Carney, of Cleveland, called him a "moral rapist," and when Frederick Good, the longtime head of obstetrics at Boston City Hospital, went to Boston's Cardinal Richard Cushing to

have Rock excommunicated, Rock was unmoved. "You should be afraid to meet your Maker," one angry woman wrote to him, soon after the Pill was approved. "My dear madam," Rock wrote back, "in my faith, we are taught that the Lord is with us always. When my time comes, there will be no need for introductions."

In the years immediately after the Pill was approved by the FDA, in 1960, Rock was everywhere. He appeared in interviews and documentaries on CBS and NBC, in *Time, Newsweek, Life, The Saturday Evening Post*. He toured the country tirelessly. He wrote a widely discussed book, *The Time Has Come: A Catholic Doctor's Proposals to End the Battle over Birth Control*, which was translated into French, German, and Dutch. Rock was six feet three and rail-thin, with impeccable manners; he held doors open for his patients and addressed them as "Mrs." or "Miss." His mere association with the Pill helped make it seem respectable. "He was a man of great dignity," Dr. Sheldon J. Segal, of the Population Council, recalls. "Even if the occasion called for an open collar, you'd never find him without an ascot. He had the shock of white hair to go along with that. And posture, straight as an arrow, even to his last year." At Harvard Medical School, he was a giant, teaching obstetrics for more than three decades. He was a pioneer in in-vitro fertilization and the freezing of sperm cells, and was the first to extract an intact fertilized egg. The Pill was his crowning achievement. His two collaborators, Gregory Pincus and Min-Cheuh Chang, worked out the mechanism. He shepherded the drug through its clinical trials. "It was his name and his reputation that gave ultimate validity to the claims that the pill would protect women against unwanted pregnancy," Loretta McLaughlin writes in her marvelous 1982

biography of Rock. Not long before the Pill's approval, Rock traveled to Washington to testify before the FDA about the drug's safety. The agency examiner, Pasquale DeFelice, was a Catholic obstetrician from Georgetown University, and at one point, the story goes, DeFelice suggested the unthinkable — that the Catholic Church would never approve of the birth-control pill. "I can still see Rock standing there, his face composed, his eyes riveted on DeFelice," a colleague recalled years later, "and then, in a voice that would congeal your soul, he said, 'Young man, don't you sell *my* church short.'"

In the end, of course, John Rock's church disappointed him. In 1968, in the encyclical "Humanae Vitae," Pope Paul VI outlawed oral contraceptives and all other "artificial" methods of birth control. The passion and urgency that animated the birth-control debates of the sixties are now a memory. John Rock still matters, though, for the simple reason that in the course of reconciling his church and his work he made an error. It was not a deliberate error. It became manifest only after his death, and through scientific advances he could not have anticipated. But because that mistake shaped the way he thought about the Pill — about what it was, and how it worked, and most of all what it meant — and because John Rock was one of those responsible for the way the Pill came into the world, his error has colored the way people have thought about contraception ever since.

John Rock believed that the Pill was a "natural" method of birth control. By that, he didn't mean that it *felt* natural, because it obviously didn't for many women, particularly not in its earliest days, when the doses of hormone were many times as high as they are today. He meant that it worked by natural means. Women can get pregnant only during a certain interval each month, because after

ovulation their bodies produce a surge of the hormone progesterone. Progesterone — one of a class of hormones known as progestin — prepares the uterus for implantation and stops the ovaries from releasing new eggs; it favors gestation. "It is progesterone, in the healthy woman, that prevents ovulation and establishes the pre- and postmenstrual 'safe' period," Rock wrote. When a woman is pregnant, her body produces a stream of progestin in part for the same reason, so that another egg can't be released and threaten the pregnancy already under way. Progestin, in other words, is nature's contraceptive. And what was the Pill? Progestin in tablet form. When a woman was on the Pill, of course, these hormones weren't coming in a sudden surge after ovulation and weren't limited to certain times in her cycle. They were being given in a steady dose, so that ovulation was permanently shut down. They were also being given with an additional dose of estrogen, which holds the endometrium together and — as we've come to learn — helps maintain other tissues as well. But to Rock, the timing and combination of hormones wasn't the issue. The key fact was that the Pill's ingredients duplicated what could be found in the body naturally. And in that naturalness he saw enormous theological significance.

In 1951, for example, Pope Pius XII had sanctioned the rhythm method for Catholics because he deemed it a "natural" method of regulating procreation: it didn't kill the sperm, like a spermicide, or frustrate the normal process of procreation, like a diaphragm, or mutilate the organs, like sterilization. Rock knew all about the rhythm method. In the 1930s, at the Free Hospital for Women, in Brookline, Massachusetts, he had started the country's first rhythm clinic for educating Catholic couples in natural contracep-

tion. But how did the rhythm method work? It worked by limiting sex to the safe period that progestin created. And how did the Pill work? It worked by using progestin to extend the safe period to the entire month. It didn't mutilate the reproductive organs, or damage any natural process. "Indeed," Rock wrote, oral contraceptives "may be characterized as a 'pill-established safe period,' and would seem to carry the same moral implications" as the rhythm method. The Pill was, to Rock, no more than "an adjunct to nature."

In 1958, Pope Pius XII approved the Pill for Catholics, so long as its contraceptive effects were "indirect" — that is, so long as it was intended only as a remedy for conditions like painful menses or "a disease of the uterus." That ruling emboldened Rock still further. Short-term use of the Pill, he knew, could regulate the cycle of women whose periods had previously been unpredictable. Since a regular menstrual cycle was necessary for the successful use of the rhythm method — and since the rhythm method was sanctioned by the Church — shouldn't it be permissible for women with an irregular menstrual cycle to use the Pill in order to facilitate the use of rhythm? And if that was true, why not take the logic one step further? As the federal judge John T. Noonan writes in *Contraception*, his history of the Catholic position on birth control:

> If it was lawful to suppress ovulation to achieve a regularity necessary for successfully sterile intercourse, why was it not lawful to suppress ovulation without appeal to rhythm? If pregnancy could be prevented by pill plus rhythm, why not by pill alone? In each case suppression of ovulation was used as a means. How was a moral difference made by the addition of rhythm?

These arguments, as arcane as they may seem, were central to the development of oral contraception. It was John Rock and Gregory Pincus who decided that the Pill ought to be taken over a four-week cycle — a woman would spend three weeks on the Pill and the fourth week off the drug (or on a placebo), to allow for menstruation. There was and is no medical reason for this. A typical woman of childbearing age has a menstrual cycle of around twenty-eight days, determined by the cascades of hormones released by her ovaries. As first estrogen and then a combination of estrogen and progestin flood the uterus, its lining becomes thick and swollen, preparing for the implantation of a fertilized egg. If the egg is not fertilized, hormone levels plunge and cause the lining — the endometrium — to be sloughed off in a menstrual bleed. When a woman is on the Pill, however, no egg is released, because the Pill suppresses ovulation. The fluxes of estrogen and progestin that cause the lining of the uterus to grow are dramatically reduced, because the Pill slows down the ovaries. Pincus and Rock knew that the effect of the Pill's hormones on the endometrium was so modest that women could conceivably go for months without having to menstruate. "In view of the ability of this compound to prevent menstrual bleeding as long as it is taken," Pincus acknowledged in 1958, "a cycle of any desired length could presumably be produced." But he and Rock decided to cut the hormones off after three weeks and trigger a menstrual period because they believed that women would find the continuation of their monthly bleeding reassuring. More to the point, if Rock wanted to demonstrate that the Pill was no more than a natural variant of the rhythm method, he couldn't very well do away

with the monthly menses. Rhythm required "regularity," and so the Pill had to produce regularity as well.

It has often been said of the Pill that no other drug has ever been so instantly recognizable by its packaging: that small, round plastic dial pack. But what was the dial pack if not the physical embodiment of the twenty-eight-day cycle? It was, in the words of its inventor, meant to fit into a case "indistinguishable" from a woman's cosmetics compact, so that it might be carried "without giving a visual clue as to matters which are of no concern to others." Today, the Pill is still often sold in dial packs and taken in twenty-eight-day cycles. It remains, in other words, a drug shaped by the dictates of the Catholic Church — by John Rock's desire to make this new method of birth control seem as natural as possible. This was John Rock's error. He was consumed by the idea of the natural. But what he thought was natural wasn't so natural after all, and the Pill he ushered into the world turned out to be something other than what he thought it was. In John Rock's mind the dictates of religion and the principles of science got mixed up, and only now are we beginning to untangle them.

2.

In 1986, a young scientist named Beverly Strassmann traveled to Africa to live with the Dogon tribe of Mali. Her research site was the village of Sangui in the Sahel, about 120 miles south of Timbuktu. The Sahel is thorn savannah, green in the rainy season and semi-arid the rest of the year. The Dogon grow millet, sorghum, and onions, raise livestock, and live in adobe houses on the Bandiagara escarpment. They use no contraception. Many of them have held

on to their ancestral customs and religious beliefs. Dogon farmers, in many respects, live much as people of that region have lived since antiquity. Strassmann wanted to construct a precise reproductive profile of the women in the tribe, in order to understand what female biology might have been like in the millennia that preceded the modern age. In a way, Strassmann was trying to answer the same question about female biology that John Rock and the Catholic Church had struggled with in the early sixties: what is natural? Only, her sense of *natural* was not theological but evolutionary. In the era during which natural selection established the basic patterns of human biology — the natural history of our species — how often did women have children? How often did they menstruate? When did they reach puberty and menopause? What impact did breast-feeding have on ovulation? These questions had been studied before, but never so thoroughly that anthropologists felt they knew the answers with any certainty.

Strassmann, who teaches at the University of Michigan at Ann Arbor, is a slender, soft-spoken woman with red hair, and she recalls her time in Mali with a certain wry humor. The house she stayed in while in Sangui had been used as a shelter for sheep before she came and was turned into a pigsty after she left. A small brown snake lived in her latrine, and would curl up in a camouflaged coil on the seat she sat on while bathing. The villagers, she says, were of two minds: was it a deadly snake — *Kere me jongolo,* literally, "My bite cannot be healed" — or a harmless mouse snake? (It turned out to be the latter.) Once, one of her neighbors and best friends in the tribe roasted her a rat as a special treat. "I told him that white people aren't allowed to eat rat because rat is our totem," Strassmann

says. "I can still see it. Bloated and charred. Stretched by its paws. Whiskers singed. To say nothing of the tail." Strassmann meant to live in Sangui for eighteen months, but her experiences there were so profound and exhilarating that she stayed for two and a half years. "I felt incredibly privileged," she says. "I just couldn't tear myself away."

Part of Strassmann's work focused on the Dogon's practice of segregating menstruating women in special huts on the fringes of the village. In Sangui, there were two menstrual huts — dark, cramped, one-room adobe structures, with boards for beds. Each accommodated three women, and when the rooms were full, latecomers were forced to stay outside on the rocks. "It's not a place where people kick back and enjoy themselves," Strassmann says. "It's simply a nighttime hangout. They get there at dusk, and get up early in the morning and draw their water." Strassmann took urine samples from the women using the hut, to confirm that they were menstruating. Then she made a list of all the women in the village, and for her entire time in Mali — 736 consecutive nights — she kept track of everyone who visited the hut. Among the Dogon, she found a woman on average has her first period at the age of sixteen and gives birth eight or nine times. From menarche, the onset of menstruation, to the age of twenty, she averages seven periods a year. Over the next decade and a half, from the age of twenty to the age of thirty-four, she spends so much time either pregnant or breast-feeding (which, among the Dogon, suppresses ovulation for an average of twenty months) that she averages only slightly more than one period per year. Then, from the age of thirty-five until menopause, at around fifty, as her fertility rapidly declines, she averages four menses a year. All told, Dogon women menstruate about a hundred times

in their lives. (Those who survive early childhood typically live into their seventh or eighth decade.) By contrast, the average for contemporary Western women is somewhere between three hundred and fifty and four hundred times.

Strassmann's office is in the basement of a converted stable next to the Natural History Museum on the University of Michigan campus. Behind her desk is a row of battered filing cabinets, and as she was talking, she turned and pulled out a series of yellowed charts. Each page listed, on the left, the first names and identification numbers of the Sangui women. Across the top was a time line, broken into thirty-day blocks. Every menses of every woman was marked with an X. In the village, Strassmann explained, there were two women who were sterile, and, because they couldn't get pregnant, they were regulars at the menstrual hut. She flipped through the pages until she found them. "Look, she had twenty-nine menses over two years, and the other had twenty-three." Next to each of their names was a solid line of x's. "Here's a woman approaching menopause," Strassmann went on, running her finger down the page. "She's cycling but is a little bit erratic. Here's another woman of prime childbearing age. Two periods. Then pregnant. I never saw her again at the menstrual hut. This woman here didn't go to the menstrual hut for twenty months after giving birth, because she was breast-feeding. Two periods. Got pregnant. Then she miscarried, had a few periods, then got pregnant again. This woman had three menses in the study period." There weren't a lot of x's on Strassmann's sheets. Most of the boxes were blank. She flipped back through her sheets to the two anomalous women who were menstruating every month. "If this were a menstrual chart of undergraduates here at the University of Michigan, all the rows would be like this."

Strassmann does not claim that her statistics apply to every preindustrial society. But she believes — and other anthropological work backs her up — that the number of lifetime menses isn't greatly affected by differences in diet or climate or method of subsistence (foraging versus agriculture, say). The more significant factors, Strassmann says, are things like the prevalence of wet-nursing or sterility. But overall she believes that the basic pattern of late menarche, many pregnancies, and long menstrual-free stretches caused by intensive breast-feeding was virtually universal up until the "demographic transition" of a hundred years ago from high to low fertility. In other words, what we think of as normal — frequent menses — is in evolutionary terms abnormal. "It's a pity that gynecologists think that women have to menstruate every month," Strassmann went on. "They just don't understand the real biology of menstruation."

To Strassmann and others in the field of evolutionary medicine, this shift from a hundred to four hundred lifetime menses is enormously significant. It means that women's bodies are being subjected to changes and stresses that they were not necessarily designed by evolution to handle. In a brilliant and provocative book, *Is Menstruation Obsolete?*, Drs. Elsimar Coutinho and Sheldon S. Segal, two of the world's most prominent contraceptive researchers, argue that this recent move to what they call "incessant ovulation" has become a serious problem for women's health. It doesn't mean that women are always better off the less they menstruate. There are times — particularly in the context of certain medical conditions — when women ought to be concerned if they aren't menstruating: In obese women, a failure to menstruate can signal an increased risk of uterine cancer. In female athletes, a failure to menstruate

can signal an increased risk of osteoporosis. But for most women, Coutinho and Segal say, incessant ovulation serves no purpose except to increase the occurence of abdominal pain, mood shifts, migraines, endometriosis, fibroids, and anemia — the last of which, they point out, is "one of the most serious health problems in the world."

Most serious of all is the greatly increased risk of some cancers. Cancer, after all, occurs because as cells divide and reproduce they sometimes make mistakes that cripple the cells' defenses against runaway growth. That's one of the reasons that our risk of cancer generally increases as we age: our cells have more time to make mistakes. But this also means that *any* change promoting cell division has the potential to increase cancer risk, and ovulation appears to be one of those changes. Whenever a woman ovulates, an egg literally bursts through the walls of her ovaries. To heal that puncture, the cells of the ovary wall have to divide and reproduce. Every time a woman gets pregnant and bears a child, her lifetime risk of ovarian cancer drops 10 percent. Why? Possibly because, between nine months of pregnancy and the suppression of ovulation associated with breast-feeding, she stops ovulating for twelve months — and saves her ovarian walls from twelve bouts of cell division. The argument is similar for endometrial cancer. When a woman is menstruating, the estrogen that flows through her uterus stimulates the growth of the uterine lining, causing a flurry of potentially dangerous cell division. Women who do not menstruate frequently spare the endometrium that risk. Ovarian and endometrial cancer are characteristically modern diseases, consequences, in part, of a century in which women have come to menstruate four hundred times in a lifetime.

In this sense, the Pill really does have a natural effect.

By blocking the release of new eggs, the progestin in oral contraceptives reduces the rounds of ovarian cell division. Progestin also counters the surges of estrogen in the endometrium, restraining cell division there. A woman who takes the Pill for ten years cuts her ovarian-cancer risk by around 70 percent and her endometrial-cancer risk by around 60 percent. But here *natural* means something different from what Rock meant. He assumed that the Pill was natural because it was an unobtrusive variant of the body's own processes. In fact, as more recent research suggests, the Pill is really only natural in so far as it's *radical* — rescuing the ovaries and endometrium from modernity. That Rock insisted on a twenty-eight-day cycle for his pill is evidence of just how deep his misunderstanding was: the real promise of the Pill was not that it could preserve the menstrual rhythms of the twentieth century but that it could disrupt them.

Today, a growing movement of reproductive specialists has begun to campaign loudly against the standard twenty-eight-day pill regimen. The drug company Organon has come out with a new oral contraceptive, called Mircette, that cuts the seven-day placebo interval to two days. Patricia Sulak, a medical researcher at Texas A&M University, has shown that most women can probably stay on the Pill, straight through, for six to twelve weeks before they experience breakthrough bleeding or spotting. More recently, Sulak has documented precisely what the cost of the Pill's monthly "off" week is. In a paper in the February issue of the journal *Obstetrics and Gynecology,* she and her colleagues documented something that will come as no surprise to most women on the Pill: during the placebo week, the number of users experiencing pelvic pain, bloating, and swelling

more than triples, breast tenderness more than doubles, and headaches increase by almost 50 percent. In other words, some women on the Pill continue to experience the kinds of side effects associated with normal menstruation. Sulak's paper is a short, dry, academic work, of the sort intended for a narrow professional audience. But it is impossible to read it without being struck by the consequences of John Rock's desire to please his Church. In the past forty years, millions of women around the world have been given the Pill in such a way as to maximize their pain and suffering. And to what end? To pretend that the Pill was no more than a pharmaceutical version of the rhythm method?

3.

In 1980 and 1981, Malcolm Pike, a medical statistician at the University of Southern California, traveled to Japan for six months to study at the Atomic Bomb Casualties Commission. Pike wasn't interested in the effects of the bomb. He wanted to examine the medical records that the commission had been painstakingly assembling on the survivors of Hiroshima and Nagasaki. He was investigating a question that would ultimately do as much to complicate our understanding of the Pill as Strassmann's research would a decade later: why did Japanese women have breast-cancer rates six times lower than American women?

In the late forties, the World Health Organization began to collect and publish comparative health statistics from around the world, and the breast-cancer disparity between Japan and America had come to obsess cancer specialists. The obvious answer — that Japanese women were somehow genetically protected against breast cancer — didn't make

sense, because once Japanese women moved to the United States they began to get breast cancer almost as often as American women did. As a result, many experts at the time assumed that the culprit had to be some unknown toxic chemical or virus unique to the West. Brian Henderson, a colleague of Pike's at USC and his regular collaborator, says that when he entered the field in 1970, "the whole viral- and chemical-carcinogenesis idea was huge — it dominated the literature." As he recalls, "Breast cancer fell into this large, unknown box that said it was something to do with the environment — and that word *environment* meant a lot of different things to a lot of different people. They might be talking about diet or smoking or pesticides."

Henderson and Pike, however, became fascinated by a number of statistical peculiarities. For one thing, the rate of increase in breast-cancer risk rises sharply throughout women's thirties and forties and then, at menopause, it starts to slow down. If a cancer is caused by some toxic outside agent, you'd expect that rate to rise steadily with each advancing year, as the number of mutations and genetic mistakes steadily accumulates. Breast cancer, by contrast, looked as if it were being driven by something specific to a woman's reproductive years. What was more, younger women who had had their ovaries removed had a markedly lower risk of breast cancer; when their bodies weren't producing estrogen and progestin every month, they got far fewer tumors. Pike and Henderson became convinced that breast cancer was linked to a process of cell division similar to that of ovarian and endometrial cancer. The female breast, after all, is just as sensitive to the level of hormones in a woman's body as the reproductive system. When the breast is exposed to estrogen, the cells of the terminal-duct lobular unit — where

most breast cancer arises — undergo a flurry of division. And during the mid-to-late stage of the menstrual cycle, when the ovaries start producing large amounts of progestin, the pace of cell division in that region doubles.

It made intuitive sense, then, that a woman's risk of breast cancer would be linked to the amount of estrogen and progestin her breasts have been exposed to during her lifetime. How old a woman is at menarche should make a big difference, because the beginning of puberty results in a hormonal surge through a woman's body, and the breast cells of an adolescent appear to be highly susceptible to the errors that result in cancer. (For more complicated reasons, bearing children turns out to be protective against breast cancer, perhaps because in the last two trimesters of pregnancy the cells of the breast mature and become much more resistant to mutations.) How old a woman is at menopause should matter, and so should how much estrogen and progestin her ovaries actually produce, and even how much she weighs after menopause, because fat cells turn other hormones into estrogen.

Pike went to Hiroshima to test the cell-division theory. With other researchers at the medical archive, he looked first at the age when Japanese women got their period. A Japanese woman born at the turn of the century had her first period at sixteen and a half. American women born at the same time had their first period at fourteen. That difference alone, by their calculation, was sufficient to explain 40 percent of the gap between American and Japanese breast-cancer rates. "They had collected amazing records from the women of that area," Pike said. "You could follow precisely the change in age of menarche over the century. You could even see the effects of the Second World War.

The age of menarche of Japanese girls went up right at that point because of poor nutrition and other hardships. And then it started to go back down after the war. That's what convinced me that the data were wonderful."

Pike, Henderson, and their colleagues then folded in the other risk factors. Age at menopause, age at first pregnancy, and number of children weren't sufficiently different between the two countries to matter. But weight was. The average post-menopausal Japanese woman weighed a hundred pounds; the average American woman weighed a hundred and forty-five pounds. That fact explained another 25 percent of the difference. Finally, the researchers analyzed blood samples from women in rural Japan and China, and found that their ovaries — possibly because of their extremely low-fat diet — were producing about 75 percent the amount of estrogen that American women were producing. Those three factors, added together, seemed to explain the breast-cancer gap. They also appeared to explain why the rates of breast cancer among Asian women began to increase when they came to America: on an American diet, they started to menstruate earlier, gained more weight, and produced more estrogen. The talk of chemicals and toxins and power lines and smog was set aside. "When people say that what we understand about breast cancer explains only a small amount of the problem, that it is somehow a mystery, it's absolute nonsense," Pike says flatly. He is a South African in his sixties, with graying hair and a salt-and-pepper beard. Along with Henderson, he is an eminent figure in cancer research, but no one would ever accuse him of being tentative in his pronouncements. "We understand breast cancer extraordinarily well. We understand it as well as we understand cigarettes and lung cancer."

What Pike discovered in Japan led him to think about the Pill, because a tablet that suppressed ovulation — and the monthly tides of estrogen and progestin that come with it — obviously had the potential to be a powerful anti-breast-cancer drug. But the breast was a little different from the reproductive organs. Progestin prevented ovarian cancer because it suppressed ovulation. It was good for preventing endometrial cancer because it countered the stimulating effects of estrogen. But in breast cells, Pike believed, progestin wasn't the solution; it was one of the hormones that *caused* cell division. This is one explanation for why, after years of studying the Pill, researchers have concluded that it has no effect one way or the other on breast cancer: whatever beneficial effect results from what the Pill does is canceled out by how it does it. John Rock touted the fact that the Pill used progestin, because progestin was the body's own contraceptive. But Pike saw nothing "natural" about subjecting the breast to that heavy a dose of progestin. In his view, the amount of progestin and estrogen needed to make an effective contraceptive was much greater than the amount needed to keep the reproductive system healthy — and that excess was unnecessarily raising the risk of breast cancer. A truly natural Pill might be one that found a way to suppress ovulation *without* using progestin. Throughout the 1980s, Pike recalls, this was his obsession. "We were all trying to work out how the hell we could fix the Pill. We thought about it day and night."

4.

Pike's proposed solution is a class of drugs known as GnRHAs, which has been around for many years.

GnRHAs disrupt the signals that the pituitary gland sends when it is attempting to order the manufacture of sex hormones. It's a circuit breaker. "We've got substantial experience with this drug," Pike says. Men suffering from prostate cancer are sometimes given a GnRHA to temporarily halt the production of testosterone, which can exacerbate their tumors. Girls suffering from what's called precocious puberty — puberty at seven or eight, or even younger — are sometimes given the drug to forestall sexual maturity. If you give GnRHA to women of childbearing age, it stops their ovaries from producing estrogen and progestin. If the conventional Pill works by convincing the body that it is, well, a little bit pregnant, Pike's pill would work by convincing the body that it was menopausal.

In the form Pike wants to use it, GnRHA will come in a clear glass bottle the size of a saltshaker, with a white plastic mister on top. It will be inhaled nasally. It breaks down in the body very quickly. A morning dose simply makes a woman menopausal for a while. Menopause, of course, has its risks. Women need estrogen to keep their hearts and bones strong. They also need progestin to keep the uterus healthy. So Pike intends to add back just enough of each hormone to solve these problems, but much less than women now receive on the Pill. Ideally, Pike says, the estrogen dose would be adjustable: women would try various levels until they found one that suited them. The progestin would come in four twelve-day stretches a year. When someone on Pike's regimen stopped the progestin, she would have one of four annual menses.

Pike and an oncologist named Darcy Spicer have joined forces with another oncologist, John Daniels, in a startup called Balance Pharmaceuticals. The firm operates

out of a small white industrial strip mall next to the freeway in Santa Monica. One of the tenants is a paint store, another looks like some sort of export company. Balance's offices are housed in an oversized garage with a big overhead door and concrete floors. There is a tiny reception area, a little coffee table and a couch, and a warren of desks, bookshelves, filing cabinets, and computers. Balance is testing its formulation on a small group of women at high risk for breast cancer, and if the results continue to be encouraging, it will one day file for FDA approval.

"When I met Darcy Spicer a couple of years ago," Pike said recently, as he sat at a conference table deep in the Balance garage, "he said, 'Why don't we just try it out? By taking mammograms, we should be able to see changes in the breasts of women on this drug, even if we add back a little estrogen to avoid side effects.' So we did a study, and we found that there were huge changes." Pike pulled out a paper he and Spicer had published in the *Journal of the National Cancer Institute*, showing breast X-rays of three young women. "These are the mammograms of the women before they start," he said. Amid the grainy black outlines of the breast were large white fibrous clumps — clumps that Pike and Spicer believe are indicators of the kind of relentless cell division that increases breast-cancer risk. Next to those X-rays were three mammograms of the same women taken after a year on the GnRHA regimen. The clumps were almost entirely gone. "This to us represents that we have actually stopped the activity inside the breasts," Pike went on. "White is a proxy for cell proliferation. We're slowing down the breast."

Pike stood up from the table and turned to a sketch pad on an easel behind him. He quickly wrote a series of numbers on the paper. "Suppose a woman reaches menarche at

fifteen and menopause at fifty. That's thirty-five years of stimulating the breast. If you cut that time in half, you will change her risk not by half but by half raised to the power of 4.5." He was working with a statistical model he had developed to calculate breast-cancer risk. "That's one-twenty-third. Your risk of breast cancer will be one-twenty-third of what it would be otherwise. It won't be zero. You can't get to zero. If you use this for ten years, your risk will be cut by at least half. If you use it for five years, your risk will be cut by at least a third. It's as if your breast were to be five years younger, or ten years younger — *forever.*" The regimen, he says, should also provide protection against ovarian cancer.

Pike gave the sense that he had made this little speech many times before, to colleagues, to his family and friends — and to investors. He knew by now how strange and unbelievable what he was saying sounded. Here he was, in a cold, cramped garage in the industrial section of Santa Monica, arguing that he knew how to save the lives of hundreds of thousands of women around the world. And he wanted to do that by making young women menopausal through a chemical regimen sniffed every morning out of a bottle. This was, to say the least, a bold idea. Could he strike the right balance between the hormone levels women need to stay healthy and those that ultimately make them sick? Was progestin really so important in breast cancer? There are cancer specialists who remain skeptical. And, most of all, what would women think? John Rock, at least, had lent the cause of birth control his Old World manners and distinguished white hair and appeals from theology; he took pains to make the Pill seem like the least radical of interventions — nature's contraceptive, something that could be slipped inside a woman's purse and pass without notice. Pike was going to

take the whole forty-year mythology of *natural* and sweep it aside. "Women are going to think, I'm being manipulated here. And it's a perfectly reasonable thing to think." Pike's South African accent gets a little stronger as he becomes more animated. "But the modern way of living represents an extraordinary change in female biology. Women are going out and becoming lawyers, doctors, presidents of countries. They need to understand that what we are trying to do isn't abnormal. It's just as normal as when someone hundreds of years ago had menarche at seventeen and had five babies and had three hundred fewer menstrual cycles than most women have today. The world is not the world it was. And some of the risks that go with the benefits of a woman getting educated and not getting pregnant all the time are breast cancer and ovarian cancer, and we need to deal with it. I have three daughters. The earliest grandchild I had was when one of them was thirty-one. That's the way many women are now. They ovulate from twelve or thirteen until their early thirties. Twenty years of uninterrupted ovulation before their first child! That's a brand-new phenomenon!"

5.

John Rock's long battle on behalf of his birth-control pill forced the Church to take notice. In the spring of 1963, just after Rock's book was published, a meeting was held at the Vatican between high officials of the Catholic Church and Donald B. Straus, the chairman of Planned Parenthood. That summit was followed by another, on the campus of the University of Notre Dame. In the summer of 1964, on the eve of the feast of St. John the Baptist, Pope Paul VI announced that he would ask a committee of Church officials to reex-

amine the Vatican's position on contraception. The group met first at the Collegio San Jose, in Rome, and it was clear that a majority of the committee were in favor of approving the Pill. Committee reports leaked to the *National Catholic Register* confirmed that Rock's case appeared to be winning. Rock was elated. *Newsweek* put him on its cover, and ran a picture of the Pope inside. "Not since the Copernicans suggested in the sixteenth century that the sun was the center of the planetary system has the Roman Catholic Church found itself on such a perilous collision course with a new body of knowledge," the article concluded. Paul VI, however, was unmoved. He stalled, delaying a verdict for months, and then years. Some said he fell under the sway of conservative elements within the Vatican. In the interim, theologians began exposing the holes in Rock's arguments. The rhythm method "'prevents' conception by abstinence, that is, by the non-performance of the conjugal act during the fertile period," the Catholic journal *America* concluded in a 1964 editorial. "The Pill prevents conception by suppressing ovulation and by thus abolishing the fertile period. No amount of word juggling can make abstinence from sexual relations and the suppression of ovulation one and the same thing." On July 29, 1968, in the "Humanae Vitae" encyclical, the Pope broke his silence, declaring all "artificial" methods of contraception to be against the teachings of the Church.

In hindsight, it is possible to see the opportunity that Rock missed. If he had known what we know now and had talked about the Pill not as a contraceptive but as a cancer drug — not as a drug to prevent life but as one that would save life — the Church might well have said yes. Hadn't Pius XII already approved the Pill for therapeutic purposes? Rock would only have had to think of the Pill

as Pike thinks of it: as a drug whose contraceptive aspects are merely a means of attracting users, of getting, as Pike put it, "people who are young to take a lot of stuff they wouldn't otherwise take."

But Rock did not live long enough to understand how things might have been. What he witnessed, instead, was the terrible time at the end of the sixties when the Pill suddenly stood accused — wrongly — of causing blood clots, strokes, and heart attacks. Between the midseventies and the early eighties, the number of women in the United States using the Pill fell by half. Harvard Medical School, meanwhile, took over Rock's Reproductive Clinic and pushed him out. His Harvard pension paid him only seventy-five dollars a year. He had almost no money in the bank and had to sell his house in Brookline. In 1971, Rock left Boston and retreated to a farmhouse in the hills of New Hampshire. He swam in the stream behind the house. He listened to John Philip Sousa marches. In the evening, he would sit in the living room with a pitcher of martinis. In 1983, he gave his last public interview, and it was as if the memory of his achievements were now so painful that he had blotted it out.

He was asked what the most gratifying time of his life was. "Right now," the inventor of the Pill answered, incredibly. He was sitting by the fire in a crisp white shirt and tie, reading *The Origin*, Irving Stone's fictional account of the life of Darwin. "It frequently occurs to me, gosh, what a lucky guy I am. I have no responsibilities, and I have everything I want. I take a dose of equanimity every twenty minutes. I will not be disturbed about things."

Once, John Rock had gone to seven-o'clock Mass every morning and kept a crucifix above his desk. His

interviewer, the writer Sara Davidson, moved her chair closer to his and asked him whether he still believed in an afterlife.

"Of course I don't," Rock answered abruptly. Though he didn't explain why, his reasons aren't hard to imagine. The Church could not square the requirements of its faith with the results of his science, and if the Church couldn't reconcile them, how could Rock be expected to? John Rock always stuck to his conscience, and in the end his conscience forced him away from the thing he loved most. This was not John Rock's error. Nor was it his Church's. It was the fault of the haphazard nature of science, which all too often produces progress in advance of understanding. If the order of events in the discovery of what was natural had been reversed, his world, and our world, too, would have been a different place.

"Heaven and Hell, Rome, all the Church stuff — that's for the solace of the multitude," Rock said. He had only a year to live. "I was an ardent practicing Catholic for a long time, and I really believed it all then, you see."*

March 13, 2000

---

* Sometimes the gap between hearing an idea and figuring out how to write about it is substantial. In this case, it was almost a decade. While he was in medical school, my friend Chris Grover once pointed out to me that, from an evolutionary perspective, the experience of modern women was profoundly unusual. Up until the beginning of the nineteenth century, women of childbearing age rarely menstruated. Today, they menstruate all the time. I found that fascinating. But how on earth do you fashion a story around that fact? Then I discovered John Rock.

What the Dog Saw

CESAR MILLAN AND THE MOVEMENTS
OF MASTERY

1.

In the case of *Sugar v. Forman,* Cesar Millan knew none of
the facts before arriving at the scene of the crime. That is
the way Cesar prefers it. His job was to reconcile Forman
with Sugar, and, since Sugar was a good deal less adept in
making her case than Forman, whatever he learned beforehand might bias him in favor of the aggrieved party.

The Forman residence was in a trailer park in Mission
Hills, just north of Los Angeles. Dark wood paneling,
leather couches, deep-pile carpeting. The air-conditioning
was on, even though it was one of those ridiculously pris-
tine Southern California days. Lynda Forman was in her
sixties, possibly older, a handsome woman with a winning
sense of humor. Her husband, Ray, was in a wheelchair,
and looked vaguely ex-military. Cesar sat across from
them, in black jeans and a blue shirt, his posture characteristically perfect.

"So how can I help?" he said.

"You can help our monster turn into a sweet, lovable

dog," Lynda replied. It was clear that she had been thinking about how to describe Sugar to Cesar for a long time. "She's ninety percent bad, ten percent the love....She sleeps with us at night. She cuddles." Sugar meant a lot to Lynda. "But she grabs anything in sight that she can get, and tries to destroy it. My husband is disabled, and she destroys his room. She tears clothes. She's torn our carpet. She bothers my grandchildren. If I open the door, she will run." Lynda pushed back her sleeves and exposed her forearms. They were covered in so many bites and scratches and scars and scabs that it was as if she had been tortured. "But I love her. What can I say?"

Cesar looked at her arms and blinked. "Wow."

Cesar is not a tall man. He is built like a soccer player. He is in his midthirties, and has large, wide eyes, olive skin, and white teeth. He crawled across the border from Mexico fourteen years ago, but his English is exceptional, except when he gets excited and starts dropping his articles — which almost never happens, because he rarely gets excited. He saw the arms and he said, "Wow," but it was a "wow" in the same calm tone of voice as "So how can I help?"

Cesar began to ask questions. Did Sugar urinate in the house? She did. She had a particularly destructive relationship with newspapers, television remotes, and plastic cups. Cesar asked about walks. Did Sugar travel, or did she track — and when he said *track* he did an astonishing impersonation of a dog sniffing. Sugar tracked. What about discipline?

"Sometimes I put her in a crate," Lynda said. "And it's only for a fifteen-minute period. Then she lays down and she's fine. I don't know how to give discipline. Ask my kids."

"Did your parents discipline you?"

"I didn't need discipline. I was perfect."

"So you had no rules.... What about using physical touch with Sugar?"

"I have used it. It bothers me."

"What about the bites?"

"I can see it in the head. She gives me that look."

"She's reminding you who rules the roost."

"Then she will lick me for half an hour where she has bit me."

"She's not apologizing. Dogs lick each other's wounds to heal the pack, you know."

Lynda looked a little lost. "I thought she was saying sorry."

"If she was sorry," Cesar said softly, "she wouldn't do it in the first place."

It was time for the defendant. Lynda's granddaughter, Carly, came in, holding a beagle as if it were a baby. Sugar was cute, but she had a mean, feral look in her eyes. Carly put Sugar on the carpet, and Sugar swaggered over to Cesar, sniffing his shoes. In front of her, Cesar placed a newspaper, a plastic cup, and a television remote.

Sugar grabbed the newspaper. Cesar snatched it back. Sugar picked up the newspaper again. She jumped on the couch. Cesar took his hand and "bit" Sugar on the shoulder, firmly and calmly. "My hand is the mouth," he explained. "My fingers are the teeth." Sugar jumped down. Cesar stood, and firmly and fluidly held Sugar down for an instant. Sugar struggled, briefly, then relaxed. Cesar backed off. Sugar lunged at the remote. Cesar looked at her and said, simply and briefly, "Sh-h-h." Sugar hesitated. She went for the plastic cup. Cesar said, "Sh-h-h." She dropped it. Cesar motioned

for Lynda to bring a jar of treats into the room. He placed it in the middle of the floor and hovered over it. Sugar looked at the treats and then at Cesar. She began sniffing, inching closer, but an invisible boundary now stood between her and the prize. She circled and circled but never came closer than three feet. She looked as if she were about to jump on the couch. Cesar shifted his weight, and blocked her. He took a step toward her. She backed up, head lowered, into the furthest corner of the room. She sank down on her haunches, then placed her head flat on the ground. Cesar took the treats, the remote, the plastic cup, and the newspaper and placed them inches from her lowered nose. Sugar, the onetime terror of Mission Hills, closed her eyes in surrender.

"She has no rules in the outside world, no boundaries," Cesar said, finally. "You practice exercise and affection. But you're not practicing exercise, discipline, and affection. When we love someone, we fulfill everything about them. That's loving. And you're not loving your dog." He stood up. He looked around.

"Let's go for a walk."

Lynda staggered into the kitchen. In five minutes, her monster had turned into an angel. "Unbelievable," she said.

2.

Cesar Millan runs the Dog Psychology Center out of a converted auto mechanic's shop in the industrial zone of South-Central Los Angeles. The center is situated at the end of a long narrow alley, off a busy street lined with bleak warehouses and garages. Behind a high green chain-link fence is a large concrete yard, and everywhere around the yard there are dogs. Dogs basking in the sun. Dogs

splashing in a pool. Dogs lying on picnic tables. Cesar takes in people's problem dogs; he keeps them for a minimum of two weeks, integrating them into the pack. He has no formal training. He learned what he knows growing up in Mexico on his grandfather's farm in Sinaloa. As a child, he was called el Perrero, "the dog boy," watching and studying until he felt that he could put himself inside the mind of a dog. In the mornings, Cesar takes the pack on a four-hour walk in the Santa Monica mountains: Cesar in front, the dogs behind him; the pit bulls and the Rottweilers and the German shepherds with backpacks, so that when the little dogs get tired Cesar can load them up on the big dogs' backs. Then they come back and eat. Exercise, then food. Work, then reward.

"I have forty-seven dogs right now," Cesar said. He opened the door, and they came running over, a jumble of dogs, big and small. Cesar pointed to a bloodhound. "He was aggressive with humans, really aggressive," he said. In a corner of the compound, a Wheaton terrier had just been given a bath. "She's stayed here six months because she could not trust men," Cesar explained. "She was beat up severely." He idly scratched a big German shepherd. "My girlfriend here, Beauty. If you were to see the relationship between her and her owner." He shook his head. "A very sick relationship. A *Fatal Attraction* kind of thing. Beauty sees her and she starts scratching her and biting her, and the owner is, like, 'I love you, too.' That one killed a dog. That one killed a dog, too. Those two guys came from New Orleans. They attacked humans. That pit bull over there with a tennis ball killed a Labrador in Beverly Hills. And look at this one — one eye. Lost the eye in a dogfight. But look at him now." Now he was nuzzling a French bulldog.

He was happy, and so was the Labrador killer from Beverly Hills, who was stretched out in the sun, and so was the aggressive-toward-humans bloodhound, who was lingering by a picnic table with his tongue hanging out. Cesar stood in the midst of all the dogs, his back straight and his shoulders square. It was a prison yard. But it was the most peaceful prison yard in all of California. "The whole point is that everybody has to stay calm, submissive, no matter what," he said. "What you are witnessing right now is a group of dogs who all have the same state of mind."

Cesar Millan is the host of *Dog Whisperer*, on the National Geographic television channel. In every episode, he arrives amid canine chaos and leaves behind peace. He is the teacher we all had in grade school who could walk into a classroom filled with rambunctious kids and get everyone to calm down and behave. But what did that teacher have? If you'd asked us back then, we might have said that we behaved for Mr. Exley because Mr. Exley had lots of rules and was really strict. But the truth is that we behaved for Mr. DeBock as well, and he wasn't strict at all. What we really mean is that both of them had that indefinable thing called presence — and if you are going to teach a classroom full of headstrong ten-year-olds, or run a company, or command an army, or walk into a trailer home in Mission Hills where a beagle named Sugar is terrorizing its owners, you have to have presence or you're lost.

Behind the Dog Psychology Center, between the back fence and the walls of the adjoining buildings, Cesar has built a dog run — a stretch of grass and dirt as long as a city block. "This is our Chuck E. Cheese," Cesar said. The dogs saw Cesar approaching the back gate, and they ran, expectantly, toward him, piling through the narrow door

in a hodgepodge of whiskers and wagging tails. Cesar had a bag over his shoulder, filled with tennis balls, and a long orange plastic ball scoop in his right hand. He reached into the bag with the scoop, grabbed a tennis ball, and flung it in a smooth practiced motion off the wall of an adjoining warehouse. A dozen dogs set off in ragged pursuit. Cesar wheeled and threw another ball, in the opposite direction, and then a third, and then a fourth, until there were so many balls in the air and on the ground that the pack had turned into a yelping, howling, leaping, charging frenzy. Woof. Woof, woof, woof. Woof.

"The game should be played five or ten minutes, maybe fifteen minutes," Cesar said. "You begin. You end. And you don't ask, 'Please stop.' You demand that it stop." With that, Cesar gathered himself, stood stock still, and let out a short whistle: not a casual whistle but a whistle of authority. Suddenly, there was absolute quiet. All forty-seven dogs stopped charging and jumping and stood as still as Cesar, their heads erect, eyes trained on their ring-leader. Cesar nodded, almost imperceptibly, toward the enclosure, and all forty-seven dogs turned and filed happily back through the gate.

3.

In the fall of 2005, Cesar filmed an episode of *Dog Whisperer* at the Los Angeles home of a couple named Patrice and Scott. They had a Korean jindo named JonBee, a stray that they had found and adopted. Outside, and on walks, JonBee was well behaved and affectionate. Inside the house, he was a terror, turning viciously on Scott whenever he tried to get the dog to submit.

"Help us tame the wild beast," Scott says to Cesar. "We've had two trainers come out, one of whom was doing this domination thing, where he would put JonBee on his back and would hold him until he submits. It went on for a good twenty minutes. This dog never let up. But, as soon as he let go, JonBee bit him four times.... The guy was bleeding, both hands and his arms. I had another trainer come out, too, and they said, 'You've got to get rid of this dog.'"

Cesar goes outside to meet JonBee. He walks down a few steps to the backyard. Cesar crouches down next to the dog. "The owner was a little concerned about me coming here by myself," he says. "To tell you the truth, I feel more comfortable with aggressive dogs than insecure dogs, or fearful dogs, or panicky dogs. These are actually the guys who put me on the map."

JonBee comes up and sniffs him. Cesar puts a leash on him. JonBee eyes Cesar nervously and starts to poke around. Cesar then walks JonBee into the living room. Scott puts a muzzle on him. Cesar tries to get the dog to lie on its side — and all hell breaks loose. JonBee turns and snaps and squirms and spins and jumps and lunges and struggles. His muzzle falls off. He bites Cesar. He twists his body up into the air, in a cold, vicious fury. The struggle between the two goes on and on. Patrice covers her face. Cesar asks her to leave the room. He is standing up, leash extended. He looks like a wrangler, taming a particularly ornery rattlesnake. Sweat is streaming down his face. Finally, Cesar gets the dog to sit, then to lie down, and then, somehow, to lie on its side. JonBee slumps, defeated. Cesar massages Jon-Bee's stomach. "That's all we wanted," he says.

What happened between Cesar and JonBee? One explanation is that they had a fight, alpha male versus alpha

male. But fights don't come out of nowhere. JonBee was clearly reacting to something in Cesar. Before he fought, he sniffed and explored and watched Cesar — the last of which is most important, because everything we know about dogs suggests that, in a way that is true of almost no other animals, dogs are students of human movement.

The anthropologist Brian Hare has done experiments with dogs, for example, where he puts a piece of food under one of two cups, placed several feet apart. The dog knows that there is food to be had, but has no idea which of the cups holds the prize. Then Hare points at the right cup, taps on it, looks directly at it. What happens? The dog goes to the right cup virtually every time. Yet when Hare did the same experiment with chimpanzees — an animal that shares 98.6 percent of our genes — the chimps couldn't get it right. A dog will look at you for help, and a chimp won't.

"Primates are very good at using the cues of the same species," Hare explained. "So if we were able to do a similar game, and it was a chimp or another primate giving a social cue, they might do better. But they are not good at using human cues when you are trying to cooperate with them. They don't get it: 'Why would you ever tell me where the food is?' The key specialization of dogs, though, is that dogs pay attention to humans, when humans are doing something very human, which is sharing information about something that someone else might actually want." Dogs aren't smarter than chimps; they just have a different attitude toward people. "Dogs are really interested in humans," Hare went on. " Interested to the point of obsession. To a dog, you are a giant walking tennis ball."

A dog cares, deeply, which way your body is leaning. Forward or backward? Forward can be seen as aggressive;

backward — even a quarter of an inch — means nonthreatening. It means you've relinquished what ethologists call an *intention movement* to proceed forward. Cock your head, even slightly, to the side, and a dog is disarmed. Look at him straight on and he'll read it like a red flag. Standing straight, with your shoulders squared, rather than slumped, can mean the difference between whether your dog obeys a command or ignores it. Breathing even and deeply — rather than holding your breath — can mean the difference between defusing a tense situation and igniting it. "I think they are looking at our eyes and where our eyes are looking, and what our eyes look like," the ethologist Patricia McConnell, who teaches at the University of Wisconsin, Madison, says. "A rounded eye with a dilated pupil is a sign of high arousal and aggression in a dog. I believe they pay a tremendous amount of attention to how relaxed our face is and how relaxed our facial muscles are, because that's a big cue for them with each other. Is the jaw relaxed? Is the mouth slightly open? And then the arms. They pay a tremendous amount of attention to where our arms go."

In the book *The Other End of the Leash,* McConnell decodes one of the most common of all human-dog interactions — the meeting between two leashed animals on a walk. To us, it's about one dog sizing up another. To her, it's about two dogs sizing up each other after first sizing up their respective owners. The owners "are often anxious about how well the dogs will get along," she writes, "and if you watch them instead of the dogs, you'll often notice that the humans will hold their breath and round their eyes and mouths in an 'on alert' expression. Since these behaviors are expressions of offensive aggression in canine culture, I suspect that the humans are unwittingly

signaling tension. If you exaggerate this by tightening the leash, as many owners do, you can actually cause the dogs to attack each other. Think of it: the dogs are in a tense social encounter, surrounded by support from their own pack, with the humans forming a tense, staring, breathless circle around them. I don't know how many times I've seen dogs shift their eyes toward their owner's frozen faces, and then launch growling at the other dog."

When Cesar walked down the stairs of Patrice and Scott's home, then, and crouched down in the backyard, JonBee looked at him, intently. And what he saw was someone who moved in a very particular way. Cesar is fluid. "He's beautifully organized intraphysically," Karen Bradley, who heads the graduate dance program at the University of Maryland, said when she first saw tapes of Cesar in action. "That lower-unit organization — I wonder whether he was a soccer player." Movement experts like Bradley use something called Laban Movement Analysis to make sense of movement, describing, for instance, how people shift their weight, or how fluid and symmetrical they are when they move, or what kind of *effort* it involves. Is it direct or indirect — that is, what kind of attention does the movement convey? Is it quick or slow? Is it strong or light — that is, what is its intention? Is it bound or free — that is, how much precision is involved? If you want to emphasize a point, you might bring your hand down across your body in a single, smooth motion. But how you make that motion greatly affects how your point will be interpreted by your audience. Ideally, your hand would come down in an explosive, bound movement — that is, with accelerating force, ending abruptly and precisely — and your head and shoulders would

descend simultaneously, so posture and gesture would be in harmony. Suppose, though, that your head and shoulders moved upward as your hand came down, or your hand came down in a free, implosive manner — that is, with a kind of a vague, decelerating force. Now your movement suggests that you are making a point on which we all agree, which is the opposite of your intention. Combinations of posture and gesture are called *phrasing*, and the great communicators are those who match their phrasing with their communicative intentions — who understand, for instance, that emphasis requires them to be bound and explosive. To Bradley, Cesar had beautiful phrasing.

There he is, talking to Patrice and Scott. He has his hands in front of him, in what Laban analysts call the sagittal plane — that is, the area directly in front of and behind the torso. He then leans forward for emphasis. But as he does, he lowers his hands to waist level, and draws them toward his body, to counterbalance the intrusion of his posture. And, when he leans backward again, the hands rise up, to fill the empty space. It's not the kind of thing you'd ever notice. But, when it's pointed out, its emotional meaning is unmistakable. It is respectful and reassuring. It communicates without being intrusive. Bradley was watching Cesar with the sound off, and there was one sequence she returned to again and again, in which Cesar was talking to a family, and his right hand swung down in a graceful arc across his chest. "He's dancing," Bradley said. "Look at that. It's gorgeous. It's such a gorgeous little dance.

"The thing is, his phrases are of mixed length," she went on. "Some of them are long. Some of them are very short. Some of them are explosive phrases, loaded up in the beginning and then trailing off. Some of them are

impactive — building up, and then coming to a sense of impact at the end. What they are is appropriate to the task. That's what I mean by *versatile.*"

Movement analysts tend to like watching, say, Bill Clinton or Ronald Reagan; they had great phrasing. George W. Bush does not. During this year's State of the Union address, Bush spent the entire speech swaying metronomically, straight down through his lower torso, a movement underscored, unfortunately, by the presence of a large vertical banner behind him. "Each shift ended with this focus that channels toward a particular place in the audience," Bradley said. She mimed, perfectly, the Bush gaze — the squinty, fixated look he reserves for moments of great solemnity — and gently swayed back and forth. "It's a little primitive, a little regressed." The combination of the look, the sway, and the gaze was, to her mind, distinctly adolescent. When people say of Bush that he seems eternally boyish, this is in part what they're referring to. He moves like a boy, which is fine, except that, unlike such movement masters as Reagan and Clinton, he can't stop moving like a boy when the occasion demands a more grown-up response.

"Mostly what we see in the normal population is undifferentiated phrasing," Bradley said. "And then you have people who are clearly preferential in their phrases, like my husband. He's Mr. Horizontal. When he's talking in a meeting, he's back. He's open. He just goes into this, this same long thing" — she leaned back, and spread her arms out wide and slowed her speech — "and it doesn't change very much. He works with people who understand him, fortunately." She laughed. "When we meet someone like this" — she nodded at Cesar, on the television screen — "what do we do? We give them their own TV series. Seriously. We reward

them. We are drawn to them, because we can trust that we can get the message. It's not going to be hidden. It contributes to a feeling of authenticity."

4.

Back to JonBee, from the beginning — only this time with the sound off. Cesar walks down the stairs. It's not the same Cesar who whistled and brought forty-seven dogs to attention. This occasion calls for subtlety. "Did you see the way he walks? He drops his hands. They're close to his side." The analyst this time was Suzi Tortora, the author of *The Dancing Dialogue*. Tortora is a New York dance-movement psychotherapist, a tall, lithe woman with long dark hair and beautiful phrasing. She was in her office on lower Broadway, a large, empty, paneled room. "He's very vertical," Tortora said. "His legs are right under his torso. He's not taking up any space. And he slows down his gait. He's telling the dog, 'I'm here by myself. I'm not going to rush. I haven't introduced myself yet. Here I am. You can feel me.'" Cesar crouches down next to JonBee. His body is perfectly symmetrical, the center of gravity low. He looks stable, as though you couldn't knock him over, which conveys a sense of calm.

JonBee was investigating Cesar, squirming nervously. When JonBee got too jumpy, Cesar would correct him, with a tug on the leash. Because Cesar was talking and the correction was so subtle, it was easy to miss. Stop. Rewind. Play. "Do you see how rhythmic it is?" Tortora said. "He pulls. He waits. He pulls. He waits. He pulls. He waits. The phrasing is so lovely. It's predictable. To a dog that is all over the place, he's bringing a rhythm. But it isn't a

panicked rhythm. It has a moderate tempo to it. There was room to wander. And it's not attack, attack. It wasn't long and sustained. It was quick and light. I would bet that with dogs like this, where people are so afraid of them being aggressive and so defensive around them, there is a lot of aggressive strength directed at them. There is no aggression here. He's using strength without it being aggressive."

Cesar moves into the living room. The fight begins. "Look how he involves the dog," Tortora said. "He's letting the dog lead. He's giving the dog room." This was not a Secret Service agent wrestling an assailant to the ground. Cesar had his body vertical, and his hand high above JonBee holding the leash, and, as JonBee turned and snapped and squirmed and spun and jumped and lunged and struggled, Cesar seemed to be moving along with him, providing a loose structure for his aggression. It may have looked like a fight, but Cesar wasn't fighting. And what was JonBee doing? Child psychologists talk about the idea of regulation. If you expose healthy babies, repeatedly, to a very loud noise, eventually they will be able to fall asleep. They'll become habituated to the noise: the first time the noise is disruptive, but, by the second or third time, they've learned to handle the disruption, and block it out. They've regulated themselves. Children throwing tantrums are said to be in a state of dysregulation. They've been knocked off kilter in some way, and cannot bring themselves back to baseline. JonBee was dysregulated. He wasn't fighting; he was throwing a tantrum. And Cesar was the understanding parent. When JonBee paused, to catch his breath, Cesar paused with him. When JonBee bit Cesar, Cesar brought his finger to his mouth, instinctively, but in a smooth and fluid and calm motion that betrayed

no anxiety. "Timing is a big part of Cesar's repertoire," Tortora went on. "His movements right now aren't complex. There aren't a lot of efforts together at one time. His range of movement qualities is limited. Look at how he's narrowing. Now he's enclosing." As JonBee calmed down, Cesar began caressing him. His touch was firm but not aggressive; not so strong as to be abusive and not so light as to be insubstantial and irritating. Using the language of movement — the plainest and most transparent of all languages — Cesar was telling JonBee that he was safe. Now JonBee was lying on his side, mouth relaxed, tongue out. "Look at that, look at the dog's face," Tortora said. This was not defeat; this was relief.

Later, when Cesar tried to show Scott how to placate JonBee, Scott couldn't do it, and Cesar made him stop. "You're still nervous," Cesar told him. "You are still unsure. That's how you become a target." It isn't as easy as it sounds to calm a dog. "There, there" in a soothing voice, accompanied by a nice belly scratch, wasn't enough for JonBee, because he was reading gesture and posture and symmetry and the precise meaning of touch. He was looking for clarity and consistency. Scott didn't have it. "Look at the tension and aggression in his face," Tortora said, when the camera turned to Scott. It was true. Scott had a long and craggy face, with high, wide cheekbones and pronounced lips, and his movements were taut and twitchy. "There's a bombardment of actions, quickness combined with tension, a quality in how he is using his eyes and focus — a darting," Tortora said. "He gesticulates in a way that is complex. There is a lot going on. So many different qualities of movement happening at the same time. It leads those who watch him to get distracted." Scott is a character actor, with a list of credits

going back thirty years. The tension and aggression in his manner made him interesting and complicated — which works for Hollywood but doesn't work for a troubled dog. Scott said he loved JonBee, but the quality of his movement did not match his emotions.

For a number of years, Tortora has worked with Eric (not his real name), an autistic boy with severe language and communication problems. Tortora videotaped some of their sessions, and in one, four months after they started to work together, Eric is standing in the middle of Tortora's studio in Cold Spring, New York, a beautiful dark-haired three-and-a-half-year-old wearing only a diaper. His mother is sitting to the side, against the wall. In the background, you can hear the sound track to *Riverdance,* which happens to be Eric's favorite album. Eric is having a tantrum.

He gets up and runs toward the stereo. Then he runs back and throws himself down on his stomach, arms and legs flailing. Tortora throws herself down on the ground, just as he did. He sits up. She sits up. He twists. She twists. He squirms. She squirms. "When Eric is running around, I didn't say, 'Let's put on quiet music.' I can't turn him off, because he can't turn off," Tortora said. "He can't go from zero to sixty and then back down to zero. With a typical child, you might say, 'Take a deep breath. Reason with me' — and that might work. But not with children like this. They are in their world by themselves. I have to go in there and meet them and bring them back out."

Tortora sits up on her knees, and faces Eric. His legs are moving in every direction, and she takes his feet in her hands. Slowly, and subtly, she begins to move his legs in time with the music. Eric gets up and runs to the corner

of the room and back again. Tortora gets up and mirrors his action, but this time she moves more fluidly and gracefully than he did. She takes his feet again. This time, she moves Eric's entire torso, opening the pelvis in a contralateral twist. "I'm standing above him, looking directly at him. I am very symmetrical. So I'm saying to him, 'I'm stable. I'm here. I'm calm.' I'm holding him at the knees and giving him sensory input. It's firm and clear. Touch is an incredible tool. It's another way to speak."

She starts to rock his knees from side to side. Eric begins to calm down. He begins to make slight adjustments to the music. His legs move more freely, more lyrically. His movement is starting to get organized. He goes back into his mother's arms. He's still upset, but his cry has softened. Tortora sits and faces him — stable, symmetrical, direct eye contact.

His mother says, "You need a tissue?"

Eric nods.

Tortora brings him a tissue. Eric's mother says that she needs a tissue. Eric gives his tissue to his mother.

"Can we dance?" Tortora asks him.

"OK," he says in a small voice.

It was impossible to see Tortora with Eric and not think of Cesar with JonBee: here was the same extraordinary energy and intelligence and personal force marshaled on behalf of the helpless, the same calm in the face of chaos, and, perhaps most surprising, the same gentleness. When we talk about people with presence, we often assume that they have a strong personality — that they sweep us all up in their own personal whirlwind. Our model is the Pied Piper, who played his irresistible tune and every child in Hamelin blindly followed. But Cesar

Millan and Suzi Tortora play different tunes, in different situations. And they don't turn their back, and expect others to follow. Cesar let JonBee lead; Tortora's approaches to Eric were dictated by Eric. Presence is not just versatile; it's also reactive. Certain people, we say, "command our attention," but the verb is all wrong. There is no commanding, only soliciting. The dogs in the dog run wanted someone to tell them when to start and stop; they were refugees from anarchy and disorder. Eric wanted to enjoy *Riverdance*. It was his favorite music. Tortora did not say, "Let us dance." She asked, "Can we dance?"

Then Tortora gets a drum and starts to play. Eric's mother stands up and starts to circle the room, in an Irish step dance. Eric is lying on the ground, and slowly his feet start to tap in time with the music. He gets up. He walks to the corner of the room, disappears behind a partition, and then reenters, triumphant. He begins to dance, playing an imaginary flute as he circles the room.

5.

When Cesar was twenty-one, he traveled from his hometown to Tijuana, and a "coyote" took him across the border for a hundred dollars. They waited in a hole, up to their chests in water, and then ran over the mudflats, through a junkyard, and across a freeway. A taxi took him to San Diego. After a month on the streets, grimy and dirty, he walked into a dog-grooming salon and got a job, working with the difficult cases and sleeping in the offices at night. He moved to Los Angeles, and took a day job detailing limousines while he ran his dog-psychology business out of a white Chevy Astrovan. When he was twenty-three,

he fell in love with an American girl named Illusion. She was seventeen, small, dark, and very beautiful. A year later, they got married.

"Cesar was a machoistic, egocentric person who thought the world revolved around him," Illusion recalled, of their first few years together. "His view was that marriage was where a man tells a woman what to do. Never give affection. Never give compassion or understanding. Marriage is about keeping the man happy, and that's where it ends."

Early in their marriage, Illusion got sick, and was in the hospital for three weeks. "Cesar visited once, for less than two hours," she said. "I thought to myself, This relationship is not working out. He just wanted to be with his dogs." They had a new baby and no money. They separated. Illusion told Cesar that she would divorce him if he didn't get into therapy. He agreed, reluctantly. "The therapist's name was Wilma," Illusion went on. "She was a strong African American woman. She said, 'You want your wife to take care of you, to clean the house. Well, she wants something, too. She wants your affection and love.'" Illusion remembers Cesar scribbling furiously on a pad. "He wrote that down. He said, 'That's it! It's like the dogs. They need exercise, discipline, and affection.'" Illusion laughed. "I looked at him, upset, because why the hell are you talking about your dogs when you should be talking about us?"

"I was fighting it," Cesar said. "Two women against me, blah, blah, blah. I had to get rid of the fight in my mind. That was very difficult. But that's when the light-bulb came on. Women have their own psychology."

Cesar could calm a stray off the street, yet, at least in the beginning, he did not grasp the simplest of truths about

his own wife. "Cesar related to dogs because he didn't feel connected to people," Illusion said. "His dogs were his way of feeling like he belonged in the world, because he wasn't people-friendly. And it was hard for him to get out of that." In Mexico, on his grandfather's farm, dogs were dogs and humans were humans: each knew its place. But in America, dogs were treated like children, and owners had shaken up the hierarchy of human and animal. Sugar's problem was Lynda. JonBee's problem was Scott. Cesar calls that epiphany in the therapist's office the most important moment in his life, because it was the moment when he understood that to succeed in the world he could not be just a dog whisperer. He needed to be a people whisperer.

For his show, Cesar once took a case involving a Chihuahua named Bandit. Bandit had a large, rapper-style diamond-encrusted necklace around his neck spelling "Stud." His owner was Lori, a voluptuous woman with an oval face and large, pleading eyes. Bandit was out of control, terrorizing guests and menacing other dogs. Three trainers had failed to get him under control.

Lori was on the couch in her living room as she spoke to Cesar. Bandit was sitting in her lap. Her teenage son, Tyler, was sitting next to her.

"About two weeks after his first visit with the vet, he started to lose a lot of hair," Lori said. "They said that he had Demodex mange." Bandit had been sold to her as a show-quality dog, she recounted, but she had the bloodline checked and learned that he had come from a puppy mill. "He didn't have any human contact," she went on. "So for three months he was getting dipped every week to try to get rid of the symptoms." As she spoke, her hands gently encased Bandit. "He would hide inside my shirt

and lay his head right by my heart, and stay there." Her eyes were moist. "He was right here on my chest."

"So your husband cooperated?" Cesar asked. He was focused on Lori, not on Bandit. This is what the new Cesar understood that the old Cesar did not.

"He was our baby. He was in need of being nurtured and helped and he was so scared all the time."

"Do you still feel the need of feeling sorry about him?"

"Yeah. He's so cute."

Cesar seemed puzzled. He didn't know why Lori would still feel sorry for her dog.

Lori tried to explain. "He's so small and he's helpless."

"But do you believe that he feels helpless?"

Lori still had her hands over the dog, stroking him. Tyler was looking at Cesar, and then at his mother, and then down at Bandit. Bandit tensed. Tyler reached over to touch the dog, and Bandit leaped out of Lori's arms and attacked him, barking and snapping and growling. Tyler, startled, jumped back. Lori, alarmed, reached out, and — this was the critical thing — put her hands around Bandit in a worried, caressing motion, and lifted him back into her lap. It happened in an instant.

Cesar stood up. "Give me the space," he said, gesturing for Tyler to move aside. "Enough dogs attacking humans, and humans not really blocking him, so he is only becoming more narcissistic. It is all about him. He owns you." Cesar was about as angry as he ever gets. "It seems like you are favoring the dog, and hopefully that is not the truth....If Tyler kicked the dog, you would correct him. The dog is biting your son, and you are not correcting hard enough." Cesar was in emphatic mode now,

his phrasing sure and unambiguous. "I don't understand why you are not putting two and two together."

Bandit was nervous. He started to back up on the couch. He started to bark. Cesar gave him a look out of the corner of his eye. Bandit shrank. Cesar kept talking. Bandit came at Cesar. Cesar stood up. "I have to touch," he said, and he gave Bandit a sharp nudge with his elbow. Lori looked horrifed.

Cesar laughed, incredulously. "You are saying that it is fair for him to touch us but not fair for us to touch him?" he asked. Lori leaned forward to object. "You don't like that, do you?" Cesar said, in his frustration speaking to the whole room now. "It's not going to work. This is a case that is not going to work, because the owner doesn't want to allow what you normally do with your kids.... The hardest part for me is that the father or mother chooses the dog instead of the son. That's hard for me. I love dogs. I'm the dog whisperer. You follow what I'm saying? But I would never choose a dog over my son."

He stopped. He had had enough of talking. There was too much talking anyhow. People saying "I love you" with a touch that didn't mean "I love you." People saying "There, there" with gestures that did not soothe. People saying "I'm your mother" while reaching out to a Chihuahua instead of their own flesh and blood. Tyler looked stricken. Lori shifted nervously in her seat. Bandit growled. Cesar turned to the dog and said "Sh-h-h." And everyone was still.

May 22, 2006

Part Two

THEORIES, PREDICTIONS, AND DIAGNOSES

*"It was like driving down an interstate
looking through a soda straw."*

Open Secrets

ENRON, INTELLIGENCE, AND THE PERILS OF
TOO MUCH INFORMATION

1.

On the afternoon of October 23, 2006, Jeffrey Skilling sat at a table at the front of a federal courtroom in Houston, Texas. He was wearing a navy blue suit and a tie. He was fifty-two years old, but looked older. Huddled around him were eight lawyers from his defense team. Outside, television-satellite trucks were parked up and down the block.

"We are here this afternoon," Judge Simeon Lake began, "for sentencing in *United States of America versus Jeffrey K. Skilling*, Criminal Case Number H-04-25." He addressed the defendant directly: "Mr. Skilling, you may now make a statement and present any information in mitigation."

Skilling stood up. Enron, the company he had built into an energy-trading leviathan, had collapsed into bankruptcy almost exactly five years before. In May, he had been convicted by a jury of fraud. Under a settlement agreement, almost everything he owned had been turned over to a fund to compensate former shareholders.

He spoke haltingly, stopping in midsentence. "In terms of remorse, Your Honor, I can't imagine more remorse," he said. He had "friends who have died, good men." He was innocent — "innocent of every one of these charges." He spoke for two or three minutes and sat down.

Judge Lake called on Anne Beliveaux, who worked as the senior administrative assistant in Enron's tax department for eighteen years. She was one of nine people who had asked to address the sentencing hearing.

"How would you like to be facing living off of sixteen hundred dollars a month, and that is what I'm facing," she said to Skilling. Her retirement savings had been wiped out by the Enron bankruptcy. "And, Mr. Skilling, that only is because of greed, nothing but greed. And you should be ashamed of yourself."

The next witness said that Skilling had destroyed a good company, the third witness that Enron had been undone by the misconduct of its management; another lashed out at Skilling directly. "Mr. Skilling has proven to be a liar, a thief, and a drunk," a woman named Dawn Powers Martin, a twenty-two-year veteran of Enron, told the court. "Mr. Skilling has cheated me and my daughter of our retirement dreams. Now it's his time to be robbed of his freedom to walk the earth as a free man." She turned to Skilling and said, "While you dine on Chateaubriand and champagne, my daughter and I clip grocery coupons and eat leftovers." And on and on it went.

The judge asked Skilling to rise.

"The evidence established that the defendant repeatedly lied to investors, including Enron's own employees, about various aspects of Enron's business," the judge said. He had no choice but to be harsh: Skilling would serve

292 months in prison — twenty-four years. The man who headed a firm that *Fortune* ranked among the "most admired" in the world had received one of the heaviest sentences ever given to a white-collar criminal. He would leave prison an old man, if he left prison at all.

"I only have one request, Your Honor," Daniel Petrocelli, Skilling's lawyer, said. "If he received ten fewer months, which shouldn't make a difference in terms of the goals of sentencing, if you do the math and you subtract fifteen percent for good time, he then qualifies under Bureau of Prisons policies to be able to serve his time at a lower facility. Just a ten-month reduction in sentence…"

It was a plea for leniency. Skilling wasn't a murderer or a rapist. He was a pillar of the Houston community, and a small adjustment in his sentence would keep him from spending the rest of his life among hardened criminals.

"No," Judge Lake said.

2.

The national security expert Gregory Treverton has famously made a distinction between puzzles and mysteries. Osama bin Laden's whereabouts are a puzzle. We can't find him because we don't have enough information. The key to the puzzle will probably come from someone close to bin Laden, and until we can find that source, bin Laden will remain at large.

The problem of what would happen in Iraq after the toppling of Saddam Hussein was, by contrast, a mystery. It wasn't a question that had a simple, factual answer. Mysteries require judgments and the assessment of uncertainty, and the hard part is not that we have too little information

but that we have too much. The CIA had a position on what a post-invasion Iraq would look like, and so did the Pentagon and the State Department and Colin Powell and Dick Cheney and any number of political scientists and journalists and think tank fellows. For that matter, so did every cabdriver in Baghdad.

The distinction is not trivial. If you consider the motivation and methods behind the attacks of September 11 to be mainly a puzzle, for instance, then the logical response is to increase the collection of intelligence, recruit more spies, add to the volume of information we have about Al Qaeda. If you consider September 11 a mystery, though, you'd have to wonder whether adding to the volume of information will only make things worse. You'd want to improve the analysis within the intelligence community; you'd want more thoughtful and skeptical people with the skills to look more closely at what we already know about Al Qaeda. You'd want to send the counterterrorism team from the CIA on a golfing trip twice a month with the counterterrorism teams from the FBI and the NSA and the Defense Department, so they could get to know one another and compare notes.

If things go wrong with a puzzle, identifying the culprit is easy: it's the person who withheld information. Mysteries, though, are a lot murkier: sometimes the information we've been given is inadequate, and sometimes we aren't very smart about making sense of what we've been given, and sometimes the question itself cannot be answered. Puzzles come to satisfying conclusions. Mysteries often don't.

If you sat through the trial of Jeffrey Skilling, you'd think that the Enron scandal was a puzzle. The company,

the prosecution said, conducted shady side deals that no one quite understood. Senior executives withheld critical information from investors. Skilling, the architect of the firm's strategy, was a liar, a thief, and a drunk. *We were not told enough* — the classic puzzle premise — was the central assumption of the Enron prosecution.

"This is a simple case, ladies and gentlemen," the lead prosecutor for the Department of Justice said in his closing arguments to the jury:

> Because it's so simple, I'm probably going to end before my allotted time. It's black-and-white. Truth and lies. The shareholders, ladies and gentlemen…buy a share of stock, and for that they're not entitled to much but they're entitled to the truth. They're entitled for the officers and employees of the company to put their interests ahead of their own. They're entitled to be told what the financial condition of the company is. They are entitled to honesty, ladies and gentlemen.

But the prosecutor was wrong. Enron wasn't really a puzzle. It was a mystery.

3.

In late July of 2000, Jonathan Weil, a reporter at the Dallas bureau of the *Wall Street Journal,* got a call from someone he knew in the investment-management business. Weil wrote the stock column called "Heard in Texas" for the paper's regional edition, and he had been closely following the big energy firms based in Houston — Dynegy, El Paso, and Enron. His caller had a suggestion. "He said,

'You really ought to check out Enron and Dynegy and see where their earnings come from,'" Weil recalled. "So I did."

Weil was interested in Enron's use of what is called *mark-to-market accounting*, which is a technique used by companies that engage in complicated financial trading. Suppose, for instance, that you are an energy company and you enter into a $100 million contract with the state of California to deliver a billion kilowatt hours of electricity in 2016. How much is that contract worth? You aren't going to get paid for another ten years, and you aren't going to know until then whether you'll show a profit on the deal or a loss. Nonetheless, that $100 million promise clearly matters to your bottom line. If electricity steadily drops in price over the next several years, the contract is going to become a hugely valuable asset. But if electricity starts to get more expensive as 2016 approaches, you could be out tens of millions of dollars. With mark-to-market accounting, you estimate how much revenue the deal is going to bring in and put that number in your books at the moment you sign the contract. If, down the line, the estimate changes, you adjust the balance sheet accordingly.

When a company using mark-to-market accounting says it has made a profit of $10 million on revenues of $100 million, then, it could mean one of two things. The company may actually have $100 million in its bank accounts, of which $10 million will remain after it has paid its bills. Or it may be guessing that it will make $10 million on a deal where money may not actually change hands for years. Weil's source wanted him to see how much of the money Enron said it was making was "real."

Weil got copies of the firm's annual reports and quar-

terly filings and began comparing the income statements and the cash-flow statements. "It took me a while to figure out everything I needed to," Weil said. "It probably took a good month or so. There was a lot of noise in the financial statements, and to zero in on this particular issue you needed to cut through a lot of that." Weil spoke to Thomas Linsmeier, then an accounting professor at Michigan State, and they talked about how some finance companies in the 1990s had used mark-to-market accounting on subprime loans — that is, loans made to higher-credit-risk consumers — and when the economy declined and consumers defaulted or paid off their loans more quickly than expected, the lenders suddenly realized that their estimates of how much money they were going to make were far too generous. Weil spoke to someone at the Financial Accounting Standards Board, to an analyst at the Moody's investment-rating agency, and to a dozen or so others. Then he went back to Enron's financial statements. His conclusions were sobering. In the second quarter of 2000, $747 million of the money Enron said it had made was *unrealized* — that is, it was money that executives thought they were going to make at some point in the future. If you took that imaginary money away, Enron had shown a significant loss in the second quarter. This was one of the most admired companies in the United States, a firm that was then valued by the stock market as the seventh-largest corporation in the country, and there was practically no cash coming into its coffers.

Weil's story ran in the *Journal* on September 20, 2000. A few days later, it was read by a Wall Street financier named James Chanos. Chanos is a *short-seller* — an investor who tries to make money by betting that a company's

stock will fall. "It pricked up my ears," Chanos said. "I read the 10-K and the 10-Q that first weekend," he went on, referring to the financial statements that public companies are required to file with federal regulators. "I went through it pretty quickly. I flagged right away the stuff that was questionable. I circled it. That was the first run-through. Then I flagged the pages and read the stuff I didn't understand, and reread it two or three times. I remember I spent a couple hours on it." Enron's profit margins and its return on equity were plunging, Chanos saw. Cash flow — the lifeblood of any business — had slowed to a trickle, and the company's rate of return was less than its cost of capital: it was as if you had borrowed money from the bank at 9 percent interest and invested it in a savings bond that paid you 7 percent interest. "They were basically liquidating themselves," Chanos said.

In November of that year, Chanos began shorting Enron stock. Over the next few months, he spread the word that he thought the company was in trouble. He tipped off a reporter for *Fortune*, Bethany McLean. She read the same reports that Chanos and Weil had, and came to the same conclusion. Her story, under the headline "IS ENRON OVERPRICED?," ran in March of 2001. More and more journalists and analysts began taking a closer look at Enron, and the stock began to fall. In August, Skilling resigned. Enron's credit rating was downgraded. Banks became reluctant to lend Enron the money it needed to make its trades. By December, the company had filed for bankruptcy.

Enron's downfall has been documented so extensively that it is easy to overlook how peculiar it was. Compare Enron, for instance, with Watergate, the prototypical

scandal of the 1970s. To expose the White House cover-up, Bob Woodward and Carl Bernstein used a source — Deep Throat — who had access to many secrets, and whose identity had to be concealed. He warned Woodward and Bernstein that their phones might be tapped. When Woodward wanted to meet with Deep Throat, he would move a flowerpot with a red flag in it to the back of his apartment balcony. That evening, he would leave by the back stairs, take multiple taxis to make sure he wasn't being followed, and meet his source in an underground parking garage at 2 a.m. Here, from *All the President's Men,* is Woodward's climactic encounter with Deep Throat:

"Okay," he said softly. "This is very serious. You can safely say that fifty people worked for the White House and CRP to play games and spy and sabotage and gather intelligence. Some of it is beyond belief, kicking at the opposition in every imaginable way."

Deep Throat nodded confirmation as Woodward ran down items on a list of tactics that he and Bernstein had heard were used against the political opposition: bugging, following people, false press leaks, fake letters, cancelling campaign rallies, investigating campaign workers' private lives, planting spies, stealing documents, planting provocateurs in political demonstrations.

"It's all in the files," Deep Throat said. "Justice and the Bureau know about it, even though it wasn't followed up."

Woodward was stunned. Fifty people directed by the White House and CRP to destroy the opposition, no holds barred?

Deep Throat nodded.

The White House had been willing to subvert — was

that the right word? — the whole electoral process? Had actually gone ahead and tried to do it?

Another nod. Deep Throat looked queasy.

And hired fifty agents to do it?

"You can safely say more than fifty," Deep Throat said. Then he turned, walked up the ramp and out. It was nearly 6:00 a.m.

Watergate was a classic puzzle: Woodward and Bernstein were searching for a buried secret, and Deep Throat was their guide.

Did Jonathan Weil have a Deep Throat? Not really. He had a friend in the investment-management business with some suspicions about energy-trading companies like Enron, but the friend wasn't an insider. Nor did Weil's source direct him to files detailing the clandestine activities of the company. He just told Weil to read a series of public documents that had been prepared and distributed by Enron itself. Woodward met with his secret source in an underground parking garage in the hours before dawn. Weil called up an accounting expert at Michigan State.

When Weil had finished his reporting, he called Enron for comment. "They had their chief accounting officer and six or seven people fly up to Dallas," Weil says. They met in a conference room at the *Journal*'s offices. The Enron officials acknowledged that the money they said they earned was virtually all money that they *hoped* to earn. Weil and the Enron officials then had a long conversation about how certain Enron was about its estimates of future earnings. "They were telling me how brilliant the people who put together their mathematical models were," Weil says. "These were MIT PhDs. I said, 'Were your math-

ematical models last year telling you that the California electricity markets would be going berserk this year? No? Why not?' They said, 'Well, this is one of those crazy events.' It was late September 2000 so I said, 'Who do you think is going to win? Bush or Gore?' They said, 'We don't know.' I said, 'Don't you think it will make a difference to the market whether you have an environmentalist Democrat in the White House or a Texas oilman?'" It was all very civil. "There was no dispute about the numbers," Weil went on. "There was only a difference in how you should interpret them."

Of all the moments in the Enron unraveling, this meeting is surely the strangest. The prosecutor in the Enron case told the jury to send Jeffrey Skilling to prison because Enron had hidden the truth: You're "entitled to be told what the financial condition of the company is," the prosecutor had said. But what truth was Enron hiding here? Everything Weil learned for his Enron exposé came from Enron, and when he wanted to confirm his numbers, the company's executives got on a plane and sat down with him in a conference room in Dallas.

Nixon never went to see Woodward and Bernstein at the *Washington Post*. He hid in the White House.

4.

The second, and perhaps more consequential, problem with Enron's accounting was its heavy reliance on what are called *special-purpose entities*, or SPEs.

An SPE works something like this. Your company isn't doing well; sales are down and you are heavily in debt. If you go to a bank to borrow $100 million, it will

probably charge you an extremely high interest rate, if it agrees to lend to you at all. But you've got a bundle of oil leases that over the next four or five years are almost certain to bring in $100 million. So you hand them over to a partnership — the SPE — that you have set up with some outside investors. The bank then lends $100 million to the partnership, and the partnership gives the money to you. That bit of financial maneuvering makes a big difference. This kind of transaction did not (at the time) have to be reported in the company's balance sheet. So a company could raise capital without increasing its indebtedness. And because the bank is almost certain the leases will generate enough money to pay off the loan, it's willing to lend its money at a much lower interest rate. SPEs have become commonplace in corporate America.

Enron introduced all kinds of twists into the SPE game. It didn't always put blue-chip assets into the partnerships — like oil leases that would reliably generate income. It sometimes sold off less-than-sterling assets. Nor did it always sell those assets to outsiders, who presumably would raise questions about the value of what they were buying. Enron had its own executives manage these partnerships. And the company would make the deals work — that is, get the partnerships and the banks to play along — by guaranteeing that, if whatever they had to sell declined in value, Enron would make up the difference with its own stock. In other words, Enron didn't sell parts of itself to an outside entity; it effectively sold parts of itself to itself — a strategy that was not only legally questionable but extraordinarily risky. It was Enron's tangle of financial obligations to the SPEs that ended up triggering the collapse.

When the prosecution in the Skilling case argued that the company had misled its investors, they were referring, in part, to these SPEs. Enron's management, the argument went, had an obligation to reveal the extent to which it had staked its financial livelihood on these shadowy side deals. As the Powers Committee, a panel charged with investigating Enron's demise, noted, the company "failed to achieve a fundamental objective: they did not communicate the essence of the transactions in a sufficiently clear fashion to enable a reader of [Enron's] financial statements to understand what was going on." In short, we weren't told enough.

Here again, though, the lessons of the Enron case aren't nearly so straightforward. The public became aware of the nature of these SPEs through the reporting of several of Weil's colleagues at the *Wall Street Journal* — principally John Emshwiller and Rebecca Smith — starting in the late summer of 2001. And how was Emshwiller tipped off to Enron's problems? The same way Jonathan Weil and Jim Chanos were: he read what Enron had reported in its own public filings. Here is the description of Emshwiller's epiphany, as described in Kurt Eichenwald's *Conspiracy of Fools*, the definitive history of the Enron debacle. (Note the verb *scrounged*, which Eichenwald uses to describe how Emshwiller found the relevant Enron documents. What he means by that is *downloaded*.)

It was section eight, called "Related Party Transactions," that got John Emshwiller's juices flowing.

After being assigned to follow the Skilling resignation, Emshwiller had put in a request for an interview, then scrounged up a copy of Enron's most recent SEC filing in search of any nuggets.

What he found startled him. Words about some
partnerships run by an unidentified "senior officer."
Arcane stuff, maybe, but the numbers were huge. Enron
reported more than $240 million in revenues in the first
six months of the year from its dealings with them.

Enron's SPEs were, by any measure, evidence of
extraordinary recklessness and incompetence. But you
can't blame Enron for covering up the existence of its side
deals. It didn't; it disclosed them. The argument against
the company, then, is more accurately that it didn't tell
its investors *enough* about its SPEs. But what is enough?
Enron had some three thousand SPEs, and the paperwork for each one probably ran in excess of a thousand
pages. It scarcely would have helped investors if Enron
had made all three million pages public. What about an
edited version of each deal? Steven Schwarcz, a professor
at Duke Law School, recently examined a random sample
of twenty SPE disclosure statements from various corporations — that is, summaries of the deals put together for
interested parties — and found that on average they ran
to forty single-spaced pages. So a summary of Enron's
SPEs would have come to a hundred and twenty thousand single-spaced pages. What about a summary of all
those summaries? That's what the bankruptcy examiner
in the Enron case put together, and it took up a thousand
pages. Well, then, what about a summary of the summary
of the summaries? That's what the Powers Committee put
together. The committee looked only at the "substance of
the most significant transactions," and its accounting still
ran to two hundred numbingly complicated pages and, as
Schwarcz points out, that was "with the benefit of hind-

sight and with the assistance of some of the finest legal talent in the nation."

A puzzle grows simpler with the addition of each new piece of information: if I tell you that Osama bin Laden is hiding in Peshawar, I make the problem of finding him an order of magnitude easier, and if I add that he's hiding in a neighborhood in the northwest corner of the city, the problem becomes simpler still. But here the rules seem different. According to the Powers report, many on Enron's board of directors failed to understand "the economic rationale, the consequences, and the risks" of their company's SPE deals — and the directors sat in meetings where those deals were discussed in detail. In *Conspiracy of Fools,* Eichenwald convincingly argues that Andrew Fastow, Enron's chief financial officer, didn't understand the full economic implications of the deals, either, and he was the one who put them together.

"These were very, very sophisticated, complex transactions," says Anthony Catanach, who teaches accounting at the Villanova University School of Business and has written extensively on the Enron case. Referring to Enron's accounting firm, he said, "I'm not even sure any of Arthur Andersen's field staff at Enron would have been able to understand them, even if it was all in front of them. This is senior-management-type stuff. I spent *two months* looking at the Powers report, just diagramming it. These deals were really convoluted."

Enron's SPEs, it should be noted, would have been this hard to understand even if they were standard issue. SPEs are by nature difficult. A company creates an SPE because it wants to reassure banks about the risks of making a loan. To provide that reassurance, the company gives

its lenders and partners very detailed information about a specific portion of its business. And the more certainty a company creates for the lender — the more guarantees and safeguards and explanations it writes into the deal — the less comprehensible the transaction becomes to outsiders. Schwarcz writes that Enron's disclosure was "necessarily imperfect." You can try to make financial transactions understandable by simplifying them, in which case you run the risk of smoothing over some of their potential risks, or you can try to disclose every potential pitfall, in which case you'll make the disclosure so unwieldy that no one will be able to understand it. To Schwarcz, all Enron proves is that in an age of increasing financial complexity, the "disclosure paradigm" — the idea that the more a company tells us about its business, the better off we are — has become an anachronism.

5.

During the summer of 1943, Nazi propaganda broadcasts boasted that the German military had developed a devastating "super weapon." Immediately, the Allied intelligence services went to work. Spies confirmed that the Germans had built a secret weapons factory. Aerial photographs taken over northern France showed a strange new concrete installation pointed in the direction of England. The Allies were worried. Bombing missions were sent to try to disrupt the mysterious operation, and plans were drawn up to deal with the prospect of devastating new attacks on English cities. Nobody was sure, though, whether the weapon was real. There seemed to be weapons factories there, but it wasn't evident what was happening

inside them. And there was a launching pad in northern France, but it might have been just a decoy, designed to distract the Allies from bombing real targets. The German secret weapon was a puzzle, and the Allies didn't have enough information to solve it. There was another way to think about the problem, though, which ultimately proved far more useful: treat the German secret weapon as a mystery.

The mystery solvers of the Second World War were small groups of analysts whose job was to listen to the overseas and domestic propaganda broadcasts of Japan and Germany. The British outfit had been around since shortly before the First World War and was run by the BBC. The American operation was known as the Screwball Division, the historian Stephen Mercado writes, and in the early 1940s had been housed in a nondescript office building on K Street, in Washington. The analysts listened to the same speeches that anyone with a shortwave radio could listen to. They simply sat at their desks with headphones on, working their way through hours and hours of Nazi broadcasts. Then they tried to figure out how what the Nazis said publicly — about, for instance, the possibility of a renewed offensive against Russia — revealed what they felt about, say, invading Russia. One journalist at the time described the propaganda analysts as "the greatest collection of individualists, international rolling stones, and slightly batty geniuses ever gathered together in one organization." And they had very definite thoughts about the Nazis' secret weapon.

The German leadership, first of all, was boasting about the secret weapon in domestic broadcasts. That was important. Propaganda was supposed to boost morale. If

the Nazi leadership said things that turned out to be misleading, its credibility would fall. When German U-boats started running into increasingly effective Allied resistance in the spring of 1943, for example, Joseph Goebbels, the Nazi minister of propaganda, tacitly acknowledged the bad news, switching his emphasis from trumpeting recent victories to predicting long-term success, and blaming the weather for hampering U-boat operations. Up to that point, Goebbels had never lied to his own people about that sort of news. So if he said that Germany had a devastating secret weapon it meant, in all likelihood, that Germany had a devastating secret weapon.

Starting from that premise, the analysts then mined the Nazis' public pronouncements for more insights. It was, they concluded, "beyond reasonable doubt" that as of November 1943 the weapon existed, that it was of an entirely new type, that it could not be easily countered, that it would produce striking results, and that it would shock the civilian population upon whom it would be used. It was, furthermore, "highly probable" that the Germans were past the experimental stage as of May of 1943, and that something had happened in August of that year that significantly delayed deployment. The analysts based this inference, in part, on the fact that, in August, the Nazis abruptly stopped mentioning their secret weapon for ten days, and that when they started again, their threats took on a new, less certain, tone. Finally, it could be tentatively estimated that the weapon would be ready between the middle of January and the middle of April, with a month's margin of error on either side. That inference, in part, came from Nazi propaganda in late 1943, which suddenly became more serious and specific in tone, and it seemed

unlikely that Goebbels would raise hopes in this way if he couldn't deliver within a few months. The secret weapon was the Nazis' fabled V-1 rocket, and virtually every one of the propaganda analysts' predictions turned out to be true.

The political scientist Alexander George described the sequence of V-1 rocket inferences in his 1959 book *Propaganda Analysis,* and the striking thing about his account is how contemporary it seems. The spies were fighting a nineteenth-century war. The analysts belonged to our age, and the lesson of their triumph is that the complex, uncertain issues that the modern world throws at us require the mystery paradigm.

Diagnosing prostate cancer used to be a puzzle, for example: the doctor would do a rectal exam and feel for a lumpy tumor on the surface of the patient's prostate. These days, though, we don't wait for patients to develop the symptoms of prostate cancer. Doctors now regularly test middle-aged men for elevated levels of PSA, a substance associated with prostate changes, and, if the results look problematic, they use ultrasound imaging to take a picture of the prostate. Then they perform a biopsy, removing tiny slices of the gland and examining the extracted tissue under a microscope. Much of that flood of information, however, is inconclusive: elevated levels of PSA don't always mean that you have cancer, and normal levels of PSA don't always mean that you don't — and, in any case, there's debate about what constitutes a normal PSA level. Nor is the biopsy definitive: because what a pathologist is looking for is early evidence of cancer — and in many cases merely something that might one day turn into cancer — two equally skilled pathologists can easily look at the same sample and disagree

about whether there is any cancer present. Even if they do agree, they may disagree about the benefits of treatment, given that most prostate cancers grow so slowly that they never cause problems. The urologist is now charged with the task of making sense of a maze of unreliable and conflicting claims. He is no longer confirming the presence of a malignancy. He's predicting it, and the certainties of his predecessors have been replaced with outcomes that can only be said to be "highly probable" or "tentatively estimated." What medical progress has meant for prostate cancer — and, as the physician H. Gilbert Welch argues in his book *Should I Be Tested for Cancer?*, for virtually every other cancer as well — is the transformation of diagnosis from a puzzle to a mystery.

That same transformation is happening in the intelligence world as well. During the Cold War, the broad context of our relationship with the Soviet bloc was stable and predictable. What we didn't know was details. As Gregory Treverton, who was a former vice-chair of the National Intelligence Council, writes in his book *Reshaping National Intelligence for an Age of Information*:

> Then the pressing questions that preoccupied intelligence were puzzles, ones that could, in principle, have been answered definitively if only the information had been available: How big was the Soviet economy? How many missiles did the Soviet Union have? Had it launched a "bolt from the blue" attack? These puzzles were intelligence's stock-in-trade during the Cold War.

With the collapse of the Eastern bloc, Treverton and others have argued that the situation facing the intelligence

community has turned upside down. Now most of the world is open, not closed. Intelligence officers aren't dependent on scraps from spies. They are inundated with information. Solving puzzles remains critical: we still want to know precisely where Osama bin Laden is hiding and where North Korea's nuclear-weapons facilities are situated. But mysteries increasingly take center stage. The stable and predictable divisions of East and West have been shattered. Now the task of the intelligence analyst is to help policymakers navigate the disorder. Several years ago, Admiral Bobby R. Inman was asked by a congressional commission what changes he thought would strengthen America's intelligence system. Inman used to head the National Security Agency, the nation's premier puzzle-solving authority, and was once the deputy director of the CIA. He was the embodiment of the Cold War intelligence structure. His answer: revive the State Department, the one part of the US foreign-policy establishment that isn't considered to be in the intelligence business at all. In a post–Cold War world of "openly available information," Inman said, "what you need are observers with language ability, with understanding of the religions, cultures of the countries they're observing." Inman thought we needed fewer spies and more slightly batty geniuses.

6.

Enron revealed that the financial community needs to make the same transition. "In order for an economy to have an adequate system of financial reporting, it is not enough that companies make disclosures of financial information," the Yale law professor Jonathan Macey

wrote in a landmark law review article that encouraged many to rethink the Enron case. "In addition, it is vital that there be a set of financial intermediaries, who are at least as competent and sophisticated at receiving, processing, and interpreting financial information…as the companies are at delivering it." Puzzles are "transmitter-dependent"; they turn on what we are told. Mysteries are "receiver-dependent"; they turn on the skills of the listener, and Macey argues that, as Enron's business practices grew more complicated, it was Wall Street's responsibility to keep pace.

Victor Fleischer, who teaches at the University of Colorado Law School, points out that one of the critical clues about Enron's condition lay in the fact that it paid no income tax in four of its last five years. Enron's use of mark-to-market accounting and SPEs was an accounting game that made the company look as though it were earning far more money than it was. But the IRS doesn't accept mark-to-market accounting; you pay tax on income when you actually receive that income. And, from the IRS's perspective, all of Enron's fantastically complex maneuvering around its SPEs was, as Fleischer puts it, "a non-event": until the partnership actually sells the asset — and makes either a profit or a loss — an SPE is just an accounting fiction. Enron wasn't paying any taxes because, in the eyes of the IRS, Enron wasn't making any money.

If you looked at Enron from the perspective of the tax code, that is, you would have seen a very different picture of the company than if you had looked through the more traditional lens of the accounting profession. But in order to do that you would have to be trained in the tax code

and be familiar with its particular conventions and intricacies, and know what questions to ask. "The fact of the gap between [Enron's] accounting income and taxable income was easily observed," Fleischer notes, but not the source of the gap. "The tax code requires special training."

Woodward and Bernstein didn't have any special training. They were in their twenties at the time of Watergate. In *All the President's Men,* they even joke about their inexperience: Woodward's expertise was mainly in office politics; Bernstein was a college dropout. But it hardly mattered, because cover-ups, whistle-blowers, secret tapes, and exposés — the principal elements of the puzzle — all require the application of energy and persistence, which are the virtues of youth. Mysteries demand experience and insight. Woodward and Bernstein would never have broken the Enron story.

"There have been scandals in corporate history where people are really making stuff up, but this wasn't a criminal enterprise of that kind," Macey says. "Enron was vanishingly close, in my view, to having complied with the accounting rules. They were going over the edge, just a little bit. And this kind of financial fraud — where people are simply stretching the truth — falls into the area that analysts and short-sellers are supposed to ferret out. The truth wasn't hidden. But you'd have to look at their financial statements, and you would have to say to yourself, 'What's that about?' It's almost as if they were saying, 'We're doing some really sleazy stuff in footnote 42, and if you want to know more about it, ask us.' And that's the thing. Nobody did."

Alexander George, in his history of propaganda

analysis, looked at hundreds of the inferences drawn by the American analysts about the Nazis, and concluded that an astonishing 81 percent of them were accurate. George's account, however, spends almost as much time on the propaganda analysts' failures as on their successes. It was the British, for example, who did the best work on the V-1 rocket problem. They systematically tracked the "occurrence and volume" of Nazi reprisal threats, which is how they were able to pinpoint things like the setback suffered by the V-1 program in August of 1943 (it turned out that Allied bombs had caused serious damage) and the date of the Nazi V-1 rocket launch. K Street's analysis was lackluster in comparison. George writes that the Americans "did not develop analytical techniques and hypotheses of sufficient refinement," relying instead on "impressionistic" analysis. George was himself one of the slightly batty geniuses of K Street, and, of course, he could easily have excused his former colleagues. They never left their desks, after all. All they had to deal with was propaganda, and their big source was Goebbels, who was a liar, a thief, and a drunk. But that is puzzle thinking. In the case of puzzles, we put the offending target, the CEO, in jail for twenty-four years and assume that our work is done. Mysteries require that we revisit our list of culprits and be willing to spread the blame a little more broadly. Because if you can't find the truth in a mystery — even a mystery shrouded in propaganda — it's not just the fault of the propagandist. It's your fault as well.

In the spring of 1998, Macey notes, a group of six students at Cornell University's business school decided to do their term project on Enron. "It was for an advanced

financial-statement-analysis class taught by a guy at Cornell called Charles Lee, who is pretty famous in financial circles," one member of the group, Jay Krueger, recalls. In the first part of the semester, Lee had led his students through a series of intensive case studies, teaching them techniques and sophisticated tools to make sense of the vast amounts of information that companies disclose in their annual reports and SEC filings. Then the students picked a company and went off on their own. "One of the second-years had a summer-internship interview with Enron, and he was very interested in the energy sector," Krueger went on. "So he said, 'Let's do them.' It was about a six-week project, half a semester. Lots of group meetings. It was a ratio analysis, which is pretty standard business-school fare. You know, take fifty different financial ratios, then lay that on top of every piece of information you could find out about the company, the businesses, how their performance compared to other competitors."

The people in the group reviewed Enron's accounting practices as best they could. They analyzed each of Enron's businesses, in succession. They used statistical tools, designed to find telltale patterns in the company's financial performance — the Beneish model, the Lev and Thiagarajan indicators, the Edwards-Bell-Ohlsen analysis — and made their way through pages and pages of footnotes. "We really had a lot of questions about what was going on with their business model," Krueger said. The students' conclusions were straightforward. Enron was pursuing a far riskier strategy than its competitors. There were clear signs that "Enron may be manipulating its earnings." The stock was then at $48 — at its peak, two years later, it was

almost double that — but the students found it overvalued. The report was posted on the website of the Cornell University business school, where it has been, ever since, for anyone who cares to read twenty-three pages of analysis. The students' recommendation was on the first page, in boldfaced type: "Sell."*

January 8, 2007

---

* By today's standards, of course, Enron barely meets the threshold for financial scandal — not after the multitrillion-dollar financial meltdown of the past few years. But I wrote about it twice — here and a few years earlier in "The Talent Myth" (which you can find in part 3), because I felt it was really the paradigmatic scandal of the information age. History has borne this out. Had we taken the lessons of Enron more seriously, would we have had the financial crisis of 2008?

Million-Dollar Murray

WHY PROBLEMS LIKE HOMELESSNESS MAY BE
EASIER TO SOLVE THAN TO MANAGE

1.

Murray Barr was a bear of a man, an ex-Marine, six feet tall and heavyset, and when he fell down — which he did nearly every day — it could take two or three grown men to pick him up. He had straight black hair and olive skin. On the street, they called him Smokey. He was missing most of his teeth. He had a wonderful smile. People loved Murray.

His chosen drink was vodka. Beer he called "horse piss." On the streets of downtown Reno, where he lived, he could buy a 250-milliliter bottle of cheap vodka for $1.50. If he was flush, he could go for the 750-milliliter bottle, and if he was broke, he could always do what many of the other homeless people of Reno did, which is to walk through the casinos and finish off the half-empty glasses of liquor left at the gaming tables.

"If he was on a runner, we could pick him up several times a day," Patrick O'Bryan, who is a bicycle cop in downtown Reno, said. "And he's gone on some amazing

runners. He would get picked up, get detoxed, then get back out a couple of hours later and start up again. A lot of the guys on the streets who've been drinking, they get so angry. They are so incredibly abrasive, so violent, so abusive. Murray was such a character and had such a great sense of humor that we somehow got past that. Even when he was abusive, we'd say, 'Murray, you know you love us,' and he'd say, 'I know' — and go back to swearing at us."

"I've been a police officer for fifteen years," O'Bryan's partner, Steve Johns, said. "I picked up Murray my whole career. Literally."

Johns and O'Bryan pleaded with Murray to quit drinking. A few years ago, he was assigned to a treatment program in which he was under the equivalent of house arrest, and he thrived. He got a job and worked hard. But then the program ended. "Once he graduated out, he had no one to report to, and he needed that," O'Bryan said. "I don't know whether it was his military background. I suspect that it was. He was a good cook. One time, he accumulated savings of over six thousand dollars. Showed up for work religiously. Did everything he was supposed to do. They said, 'Congratulations,' and put him back on the street. He spent that six thousand in a week or so."

Often, he was too intoxicated for the drunk tank at the jail, and he'd get sent to the emergency room at either Saint Mary's or Washoe Medical Center. Marla Johns, who was a social worker in the emergency room at Saint Mary's, saw him several times a week. "The ambulance would bring him in. We would sober him up, so he would be sober enough to go to jail. And we would call the police to pick him up. In fact, that's how I met my husband." Marla Johns is married to Steve Johns.

"He was like the one constant in an environment that was ever changing," she went on. "In he would come. He would grin that half-toothless grin. He called me 'my angel.' I would walk in the room, and he would smile and say, 'Oh, my angel, I'm so happy to see you.' We would joke back and forth, and I would beg him to quit drinking and he would laugh it off. And when time went by and he didn't come in, I would get worried and call the coroner's office. When he was sober, we would find out, oh, he's working someplace, and my husband and I would go and have dinner where he was working. When my husband and I were dating, and we were going to get married, he said, 'Can I come to the wedding?' And I almost felt like he should. My joke was 'If you are sober you can come, because I can't afford your bar bill.' When we started a family, he would lay a hand on my pregnant belly and bless the child. He really was this kind of light."

In the fall of 2003, the Reno Police Department started an initiative designed to limit panhandling in the downtown core. There were articles in the newspapers, and the police department came under harsh criticism on local talk radio. The crackdown on panhandling amounted to harassment, the critics said. The homeless weren't an imposition on the city; they were just trying to get by. "One morning, I'm listening to one of the talk shows, and they're just trashing the police department and going on about how unfair it is," O'Bryan said. "And I thought, Wow, I've never seen any of these critics in one of the alleyways in the middle of the winter looking for bodies." O'Bryan was angry. In downtown Reno, food for the homeless was plentiful: there was a Gospel kitchen and Catholic Services, and even the local McDonald's

fed the hungry. The panhandling was for liquor, and the liquor was anything but harmless. He and Johns spent at least half their time dealing with people like Murray; they were as much caseworkers as police officers. And they knew they weren't the only ones involved. When someone passed out on the street, there was a "One down" call to the paramedics. There were four people in an ambulance, and the patient sometimes stayed at the hospital for days, because living on the streets in a state of almost constant intoxication was a reliable way of getting sick. None of that, surely, could be cheap.

O'Bryan and Johns called someone they knew at an ambulance service and then contacted the local hospitals. "We came up with three names that were some of our chronic inebriates in the downtown area, that got arrested the most often," O'Bryan said. "We tracked those three individuals through just one of our two hospitals. One of the guys had been in jail previously, so he'd only been on the streets for six months. In those six months, he had accumulated a bill of a hundred thousand dollars — and that's at the smaller of the two hospitals near downtown Reno. It's pretty reasonable to assume that the other hospital had an even larger bill. Another individual came from Portland and had been in Reno for three months. In those three months, he had accumulated a bill for sixty-five thousand dollars. The third individual actually had some periods of being sober, and had accumulated a bill of fifty thousand."

The first of those people was Murray Barr, and Johns and O'Bryan realized that if you toted up all his hospital bills for the ten years that he had been on the streets — as well as substance-abuse-treatment costs, doctors' fees, and

other expenses — Murray Barr probably ran up a medical bill as large as anyone in the state of Nevada.

"It cost us one million dollars not to do something about Murray," O'Bryan said.

2.

In the wake of the Rodney King beating, the Los Angeles Police Department was in crisis. It was accused of racial insensitivity and ill discipline and violence, and the assumption was that those problems had spread broadly throughout the rank and file. In the language of statisticians, it was thought that the LAPD's troubles had a "normal" distribution — that if you graphed them, the result would look like a bell curve, with a small number of officers at one end of the curve, a small number at the other end, and the bulk of the problem situated in the middle. The bell-curve assumption has become so much a part of our mental architecture that we tend to use it to organize experience automatically.

But when the LAPD was investigated by a special commission headed by Warren Christopher, a very different picture emerged. Between 1986 and 1990, allegations of excessive force or improper tactics were made against eighteen hundred of the eighty-five hundred officers in the LAPD. The broad middle had scarcely been accused of anything. Furthermore, more than fourteen hundred officers had only one or two allegations made against them — and bear in mind that these were not proven charges, that they happened in a four-year period, and that allegations of excessive force are an inevitable feature of urban police work. (The NYPD receives about

three thousand such complaints a year.) A hundred and eighty-three officers, however, had four or more complaints against them, forty-four officers had six or more complaints, sixteen had eight or more, and one had sixteen complaints. If you were to graph the troubles of the LAPD, it wouldn't look like a bell curve. It would look more like a hockey stick. It would follow what statisticians call a *power law* distribution — where all the activity is not in the middle but at one extreme.

The Christopher Commission's report repeatedly comes back to what it describes as the extreme concentration of problematic officers. One officer had been the subject of thirteen allegations of excessive use of force, five other complaints, twenty-eight "use of force reports" (that is, documented internal accounts of inappropriate behavior), and one shooting. Another had six excessive-force complaints, nineteen other complaints, ten use-of-force reports, and three shootings. A third had twenty-seven use-of-force reports, and a fourth had thirty-five. Another had a file full of complaints for doing things like "striking an arrestee on the back of the neck with the butt of a shotgun for no apparent reason while the arrestee was kneeling and handcuffed," beating up a thirteen-year-old juvenile, and throwing an arrestee from his chair and kicking him in the back and side of the head while he was handcuffed and lying on his stomach.

The report gives the strong impression that if you fired those forty-four cops, the LAPD would suddenly become a pretty well-functioning police department. But the report also suggests that the problem is tougher than it seems, because those forty-four bad cops were *so* bad that the institutional mechanisms in place to get rid of bad

apples clearly weren't working. If you made the mistake of assuming that the department's troubles fell into a normal distribution, you'd propose solutions that would raise the performance of the middle — like better training or better hiring — when the middle didn't need help. For those hard-core few who did need help, meanwhile, the medicine that helped the middle wouldn't be nearly strong enough.

In the 1980s, when homelessness first surfaced as a national issue, the assumption was that the problem fit a normal distribution: that the vast majority of the homeless were in the same state of semipermanent distress. It was an assumption that bred despair: if there were so many home-less, with so many problems, what could be done to help them? Then, in the early 1990s, a young Boston College graduate student named Dennis Culhane lived in a shel-ter in Philadelphia for seven weeks as part of the research for his dissertation. A few months later he went back and was surprised to discover that he couldn't find any of the people he had recently spent so much time with. "It made me realize that most of these people were getting on with their own lives," he said.

Culhane then put together a database — the first of its kind — to track who was coming in and out of the shelter system. What he discovered profoundly changed the way homelessness is understood. Homelessness doesn't have a normal distribution, it turned out. It has a power-law dis-tribution. "We found that eighty percent of the homeless were in and out really quickly," he said. "In Philadelphia, the most common length of time that someone is homeless is one day. And the second most common length is two days. And they never come back. Anyone who ever has

to stay in a shelter involuntarily knows that all you think about is how to make sure you never come back."

The next 10 percent were what Culhane calls episodic users. They would come for three weeks at a time, and return periodically, particularly in the winter. They were quite young, and they were often heavy drug users. It was the last 10 percent — the group at the farthest edge of the curve — that interested Culhane the most. They were the chronically homeless, who lived in the shelters, sometimes for years at a time. They were older. Many were mentally ill or physically disabled, and when we think about home-lessness as a social problem — the people sleeping on the sidewalk, aggressively panhandling, lying drunk in door-ways, huddled on subway grates and under bridges — it's this group that we have in mind. In the early 1990s, Cul-hane's database suggested that New York City had a quar-ter of a million people who were homeless at some point in the previous half decade — which was a surprisingly high number. But only about twenty-five hundred were *chroni-cally* homeless.

It turns out, furthermore, that this group costs the health-care and social-services systems far more than any-one had ever anticipated. Culhane estimates that in New York at least $62 million was being spent annually to shel-ter just those twenty-five hundred hard-core homeless. "It costs twenty-four thousand dollars a year for one of these shelter beds," Culhane said. "We're talking about a cot eighteen inches away from the next cot." Boston Health Care for the Homeless Program, a leading service group for the homeless in Boston, recently tracked the medical expenses of a hundred and nineteen chronically homeless people. In the course of five years, thirty-three people died

and seven more were sent to nursing homes, and the group still accounted for 18,834 emergency-room visits — at a minimum cost of $1,000 a visit. The University of California, San Diego, Medical Center followed fifteen chronically homeless inebriates and found that over eighteen months, those fifteen people were treated at the hospital's emergency room 417 times, and ran up bills that averaged $100,000 each. One person — San Diego's counterpart to Murray Barr — came to the emergency room eighty-seven times.

"If it's a medical admission, it's likely to be the guys with the really complex pneumonia," James Dunford, the city of San Diego's emergency medical director and the author of the observational study, said. "They are drunk and they aspirate and get vomit in their lungs and develop a lung abscess, and they get hypothermia on top of that, because they're out in the rain. They end up in the intensive-care unit with these very complicated medical infections. These are the guys who typically get hit by cars and buses and trucks. They often have a neurosurgical catastrophe as well. So they are very prone to just falling down and cracking their head and getting a subdural hematoma, which, if not drained, could kill them, and it's the guy who falls down and hits his head who ends up costing you at least fifty thousand dollars. Meanwhile, they are going through alcohol withdrawal and have devastating liver disease that only adds to their inability to fight infections. There is no end to the issues. We do this huge drill. We run up big lab fees, and the nurses want to quit, because they see the same guys come in over and over, and all we're doing is making them capable of walking down the block."

The homelessness problem is like the LAPD's bad-cop

problem. It's a matter of a few hard cases, and that's good news, because when a problem is that concentrated you can wrap your arms around it and think about solving it. The bad news is that those few hard cases are *hard*. They are falling-down drunks with liver disease and complex infections and mental illness. They need time and attention and lots of money. But enormous sums of money are already being spent on the chronically homeless, and Culhane saw that the kind of money it would take to solve the homeless problem could well be less than the kind of money it took to ignore it. Murray Barr used more health-care dollars, after all, than almost anyone in the state of Nevada. It would probably have been cheaper to give him a full-time nurse and his own apartment.

The leading exponent for the power-law theory of homelessness is Philip Mangano, who, since he was appointed by President Bush in 2002, has been the executive director of the US Interagency Council on Homelessness, a group that oversees the programs of twenty federal agencies. Mangano is a slender man, with a mane of white hair and a magnetic presence, who got his start as an advocate for the homeless in Massachusetts. He is on the road constantly, crisscrossing the United States, educating local mayors and city councils about the real shape of the homelessness curve. Simply running soup kitchens and shelters, he argues, allows the chronically homeless to remain chronically homeless. You build a shelter and a soup kitchen if you think that homelessness is a problem with a broad and unmanageable middle. But if it's a problem at the fringe it can be solved. So far, Mangano has convinced more than two hundred cities to radically reevaluate their policy for dealing with the homeless.

"I was in St. Louis recently," Mangano said, back in June, when he dropped by New York on his way to Boise, Idaho. "I spoke with people doing services there. They had a very difficult group of people they couldn't reach no matter what they offered. So I said, 'Take some of your money and rent some apartments and go out to those people, and literally go out there with the key and say to them, "This is the key to an apartment. If you come with me right now I am going to give it to you, and you are going to have that apartment."' And so they did. And one by one those people were coming in. Our intent is to take homeless policy from the old idea of funding programs that serve homeless people endlessly and invest in results that actually end homelessness."

Mangano is a history buff, a man who sometimes falls asleep listening to old Malcolm X speeches, and who peppers his remarks with references to the civil-rights movement and the Berlin Wall and, most of all, the fight against slavery. "I am an abolitionist," he says. "My office in Boston was opposite the monument to the 54th Regiment on the Boston Common, up the street from the Park Street Church, where William Lloyd Garrison called for immediate abolition, and around the corner from where Frederick Douglass gave that famous speech at the Tremont Temple. It is very much ingrained in me that you do not manage a social wrong. You should be ending it."

3.

The old YMCA in downtown Denver is on Sixteenth Street, just east of the central business district. The main building is a handsome six-story stone structure that was

erected in 1906, and next door is an annex that was added in the 1950s. On the ground floor are a gym and exercise rooms. On the upper floors there are several hundred apartments — brightly painted one bedrooms, efficiencies, and SRO-style rooms with microwaves and refrigerators and central air-conditioning — and for the past several years those apartments have been owned and managed by the Colorado Coalition for the Homeless.

Even by big-city standards, Denver has a serious homelessness problem. The winters are relatively mild, and the summers aren't nearly as hot as those of neighboring New Mexico or Utah, which has made the city a magnet for the indigent. By the city's estimates, it has roughly a thousand chronically homeless people, of whom three hundred spend their time downtown, along the central Sixteenth Street shopping corridor or in nearby Civic Center Park. Many of the merchants downtown worry that the presence of the homeless is scaring away customers. A few blocks north, near the hospital, a modest, low-slung detox center handles twenty-eight thousand admissions a year, many of them homeless people who have passed out on the streets, either from liquor or — as is increasingly the case — from mouthwash. "Dr. —, Dr. Tich, they call it — is the brand of mouthwash they use," says Roxane White, the manager of the city's social services. "You can imagine what that does to your gut."

Eighteen months ago the city signed up with Mangano. With a mixture of federal and local funds, the CCH inaugurated a new program that has so far enrolled 106 people. It is aimed at the Murray Barrs of Denver, the people costing the system the most. CCH went after the people who had been on the streets the longest, who

had a criminal record, who had a problem with substance abuse or mental illness. "We have one individual in her early sixties, but looking at her you'd think she's eighty," Rachel Post, the director of substance treatment at the CCH, said. (Post changed some details about her clients in order to protect their identity.) "She's a chronic alcoholic. A typical day for her is, she gets up and tries to find whatever she's going to drink that day. She falls down a lot. There's another person who came in during the first week. He was on methadone maintenance. He'd had psychiatric treatment. He was incarcerated for eleven years, and lived on the streets for three years after that, and, if that's not enough, he had a hole in his heart."

The recruitment strategy was as simple as the one that Mangano had laid out in St. Louis: Would you like a free apartment? The enrollees got either an efficiency at the YMCA or an apartment rented for them in a building somewhere else in the city, provided they agreed to work within the rules of the program. In the basement of the Y, where the racquetball courts used to be, the coalition built a command center, staffed with ten caseworkers. Five days a week, between eight-thirty and ten in the morning, the caseworkers meet and painstakingly review the status of everyone in the program. On the wall around the conference table are several large whiteboards, with lists of doctor's appointments and court dates and medication schedules. "We need a staffing ratio of one to ten to make it work," Post said. "You go out there and you find people and assess how they're doing in their residence. Sometimes we're in contact with someone every day. Ideally, we want to be in contact every couple of days. We've got about fifteen people we're really worried about now."

The cost of services comes to about $10,000 per homeless client per year. An efficiency apartment in Denver averages $376 a month, or just over $4,500 a year, which means that you can house and care for a chronically homeless person for at most $15,000, or about a third of what he or she would cost on the street. The idea is that once the people in the program get stabilized, they will find jobs, and start to pick up more and more of their own rent, which would bring someone's annual cost to the program closer to $6,000 dollars. As of today, seventy-five supportive housing slots have already been added, and the city's homeless plan calls for eight hundred more over the next ten years.

The reality, of course, is hardly that neat and tidy. The idea that the very sickest and most troubled of the homeless can be stabilized and eventually employed is only a hope. Some of them plainly won't be able to get there: these are, after all, hard cases. "We've got one man, he's in his twenties," Post said. "Already, he has cirrhosis of the liver. One time he blew a blood alcohol of .49, which is enough to kill most people. The first place we had, he brought over all his friends, and they partied and trashed the place and broke a window. Then we gave him another apartment, and he did the same thing."

Post said that the man had been sober for several months. But he could relapse at some point and perhaps trash another apartment, and they'd have to figure out what to do with him next. Post had just been on a conference call with some people in New York City who run a similar program, and they talked about whether giving clients so many chances simply encourages them to behave irresponsibly. For some people, it probably does. But what was the alter-

native? If this young man was put back on the streets, he would cost the system even more money. The current philosophy of welfare holds that government assistance should be temporary and conditional, to avoid creating dependency. But someone who blows .49 on a Breathalyzer and has cirrhosis of the liver at the age of twenty-seven doesn't respond to incentives and sanctions in the usual way. "The most complicated people to work with are those who have been homeless for so long that going back to the streets just isn't scary to them," Post said. "The summer comes along and they say, 'I don't need to follow your rules.'" Power-law homeless policy has to do the opposite of normal-distribution social policy. It *should* create dependency: you want people who have been outside the system to come inside and rebuild their lives under the supervision of those ten caseworkers in the basement of the YMCA.

That is what is so perplexing about power-law homeless policy. From an economic perspective the approach makes perfect sense. But from a moral perspective it doesn't seem fair. Thousands of people in the Denver area no doubt live day to day, work two or three jobs, and are eminently deserving of a helping hand — and no one offers them the key to a new apartment. Yet that's just what the guy screaming obscenities and swigging Dr. Tich gets. When the welfare mom's time on public assistance runs out, we cut her off. Yet when the homeless man trashes his apartment, we give him another. Social benefits are supposed to have some kind of moral justification. We give them to widows and disabled veterans and poor mothers with small children. Giving the homeless guy passed out on the sidewalk an apartment has a different rationale. It's simply about efficiency.

We also believe that the distribution of social benefits should not be arbitrary. We don't give only to some poor mothers, or to a random handful of disabled veterans. We give to everyone who meets a formal criterion, and the moral credibility of government assistance derives, in part, from this universality. But the Denver homelessness program doesn't help every chronically homeless person in Denver. There is a waiting list of six hundred for the supportive-housing program; it will be years before all those people get apartments, and some may never get one. There isn't enough money to go around, and to try to help everyone a little bit — to observe the principle of universality — isn't as cost-effective as helping a few people a lot. Being fair, in this case, means providing shelters and soup kitchens, and shelters and soup kitchens don't solve the problem of homelessness. Our usual moral intuitions are of little use, then, when it comes to a few hard cases. Power-law problems leave us with an unpleasant choice. We can be true to our principles or we can fix the problem. We cannot do both.

4.

A few miles northwest of the old YMCA in downtown Denver, on the Speer Boulevard off-ramp from I-25, there is a big electronic sign by the side of the road, connected to a device that remotely measures the emissions of the vehicles driving past. When a car with properly functioning pollution-control equipment passes, the sign flashes "Good." When a car passes that is well over the acceptable limits, the sign flashes "Poor." If you stand at the Speer Boulevard exit and watch the sign for any length of

time, you'll find that virtually every car scores "Good."
An Audi A4 — "Good." A Buick Century — "Good." A
Toyota Corolla — "Good." A Ford Taurus — "Good." A
Saab 9-5 — "Good," and on and on, until after twenty
minutes or so, some beat-up old Ford Escort or tricked-
out Porsche drives by and the sign flashes "Poor." The
picture of the smog problem you get from watching the
Speer Boulevard sign and the picture of the homelessness
problem you get from listening in on the morning staff
meetings at the YMCA are pretty much the same. Auto
emissions follow a power-law distribution, and the air-
pollution example offers another look at why we struggle
so much with problems centered on a few hard cases.

Most cars, especially new ones, are extraordinarily
clean. A 2004 Subaru in good working order has an
exhaust stream that's just .06 percent carbon monoxide,
which is negligible. But on almost any highway, for whatever reason — age, ill repair, deliberate tampering by the
owner — a small number of cars have carbon-monoxide
levels in excess of 10 percent, which is almost two hundred times higher. In Denver, 5 percent of the vehicles on
the road produce 55 percent of the automobile pollution.

"Let's say a car is fifteen years old," Donald Stedman
says. Stedman is a chemist and automobile-emissions specialist at the University of Denver. His laboratory put up
the sign on Speer Avenue. "Obviously, the older a car is,
the more likely it is to become broken. It's the same as
human beings. And by *broken* we mean any number of
mechanical malfunctions — the computer's not working
anymore, fuel injection is stuck open, the catalyst died. It's
not unusual that these failure modes result in high emissions. We have at least one car in our database which was

emitting seventy grams of hydrocarbon per mile, which means that you could almost drive a Honda Civic on the exhaust fumes from that car. It's not just old cars. It's new cars with high mileage, like taxis. One of the most successful and least publicized control measures was done by a district attorney in L.A. back in the nineties. He went to LAX and discovered that all of the Bell Cabs were gross emitters. One of those cabs emitted more than its own weight of pollution every year."

In Stedman's view, the current system of smog checks makes little sense. A million motorists in Denver have to go to an emissions center every year — take time from work, wait in line, pay $15 or $25 — for a test that more than 90 percent of them don't need. "Not everybody gets tested for breast cancer," Stedman says. "Not everybody takes an AIDS test." On-site smog checks, furthermore, do a pretty bad job of finding and fixing the few outliers. Car enthusiasts — with high-powered, high-polluting sports cars — have been known to drop a clean engine into their car on the day they get it tested. Others register their car in a faraway town without emissions testing or arrive at the test site "hot" — having just come off hard driving on the freeway — which is a good way to make a dirty engine appear to be clean. Still others randomly pass the test when they shouldn't, because dirty engines are highly variable and sometimes burn cleanly for short durations. There is little evidence, Stedman says, that the city's regime of inspections makes any difference in air quality.

He proposes mobile testing instead. In the early 1980s, he invented a device the size of a suitcase that uses infrared light to instantly measure and then analyze the emissions of cars as they drive by on the highway. The Speer Avenue sign

is attached to one of Stedman's devices. He says that cities should put half a dozen or so of his devices in vans, park them on freeway off-ramps around the city, and have a police car poised to pull over anyone who fails the test. A half-dozen vans could test thirty thousand cars a day. For the same $25 million that Denver's motorists now spend on on-site testing, Stedman estimates, the city could identify and fix twenty-five thousand truly dirty vehicles every year, and within a few years cut automobile emissions in the Denver metropolitan area by somewhere between 35 and 40 percent. The city could stop managing its smog problem and start ending it.

Why don't we all adopt the Stedman method? There's no moral impediment here. We're used to the police pulling people over for having a blown headlight or a broken side mirror, and it wouldn't be difficult to have them add pollution-control devices to their list. Yet it does run counter to an instinctive social preference for thinking of pollution as a problem to which we all contribute equally. We have developed institutions that move reassuringly quickly and forcefully on collective problems. Congress passes a law. The Environmental Protection Agency promulgates a regulation. The auto industry makes its cars a little cleaner, and — presto — the air gets better. But Stedman doesn't much care about what happens in Washington and Detroit. The challenge of controlling air pollution isn't so much about the laws as it is about compliance with them. It's a policing problem, rather than a policy problem, and there is something ultimately unsatisfying about his proposed solution. He wants to end air pollution in Denver with a half-dozen vans outfitted with a contraption about the size of a suitcase. Can such a big problem have such a small-bore solution?

That's what made the findings of the Christopher Commission so unsatisfying. We put together blue-ribbon panels when we're faced with problems that seem too large for the normal mechanisms of bureaucratic repair. We want sweeping reforms. But what was the commission's most memorable observation? It was the story of an officer with a known history of doing things like beating up handcuffed suspects who nonetheless received a performance review from his superior stating that he "usually conducts himself in a manner that inspires respect for the law and instills public confidence." This is what you say about an officer when you haven't actually read his file, and the implication of the Christopher Commission's report was that the LAPD might help solve its problem simply by getting its police captains to read the files of their officers. The LAPD's problem was a matter not of policy but of compliance. The department needed to adhere to the rules it already had in place, and that's not what a public hungry for institutional transformation wants to hear. Solving problems that have power-law distributions doesn't just violate our moral intuitions; it violates our political intuitions as well. It's hard not to conclude, in the end, that the reason we treated the homeless as one hopeless undifferentiated group for so long is not simply that we didn't know better. It's that we didn't want to know better. It was easier the old way.

Power-law solutions have little appeal to the right, because they involve special treatment for people who do not deserve special treatment; and they have little appeal to the left, because their emphasis on efficiency over fairness suggests the cold number-crunching of Chicago school cost-benefit analysis. Even the promise of millions

of dollars in savings or cleaner air or better police departments cannot entirely compensate for such discomfort. In
Denver, John Hickenlooper, the city's enormously popular mayor, has worked on the homelessness issue tirelessly
during the past couple of years. He spent more time on
the subject in his annual State of the City address this
past summer than on any other topic. He gave the speech,
with deliberate symbolism, in the city's downtown Civic
Center Park, where homeless people gather every day
with their shopping carts and garbage bags. He has gone
on local talk radio on many occasions to discuss what the
city is doing about the issue. He has commissioned studies to show what a drain on the city's resources the homeless population has become. But, he says, "there are still
people who stop me going into the supermarket and say,
'I can't believe you're going to help those homeless people,
those bums.'"

5.

Early one morning, a few years ago, Marla Johns got a
call from her husband, Steve. He was at work. "He called
and woke me up," Johns remembers. "He was choked up
and crying on the phone. And I thought that something
had happened with another police officer. I said, 'Oh, my
gosh, what happened?' He said, 'Murray died last night.'"
He died of intestinal bleeding. At the police department
that morning, some of the officers gave Murray a moment
of silence.

"There are not many days that go by that I don't have
a thought of him," she went on. "Christmas comes — and
I used to buy him a Christmas present. Make sure he had

warm gloves and a blanket and a coat. There was this mutual respect. There was a time when another intoxicated patient jumped off the gurney and was coming at me, and Murray jumped off his gurney and shook his fist and said, 'Don't you touch my angel.' You know, when he was monitored by the system, he did fabulously. He would be on house arrest and he would get a job and he would save money and go to work every day, and he wouldn't drink. He would do all the things he was supposed to do. There are some people who can be very successful members of society if someone monitors them. Murray needed someone to be in charge of him."

But, of course, Reno didn't have a place where Murray could be given the structure he needed. Someone must have decided that it cost too much.

"I told my husband that I would claim his body if no one else did," she said. "I would not have him in an unmarked grave."

February 13, 2006

The Picture Problem

1.

At the beginning of the first Gulf war, the United States Air Force dispatched two squadrons of F-15E Strike Eagle fighter jets to find and destroy the Scud missiles that Iraq was firing at Israel. The rockets were being launched, mostly at night, from the backs of modified flatbed tractor-trailers, moving stealthily around a four-hundred-square-mile "Scud box" in the western desert. The plan was for the fighter jets to patrol the box from sunset to sunrise. When a Scud was launched, it would light up the night sky. An F-15E pilot would fly toward the launch point, follow the roads that crisscrossed the desert, and then locate the target using a state-of-the-art, $4.6 million device called a LANTIM navigation and targeting pod, capable of taking a high-resolution infrared photograph of a four-and-a-half-mile swath below the plane. How hard could it be to pick up a hulking tractor-trailer in the middle of an empty desert?

Almost immediately, reports of Scud kills began to come back from the field. The Desert Storm commanders

were elated. "I remember going out to Nellis Air Force Base after the war," Barry Watts, a former Air Force colonel, says. "They did a big static display, and they had all the Air Force jets that flew in Desert Storm, and they had little placards in front of them, with a box score, explaining what this plane did and that plane did in the war. And, when you added up how many Scud launchers they claimed each got, the total was about a hundred." Air Force officials were not guessing at the number of Scud launchers hit; as far as they were concerned, they *knew*. They had a $4 million camera that took a nearly perfect picture, and there are few cultural reflexes more deeply ingrained than the idea that a picture has the weight of truth. "That photography not only does not, but cannot, lie is a matter of belief, an article of faith," Charles Rosen and Henri Zerner have written. "We tend to trust the camera more than our own eyes." Thus was victory declared in the Scud hunt — until hostilities ended and the Air Force appointed a team to determine the effectiveness of the air campaigns in Desert Storm. The actual number of definite Scud kills, the team said, was zero.

The problem was that the pilots were operating at night, when depth perception is impaired. LANTIM could see in the dark, but the camera worked only when it was pointed in the right place, and the right place wasn't obvious. Meanwhile, the pilot had only about five minutes to find his quarry, because after launch the Iraqis would immediately hide in one of the many culverts underneath the highway between Baghdad and Jordan, and the screen the pilot was using to scan all that desert measured just six inches by six inches. "It was like driving down an interstate looking through a soda straw," Major General

Mike DeCuir, who flew numerous Scud-hunt missions throughout the war, recalled. Nor was it clear what a Scud launcher looked like on that screen. "We had an intelligence photo of one on the ground. But you had to imagine what it would look like on a black-and-white screen from twenty thousand feet up and five or more miles away," DeCuir went on. "With the resolution we had at the time, you could tell something was a big truck and that it had wheels, but at that altitude it was hard to tell much more than that." The postwar analysis indicated that a number of the targets the pilots had hit were actually decoys, constructed by the Iraqis from old trucks and spare missile parts. Others were tanker trucks transporting oil on the highway to Jordan. A tanker truck, after all, is a tractor-trailer hauling a long, shiny cylindrical object, and, from twenty thousand feet up at four hundred miles an hour on a six-by-six-inch screen, a long, shiny cylindrical object can look a lot like a missile. "It's a problem we've always had," Watts, who served on the team that did the Gulf war analysis, said. "It's night out. You think you've got something on the sensor. You roll out your weapons. Bombs go off. It's really hard to tell what you did."

You can build a high-tech camera capable of taking pictures in the middle of the night, in other words, but the system works only if the camera is pointed in the right place, and even then the pictures are not self-explanatory. They need to be interpreted, and the human task of interpretation is often a bigger obstacle than the technical task of picture taking. This was the lesson of the Scud hunt: pictures promise to clarify but often confuse. The Zapruder film intensified rather than dispelled the controversy surrounding John F. Kennedy's assassination. The videotape

of the beating of Rodney King led to widespread uproar
about police brutality; it also served as the basis for a jury's
decision to acquit the officers charged with the assault.
Perhaps nowhere have these issues been so apparent, however, as in the arena of mammography. Radiologists developed state-of-the-art X-ray cameras and used them to scan
women's breasts for tumors, reasoning that, if you can take
a nearly perfect picture, you can find and destroy tumors
before they go on to do serious damage. Yet there remains
a great deal of confusion about the benefits of mammography. Is it possible that we place too much faith in pictures?

2.

The head of breast imaging at Memorial Sloan-Kettering
Cancer Center, in New York City, is a physician named
David Dershaw, a youthful man in his fifties, who bears
a striking resemblance to the actor Kevin Spacey. One
morning not long ago, he sat down in his office at the back
of the Sloan-Kettering Building and tried to explain how
to read a mammogram.

Dershaw began by putting an X-ray on a light box
behind his desk. "Cancer shows up as one of two patterns," he said. "You look for lumps and bumps, and you
look for calcium. And, if you find it, you have to make a
determination: is it acceptable, or is it a pattern that might
be due to cancer?" He pointed at the X-ray. "This woman
has cancer. She has these tiny little calcifications. Can you
see them? Can you see how small they are?" He took out a
magnifying glass and placed it over a series of white flecks;
as a cancer grows, it produces calcium deposits. "That's
the stuff we are looking for," he said.

Then Dershaw added a series of slides to the light box and began to explain all the varieties that those white flecks came in. Some calcium deposits are oval and lucent. "They're called eggshell calcifications," Dershaw said. "And they're basically benign." Another kind of calcium runs like a railway track on either side of the breast's many blood vessels — that's benign, too. "Then there's calcium that's thick and heavy and looks like popcorn," Dershaw went on. "That's just dead tissue. That's benign. There's another calcification that's little sacs of calcium floating in liquid. It's called 'milk of calcium.' That's another kind of calcium that's always benign." He put a new set of slides against the light. "Then we have calcium that looks like this — irregular. All of these are of different density and different sizes and different configurations. Those are usually benign, but sometimes they are due to cancer. Remember you saw those railway tracks? This is calcium laid down inside a tube as well, but you can see that the outside of the tube is irregular. That's cancer." Dershaw's explanations were beginning to be confusing. "There are certain calcifications in benign tissues that are always benign," he said. "There are certain kinds that are always associated with cancer. But those are the ends of the spectrum, and the vast amount of calcium is somewhere in the middle. And making that differentiation, between whether the calcium is acceptable or not, is not clear-cut."

The same is true of lumps. Some lumps are simply benign clumps of cells. You can tell they are benign because the walls of the mass look round and smooth; in a cancer, cells proliferate so wildly that the walls of the tumor tend to be ragged and to intrude into the surrounding tissue. But sometimes benign lumps resemble tumors, and sometimes

tumors look a lot like benign lumps. And sometimes you have lots of masses that, taken individually, would be suspicious but are so pervasive that the reasonable conclusion is that this is just how the woman's breast looks. "If you have a CAT scan of the chest, the heart always looks like the heart, the aorta always looks like the aorta," Dershaw said. "So when there's a lump in the middle of that, it's clearly abnormal. Looking at a mammogram is conceptually different from looking at images elsewhere in the body. Everything else has anatomy — anatomy that essentially looks the same from one person to the next. But we don't have that kind of standardized information on the breast. The most difficult decision I think anybody needs to make when we're confronted with a patient is: Is this person normal? And we have to decide that without a pattern that is reasonably stable from individual to individual, and sometimes even without a pattern that is the same from the left side to the right."

Dershaw was saying that mammography doesn't fit our normal expectations of pictures. In the days before the invention of photography, for instance, a horse in motion was represented in drawings and paintings according to the convention of *ventre à terre,* or "belly to the ground." Horses were drawn with their front legs extended beyond their heads, and their hind legs stretched straight back, because that was the way, in the blur of movement, a horse seemed to gallop. Then, in the 1870s, came Eadweard Muybridge, with his famous sequential photographs of a galloping horse, and that was the end of *ventre à terre.* Now we knew how a horse galloped. The photograph promised that we would now be able to capture reality itself.

The situation with mammography is different. The way in which we ordinarily speak about calcium and lumps

is clear and unambiguous. But the picture demonstrates how blurry those seemingly distinct categories actually are. Joann Elmore, a physician and epidemiologist at the University of Washington Harborview Medical Center, once asked ten board-certified radiologists to look at 150 mammograms — of which 27 had come from women who developed breast cancer, and 123 from women who were known to be healthy. One radiologist caught 85 percent of the cancers the first time around. Another caught only 37 percent. One looked at the same X-rays and saw suspicious masses in 78 percent of the cases. Another doctor saw "focal asymmetric density" in half of the cancer cases; yet another saw no "focal asymmetric density" at all. There was one particularly perplexing mammogram that three radiologists thought was normal, two thought was abnormal but probably benign, four couldn't make up their minds about, and one was convinced was cancer. (The patient was fine.) Some of these differences are a matter of skill, and there is good evidence that with more rigorous training and experience radiologists can become better at reading breast X-rays. But so much of what can be seen on an X-ray falls into a gray area that interpreting a mammogram is also, in part, a matter of temperament. Some radiologists see something ambiguous and are comfortable calling it normal. Others see something ambiguous and get suspicious.

Does that mean radiologists ought to be as suspicious as possible? You might think so, but caution simply creates another kind of problem. The radiologist in the Elmore study who caught the most cancers also recommended immediate workups — a biopsy, an ultrasound, or additional X-rays — on 64 percent of the women who didn't have cancer. In the real world, a radiologist who needlessly

subjected such an extraordinary percentage of healthy patients to the time, expense, anxiety, and discomfort of biopsies and further testing would find himself seriously out of step with his profession. Mammography is not a form of medical treatment, where doctors are justified in going to heroic lengths on behalf of their patients. Mammography is a form of medical *screening:* it is supposed to exclude the healthy, so that more time and attention can be given to the sick. If screening doesn't screen, it ceases to be useful.

Gilbert Welch, a medical-outcomes expert at Dartmouth Medical School, has pointed out that, given current breast-cancer mortality rates, nine out of every thousand sixty-year-old women will die of breast cancer in the next ten years. If every one of those women had a mammogram every year, that number would fall to six. The radiologist seeing those thousand women, in other words, would read ten thousand X-rays over a decade in order to save three lives — and that's using the most generous possible estimate of mammography's effectiveness. The reason a radiologist is required to assume that the overwhelming number of ambiguous things are normal, in other words, is that the overwhelming number of ambiguous things really are normal. Radiologists are, in this sense, a lot like baggage screeners at airports. The chances are that the dark mass in the middle of the suitcase isn't a bomb, because you've seen a thousand dark masses like it in suitcases before, and none of those were bombs — and if you flagged every suitcase with something ambiguous in it, no one would ever make his flight. But that doesn't mean, of course, that it isn't a bomb. All you have to go on is what it looks like on the X-ray screen — and the screen seldom gives you quite enough information.

3.

Dershaw picked up a new X-ray and put it on the light box. It belonged to a forty-eight-year-old woman. Mammograms indicate density in the breast: the denser the tissue is, the more the X-rays are absorbed, creating the variations in black and white that make up the picture. Fat hardly absorbs the beam at all, so it shows up as black. Breast tissue, particularly the thick breast tissue of younger women, shows up on an X-ray as shades of light gray or white. This woman's breasts consisted of fat at the back of the breast and more dense, glandular tissue toward the front, so the X-ray was entirely black, with what looked like a large, white, dense cloud behind the nipple. Clearly visible, in the black, fatty portion of the left breast, was a white spot. "Now, that looks like a cancer, that little smudgy, irregular, infiltrative thing," Dershaw said. "It's about five millimeters across." He looked at the X-ray for a moment. This was mammography at its best: a clear picture of a problem that needed to be fixed. Then he took a pen and pointed to the thick cloud just to the right of the tumor. The cloud and the tumor were exactly the same color. "That cancer only shows up because it's in the fatty part of the breast," he said. "If you take that cancer and put it in the dense part of the breast, you'd never see it, because the whiteness of the mass is the same as the whiteness of normal tissue. If the tumor was over there, it could be four times as big and we still wouldn't see it."

What's more, mammography is especially likely to miss the tumors that do the most harm. A team led by the research pathologist Peggy Porter analyzed 429 breast cancers that had been diagnosed over five years at the Group

Health Cooperative of Puget Sound. Of those, 279 were picked up by mammography, and the bulk of them were detected very early, at what is called Stage One. (Cancer is classified into four stages, according to how far the tumor has spread from its original position.) Most of the tumors were small, less than two centimeters. Pathologists grade a tumor's aggression according to such measures as the "mitotic count" — the rate at which the cells are dividing — and the screen-detected tumors were graded "low" in almost 70 percent of the cases. These were the kinds of cancers that could probably be treated successfully. "Most tumors develop very, very slowly, and those tend to lay down calcium deposits — and what mammograms are doing is picking up those calcifications," Leslie Laufman, a hematologist-oncologist in Ohio, who served on a recent National Institutes of Health breast-cancer advisory panel, said. "Almost by definition, mammograms are picking up slow-growing tumors."

A hundred and fifty cancers in Porter's study, however, were missed by mammography. Some of these were tumors the mammogram couldn't see — that were, for instance, hiding in the dense part of the breast. The majority, though, simply didn't exist at the time of the mammogram. These cancers were found in women who had had regular mammograms, and who were legitimately told that they showed no sign of cancer on their last visit. In the interval between X-rays, however, either they or their doctor had manually discovered a lump in their breast, and these "interval" cancers were twice as likely to be in Stage Three and three times as likely to have high mitotic counts; 28 percent had spread to the lymph nodes, as opposed to 18 percent of the screen-detected cancers.

These tumors were so aggressive that they had gone from undetectable to detectable in the interval between two mammograms.

The problem of interval tumors explains why the overwhelming majority of breast-cancer experts insist that women in the critical fifty-to-sixty-nine age group get regular mammograms. In Porter's study, the women were X-rayed at intervals as great as every three years, and that created a window large enough for interval cancers to emerge. Interval cancers also explain why many breast-cancer experts believe that mammograms must be supplemented by regular and thorough clinical breast exams. (*Thorough* is defined as palpation of the area from the collarbone to the bottom of the rib cage, one dime-size area at a time, at three levels of pressure — just below the skin, the midbreast, and up against the chest wall — by a specially trained practitioner for a period not less than five minutes per breast.) In a major study of mammography's effectiveness — one of a pair of Canadian trials conducted in the 1980s — women who were given regular, thorough breast exams but no mammograms were compared with those who had thorough breast exams and regular mammograms, and no difference was found in the death rates from breast cancer between the two groups. The Canadian studies are controversial, and some breast-cancer experts are convinced that they may have understated the benefits of mammography. But there is no denying the basic lessons of the Canadian trials: that a skilled pair of fingertips can find out an extraordinary amount about the health of a breast, and that we should not automatically value what we see in a picture over what we learn from our other senses.

"The finger has hundreds of sensors per square

centimeter," says Mark Goldstein, a sensory psychophysicist who cofounded MammaCare, a company devoted to training nurses and physicians in the art of the clinical exam. "There is nothing in science or technology that has even come close to the sensitivity of the human finger with respect to the range of stimuli it can pick up. It's a brilliant instrument. But we simply don't trust our tactile sense as much as our visual sense."

4.

On the night of August 17, 1943, two hundred B-17 bombers from the United States Eighth Air Force set out from England for the German city of Schweinfurt. Two months later, 228 B-17s set out to strike Schweinfurt a second time. The raids were two of the heaviest nights of bombing in the war, and the Allied experience at Schweinfurt is an example of a more subtle — but in some cases more serious — problem with the picture paradigm.

The Schweinfurt raids grew out of the United States military's commitment to bombing accuracy. As Stephen Budiansky writes in his wonderful recent book *Air Power,* the chief lesson of aerial bombardment in the First World War was that hitting a target from eight or ten thousand feet was a prohibitively difficult task. In the thick of battle, the bombardier had to adjust for the speed of the plane, the speed and direction of the prevailing winds, and the pitching and rolling of the plane, all while keeping the bombsight level with the ground. It was an impossible task, requiring complex trigonometric calculations. For a variety of reasons, including the technical challenges, the British simply abandoned the quest for precision: in both

the First World War and the Second, the British military pursued a strategy of *morale* or *area bombing,* in which bombs were simply dropped, indiscriminately, on urban areas, with the intention of killing, dispossessing, and dispiriting the German civilian population.

But the American military believed that the problem of bombing accuracy was solvable, and a big part of the solution was something called the *Norden bombsight.* This breakthrough was the work of a solitary, cantankerous genius named Carl Norden, who operated out of a factory in New York City. Norden built a fifty-pound mechanical computer called the Mark XV, which used gears and wheels and gyroscopes to calculate airspeed, altitude, and crosswinds in order to determine the correct bomb-release point. The Mark XV, Norden's business partner boasted, could put a bomb in a pickle barrel from twenty thousand feet. The United States spent $1.5 billion developing it, which, as Budiansky points out, was more than half the amount that was spent building the atomic bomb. "At air bases, the Nordens were kept under lock and key in secure vaults, escorted to their planes by armed guards, and shrouded in a canvas cover until after takeoff," Budiansky recounts. The American military, convinced that its bombers could now hit whatever they could see, developed a strategic approach to bombing, identifying, and selectively destroying targets that were critical to the Nazi war effort. In early 1943, General Henry (Hap) Arnold — the head of the Army Air Forces — assembled a group of prominent civilians to analyze the German economy and recommend critical targets. The Advisory Committee on Bombardment, as it was called, determined that the United States should target Germany's ball-bearing factories, since ball

bearings were critical to the manufacture of airplanes. And the center of the German ball-bearing industry was Schweinfurt. Allied losses from the two raids were staggering. Thirty-six B-17s were shot down in the August attack, 62 bombers were shot down in the October raid, and between the two operations, a further 138 planes were badly damaged. Yet, with the war in the balance, this was considered worth the price. When the damage reports came in, Arnold exulted, "Now we have got Schweinfurt!" He was wrong.

The problem was not, as in the case of the Scud hunt, that the target could not be found, or that what was thought to be the target was actually something else. The B-17s, aided by their Norden Mark XVs, hit the ball-bearing factories hard. The problem was that the picture Air Force officers had of their target didn't tell them what they really needed to know. The Germans, it emerged, had ample stockpiles of ball bearings. They also had no difficulty increasing their imports from Sweden and Switzerland, and, through a few simple design changes, they were able to greatly reduce their need for ball bearings in aircraft production. What's more, although the factory buildings were badly damaged by the bombing, the machinery inside wasn't. Ball-bearing equipment turned out to be surprisingly hardy. "As it was, not a tank, plane, or other piece of weaponry failed to be produced because of lack of ball bearings," Albert Speer, the Nazi production chief, wrote after the war. Seeing a problem and understanding it, then, are two different things.

In recent years, with the rise of highly accurate long-distance weaponry, the Schweinfurt problem has become even more acute. If you can aim at and hit the kitchen at the back of a house, after all, you don't have to bomb

the whole building. So your bomb can be two hundred pounds rather than a thousand. That means, in turn, that you can fit five times as many bombs on a single plane and hit five times as many targets in a single sortie, which sounds good — except that now you need to get intelligence on five times as many targets. And that intelligence has to be five times more specific, because if the target is in the bedroom and not the kitchen, you've missed him.

This is the issue that the US command faced in the most recent Iraq war. Early in the campaign, the military mounted a series of air strikes against specific targets, where Saddam Hussein or other senior Baathist officials were thought to be hiding. There were fifty of these so-called decapitation attempts, each taking advantage of the fact that modern-day GPS-guided bombs can be delivered from a fighter to within thirteen meters of their intended target. The strikes were dazzling in their precision. In one case, a restaurant was leveled. In another, a bomb burrowed down into a basement. But, in the end, every single strike failed. "The issue isn't accuracy," Watts, who has written extensively on the limitations of high-tech weaponry, says. "The issue is the quality of targeting information. The amount of information we need has gone up an order of magnitude or two in the last decade."

5.

Mammography has a Schweinfurt problem as well. Nowhere is that more evident than in the case of the breast lesion known as ductal carcinoma in situ, or DCIS, which shows up as a cluster of calcifications inside the ducts that carry milk to the nipple. It's a tumor that hasn't spread

beyond those ducts, and it is so tiny that without mammography few women with DCIS would ever know they have it. In the past couple of decades, as more and more people have received regular breast X-rays and the resolution of mammography has increased, diagnoses of DCIS have soared. About fifty thousand new cases are now found every year in the United States, and virtually every DCIS lesion detected by mammography is promptly removed. But what has the targeting and destruction of DCIS meant for the battle against breast cancer? You'd expect that if we've been catching fifty thousand early-stage cancers every year, we should be seeing a corresponding decrease in the number of late-stage invasive cancers. It's not clear whether we have. During the past twenty years, the incidence of invasive breast cancer has continued to rise by the same small, steady increment every year.

In 1987, pathologists in Denmark performed a series of autopsies on women in their forties who had not been known to have breast cancer when they died of other causes. The pathologists looked at an average of 275 samples of breast tissue in each case, and found some evidence of cancer — usually DCIS — in nearly 40 percent of the women. Since breast cancer accounts for less than 4 percent of female deaths, clearly the overwhelming majority of these women, had they lived longer, would never have died of breast cancer. "To me, that indicates that these kinds of genetic changes happen really frequently, and that they can happen without having an impact on women's health," Karla Kerlikowske, a breast-cancer expert at the University of California at San Francisco, says. "The body has this whole mechanism to repair things, and maybe that's what happened with these tumors." Gilbert

Welch, the medical-outcomes expert, thinks that we fail to understand the hit-or-miss nature of cancerous growth, and assume it to be a process that, in the absence of intervention, will eventually kill us. "A pathologist from the International Agency for Research on Cancer once told me that the biggest mistake we ever made was attaching the word 'carcinoma' to DCIS," Welch says. "The minute carcinoma got linked to it, it all of a sudden drove doctors to recommend therapy, because what was implied was that this was a lesion that would inexorably progress to invasive cancer. But we know that that's not always the case."

In some percentage of cases, however, DCIS does progress to something more serious. Some studies suggest that this happens very infrequently. Others suggest that it happens frequently enough to be of major concern. There is no definitive answer, and it's all but impossible to tell, simply by looking at a mammogram, whether a given DCIS tumor is among those lesions that will grow out from the duct, or part of the majority that will never amount to anything. That's why some doctors feel that we have no choice but to treat every DCIS as life-threatening, and in 30 percent of cases that means a mastectomy, and in another 35 percent it means a lumpectomy and radiation. Would taking a better picture solve the problem? Not really, because the problem is that we don't know for sure what we're seeing, and as pictures have become better we have put ourselves in a position where we see more and more things that we don't know how to interpret. When it comes to DCIS, the mammogram delivers information without true understanding. "Almost half a million women have been diagnosed and treated for DCIS since the early nineteen-eighties — a diagnosis virtually unknown before

then," Welch writes in his new book, *Should I Be Tested for Cancer?*, a brilliant account of the statistical and medical uncertainties surrounding cancer screening. "This increase is the direct result of looking harder — in this case with 'better' mammography equipment. But I think you can see why it is a diagnosis that some women might reasonably prefer not to know about."

6.

The disturbing thing about DCIS, of course, is that our approach to this tumor seems like a textbook example of how the battle against cancer is supposed to work. Use a powerful camera. Take a detailed picture. Spot the tumor as early as possible. Treat it immediately and aggressively. The campaign to promote regular mammograms has used this early-detection argument with great success because it makes intuitive sense. The danger posed by a tumor is represented visually. Large is bad; small is better — less likely to have metastasized. But here, too, tumors defy our visual intuitions.

According to Donald Berry, who is the chairman of the Department of Biostatistics and Applied Mathematics at M. D. Anderson Cancer Center, in Houston, a woman's risk of death increases only by about 10 percent for every additional centimeter in tumor length. "Suppose there is a tumor size above which the tumor is lethal, and below which it's not," Berry says. "The problem is that the threshold varies. When we find a tumor, we don't know whether it has metastasized already. And we don't know whether it's tumor size that drives the metastatic process or whether all you need is a few million cells to start

sloughing off to other parts of the body. We do observe that it's worse to have a bigger tumor. But not amazingly worse. The relationship is not as great as you'd think."

In a recent genetic analysis of breast-cancer tumors, scientists selected women with breast cancer who had been followed for many years, and divided them into two groups — those whose cancer had gone into remission, and those whose cancer had spread to the rest of their body. Then the scientists went back to the earliest moment that each cancer became apparent and analyzed thousands of genes in order to determine whether it was possible to predict, at that moment, who was going to do well and who wasn't. Early detection presumes that it isn't possible to make that prediction: a tumor is removed before it becomes truly dangerous. But scientists discovered that even with tumors in the one-centimeter range — the range in which cancer is first picked up by a mammogram — the fate of the cancer seems already to have been set. "What we found is that there is biology that you can glean from the tumor, at the time you take it out, that is strongly predictive of whether or not it will go on to metastasize," Stephen Friend, a member of the gene-expression team at Merck, says. "We like to think of a small tumor as an innocent. The reality is that in that innocent lump are a lot of behaviors that spell a potential poor or good prognosis."

The good news here is that it might eventually be possible to screen breast cancers on a genetic level, using other kinds of tests — even blood tests — to look for the biological traces of those genes. This might also help with the chronic problem of overtreatment in breast cancer. If we can single out that small percentage of women whose tumors will metastasize, we can spare the rest the usual

regimen of surgery, radiation, and chemotherapy. Gene-signature research is one of a number of reasons that many scientists are optimistic about the fight against breast cancer. But it is an advance that has nothing to do with taking more pictures, or taking better pictures. It has to do with going beyond the picture.

Under the circumstances, it is not hard to understand why mammography draws so much controversy. The picture promises certainty, and it cannot deliver on that promise. Even after forty years of research, there remains widespread disagreement over how much benefit women in the critical fifty-to-sixty-nine age bracket receive from breast X-rays, and further disagreement about whether there is enough evidence to justify regular mammography in women under fifty and over seventy. Is there any way to resolve the disagreement? Donald Berry says that there probably isn't — that a clinical trial that could definitively answer the question of mammography's precise benefits would have to be so large (involving more than five hundred thousand women) and so expensive (costing billions of dollars) as to be impractical. The resulting confusion has turned radiologists who do mammograms into one of the chief targets of malpractice litigation. "The problem is that mammographers — radiology groups — do hundreds of thousands of these mammograms, giving women the illusion that these things work and they are good, and if a lump is found and in most cases if it is found early, they tell women they have the probability of a higher survival rate," says E. Clay Parker, a Florida plaintiff's attorney, who recently won a $5.1 million judgment against an Orlando radiologist. "But then, when it comes to defending themselves, they tell you that the reality is that it

doesn't make a difference when you find it. So you scratch your head and say, 'Well, why do you do mammography, then?'"

The answer is that mammograms do not have to be infallible to save lives. A modest estimate of mammography's benefit is that it reduces the risk of dying from breast cancer by about 10 percent — which works out, for the average woman in her fifties, to be about three extra days of life, or, to put it another way, a health benefit on a par with wearing a helmet on a ten-hour bicycle trip. That is not a trivial benefit. Multiplied across the millions of adult women in the United States, it amounts to thousands of lives saved every year, and, in combination with a medical regimen that includes radiation, surgery, and new and promising drugs, it has helped brighten the prognosis for women with breast cancer. Mammography isn't as good as we'd like it to be. But we are still better off than we would be without it.

"There is increasingly an understanding among those of us who do this a lot that our efforts to sell mammography may have been overvigorous," Dershaw said, "and that although we didn't intend to, the perception may have been that mammography accomplishes even more than it does." He was looking, as he spoke, at the mammogram of the woman whose tumor would have been invisible had it been a few centimeters to the right. Did looking at an X-ray like that make him nervous? Dershaw shook his head. "You have to respect the limitations of the technology," he said. "My job with the mammogram isn't to find what I can't find with a mammogram. It's to find what I can find with a mammogram. If I'm not going to accept that, then I shouldn't be reading mammograms."

7.

In February of 2002, just before the start of the Iraq war, Secretary of State Colin Powell went before the United Nations to declare that Iraq was in defiance of international law. He presented transcripts of telephone conversations between senior Iraqi military officials, purportedly discussing attempts to conceal weapons of mass destruction. He told of eyewitness accounts of mobile biological-weapons facilities. And, most persuasive, he presented a series of images — carefully annotated, high-resolution satellite photographs of what he said was the Taji Iraqi chemical-munitions facility.

"Let me say a word about satellite images before I show a couple," Powell began. "The photos that I am about to show you are sometimes hard for the average person to interpret, hard for me. The painstaking work of photo analysis takes experts with years and years of experience, poring for hours and hours over light tables. But as I show you these images, I will try to capture and explain what they mean, what they indicate, to our imagery specialists." The first photograph was dated November 10, 2002, just three months earlier, and years after the Iraqis were supposed to have rid themselves of all weapons of mass destruction. "Let me give you a closer look," Powell said as he flipped to a closeup of the first photograph. It showed a rectangular building, with a vehicle parked next to it. "Look at the image on the left. On the left is a closeup of one of the four chemical bunkers. The two arrows indicate the presence of sure signs that the bunkers are storing chemical munitions. The arrow at the top that says 'Security' points to a facility that is a signature item for this kind of bunker. Inside that

facility are special guards and special equipment to monitor any leakage that might come out of the bunker." Then he moved to the vehicle next to the building. It was, he said, another signature item. "It's a decontamination vehicle in case something goes wrong....It is moving around those four and it moves as needed to move as people are working in the different bunkers."

Powell's analysis assumed, of course, that you could tell from the picture what kind of truck it was. But pictures of trucks, taken from above, are not always as clear as we would like; sometimes trucks hauling oil tanks look just like trucks hauling Scud launchers, and, while a picture is a good start, if you really want to know what you're looking at, you probably need more than a picture. I looked at the photographs with Patrick Eddington, who for many years was an imagery analyst with the CIA. Eddington examined them closely. "They're trying to say that those are decontamination vehicles," he told me. He had a photo up on his laptop, and he peered closer to get a better look. "But the resolution is sufficient for me to say that I don't think it is — and I don't see any other decontamination vehicles down there that I would recognize." The standard decontamination vehicle was a Soviet-made box-body van, Eddington said. This truck was too long. For a second opinion, Eddington recommended Ray McGovern, a twenty-seven-year CIA analyst, who had been one of George H. W. Bush's personal intelligence briefers when he was vice president. "If you're an expert, you can tell one hell of a lot from pictures like this," McGovern said. He'd heard another interpretation. "I think," he said, "that it's a fire truck."

December 13, 2004

Something Borrowed

1.

One day in the spring of 2004, a psychiatrist named Dorothy Lewis got a call from her friend Betty, who works in New York City. Betty had just seen a Broadway play called *Frozen,* written by the British playwright Bryony Lavery. "She said, 'Somehow it reminded me of you. You really ought to see it,'" Lewis recalled. Lewis asked Betty what the play was about, and Betty said that one of the characters was a psychiatrist who studied serial killers. "And I told her, 'I need to see that as much as I need to go to the moon.'"

Lewis has studied serial killers for the past twenty-five years. With her collaborator, the neurologist Jonathan Pincus, she has published a great many research papers, showing that serial killers tend to suffer from predictable patterns of psychological, physical, and neurological dysfunction: that they were almost all the victims of harrowing physical and sexual abuse as children, and that almost all of them have suffered some kind of brain injury

or mental illness. In 1998, she published a memoir of her life and work entitled *Guilty by Reason of Insanity*. She was the last person to visit Ted Bundy before he went to the electric chair. Few people in the world have spent as much time thinking about serial killers as Dorothy Lewis, so when her friend Betty told her that she needed to see *Frozen* it struck her as a busman's holiday.

But the calls kept coming. *Frozen* was winning raves on Broadway, and it had been nominated for a Tony. Whenever someone who knew Dorothy Lewis saw it, they would tell her that she really ought to see it, too. In June, she got a call from a woman at the theater where *Frozen* was playing. "She said she'd heard that I work in this field, and that I see murderers, and she was wondering if I would do a talk-back after the show," Lewis said. "I had done that once before, and it was a delight, so I said sure. And I said, 'Would you please send me the script, because I want to read the play.'"

The script came, and Lewis sat down to read it. Early in the play, something caught her eye, a phrase: "it was one of those days." One of the murderers Lewis had written about in her book had used that same expression. But she thought it was just a coincidence. "Then, there's a scene of a woman on an airplane, typing away to her friend. Her name is Agnetha Gottmundsdottir. I read that she's writing to her colleague, a neurologist called David Nabkus. And with that I realized that more was going on, and I realized as well why all these people had been telling me to see the play."

Lewis began underlining line after line. She had worked at New York University School of Medicine. The psychiatrist in *Frozen* worked at New York School of

Medicine. Lewis and Pincus did a study of brain injuries among fifteen death-row inmates. Gottmundsdottir and Nabkus did a study of brain injuries among fifteen death-row inmates. Once, while Lewis was examining the serial killer Joseph Franklin, he sniffed her, in a grotesque, sexual way. Gottmundsdottir is sniffed by the play's serial killer, Ralph. Once, while Lewis was examining Ted Bundy, she kissed him on the cheek. Gottmundsdottir, in some productions of *Frozen*, kisses Ralph. "The whole thing was right there," Lewis went on. "I was sitting at home reading the play, and I realized that it was I. I felt robbed and violated in some peculiar way. It was as if someone had stolen — I don't believe in the soul, but, if there was such a thing, it was as if someone had stolen my essence."

Lewis never did the talk-back. She hired a lawyer. And she came down from New Haven to see *Frozen*. "In my book," she said, "I talk about where I rush out of the house with my black carry-on, and I have two black pocketbooks, and the play opens with her" — Agnetha — "with one big black bag and a carry-on, rushing out to do a lecture." Lewis had written about biting her sister on the stomach as a child. Onstage, Agnetha fantasized out loud about attacking a stewardess on an airplane and "biting out her throat." After the play was over, the cast came onstage and took questions from the audience. "Somebody in the audience said, 'Where did Bryony Lavery get the idea for the psychiatrist?' " Lewis recounted. "And one of the cast members, the male lead, said, 'Oh, she said that she read it in an English medical magazine.' " Lewis is a tiny woman, with enormous, childlike eyes, and they were wide open now with the memory. "I wouldn't have cared if she did a play about a shrink who's interested in the frontal lobe and

the limbic system. That's out there to do. I see things week after week on television, on *Law & Order* or *C.S.I.*, and I see that they are using material that Jonathan and I brought to light. And it's wonderful. That would have been acceptable. But she did more than that. She took things about my own life, and that is the part that made me feel violated."

At the request of her lawyer, Lewis sat down and made up a chart detailing what she felt were the questionable parts of Lavery's play. The chart was fifteen pages long. The first part was devoted to thematic similarities between *Frozen* and Lewis's book *Guilty by Reason of Insanity*. The other, more damning section listed twelve instances of almost verbatim similarities — totaling perhaps 675 words — between passages from *Frozen* and passages from a 1997 magazine profile of Lewis. The profile was called "Damaged." It appeared in the February 24, 1997, issue of *The New Yorker*. It was written by me.

2.

Words belong to the person who wrote them. There are few simpler ethical notions than this one, particularly as society directs more and more energy and resources toward the creation of intellectual property. In the past thirty years, copyright laws have been strengthened. Courts have become more willing to grant intellectual-property protections. Fighting piracy has become an obsession with Hollywood and the recording industry, and, in the worlds of academia and publishing, plagiarism has gone from being bad literary manners to something much closer to a crime. When, two years ago, Doris Kearns Goodwin was found to have lifted passages from several other historians, she

was asked to resign from the board of the Pulitzer Prize committee. And why not? If she had robbed a bank, she would have been fired the next day.

I'd worked on "Damaged" through the fall of 1996. I would visit Dorothy Lewis in her office at Bellevue Hospital and watch the videotapes of her interviews with serial killers. At one point, I met up with her in Missouri. Lewis was testifying at the trial of Joseph Franklin, who claims responsibility for shooting, among others, the civil-rights leader Vernon Jordan and the pornographer Larry Flynt. In the trial, a videotape was shown of an interview that Franklin once gave to a television station. He was asked whether he felt any remorse. I wrote:

> "I can't say that I do," he said. He paused again, then added, "The only thing I'm sorry about is that it's not legal."
>
> "What's not legal?"
>
> Franklin answered as if he'd been asked the time of day: "Killing Jews."

That exchange, almost to the word, was reproduced in *Frozen*.

Lewis, the article continued, didn't feel that Franklin was fully responsible for his actions. She viewed him as a victim of neurological dysfunction and childhood physical abuse. "The difference between a crime of evil and a crime of illness," I wrote, "is the difference between a sin and a symptom." That line was in *Frozen,* too — not once but twice. I faxed Bryony Lavery a letter:

> I am happy to be the source of inspiration for other writers, and had you asked for my permission to quote — even

liberally — from my piece, I would have been delighted to oblige. But to lift material, without my approval, is theft.

Almost as soon as I'd sent the letter, though, I began to have second thoughts. The truth was that, although I said I'd been robbed, I didn't feel that way. Nor did I feel particularly angry. One of the first things I had said to a friend after hearing about the echoes of my article in *Frozen* was that this was the only way I was ever going to get to Broadway — and I was only half joking. On some level, I considered Lavery's borrowing to be a compliment. A savvier writer would have changed all those references to Lewis, and rewritten the quotes from me, so that their origin was no longer recognizable. But how would I have been better off if Lavery had disguised the source of her inspiration?

Dorothy Lewis, for her part, was understandably upset. She was considering a lawsuit. And, to increase her odds of success, she asked me to assign her the copyright to my article. I agreed, but then I changed my mind. Lewis had told me that she "wanted her life back." Yet in order to get her life back, it appeared, she first had to acquire it from me. That seemed a little strange.

Then I got a copy of the script for *Frozen*. I found it breathtaking. I realize that this isn't supposed to be a relevant consideration. And yet it was: instead of feeling that my words had been taken from me, I felt that they had become part of some grander cause. In late September, the story broke. The *Times*, the *Observer* in England, and the Associated Press all ran stories about Lavery's alleged plagiarism, and the articles were picked up by newspapers around the world. Bryony Lavery had seen one of my articles, responded to what she read, and used it as she

constructed a work of art. And now her reputation was in tatters. Something about that didn't seem right.

3.

In 1992, the Beastie Boys released a song called "Pass the Mic," which begins with a six-second sample taken from the 1976 composition "Choir" by the jazz flutist James Newton. The sample was an exercise in what is called multiphonics, where the flutist "overblows" into the instrument while simultaneously singing in a falsetto. In the case of "Choir," Newton played a C on the flute, then sang C, D-flat, C — and the distortion of the overblown C combined with his vocalizing created a surprisingly complex and haunting sound. In "Pass the Mic," the Beastie Boys repeated the Newton sample more than forty times. The effect was riveting.

In the world of music, copyrighted works fall into two categories — the recorded performance and the composition underlying that performance. If you write a rap song, and you want to sample the chorus from Billy Joel's "Piano Man," you have to first get permission from the record label to use the "Piano Man" recording, and then get permission from Billy Joel (or whoever owns his music) to use the underlying composition. In the case of "Pass the Mic," the Beastie Boys got the first kind of permission — the rights to use the recording of "Choir" — but not the second. Newton sued, and he lost — and the reason he lost serves as a useful introduction to how to think about intellectual property.

At issue in the case wasn't the distinctiveness of Newton's performance. The Beastie Boys, everyone agreed, had properly licensed Newton's performance when they

paid the copyright recording fee. And there was no question about whether they had copied the underlying music to the sample. At issue was simply whether the Beastie Boys were required to ask for that secondary permission: was the composition underneath those six seconds so distinctive and original that Newton could be said to own it? The court said that it wasn't.

The chief expert witness for the Beastie Boys in the "Choir" case was Lawrence Ferrara, who is a professor of music at New York University, and when I asked him to explain the court's ruling, he walked over to the piano in the corner of his office and played those three notes: C, D-flat, C. "That's it!" he shouted. "There ain't nothing else! That's what was used. You know what this is? It's no more than a mordent, a turn. It's been done thousands upon thousands of times. No one can say they own that."

Ferrara then played the most famous four-note sequence in classical music, the opening of Beethoven's Fifth: G, G, G, E-flat. This was unmistakably Beethoven. But was it original? "That's a harder case," Ferrara said. "Actually, though, other composers wrote that. Beethoven himself wrote that in a piano sonata, and you can find figures like that in composers who predate Beethoven. It's one thing if you're talking about *da-da-da dummm, da-da-da dummm* — those notes, with those durations. But just the four pitches, G, G, G, E-flat? Nobody owns those."

Ferrara once served as an expert witness for Andrew Lloyd Webber, who was being sued by Ray Repp, a composer of Catholic folk music. Repp said that the opening few bars of Lloyd Webber's 1984 "Phantom Song," from *The Phantom of the Opera,* bore an overwhelming resemblance to his composition "Till You," written six years

earlier, in 1978. As Ferrara told the story, he sat down at the piano again and played the beginning of both songs, one after the other; sure enough, they sounded strikingly similar. "Here's Lloyd Webber," he said, calling out each note as he played it. "Here's Repp. Same sequence. The only difference is that Andrew writes a perfect fourth and Repp writes a sixth."

But Ferrara wasn't quite finished. "I said, let me have everything Andrew Lloyd Webber wrote prior to 1978 — *Jesus Christ Superstar, Joseph, Evita*." He combed through every score, and in *Joseph and the Amazing Technicolor Dreamcoat* he found what he was looking for. "It's the song 'Benjamin Calypso.'" Ferrara started playing it. It was immediately familiar. "It's the first phrase of 'Phantom Song.' It's even using the same notes. But wait — it gets better. Here's 'Close Every Door,' from a 1969 concert performance of *Joseph*." Ferrara is a dapper, animated man, with a thin, well-manicured mustache, and thinking about the Lloyd Webber case was almost enough to make him jump up and down. He began to play again. It was the second phrase of "Phantom." "The first half of 'Phantom' is in 'Benjamin Calypso.' The second half is in 'Close Every Door.' They are identical. On the button. In the case of the first theme, in fact, 'Benjamin Calypso' is closer to the first half of the theme at issue than the plaintiff's song. Lloyd Webber writes something in 1984, and he borrows from himself."

In the "Choir" case, the Beastie Boys' copying didn't amount to theft because it was too trivial. In the "Phantom" case, what Lloyd Webber was alleged to have copied didn't amount to theft because the material in question wasn't original to his accuser. Under copyright law,

what matters is not that you copied someone else's work. What matters is *what* you copied, and *how much* you copied. Intellectual-property doctrine isn't a straightforward application of the ethical principle "Thou shalt not steal." At its core is the notion that there are certain situations where you *can* steal. The protections of copyright, for instance, are time-limited; once something passes into the public domain, anyone can copy it without restriction. Or suppose that you invented a cure for breast cancer in your basement lab. Any patent you received would protect your intellectual property for twenty years, but after that anyone could take your invention. You get an initial monopoly on your creation because we want to provide economic incentives for people to invent things like cancer drugs. But everyone gets to steal your breast-cancer cure — after a decent interval — because it is also in society's interest to let as many people as possible copy your invention; only then can others learn from it, and build on it, and come up with better and cheaper alternatives. This balance between the protecting and the limiting of intellectual property is, in fact, enshrined in the Constitution: "Congress shall have the power to promote the Progress of Science and useful Arts, by securing for limited" — note that specification, *limited* — "Times to Authors and Inventors the exclusive Right to their respective Writings and Discoveries."

4.

So is it true that words belong to the person who wrote them, just as other kinds of property belong to their owners? Actually, no. As the Stanford law professor Lawrence Lessig argues in his book *Free Culture*:

In ordinary language, to call a copyright a "property" right is a bit misleading, for the property of copyright is an odd kind of property.... I understand what I am taking when I take the picnic table you put in your backyard. I am taking a thing, the picnic table, and after I take it, you don't have it. But what am I taking when I take the good idea you had to put a picnic table in the backyard — by, for example, going to Sears, buying a table, and putting it in my backyard? What is the thing that I am taking then?

The point is not just about the thingness of picnic tables versus ideas, though that is an important difference. The point instead is that in the ordinary case — indeed, in practically every case except for a narrow range of exceptions — ideas released to the world are free. I don't take anything from you when I copy the way you dress — though I might seem weird if I do it every day.... Instead, as Thomas Jefferson said (and this is especially true when I copy the way someone dresses), "He who receives an idea from me, receives instruction himself without lessening mine; as he who lights his taper at mine, receives light without darkening me."

Lessig argues that, when it comes to drawing this line between private interests and public interests in intellectual property, the courts and Congress have, in recent years, swung much too far in the direction of private interests. He writes, for instance, about the fight by some developing countries to get access to inexpensive versions of Western drugs through what is called *parallel importation* — buying drugs from another developing country that has been licensed to produce patented medicines. The move would save countless lives. But it has been opposed by the United States not on the ground

that it would cut into the profits of Western pharmaceutical companies (they don't sell that many patented drugs in developing countries anyway) but on the ground that it violates the sanctity of intellectual property. "We as a culture have lost this sense of balance," Lessig writes. "A certain property fundamentalism, having no connection to our tradition, now reigns in this culture."

Even what Lessig decries as intellectual-property extremism, however, acknowledges that intellectual property has its limits. The United States didn't say that developing countries could never get access to cheap versions of American drugs. It said only that they would have to wait until the patents on those drugs expired. The arguments that Lessig has with the hard-core proponents of intellectual property are almost all arguments about *where* and *when* the line should be drawn between the right to copy and the right to protection from copying, not *whether* a line should be drawn.

But plagiarism is different, and that's what's so strange about it. The ethical rules that govern when it's acceptable for one writer to copy another are even more extreme than the most extreme position of the intellectual-property crowd: when it comes to literature, we have somehow decided that copying is *never* acceptable. Not long ago, the Harvard law professor Laurence Tribe was accused of lifting material from the historian Henry Abraham for his 1985 book, *God Save This Honorable Court*. What did the charge amount to? In an exposé that appeared in the conservative publication *The Weekly Standard*, Joseph Bottum produced a number of examples of close paraphrasing, but his smoking gun was this one borrowed sentence: "Taft publicly pronounced Pitney to be a 'weak

member' of the Court to whom he could not assign cases."
That's it. Nineteen words.

Not long after I learned about *Frozen*, I went to see a
friend of mine who works in the music industry. We sat in
his living room on the Upper East Side, facing each other
in easy chairs, as he worked his way through a mountain
of CDs. He played "Angel," by the reggae singer Shaggy,
and then "The Joker," by the Steve Miller Band, and told
me to listen very carefully to the similarity in bass lines.
He played Led Zeppelin's "Whole Lotta Love" and then
Muddy Waters's "You Need Love," to show the extent to
which Led Zeppelin had mined the blues for inspiration.
He played "Twice My Age," by Shabba Ranks and Krys-
tal, and then the saccharine '70s pop standard "Seasons
in the Sun," until I could hear the echoes of the second
song in the first. He played "Last Christmas," by Wham!
followed by Barry Manilow's "Can't Smile Without You"
to explain why Manilow might have been startled when
he first heard that song, and then "Joanna," by Kool and
the Gang, because, in a different way, "Last Christmas"
was an homage to Kool and the Gang as well. "That sound
you hear in Nirvana," my friend said at one point, "that
soft and then loud kind of exploding thing, a lot of that
was inspired by the Pixies. Yet Kurt Cobain" — Nirvana's lead singer and songwriter — "was such a genius
that he managed to make it his own. And 'Smells Like
Teen Spirit'?" — here he was referring to perhaps the
best-known Nirvana song. "That's Boston's 'More Than
a Feeling.'" He began to hum the riff of the Boston hit,
and said, "The first time I heard 'Teen Spirit,' I said, 'That
guitar lick is from "More Than a Feeling."' But it was different — it was urgent and brilliant and new."

He played another CD. It was Rod Stewart's "Do Ya Think I'm Sexy," a huge hit from the 1970s. The chorus has a distinctive, catchy hook — the kind of tune that millions of Americans probably hummed in the shower the year it came out. Then he put on "Taj Mahal," by the Brazilian artist Jorge Ben Jor, which was recorded several years before the Rod Stewart song. In his twenties, my friend was a DJ at various downtown clubs, and at some point he'd become interested in world music. "I caught it back then," he said. A small, sly smile spread across his face. The opening bars of "Taj Mahal" were very South American, a world away from what we had just listened to. And then I heard it. It was so obvious and unambiguous that I laughed out loud; virtually note for note, it was the hook from "Do Ya Think I'm Sexy." It was possible that Rod Stewart had independently come up with that riff, because resemblance is not proof of influence. It was also possible that he'd been in Brazil, listened to some local music, and liked what he heard.

My friend had hundreds of these examples. We could have sat in his living room playing at musical genealogy for hours. Did the examples upset him? Of course not, because he knew enough about music to know that these patterns of influence — cribbing, tweaking, transforming — were at the very heart of the creative process. True, copying could go too far. There were times when one artist was simply replicating the work of another, and to let that pass inhibited true creativity. But it was equally dangerous to be overly vigilant in policing creative expression, because if Led Zeppelin hadn't been free to mine the blues for inspiration, we wouldn't have got "Whole Lotta Love," and if Kurt Cobain couldn't listen to "More Than a Feeling" and pick out and transform the part he really

liked, we wouldn't have "Smells Like Teen Spirit" — and, in the evolution of rock, "Smells Like Teen Spirit" was a real step forward from "More Than a Feeling." A successful music executive has to understand the distinction between borrowing that is transformative and borrowing that is merely derivative, and that distinction, I realized, was what was missing from the discussion of Bryony Lavery's borrowings. Yes, she had copied my work. But no one was asking why she had copied it, or what she had copied, or whether her copying served some larger purpose.

5.

Bryony Lavery came to see me in early October of that year. It was a beautiful Saturday afternoon, and we met at my apartment. She is in her fifties, with short, tousled blond hair and pale blue eyes, and was wearing jeans and a loose green shirt and clogs. There was something rugged and raw about her. In the *Times* the previous day, the theater critic Ben Brantley had not been kind to her new play, *Last Easter.* This was supposed to be her moment of triumph. *Frozen* had been nominated for a Tony. *Last Easter* had opened Off Broadway. And now? She sat down heavily at my kitchen table. "I've had the absolute gamut of emotions," she said, playing nervously with her hands as she spoke, as if she needed a cigarette. "I think when one's working, one works between absolute confidence and absolute doubt, and I got a huge dollop of each. I was terribly confident that I could write well after *Frozen,* and then this opened a chasm of doubt." She looked up at me. "I'm terribly sorry," she said.

Lavery began to explain: "What happens when I write is that I find that I'm somehow zoning in on a number

of things. I find that I've cut things out of newspapers because the story or something in them is interesting to me, and seems to me to have a place onstage. Then it starts coagulating. It's like the soup starts thickening. And then a story, which is also a structure, starts emerging. I'd been reading thrillers like *The Silence of the Lambs,* about fiendishly clever serial killers. I'd also seen a documentary of the victims of the Yorkshire killers, Myra Hindley and Ian Brady, who were called the Moors Murderers. They spirited away several children. It seemed to me that killing somehow wasn't fiendishly clever. It was the opposite of clever. It was as banal and stupid and destructive as it could be. There are these interviews with the survivors, and what struck me was that they appeared to be frozen in time. And one of them said, 'If that man was out now, I'm a forgiving man but I couldn't forgive him. I'd kill him.' That's in *Frozen.* I was thinking about that. Then my mother went into hospital for a very simple operation, and the surgeon punctured her womb, and therefore her intestine, and she got peritonitis and died."

When Lavery started talking about her mother, she stopped, and had to collect herself. "She was seventy-four, and what occurred to me is that I utterly forgave him. I thought it was an honest mistake. I'm very sorry it happened to my mother, but it's an honest mistake." Lavery's feelings confused her, though, because she could think of people in her own life whom she had held grudges against for years, for the most trivial of reasons. "In a lot of ways, *Frozen* was an attempt to understand the nature of forgiveness," she said.

Lavery settled, in the end, on a play with three characters. The first is a serial killer named Ralph who kidnaps

and murders a young girl. The second is the murdered girl's mother, Nancy. The third is a psychiatrist from New York, Agnetha, who goes to England to examine Ralph. In the course of the play, the three lives slowly intersect — and the characters gradually change and become "unfrozen" as they come to terms with the idea of forgiveness. For the character of Ralph, Lavery says that she drew on a book about a serial killer titled *The Murder of Childhood*, by Ray Wyre and Tim Tate. For the character of Nancy, she drew on an article written in the *Guardian* by a woman named Marian Partington, whose sister had been murdered by the serial killers Frederick and Rosemary West. And, for the character of Agnetha, Lavery drew on a reprint of my article that she had read in a British publication. "I wanted a scientist who would understand," Lavery said — a scientist who could explain how it was possible to forgive a man who had killed your daughter, who could explain that a serial killing was not a crime of evil but a crime of illness. "I wanted it to be *accurate*," she added.

So why didn't she credit me and Lewis? How could she have been so meticulous about accuracy but not about attribution? Lavery didn't have an answer. "I thought it was OK to use it," she said with an embarrassed shrug. "It never occurred to me to ask you. I thought it was *news*."

She was aware of how hopelessly inadequate that sounded, and when she went on to say that my article had been in a big folder of source material that she had used in the writing of the play, and that the folder had got lost during the play's initial run, in Birmingham, she was aware of how inadequate that sounded, too.

But then Lavery began to talk about Marian Partington, her other important inspiration, and her story became

more complicated. While she was writing *Frozen*, Lavery said, she wrote to Partington to inform her of how much she was relying on Partington's experiences. And when *Frozen* opened in London, she and Partington met and talked. In reading through articles on Lavery in the British press, I found this, from the *Guardian* two years ago, long before the accusations of plagiarism surfaced:

> Lavery is aware of the debt she owes to Partington's writing and is eager to acknowledge it. "I always mention it, because I am aware of the enormous debt that I owe to the generosity of Marian Partington's piece.... You have to be hugely careful when writing something like this, because it touches on people's shattered lives and you wouldn't want them to come across it unawares."

Lavery wasn't indifferent to other people's intellectual property, then; she was just indifferent to my intellectual property. That's because, in her eyes, what she took from me was different. It was, as she put it, "news." She copied my description of Dorothy Lewis's collaborator, Jonathan Pincus, conducting a neurological examination. She copied the description of the disruptive neurological effects of prolonged periods of high stress. She copied my transcription of the television interview with Franklin. She reproduced a quote that I had taken from a study of abused children, and she copied a quotation from Lewis on the nature of evil. She didn't copy my musings, or conclusions, or structure. She lifted sentences like "It is the function of the cortex — and, in particular, those parts of the cortex beneath the forehead, known as the frontal lobes — to modify the impulses that surge up from within

the brain, to provide judgment, to organize behavior and decision-making, to learn and adhere to rules of everyday life." It is difficult to have pride of authorship in a sentence like that. My guess is that it's a reworked version of something I read in a textbook. Lavery knew that failing to credit Partington would have been wrong. Borrowing the personal story of a woman whose sister was murdered by a serial killer matters because that story has real emotional value to its owner. As Lavery put it, it touches on someone's shattered life. Are boilerplate descriptions of physiological functions in the same league?

It also matters *how* Lavery chose to use my words. Borrowing crosses the line when it is used for a derivative work. It's one thing if you're writing a history of the Kennedys, like Doris Kearns Goodwin, and borrow, without attribution, from another history of the Kennedys. But Lavery wasn't writing another profile of Dorothy Lewis. She was writing a play about something entirely new — about what would happen if a mother met the man who killed her daughter. And she used my descriptions of Lewis's work and the outline of Lewis's life as a building block in making that confrontation plausible. Isn't that the way creativity is supposed to work? Old words in the service of a new idea aren't the problem. What inhibits creativity is new words in the service of an old idea.

And this is the second problem with plagiarism. It is not merely extremist. It has also become disconnected from the broader question of what does and does not inhibit creativity. We accept the right of one writer to engage in a full-scale knockoff of another — think how many serial-killer novels have been cloned from *The Silence of the Lambs*. Yet, when Kathy Acker incorporated parts of a

Harold Robbins sex scene verbatim in a satiric novel, she was denounced as a plagiarist (and threatened with a lawsuit). When I worked at a newspaper, we were routinely dispatched to "match" a story from the *Times:* to do a new version of someone else's idea. But had we "matched" any of the *Times'* words — even the most banal of phrases — it could have been a firing offense. The ethics of plagiarism have turned into the narcissism of small differences: because journalism cannot own up to its heavily derivative nature, it must enforce originality on the level of the sentence.

Dorothy Lewis says that one of the things that hurt her most about *Frozen* was that Agnetha turns out to have had an affair with her collaborator, David Nabkus. Lewis feared that people would think she had had an affair with her collaborator, Jonathan Pincus. "That's slander," Lewis told me. "I'm recognizable in that. Enough people have called me and said, 'Dorothy, it's about you,' and if everything up to that point is true, then the affair becomes true in the mind. So that is another reason that I feel violated. If you are going to take the life of somebody, and make them absolutely identifiable, you don't create an affair, and you certainly don't have that as a climax of the play."

It is easy to understand how shocking it must have been for Lewis to sit in the audience and see her "character" admit to that indiscretion. But the truth is that Lavery has every right to create an affair for Agnetha, because Agnetha is not Dorothy Lewis. She is a fictional character, drawn from Lewis's life but endowed with a completely imaginary set of circumstances and actions. In real life, Lewis kissed Ted Bundy on the cheek, and in some versions of *Frozen,* Agnetha kisses Ralph. But Lewis kissed Bundy only because he kissed her first, and there's a big

difference between responding to a kiss from a killer and initiating one. When we first see Agnetha, she's rushing out of the house and thinking murderous thoughts on the airplane. Dorothy Lewis also charges out of her house and thinks murderous thoughts. But the dramatic function of that scene is to make us think, in that moment, that Agnetha is crazy. And the one inescapable fact about Lewis is that she is not crazy: she has helped get people to rethink their notions of criminality because of her unshakable command of herself and her work. Lewis is upset not just about how Lavery copied her life story, in other words, but about how Lavery *changed* her life story. She's not merely upset about plagiarism. She's upset about art — about the use of old words in the service of a new idea — and her feelings are perfectly understandable, because the alterations of art can be every bit as unsettling and hurtful as the thievery of plagiarism. It's just that art is not a breach of ethics.

When I read the original reviews of *Frozen,* I noticed that time and again critics would use, without attribution, some version of the sentence "The difference between a crime of evil and a crime of illness is the difference between a sin and a symptom." That's my phrase, of course. I wrote it. Lavery borrowed it from me, and now the critics were borrowing it from her. The plagiarist was being plagiarized. In this case, there is no "art" defense: nothing new was being done with that line. And this was not "news." Yet do I really own "sins and symptoms"? There is a quote by Gandhi, it turns out, using the same two words, and I'm sure that if I were to plow through the body of English literature I would find the path littered with crimes of evil and crimes of illness. The central

fact about the "Phantom" case is that Ray Repp, if he was borrowing from Andrew Lloyd Webber, certainly didn't realize it, and Andrew Lloyd Webber didn't realize that he was borrowing from himself. Creative property, Lessig reminds us, has many lives — the newspaper arrives at our door, it becomes part of the archive of human knowledge, then it wraps fish. And, by the time ideas pass into their third and fourth lives, we lose track of where they came from, and we lose control of where they are going. The final dishonesty of the plagiarism fundamentalists is to encourage us to pretend that these chains of influence and evolution do not exist, and that a writer's words have a virgin birth and an eternal life. I suppose that I could get upset about what happened to my words. I could also simply acknowledge that I had a good, long ride with that line — and let it go.

"It's been absolutely bloody, really, because it attacks my own notion of my character," Lavery said, sitting at my kitchen table. A bouquet of flowers she had brought were on the counter behind her. "It feels absolutely terrible. I've had to go through the pain for being careless. I'd like to repair what happened, and I don't know how to do that. I just didn't think I was doing the wrong thing…and then the article comes out in the *New York Times* and every continent in the world." There was a long silence. She was heartbroken. But, more than that, she was confused, because she didn't understand how 675 rather ordinary words could bring the walls tumbling down. "It's been horrible and bloody." She began to cry. "I'm still composting what happened. It will be for a purpose…whatever that purpose is."

November 22, 2004

Connecting the Dots

THE PARADOXES OF
INTELLIGENCE REFORM

1.

In the fall of 1973, the Syrian army began to gather a large number of tanks, artillery batteries, and infantry along its border with Israel. Simultaneously, to the south, the Egyptian army canceled all leaves, called up thousands of reservists, and launched a massive military exercise, building roads and preparing anti-aircraft and artillery positions along the Suez Canal. On October 4, an Israeli aerial reconnaissance mission showed that the Egyptians had moved artillery into offensive positions. That evening, Aman, the Israeli military intelligence agency, learned that portions of the Soviet fleet near Port Said and Alexandria had set sail, and that the Soviet government had begun airlifting the families of Soviet advisers out of Cairo and Damascus. Then, at four o'clock in the morning on October 6, Israel's director of military intelligence received an urgent telephone call from one of the country's most trusted intelligence sources. Egypt and Syria, the source said, would attack later that day. Top Israeli offi-

cials immediately called a meeting. Was war imminent? The head of Aman, Major General Eli Zeira, looked over the evidence and said he didn't think so. He was wrong. That afternoon, Syria attacked from the east, overwhelming the thin Israeli defenses in the Golan Heights, and Egypt attacked from the south, bombing Israeli positions and sending eight thousand infantry streaming across the Suez. Despite all the warnings of the previous weeks, Israeli officials were caught by surprise. Why couldn't they connect the dots?

If you start on the afternoon of October 6 and work backward, the trail of clues pointing to an attack seems obvious; you'd have to conclude that something was badly wrong with the Israeli intelligence service. On the other hand, if you start several years before the Yom Kippur War and work forward, re-creating what people in Israeli intelligence knew in the same order that they knew it, a very different picture emerges. In the fall of 1973, Egypt and Syria certainly looked as if they were preparing to go to war. But, in the Middle East of the time, countries always looked as if they were going to war. In the fall of 1971, for instance, both Egypt's president and its minister of war stated publicly that the hour of battle was approaching. The Egyptian army was mobilized. Tanks and bridging equipment were sent to the canal. Offensive positions were readied. And nothing happened. In December of 1972, the Egyptians mobilized again. The army furiously built fortifications along the canal. A reliable source told Israeli intelligence that an attack was imminent. Nothing happened. In the spring of 1973, the president of Egypt told *Newsweek* that everything in his country "is now being mobilized in earnest for the

resumption of battle." Egyptian forces were moved closer to the canal. Extensive fortifications were built along the Suez. Blood donors were rounded up. Civil-defense personnel were mobilized. Blackouts were imposed throughout Egypt. A trusted source told Israeli intelligence that an attack was imminent. It didn't come. Between January and October of 1973, the Egyptian army mobilized *nineteen times* without going to war. The Israeli government couldn't mobilize its army every time its neighbors threatened war. Israel is a small country with a citizen army. Mobilization was disruptive and expensive, and the Israeli government was acutely aware that if its army was mobilized and Egypt and Syria weren't serious about war, the very act of mobilization might cause them to become serious about war.

Nor did the other signs seem remarkable. The fact that the Soviet families had been sent home could have signified nothing more than a falling-out between the Arab states and Moscow. Yes, a trusted source called at four in the morning, with definite word of a late-afternoon attack, but his last two attack warnings had been wrong. What's more, the source said that the attack would come at sunset, and an attack so late in the day wouldn't leave enough time for opening air strikes. Israeli intelligence didn't see the pattern of Arab intentions, in other words, because, until Egypt and Syria actually attacked, on the afternoon of October 6, 1973, their intentions didn't form a pattern. They formed a Rorschach blot. What is clear in hindsight is rarely clear before the fact. It's an obvious point, but one that nonetheless bears repeating, particularly when we're in the midst of assigning blame for the surprise attack of September 11.

2.

Of the many postmortems conducted after September 11, the one that has received the most attention is *The Cell: Inside the 9/11 Plot, and Why the F.B.I. and C.I.A. Failed to Stop It* by John Miller, Michael Stone, and Chris Mitchell. The authors begin their tale with El Sayyid Nosair, the Egyptian who was arrested in November of 1990 for shooting Rabbi Meir Kahane, the founder of the Jewish Defense League, in the ballroom of the Marriott Hotel in midtown Manhattan. Nosair's apartment in New Jersey was searched, and investigators found sixteen boxes of files, including training manuals from the Army Special Warfare School; copies of teletypes that had been routed to the Joint Chiefs of Staff; bomb-making manuals; and maps, annotated in Arabic, of landmarks like the Statue of Liberty, Rockefeller Center, and the World Trade Center. According to *The Cell,* Nosair was connected to gunrunners and to Islamic radicals in Brooklyn, who were in turn behind the World Trade Center bombing two and a half years later, which was masterminded by Ramzi Yousef, who then showed up in Manila in 1994, apparently plotting to kill the pope, crash a plane into the Pentagon or the CIA, and bomb as many as twelve transcontinental airliners simultaneously. And who was Yousef associating with in the Philippines? Mohammed Khalifa, Wali Khan Amin-Shah, and Ibrahim Munir, all of whom had fought alongside, pledged a loyalty oath to, or worked for a shadowy Saudi Arabian millionaire named Osama bin Laden.

Miller was a network-television correspondent throughout much of the past decade, and the best parts of *The Cell* recount his own experiences in covering the

terrorist story. He is an extraordinary reporter. At the time of the first World Trade Center attack, in February of 1993, he clapped a flashing light on the dashboard of his car and followed the wave of emergency vehicles downtown. (At the bombing site, he was continuously trailed by a knot of reporters — I was one of them — who had concluded that the best way to learn what was going on was to try to overhear his conversations.) Miller became friends with the FBI agents who headed the New York counterterrorist office — Neil Herman and John O'Neill, in particular — and he became as obsessed with Al Qaeda as they were. He was in Yemen, with the FBI, after Al Qaeda bombed the U.S.S. *Cole.* In 1998, at the Marriott in Islamabad, he and his cameraman met someone known to them only as Akhtar, who spirited them across the border into the hills of Afghanistan to interview Osama bin Laden. In *The Cell*, the period from 1990 through September 11 becomes a seamless, devastating narrative: the evolution of Al Qaeda. "How did this happen to us?" the book asks in its opening pages. The answer, the authors argue, can be found by following the "thread" connecting Kahane's murder to September 11. In the events of the past decade, they declare, there is a clear "recurring pattern."

The same argument is made by Senator Richard Shelby, vice chairman of the Senate Select Committee on Intelligence, in his investigative report on September 11, released this past December. The report is a lucid and powerful document, in which Shelby painstakingly points out all the missed or misinterpreted signals pointing to a major terrorist attack. The CIA knew that two suspected Al Qaeda operatives, Khalid al-Mihdhar and Nawaf al-Hazmi, had entered the country, but the CIA

didn't tell the FBI or the NSC. An FBI agent in Phoenix sent a memo to headquarters that began with the sentence "The purpose of this communication is to advise the Bureau and New York of the possibility of a coordinated effort by Osama Bin Laden to send students to the United States to attend civilian aviation universities and colleges." But the FBI never acted on the information, and failed to connect it with reports that terrorists were interested in using airplanes as weapons. The FBI took into custody the suspected terrorist Zacarias Moussaoui, on account of his suspicious behavior at flight school, but was unable to integrate his case into a larger picture of terrorist behavior. "The most fundamental problem...is our Intelligence Community's inability to 'connect the dots' available to it before September 11, 2001, about terrorists' interest in attacking symbolic American targets," the Shelby report states. The phrase "connect the dots" appears so often in the report that it becomes a kind of mantra. There was a pattern, as plain as day in retrospect, yet the vaunted American intelligence community simply could not see it.

None of these postmortems, however, answer the question raised by the Yom Kippur War: was this pattern obvious *before* the attack? This question — whether we revise our judgment of events after the fact — is something that psychologists have paid a great deal of attention to. For example, on the eve of Richard Nixon's historic visit to China, the psychologist Baruch Fischhoff asked a group of people to estimate the probability of a series of possible outcomes of the trip. What were the chances that the trip would lead to permanent diplomatic relations between China and the United States? That Nixon would meet with the leader of China, Mao Tse-tung, at

least once? That Nixon would call the trip a success? As it turned out, the trip was a diplomatic triumph, and Fischhoff then went back to the same people and asked them to recall what their estimates of the different outcomes of the visit had been. He found that the subjects now, overwhelmingly, "remembered" being more optimistic than they had actually been. If you originally thought that it was unlikely that Nixon would meet with Mao, afterward, when the press was full of accounts of Nixon's meeting with Mao, you'd "remember" that you had thought the chances of a meeting were pretty good. Fischhoff calls this phenomenon "creeping determinism" — the sense that grows on us, in retrospect, that what has happened was actually inevitable — and the chief effect of creeping determinism, he points out, is that it turns unexpected events into expected events. As he writes, "The occurrence of an event increases its reconstructed probability and makes it less surprising than it would have been had the original probability been remembered."

To read the Shelby report, or the seamless narrative from Nosair to bin Laden in *The Cell,* is to be convinced that if the CIA and the FBI had simply been able to connect the dots, what happened on September 11 should not have been a surprise at all. Is this a fair criticism or is it just a case of creeping determinism?

3.

On August 7, 1998, two Al Qaeda terrorists detonated a cargo truck filled with explosives outside the US embassy in Nairobi, killing 213 people and injuring more than four

thousand. Miller, Stone, and Mitchell see the Kenyan embassy bombing as a textbook example of intelligence failure. The CIA, they tell us, had identified an Al Qaeda cell in Kenya well before the attack, and its members were under surveillance. They had an eight-page letter, written by an Al Qaeda operative, speaking of the imminent arrival of "engineers" — the code word for bomb makers — in Nairobi. The US ambassador to Kenya, Prudence Bushnell, had begged Washington for more security. A prominent Kenyan lawyer and legislator says that the Kenyan intelligence service warned US intelligence about the plot several months before August 7, and in November of 1997 a man named Mustafa Mahmoud Said Ahmed, who worked for one of Osama bin Laden's companies, walked into the US embassy in Nairobi and told American intelligence of a plot to blow up the building. What did our officials do? They forced the leader of the Kenyan cell — a US citizen — to return home, and then abruptly halted their surveillance of the group. They ignored the eight-page letter. They allegedly showed the Kenyan intelligence service's warning to the Mossad, which dismissed it, and after questioning Ahmed, they decided that he wasn't credible. After the bombing, *The Cell* tells us, a senior State Department official phoned Bushnell and asked, "How could this have happened?"

"For the first time since the blast," Miller, Stone, and Mitchell write, "Bushnell's horror turned to anger. There was too much history. 'I wrote you a letter,' she said."

This is all very damning, but doesn't it fall into the creeping-determinism trap? It is not at all clear that it passes the creeping-determinism test. It's an edited version

of the past. What we don't hear about is all the other people whom American intelligence had under surveillance, how many other warnings they received, and how many other tips came in that seemed promising at the time but led nowhere. The central challenge of intelligence gathering has always been the problem of "noise": the fact that useless information is vastly more plentiful than useful information. Shelby's report mentions that the FBI's counterterrorism division has *sixty-eight thousand* outstanding and unassigned leads dating back to 1995. And, of those, probably no more than a few hundred are useful. Analysts, in short, must be selective, and the decisions made in Kenya, by that standard, do not seem unreasonable. Surveillance on the cell was shut down, but, then, its leader had left the country. Bushnell warned Washington — but, as *The Cell* admits, there were bomb warnings in Africa all the time. Officials at the Mossad thought the Kenyan intelligence was dubious, and the Mossad ought to know. Ahmed may have worked for bin Laden but he failed a polygraph test, and it was also learned that he had previously given similar — groundless — warnings to other embassies in Africa. When a man comes into your office, fails a lie-detector test, and is found to have shopped the same unsubstantiated story all over town, can you be blamed for turning him out?

Miller, Stone, and Mitchell make the same mistake when they quote from a transcript of a conversation that was recorded by Italian intelligence in August of 2001 between two Al Qaeda operatives, Abdel Kader Es Sayed and a man known as al Hilal. This, they say, is yet another piece of intelligence that "seemed to forecast the September 11 attacks."

"I've been studying airplanes," al Hilal tells Es Sayed. "If God wills, I hope to be able to bring you a window or a piece of a plane the next time I see you."

"What, is there a jihad planned?" Es Sayed asks.

"In the future, listen to the news and remember these words: 'Up above,'" al Hilal replies. Es Sayed thinks that al Hilal is referring to an operation in his native Yemen, but al Hilal corrects him: "But the surprise attack will come from the other country, one of those attacks you will never forget."

A moment later al Hilal says about the plan, "It is something terrifying that goes from south to north, east to west. The person who devised this plan is a madman, but a genius. He will leave them frozen [in shock]."

This is a tantalizing exchange. It would now seem that it refers to September 11. But in what sense was it a "forecast"? It gave neither time nor place nor method nor target. It suggested only that there were terrorists out there who liked to talk about doing something dramatic with an airplane — which did not, it must be remembered, reliably distinguish them from any other terrorists of the past thirty years.

In the real world, intelligence is invariably ambiguous. Information about enemy intentions tends to be short on detail. And information that's rich in detail tends to be short on intentions. In April of 1941, for instance, the Allies learned that Germany had moved a huge army up to the Russian front. The intelligence was beyond dispute: the troops could be seen and counted. But what did it mean? Churchill concluded that Hitler wanted to attack Russia. Stalin concluded that Hitler was serious about attacking, but only if the Soviet Union didn't meet the

terms of the German ultimatum. The British foreign secretary, Anthony Eden, thought that Hitler was bluffing,
in the hope of winning further Russian concessions. British intelligence thought — at least, in the beginning — that
Hitler simply wanted to reinforce his eastern frontier
against a possible Soviet attack. The only way for this piece
of intelligence to have been definitive would have been if
the Allies had had a second piece of intelligence — like the
phone call between al Hilal and Es Sayed — that demonstrated Germany's true purpose. Similarly, the only way
the al Hilal phone call would have been definitive is if we'd
also had intelligence as detailed as the Allied knowledge of
German troop movements. But rarely do intelligence services have the luxury of both kinds of information. Nor
are their analysts mind readers. It is only with hindsight
that human beings acquire that skill.

The Cell tells us that, in the final months before September 11, Washington was frantic with worry:

> A spike in phone traffic among suspected Al Qaeda mem-
> bers in the early part of the summer [of 2001], as well as
> debriefings of [an Al Qaeda operative in custody] who
> had begun cooperating with the government, convinced
> investigators that bin Laden was planning a significant
> operation — one intercepted Al Qaeda message spoke of
> a "Hiroshima-type" event — and that he was planning it
> soon. Through the summer, the CIA repeatedly warned
> the White House that attacks were imminent.

The fact that these worries did not protect us is not
evidence of the limitations of the intelligence community.
It is evidence of the limitations of intelligence.

4.

In the early 1970s, a professor of psychology at Stanford University named David L. Rosenhan gathered together a painter, a graduate student, a pediatrician, a psychiatrist, a housewife, and three psychologists. He told them to check into different psychiatric hospitals under aliases, with the complaint that they had been hearing voices. They were instructed to say that the voices were unfamiliar, and that they heard words like *empty, thud,* and *hollow.* Apart from that initial story, the pseudo patients were instructed to answer every question truthfully, to behave as they normally would, and to tell the hospital staff — at every opportunity — that the voices were gone and that they had experienced no further symptoms. The eight subjects were hospitalized, on average, for nineteen days. One was kept for almost two months. Rosenhan wanted to find out if the hospital staffs would ever see through the ruse. They never did.

Rosenhan's test is, in a way, a classic intelligence problem. Here was a signal (a sane person) buried in a mountain of conflicting and confusing noise (a mental hospital), and the intelligence analysts (the doctors) were asked to connect the dots — and they failed spectacularly. In the course of their hospital stay, the eight pseudo patients were given a total of twenty-one hundred pills. They underwent psychiatric interviews, and sober case summaries documenting their pathologies were written up. They were asked by Rosenhan to take notes documenting how they were treated, and this quickly became part of their supposed pathology. "Patient engaging in writing behavior," one nurse ominously wrote in her notes. Having been labeled

as ill upon admission, they could not shake the diagnosis. "Nervous?" a friendly nurse asked one of the subjects as he paced the halls one day. "No," he corrected her, to no avail, "bored."

The solution to this problem seems obvious enough. Doctors and nurses need to be made alert to the possibility that sane people sometimes get admitted to mental hospitals. So Rosenhan went to a research-and-teaching hospital and informed the staff that at some point in the next three months, he would once again send over one or more of his pseudo patients. This time, of the 193 patients admitted in the three-month period, 41 were identified by at least one staff member as being almost certainly sane. Once again, however, they were wrong. Rosenhan hadn't sent anyone over. In attempting to solve one kind of intelligence problem (overdiagnosis), the hospital simply created another problem (underdiagnosis). This is the second, and perhaps more serious, consequence of creeping determinism: in our zeal to correct what we believe to be the problems of the past, we end up creating new problems for the future.

Pearl Harbor, for example, was widely considered to be an organizational failure. The United States had all the evidence it needed to predict the Japanese attack, but the signals were scattered throughout the various intelligence services. The army and the navy didn't talk to each other. They spent all their time arguing and competing. This was, in part, why the Central Intelligence Agency was created, in 1947 — to ensure that all intelligence would be collected and processed in one place. Twenty years after Pearl Harbor, the United States suffered another catastrophic intelligence failure, at the Bay of Pigs: the Kennedy administration grossly underestimated the Cubans'

capacity to fight and their support for Fidel Castro. This time, however, the diagnosis was completely different. As Irving L. Janis concluded in his famous study of "groupthink," the root cause of the Bay of Pigs fiasco was that the operation was conceived by a small, highly cohesive group whose close ties inhibited the beneficial effects of argument and competition. Centralization was now the problem. One of the most influential organizational sociologists of the postwar era, Harold Wilensky, went out of his way to praise the "constructive rivalry" fostered by Franklin D. Roosevelt, which, he says, is why the President had such formidable intelligence on how to attack the economic ills of the Great Depression. In his classic 1967 work *Organizational Intelligence,* Wilensky pointed out that Roosevelt would

> use one anonymous informant's information to challenge and check another's, putting both on their toes; he recruited strong personalities and structured their work so that clashes would be certain.... In foreign affairs, he gave Moley and Welles tasks that overlapped those of Secretary of State Hull; in conservation and power, he gave Ickes and Wallace identical missions; in welfare, confusing both functions and initials, he assigned PWA to Ickes, WPA to Hopkins; in politics, Farley found himself competing with other political advisors for control over patronage. The effect: the timely advertisement of arguments, with both the experts and the President pressured to consider the main choices as they came boiling up from below.

The intelligence community that we had prior to September 11 was the direct result of this philosophy. The FBI

and the CIA were supposed to be rivals, just as Ickes and Wallace were rivals. But now we've changed our minds. The FBI and the CIA, Senator Shelby tells us disapprovingly, argue and compete with one another. The September 11 story, his report concludes, "should be an object lesson in the perils of failing to share information promptly and efficiently between (and within) organizations." Shelby wants recentralization and more focus on cooperation. He wants a "central national level knowledge-compiling entity standing above and independent from the disputatious bureaucracies." He thinks the intelligence service should be run by a small, highly cohesive group, and so he suggests that the FBI be removed from the counterterrorism business entirely. The FBI, according to Shelby, is governed by

> deeply entrenched individual mind-sets that prize the production of evidence-supported narratives of defendant wrongdoing over the drawing of probabilistic inferences based on incomplete and fragmentary information in order to support decision-making.... Law enforcement organizations handle information, reach conclusions, and ultimately just *think* differently than intelligence organizations. Intelligence analysts would doubtless make poor policemen, and it has become very clear that policemen make poor intelligence analysts.

In his 2003 State of the Union message, President George W. Bush did what Shelby wanted, and announced the formation of the Terrorist Threat Integration Center — a special unit combining the antiterrorist activities of the FBI and the CIA. The cultural and organizational diversity of the intelligence business, once prized, is now despised.

The truth is, though, that it is just as easy, in the wake of September 11, to make the case for the old system. Isn't it an advantage that the FBI doesn't think like the CIA? It was the FBI, after all, that produced two of the most prescient pieces of analysis — the request by the Minneapolis office for a warrant to secretly search Zacarias Moussaoui's belongings, and the now famous Phoenix memo. In both cases, what was valuable about the FBI's analysis was precisely the way in which it differed from the traditional "big picture," probabilistic inference making of the analyst. The FBI agents in the field focused on a single case, dug deep, and came up with an "evidence-supported narrative of defendant wrongdoing" that spoke volumes about a possible Al Qaeda threat.

The same can be said for the alleged problem of rivalry. *The Cell* describes what happened after police in the Philippines searched the apartment that Ramzi Yousef shared with his coconspirator, Abdul Hakim Murad. Agents from the FBI's counterterrorism unit immediately flew to Manila and "bumped up against the CIA." As the old adage about the Bureau and the Agency has it, the FBI wanted to string Murad up, and the CIA wanted to string him along. The two groups eventually worked together, but only because they had to. It was a relationship "marred by rivalry and mistrust." But what's wrong with this kind of rivalry? As Miller, Stone, and Mitchell tell us, the real objection of Neil Herman — the FBI's former domestic counterterrorism chief — to "working with the CIA had nothing to do with procedure. He just didn't think the Agency was going to be of any help in finding Ramzi Yousef. 'Back then, I don't think the CIA could have found a person in a bathroom,' " Herman says.

" 'Hell, I don't think they could have found the bathroom.' " The assumption of the reformers is always that the rivalry between the FBI and the CIA is essentially marital, that it is the dysfunction of people who ought to work together but can't. But it could equally be seen as a version of the marketplace rivalry that leads to companies working harder and making better products.

There is no such thing as a perfect intelligence system, and every seeming improvement involves a trade-off. A couple of months ago, for example, a suspect in custody in Canada, who was wanted in New York on forgery charges, gave police the names and photographs of five Arab immigrants, who he said had crossed the border into the United States. The FBI put out an alert on December 29, posting the names and photographs on its website, in the "war on terrorism" section. Even President Bush joined in, saying, "We need to know why they have been smuggled into the country, what they're doing in the country." As it turned out, the suspect in Canada had made the story up. Afterward, an FBI official said that the agency circulated the photographs in order to "err on the side of caution." Our intelligence services today are highly sensitive. But this kind of sensitivity is not without its costs. As the political scientist Richard K. Betts wrote in his essay "Analysis, War, and Decision: Why Intelligence Failures Are Inevitable," "Making warning systems more sensitive reduces the risk of surprise, but increases the number of false alarms, which in turn reduces sensitivity." When we run out and buy duct tape to seal our windows against chemical attack, and nothing happens, and when the government's warning light is orange for weeks on end, and nothing happens, we soon begin to doubt every warning that comes our way.

Why was the Pacific fleet at Pearl Harbor so unresponsive to signs of an impending Japanese attack? Because, in the week before December 7, 1941, they had checked out seven reports of Japanese submarines in the area — and all seven were false. Rosenhan's psychiatrists used to miss the sane; then they started to see sane people everywhere. That is a change, but it is not exactly progress.

5.

In the wake of the Yom Kippur War, the Israeli government appointed a special investigative commission, and one of the witnesses called was Major General Zeira, the head of Aman. Why, they asked, had he insisted that war was not imminent? His answer was simple:

> The Chief of Staff has to make decisions, and his decisions must be clear. The best support that the head of Aman can give the Chief of Staff is to give a clear and unambiguous estimate, provided that it is done in an objective fashion. To be sure, the clearer and sharper the estimate, the clearer and sharper the mistake — but this is a professional hazard for the head of Aman.

The historians Eliot A. Cohen and John Gooch, in their book *Military Misfortunes,* argue that it was Zeira's certainty that had proved fatal: "The culpable failure of Aman's leaders in September and October 1973 lay not in their belief that Egypt would not attack but in their supreme confidence, which dazzled decision-makers....Rather than impress upon the prime minister, the chief of staff and the minister of defense the ambiguity of the situation, they insisted — until the last day — that there would be no war, period."

But, of course, Zeira gave an unambiguous answer to the question of war because that is what politicians and the public demanded of him. No one wants ambiguity. Today, the FBI gives us color-coded warnings and speaks of increased chatter among terrorist operatives, and the information is infuriating to us because it is so vague. What does *increased chatter* mean? We want a prediction. We want to believe that the intentions of our enemies are a puzzle that intelligence services can piece together, so that a clear story emerges. But there rarely is a clear story — at least, not until afterward, when some enterprising journalist or investigative committee decides to write one.

March 10, 2003

The Art of Failure

WHY SOME PEOPLE CHOKE
AND OTHERS PANIC

1.

There was a moment in the third and deciding set of the 1993 Wimbledon final when Jana Novotna seemed invincible. She was leading 4–1 and serving at 40–30, meaning that she was one point from winning the game, and just five points from the most coveted championship in tennis. She had just hit a backhand to her opponent, Steffi Graf, that skimmed the net and landed so abruptly on the far side of the court that Graf could only watch, in flat-footed frustration. The stands at Center Court were packed. The Duke and Duchess of Kent were in their customary places in the royal box. Novotna was in white, poised and confident, her blond hair held back with a headband — and then something happened. She served the ball straight into the net. She stopped and steadied herself for the second serve — the toss, the arch of the back — but this time it was worse. Her swing seemed halfhearted, all arm and no legs and torso. Double fault. On the next point, she was slow to react to a high shot by Graf and badly missed on a forehand

volley. At game point, she hit an overhead straight into the net. Instead of 5–1, it was now 4–2. Graf to serve: an easy victory, 4–3. Novotna to serve. She wasn't tossing the ball high enough. Her head was down. Her movements had slowed markedly. She double-faulted once, twice, three times. Pulled wide by a Graf forehand, Novotna inexplicably hit a low, flat shot directly at Graf, instead of a high crosscourt forehand that would have given her time to get back into position: 4–4. Did she suddenly realize how terrifyingly close she was to victory? Did she remember that she had never won a major tournament before? Did she look across the net and see Steffi Graf — Steffi Graf! — the greatest player of her generation?

On the baseline, awaiting Graf's serve, Novotna was now visibly agitated, rocking back and forth, jumping up and down. She talked to herself under her breath. Her eyes darted around the court. Graf took the game at love; Novotna, moving as if in slow motion, did not win a single point: 5–4 Graf. On the sidelines, Novotna wiped her racquet and her face with a towel, and then each finger individually. It was her turn to serve. She missed a routine volley wide, shook her head, talked to herself. She missed her first serve, made the second, then, in the resulting rally, mishit a backhand so badly that it sailed off her racquet as if launched into flight. Novotna was unrecognizable, not an elite tennis player but a beginner again. She was crumbling under pressure, but exactly why was as baffling to her as it was to all those looking on. Isn't pressure supposed to bring out the best in us? We try harder. We concentrate harder. We get a boost of adrenaline. We care more about how well we perform. So what was happening to her?

At championship point, Novotna hit a low, cautious,

and shallow lob to Graf. Graf answered with an unreturn-
able overhead smash, and, mercifully, it was over. Stunned,
Novotna moved to the net. Graf kissed her twice. At the
awards ceremony, the Duchess of Kent handed Novotna
the runner-up's trophy, a small silver plate, and whispered
something in her ear, and what Novotna had done finally
caught up with her. There she was, sweaty and exhausted,
looming over the delicate white-haired Duchess in her
pearl necklace. The Duchess reached up and pulled her
head down onto her shoulder, and Novotna started to sob.

2.

Human beings sometimes falter under pressure. Pilots
crash and divers drown. Under the glare of competition,
basketball players cannot find the basket and golfers cannot find the pin. When that happens, we say variously that
people have *panicked* or, to use the sports colloquialism,
choked. But what do those words mean? Both are pejo-
ratives. To choke or panic is considered to be as bad as
to quit. But are all forms of failure equal? And what do
the forms in which we fail say about who we are and how
we think? We live in an age obsessed with success, with
documenting the myriad ways by which talented people
overcome challenges and obstacles. There is as much to be
learned, though, from documenting the myriad ways in
which talented people sometimes fail.

Choking sounds like a vague and all-encompassing
term, yet it describes a very specific kind of failure. For
example, psychologists often use a primitive video game
to test motor skills. They'll sit you in front of a computer with a screen that shows four boxes in a row, and

a keyboard that has four corresponding buttons in a row. One at a time, *x*'s start to appear in the boxes on the screen, and you are told that every time this happens you are to push the key corresponding to the box. According to Daniel Willingham, a psychologist at the University of Virginia, if you're told ahead of time about the pattern in which those x's will appear, your reaction time in hitting the right key will improve dramatically. You'll play the game very carefully for a few rounds, until you've learned the sequence, and then you'll get faster and faster. Willingham calls this *explicit learning*. But suppose you're not told that the x's appear in a regular sequence, and even after playing the game for a while, you're not aware that there is a pattern. You'll still get faster: you'll learn the sequence unconsciously. Willingham calls that *implicit learning* — learning that takes place outside of awareness. These two learning systems are quite separate, based in different parts of the brain. Willingham says that when you are first taught something — say, how to hit a backhand or an overhead forehand — you think it through in a very deliberate, mechanical manner. But as you get better, the implicit system takes over: you start to hit a backhand fluidly, without thinking. The basal ganglia, where implicit learning partially resides, are concerned with force and timing, and when that system kicks in, you begin to develop touch and accuracy, the ability to hit a drop shot or place a serve at a hundred miles per hour. "This is something that is going to happen gradually," Willingham says. "You hit several thousand forehands, after a while you may still be attending to it. But not very much. In the end, you don't really notice what your hand is doing at all."

Under conditions of stress, however, the explicit sys-

tem sometimes takes over. That's what it means to choke. When Jana Novotna faltered at Wimbledon, it was because she began thinking about her shots again. She lost her fluidity, her touch. She double-faulted on her serves and mis-hit her overheads, the shots that demand the greatest sensitivity in force and timing. She seemed like a different person — playing with the slow, cautious deliberation of a beginner — because, in a sense, she was a beginner again: she was relying on a learning system that she hadn't used to hit serves and overhead forehands and volleys since she was first taught tennis, as a child. The same thing has happened to Chuck Knoblauch, the New York Yankees' second baseman, who inexplicably has had trouble throwing the ball to first base. Under the stress of playing in front of forty thousand fans at Yankee Stadium, Knoblauch finds himself reverting to explicit mode, throwing like a Little Leaguer again.

Panic is something else altogether. Consider the following account of a scuba-diving accident, recounted to me by Ephimia Morphew, a human-factors specialist at NASA: "It was an open-water certification dive, Monterey Bay, California, about ten years ago. I was nineteen. I'd been diving for two weeks. This was my first time in the open ocean without the instructor. Just my buddy and I. We had to go about forty feet down, to the bottom of the ocean, and do an exercise where we took our regulators out of our mouth, picked up a spare one that we had on our vest, and practiced breathing out of the spare. My buddy did hers. Then it was my turn. I removed my regulator. I lifted up my secondary regulator. I put it in my mouth, exhaled, to clear the lines, and then I inhaled, and, to my surprise, it was water. I inhaled water. Then the hose that connected

that mouthpiece to my tank, my air source, came unlatched and air from the hose came exploding into my face.

"Right away, my hand reached out for my partner's air supply, as if I was going to rip it out. It was without thought. It was a physiological response. My eyes are seeing my hand do something irresponsible. I'm fighting with myself. Don't do it. Then I searched my mind for what I could do. And nothing came to mind. All I could remember was one thing: if you can't take care of yourself, let your buddy take care of you. I let my hand fall back to my side, and I just stood there."

This is a textbook example of panic. In that moment, Morphew stopped thinking. She forgot that she had another source of air, one that worked perfectly well and that, moments before, she had taken out of her mouth. She forgot that her partner had a working air supply as well, which could easily be shared, and she forgot that grabbing her partner's regulator would imperil both of them. All she had was her most basic instinct: get air. Stress wipes out short-term memory. People with lots of experience tend not to panic, because when the stress suppresses their short-term memory they still have some residue of experience to draw on. But what did a novice like Morphew have? *I searched my mind for what I could do. And nothing came to mind.*

Panic also causes what psychologists call perceptual narrowing. In one study, from the early seventies, a group of subjects were asked to perform a visual-acuity task while undergoing what they thought was a sixty-foot dive in a pressure chamber. At the same time, they were asked to push a button whenever they saw a small light flash on and off in their peripheral vision. The subjects in

the pressure chamber had much higher heart rates than the control group, indicating that they were under stress. That stress didn't affect their accuracy at the visual-acuity task, but they were only half as good as the control group at picking up the peripheral light. "You tend to focus or obsess on one thing," Morphew says. "There's a famous airplane example, where the landing light went off, and the pilots had no way of knowing if the landing gear was down. The pilots were so focused on that light that no one noticed the autopilot had been disengaged, and they crashed the plane." Morphew reached for her buddy's air supply because it was the only air supply she could see.

Panic, in this sense, is the opposite of choking. Choking is about thinking too much. Panic is about thinking too little. Choking is about loss of instinct. Panic is reversion to instinct. They may look the same, but they are worlds apart.

3.

Why does this distinction matter? In some instances, it doesn't much. If you lose a close tennis match, it's of little moment whether you choked or panicked; either way, you lost. But there are clearly cases when how failure happens is central to understanding why failure happens.

Take the plane crash in which John F. Kennedy, Jr., was killed. The details of the flight are well known. On a Friday evening in July of 1999, Kennedy took off with his wife and sister-in-law for Martha's Vineyard. The night was hazy, and Kennedy flew along the Connecticut coastline, using the trail of lights below him as a guide. At Westerly, Rhode Island, he left the shoreline, heading

straight out over Rhode Island Sound, and at that point, apparently disoriented by the darkness and haze, he began a series of curious maneuvers: He banked his plane to the right, farther out into the ocean, and then to the left. He climbed and descended. He sped up and slowed down. Just a few miles from his destination, Kennedy lost control of the plane, and it crashed into the ocean.

Kennedy's mistake, in technical terms, was that he failed to keep his wings level. That was critical, because when a plane banks to one side it begins to turn and its wings lose some of their vertical lift. Left unchecked, this process accelerates. The angle of the bank increases, the turn gets sharper and sharper, and the plane starts to dive toward the ground in an ever-narrowing corkscrew. Pilots call this the graveyard spiral. And why didn't Kennedy stop the dive? Because, in times of low visibility and high stress, keeping your wings level — indeed, even knowing whether you are in a graveyard spiral — turns out to be surprisingly difficult. Kennedy failed under pressure.

Had Kennedy been flying during the day or with a clear moon, he would have been fine. If you are the pilot, looking straight ahead from the cockpit, the angle of your wings will be obvious from the straight line of the horizon in front of you. But when it's dark outside, the horizon disappears. There is no external measure of the plane's bank. On the ground, we know whether we are level even when it's dark, because of the motion-sensing mechanisms in the inner ear. In a spiral dive, though, the effect of the plane's G-force on the inner ear means that the pilot feels perfectly level even if his plane is not. Similarly, when you are in a jetliner that is banking at thirty degrees after takeoff, the book on your neighbor's lap does not slide into your

lap, nor will a pen on the floor roll toward the "down" side of the plane. The physics of flying is such that an airplane in the midst of a turn always feels perfectly level to someone inside the cabin.

This is a difficult notion, and to understand it I went flying with William Langewiesche, the author of a superb book on flying, *Inside the Sky*. We met at San Jose Airport, in the jet center where the Silicon Valley billionaires keep their private planes. Langewiesche is a rugged man in his forties, deeply tanned, and handsome in the way that pilots (at least since the movie *The Right Stuff*) are supposed to be. We took off at dusk, heading out toward Monterey Bay, until we had left the lights of the coast behind and night had erased the horizon. Langewiesche let the plane bank gently to the left. He took his hands off the stick. The sky told me nothing now, so I concentrated on the instruments. The nose of the plane was dropping. The gyroscope told me that we were banking, first fifteen, then thirty, then forty-five degrees. "We're in a spiral dive," Langewiesche said calmly. Our airspeed was steadily accelerating, from 180 to 190 to 200 knots. The needle on the altimeter was moving down. The plane was dropping like a stone, at three thousand feet per minute. I could hear, faintly, a slight increase in the hum of the engine, and the wind noise as we picked up speed. But if Langewiesche and I had been talking, I would have caught none of that. Had the cabin been unpressurized, my ears might have popped, particularly as we went into the steep part of the dive. But beyond that? Nothing at all. In a spiral dive, the G-load — the force of inertia — is normal. As Langewiesche puts it, the plane likes to spiral-dive. The total time elapsed since we started diving was no more than six or seven seconds. Suddenly,

Langewiesche straightened the wings and pulled back on the stick to get the nose of the plane up, breaking out of the dive. Only now did I feel the full force of the G-load, pushing me back in my seat. "You feel no G-load in a bank," Langewiesche said. "There's nothing more confusing for the uninitiated."

I asked Langewiesche how much longer we could have fallen. "Within five seconds, we would have exceeded the limits of the airplane," he replied, by which he meant that the force of trying to pull out of the dive would have broken the plane into pieces. I looked away from the instruments and asked Langewiesche to spiral-dive again, this time without telling me. I sat and waited. I was about to tell Langewiesche that he could start diving anytime, when, suddenly, I was thrown back in my chair. "We just lost a thousand feet," he said.

This inability to sense, experientially, what your plane is doing is what makes night flying so stressful. And this was the stress that Kennedy must have felt when he turned out across the water at Westerly, leaving the guiding lights of the Connecticut coastline behind him. A pilot who flew into Nantucket that night told the National Transportation Safety Board that when he descended over Martha's Vineyard, he looked down and there was "nothing to see. There was no horizon and no light....I thought the island might [have] suffered a power failure." Kennedy was now blind, in every sense, and he must have known the danger he was in. He had very little experience in flying strictly by instruments. Most of the time when he had flown up to the Vineyard, the horizon or lights had still been visible. That strange, final sequence of maneuvers was Kennedy's frantic search for a clearing in the haze. He was trying to

pick up the lights of Martha's Vineyard, to restore the lost horizon. Between the lines of the National Transportation Safety Board's report on the crash, you can almost feel his desperation:

> About 2138 the target began a right turn in a southerly direction. About 30 seconds later, the target stopped its descent at 2200 feet and began a climb that lasted another 30 seconds. During this period of time, the target stopped the turn, and the airspeed decreased to about 153 KIAS. About 2139, the target leveled off at 2500 feet and flew in a southeasterly direction. About 50 seconds later, the target entered a left turn and climbed to 2600 feet. As the target continued in the left turn, it began a descent that reached a rate of about 900 fpm.

But was he choking or panicking? Here the distinction between those two states is critical. Had he choked, he would have reverted to the mode of explicit learning. His movements in the cockpit would have become markedly slower and less fluid. He would have gone back to the mechanical, self-conscious application of the lessons he had first received as a pilot — and that might have been a good thing. Kennedy needed to think, to concentrate on his instruments, to break away from the instinctive flying that served him when he had a visible horizon.

But instead, from all appearances, he panicked. At the moment when he needed to remember the lessons he had been taught about instrument flying, his mind — like Morphew's when she was underwater — must have gone blank. Instead of reviewing the instruments, he seems to have been focused on one question: Where are the lights of

Martha's Vineyard? His gyroscope and his other instruments may well have become as invisible as the peripheral lights in the underwater-panic experiments. He had fallen back on his instincts — on the way the plane felt — and in the dark, of course, instinct can tell you nothing. The NTSB report says that the last time the Piper's wings were level was seven seconds past 9:40, and the plane hit the water at about 9:41, so the critical period here was less than sixty seconds. At twenty-five seconds past the minute, the plane was tilted at an angle greater than forty-five degrees. Inside the cockpit it would have felt normal. At some point, Kennedy must have heard the rising wind outside, or the roar of the engine as it picked up speed. Again, relying on instinct, he might have pulled back on the stick, trying to raise the nose of the plane. But pulling back on the stick without first leveling the wings only makes the spiral tighter and the problem worse. It's also possible that Kennedy did nothing at all, and that he was frozen at the controls, still frantically searching for the lights of the Vineyard, when his plane hit the water. Sometimes pilots don't even try to make it out of a spiral dive. Langewiesche calls that "one G all the way down."

4.

What happened to Kennedy that night illustrates a second major difference between panicking and choking. Panicking is conventional failure, of the sort we tacitly understand. Kennedy panicked because he didn't know enough about instrument flying. If he'd had another year in the air, he might not have panicked, and that fits with what we believe — that performance ought to improve with experi-

ence, and that pressure is an obstacle that the diligent can overcome. But choking makes little intuitive sense. Novotna's problem wasn't lack of diligence; she was as superbly conditioned and schooled as anyone on the tennis tour. And what did experience do for her? In 1995, in the third round of the French Open, Novotna choked even more spectacularly than she had against Graf, losing to Chanda Rubin after surrendering a 5–0 lead in the third set. There seems little doubt that part of the reason for her collapse against Rubin was her collapse against Graf — that the second failure built on the first, making it possible for her to be up 5–0 in the third set and yet entertain the thought I can still lose. If panicking is conventional failure, choking is paradoxical failure.

Claude Steele, a psychologist at Stanford University, and his colleagues have done a number of experiments in recent years looking at how certain groups perform under pressure, and their findings go to the heart of what is so strange about choking. Steele and Joshua Aronson found that when they gave a group of Stanford undergraduates a standardized test and told them that it was a measure of their intellectual ability, the white students did much better than their black counterparts. But when the same test was presented simply as an abstract laboratory tool, with no relevance to ability, the scores of blacks and whites were virtually identical. Steele and Aronson attribute this disparity to what they call "stereotype threat": when black students are put into a situation where they are directly confronted with a stereotype about their group — in this case one having to do with intelligence — the resulting pressure causes their performance to suffer.

Steele and others have found stereotype threat at

work in any situation where groups are depicted in negative ways. Give a group of qualified women a math test and tell them it will measure their quantitative ability and they'll do much worse than equally skilled men will; present the same test simply as a research tool and they'll do just as well as the men. Or consider a handful of experiments conducted by one of Steele's former graduate students, Julio Garcia, a professor at Tufts University. Garcia gathered together a group of white, athletic students and had a white instructor lead them through a series of physical tests: to jump as high as they could, to do a standing broad jump, and to see how many pushups they could do in twenty seconds. The instructor then asked them to do the tests a second time, and, as you'd expect, Garcia found that the students did a little better on each of the tasks the second time around. Then Garcia ran a second group of students through the tests, this time replacing the instructor between the first and second trials with an African-American. Now the white students ceased to improve on their vertical leaps. He did the experiment again, only this time he replaced the white instructor with a black instructor who was much taller and heavier than the previous black instructor. In this trial, the white students actually jumped less high than they had the first time around. Their performance on the pushups, though, was unchanged in each of the conditions. There is no stereotype, after all, that suggests that whites can't do as many pushups as blacks. The task that was affected was the vertical leap, because of what our culture says: white men can't jump.

It doesn't come as news, of course, that black students aren't as good at test-taking as white students, or that white students aren't as good at jumping as black students. The

problem is that we've always assumed that this kind of failure under pressure is panic. What is it we tell underperform-
ing athletes and students? The same thing we tell novice
pilots or scuba divers: to work harder, to buckle down, to
take the tests of their ability more seriously. But Steele says
that when you look at the way black or female students perform under stereotype threat, you don't see the wild guessing
of a panicked test taker. "What you tend to see is careful-
ness and second-guessing," he explains. "When you go and
interview them, you have the sense that when they are in the
stereotype-threat condition they say to themselves, 'Look,
I'm going to be careful here. I'm not going to mess things up.'
Then, after having decided to take that strategy, they calm
down and go through the test. But that's not the way to succeed on a standardized test. The more you do that, the more
you will get away from the intuitions that help you, the quick
processing. They think they did well, and they are trying to
do well. But they are not." This is choking, not panicking.
Garcia's athletes and Steele's students are like Novotna, not
Kennedy. They failed because they were good at what they
did: only those who care about how well they perform ever
feel the pressure of stereotype threat. The usual prescrip-
tion for failure — to work harder and take the test more seriously — would only make their problems worse.

That is a hard lesson to grasp, but harder still is the fact
that choking requires us to concern ourselves less with the performer and more with the situation in which the performance
occurs. Novotna herself could do nothing to prevent her collapse against Graf. The only thing that could have saved her
is if — at that critical moment in the third set — the television
cameras had been turned off, the Duke and Duchess had gone
home, and the spectators had been told to wait outside. In

sports, of course, you can't do that. Choking is a central part of the drama of athletic competition, because the spectators have to be there — and the ability to overcome the pressure of the spectators is part of what it means to be a champion. But the same ruthless inflexibility need not govern the rest of our lives. We have to learn that sometimes a poor performance reflects not the innate ability of the performer but the complexion of the audience; and that sometimes a poor test score is the sign not of a poor student but of a good one.

5.

Through the first three rounds of the 1996 Masters golf tournament, Greg Norman held a seemingly insurmountable lead over his nearest rival, the Englishman Nick Faldo. He was the best player in the world. His nickname was the Shark. He didn't saunter down the fairways; he stalked the course, blond and broad-shouldered, his caddy behind him, struggling to keep up. But then came the ninth hole on the tournament's final day. Norman was paired with Faldo, and the two hit their first shots well. They were now facing the green. In front of the pin, there was a steep slope, so that any ball hit short would come rolling back down the hill into oblivion. Faldo shot first, and the ball landed safely long, well past the cup.

Norman was next. He stood over the ball. "The one thing you guard against here is short," the announcer said, stating the obvious. Norman swung and then froze, his club in midair, following the ball in flight. It was short. Norman watched, stone-faced, as the ball rolled thirty yards back down the hill, and with that error something inside of him broke.

At the tenth hole, he hooked the ball to the left, hit his third shot well past the cup, and missed a makeable putt. At eleven, Norman had a three-and-a-half-foot putt for par — the kind he had been making all week. He shook out his hands and legs before grasping the club, trying to relax. He missed: his third straight bogey. At twelve, Norman hit the ball straight into the water. At thirteen, he hit it into a patch of pine needles. At sixteen, his movements were so mechanical and out of synch that, when he swung, his hips spun out ahead of his body and the ball sailed into another pond. At that, he took his club and made a frustrated scythelike motion through the grass, because what had been obvious for twenty minutes was now official: he had fumbled away the chance of a lifetime.

Faldo had begun the day six strokes behind Norman. By the time the two started their slow walk to the eighteenth hole, through the throng of spectators, Faldo had a four-stroke lead. But he took those final steps quietly, giving only the smallest of nods, keeping his head low. He understood what had happened on the greens and fairways that day. And he was bound by the particular etiquette of choking, the understanding that what he had earned was something less than a victory and what Norman had suffered was something less than a defeat.

When it was all over, Faldo wrapped his arms around Norman. "I don't know what to say — I just want to give you a hug," he whispered, and then he said the only thing you can say to a choker: "I feel horrible about what happened. I'm so sorry." With that, the two men began to cry.

August 21 and 28, 2000

Blowup

WHO CAN BE BLAMED FOR A DISASTER LIKE
THE *CHALLENGER* EXPLOSION? NO ONE, AND
WE'D BETTER GET USED TO IT

1.

In the technological age, there is a ritual to disaster. When planes crash or chemical plants explode, each piece of physical evidence — of twisted metal or fractured concrete — becomes a kind of fetish object, painstakingly located, mapped, tagged, and analyzed, with findings submitted to boards of inquiry that then probe and interview and soberly draw conclusions. It is a ritual of reassurance, based on the principle that what we learn from one accident can help us prevent another, and a measure of its effectiveness is that Americans did not shut down the nuclear industry after Three Mile Island and do not abandon the skies after each new plane crash. But the rituals of disaster have rarely been played out so dramatically as they were in the case of the *Challenger* space shuttle, which blew up over southern Florida on January 28, 1986.

Fifty-five minutes after the explosion, when the last of the debris had fallen into the ocean, recovery ships

were on the scene. They remained there for the next three months, as part of what turned into the largest maritime salvage operation in history, combing a hundred and fifty thousand square nautical miles for floating debris, while the ocean floor surrounding the crash site was inspected by submarines. In mid-April of 1986, the salvage team found several chunks of charred metal that confirmed what had previously been only suspected: the explosion was caused by a faulty seal in one of the shuttle's rocket boosters, which had allowed a stream of flame to escape and ignite an external fuel tank.

Armed with this confirmation, a special presidential investigative commission concluded the following June that the deficient seal reflected shoddy engineering and lax management at NASA and its prime contractor, Morton Thiokol. Properly chastised, NASA returned to the drawing board, to emerge thirty-two months later with a new shuttle — *Discovery* — redesigned according to the lessons learned from the disaster. During that first post-*Challenger* flight, as America watched breathlessly, the crew of the *Discovery* held a short commemorative service. "Dear friends," the mission commander, Captain Frederick H. Hauck, said, addressing the seven dead *Challenger* astronauts, "your loss has meant that we could confidently begin anew." The ritual was complete. NASA was back.

But what if the assumptions that underlie our disaster rituals aren't true? What if these public postmortems don't help us avoid future accidents? Over the past few years, a group of scholars has begun making the unsettling argument that the rituals that follow things like plane crashes or the Three Mile Island crisis are as much exercises in self-deception as they are genuine opportunities

for reassurance. For these revisionists, high-technology accidents may not have clear causes at all. They may be inherent in the complexity of the technological systems we have created.

This revisionism has now been extended to the *Challenger* disaster, with the publication of *The Challenger Launch Decision,* by the sociologist Diane Vaughan, which is the first truly definitive analysis of the events leading up to January 28, 1986. The conventional view is that the *Challenger* accident was an anomaly, that it happened because people at NASA had not done their job. But the study's conclusion is the opposite: it says that the accident happened because people at NASA had done exactly what they were supposed to do. "No fundamental decision was made at NASA to do evil," Vaughan writes. "Rather, a series of seemingly harmless decisions were made that incrementally moved the space agency toward a catastrophic outcome."

No doubt Vaughan's analysis will be hotly disputed, but even if she is only partly right, the implications of this kind of argument are enormous. We have surrounded ourselves in the modern age with things like power plants and nuclear weapons systems and airports that handle hundreds of planes an hour, on the understanding that the risks they represent are, at the very least, manageable. But if the potential for catastrophe is actually found in the normal functioning of complex systems, this assumption is false. Risks are not easily manageable, accidents are not easily preventable, and the rituals of disaster have no meaning. The first time around, the story of the *Challenger* was tragic. In its retelling, a decade later, it is merely banal.

2.

Perhaps the best way to understand the argument over the *Challenger* explosion is to start with an accident that preceded it — the near disaster at the Three Mile Island (TMI) nuclear-power plant in March of 1979. The conclusion of the president's commission that investigated the TMI accident was that it was the result of human error, particularly on the part of the plant's operators. But the truth of what happened there, the revisionists maintain, is a good deal more complicated than that, and their arguments are worth examining in detail.

The trouble at TMI started with a blockage in what is called the plant's polisher — a kind of giant water filter. Polisher problems were not unusual at TMI, or particularly serious. But in this case the blockage caused moisture to leak into the plant's air system, inadvertently tripping two valves and shutting down the flow of cold water into the plant's steam generator.

As it happens, TMI had a backup cooling system for precisely this situation. But on that particular day, for reasons that no one really knows, the valves for the backup system weren't open. They had been closed, and an indicator in the control room showing they were closed was blocked by a repair tag hanging from a switch above it. That left the reactor dependent on another backup system, a special sort of relief valve. But, as luck would have it, the relief valve wasn't working properly that day, either. It stuck open when it was supposed to close, and, to make matters even worse, a gauge in the control room which should have told the operators that the relief valve wasn't working was itself not working. By the time TMI's

engineers realized what was happening, the reactor had come dangerously close to a meltdown.

Here, in other words, was a major accident caused by five discrete events. There is no way the engineers in the control room could have known about any of them. No glaring errors or spectacularly bad decisions were made that exacerbated those events. And all the malfunctions — the blocked polisher, the shut valves, the obscured indicator, the faulty relief valve, and the broken gauge — were in themselves so trivial that individually they would have created no more than a nuisance. What caused the accident was the way minor events unexpectedly interacted to create a major problem.

This kind of disaster is what the Yale University sociologist Charles Perrow has famously called a *normal accident*. By *normal,* Perrow does not mean that it is frequent; he means that it is the kind of accident one can expect in the normal functioning of a technologically complex operation. Modern systems, Perrow argues, are made up of thousands of parts, all of which interrelate in ways that are impossible to anticipate. Given that complexity, he says, it is almost inevitable that some combinations of minor failures will eventually amount to something catastrophic. In a classic 1984 treatise on accidents, Perrow takes examples of well-known plane crashes, oil spills, chemical-plant explosions, and nuclear-weapons mishaps and shows how many of them are best understood as normal. If you saw the movie *Apollo 13,* in fact, you have seen a perfect illustration of one of the most famous of all normal accidents: the Apollo flight went awry because of the interaction of failures of the spacecraft's oxygen and hydrogen tanks, and an indicator light that diverted the astronauts' attention from the real problem.

Had this been a "real" accident — if the mission had run into trouble because of one massive or venal error — the story would have made for a much inferior movie. In real accidents, people rant and rave and hunt down the culprit. They do, in short, what people in Hollywood thrillers always do. But what made *Apollo 13* unusual was that the dominant emotion was not anger but bafflement — bafflement that so much could go wrong for so little apparent reason. There was no one to blame, no dark secret to unearth, no recourse but to re-create an entire system in place of one that had inexplicably failed. In the end, the normal accident was the more terrifying one.

3.

Was the *Challenger* explosion a normal accident? In a narrow sense, the answer is no. Unlike what happened at TMI, its explosion was caused by a single, catastrophic malfunction: the so-called O-rings that were supposed to prevent hot gases from leaking out of the rocket boosters didn't do their job. But Vaughan argues that the O-ring problem was really just a symptom. The cause of the accident was the culture of NASA, she says, and that culture led to a series of decisions about the *Challenger* that very much followed the contours of a normal accident.

The heart of the question is how NASA chose to evaluate the problems it had been having with the rocket boosters' O-rings. These are the thin rubber bands that run around the lips of each of the rocket's four segments, and each O-ring was meant to work like the rubber seal on the top of a bottle of preserves, making the fit between each part of the rocket snug and airtight. But from as far back

as 1981, on one shuttle flight after another, the O-rings
had shown increasing problems. In a number of instances,
the rubber seal had been dangerously eroded — a condition suggesting that hot gases had almost escaped. What's
more, O-rings were strongly suspected to be less effective in cold weather, when the rubber would harden and
not give as tight a seal. On the morning of January 28,
1986, the shuttle launchpad was encased in ice, and the
temperature at liftoff was just above freezing. Anticipat-
ing these low temperatures, engineers at Morton Thiokol,
the manufacturer of the shuttle's rockets, recommended
that the launch be delayed. Morton Thiokol brass and
NASA, however, overruled the recommendation, and that
decision led both the president's commission and numerous critics since to accuse NASA of egregious — if not
criminal — misjudgment.

Vaughan doesn't dispute that the decision was fatally
flawed. But, after reviewing thousands of pages of transcripts and internal NASA documents, she can't find any
evidence of people acting negligently, or nakedly sacri-
ficing safety in the name of politics or expediency. The
mistakes that NASA made, she says, were made in the
normal course of operation. For example, in retrospect it
may seem obvious that cold weather impaired O-ring performance. But it wasn't obvious at the time. A previous
shuttle flight that had suffered worse O-ring damage had
been launched in 75-degree heat. And on a series of previous occasions when NASA had proposed — but eventually
scrubbed for other reasons — shuttle launches in weather
as cold as 41 degrees, Morton Thiokol had not said a word
about the potential threat posed by the cold, so its pre-
Challenger objection had seemed to NASA not reasonable

but arbitrary. Vaughan confirms that there was a dispute between managers and engineers on the eve of the launch but points out that in the shuttle program, disputes of this sort were commonplace. And, while the president's commission was astonished by NASA's repeated use of the phrases *acceptable risk* and *acceptable erosion* in internal discussion of the rocket-booster joints, Vaughan shows that flying with acceptable risks was a standard part of NASA culture. The lists of acceptable risks on the space shuttle, in fact, filled six volumes. "Although [O-ring] erosion itself had not been predicted, its occurrence conformed to engineering expectations about large-scale technical systems," she writes. "At NASA, problems were the norm. The word *anomaly* was part of everyday talk.... The whole shuttle system operated on the assumption that deviation could be controlled but not eliminated."

What NASA had created was a closed culture that, in her words, "normalized deviance" so that to the outside world, decisions that were obviously questionable were seen by NASA's management as prudent and reasonable. It is her depiction of this internal world that makes her book so disquieting: when she lays out the sequence of decisions that led to the launch — each decision as trivial as the string of failures that led to the near disaster at TMI — it is difficult to find any precise point where things went wrong or where things might be improved next time. "It can truly be said that the *Challenger* launch decision was a rule-based decision," she concludes. "But the cultural understandings, rules, procedures, and norms that always had worked in the past did not work this time. It was not amorally calculating managers violating rules that were responsible for the tragedy. It was conformity."

4.

There is another way to look at this problem, and that is from the standpoint of how human beings handle risk. One of the assumptions behind the modern disaster ritual is that when a risk can be identified and eliminated, a system can be made safer. The new booster joints on the shuttle, for example, are so much better than the old ones that the overall chances of a *Challenger*-style accident's ever happening again must be lower, right? This is such a straightforward idea that questioning it seems almost impossible. But that is just what another group of scholars has done, under what is called the theory of *risk homeostasis*. It should be said that within the academic community, there are huge debates over how widely the theory of risk homeostasis can and should be applied. But the basic idea, which has been laid out brilliantly by the Canadian psychologist Gerald Wilde in his book *Target Risk,* is quite simple: under certain circumstances, changes that appear to make a system or an organization safer in fact don't. Why? Because human beings have a seemingly fundamental tendency to compensate for lower risks in one area by taking greater risks in another.

Consider, for example, the results of a famous experiment conducted several years ago in Germany. Part of a fleet of taxicabs in Munich was equipped with antilock brake systems (ABS), a technological innovation that vastly improves braking, particularly on slippery surfaces. The rest of the fleet was left alone, and the two groups — which were otherwise perfectly matched — were placed under careful and secret observation for three years. You would expect the better brakes to make for safer driving.

But that is exactly the opposite of what happened. Giving some drivers ABS made no difference at all in their accident rate; in fact, it turned them into markedly inferior drivers. They drove faster. They made sharper turns. They showed poorer lane discipline. They braked harder. They were more likely to tailgate. They didn't merge as well, and they were involved in more near misses. In other words, the ABS systems were not used to reduce accidents; instead, the drivers used the additional element of safety to enable them to drive faster and more recklessly without increasing their risk of getting into an accident. As economists would say, they *consumed* the risk reduction, they didn't save it.

Risk homeostasis doesn't happen all the time. Often — as in the case of seat belts, say — compensatory behavior only partly offsets the risk reduction of a safety measure. But it happens often enough that it must be given serious consideration. Why are more pedestrians killed crossing the street at marked crosswalks than at unmarked crosswalks? Because they compensate for the "safe" environment of a marked crossing by being less vigilant about oncoming traffic. Why did the introduction of childproof lids on medicine bottles lead, according to one study, to a substantial increase in fatal child poisonings? Because adults became less careful in keeping pill bottles out of the reach of children.

Risk homeostasis also works in the opposite direction. In the late 1960s, Sweden changed over from driving on the left-hand side of the road to driving on the right, a switch that one would think would create an epidemic of accidents. But, in fact, the opposite was true. People compensated for their unfamiliarity with the new traffic

patterns by driving more carefully. During the next twelve months, traffic fatalities dropped 17 percent before returning slowly to their previous levels. As Wilde only half-facetiously argues, countries truly interested in making their streets and highways safer should think about switching over from one side of the road to the other on a regular basis.

It doesn't take much imagination to see how risk homeostasis applies to NASA and the space shuttle. In one frequently quoted phrase, Richard Feynman, the Nobel Prize–winning physicist who served on the *Challenger* commission, said that at NASA decision-making was "a kind of Russian roulette." When the O-rings began to have problems and nothing happened, the agency began to believe that "the risk is no longer so high for the next flights," Feynman said, and that "we can lower our standards a little bit because we got away with it last time." But fixing the O-rings doesn't mean that this kind of risk-taking stops. There are six whole volumes of shuttle components that are deemed by NASA to be as risky as O-rings. It is entirely possible that better O-rings just give NASA the confidence to play Russian roulette with something else.

This is a depressing conclusion, but it shouldn't come as a surprise. The truth is that our stated commitment to safety, our faithful enactment of the rituals of disaster, has always masked a certain hypocrisy. We don't really want the safest of all possible worlds. The national 55-mile-per-hour speed limit probably saved more lives than any other single government intervention of the past generation. But the fact that Congress lifted it last month with a minimum of argument proves that we would rather consume the

recent safety advances of things like seat belts and air bags than save them. The same is true of the dramatic improvements that have been made in recent years in the design of aircraft and flight-navigation systems. Presumably, these innovations could be used to bring down the airline accident rate as low as possible. But that is not what consumers want. They want air travel to be cheaper, more reliable, or more convenient, and so those safety advances have been at least partly consumed by flying and landing planes in worse weather and heavier traffic conditions.

What accidents like the *Challenger* should teach us is that we have constructed a world in which the potential for high-tech catastrophe is embedded in the fabric of day-to-day life. At some point in the future — for the most mundane of reasons, and with the very best of intentions — a NASA spacecraft will again go down in flames. We should at least admit this to ourselves now. And if we cannot — if the possibility is too much to bear — then our only option is to start thinking about getting rid of things like space shuttles altogether.

January 22, 1996

Part Three

PERSONALITY, CHARACTER, AND INTELLIGENCE

"'He'll be wearing a double-breasted suit.
Buttoned.' — And he was."

Late Bloomers

WHY DO WE EQUATE GENIUS
WITH PRECOCITY?

1.

Ben Fountain was an associate in the real-estate practice at the Dallas offices of Akin, Gump, Strauss, Hauer & Feld, just a few years out of law school, when he decided he wanted to write fiction. The only thing Fountain had ever published was a law-review article. His literary training consisted of a handful of creative-writing classes in college. He had tried to write when he came home at night from work, but usually he was too tired to do much. He decided to quit his job.

"I was tremendously apprehensive," Fountain recalls. "I felt like I'd stepped off a cliff and I didn't know if the parachute was going to open. Nobody wants to waste their life, and I was doing well at the practice of law. I could have had a good career. And my parents were very proud of me — my dad was so proud of me.... It was crazy."

He began his new life on a February morning — a Monday. He sat down at his kitchen table at 7:30 a.m. He made a plan. Every day, he would write until lunchtime.

Then he would lie down on the floor for twenty minutes to rest his mind. Then he would return to work for a few more hours. He was a lawyer. He had discipline. "I figured out very early on that if I didn't get my writing done I felt terrible. So I always got my writing done. I treated it like a job. I did not procrastinate." His first story was about a stockbroker who uses inside information and crosses a moral line. It was sixty pages long and took him three months to write. When he finished that story, he went back to work and wrote another — and then another.

In his first year, Fountain sold two stories. He gained confidence. He wrote a novel. He decided it wasn't very good, and he ended up putting it in a drawer. Then came what he describes as his dark period, when he adjusted his expectations and started again. He got a short story published in *Harper's*. A New York literary agent saw it and signed him up. He put together a collection of short stories titled *Brief Encounters with Che Guevara*, and Ecco, a HarperCollins imprint, published it. The reviews were sensational. The *Times Book Review* called it "heartbreaking." It won the Hemingway Foundation/PEN award. It was named a No. 1 Book Sense Pick. It made major regional bestseller lists, was named one of the best books of the year by the San Francisco *Chronicle*, the Chicago *Tribune*, and *Kirkus Reviews*, and drew comparisons to Graham Greene, Evelyn Waugh, Robert Stone, and John le Carré.

Ben Fountain's rise sounds like a familiar story: the young man from the provinces suddenly takes the literary world by storm. But Ben Fountain's success was far from sudden. He quit his job at Akin, Gump in 1988. For every story he published in those early years, he had at least thirty rejections. The novel that he put away in a drawer took him

four years. The dark period lasted for the entire second half of the 1990s. His breakthrough with *Brief Encounters* came in 2006, eighteen years after he first sat down to write at his kitchen table. The "young" writer from the provinces took the literary world by storm at the age of forty-eight.

2.

Genius, in the popular conception, is inextricably tied up with precocity — doing something truly creative, we're inclined to think, requires the freshness and exuberance and energy of youth. Orson Welles made his masterpiece, *Citizen Kane,* at twenty-five. Herman Melville wrote a book a year through his late twenties, culminating, at age thirty-two, with *Moby-Dick.* Mozart wrote his breakthrough Piano Concerto No. 9 in E-flat major at the age of twenty-one. In some creative forms, like lyric poetry, the importance of precocity has hardened into an iron law. How old was T. S. Eliot when he wrote "The Love Song of J. Alfred Prufrock" ("I grow old...I grow old")? Twenty-three. "Poets peak young," the creativity researcher James Kaufman maintains. Mihály Csíkszentmihályi, the author of "Flow," agrees: "The most creative lyric verse is believed to be that written by the young." According to the Harvard psychologist Howard Gardner, a leading authority on creativity, "Lyric poetry is a domain where talent is discovered early, burns brightly, and then peters out at an early age."

A few years ago, an economist at the University of Chicago named David Galenson decided to find out whether this assumption about creativity was true. He looked through forty-seven major poetry anthologies published since 1980 and counted the poems that appear most fre-

quently. Some people, of course, would quarrel with the notion that literary merit can be quantified. But Galenson simply wanted to poll a broad cross-section of literary scholars about which poems they felt were the most important in the American canon. The top eleven are, in order, T. S. Eliot's "Prufrock," Robert Lowell's "Skunk Hour," Robert Frost's "Stopping by Woods on a Snowy Evening," William Carlos Williams's "Red Wheelbarrow," Elizabeth Bishop's "The Fish," Ezra Pound's "The River Merchant's Wife," Sylvia Plath's "Daddy," Pound's "In a Station of the Metro," Frost's "Mending Wall," Wallace Stevens's "The Snow Man," and Williams's "The Dance." Those eleven were composed at the ages of twenty-three, forty-one, forty-eight, forty, twenty-nine, thirty, thirty, twenty-eight, thirty-eight, forty-two, and fifty-nine, respectively. There is no evidence, Galenson concluded, for the notion that lyric poetry is a young person's game. Some poets do their best work at the beginning of their careers. Others do their best work decades later. Forty-two percent of Frost's anthologized poems were written after the age of fifty. For Williams, it's 44 percent. For Stevens, it's 49 percent.

The same was true of film, Galenson points out in his study "Old Masters and Young Geniuses: The Two Life Cycles of Artistic Creativity." Yes, there was Orson Welles, peaking as a director at twenty-five. But then there was Alfred Hitchcock, who made *Dial M for Murder, Rear Window, To Catch a Thief, The Trouble with Harry, Vertigo, North by Northwest,* and *Psycho* — one of the greatest runs by a director in history — between his fifty-fourth and sixty-first birthdays. Mark Twain published *Adventures of Huckleberry Finn* at forty-nine. Daniel Defoe wrote *Robinson Crusoe* at fifty-eight.

The examples that Galenson could not get out of his head, however, were Picasso and Cézanne. He was an art lover, and he knew their stories well. Picasso was the incandescent prodigy. His career as a serious artist began with a masterpiece, *Evocation: The Burial of Casagemas*, produced at age twenty. In short order, he painted many of the greatest works of his career — including *Les Demoiselles d'Avignon*, at the age of twenty-six. Picasso fit our usual ideas about genius perfectly.

Cézanne didn't. If you go to the Cézanne room at the Musée d'Orsay, in Paris — the finest collection of Cézannes in the world — the array of masterpieces you'll find along the back wall were all painted at the end of his career. Galenson did a simple economic analysis, tabulating the prices paid at auction for paintings by Picasso and Cézanne with the ages at which they created those works. A painting done by Picasso in his midtwenties was worth, he found, an average of four times as much as a painting done in his sixties. For Cézanne, the opposite was true. The paintings he created in his midsixties were valued fifteen times as highly as the paintings he created as a young man. The freshness, exuberance, and energy of youth did little for Cézanne. He was a late bloomer — and for some reason in our accounting of genius and creativity we have forgotten to make sense of the Cézannes of the world.

3.

The first day that Ben Fountain sat down to write at his kitchen table went well. He knew how the story about the stockbroker was supposed to start. But the second day, he says, he "completely freaked out." He didn't know how

to describe things. He felt as if he were back in first grade. He didn't have a fully formed vision, waiting to be emptied onto the page. "I had to create a mental image of a building, a room, a facade, haircut, clothes — just really basic things," he says. "I realized I didn't have the facility to put those into words. I started going out and buying visual dictionaries, architectural dictionaries, and going to school on those."

He began to collect articles about things he was interested in, and before long he realized that he had developed a fascination with Haiti. "The Haiti file just kept getting bigger and bigger," Fountain says. "And I thought, OK, here's my novel. For a month or two I said, I really don't need to go there, I can imagine everything. But after a couple of months I thought, Yeah, you've got to go there, and so I went, in April or May of 'ninety-one."

He spoke little French, let alone Haitian Creole. He had never been abroad. Nor did he know anyone in Haiti. "I got to the hotel, walked up the stairs, and there was this guy standing at the top of the stairs," Fountain recalls. "He said, 'My name is Pierre. You need a guide.' I said, 'You're sure as hell right, I do.' He was a very genuine person, and he realized pretty quickly I didn't want to go see the girls, I didn't want drugs, I didn't want any of that other stuff," Fountain went on. "And then it was, *boom,* 'I can take you there. I can take you to this person.'"

Fountain was riveted by Haiti. "It's like a laboratory, almost," he says. "Everything that's gone on in the last five hundred years — colonialism, race, power, politics, ecological disasters — it's all there in very concentrated form. And also I just felt, viscerally, pretty comfortable there." He made more trips to Haiti, sometimes for

a week, sometimes for two weeks. He made friends. He invited them to visit him in Dallas. ("You haven't lived until you've had Haitians stay in your house," Fountain says.) "I mean, I was involved. I couldn't just walk away. There's this very nonrational, nonlinear part of the whole process. I had a pretty specific time era that I was writing about, and certain things that I needed to know. But there were other things I didn't really need to know. I met a fellow who was with Save the Children, and he was on the Central Plateau, which takes about twelve hours to get to on a bus, and I had no reason to go there. But I went up there. Suffered on that bus, and ate dust. It was a hard trip, but it was a glorious trip. It had nothing to do with the book, but it wasn't wasted knowledge."

In *Brief Encounters with Che Guevara*, four of the stories are about Haiti, and they are the strongest in the collection. They feel like Haiti; they feel as if they've been written from the inside looking out, not the outside looking in. "After the novel was done, I don't know, I just felt like there was more for me, and I could keep going, keep going deeper there," Fountain recalls. "Always there's something — always something — here for me. How many times have I been? At least thirty times."

Prodigies like Picasso, Galenson argues, rarely engage in that kind of open-ended exploration. They tend to be "conceptual," Galenson says, in the sense that they start with a clear idea of where they want to go, and then they execute it. "I can hardly understand the importance given to the word *research*," Picasso once said in an interview with the artist Marius de Zayas. "In my opinion, to search means nothing in painting. To find is the thing." He continued, "The several manners I have used in my art must

not be considered as an evolution or as steps toward an unknown ideal of painting....I have never made trials or experiments."

But late bloomers, Galenson says, tend to work the other way around. Their approach is experimental. "Their goals are imprecise, so their procedure is tentative and incremental," Galenson writes in "Old Masters and Young Geniuses," and he goes on:

> The imprecision of their goals means that these artists rarely feel they have succeeded, and their careers are consequently often dominated by the pursuit of a single objective. These artists repeat themselves, painting the same subject many times, and gradually changing its treatment in an experimental process of trial and error. Each work leads to the next, and none is generally privileged over others, so experimental painters rarely make specific preparatory sketches or plans for a painting. They consider the production of a painting as a process of searching, in which they aim to discover the image in the course of making it; they typically believe that learning is a more important goal than making finished paintings. Experimental artists build their skills gradually over the course of their careers, improving their work slowly over long periods. These artists are perfectionists and are typically plagued by frustration at their inability to achieve their goal.

Where Picasso wanted to find, not search, Cézanne said the opposite: "I seek in painting."

An experimental innovator *would* go back to Haiti thirty times. That's how that kind of mind figures out what it wants to do. When Cézanne was painting a portrait

of the critic Gustave Geffroy, he made him endure eighty sittings, over three months, before announcing the project a failure. (The result is one of that string of masterpieces in the Musée d'Orsay.) When Cézanne painted his dealer, Ambrose Vollard, he made Vollard arrive at eight in the morning and sit on a rickety platform until eleven-thirty, without a break, on 150 occasions — before abandoning the portrait. He would paint a scene, then repaint it, then paint it again. He was notorious for slashing his canvases to pieces in fits of frustration.

Mark Twain was the same way. Galenson quotes the literary critic Franklin Rogers on Twain's trial-and-error method: "His routine procedure seems to have been to start a novel with some structural plan which ordinarily soon proved defective, whereupon he would cast about for a new plot which would overcome the difficulty, rewrite what he had already written, and then push on until some new defect forced him to repeat the process once again." Twain fiddled and despaired and revised and gave up on *Huckleberry Finn* so many times that the book took him nearly a decade to complete. The Cézannes of the world bloom late not as a result of some defect in character, or distraction, or lack of ambition, but because the kind of creativity that proceeds through trial and error necessarily takes a long time to come to fruition.

One of the best stories in *Brief Encounters* is called "Near-Extinct Birds of the Central Cordillera." It's about an ornithologist taken hostage by the FARC guerrillas of Colombia. Like so much of Fountain's work, it reads with an easy grace. But there was nothing easy or graceful about its creation. "I struggled with that story," Fountain says. "I always try to do too much. I mean, I probably

wrote five hundred pages of it in various incarnations."
Fountain is at work right now on a novel. It was supposed
to come out this year. It's late.

4.

Galenson's idea that creativity can be divided into these
types — conceptual and experimental — has a number of
important implications. For example, we sometimes think
of late bloomers as late starters. They don't realize they're
good at something until they're fifty, so of course they
achieve late in life. But that's not quite right. Cézanne was
painting almost as early as Picasso was. We also sometimes think of them as artists who are *discovered* late; the
world is just slow to appreciate their gifts. In both cases,
the assumption is that the prodigy and the late bloomer
are fundamentally the same, and that late blooming is
simply genius under conditions of market failure. What
Galenson's argument suggests is something else — that
late bloomers bloom late because they simply aren't much
good until late in their careers.

"All these qualities of his inner vision were continu-
ally hampered and obstructed by Cézanne's incapacity to
give sufficient verisimilitude to the personae of his drama,"
the great English art critic Roger Fry wrote of the early
Cézanne. "With all his rare endowments, he happened to
lack the comparatively common gift of illustration, the gift
that any draughtsman for the illustrated papers learns in a
school of commercial art; whereas, to realize such visions as
Cézanne's required this gift in high degree." In other words,
the young Cézanne couldn't draw. Of *The Banquet,* which
Cézanne painted at thirty-one, Fry writes, "It is no use to

deny that Cézanne has made a very poor job of it." Fry goes on, "More happily endowed and more integral personalities have been able to express themselves harmoniously from the very first. But such rich, complex, and conflicting natures as Cézanne's require a long period of fermentation." Cézanne was trying something so elusive that he couldn't master it until he'd spent decades practicing.

This is the vexing lesson of Fountain's long attempt to get noticed by the literary world. On the road to great achievement, the late bloomer will resemble a failure: while the late bloomer is revising and despairing and changing course and slashing canvases to ribbons after months or years, what he or she produces will look like the kind of thing produced by the artist who will never bloom at all. Prodigies are easy. They advertise their genius from the get-go. Late bloomers are hard. They require forbearance and blind faith. (Let's just be thankful that Cézanne didn't have a guidance counselor in high school who looked at his primitive sketches and told him to try accounting.) Whenever we find a late bloomer, we can't but wonder how many others like him or her we have thwarted because we prematurely judged their talents. But we also have to accept that there's nothing we can do about it. How can we ever know which of the failures will end up blooming?

Not long after meeting Ben Fountain, I went to see the novelist Jonathan Safran Foer, the author of the 2002 bestseller *Everything Is Illuminated*. Fountain is a graying man, slight and modest, who looks, in the words of a friend of his, like a "golf pro from Augusta, Georgia." Foer is in his early thirties and looks barely old enough to drink. Fountain has a softness to him, as if years of struggle have worn away whatever sharp edges he once had. Foer gives

the impression that if you touched him while he was in full conversational flight, you would get an electric shock.

"I came to writing really by the back door," Foer said. "My wife is a writer, and she grew up keeping journals — you know, parents said, 'Lights out, time for bed,' and she had a little flashlight under the covers, reading books. I don't think I *read* a book until much later than other people. I just wasn't interested in it."

Foer went to Princeton and took a creative-writing class in his freshman year with Joyce Carol Oates. It was, he explains, "sort of on a whim, maybe out of a sense that I should have a diverse course load." He'd never written a story before. "I didn't really think anything of it, to be honest, but halfway through the semester I arrived to class early one day, and she said, 'Oh, I'm glad I have this chance to talk to you. I'm a fan of your writing.' And it was a *real* revelation for me."

Oates told him that he had the most important of writerly qualities, which was energy. He had been writing fifteen pages a week for that class, an entire story for each seminar.

"Why does a dam with a crack in it leak so much?" he said, with a laugh. "There was just something in me, there was like a pressure."

As a sophomore, he took another creative-writing class. During the following summer, he went to Europe. He wanted to find the village in Ukraine where his grandfather had come from. After the trip, he went to Prague. There he read Kafka, as any literary undergraduate would, and sat down at his computer.

"I was just writing," he said. "I didn't know that I was writing until it was happening. I didn't go with the

intention of writing a book. I wrote three hundred pages in ten weeks. I *really* wrote. I'd never done it like that."

It was a novel about a boy named Jonathan Safran Foer who visits the village in Ukraine where his grandfather had come from. Those three hundred pages were the first draft of *Everything Is Illuminated* — the exquisite and extraordinary novel that established Foer as one of the most distinctive literary voices of his generation. He was nineteen years old.

Foer began to talk about the other way of writing books, where you painstakingly honed your craft, over years and years. "I couldn't do that," he said. He seemed puzzled by it. It was clear that he had no understanding of how being an experimental innovator would work. "I mean, imagine if the craft you're trying to learn is to be an original. How could you learn the craft of being an original?"

He began to describe his visit to Ukraine. "I went to the shtetl where my family came from. It's called Trachimbrod, the name I use in the book. It's a real place. But you know what's funny? It's the single piece of research that made its way into the book." He wrote the first sentence, and he was proud of it, and then he went back and forth in his mind about where to go next. "I spent the first week just having this debate with myself about what to do with this first sentence. And once I made the decision, I felt liberated to just create — and it was very explosive after that."

If you read *Everything Is Illuminated*, you end up with the same feeling you get when you read *Brief Encounters with Che Guevara* — the sense of transport you experience when a work of literature draws you into its own world. Both are works of art. It's just that, as artists, Fountain and Foer could not be less alike. Fountain

went to Haiti thirty times. Foer went to Trachimbrod just once. "I mean, it was nothing," Foer said. "I had absolutely no experience there at all. It was just a springboard for my book. It was like an empty swimming pool that had to be filled up." Total time spent getting inspiration for his novel: three days.

5.

Ben Fountain did not make the decision to quit the law and become a writer all by himself. He is married and has a family. He met his wife, Sharon, when they were both in law school at Duke. When he was doing real-estate work at Akin, Gump, she was on the partner track in the tax practice at Thompson & Knight. The two actually worked in the same building in downtown Dallas. They got married in 1985, and had a son in April of 1987. Sharie, as Fountain calls her, took four months of maternity leave before returning to work. She made partner by the end of that year.

"We had our son in a day care downtown," she recalls. "We would drive in together, one of us would take him to day care, the other one would go to work. One of us would pick him up, and then, somewhere around eight o'clock at night, we would have him bathed, in bed, and then we hadn't even eaten yet, and we'd be looking at each other, going, 'This is just the beginning.'" She made a face. "That went on for maybe a month or two, and Ben's like, 'I don't know how people do this.' We both agreed that continuing at that pace was probably going to make us all miserable. Ben said to me, 'Do you want to stay home?' Well, I was pretty happy in my job, and he wasn't, so as far as I was concerned it didn't make any sense for me to stay

home. And I didn't have anything besides practicing law that I really wanted to do, and he did. So I said, 'Look, can we do this in a way that we can still have some day care and so you can write?' And so we did that."

Ben could start writing at seven-thirty in the morning because Sharie took their son to day care. He stopped working in the afternoon because that was when he had to pick him up, and then he did the shopping and the household chores. In 1989, they had a second child, a daughter. Fountain was a full-fledged North Dallas stay-at-home dad.

"When Ben first did this, we talked about the fact that it might not work, and we talked about, generally, 'When will we know that it really isn't working?' and I'd say, 'Well, give it ten years,'" Sharie recalled. To her, ten years didn't seem unreasonable. "It takes a while to decide whether you like something or not," she says. And when ten years became twelve and then fourteen and then sixteen, and the kids were off in high school, she stood by him, because, even during that long stretch when Ben had nothing published at all, she was confident that he was getting better. She was fine with the trips to Haiti, too. "I can't imagine writing a novel about a place you haven't at least tried to visit," she says. She even went with him once, and on the way into town from the airport there were people burning tires in the middle of the road.

"I was making pretty decent money, and we didn't need two incomes," Sharie went on. She has a calm, unflappable quality about her. "I mean, it would have been nice, but we could live on one."

Sharie was Ben's wife. But she was also — to borrow a term from long ago — his patron. That word has a condescending edge to it today, because we think it far more

appropriate for artists (and everyone else for that matter) to be supported by the marketplace. But the marketplace works only for people like Jonathan Safran Foer, whose art emerges, fully realized, at the beginning of their career, or Picasso, whose talent was so blindingly obvious that an art dealer offered him a hundred-and-fifty-franc-a-month stipend the minute he got to Paris, at age twenty. If you are the type of creative mind that starts without a plan, and has to experiment and learn by doing, you need someone to see you through the long and difficult time it takes for your art to reach its true level.

This is what is so instructive about any biography of Cézanne. Accounts of his life start out being about Cézanne, and then quickly turn into the story of Cézanne's circle. First and foremost is always his best friend from childhood, the writer Emile Zola, who convinces the awkward misfit from the provinces to come to Paris, and who serves as his guardian and protector and coach through the long, lean years.

Here is Zola, already in Paris, in a letter to the young Cézanne back in Provence. Note the tone, more paternal than fraternal:

> You ask me an odd question. Of course one can work here, as anywhere else, if one has the will. Paris offers, further, an advantage you can't find elsewhere: the museums in which you can study the old masters from 11 to 4. This is how you must divide your time. From 6 to 11 you go to a studio to paint from a live model; you have lunch, then from 12 to 4 you copy, in the Louvre or the Luxembourg, whatever masterpiece you like. That will make up nine hours of work. I think that ought to be enough.

Zola goes on, detailing exactly how Cézanne could manage financially on a monthly stipend of a hundred and twenty-five francs:

> I'll reckon out for you what you should spend. A room at 20 francs a month; lunch at 18 sous and dinner at 22, which makes two francs a day, or 60 francs a month.... Then you have the studio to pay for: the Atelier Suisse, one of the least expensive, charges, I think, 10 francs. Add 10 francs for canvas, brushes, colors; that makes 100. So you'll have 25 francs left for laundry, light, the thousand little needs that turn up.

Camille Pissarro was the next critical figure in Cézanne's life. It was Pissarro who took Cézanne under his wing and taught him how to be a painter. For years, there would be periods in which they went off into the country and worked side by side.

Then there was Ambrose Vollard, the sponsor of Cézanne's first one-man show, at the age of fifty-six. At the urging of Pissarro, Renoir, Degas, and Monet, Vollard hunted down Cézanne in Aix. He spotted a still-life in a tree, where it had been flung by Cézanne in disgust. He poked around the town, putting the word out that he was in the market for Cézanne's canvases. In *Lost Earth: A Life of Cézanne,* the biographer Philip Callow writes about what happened next:

> Before long someone appeared at his hotel with an object wrapped in a cloth. He sold the picture for 150 francs, which inspired him to trot back to his house with the dealer to inspect several more magnificent Cézannes. Vollard paid a thousand francs for the job lot, then on

the way out was nearly hit on the head by a canvas that had been overlooked, dropped out the window by the man's wife. All the pictures had been gathering dust, half buried in a pile of junk in the attic.

All this came before Vollard agreed to sit 150 times, from eight in the morning to eleven-thirty, without a break, for a picture that Cézanne disgustedly abandoned. Once, Vollard recounted in his memoir, he fell asleep, and toppled off the makeshift platform. Cézanne berated him, incensed: "Does an apple move?" This is called friendship.

Finally, there was Cézanne's father, the banker Louis-Auguste. From the time Cézanne first left Aix, at the age of twenty-two, Louis-Auguste paid his bills, even when Cézanne gave every indication of being nothing more than a failed dilettante. But for Zola, Cézanne would have remained an unhappy banker's son in Provence; but for Pissarro, he would never have learned how to paint; but for Vollard (at the urging of Pissarro, Renoir, Degas, and Monet), his canvases would have rotted away in some attic; and, but for his father, Cézanne's long apprentice-ship would have been a financial impossibility. That is an extraordinary list of patrons. The first three — Zola, Pissarro, and Vollard — would have been famous even if Cézanne never existed, and the fourth was an unusually gifted entrepreneur who left Cézanne four hundred thousand francs when he died. Cézanne didn't just have help. He had a dream team in his corner.

This is the final lesson of the late bloomer: his or her success is highly contingent on the efforts of others. In biographies of Cézanne, Louis-Auguste invariably comes across as a kind of grumpy philistine, who didn't

appreciate his son's genius. But Louis-Auguste didn't have to support Cézanne all those years. He would have been within his rights to make his son get a real job, just as Sharie might well have said no to her husband's repeated trips to the chaos of Haiti. She could have argued that she had some right to the lifestyle of her profession and status — that she deserved to drive a BMW, which is what power couples in North Dallas drive, instead of a Honda Accord, which is what she settled for.

But she believed in her husband's art, or perhaps, more simply, she believed in her husband, the same way Zola and Pissarro and Vollard and — in his own querulous way — Louis-Auguste must have believed in Cézanne. Late bloomers' stories are invariably love stories, and this may be why we have such difficulty with them. We'd like to think that mundane matters like loyalty, steadfastness, and the willingness to keep writing checks to support what looks like failure have nothing to do with something as rarefied as genius. But sometimes genius is anything but rarefied; sometimes it's just the thing that emerges after twenty years of working at your kitchen table.

"Sharie never once brought up money, not once — never," Fountain said. She was sitting next to him, and he looked at her in a way that made it plain that he understood how much of the credit for *Brief Encounters* belonged to his wife. His eyes welled up with tears. "I never felt any pressure from her," he said. "Not even covert, not even implied."

October 20, 2008

Most Likely to Succeed

HOW DO WE HIRE WHEN WE CAN'T TELL
WHO'S RIGHT FOR THE JOB?

1.

On the day of the big football game between the University of Missouri Tigers and the Cowboys of Oklahoma State, a football scout named Dan Shonka sat in his hotel in Columbia, Missouri, with a portable DVD player. Shonka has worked for three National Football League teams. Before that, he was a football coach, and before that, he played linebacker — although, he says, "that was three knee operations and a hundred pounds ago." Every year, he evaluates somewhere between eight hundred and twelve hundred players around the country, helping professional teams decide whom to choose in the college draft, which means that over the last thirty years he has probably seen as many football games as anyone else in America. In his DVD player was his homework for the evening's big game — an edited video of the Tigers' previous contest, against the University of Nebraska Cornhuskers.

Shonka methodically made his way through the video, stopping and rewinding whenever he saw something

that caught his eye. He liked Jeremy Maclin and Chase Coffman, two of the Mizzou receivers. He loved William Moore, the team's bruising strong safety. But most of all, he was interested in the Tigers' quarterback and star, a stocky, strong-armed senior named Chase Daniel.

"I like to see that the quarterback can hit a receiver in stride so he doesn't have to slow for the ball," Shonka began. He had a stack of evaluation forms next to him, and as he watched the game, he was charting and grading every throw that Daniel made. "Then judgment. Hey, if it's not there, throw it away and play another day. Will he stand in there and take a hit, with a guy breathing down his face? Will he be able to step right in there, throw, and still take that hit? Does the guy throw better when he's in the pocket, or does he throw equally well when he's on the move? You want a great competitor. Durability. Can they hold up, their strength, toughness? Can they make big plays? Can they lead a team down the field and score late in the game? Can they see the field? When your team's way ahead, that's fine. But when you're getting your ass kicked, I want to see what you're going to do."

He pointed to his screen. Daniel had thrown a dart, and, just as he did, a defensive player had hit him squarely. "See how he popped up?" Shonka said. "He stood right there and threw the ball in the face of that rush. This kid has got a lot of courage." Daniel was six feet tall and weighed 225 pounds: thick through the chest and trunk. He carried himself with a self-assurance that bordered on cockiness. He threw quickly and in rhythm. He nimbly evaded defenders. He made short throws with touch and longer throws with accuracy. By the game's end, he had completed an astonishing 78 percent of his passes,

and handed Nebraska its worst home defeat in fifty-three years. "He can zip it," Shonka said. "He can really gun when he has to." Shonka had seen all the promising college quarterbacks, charted and graded their throws, and to his mind Daniel was special: "He might be one of the best college quarterbacks in the country."

But then Shonka began to talk about when he was on the staff of the Philadelphia Eagles, in 1999. Five quarterbacks were taken in the first round of the college draft that year, and each looked as promising as Chase Daniel did now. But only one of them, Donovan McNabb, ended up fulfilling that promise. Of the rest, one descended into mediocrity after a decent start. Two were complete busts, and the last was so awful that after failing out of the NFL he ended up failing out of the Canadian Football League as well.

The year before, the same thing happened with Ryan Leaf, who was the Chase Daniel of 1998. The San Diego Chargers made him the second player taken over all in the draft, and gave him an $11 million signing bonus. Leaf turned out to be terrible. In 2002, it was Joey Harrington's turn. Harrington was a golden boy out of the University of Oregon, and the third player taken in the draft. Shonka still can't get over what happened to him.

"I tell you, I saw Joey live," he said. "This guy threw lasers, he could throw under tight spots, he had the arm strength, he had the size, he had the intelligence." Shonka got as misty as a 280-pound ex-linebacker in a black track-suit can get. "He's a concert pianist, you know? I really — I mean, I *really* — liked Joey." And yet Harrington's career consisted of a failed stint with the Detroit Lions and a slide into obscurity. Shonka looked back at the screen, where the young man he felt might be the best quarterback in

the country was marching his team up and down the field. "How will that ability translate to the National Football League?" He shook his head slowly. "Shoot."

This is the quarterback problem. There are certain jobs where almost nothing you can learn about candidates before they start predicts how they'll do once they're hired. So how do we know whom to choose in cases like that? In recent years, a number of fields have begun to wrestle with this problem, but none with such profound social consequences as the profession of teaching.

2.

One of the most important tools in contemporary educational research is *value added* analysis. It uses standardized test scores to look at how much the academic performance of students in a given teacher's classroom changes between the beginning and the end of the school year. Suppose that Mrs. Brown and Mr. Smith both teach a classroom of third graders who score at the fiftieth percentile on math and reading tests on the first day of school in September. When the students are retested in June, Mrs. Brown's class scores at the seventieth percentile, while Mr. Smith's students have fallen to the fortieth percentile. That change in the students' rankings, value-added theory says, is a meaningful indicator of how much more effective Mrs. Brown is as a teacher than Mr. Smith.

It's only a crude measure, of course. A teacher is not solely responsible for how much is learned in a classroom, and not everything of value that a teacher imparts to his or her students can be captured on a standardized test. Nonetheless, if you follow Brown and Smith for three or

four years, their effect on their students' test scores starts to become predictable: with enough data, it is possible to identify who the very good teachers are and who the very poor teachers are. What's more — and this is the finding that has galvanized the educational world — the difference between good teachers and poor teachers turns out to be vast.

Eric Hanushek, an economist at Stanford, estimates that the students of a very bad teacher will learn, on average, half a year's worth of material in one school year. The students in the class of a very good teacher will learn a year and a half's worth of material. That difference amounts to a year's worth of learning in a single year. Teacher effects dwarf school effects: your child is actually better off in a bad school with an excellent teacher than in an excellent school with a bad teacher. Teacher effects are also much stronger than class-size effects. You'd have to cut the average class almost in half to get the same boost that you'd get if you switched from an average teacher to a teacher in the eighty-fifth percentile. And remember that a good teacher costs as much as an average one, whereas halving class size would require that you build twice as many classrooms and hire twice as many teachers.

Hanushek recently did a back-of-the-envelope calculation about what even a rudimentary focus on teacher quality could mean for the United States. If you rank the countries of the world in terms of the academic performance of their schoolchildren, the United States is just below average, half a standard deviation below a clump of relatively high-performing countries like Canada and Belgium. According to Hanushek, the United States could close that gap simply by replacing the bottom 6 percent to 10 percent of public-school teachers with teachers of

average quality. After years of worrying about issues like school funding levels, class size, and curriculum design, many reformers have come to the conclusion that nothing matters more than finding people with the potential to be great teachers. But there's a hitch: no one knows what a person with the potential to be a great teacher looks like. The school system has a quarterback problem.

3.

Kickoff time for Missouri's game against Oklahoma State was seven o'clock. It was a perfect evening for football: cloudless skies and a light fall breeze. For hours, fans had been tailgating in the parking lots around the stadium. Cars lined the roads leading to the university, many with fuzzy yellow-and-black Tiger tails hanging from their trunks. It was one of Mizzou's biggest games in years. The Tigers were undefeated and had a chance to become the No. 1 college football team in the country. Shonka made his way through the milling crowds and took a seat in the press box. Below him, the players on the field looked like pieces on a chessboard.

The Tigers held the ball first. Chase Daniel stood a good seven yards behind his offensive line. He had five receivers, two to his left and three to his right, spaced from one side of the field to the other. His linemen were widely spaced as well. In play after play, Daniel caught the snap from his center, planted his feet, and threw the ball in quick seven- and eight-yard diagonal passes to one of his five receivers.

The style of offense that the Tigers run is called the *spread*, and most of the top quarterbacks in college foot-

ball — the players who will be drafted into the pros — are spread quarterbacks. By spacing out the offensive linemen and wide receivers, the system makes it easy for the quarterback to figure out the intentions of the opposing defense before the ball is snapped: he can look up and down the line, "read" the defense, and decide where to throw the ball before anyone has moved a muscle. Daniel had been playing in the spread since high school; he was its master. "Look how quickly he gets the ball out," Shonka said. "You can hardly go a thousand and one, a thousand and two, and it's out of his hand. He knows right where he's going. When everyone is spread out like that, the defense can't disguise its coverage. Chase knows right away what they are going to do. The system simplifies the quarterback's decisions."

But for Shonka this didn't help matters. It had always been hard to predict how a college quarterback would fare in the pros. The professional game was, simply, faster and more complicated. With the advent of the spread, though, the correspondence between the two levels of play had broken down almost entirely. NFL teams don't run the spread. They can't. The defenders in the pros are so much faster than their college counterparts that they would shoot through those big gaps in the offensive line and flatten the quarterback. In the NFL, the offensive line is bunched closely together. Daniel wouldn't have five receivers. Most of the time, he'd have just three or four. He wouldn't have the luxury of standing seven yards behind the center, planting his feet, and knowing instantly where to throw. He'd have to crouch right behind the center, take the snap directly, and run backward before planting

his feet to throw. The onrushing defenders wouldn't be seven yards away. They would be all around him, from the start. The defense would no longer have to show its hand, because the field would not be so spread out. It could now disguise its intentions. Daniel wouldn't be able to read the defense before the snap was taken. He'd have to read it in the seconds after the play began.

"In the spread, you see a lot of guys wide open," Shonka said. "But when a guy like Chase goes to the NFL, he's never going to see his receivers that open — only in some rare case, like someone slips or there's a bust in the coverage. When that ball's leaving your hands in the pros, if you don't use your eyes to move the defender a little bit, they'll break on the ball and intercept it. The athletic ability that they're playing against in the league is unbelievable."

As Shonka talked, Daniel was moving his team down the field. But he was almost always throwing those quick, diagonal passes. In the NFL, he would have to do much more than that — he would have to throw long, vertical passes over the top of the defense. Could he make that kind of throw? Shonka didn't know. There was also the matter of his height. Six feet was fine in a spread system, where the big gaps in the offensive line gave Daniel plenty of opportunity to throw the ball and see downfield. But in the NFL, there wouldn't be gaps, and the linemen rushing at him would be six five, not six one.

"I wonder," Shonka went on. "Can he see? Can he be productive in a new kind of offense? How will he handle that? I'd like to see him set up quickly from center. I'd like to see his ability to read coverages that are not in the spread. I'd like to see him in the pocket. I'd like to see him

move his feet. I'd like to see him do a deep dig, or deep comeback. You know, like a throw twenty to twenty-five yards down the field."

It was clear that Shonka didn't feel the same hesitancy in evaluating the other Mizzou stars — the safety Moore, the receivers Maclin and Coffman. The game that they would play in the pros would also be different from the game they were playing in college, but the difference was merely one of degree. They had succeeded at Missouri because they were strong and fast and skilled, and these traits translate in kind to professional football.

A college quarterback joining the NFL, by contrast, has to learn to play an entirely new game. Shonka began to talk about Tim Couch, the quarterback taken first in that legendary draft of 1999. Couch set every record imaginable in his years at the University of Kentucky. "They used to put five garbage cans on the field," Shonka recalled, shaking his head, "and Couch would stand there and throw and just drop the ball into every one." But Couch was a flop in the pros. It wasn't that professional quarterbacks didn't need to be accurate. It was that the kind of accuracy required to do the job well could be measured only in a real NFL game.

Similarly, all quarterbacks drafted into the pros are required to take an IQ test — the Wonderlic Personnel Test. The theory behind the test is that the pro game is so much more cognitively demanding than the college game that high intelligence should be a good predictor of success. But when the economists David Berri and Rob Simmons analyzed the scores — which are routinely leaked to the press — they found that Wonderlic scores are all but useless as predictors. Of the five quarterbacks taken in round one of the 1999 draft, Donovan McNabb, the only

one of the five with a shot at the Hall of Fame, had the lowest Wonderlic score. And who else had IQ scores in the same range as McNabb? Dan Marino and Terry Bradshaw, two of the greatest quarterbacks ever to play the game.

We're used to dealing with prediction problems by going back and looking for better predictors. We now realize that being a good doctor requires the ability to communicate, listen, and empathize — and so there is increasing pressure on medical schools to pay attention to interpersonal skills as well as to test scores. We can have better physicians if we're just smarter about how we choose medical school students. But no one is saying that Dan Shonka is somehow missing some key ingredient in his analysis; that if he were only more perceptive he could predict Chase Daniel's career trajectory. The problem with picking quarterbacks is that Chase Daniel's performance can't be predicted. The job he's being groomed for is so particular and specialized that there is no way to know who will succeed at it and who won't. In fact, Berri and Simmons found no connection between where a quarterback was taken in the draft — that is, how highly he was rated on the basis of his college performance — and how well he played in the pros.

The entire time that Chase Daniel was on the field against Oklahoma State, his backup, Chase Patton, stood on the sidelines, watching. Patton didn't play a single down. In his four years at Missouri, up to that point, he had thrown a total of twenty-six passes. And yet there were people in Shonka's world who thought that Patton would end up as a better professional quarterback than Daniel. The week of the Oklahoma State game, the

national sports magazine *ESPN* even put the two players on its cover, with the title "CHASE DANIEL MIGHT WIN THE HEISMAN" — referring to the trophy given to college football's best player. "HIS BACKUP COULD WIN THE SUPER BOWL." Why did everyone like Patton so much? It wasn't clear. Maybe he looked good in practice. Maybe it was because this season in the NFL a quarterback who had also never started in a single college game is playing superbly for the New England Patriots. It sounds absurd to put an athlete on the cover of a magazine for no particular reason. But perhaps that's just the quarterback problem taken to an extreme. If college performance doesn't tell us anything, why shouldn't we value someone who hasn't had the chance to play as highly as we do someone who plays as well as anyone in the land?

4.

Picture a young preschool teacher, sitting on a classroom floor surrounded by seven children. She is holding an alphabet book, and working through the letters with the children, one by one: "*A* is for apple.... *C* is for cow." The session was taped, and the videotape is being watched by a group of experts, who are charting and grading each of the teacher's moves.

After thirty seconds, the leader of the group — Bob Pianta, the dean of the University of Virginia's Curry School of Education — stops the tape. He points to two little girls on the right side of the circle. They are unusually active, leaning into the circle and reaching out to touch the book.

"What I'm struck by is how lively the affect is in this

room," Pianta said. "One of the things the teacher is doing is creating a holding space for that. And what distinguishes her from other teachers is that she flexibly allows the kids to move and point to the book. She's not rigidly forcing the kids to sit back."

Pianta's team has developed a system for evaluating various competencies relating to student-teacher interaction. Among them is "regard for student perspective"; that is, a teacher's knack for allowing students some flexibility in how they become engaged in the classroom. Pianta stopped and rewound the tape twice, until what the teacher had managed to achieve became plain: the children were active, but somehow the class hadn't become a free-for-all.

"A lesser teacher would have responded to the kids' leaning over as misbehavior," Pianta went on. "'We can't do this right now. You need to be sitting still.' She would have turned this off."

Bridget Hamre, one of Pianta's colleagues, chimed in: "These are three- and four-year-olds. At this age, when kids show their engagement it's not like the way we show our engagement, where we look alert. They're leaning forward and wriggling. That's their way of doing it. And a good teacher doesn't interpret that as bad behavior. You can see how hard it is to teach new teachers this idea, because the minute you teach them to have regard for the student's perspective, they think you have to give up control of the classroom."

The lesson continued. Pianta pointed out how the teacher managed to personalize the material. "C is for cow" turned into a short discussion of which of the kids had ever visited a farm. "Almost every time a child says

something, she responds to it, which is what we describe as teacher sensitivity," Hamre said.

The teacher then asked the children if anyone's name began with that letter. "Calvin," a boy named Calvin says. The teacher nods, and says, "Calvin starts with *C*." A little girl in the middle says, "Me!" The teacher turns to her. "Your name's Venisha. Letter *V*. Venisha."

It was a key moment. Of all the teacher elements analyzed by the Virginia group, feedback — a direct, personal response by a teacher to a specific statement by a student — seems to be most closely linked to academic success. Not only did the teacher catch the "Me!" amid the wiggling and tumult; she addressed it directly.

"Mind you, that's not *great* feedback," Hamre said. "High-quality feedback is where there is a back-and-forth exchange to get a deeper understanding." The perfect way to handle that moment would have been for the teacher to pause and pull out Venisha's name card, point to the letter *V*, show her how different it is from *C*, and make the class sound out both letters. But the teacher didn't do that — either because it didn't occur to her or because she was distracted by the wiggling of the girls to her right.

"On the other hand, she could have completely ignored the girl, which happens a lot," Hamre went on. "The other thing that happens a lot is the teacher will just say, 'You're wrong.' Yes-no feedback is probably the predominant kind of feedback, which provides almost no information for the kid in terms of learning."

Pianta showed another tape, of a nearly identical situation: a circle of preschoolers around a teacher. The lesson was about how we can tell when someone is happy or sad. The teacher began by acting out a short conversation

between two hand puppets, Henrietta and Twiggle: Twiggle is sad until Henrietta shares some watermelon with him.

"The idea that the teacher is trying to get across is that you can tell by looking at somebody's face how they're feeling, whether they're feeling sad or happy," Hamre said. "What kids of this age tend to say is you can tell how they're feeling because of something that happened to them. They lost their puppy and that's why they're sad. They don't really get this idea. So she's been challenged, and she's struggling."

The teacher begins, "Remember when we did something and we drew our face?" She touches her face, pointing out her eyes and mouth. "When somebody is happy, their face tells us that they're happy. And their eyes tell us." The children look on blankly. The teacher plunges on: "Watch, watch." She smiles broadly. "This is happy! How can you tell that I'm happy? Look at my face. Tell me what changes about my face when I'm happy. No, no, look at my face....No...."

A little girl next to her says, "Eyes," providing the teacher with an opportunity to use one of her students to draw the lesson out. But the teacher doesn't hear her. Again, she asks, "What's changed about my face?" She smiles and she frowns, as if she can reach the children by sheer force of repetition. Pianta stopped the tape. One problem, he pointed out, was that Henrietta made Twiggle happy by sharing watermelon with him, which doesn't illustrate what the lesson is about.

"You know, a better way to handle this would be to anchor something around the kids," Pianta said. "She should ask, 'What makes you feel happy?' The kids could

answer. Then she could say, 'Show me your face when you have that feeling. OK, what does So-and-So's face look like? Now tell me what makes you sad. Show me your face when you're sad. Oh, look, her face changed!' You've basically made the point. And then you could have the kids practice, or something. But this is going to go nowhere."

"What's changed about my face?" the teacher repeated, for what seemed like the hundredth time. One boy leaned forward into the circle, trying to engage himself in the lesson, in the way that little children do. His eyes were on the teacher. "Sit up!" she snapped at him.

As Pianta played one tape after another, the patterns started to become clear. Here was a teacher who read out sentences in a spelling test, and every sentence came from her own life — "I went to a wedding last week" — which meant she was missing an opportunity to say something that engaged her students. Another teacher walked over to a computer to do a PowerPoint presentation, only to realize that she hadn't turned it on. As she waited for it to boot up, the classroom slid into chaos.

Then there was the superstar — a young high-school math teacher in jeans and a green polo shirt. "So let's see," he began, standing up at the blackboard. "Special right triangles. We're going to do practice with this, just throwing out ideas." He drew two triangles. "Label the length of the side, if you can. If you can't, we'll all do it." He was talking and moving quickly, which Pianta said might be interpreted as a bad thing, because this was trigonometry. It wasn't easy material. But his energy seemed to infect the class. And all the time he offered the promise of help. *If you can't, we'll all do it.* In a corner of the room was a student named Ben, who'd evidently missed a few classes.

"See what you can remember, Ben," the teacher said. Ben was lost. The teacher quickly went to his side: "I'm going to give you a way to get to it." He made a quick suggestion: "How about that?" Ben went back to work. The teacher slipped over to the student next to Ben, and glanced at her work. "That's all right!" He went to a third student, then a fourth. Two and a half minutes into the lesson — the length of time it took that subpar teacher to turn on the computer — he had already laid out the problem, checked in with nearly every student in the class, and was back at the blackboard, to take the lesson a step further.

"In a group like this, the standard MO would be: he's at the board, broadcasting to the kids, and has no idea who knows what he's doing and who doesn't know," Pianta said. "But he's giving individualized feedback. He's off the charts on feedback." Pianta and his team watched in awe.

5.

Educational-reform efforts typically start with a push for higher standards for teachers — that is, for the academic and cognitive requirements for entering the profession to be as stiff as possible. But after you've watched Pianta's tapes and seen how complex the elements of effective teaching are, this emphasis on book smarts suddenly seems peculiar. The preschool teacher with the alphabet book was sensitive to her students' needs and knew how to let the two girls on the right wiggle and squirm without disrupting the rest of the students; the trigonometry teacher knew how to complete a circuit of his classroom in two and a half minutes and make everyone feel that he or she was getting his personal attention. But these aren't cognitive skills.

A group of researchers — Thomas J. Kane, an economist at Harvard's school of education; Douglas Staiger, an
economist at Dartmouth; and Robert Gordon, a policy
analyst at the Center for American Progress — have investigated whether it helps to have a teacher who has earned
a teaching certification or a master's degree. Both are
expensive, time-consuming credentials that almost every
district expects teachers to acquire; neither makes a difference in the classroom. Test scores, graduate degrees, and
certifications — as much as they appear related to teaching prowess — turn out to be about as useful in predicting success as having a quarterback throw footballs into a
bunch of garbage cans.

Another educational researcher, Jacob Kounin, once
did an analysis of "desist" events, in which a teacher has
to stop some kind of misbehavior. In one instance, "Mary
leans toward the table to her right and whispers to Jane.
Both she and Jane giggle. The teacher says, 'Mary and
Jane, stop that!'" That's a desist event. But how a teacher
desists — her tone of voice, her attitudes, her choice of
words — appears to make no difference at all in maintain-
ing an orderly classroom. How can that be? Kounin went
back over the videotape and noticed that forty-five seconds before Mary whispered to Jane, Lucy and John had
started whispering. Then Robert had noticed and joined
in, making Jane giggle, whereupon Jane said something to
John. Then Mary whispered to Jane. It was a contagious
chain of misbehavior, and what really was significant was
not how a teacher stopped the deviancy at the end of the
chain but whether she was able to stop the chain before
it started. Kounin called that ability *withitness*, which he
defined as "a teacher's communicating to the children by

her actual behavior (rather than by verbally announcing: 'I know what's going on') that she knows what the children are doing, or has the proverbial eyes in the back of her head." It stands to reason that to be a great teacher you have to have withitness. But how do you know whether someone has withitness until she stands up in front of a classroom of twenty-five wiggly Janes, Lucys, Johns, and Roberts and tries to impose order?

6.

Perhaps no profession has taken the implications of the quarterback problem more seriously than the financial-advice field, and the experience of financial advisers is a useful guide to what could happen in teaching as well. There are no formal qualifications for entering the field except a college degree. Financial-services firms don't look for only the best students or require graduate degrees or specify a list of prerequisites. No one knows beforehand what makes a high-performing financial adviser different from a low-performing one, so the field throws the door wide open.

"A question I ask is, 'Give me a typical day,'" Ed Deutschlander, the co-president of North Star Resource Group, in Minneapolis, says. "If that person says, 'I get up at five-thirty, hit the gym, go to the library, go to class, go to my job, do homework until eleven,' that person has a chance." Deutschlander, in other words, begins by looking for the same general traits that every corporate recruiter looks for.

Deutschlander says that last year his firm interviewed about a thousand people, and found forty-nine it liked, a

ratio of twenty interviewees to one candidate. Those candidates were put through a four-month "training camp," in which they tried to act like real financial advisers. "They should be able to obtain in that four-month period a minimum of ten official clients," Deutschlander said. "If someone can obtain ten clients, and is able to maintain a minimum of ten meetings a week, that means that person has gathered over a hundred introductions in that four-month period. Then we know that person is at least fast enough to play this game."

Of the forty-nine people invited to the training camp, twenty-three made the cut and were hired as apprentice advisers. Then the real sorting began. "Even with the top performers, it really takes three to four years to see whether someone can make it," Deutschlander says. "You're just scratching the surface at the beginning. Four years from now, I expect to hang on to at least thirty to forty percent of that twenty-three."

People like Deutschlander are referred to as *gatekeepers,* a title that suggests that those at the door of a profession are expected to discriminate — to select who gets through the gate and who doesn't. But Deutschlander sees his role as keeping the gate as wide open as possible: to find ten new financial advisers, he's willing to interview a thousand people. The equivalent of that approach in the NFL would be for a team to give up trying to figure out who the best college quarterback is, and, instead, try out three or four good candidates.

In teaching, the implications are even more profound. They suggest that we shouldn't be raising standards. We should be lowering them, because there is no point in raising standards if standards don't track with what we care

about. Teaching should be open to anyone with a pulse and a college degree — and teachers should be judged after they have started their jobs, not before. That means that the profession needs to start the equivalent of Ed Deutschlander's training camp. It needs an apprenticeship system that allows candidates to be rigorously evaluated. Kane and Staiger have calculated that, given the enormous differences between the top and the bottom of the profession, you'd probably have to try out four candidates to find one good teacher. That means tenure can't be routinely awarded, the way it is now. Currently, the salary structure of the teaching profession is highly rigid, and that would also have to change in a world where we want to rate teachers on their actual performance. An apprentice should get apprentice wages. But if we find eighty-fifth-percentile teachers who can teach a year and a half's material in one year, we're going to have to pay them a lot — both because we want them to stay and because the only way to get people to try out for what will suddenly be a high-risk profession is to offer those who survive the winnowing a healthy reward.

Is this solution to teaching's quarterback problem politically possible? Taxpayers might well balk at the costs of trying out four teachers to find one good one. Teachers' unions have been resistant to even the slightest move away from the current tenure arrangement. But all the reformers want is for the teaching profession to copy what firms like North Star have been doing for years. Deutschlander interviews a thousand people to find ten advisers. He spends large amounts of money to figure out who has the particular mixture of abilities to do the job. "Between hard and soft costs," he says, "most firms sink between a hun-

dred thousand dollars and two hundred and fifty thousand dollars on someone in their first three or four years," and in most cases, of course, that investment comes to naught. But if you are willing to make that kind of investment and show that kind of patience, you wind up with a truly high-performing financial adviser. "We have a hundred and twenty-five full-time advisers," Deutschlander says. "Last year, we had seventy-one of them qualify for the Million Dollar Round Table" — the industry's association of its most successful practitioners. "We're seventy-one out of a hundred and twenty-five in that elite group." What does it say about a society that it devotes more care and patience to the selection of those who handle its money than of those who handle its children?

7.

Midway through the fourth quarter of the Oklahoma State–Missouri game, the Tigers were in trouble. For the first time all year, they were behind late in the game. They needed to score, or they'd lose any chance of a national championship. Daniel took the snap from his center and planted his feet to pass. His receivers were covered. He began to run. The Oklahoma State defenders closed in on him. He was under pressure, something that rarely happened to him in the spread. Desperate, he heaved the ball downfield, right into the arms of a Cowboy defender.

Shonka jumped up. "That's not like him!" he cried out. "He doesn't throw stuff up like that."

Next to Shonka, a scout for the Kansas City Chiefs looked crestfallen. "Chase never throws something up for grabs!"

It was tempting to see Daniel's mistake as definitive. The spread had broken down. He was finally under pressure. This was what it would be like to be an NFL quarterback, wasn't it? But there is nothing like being an NFL quarterback except being an NFL quarterback. A prediction, in a field where prediction is not possible, is no more than a prejudice. Maybe that interception means that Daniel won't be a good professional quarterback, or maybe he made a mistake that he'll learn from. "In a great big piece of pie," Shonka said, "that was just a little slice."*

December 15, 2008

---

*This article was written during the 2008 college football season. Missouri ended up finishing 10–4, and Chase Daniel — who at one point was considered one of the favorites to win the Heisman Trophy — faded down the stretch. He was not selected in the 2009 NFL draft but signed as a free agent with the Washington Redskins.

Dangerous Minds

CRIMINAL PROFILING MADE EASY

1.

On November 16, 1940, workers at the Consolidated Edison building on West 64th Street in Manhattan found a homemade pipe bomb on a windowsill. Attached was a note: "Con Edison crooks, this is for you." In September of 1941, a second bomb was found, on 19th Street, just a few blocks from Con Edison's headquarters, near Union Square. It had been left in the street, wrapped in a sock. A few months later, the New York police received a letter promising to "bring the Con Edison to justice — they will pay for their dastardly deeds." Sixteen other letters followed, between 1941 and 1946, all written in block letters, many repeating the phrase *dastardly deeds* and all signed with the initials *F.P.* In March of 1950, a third bomb — larger and more powerful than the others — was found on the lower level of Grand Central Terminal. The next was left in a phone booth at the New York Public Library. It exploded, as did one placed in a phone booth in Grand Central. In 1954, the Mad Bomber — as he came to be known — struck four times, once in Radio City

Music Hall, sending shrapnel throughout the audience. In 1955, he struck six times. The city was in an uproar. The police were getting nowhere. Late in 1956, in desperation, Inspector Howard Finney, of the New York City Police Department's crime laboratory, and two plainclothesmen paid a visit to a psychiatrist by the name of James Brussel.

Brussel was a Freudian. He lived on 12th Street, in the West Village, and smoked a pipe. In Mexico, early in his career, he had done counterespionage work for the FBI. He wrote many books, including *Instant Shrink: How to Become an Expert Psychiatrist in Ten Easy Lessons.* Finney put a stack of documents on Brussel's desk: photographs of unexploded bombs, pictures of devastation, photostats of F.P.'s neatly lettered missives. "I didn't miss the look in the two plainclothesmen's eyes," Brussel writes in his memoir, *Casebook of a Crime Psychiatrist.* "I'd seen that look before, most often in the Army, on the faces of hard, old-line, field-grade officers who were sure this newfangled psychiatry business was all nonsense."

He began to leaf through the case materials. For sixteen years, F.P. had been fixated on the notion that Con Ed had done him some terrible injustice. Clearly, he was clinically paranoid. But paranoia takes some time to develop. F.P. had been bombing since 1940, which suggested that he was now middle-aged. Brussel looked closely at the precise lettering of F.P.'s notes to the police. This was an orderly man. He would be cautious. His work record would be exemplary. Further, the language suggested some degree of education. But there was a stilted quality to the word choice and the phrasing. Con Edison was often referred to as *the* Con Edison. And who still used the expression *dastardly deeds*? F.P. seemed to be foreign-born. Brussel

looked more closely at the letters and noticed that they were all perfect block capitals, except the Ws. They were misshapen, like two U's. To Brussel's eye, those Ws looked like a pair of breasts. He flipped to the crime-scene descriptions. When F.P. planted his bombs in movie theaters, he would slit the underside of the seat with a knife and stuff his explosives into the upholstery. Didn't that seem like a symbolic act of penetrating a woman, or castrating a man — or perhaps both? F.P. had probably never progressed beyond the Oedipal stage. He was unmarried, a loner. Living with a mother figure. Brussel made another leap. F.P. was a Slav. Just as the use of a garrote would have suggested someone of Mediterranean extraction, the bomb-knife combination struck him as Eastern European. Some of the letters had been posted from Westchester County, but F.P. wouldn't have mailed the letters from his hometown. Still, a number of cities in southeastern Connecticut had a large Slavic population. And didn't you have to pass through Westchester to get to the city from Connecticut?

Brussel waited a moment, and then, in a scene that has become legendary among criminal profilers, he made a prediction:

"One more thing." I closed my eyes because I didn't want to see their reaction. I saw the Bomber: impeccably neat, absolutely proper. A man who would avoid the newer styles of clothing until long custom had made them conservative. I saw him clearly — much more clearly than the facts really warranted. I knew I was letting my imagination get the better of me, but I couldn't help it.

"One more thing," I said, my eyes closed tight.

"When you catch him — and I have no doubt you will — he'll be wearing a double-breasted suit."

"Jesus!" one of the detectives whispered.

"And it will be buttoned," I said. I opened my eyes. Finney and his men were looking at each other.

"A double-breasted suit," said the Inspector.

"Yes."

"Buttoned."

"Yes."

He nodded. Without another word, they left.

A month later, George Metesky was arrested by police in connection with the New York City bombings. His name had been changed from Milauskas. He lived in Waterbury, Connecticut, with his two older sisters. He was unmarried. He was unfailingly neat. He attended Mass regularly. He had been employed by Con Edison from 1929 to 1931, and claimed to have been injured on the job. When he opened the door to the police officers, he said, "I know why you fellows are here. You think I'm the Mad Bomber." It was midnight, and he was in his pajamas. The police asked that he get dressed. When he returned, his hair was combed into a pompadour and his shoes were newly shined. He was also wearing a double-breasted suit — buttoned.

2.

In *Inside the Mind of BTK,* the eminent FBI criminal profiler John Douglas tells the story of a serial killer who stalked the streets of Wichita, Kansas, in the 1970s and '80s. Douglas was the model for Agent Jack Crawford in *The Silence of the Lambs.* He was the protégé of the pioneering FBI profiler Howard Teten, who helped establish the bureau's Behavioral

Science Unit, at Quantico, in 1972, and who was a protégé of Brussel — which, in the close-knit fraternity of profilers, is like being analyzed by the analyst who was analyzed by Freud. To Douglas, Brussel was the father of criminal profiling, and, in both style and logic, *Inside the Mind of BTK* pays homage to *Casebook of a Crime Psychiatrist* at every turn.

BTK stood for "Bind, Torture, Kill" — the three words that the killer used to identify himself in his taunting notes to the Wichita police. He had struck first in January 1974, when he killed thirty-eight-year-old Joseph Otero in his home, along with his wife, Julie, their son, Joey, and their eleven-year-old daughter, who was found hanging from a water pipe in the basement with semen on her leg. The following April, he stabbed a twenty-four-year-old woman. In March 1977, he bound and strangled another young woman, and over the next few years, he committed at least four more murders. The city of Wichita was in an uproar. The police were getting nowhere. In 1984, in desperation, two police detectives from Wichita paid a visit to Quantico.

The meeting, Douglas writes, was held in a first-floor conference room of the FBI's forensic-science building. He was then nearly a decade into his career at the Behavioral Science Unit. His first two bestsellers, *Mindhunter: Inside the FBI's Elite Serial Crime Unit* and *Obsession: The FBI's Legendary Profiler Probes the Psyches of Killers, Rapists, and Stalkers and Their Victims and Tells How to Fight Back,* were still in the future. Working 150 cases a year, he was on the road constantly, but BTK was never far from his thoughts. "Some nights I'd lie awake, asking myself, 'Who the hell is this BTK?'" he writes. "What makes a guy like this do what he does? What makes him tick?"

Roy Hazelwood sat next to Douglas. A lean

chain-smoker, Hazelwood specialized in sex crimes, and went on to write the bestsellers *Dark Dreams* and *The Evil That Men Do*. Beside Hazelwood was an ex–Air Force pilot named Ron Walker. Walker, Douglas writes, was "whip smart" and an "exceptionally quick study." The three bureau men and the two detectives sat around a massive oak table. "The objective of our session was to keep moving forward until we ran out of juice," Douglas writes. They would rely on the typology developed by their colleague Robert Ressler, himself the author of the true-crime bestsellers *Whoever Fights Monsters* and *I Have Lived in the Monster*. The goal was to paint a picture of the killer — of what sort of man BTK was, and what he did, and where he worked, and what he was like — and with that scene *Inside the Mind of BTK* begins.

We are now so familiar with crime stories told through the eyes of the profiler that it is easy to lose sight of how audacious the genre is. The traditional detective story begins with the body and centers on the detective's search for the culprit. Leads are pursued. A net is cast, widening to encompass a bewilderingly diverse pool of suspects: the butler, the spurned lover, the embittered nephew, the shadowy European. That's a whodunit. In the profiling genre, the net is narrowed. The crime scene doesn't initiate our search for the killer. It defines the killer for us. The profiler sifts through the case materials, looks off into the distance, and *knows*. "Generally, a psychiatrist can study a man and make a few reasonable predictions about what the man may do in the future — how he will react to such-and-such a stimulus, how he will behave in such-and-such a situation," Brussel writes. "What I have done is reverse the terms of the prophecy. By studying a man's deeds, I have deduced what kind of man he

might be." Look for a middle-aged Slav in a double-breasted suit. Profiling stories aren't whodunits; they're hedunits.

In the hedunit, the profiler does not catch the criminal. That's for local law enforcement. He takes the meeting. Often, he doesn't write down his predictions. It's up to the visiting police officers to take notes. He does not feel the need to involve himself in the subsequent investigation, or even, it turns out, to justify his predictions. Once, Douglas tells us, he drove down to the local police station and offered his services in the case of an elderly woman who had been savagely beaten and sexually assaulted. The detectives working the crime were regular cops, and Douglas was a bureau guy, so you can imagine him perched on the edge of a desk, the others pulling up chairs around him.

"'Okay,' I said to the detectives.... 'Here's what I think,'" Douglas begins. "It's a sixteen- or seventeen-year-old high school kid.... He'll be disheveled-looking, he'll have scruffy hair, generally poorly groomed." He went on: a loner, kind of weird, no girlfriend, lots of bottled-up anger. He comes to the old lady's house. He knows she's alone. Maybe he's done odd jobs for her in the past. Douglas continues:

> I pause in my narrative and tell them there's someone who meets this description out there. If they can find him, they've got their offender.
>
> One detective looks at another. One of them starts to smile. "Are you a psychic, Douglas?"
>
> "No," I say, "but my job would be a lot easier if I were."
>
> "Because we had a psychic, Beverly Newton, in here a couple of weeks ago, and she said just about the same things."

You might think that Douglas would bridle at that comparison. He is, after all, an agent of the Federal Bureau of Investigation, who studied with Teten, who studied with Brussel. He is an ace profiler, part of a team that restored the FBI's reputation for crime-fighting, inspired countless movies, television shows, and bestselling thrillers, and brought the modern tools of psychology to bear on the savagery of the criminal mind — and some cop is calling him a *psychic*. But Douglas doesn't object. Instead, he begins to muse on the ineffable origins of his insights, at which point the question arises of what exactly this mysterious art called profiling is, and whether it can be trusted. Douglas writes,

> What I try to do with a case is to take in all the evidence I have to work with…and then put myself mentally and emotionally in the head of the offender. I try to think as he does. Exactly how this happens, I'm not sure, any more than the novelists such as Tom Harris who've consulted me over the years can say exactly how their characters come to life. If there's a psychic component to this, I won't run from it.

3.

In the late 1970s, John Douglas and his FBI colleague Robert Ressler set out to interview the most notorious serial killers in the country. They started in California, since, as Douglas says, "California has always had more than its share of weird and spectacular crimes." On weekends and days off, over the next months, they stopped by one federal prison after another, until they had interviewed thirty-six murderers.

Douglas and Ressler wanted to know whether there was a pattern that connected a killer's life and personality

with the nature of his crimes. They were looking for what psychologists would call a *homology,* an agreement between character and action, and after comparing what they learned from the killers with what they already knew about the characteristics of their murders, they became convinced that they'd found one.

Serial killers, they concluded, fall into one of two categories. Some crime scenes show evidence of logic and planning. The victim has been hunted and selected in order to fulfill a specific fantasy. The recruitment of the victim might involve a ruse or a con. The perpetrator maintains control throughout the offense. He takes his time with the victim, carefully enacting his fantasies. He is adaptable and mobile. He almost never leaves a weapon behind. He meticulously conceals the body. Douglas and Ressler, in their respective books, call that kind of crime *organized.*

In a *disorganized* crime, the victim isn't chosen logically. She's seemingly picked at random and "blitz-attacked," not stalked and coerced. The killer might grab a steak knife from the kitchen and leave the knife behind. The crime is so sloppily executed that the victim often has a chance to fight back. The crime might take place in a high-risk environment. "Moreover, the disorganized killer has no idea of, or interest in, the personalities of his victims," Ressler writes in *Whoever Fights Monsters.* "He does not want to know who they are, and many times takes steps to obliterate their personalities by quickly knocking them unconscious or covering their faces or otherwise disfiguring them."

Each of these styles, the argument goes, corresponds to a personality type. The organized killer is intelligent and articulate. He feels superior to those around him. The

disorganized killer is unattractive and has a poor self-image. He often has some kind of disability. He's too strange and withdrawn to be married or have a girlfriend. If he doesn't live alone, he lives with his parents. He has pornography stashed in his closet. If he drives at all, his car is a wreck.

"The crime scene is presumed to reflect the murderer's behavior and personality in much the same way as furnishings reveal the homeowner's character," we're told in a crime manual that Douglas and Ressler helped write. The more they learned, the more precise the associations became. If the victim was white, the killer would be white. If the victim was old, the killer would be sexually immature.

"In our research, we discovered that...frequently serial offenders had failed in their efforts to join police departments and had taken jobs in related fields, such as security guard or night watchman," Douglas writes. Given that organized rapists were preoccupied with control, it made sense that they would be fascinated by the social institution that symbolizes control. Out of that insight came another prediction: "One of the things we began saying in some of our profiles was that the UNSUB" — the unknown subject — "would drive a policelike vehicle, say a Ford Crown Victoria or Chevrolet Caprice."

4.

On the surface, the FBI's system seems extraordinarily useful. Consider a case study widely used in the profiling literature. The body of a twenty-six-year-old special-education teacher was found on the roof of her Bronx

apartment building. She was apparently abducted just after she left her house for work, at six-thirty in the morning. She had been beaten beyond recognition and tied up with her stockings and belt. The killer had mutilated her sexual organs, chopped off her nipples, covered her body with bites, written obscenities across her abdomen, masturbated, and then defecated next to the body.

Let's pretend that we're an FBI profiler. First question: race. The victim is white, so let's call the offender white. Let's say he's in his midtwenties to early thirties, which is when the thirty-six men in the FBI's sample started killing. Is the crime organized or disorganized? Disorganized, clearly. It's on a rooftop, in the Bronx, in broad daylight — high risk. So what is the killer doing in the building at six-thirty in the morning? He could be some kind of serviceman, or he could live in the neighborhood. Either way, he appears to be familiar with the building. He's disorganized, though, so he's not stable. If he is employed, it's blue-collar work at best. He probably has a prior offense, having to do with violence or sex. His relationships with women will be either nonexistent or deeply troubled. And the mutilation and the defecation are so strange that he's probably mentally ill or has some kind of substance-abuse problem. How does that sound? As it turns out, it's spot-on. The killer was Carmine Calabro, age thirty, a single, unemployed, deeply troubled actor who, when he was not in a mental institution, lived with his widowed father on the fourth floor of the building where the murder took place.

But how useful is that profile really? The police already had Calabro on their list of suspects: if you're looking for the person who killed and mutilated someone on the roof,

you don't really need a profiler to tell you to check out the disheveled, mentally ill guy living with his father on the fourth floor.

That's why the FBI's profilers have always tried to supplement the basic outlines of the organized/disorganized system with telling details — something that lets the police zero in on a suspect. In the early 1980s, Douglas gave a presentation to a roomful of police officers and FBI agents in Marin County about the Trailside Killer, who was murdering female hikers in the hills north of San Francisco. In Douglas's view, the killer was a classic disorganized offender — a blitz attacker, white, early to midthirties, blue collar, probably with "a history of bed-wetting, fire-starting, and cruelty to animals." Then he went back to how asocial the killer seemed. Why did all the killings take place in heavily wooded areas miles from the road? Douglas reasoned that the killer required such seclusion because he had some condition that he was deeply self-conscious about. Was it something physical, like a missing limb? But then how could he hike miles into the woods and physically overpower his victims? Finally, it came to him: "'Another thing,' I added after a pregnant pause, 'the killer will have a speech impediment.'"

And so he did. Now, that's a useful detail. Or is it? Douglas then tells us that he pegged the offender's age as early thirties and he turned out to be fifty. Detectives use profiles to narrow down the range of suspects. It doesn't do any good to get a specific detail right if you get general details wrong.

In the case of Derrick Todd Lee, the Baton Rouge serial killer, the FBI profile described the offender as a white male blue-collar worker between twenty-five and

thirty-five years old who "wants to be seen as someone who is attractive and appealing to women." The profile went on, "However, his level of sophistication in interacting with women, especially women who are above him in the social strata, is low. Any contact he has had with women he has found attractive would be described by these women as 'awkward.'" The FBI was right about the killer being a blue-collar male between twenty-five and thirty-five. But Lee turned out to be charming and outgoing, the sort to put on a cowboy hat and snakeskin boots and head for the bars. He was an extrovert with a number of girlfriends and a reputation as a ladies' man. And he wasn't white. He was black.

A profile isn't a test, where you pass if you get most of the answers right. It's a portrait, and all the details have to cohere in some way if the image is to be helpful. In the mid-nineties, the British Home Office analyzed 184 crimes to see how many times profiles led to the arrest of a criminal. The profile worked in five of those cases. That's just 2.7 percent, which makes sense if you consider the position of the detective on the receiving end of a profiler's list of conjectures. Do you believe the stuttering part? Or do you believe the thirty-year-old part? Or do you throw up your hands in frustration?

5.

There is a deeper problem with FBI profiling. Douglas and Ressler didn't interview a representative sample of serial killers to come up with their typology. They talked to whoever happened to be in the neighborhood. Nor did they interview their subjects according to a standardized

protocol. They just sat down and chatted, which isn't a particularly firm foundation for a psychological system. So you might wonder whether serial killers can really be categorized by their level of organization.

Not long ago, a group of psychologists at the University of Liverpool decided to test the FBI's assumptions. First, they made a list of crime-scene characteristics generally considered to show organization: perhaps the victim was alive during the sex acts, or the body was posed in a certain way, or the murder weapon was missing, or the body was concealed, or torture and restraints were involved. Then they made a list of characteristics showing disorganization: perhaps the victim was beaten, the body was left in an isolated spot, the victim's belongings were scattered, or the murder weapon was improvised.

If the FBI was right, they reasoned, the crime-scene details on each of those two lists should *co-occur* — that is, if you see one or more organized traits in a crime, there should be a reasonably high probability of seeing other organized traits. When they looked at a sample of a hundred serial crimes, however, they couldn't find any support for the FBI's distinction. Crimes don't fall into one camp or the other. It turns out that they're almost always a mixture of a few key organized traits and a random array of disorganized traits. Laurence Alison, one of the leaders of the Liverpool group and the author of *The Forensic Psychologist's Casebook*, told me, "The whole business is a lot more complicated than the FBI imagines."

Alison and another of his colleagues also looked at homology. If Douglas was right, then a certain kind of crime should correspond to a certain kind of criminal. So the Liverpool group selected a hundred stranger rapes

in the United Kingdom, classifying them according to twenty-eight variables, such as whether a disguise was worn, whether compliments were given, whether there was binding, gagging, or blindfolding, whether there was apologizing or the theft of personal property, and so on. They then looked at whether the patterns in the crimes corresponded to attributes of the criminals — like age, type of employment, ethnicity, level of education, marital status, number of prior convictions, type of prior convictions, and drug use. Were rapists who bind, gag, and blindfold more like one another than they were like rapists who, say, compliment and apologize? The answer is no — not even slightly.

"The fact is that different offenders can exhibit the same behaviors for completely different reasons," Brent Turvey, a forensic scientist who has been highly critical of the FBI's approach, says. "You've got a rapist who attacks a woman in the park and pulls her shirt up over her face. Why? What does that mean? There are ten different things it could mean. It could mean he doesn't want to see her. It could mean he doesn't want her to see him. It could mean he wants to see her breasts, he wants to imagine someone else, he wants to incapacitate her arms — all of those are possibilities. You can't just look at one behavior in isolation."

A few years ago, Alison went back to the case of the teacher who was murdered on the roof of her building in the Bronx. He wanted to know why, if the FBI's approach to criminal profiling was based on such simplistic psychology, it continues to have such a sterling reputation. The answer, he suspected, lay in the way the profiles were written, and, sure enough, when he broke down the

rooftop-killer analysis, sentence by sentence, he found that it was so full of unverifiable and contradictory and ambiguous language that it could support virtually any interpretation.

Astrologers and psychics have known these tricks for years. The magician Ian Rowland, in his classic *The Full Facts Book of Cold Reading,* itemizes them one by one, in what could easily serve as a manual for the beginner profiler. First is the Rainbow Ruse — the "statement which credits the client with both a personality trait *and* its opposite." ("I would say that on the whole you can be rather a quiet, self-effacing type, but when the circumstances are right, you can be quite the life and soul of the party if the mood strikes you.") The Jacques Statement, named for the character in *As You Like It* who gives the Seven Ages of Man speech, tailors the prediction to the age of the subject. To someone in his late thirties or early forties, for example, the psychic says, "If you are honest about it, you often get to wondering what happened to all those dreams you had when you were younger." There is the Barnum Statement, the assertion so general that anyone would agree, and the Fuzzy Fact, the seemingly factual statement couched in a way that "leaves plenty of scope to be developed into something more specific." ("I can see a connection with Europe, possibly Britain, or it could be the warmer, Mediterranean part?") And that's only the start: there is the Greener Grass technique, the Diverted Question, the Russian Doll, Sugar Lumps, not to mention Forking and the Good Chance Guess — all of which, when put together in skillful combination, can convince even the most skeptical observer that he or she is in the presence of real insight.

"Moving on to career matters, you don't work with children, do you?" Rowland will ask his subjects, in an example of what he dubs the "Vanishing Negative."

No, I don't.
"No, I thought not. That's not really your role."

Of course, if the subject answers differently, there's another way to play the question: "Moving on to career matters, you don't work with children, do you?"

I do, actually, part time.
"Yes, I thought so."

After Alison had analyzed the rooftop-killer profile, he decided to play a version of the cold-reading game. He gave the details of the crime, the profile prepared by the FBI, and a description of the offender to a group of senior police officers and forensic professionals in England. How did they find the profile? Highly accurate. Then Alison gave the same packet of case materials to another group of police officers, but this time he invented an imaginary offender, one who was altogether different from Calabro. The new killer was thirty-seven years old. He was an alcoholic. He had recently been laid off from his job with the water board and had met the victim before on one of his rounds. What's more, Alison claimed, he had a history of violent relationships with women, and prior convictions for assault and burglary. How accurate did a group of experienced police officers find the FBI's profile when it was matched with the phony offender? Every bit as accurate as when it was matched to the real offender.

James Brussel didn't really see the Mad Bomber in that pile of pictures and photostats, then. That was an illusion. As the literary scholar Donald Foster pointed out in his 2000 book *Author Unknown*, Brussel cleaned up his predictions for his memoirs. He actually told the police to look for the bomber in White Plains, sending the NYPD's bomb unit on a wild goose chase in Westchester County, sifting through local records. Brussel also told the police to look for a man with a facial scar, which Metesky didn't have. He told them to look for a man with a night job, and Metesky had been largely unemployed since leaving Con Edison in 1931. He told them to look for someone between forty and fifty, and Metesky was over fifty. He told them to look for someone who was an "expert in civil or military ordnance" and the closest Metesky came to that was a brief stint in a machine shop. And Brussel, despite what he wrote in his memoir, never said that the bomber would be a Slav. He actually told the police to look for a man "born and educated in Germany," a prediction so far off the mark that the Mad Bomber himself was moved to object. At the height of the police investigation, when the New York *Journal American* offered to print any communications from the Mad Bomber, Metesky wrote in huffily to say that "the nearest to my being 'Teutonic' is that my father boarded a liner in Hamburg for passage to this country — about sixty-five years ago."

The true hero of the case wasn't Brussel; it was a woman named Alice Kelly, who had been assigned to go through Con Edison's personnel files. In January 1957, she ran across an employee complaint from the early 1930s: a generator wiper at the Hell Gate plant had been knocked down by a backdraft of hot gases. The worker said that he

was injured. The company said that he wasn't. And in the flood of angry letters from the ex-employee Kelly spotted a threat — to "take justice in my own hands" — that had appeared in one of the Mad Bomber's letters. The name on the file was George Metesky.

Brussel did not really understand the mind of the Mad Bomber. He seems to have understood only that, if you make a great number of predictions, the ones that were wrong will soon be forgotten, and the ones that turn out to be true will make you famous. The hedunit is not a triumph of forensic analysis. It's a party trick.

6.

"Here's where I'm at with this guy," Douglas said, kicking off the profiling session with which *Inside the Mind of BTK* begins. It was 1984. The killer was still at large. Douglas, Hazelwood, and Walker and the two detectives from Wichita were all seated around the oak table. Douglas took off his suit jacket and draped it over his chair. "Back when he started in 1974, he was in his mid to late twenties," Douglas began. "It's now ten years later, so that would put him in his mid to late thirties."

It was Walker's turn: BTK had never engaged in any sexual penetration. That suggested to him someone with an "inadequate, immature sexual history." He would have a "lone-wolf type of personality. But he's not alone because he's shunned by others — it's because he chooses to be alone.…He can function in social settings, but only on the surface. He may have women friends he can talk to, but he'd feel very inadequate with a peer-group female." Hazelwood was next. BTK would be "heavily

into masturbation." He went on, "Women who have had sex with this guy would describe him as aloof, uninvolved, the type who is more interested in her servicing him than the other way around."

Douglas followed his lead. "The women he's been with are either many years younger, very naive, or much older and depend on him as their meal ticket," he ventured. What's more, the profilers determined, BTK would drive a "decent" automobile, but it would be "nondescript."

At this point, the insights began piling on. Douglas said he'd been thinking that BTK was married. But now maybe he was thinking he was divorced. He speculated that BTK was lower middle class, probably living in a rental. Walker felt BTK was in a "lower-paying white-collar job, as opposed to blue-collar." Hazelwood saw him as "middle class" and "articulate." The consensus was that his IQ was somewhere between 105 and 145. Douglas wondered whether he was connected with the military. Hazelwood called him a "now" person, who needed "instant gratification."

Walker said that those who knew him "might say they remember him, but didn't really know much about him." Douglas then had a flash — "It was a sense, almost a knowing" — and said, "I wouldn't be surprised if, in the job he's in today, that he's wearing some sort of uniform.... This guy isn't mental. But he is crazy like a fox."

They had been at it for almost six hours. The best minds in the FBI had given the Wichita detectives a blueprint for their investigation. Look for an American male with a possible connection to the military. His IQ will be above 105. He will like to masturbate and will be aloof and selfish in bed. He will drive a decent car. He will be

a "now" person. He won't be comfortable with women. But he may have women friends. He will be a lone wolf. But he will be able to function in social settings. He won't be unmemorable. But he will be unknowable. He will be either never married, divorced, or married, and if he was or is married, his wife will be younger or older. He may or may not live in a rental, and might be lower class, upper lower class, lower middle class, or middle class. And he will be crazy like a fox as opposed to being mental. If you're keeping score, that's a Jacques Statement, two Barnum Statements, four Rainbow Ruses, a Good Chance Guess, two predictions that aren't really predictions because they could never be verified — and nothing even close to the salient fact that BTK was a pillar of his community, the president of his church, and the married father of two.

"This thing is solvable," Douglas told the detectives as he stood up and put on his jacket. "Feel free to pick up the phone and call us if we can be of any further assistance." You can imagine him taking the time for an encouraging smile and a slap on the back. "You're gonna nail this guy."*

November 12, 2007

---

* Not long after this article came out, I debated John Douglas on NPR. I expected him to have some kind of well-thought-out response to the criticisms of Alison and his colleagues. But it quickly became apparent that he had no idea who Alison or any of the other academic critics of profiling were.

The Talent Myth

ARE SMART PEOPLE OVERRATED?

1.

At the height of the dot-com boom of the 1990s, several executives at McKinsey & Company, America's largest and most prestigious management-consulting firm, launched what they called the War for Talent. Thousands of questionnaires were sent to managers across the country. Eighteen companies were singled out for special attention, and the consultants spent up to three days at each firm, interviewing everyone from the CEO down to the human-resources staff. McKinsey wanted to document how the top-performing companies in America differed from other firms in the way they handled matters like hiring and promotion. But, as the consultants sifted through the piles of reports and questionnaires and interview transcripts, they grew convinced that the difference between winners and losers was more profound than they had realized. "We looked at one another and suddenly the lightbulb blinked on," the three consultants who headed the project — Ed Michaels, Helen Handfield-Jones, and Beth Axelrod — write in their book, also called *The War*

for Talent. The very best companies, they concluded, had leaders who were obsessed with the talent issue. They recruited ceaselessly, finding and hiring as many top performers as possible. They singled out and segregated their stars, rewarding them disproportionately, and pushing them into ever more senior positions. "Bet on the natural athletes, the ones with the strongest intrinsic skills," the authors approvingly quote one senior General Electric executive as saying. "Don't be afraid to promote stars without specifically relevant experience, seemingly over their heads." Success in the modern economy, according to Michaels, Handfield-Jones, and Axelrod, requires "the talent mind-set": the "deep-seated belief that having better talent at all levels is how you outperform your competitors."

This "talent mind-set" is the new orthodoxy of American management. It is the intellectual justification for why such a high premium is placed on degrees from first-tier business schools, and why the compensation packages for top executives have become so lavish. In the modern corporation, the system is considered only as strong as its stars, and in the past few years, this message has been preached by consultants and management gurus all over the world. None, however, have spread the word quite so ardently as McKinsey, and, of all its clients, one firm took the talent mind-set closest to heart. It was a company where McKinsey conducted twenty separate projects, where McKinsey's billings topped $10 million a year, where a McKinsey director regularly attended board meetings, and where the CEO himself was a former McKinsey partner. The company, of course, was Enron.

The Enron scandal is now almost a year old. The

reputations of Jeffrey Skilling and Kenneth Lay, the company's two top executives, have been destroyed. Arthur Andersen, Enron's auditor, has been all but driven out of business, and now investigators have turned their attention to Enron's investment bankers. The one Enron partner that has escaped largely unscathed is McKinsey, which is odd, given that it essentially created the blueprint for the Enron culture. Enron was the ultimate "talent" company. When Skilling started the corporate division known as Enron Capital and Trade, in 1990, he "decided to bring in a steady stream of the very best college and MBA graduates he could find to stock the company with talent," Michaels, Handfield-Jones, and Axelrod tell us. During the nineties, Enron was bringing in 250 newly minted MBAs a year. "We had these things called Super Saturdays," one former Enron manager recalls. "I'd interview some of these guys who were fresh out of Harvard, and these kids could blow me out of the water. They knew things I'd never heard of." Once at Enron, the top performers were rewarded inordinately, and promoted without regard for seniority or experience. Enron was a star system. "The only thing that differentiates Enron from our competitors is our people, our talent," Lay, Enron's former chairman and CEO, told the McKinsey consultants when they came to the company's headquarters, in Houston. Or, as another senior Enron executive put it to Richard Foster, a McKinsey partner who celebrated Enron in his 2001 book, *Creative Destruction*, "We hire very smart people and we pay them more than they think they are worth."

The management of Enron, in other words, did exactly what the consultants at McKinsey said that companies ought to do in order to succeed in the modern economy.

It hired and rewarded the very best and the very brightest — and it is now in bankruptcy. The reasons for its collapse are complex, needless to say. But what if Enron failed
not in spite of its talent mind-set but because of it? What if
smart people are overrated?

2.

At the heart of the McKinsey vision is a process that the
War for Talent advocates refer to as *differentiation and
affirmation*. Employers, they argue, need to sit down once
or twice a year and hold a "candid, probing, no-holds-
barred debate about each individual," sorting employees
into A, B, and C groups. The A's must be challenged and
disproportionately rewarded. The B's need to be encouraged and affirmed. The C's need to shape up or be shipped
out. Enron followed this advice almost to the letter, setting
up internal Performance Review Committees. The members got together twice a year, and graded each person in
their section on ten separate criteria, using a scale of 1 to 5.
The process was called *rank and yank*. Those graded at the
top of their unit received bonuses two-thirds higher than
those in the next 30 percent; those who ranked at the bottom received no bonuses and no extra stock options — and
in some cases were pushed out.

How should that ranking be done? Unfortunately, the
McKinsey consultants spend very little time discussing
the matter. One possibility is simply to hire and reward the
smartest people. But the link between, say, IQ and job performance is distinctly underwhelming. On a scale where 0.1
or below means virtually no correlation and 0.7 or above
implies a strong correlation (your height, for example, has

a 0.7 correlation with your parents' height), the correlation between IQ and occupational success is between 0.2 and 0.3. "What IQ doesn't pick up is effectiveness at common-sense sorts of things, especially working with people," Richard Wagner, a psychologist at Florida State University, says. "In terms of how we evaluate schooling, everything is about working by yourself. If you work with someone else, it's called cheating. Once you get out in the real world, everything you do involves working with other people."

Wagner and Robert Sternberg, a psychologist at Yale University, have developed tests of this practical component, which they call *tacit knowledge*. Tacit knowledge involves things like knowing how to manage yourself and others and how to navigate complicated social situations. Here is a question from one of their tests:

You have just been promoted to head of an important department in your organization. The previous head has been transferred to an equivalent position in a less important department. Your understanding of the reason for the move is that the performance of the department as a whole has been mediocre. There have not been any glaring deficiencies, just a perception of the department as so-so rather than very good. Your charge is to shape up the department. Results are expected quickly. Rate the quality of the following strategies for succeeding at your new position.

   a) Always delegate to the most junior person who can be trusted with the task.
   b) Give your superiors frequent progress reports.
   c) Announce a major reorganization of the department that includes getting rid of whomever you believe to be "dead wood."

    d) Concentrate more on your people than on the
       tasks to be done.

    e) Make people feel completely responsible for their
       work.

Wagner finds that how well people do on a test like
this predicts how well they will do in the workplace: good
managers pick (b) and (e); bad managers tend to pick (c).
Yet there's no clear connection between such tacit knowledge and other forms of knowledge and experience. The
process of assessing ability in the workplace is a lot mess-
ier than it appears.

An employer really wants to assess not potential but
performance. Yet that's just as tricky. In *The War for Talent,* the authors talk about how the Royal Air Force used
the A, B, and C ranking system for its pilots during the
Battle of Britain. But ranking fighter pilots — for whom
there are limited and relatively objective performance criteria (enemy kills, for example, and the ability to get their
formations safely home) — is a lot easier than assessing
how the manager of a new unit is doing at, say, marketing or business development. And whom do you ask to
rate the manager's performance? Studies show that there
is very little correlation between how someone's peers
rate him and how his boss rates him. The only rigorous
way to assess performance, according to human-resources
specialists, is to use criteria that are as specific as possible. Managers are supposed to take detailed notes on their
employees throughout the year, in order to remove subjective personal reactions from the process of assessment.
You can grade someone's performance only if you *know*
their performance. And, in the freewheeling culture of

Enron, this was all but impossible. People deemed talented were constantly being pushed into new jobs and given new challenges. Annual turnover from promotions was close to 20 percent. Lynda Clemmons, the so-called weather babe who started Enron's weather derivatives business, jumped, in seven quick years, from trader to associate to manager to director and, finally, to head of her own business unit. How do you evaluate someone's performance in a system where no one is in a job long enough to allow such evaluation?

The answer is that you end up doing performance evaluations that aren't based on performance. Among the many glowing books about Enron written before its fall was the bestseller *Leading the Revolution*, by the management consultant Gary Hamel, which tells the story of Lou Pai, who launched Enron's power-trading business. Pai's group began with a disaster: it lost tens of millions of dollars trying to sell electricity to residential consumers in newly deregulated markets. The problem, Hamel explains, is that the markets weren't truly deregulated: "The states that were opening their markets to competition were still setting rules designed to give their traditional utilities big advantages." It doesn't seem to have occurred to anyone that Pai ought to have looked into those rules more carefully before risking millions of dollars. He was promptly given the chance to build the commercial electricity-outsourcing business, where he ran up several more years of heavy losses before cashing out of Enron with $270 million. Because Pai had "talent," he was given new opportunities, and when he failed at those new opportunities he was given still more opportunities...because he had "talent." "At Enron, failure — even of the type that ends

up on the front page of the *Wall Street Journal* — doesn't necessarily sink a career," Hamel writes, as if that were a good thing. Presumably, companies that want to encourage risk-taking must be willing to tolerate mistakes. Yet if talent is defined as something separate from an employee's actual performance, what use is it exactly?

3.

What the War for Talent amounts to is an argument for indulging A employees, for fawning over them. "You need to do everything you can to keep them engaged and satisfied — even delighted," Michaels, Handfield-Jones, and Axelrod write. "Find out what they would most like to be doing, and shape their career and responsibilities in that direction. Solve any issues that might be pushing them out the door, such as a boss that frustrates them or travel demands that burden them." No company was better at this than Enron. In one oft-told story, Louise Kitchin, a twenty-nine-year-old gas trader in Europe, became convinced that the company ought to develop an online-trading business. She told her boss, and she began working in her spare time on the project, until she had 250 people throughout Enron helping her. After six months, Skilling was finally informed. "I was never asked for any capital," Skilling said later. "I was never asked for any people. They had already purchased the servers. They had already started ripping apart the building. They had started legal reviews in twenty-two countries by the time I heard about it." It was, Skilling went on approvingly, "exactly the kind of behavior that will continue to drive this company forward."

Kitchin's qualification for running EnronOnline, it should be pointed out, was not that she was good at it. It was that she wanted to do it, and Enron was a place where stars did whatever they wanted. "Fluid movement is absolutely necessary in our company. And the type of people we hire enforces that," Skilling told the team from McKinsey. "Not only does this system help the excitement level for each manager, it shapes Enron's business in the direction that its managers find most exciting." Here is Skilling again: "If lots of [employees] are flocking to a new business unit, that's a good sign that the opportunity is a good one.... If a business unit can't attract people very easily, that's a good sign that it's a business Enron shouldn't be in." You might expect a CEO to say that if a business unit can't attract *customers* very easily, that's a good sign it's a business the company shouldn't be in. A company's business is supposed to be shaped in the direction that its managers find most *profitable*. But at Enron the needs of the customers and the shareholders were secondary to the needs of its stars.

In the early 1990s, the psychologists Robert Hogan, Robert Raskin, and Dan Fazzini wrote a brilliant essay called "The Dark Side of Charisma." It argued that flawed managers fall into three types. One is the High Likability Floater, who rises effortlessly in an organization because he never takes any difficult decisions or makes any enemies. Another is the Homme de Ressentiment, who seethes below the surface and plots against his enemies. The most interesting of the three is the Narcissist, whose energy and self-confidence and charm lead him inexorably up the corporate ladder. Narcissists are terrible managers. They resist accepting suggestions, thinking it will

make them appear weak, and they don't believe that others have anything useful to tell them. "Narcissists are biased to take more credit for success than is legitimate," Hogan and his coauthors write, and "biased to avoid acknowledging responsibility for their failures and shortcomings for the same reasons that they claim more success than is their due." Moreover:

> Narcissists typically make judgments with greater confidence than other people…and, because their judgments are rendered with such conviction, other people tend to believe them and the narcissists become disproportionately more influential in group situations. Finally, because of their self-confidence and strong need for recognition, narcissists tend to "self-nominate"; consequently, when a leadership gap appears in a group or organization, the narcissists rush to fill it.

Tyco Corporation and WorldCom were the Greedy Corporations: they were purely interested in short-term financial gain. Enron was the Narcissistic Corporation — a company that took more credit for success than was legitimate, that did not acknowledge responsibility for its failures, that shrewdly sold the rest of us on its genius, and that substituted self-nomination for disciplined management. At one point in *Leading the Revolution*, Hamel tracks down a senior Enron executive, and what he breathlessly recounts — the braggadocio, the self-satisfaction — could be an epitaph for the talent mind-set:

> "You cannot control the atoms within a nuclear fusion reaction," said Ken Rice when he was head of Enron Capital and Trade Resources (ECT), America's largest

marketer of natural gas and largest buyer and seller of electricity. Adorned in a black T-shirt, blue jeans, and cowboy boots, Rice drew a box on an office whiteboard that pictured his business unit as a nuclear reactor. Little circles in the box represented its "contract originators," the gunslingers charged with doing deals and creating new businesses. Attached to each circle was an arrow. In Rice's diagram the arrows were pointing in all different directions. "We allow people to go in whichever direction that they want to go."

The distinction between the Greedy Corporation and the Narcissistic Corporation matters, because the way we conceive our attainments helps determine how we behave. Carol Dweck, a psychologist at Columbia University, has found that people generally hold one of two fairly firm beliefs about their intelligence: they consider it either a fixed trait or something that is malleable and can be developed over time. Dweck once did a study at the University of Hong Kong, where all classes are conducted in English. She and her colleagues approached a large group of social-sciences students, told them their English-proficiency scores, and asked them if they wanted to take a course to improve their language skills. One would expect all those who scored poorly to sign up for the remedial course. The University of Hong Kong is a demanding institution, and it is hard to do well in the social sciences without strong English skills. Curiously, however, only the ones who believed in malleable intelligence expressed interest in the class. The students who believed that their intelligence was a fixed trait were so concerned about appearing to be deficient that they preferred to stay home. "Students who hold a fixed view of their intelligence care so much about

looking smart that they act dumb," Dweck writes, "for what could be dumber than giving up a chance to learn something that is essential for your own success?"

In a similar experiment, Dweck gave a class of preadolescent students a test filled with challenging problems. After they were finished, one group was praised for its effort and another group was praised for its intelligence. Those praised for their intelligence were reluctant to tackle difficult tasks, and their performance on subsequent tests soon began to suffer. Then Dweck asked the children to write a letter to students at another school, describing their experience in the study. She discovered something remarkable: 40 percent of those students who were praised for their intelligence lied about how they had scored on the test, adjusting their grade upward. They weren't naturally deceptive people, and they weren't any less intelligent or self-confident than anyone else. They simply did what people do when they are immersed in an environment that celebrates them solely for their innate "talent." They begin to define themselves by that description, and when times get tough and that self-image is threatened, they have difficulty with the consequences. They will not take the remedial course. They will not stand up to investors and the public and admit that they were wrong. They'd sooner lie.

4.

The broader failing of McKinsey and its acolytes at Enron is their assumption that an organization's intelligence is simply a function of the intelligence of its employees. They believe in stars, because they don't believe in systems.

In a way, that's understandable, because our lives are so obviously enriched by individual brilliance. Groups don't write great novels, and a committee didn't come up with the theory of relativity. But companies work by different rules. They don't just create; they execute and compete and coordinate the efforts of many different people, and the organizations that are most successful at that task are the ones where the system *is* the star.

There is a wonderful example of this in the story of the so-called Eastern Pearl Harbor, of the Second World War. During the first nine months of 1942, the United States Navy suffered a catastrophe. German U-boats, operating just off the Atlantic coast and in the Caribbean, were sinking our merchant ships almost at will. U-boat captains marveled at their good fortune. "Before this sea of light, against this footlight glare of a carefree new world were passing the silhouettes of ships recognizable in every detail and sharp as the outlines in a sales catalogue," one U-boat commander wrote. "All we had to do was press the button."

What made this such a puzzle is that, on the other side of the Atlantic, the British had much less trouble defending their ships against U-boat attacks. The British, furthermore, eagerly passed on to the Americans everything they knew about sonar and depth-charge throwers and the construction of destroyers. And still the Germans managed to paralyze America's coastal zones.

You can imagine what the consultants at McKinsey would have concluded: they would have said that the Navy did not have a talent mind-set, that President Roosevelt needed to recruit and promote top performers into key positions in the Atlantic command. In fact, he had already

done that. At the beginning of the war, he had pushed out
the solid and unspectacular Admiral Harold R. Stark as
Chief of Naval Operations and replaced him with the
legendary Ernest Joseph King. "He was a supreme real-
ist with the arrogance of genius," Ladislas Farago writes
in *The Tenth Fleet,* a history of the Navy's U-boat battles in the Second World War. "He had unbounded faith
in himself, in his vast knowledge of naval matters and in
the soundness of his ideas. Unlike Stark, who tolerated
incompetence all around him, King had no patience with
fools."

The Navy had plenty of talent at the top, in other
words. What it didn't have was the right kind of organization. As Eliot A. Cohen, a scholar of military strategy at
Johns Hopkins, writes in his brilliant book *Military Misfortunes in the Atlantic:*

> To wage the antisubmarine war well, analysts had to
> bring together fragments of information, direction-find-
> ing fixes, visual sightings, decrypts, and the "flaming
> datum" of a U-boat attack — for use by a commander to
> coordinate the efforts of warships, aircraft, and convoy
> commanders. Such synthesis had to occur in near "real
> time" — within hours, even minutes in some cases.

The British excelled at the task because they had a cen-
tralized operational system. The controllers moved the
British ships around the Atlantic like chess pieces, in order
to outsmart U-boat "wolf packs." By contrast, Admiral
King believed strongly in a decentralized management
structure: he held that managers should never tell their sub-
ordinates "*how* as well as *what* to 'do.'" In today's jargon,

we would say he was a believer in "loose-tight" management, of the kind celebrated by the McKinsey consultants Thomas J. Peters and Robert H. Waterman in their 1982 bestseller, *In Search of Excellence*. But "loose-tight" doesn't help you find U-boats. Throughout most of 1942, the Navy kept trying to act smart by relying on technical know-how, and stubbornly refused to take operational lessons from the British. The Navy also lacked the organizational structure necessary to apply the technical knowledge it did have to the field. Only when the Navy set up the Tenth Fleet — a single unit to coordinate all antisubmarine warfare in the Atlantic — did the situation change. In the year and a half before the Tenth Fleet was formed, in May of 1943, the Navy sank thirty-six U-boats. In the six months afterward, it sank seventy-five. "The creation of the Tenth Fleet did *not* bring more talented individuals into the field of ASW" — antisubmarine warfare — "than had previous organizations," Cohen writes. "What Tenth Fleet did allow, by virtue of its organization and mandate, was for these individuals to become far more effective than previously." The talent myth assumes that people make organizations smart. More often than not, it's the other way around.

5.

There is ample evidence of this principle among America's most successful companies. Southwest Airlines hires very few MBAs, pays its managers modestly, and gives raises according to seniority, not "rank and yank." Yet it is by far the most successful of all United States airlines, because it has created a vastly more efficient organization than its competitors have. At Southwest, the time it takes

to get a plane that has just landed ready for takeoff — a key index of productivity — is, on average, twenty minutes, and requires a ground crew of four, and two people at the gate. (At United Airlines, by contrast, turnaround time is closer to thirty-five minutes, and requires a ground crew of twelve, and three agents at the gate.)

In the case of the giant retailer Wal-Mart, one of the most critical periods in its history came in 1976, when Sam Walton "unretired," pushing out his handpicked successor, Ron Mayer. Mayer was just over forty. He was ambitious. He was charismatic. He was, in the words of one Walton biographer, "the boy-genius financial officer." But Walton was convinced that Mayer was, as people at McKinsey would say, "differentiating and affirming" in the corporate suite, in defiance of Wal-Mart's inclusive culture. Mayer left, and Wal-Mart survived. After all, Wal-Mart is an organization, not an all-star team. Walton brought in David Glass, late of the Army and Southern Missouri State University, as CEO; the company is now ranked No. 1 on the Fortune 500 list.

Procter & Gamble doesn't have a star system, either. How could it? Would the top MBA graduates of Harvard and Stanford move to Cincinnati to work on detergent when they could make three times as much reinventing the world in Houston? Procter & Gamble isn't glamorous. Its CEO is a lifer — a former Navy officer who began his corporate career as an assistant brand manager for Joy dishwashing liquid — and if Procter & Gamble's best played Enron's best at Trivial Pursuit, no doubt the team from Houston would win handily. But Procter & Gamble has dominated the consumer-products field for close to a century, because it has a carefully conceived managerial

system, and a rigorous marketing methodology that has allowed it to win battles for brands like Crest and Tide decade after decade. In Procter & Gamble's Navy, Admiral Stark would have stayed. But a cross-divisional management committee would have set the Tenth Fleet in place before the war ever started.

6.

Among the most damning facts about Enron, in the end, was something its managers were proudest of. They had what, in McKinsey terminology, is called an *open market* for hiring. In the open-market system — McKinsey's assault on the very idea of a fixed organization — anyone could apply for any job that he or she wanted, and no manager was allowed to hold anyone back. Poaching was encouraged. When an Enron executive named Kevin Hannon started the company's global broadband unit, he launched what he called Project Quick Hire. A hundred top performers from around the company were invited to the Houston Hyatt to hear Hannon give his pitch. Recruiting booths were set up outside the meeting room. "Hannon had his fifty top performers for the broadband unit by the end of the week," Michaels, Handfield-Jones, and Axelrod write, "and his peers had fifty holes to fill." Nobody, not even the consultants who were paid to think about the Enron culture, seemed worried that those fifty holes might disrupt the functioning of the affected departments, that stability in a firm's existing businesses might be a good thing, that the self-fulfillment of Enron's star employees might possibly be in conflict with the best interests of the firm as a whole.

These are the sorts of concerns that management consultants ought to raise. But Enron's management consultant was McKinsey, and McKinsey was as much a prisoner of the talent myth as its clients were. In 1998, Enron hired ten Wharton MBAs; that same year, McKinsey hired forty. In 1999, Enron hired twelve from Wharton; McKinsey hired sixty-one. The consultants at McKinsey were preaching at Enron what they believed about themselves. "When we would hire them, it wouldn't just be for a week," one former Enron manager recalls, of the brilliant young men and women from McKinsey who wandered the hallways at the company's headquarters. "It would be for two to four months. They were always around." They were there looking for people who had the talent to think outside the box. It never occurred to them that, if everyone had to think outside the box, maybe it was the box that needed fixing.

July 22, 2002

The New-Boy Network

1.

Nolan Myers grew up in Houston, the elder of two boys in a middle-class family. He went to Houston's High School for the Performing and Visual Arts and then Harvard, where he intended to major in history and science. After discovering the joys of writing code, though, he switched to computer science. "Programming is one of those things you get involved in, and you just can't stop until you finish," Myers says. "You get involved in it, and all of a sudden you look at your watch and it's four in the morning! I love the elegance of it." Myers is short and slightly stocky and has pale-blue eyes. He smiles easily, and when he speaks he moves his hands and torso for emphasis. He plays in a klezmer band called the Charvard Chai Notes. He talks to his parents a lot. He gets Bs and B-pluses.

In the last stretch of his senior year, Myers spent a lot of time interviewing for jobs with technology companies. He talked to a company named Trilogy, down in Texas, but he didn't think he would fit in. "One of Trilogy's subsidiaries

put ads out in the paper saying that they were looking for the top tech students, and that they'd give them two hundred thousand dollars and a BMW," Myers said, shaking his head in disbelief. In another of his interviews, a recruiter asked him to solve a programming problem, and he made a stupid mistake and the recruiter pushed the answer back across the table to him, saying that his "solution" accomplished nothing. As he remembers the moment, Myers blushes. "I was so nervous. I thought, Hmm, that sucks!" The way he says that, though, makes it hard to believe that he really was nervous, or maybe what Nolan Myers calls nervous the rest of us call a tiny flutter in the stomach. Myers doesn't seem like the sort to get flustered. He's the kind of person you would call the night before the big test in seventh grade when nothing made sense and you had begun to panic.

I like Nolan Myers. He will, I am convinced, be very good at whatever career he chooses. I say those two things even though I have spent no more than ninety minutes in his presence. We met only once, on a sunny afternoon just before his graduation at the Au Bon Pain in Harvard Square. He was wearing sneakers and khakis and a polo shirt in a dark-green pattern. He had a big backpack, which he plopped on the floor beneath the table. I bought him an orange juice. He fished around in his wallet and came up with a dollar to try to repay me, which I refused. We sat by the window. Previously, we had talked for perhaps three minutes on the phone, setting up the interview. Then I e-mailed him, asking him how I would recognize him at Au Bon Pain. He sent me the following message, with what I'm convinced — again, on the basis of almost no evidence — to be typical Myers panache: "22ish, five foot seven, straight brown hair, very good-looking.:)." I have never talked to his father, his mother, or his little brother, or any

of his professors. I have never seen him ecstatic or angry or depressed. I know nothing of his personal habits, his tastes, or his quirks. I cannot even tell you why I feel the way I do about him. He's good-looking and smart and articulate and funny, but not *so* good-looking and smart and articulate and funny that there is some obvious explanation for the conclusions I've drawn about him. I just like him, and I'm impressed by him, and if I were an employer looking for bright young college graduates, I'd hire him in a heartbeat.

I heard about Nolan Myers from Hadi Partovi, an executive with Tellme, a highly touted Silicon Valley startup offering Internet access through the telephone. If you were a computer-science major at MIT, Harvard, Stanford, Caltech, or the University of Waterloo this spring, looking for a job in software, Tellme was probably at the top of your list. Partovi and I talked in the conference room at Tellme's offices, just off the soaring, open floor where all the firm's programmers and marketers and executives sit, some of them with bunk beds built over their desks. (Tellme recently moved into an old printing plant — a low-slung office building with a huge warehouse attached — and, in accordance with new-economy logic, promptly turned the old offices into a warehouse and the old warehouse into offices.) Partovi is a handsome man of twenty-seven, with olive skin and short curly black hair, and throughout our entire interview he sat with his chair tilted precariously at a forty-five-degree angle. At the end of a long riff about how hard it is to find high-quality people, he blurted out one name: Nolan Myers. Then, from memory, he rattled off Myers's telephone number. He very much wanted Myers to come to Tellme.

Partovi had met Myers in January of Myers's senior year, during a recruiting trip to Harvard. "It was a heinous

day," Partovi remembers. "I started at seven and went until nine. I'd walk one person out and walk the other in." The first fifteen minutes of every interview he spent talking about Tellme — its strategy, its goals, and its business. Then he gave everyone a short programming puzzle. For the rest of the hour-long meeting, Partovi asked questions. He remembers that Myers did well on the programming test, and after talking to him for thirty to forty minutes he became convinced that Myers had, as he puts it, "the right stuff." Partovi spent even less time with Myers than I did. He didn't talk to Myers's family, or see him ecstatic or angry or depressed, either. He knew that Myers had spent last summer as an intern at Microsoft and was about to graduate from an Ivy League school. But virtually everyone recruited by a place like Tellme has graduated from an elite university, and the Microsoft summer-internship program has more than six hundred people in it. Partovi didn't even know why he liked Myers so much. He just did. "It was very much a gut call," he says.

This wasn't so very different from the experience Nolan Myers had with Steve Ballmer, the CEO of Microsoft. Earlier that year, Myers attended a party for former Microsoft interns called Gradbash. Ballmer gave a speech there, and at the end of his remarks Myers raised his hand. "He was talking a lot about aligning the company in certain directions," Myers told me, "and I asked him about how that influences his ability to make bets on other directions. Are they still going to make small bets?" Afterward, a Microsoft recruiter came up to Myers and said, "Steve wants your e-mail address." Myers gave it to him, and soon he and Ballmer were e-mailing. Ballmer, it seems, badly wanted Myers to come to Microsoft. "He

did research on me," Myers says. "He knew which group I was interviewing with, and knew a lot about me personally. He sent me an e-mail saying that he'd love to have me come to Microsoft, and if I had any questions I should contact him. So I sent him a response, saying thank you. After I visited Tellme, I sent him an e-mail saying I was interested in Tellme, here were the reasons, that I wasn't sure yet, and if he had anything to say I said I'd love to talk to him. I gave him my number. So he called, and after playing phone tag we talked — about career trajectory, how Microsoft would influence my career, what he thought of Tellme. I was extremely impressed with him, and he seemed very genuinely interested in me."

What convinced Ballmer he wanted Myers? A glimpse! He caught a little slice of Nolan Myers in action and — just like that — the CEO of a $400 billion company was calling a college senior in his dorm room. Ballmer somehow knew he liked Myers, the same way Hadi Partovi knew, and the same way I knew after our little chat at Au Bon Pain. But what did we know? What could we know? By any reasonable measure, surely none of us knew Nolan Myers at all.

It is a truism of the new economy that the ultimate success of any enterprise lies with the quality of the people it hires. At many technology companies, employees are asked to all but live at the office, in conditions of intimacy that would have been unthinkable a generation ago. The artifacts of the prototypical Silicon Valley office — the videogames, the espresso bar, the bunk beds, the basketball hoops — are the elements of the rec room, not the workplace. And in the rec room you want to play only with your friends. But how do you find out who your friends are? Today, recruiters canvas the country for résumés.

They analyze employment histories and their competitors' staff listings. They call references and then do what I did with Nolan Myers: sit down with a perfect stranger for an hour and a half and attempt to draw conclusions about that stranger's intelligence and personality. The job interview has become one of the central conventions of the modern economy. But what, exactly, can you know about a stranger after sitting down and talking with him for an hour?

2.

Some years ago, an experimental psychologist at Harvard University, Nalini Ambady, together with Robert Rosenthal, set out to examine the nonverbal aspects of good teaching. As the basis of her research, she used videotapes of teaching fellows that had been made during a training program at Harvard. Her plan was to have outside observers look at the tapes with the sound off and rate the effectiveness of the teachers by their expressions and physical cues. Ambady wanted to have at least a minute of film to work with. When she looked at the tapes, though, there was really only about ten seconds when the teachers were shown apart from the students. "I didn't want students in the frame, because obviously it would bias the ratings," Ambady says. "So I went to my adviser, and I said, 'This isn't going to work.'"

But it did. The observers, presented with a ten-second silent video clip, had no difficulty rating the teachers on a fifteen-item checklist of personality traits. In fact, when Ambady cut the clips back to five seconds, the ratings were the same. They were the same even when she showed her raters just two seconds of videotape. That sounds unbelievable unless you actually watch Ambady's teacher clips, as I did,

and realize that the eight seconds that distinguish the longest clips from the shortest are superfluous: anything beyond the first flash of insight is unnecessary. When we make a snap judgment, it is made in a snap. It's also, very clearly, a judgment: we get a feeling that we have no difficulty articulating.

Ambady's next step led to an even more remarkable conclusion. She compared those snap judgments of teacher effectiveness with evaluations made, after a full semester of classes, by students of the same teachers. The correlation between the two, she found, was astoundingly high. A person watching a two-second silent video clip of a teacher he has never met will reach conclusions about how good that teacher is that are very similar to those of a student who sits in the teacher's class for an entire semester.

Recently, a comparable experiment was conducted by Frank Bernieri, a psychologist at the University of Toledo. Bernieri, working with one of his graduate students, Neha Gada-Jain, selected two people to act as interviewers, and trained them for six weeks in the proper procedures and techniques of giving an effective job interview. The two then interviewed ninety-eight volunteers of various ages and backgrounds. The interviews lasted between fifteen and twenty minutes, and afterward each interviewer filled out a six-page, five-part evaluation of the person he'd just talked to. Originally, the intention of the study was to find out whether applicants who had been coached in certain nonverbal behaviors designed to ingratiate themselves with their interviewers — like mimicking the interviewers' physical gestures or posture — would get better ratings than applicants who behaved normally. As it turns out, they didn't. But then another of Bernieri's students, an undergraduate named Tricia Prickett, decided that she

wanted to use the interview videotapes and the evaluations that had been collected to test out the adage that the handshake is everything.

"She took fifteen seconds of videotape showing the applicant as he or she knocks on the door, comes in, shakes the hand of the interviewer, sits down, and the interviewer welcomes the person," Bernieri explained. Then, like Ambady, Prickett got a series of strangers to rate the applicants based on the handshake clip, using the same criteria that the interviewers had used. Once more, against all expectations, the ratings were very similar to those of the interviewers. "On nine out of the eleven traits the applicants were being judged on, the observers significantly predicted the outcome of the interview," Bernieri says. "The strength of the correlations was extraordinary."

This research takes Ambady's conclusions one step further. In the Toledo experiment, the interviewers were trained in the art of interviewing. They weren't dashing off a teacher evaluation on their way out the door. They were filling out a formal, detailed questionnaire, of the sort designed to give the most thorough and unbiased account of an interview. And still their ratings weren't all that different from those of people off the street who saw just the greeting.

This is why Hadi Partovi, Steve Ballmer, and I all agreed on Nolan Myers. Apparently, human beings don't need to know someone in order to believe that they know someone. Nor does it make that much difference, apparently, that Partovi reached his conclusion after putting Myers through the wringer for an hour, I reached mine after ninety minutes of amiable conversation at Au Bon Pain, and Ballmer reached his after watching and listening as Myers asked a question.

Bernieri and Ambady believe that the power of first

impressions suggests that human beings have a particular kind of prerational ability for making searching judgments about others. In Ambady's teacher experiments, when she asked her observers to perform a potentially distracting cognitive task — like memorizing a set of numbers — while watching the tapes, their judgments of teacher effectiveness were unchanged. But when she instructed her observers to think hard about their ratings before they made them, their accuracy suffered substantially. Thinking only gets in the way. "The brain structures that are involved here are very primitive," Ambady speculates. "All of these affective reactions are probably governed by the lower brain structures." What we are picking up in that first instant would seem to be something quite basic about a person's character, because what we conclude after two seconds is pretty much the same as what we conclude after twenty minutes or, indeed, an entire semester. "Maybe you can tell immediately whether someone is extroverted, or gauge the person's ability to communicate," Bernieri says. "Maybe these clues or cues are immediately accessible and apparent." Bernieri and Ambady are talking about the existence of a powerful form of human intuition. In a way, that's comforting, because it suggests that we can meet a perfect stranger and immediately pick up on something important about him. It means that I shouldn't be concerned that I can't explain why I like Nolan Myers, because, if such judgments are made without thinking, then surely they defy explanation.

But there's a troubling suggestion here as well. I believe that Nolan Myers is an accomplished and likable person. But I have no idea from our brief encounter how honest he is, or whether he is self-centered, or whether he works best by himself or in a group, or any number of

other fundamental traits. That people who simply see the handshake arrive at the same conclusions as people who conduct a full interview also implies, perhaps, that those initial impressions matter too much — that they color all the other impressions that we gather over time.

For example, I asked Myers if he felt nervous about the prospect of leaving school for the workplace, which seemed like a reasonable question, since I remember how anxious I was before my first job. Would the hours scare him? Oh no, he replied, he was already working between eighty and a hundred hours a week at school. "Are there things that you think you aren't good at that, make you worry?" I continued.

His reply was sharp: "Are there things that I'm not good at, or things that I can't learn? I think that's the real question. There are a lot of things I don't know anything about, but I feel comfortable that given the right environment and the right encouragement I can do well at." In my notes, next to that reply, I wrote "Great answer!" and I can remember at the time feeling the little thrill you experience as an interviewer when someone's behavior conforms with your expectations. Because I had decided, right off, that I liked him, what I heard in his answer was toughness and confidence. Had I decided early on that I didn't like Nolan Myers, I would have heard in that reply arrogance and bluster. The first impression becomes a self-fulfilling prophecy: we hear what we expect to hear. The interview is hopelessly biased in favor of the nice.

3.

When Ballmer and Partovi and I met Nolan Myers, we made a prediction. We looked at the way he behaved in

our presence — at the way he talked and acted and seemed to think — and drew conclusions about how he would behave in other situations. I had decided, remember, that Myers was the kind of person you called the night before the big test in seventh grade. Was I right to make that kind of generalization?

This is a question that social psychologists have looked at closely. In the late 1920s, in a famous study, the psychologist Theodore Newcomb analyzed extroversion among adolescent boys at a summer camp. He found that how talkative a boy was in one setting — say, at lunch — was highly predictive of how talkative that boy would be in the same setting in the future. A boy who was curious at lunch on Monday was likely to be curious at lunch on Tuesday. But his behavior in one setting told you almost nothing about how he would behave in a different setting: from how someone behaved at lunch, you couldn't predict how he would behave during, say, afternoon playtime. In a more recent study, of conscientiousness among students at Carleton College, the researchers Walter Mischel, Neil Lutsky, and Philip K. Peake showed that how neat a student's assignments were or how punctual he was told you almost nothing about how often he attended class or how neat his room or his personal appearance was. How we behave at any one time, evidently, has less to do with some immutable inner compass than with the particulars of our situation.

This conclusion, obviously, is at odds with our intuition. Most of the time, we assume that people display the same character traits in different situations. We habitually underestimate the large role that context plays in people's behavior. In the Newcomb summer-camp experiment, for

example, the results showing how little consistency there was from one setting to another in talkativeness, curiosity, and gregariousness were tabulated from observations made and recorded by camp counselors on the spot. But when, at the end of the summer, those same counselors were asked to give their final impressions of the kids, they remembered the children's behavior as being highly consistent.

"The basis of the illusion is that we are somehow confident that we are getting what is there, that we are able to read off a person's disposition," Richard Nisbett, a psychologist at the University of Michigan, says. "When you have an interview with someone and have an hour with them, you don't conceptualize that as taking a sample of a person's behavior, let alone a possibly biased sample, which is what it is. What you think is that you are seeing a hologram, a small and fuzzy image but still the whole person."

Then Nisbett mentioned his frequent collaborator, Lee Ross, who teaches psychology at Stanford. "There was one term when he was teaching statistics and one term when he was teaching a course with a lot of humanistic psychology. He gets his teacher evaluations. The first referred to him as cold, rigid, remote, finicky, and uptight. And the second described this wonderful warmhearted guy who was so deeply concerned with questions of community and getting students to grow. It was Jekyll and Hyde. In both cases, the students thought they were seeing the real Lee Ross."

Psychologists call this tendency — to fixate on supposedly stable character traits and overlook the influence of context — the *Fundamental Attribution Error,* and if

you combine this error with what we know about snap judgments, the interview becomes an even more problematic encounter. Not only had I let my first impressions color the information I gathered about Myers, but I had also assumed that the way he behaved with me in an interview setting was indicative of the way he would always behave. It isn't that the interview is useless; what I learned about Myers — that he and I get along well — is something I could never have gotten from a résumé or by talking to his references. It's just that our conversation turns out to have been less useful, and potentially more misleading, than I had supposed. That most basic of human rituals — the conversation with a stranger — turns out to be a minefield.

4.

Not long after I met with Nolan Myers, I talked with a human-resources consultant from Pasadena named Justin Menkes. Menkes's job is to figure out how to extract meaning from face-to-face encounters, and with that in mind he agreed to spend an hour interviewing me the way he thinks interviewing ought to be done. It felt, going in, not unlike a visit to a shrink, except that instead of having months, if not years, to work things out, Menkes was set upon stripping away my secrets in one session. Consider, he told me, a commonly asked question like "Describe a few situations in which your work was criticized. How did you handle the criticism?" The problem, Menkes said, is that it's much too obvious what the interviewee is supposed to say. "There was a situation where I was working on a project, and I didn't do as well as I could have,"

he said, adopting a mock-sincere singsong. "My boss gave me some constructive criticism. And I redid the project. It hurt. Yet we worked it out." The same is true of the question "What would your friends say about you?" — to which the correct answer (preferably preceded by a pause, as if to suggest that it had never dawned on you that someone would ask such a question) is "My guess is that they would call me a people person — either that or a hard worker."

Myers and I had talked about obvious questions, too. "What is your greatest weakness?" I asked him. He answered, "I tried to work on a project my freshman year, a children's festival. I was trying to start a festival as a benefit here in Boston. And I had a number of guys working with me. I started getting concerned with the scope of the project we were working on — how much responsibility we had, getting things done. I really put the brakes on, but in retrospect I really think we could have done it and done a great job."

Then Myers grinned and said, as an aside, "Do I truly think that is a fault? Honestly, no." And, of course, he's right. All I'd really asked him was whether he could describe a personal strength as if it were a weakness, and in answering as he did, he had merely demonstrated his knowledge of the unwritten rules of the interview.

But, Menkes said, what if those questions were rephrased so that the answers weren't obvious? For example: "At your weekly team meetings, your boss unexpectedly begins aggressively critiquing your performance on a current project. What do you do?"

I felt a twinge of anxiety. What would I do? I remembered a terrible boss I'd had years ago. "I'd probably be

upset," I said. "But I doubt I'd say anything. I'd probably just walk away." Menkes gave no indication whether he was concerned or pleased by that answer. He simply pointed out that another person might well have said something like "I'd go and see my boss later in private, and confront him about why he embarrassed me in front of my team." I was saying that I would probably handle criticism — even inappropriate criticism — from a superior with stoicism; in the second case, the applicant was saying he or she would adopt a more confrontational style. Or, at least, we were telling the interviewer that the workplace demands either stoicism or confrontation — and to Menkes these are revealing and pertinent pieces of information.

Menkes moved on to another area — handling stress. A typical question in this area is something like "Tell me about a time when you had to do several things at once. How did you handle the situation? How did you decide what to do first?" Menkes says this is also too easy. "I just had to be very organized," he began again in his mock-sincere singsong. "I had to multitask. I had to prioritize and delegate appropriately. I checked in frequently with my boss." Here's how Menkes rephrased it: "You're in a situation where you have two very important responsibilities that both have a deadline that is impossible to meet. You cannot accomplish both. How do you handle that situation?"

"Well," I said, "I would look at the two and decide what I was best at, and then go to my boss and say, 'It's better that I do one well than both poorly,' and we'd figure out who else could do the other task."

Menkes immediately seized on a telling detail in my answer. I was interested in what job I would do best. But

isn't the key issue what job the *company* most needed to have done? With that comment, I had revealed something valuable: that in a time of work-related crisis I start from a self-centered consideration. "Perhaps you are a bit of a solo practitioner," Menkes said diplomatically. "That's an essential bit of information."

Menkes deliberately wasn't drawing any broad conclusions. If we are not people who are shy or talkative or outspoken but people who are shy in some contexts, talkative in other situations, and outspoken in still other areas, then what it means to know someone is to catalog and appreciate all those variations. Menkes was trying to begin that process of cataloging. This interviewing technique is known as *structured interviewing,* and in studies by industrial psychologists it has been shown to be the only kind of interviewing that has any success at all in predicting performance in the workplace. In the structured interviews, the format is fairly rigid. Each applicant is treated in precisely the same manner. The questions are scripted. The interviewers are carefully trained, and each applicant is rated on a series of predetermined scales.

What is interesting about the structured interview is how narrow its objectives are. When I interviewed Nolan Myers I was groping for some kind of global sense of who he was; Menkes seemed entirely uninterested in arriving at that same general sense of me — he seemed to realize how foolish that expectation was for an hour-long interview. The structured interview works precisely because it isn't really an interview; it isn't about getting to know someone, in a traditional sense. It's as much concerned with rejecting information as it is with collecting it.

Not surprisingly, interview specialists have found it

extraordinarily difficult to persuade most employers to adopt the structured interview. It just doesn't feel right. For most of us, hiring someone is essentially a romantic process, in which the job interview functions as a desexualized version of a date. We are looking for someone with whom we have a certain chemistry, even if the coupling that results ends in tears and the pursuer and the pursued turn out to have nothing in common. We want the unlimited promise of a love affair. The structured interview, by contrast, seems to offer only the dry logic and practicality of an arranged marriage.

5.

Nolan Myers agonized over which job to take. He spent half an hour on the phone with Steve Ballmer, and Ballmer was very persuasive. "He gave me very, very good advice," Myers says of his conversations with the Microsoft CEO. "He felt that I should go to the place that excited me the most and that I thought would be best for my career. He offered to be my mentor." Myers says he talked to his parents every day about what to do. In February, he flew out to California and spent a Saturday going from one Tellme executive to another, asking and answering questions. "Basically, I had three things I was looking for. One was long-term goals for the company. Where did they see themselves in five years? Second, what position would I be playing in the company?" He stopped and burst out laughing. "And I forget what the third one is." In March, Myers committed to Tellme.

Will Nolan Myers succeed at Tellme? I think so, although I honestly have no idea. It's a harder question to

answer now than it would have been thirty or forty years ago. If this were 1965, Nolan Myers would have gone to work at IBM and worn a blue suit and sat in a small office and kept his head down, and the particulars of his personality would not have mattered so much. It was not so important that IBM understood who you were before it hired you, because you understood what IBM was. If you walked through the door at Armonk or at a branch office in Illinois, you knew what you had to be and how you were supposed to act. But to walk through the soaring, open offices of Tellme, with the bunk beds over the desks, is to be struck by how much more demanding the culture of Silicon Valley is. Nolan Myers will not be provided with a social script, that blue suit, and organization chart. Tellme, like any technology startup these days, wants its employees to be part of a fluid team, to be flexible and innovative, to work with shifting groups in the absence of hierarchy and bureaucracy, and in that environment, where the workplace doubles as the rec room, the particulars of your personality matter a great deal.

This is part of the new economy's appeal, because Tellme's soaring warehouse is a more productive and enjoyable place to work than the little office boxes of the old IBM. But the danger here is that we will be led astray in judging these newly important particulars of character. If we let personability — some indefinable, prerational intuition, magnified by the Fundamental Attribution Error — bias the hiring process today, then all we will have done is replace the old-boy network, where you hired your nephew, with the new-boy network, where you hire whoever impressed you most when you shook his hand. Social progress, unless we're careful, can merely

be the means by which we replace the obviously arbitrary with the not so obviously arbitrary.

Myers has spent much of the past year helping to teach Introduction to Computer Science. He realized, he says, that one of the reasons that students were taking the course was that they wanted to get jobs in the software industry. "I decided that, having gone through all this interviewing, I had developed some expertise, and I would like to share that. There is a real skill and art in presenting yourself to potential employers. And so what we did in this class was talk about the kinds of things that employers are looking for — what are they looking for in terms of personality. One of the most important things is that you have to come across as being confident in what you are doing and in who you are. How do you do that? Speak clearly and smile." As he said that, Nolan Myers smiled. "For a lot of people, that's a very hard skill to learn. But for some reason I seem to understand it intuitively."

May 29, 2000

Troublemakers

WHAT PIT BULLS CAN TEACH US
ABOUT CRIME

1.

One sunny winter afternoon, Guy Clairoux picked up his two-and-a-half-year-old son, Jayden, from day care and walked him back to their house in the west end of Ottawa, Ontario. They were almost home. Jayden was straggling behind, and, as his father's back was turned, a pit bull jumped over a backyard fence and lunged at Jayden. "The dog had his head in its mouth and started to do this shake," Clairoux's wife, JoAnn Hartley, said later. As she watched in horror, two more pit bulls jumped over the fence, joining in the assault. She and Clairoux came running, and he punched the first of the dogs in the head, until it dropped Jayden, and then he threw the boy toward his mother. Hartley fell on her son, protecting him with her body. "JoAnn!" Clairoux cried out, as all three dogs descended on his wife. "Cover your neck, cover your neck." A neighbor, sitting by her window, screamed for help. Her partner and a friend, Mario Gauthier, ran outside. A neighborhood boy grabbed his hockey stick and threw it to Gauthier. He began hitting one of the dogs

over the head, until the stick broke. "They wouldn't stop," Gauthier said. "As soon as you'd stop, they'd attack again. I've never seen a dog go so crazy. They were like Tasmanian devils." The police came. The dogs were pulled away, and the Clairouxes and one of the rescuers were taken to the hospital. Five days later, the Ontario legislature banned the ownership of pit bulls. "Just as we wouldn't let a great white shark in a swimming pool," the province's attorney general, Michael Bryant, had said, "maybe we shouldn't have these animals on the civilized streets."

Pit bulls, descendants of the bulldogs used in the nineteenth century for bull baiting and dogfighting, have been bred for "gameness," and thus a lowered inhibition to aggression. Most dogs fight as a last resort, when staring and growling fail. A pit bull is willing to fight with little or no provocation. Pit bulls seem to have a high tolerance for pain, making it possible for them to fight to the point of exhaustion. Whereas guard dogs like German shepherds usually attempt to restrain those they perceive to be threats by biting and holding, pit bulls try to inflict the maximum amount of damage on an opponent. They bite, hold, shake, and tear. They don't growl or assume an aggressive facial expression as warning. They just attack. "They are often insensitive to behaviors that usually stop aggression," one scientific review of the breed states. "For example, dogs not bred for fighting usually display defeat in combat by rolling over and exposing a light underside. On several occasions, pit bulls have been reported to disembowel dogs offering this signal of submission." In epidemiological studies of dog bites, the pit bull is over-represented among dogs known to have seriously injured or killed human beings, and as a result, pit bulls have

been banned or restricted in several Western European countries, China, and numerous cities and municipalities across North America. Pit bulls are dangerous.

Of course, not all pit bulls are dangerous. Most don't bite anyone. Meanwhile, Dobermans and Great Danes and German shepherds and Rottweilers are frequent biters as well, and the dog that recently mauled a Frenchwoman so badly that she was given the world's first face transplant was, of all things, a Labrador retriever. When we say that pit bulls are dangerous, we are making a generalization, just as insurance companies use generalizations when they charge young men more for car insurance than the rest of us (even though many young men are perfectly good drivers), and doctors use generalizations when they tell overweight middle-aged men to get their cholesterol checked (even though many overweight middle-aged men won't experience heart trouble). Because we don't know which dog will bite someone or who will have a heart attack or which drivers will get in an accident, we can make predictions only by generalizing. As the legal scholar Frederick Schauer has observed, "painting with a broad brush" is "an often inevitable and frequently desirable dimension of our decision-making lives."

Another word for generalization, though, is *stereotype,* and stereotypes are usually not considered desirable dimensions of our decision-making lives. The process of moving from the specific to the general is both necessary and perilous. A doctor could, with some statistical support, generalize about men of a certain age and weight. But what if generalizing from other traits — such as high blood pressure, family history, and smoking — saved more lives? Behind each generalization is a choice of what factors to leave in and what factors to leave out, and those choices can

prove surprisingly complicated. After the attack on Jayden Clairoux, the Ontario government chose to make a generalization about pit bulls. But it could also have chosen to generalize about powerful dogs, or about the kinds of people who own powerful dogs, or about small children, or about backyard fences — or, indeed, about any number of other things to do with dogs and people and places. How do we know when we've made the right generalization?

2.

In July of 2005, following a series of bombings in subways and on buses in London, the New York City Police Department announced that it would send officers into the subways to conduct random searches of passengers' bags. On the face of it, doing random searches in the hunt for terrorists — as opposed to being guided by generalizations — seems like a silly idea. As a columnist in *New York* magazine wrote at the time, "Not just 'most' but nearly every jihadi who has attacked a Western European or American target is a young Arab or Pakistani man. In other words, you can predict with a fair degree of certainty what an Al Qaeda terrorist looks like. Just as we have always known what Mafiosi look like — even as we understand that only an infinitesimal fraction of Italian-Americans are members of the mob."

But wait: do we really know what mafiosi look like? In *The Godfather*, where most of us get our knowledge of the Mafia, the male members of the Corleone family were played by Marlon Brando, who was of Irish and French ancestry, James Caan, who is Jewish, and two Italian-Americans, Al Pacino and John Cazale. To go by *The Godfather*, mafiosi look like white men of European

descent, which, as generalizations go, isn't terribly helpful. Figuring out what an Islamic terrorist looks like isn't any easier. Muslims are not like the Amish: they don't come dressed in identifiable costumes. And they don't look like basketball players; they don't come in predictable shapes and sizes. Islam is a religion that spans the globe.

"We have a policy against racial profiling," Raymond Kelly, New York City's police commissioner, told me. "I put it in here in March of the first year I was here. It's the wrong thing to do, and it's also ineffective. If you look at the London bombings, you have three British citizens of Pakistani descent. You have Germaine Lindsay, who is Jamaican. You have the next crew, on July 21, who are East African. You have a Chechen woman in Moscow in early 2004 who blows herself up in the subway station. So whom do you profile? Look at New York City. Forty percent of New Yorkers are born outside the country. Look at the diversity here. Who am I supposed to profile?"

Kelly was pointing out what might be called profiling's "category problem." Generalizations involve matching a category of people to a behavior or trait — overweight middle-aged men to heart-attack risk, young men to bad driving. But, for that process to work, you have to be able both to define and to identify the category you are generalizing about. "You think that terrorists aren't aware of how easy it is to be characterized by ethnicity?" Kelly went on. "Look at the 9/11 hijackers. They came here. They shaved. They went to topless bars. They wanted to blend in. They wanted to look like they were part of the American dream. These are not dumb people. Could a terrorist dress up as a Hasidic Jew and walk into the subway, and not be profiled? Yes. I think profiling is just nuts."

3.

Pit bull bans involve a category problem, too, because pit bulls, as it happens, aren't a single breed. The name refers to dogs belonging to a number of related breeds, such as the American Staffordshire terrier, the Staffordshire bull terrier, and the American pit bull terrier — all of which share a square and muscular body, a short snout, and a sleek, short-haired coat. Thus the Ontario ban prohibits not only these three breeds but any "dog that has an appearance and physical characteristics that are substantially similar" to theirs; the term of art is "pit bull–type" dogs. But what does that mean? Is a cross between an American pit bull terrier and a golden retriever a pit bull–type dog or a golden retriever–type dog? If thinking about muscular terriers as pit bulls is a generalization, then thinking about dangerous dogs as anything substantially similar to a pit bull is a generalization about a generalization. "The way a lot of these laws are written, pit bulls are whatever they say they are," Lora Brashears, a kennel manager in Pennsylvania, says. "And for most people it just means big, nasty, scary dog that bites."

The goal of pit bull bans, obviously, isn't to prohibit dogs that look like pit bulls. The pit bull appearance is a proxy for the pit bull temperament — for some trait that these dogs share. But "pit bull–ness" turns out to be elusive as well. The supposedly troublesome characteristics of the pit bull type — its gameness, its determination, its insensitivity to pain — are chiefly directed toward other dogs. Pit bulls were not bred to fight humans. On the contrary: a dog that went after spectators, or its handler, or the trainer, or any of the other people involved in making a

dogfighting dog a good dogfighter was usually put down. (The rule in the pit bull world was "Man-eaters die.")

A Georgia-based group called the American Temperament Test Society has put twenty-five thousand dogs through a ten-part standardized drill designed to assess a dog's stability, shyness, aggressiveness, and friendliness in the company of people. A handler takes a dog on a six-foot lead and judges its reaction to stimuli such as gunshots, an umbrella opening, and a weirdly dressed stranger approaching in a threatening way. Eighty-four percent of the pit bulls that have been given the test have passed, which ranks pit bulls ahead of beagles, Airedales, bearded collies, and all but one variety of dachshund. "We have tested somewhere around a thousand pit bull–type dogs," Carl Herkstroeter, the president of the ATTS, says. "I've tested half of them. And of the number I've tested I have disqualified one pit bull because of aggressive tendencies. They have done extremely well. They have a good temperament. They are very good with children." It can even be argued that the same traits that make the pit bull so aggressive toward other dogs are what make it so nice to humans. "There are a lot of pit bulls these days who are licensed therapy dogs," the writer Vicki Hearne points out. "Their stability and resoluteness make them excellent for work with people who might not like a more bouncy, flibberti-gibbet sort of dog. When pit bulls set out to provide comfort, they are as resolute as they are when they fight, but what they are resolute about is being gentle. And, because they are fearless, they can be gentle with anybody."

Then which are the pit bulls that get into trouble? "The ones that the legislation is geared toward have aggressive tendencies that are either bred in by the breeder, trained in

by the trainer, or reinforced in by the owner," Herkstroeter says. A mean pit bull is a dog that has been turned mean, by selective breeding, by being cross-bred with a bigger, human-aggressive breed like German shepherds or Rott-weilers, or by being conditioned in such a way that it begins to express hostility to human beings. A pit bull is dangerous to people, then, not to the extent that it expresses its essen-tial pit bull-ness but to the extent that it deviates from it. A pit-bull ban is a generalization about a generalization about a trait that is not, in fact, general. That's a category problem.

4.

One of the puzzling things about New York City is that, after the enormous and well-publicized reductions in crime in the mid-1990s, the crime rate has continued to fall. From 2004 to 2006, for instance, murder in New York declined by almost 10 percent, rape by 12 percent, and burglary by more than 18 percent. To pick another random year, in 2005 auto theft went down 11.8 percent. On a list of two hundred and forty cities in the United States with a population of a hundred thousand or more, New York City ranks two hundred-and-twenty-second in crime, down near the bottom with Fontana, Califor-nia, and Port St. Lucie, Florida. In the 1990s, the crime decrease was attributed to big obvious changes in city life and government — the decline of the drug trade, the gen-trification of Brooklyn, the successful implementation of *broken windows policing.* But all those big changes hap-pened a decade ago. Why is crime *still* falling?

The explanation may have to do with a shift in police tactics. The NYPD has a computerized map showing,

in real time, precisely where serious crimes are being reported, and at any moment the map typically shows a few dozen constantly shifting high-crime hot spots, some as small as two or three blocks square. What the NYPD has done, under Commissioner Kelly, is to use the map to establish *impact zones,* and to direct newly graduated officers — who used to be distributed proportionally to precincts across the city — to these zones, in some cases doubling the number of officers in the immediate neighborhood. "We took two-thirds of our graduating class and linked them with experienced officers, and focused on those areas," Kelly said. "Well, what has happened is that over time we have averaged about a thirty-five-percent crime reduction in impact zones."

For years, experts have maintained that the incidence of violent crime is *inelastic* relative to police presence — that people commit serious crimes because of poverty and psychopathology and cultural dysfunction, along with spontaneous motives and opportunities. The presence of a few extra officers down the block, it was thought, wouldn't make much difference. But the NYPD experience suggests otherwise. More police means that some crimes are prevented, others are more easily solved, and still others are displaced — pushed out of the troubled neighborhood — which Kelly says is a good thing, because it disrupts the patterns and practices and social networks that serve as the basis for lawbreaking. In other words, the relation between New York City (a category) and criminality (a trait) is unstable, and this kind of instability is another way in which our generalizations can be derailed.

Why, for instance, is it a useful rule of thumb that Kenyans are good distance runners? It's not just that it's

statistically supportable today. It's that it has been true for almost half a century, and that in Kenya the tradition of distance running is sufficiently rooted that something cataclysmic would have to happen to dislodge it. By contrast, the generalization that New York City is a crime-ridden place was once true and now, manifestly, isn't. People who moved to sunny retirement communities like Port St. Lucie because they thought they were much safer there than in New York are suddenly in the position of having made the wrong bet.

The instability issue is a problem for profiling in law enforcement as well. The law professor David Cole once tallied up some of the traits that Drug Enforcement Administration agents have used over the years in making generalizations about suspected smugglers. Here is a sample:

> Arrived late at night; arrived early in the morning; arrived in afternoon; one of the first to deplane; one of the last to deplane; deplaned in the middle; purchased ticket at the airport; made reservation on short notice; bought coach ticket; bought first-class ticket; used one-way ticket; used round-trip ticket; paid for ticket with cash; paid for ticket with small denomination currency; paid for ticket with large denomination currency; made local telephone calls after deplaning; made long-distance telephone call after deplaning; pretended to make telephone call; traveled from New York to Los Angeles; traveled to Houston; carried no luggage; carried brand-new luggage; carried a small bag; carried a medium-sized bag; carried two bulky garment bags; carried two heavy suitcases; carried four pieces of luggage; overly protective of luggage; disassociated self from luggage; traveled alone; traveled with a companion; acted too nervous; acted too

calm; made eye contact with officer; avoided making eye contact with officer; wore expensive clothing and jewelry; dressed casually; went to restroom after deplaning; walked rapidly through airport; walked slowly through airport; walked aimlessly through airport; left airport by taxi; left airport by limousine; left airport by private car; left airport by hotel courtesy van.

Some of these reasons for suspicion are plainly absurd, suggesting that there's no particular rationale to the generalizations used by DEA agents in stopping suspected drug smugglers. A way of making sense of the list, though, is to think of it as a catalog of unstable traits. Smugglers may once have tended to buy one-way tickets in cash and carry two bulky suitcases. But they don't have to. They can easily switch to round-trip tickets bought with a credit card, or a single carry-on bag, without losing their capacity to smuggle. There's a second kind of instability here as well. Maybe the reason some of them switched from one-way tickets and two bulky suitcases was that law enforcement got wise to those habits, so the smugglers did the equivalent of what the jihadis seemed to have done in London when they switched to East Africans because the scrutiny of young Arab and Pakistani men grew too intense. It doesn't work to generalize about a relationship between a category and a trait when that relationship isn't stable — or when the act of generalizing may itself change the basis of the generalization.

Before Kelly became the New York City police commissioner, he served as the head of the US Customs Service, and while he was there, he overhauled the criteria that border-control officers use to identify and search suspected smugglers. There had been a list of forty-three suspicious

traits. He replaced it with a list of six broad criteria. Is there something suspicious about their physical appearance? Are they nervous? Is there specific intelligence targeting this person? Does the drug-sniffing dog raise an alarm? Is there something amiss in their paperwork or explanations? Has contraband been found that implicates this person?

You'll find nothing here about race or gender or ethnicity, and nothing here about expensive jewelry or deplaning at the middle or the end, or walking briskly or walking aimlessly. Kelly removed all the unstable generalizations, forcing customs officers to make generalizations about things that don't change from one day or one month to the next. Some percentage of smugglers will *always* be nervous, will *always* get their story wrong, and will *always* be caught by the dogs. That's why those kinds of inferences are more reliable than the ones based on whether smugglers are white or black, or carry one bag or two. After Kelly's reforms, the number of searches conducted by the Customs Service dropped by about 75 percent, but the number of successful seizures improved by 25 percent. The officers went from making fairly lousy decisions about smugglers to making pretty good ones. "We made them more efficient and more effective at what they were doing," Kelly said.

5.

Does the notion of a pit bull menace rest on a stable or an unstable generalization? The best data we have on breed dangerousness are fatal dog bites, which serve as a useful indicator of just how much havoc certain kinds of dogs are causing. Between the late 1970s and the late 1990s, more than twenty-five breeds were involved in fatal attacks in

the United States. Pit bull breeds led the pack, but the variability from year to year is considerable. For instance, in the period from 1981 to 1982, fatalities were caused by five pit bulls, three mixed breeds, two St. Bernards, two German shepherd mixes, a pure-bred German shepherd, a husky-type, a Doberman, a Chow Chow, a Great Dane, a wolf-dog hybrid, a husky mix, and a pit bull mix — but no Rottweilers. In 1995 and 1996, the list included ten Rottweilers, four pit bulls, two German shepherds, two huskies, two Chow Chows, two wolf-dog hybrids, two shepherd mixes, a Rottweiler mix, a mixed breed, a Chow Chow mix, and a Great Dane. The kinds of dogs that kill people change over time, because the popularity of certain breeds changes over time. The one thing that doesn't change is the total number of the people killed by dogs. When we have more problems with pit bulls, it's not necessarily a sign that pit bulls are more dangerous than other dogs. It could just be a sign that pit bulls have become more numerous.

"I've seen virtually every breed involved in fatalities, including Pomeranians and everything else, except a beagle or a basset hound," Randall Lockwood, a senior vice president of the ASPCA and one of the country's leading dog-bite experts, told me. "And there's always one or two deaths attributable to malamutes or huskies, although you never hear people clamoring for a ban on those breeds. When I first started looking at fatal dog attacks, they largely involved dogs like German shepherds and shepherd mixes and St. Bernards — which is probably why Stephen King chose to make Cujo a St. Bernard, not a pit bull. I haven't seen a fatality involving a Doberman for decades, whereas in the 1970s they were quite common. If you wanted a mean dog, back then, you got a Doberman. I don't think I even

saw my first pit bull case until the middle to late 1980s, and I didn't start seeing Rottweilers until I'd already looked at a few hundred fatal dog attacks. Now those dogs make up the preponderance of fatalities. The point is that it changes over time. It's a reflection of what the dog of choice is among people who want to own an aggressive dog."

There is no shortage of more stable generalizations about dangerous dogs, though. A 1991 study in Denver, for example, compared 178 dogs that had a history of biting people with a random sample of 178 dogs with no history of biting. The breeds were scattered: German shepherds, Akitas, and Chow Chows were among those most heavily represented. (There were no pit bulls among the biting dogs in the study, because Denver banned pit bulls in 1989.) But a number of other, more stable factors stand out. The biters were 6.2 times as likely to be male than female, and 2.6 times as likely to be intact than neutered. The Denver study also found that biters were 2.8 times as likely to be chained as unchained. "About twenty percent of the dogs involved in fatalities were chained at the time, and had a history of long-term chaining," Lockwood said. "Now, are they chained because they are aggressive or aggressive because they are chained? It's a bit of both. These are animals that have not had an opportunity to become socialized to people. They don't necessarily even know that children are small human beings. They tend to see them as prey."

In many cases, vicious dogs are hungry or in need of medical attention. Often, the dogs had a history of aggressive incidents, and, overwhelmingly, dog-bite victims were children (particularly small boys) who were physically vulnerable to attack and may also have unwittingly done

things to provoke the dog, like teasing it, or bothering it while it was eating. The strongest connection of all, though, is between the trait of dog viciousness and certain kinds of dog owners. In about a quarter of fatal dog-bite cases, the dog owners were previously involved in illegal fighting. The dogs that bite people are, in many cases, socially isolated because their owners are socially isolated, and they are vicious because they have owners who want a vicious dog. The junkyard German shepherd — which looks as if it would rip your throat out — and the German-shepherd guide dog are the same breed. But they are not the same dog, because they have owners with different intentions.

"A fatal dog attack is not just a dog bite by a big or aggressive dog," Lockwood went on. "It is usually a perfect storm of bad human-canine interactions — the wrong dog, the wrong background, the wrong history in the hands of the wrong person in the wrong environmental situation. I've been involved in many legal cases involving fatal dog attacks, and, certainly, it's my impression that these are generally cases where everyone is to blame. You've got the unsupervised three-year-old child wandering in the neighborhood killed by a starved, abused dog owned by the dogfighting boyfriend of some woman who doesn't know where her child is. It's not old Shep sleeping by the fire who suddenly goes bonkers. Usually there are all kinds of other warning signs."

6.

Jayden Clairoux was attacked by Jada, a pit bull terrier, and her two pit bull–bullmastiff puppies, Agua and Akasha. The dogs were owned by a twenty-one-year-old

man named Shridev Café, who worked in construction and did odd jobs. Five weeks before the Clairoux attack, Café's three dogs got loose and attacked a sixteen-year-old boy and his four-year-old half brother while they were ice skating. The boys beat back the animals with a snow shovel and escaped into a neighbor's house. Café was fined, and he moved the dogs to his seventeen-year-old girlfriend's house. This was not the only time that he had run into trouble; a few months later, he was charged with domestic assault and, in another incident, involving a street brawl, with aggravated assault. "Shridev has personal issues," Cheryl Smith, a canine-behavior specialist who consulted on the case, says. "He's certainly not a very mature person." Agua and Akasha were now about seven months old. The court order in the wake of the first attack required that they be muzzled when they were outside the home and kept in an enclosed yard. But Café did not muzzle them, because, he said later, he couldn't afford muzzles, and apparently no one from the city ever came by to force him to comply. A few times, he talked about taking his dogs to obedience classes, but he never did. The subject of neutering them also came up — particularly Agua, the male — but neutering cost a hundred dollars, which he evidently thought was too much money, and when the city temporarily confiscated his animals after the first attack, it did not neuter them, either, because Ottawa does not have a policy of preemptively neutering dogs that bite people.

On the day of the second attack, according to some accounts, a visitor came by the house of Café's girlfriend, and the dogs got wound up. They were put outside, where the snowbanks were high enough that the backyard fence

could be readily jumped. Jayden Clairoux stopped and stared at the dogs, saying, "Puppies, puppies." His mother called out to his father. His father came running, which is the kind of thing that will rile up an aggressive dog. The dogs jumped the fence, and Agua took Jayden's head in his mouth and started to shake. It was a textbook dog-biting case: unneutered, ill-trained, charged-up dogs with a history of aggression and an irresponsible owner somehow get loose and set upon a small child. The dogs had already passed through the animal bureaucracy of Ottawa, and the city could easily have prevented the second attack with the right kind of generalization — a generalization based not on breed but on the known and meaningful connection between dangerous dogs and negligent owners. But that would have required someone to track down Shridev Café and check to see whether he had bought muzzles, and someone to send the dogs to be neutered after the first attack, and an animal-control law that ensured that those whose dogs attack small children forfeit their right to have a dog. It would have required, that is, a more exacting set of generalizations to be more exactingly applied. It's always easier just to ban the breed.

February 6, 2006

Acknowledgments

Every one of these stories was rigorously perfected by the copy and fact-checking departments of *The New Yorker* magazine. They are all wizards. Thank you.

If you enjoyed this book, there's more to read from Malcolm Gladwell

...

Out from October 2013, his dazzling and provocative new book, *David and Goliath*

Why do underdogs succeed so much more than we expect? How do the weak outsmart the strong? In *David and Goliath* Malcolm Gladwell takes us on a scintillating and surprising journey through the hidden dynamics that shape the balance of power between the small and the mighty. *David and Goliath* draws on the stories of remarkable underdogs, history, science, psychology and on Malcolm Gladwell's unparalleled ability to make the connections other miss. It's a brilliant, illuminating book that overturns conventional thinking about power and advantage.

'A global phenomenon ... he has a genius for making everything he writes seem like an impossible adventure ... there is, it seems, no subject over which he cannot scatter some magic dust' *Observer*

'He is the best kind of writer - the kind who makes you feel like you're a genius, rather than he's a genius' *The Times*

'Gladwell makes the world seem fresh and exciting again' *Evening Standard*

Also by Malcolm Gladwell

Outliers

Why do some people achieve so much more than others? Can they lie so far out of the ordinary? *Outliers* reveals that the story of success is far more surprising, and more fascinating, than we could ever have imagined. It will change the way you think about your own life story, and about what makes us all unique.

'Gladwell makes the world seem fresh and exciting again'
Evening Standard

Blink

Blink is about all those moments when we 'know' something without knowing why. Here Malcolm Gladwell explores the phenomenon of 'blink', showing how a snap judgement can be far more effective than a cautious decision. By trusting your instincts, he reveals, you'll never think about thinking in the same way again.

'He has a genius for making everything he writes seem like an impossible adventure' *Observer*

He just wanted a decent book to read ...

Not too much to ask, is it? It was in 1935 when Allen Lane, Managing Director of Bodley Head Publishers, stood on a platform at Exeter railway station looking for something good to read on his journey back to London. His choice was limited to popular magazines and poor-quality paperbacks – the same choice faced every day by the vast majority of readers, few of whom could afford hardbacks. Lane's disappointment and subsequent anger at the range of books generally available led him to found a company – and change the world.

'We believed in the existence in this country of a vast reading public for intelligent books at a low price, and staked everything on it'
Sir Allen Lane, 1902–1970, founder of Penguin Books

The quality paperback had arrived – and not just in bookshops. Lane was adamant that his Penguins should appear in chain stores and tobacconists, and should cost no more than a packet of cigarettes.

Reading habits (and cigarette prices) have changed since 1935, but Penguin still believes in publishing the best books for everybody to enjoy. We still believe that good design costs no more than bad design, and we still believe that quality books published passionately and responsibly make the world a better place.

So wherever you see the little bird – whether it's on a piece of prize-winning literary fiction or a celebrity autobiography, political tour de force or historical masterpiece, a serial-killer thriller, reference book, world classic or a piece of pure escapism – you can bet that it represents the very best that the genre has to offer.

Whatever you like to read – trust Penguin.